THE PLAIN OF JARS

I couldn't stop reading, an awesome work, if indeed the mark of a great work is to inspire, educate, move and—above all—keep the reader reading from beginning to end... a great writer to this reader! **Fred Branfman,** feature writer for *Huffington Post*, editor *Voices from the Plain of Jars.*

This irresistible story jumps off the page pulling the reader into the jungle to unravel a mystery that mirrors the complexities of this covert war. To read this book is to bare witness, and in the process be uplifted and proud of the human power to transmute boundless remorse into benevolence.
Harriet Beinfield, co-author, *Between Heaven and Earth*

A well-deserved indictment of the horrors inflicted on innocents in faraway countries by politicians, bureaucrats, and generals...Not just that, Mr. Lombardi has been able to present to us an extraordinary rendering of Laotian village life.

The writing is picturesque, cinematic, vivid, and sharp...a splendid achievement, a surprisingly well-researched, finely crafted novel.

Richard Crasta, author, *The Revised Kama Sutra: A Novel,* and *I Will Not Go the F**k to Sleep,* and other books

Visit the website

http://plainofjars.net

for maps and photos related to the story

The Plain of Jars

of Jars

A Novel

"Congrats
and enjoy
nick"

The Plain
of Jars

A Novel

N. Lombardi Jr.

Winchester, UK
Washington, USA

First published by Roundfire Books, 2013
Roundfire Books is an imprint of John Hunt Publishing Ltd., Laurel House, Station Approach,
Alresford, Hants, SO24 9JH, UK
office1@jhpbooks.net
www.johnhuntpublishing.com
www.roundfire-books.com

For distributor details and how to order please visit the 'Ordering' section on our website.

Text copyright: N. Lombardi Jr. 2012

ISBN: 978 1 78099 670 7

All rights reserved. Except for brief quotations in critical articles or reviews, no part of this
book may be reproduced in any manner without prior written permission from the publishers.

The rights of N. Lombardi Jr. as author have been asserted in accordance with the Copyright,
Designs and Patents Act 1988.

A CIP catalogue record for this book is available from the British Library.

Design: Stuart Davies

Printed in the USA by Edwards Brothers Malloy

We operate a distinctive and ethical publishing philosophy in all
areas of our business, from our global network of authors to
production and worldwide distribution.

Dedicated to the people of Laos

PROLOGUE Laos 1969

"It takes twenty years or more of peace to make a man; it takes only twenty seconds of war to destroy him."
Baudouin I, King of Belgium, Address to joint session of U.S. Congress, 12 May 1959

Nothing that extraordinary really. Those things were known to happen. After all, there was a war going on.

Nevertheless, when he heard that firsthand account of what it was like to get blown out of the sky, it managed to unsettle him. It must have been just two or three days after he had shifted over to Eighth Tactical. He had walked into the Rec Room, where a serious card game was supposedly going on, though all the players had already put their cards face down on the table, absorbed in the narration of a highly animated second lieutenant in a leather bomber jacket who was standing over them.

"With death staring you in the face, you're suddenly stunned at your own mortality," the pilot was saying, "like, for the first time, you really grasp that it could all end here and now. And everything that's in your life, I mean everything, changes in a fucking flash of a moment...But the funny thing, and I know you're gonna say I'm full of shit, was...well, I could feel it, feel it coming, even before I got into the cockpit..."

The story ran on, but he had forgotten the rest of the details the young officer had so vigorously depicted. In fact, First Lieutenant Andrew Kozeny had intended to forget the whole damn thing, deeming it best not to even consider the possibility, to give no thought at all to such a disagreeable scenario, as this was the best way to rid himself of doubt and fear, emotions that tended to get in the way of what a pilot had to do.

Wanting to forget is one thing, but actually forgetting is another, for the mission briefing at 0400, only a few weeks later, reminded him of that episode in the Rec Room, and did indeed present the prospect that something dicey might happen on the next scheduled sortie. To begin with, the reconnaissance photos were practically useless. It wasn't merely the cloud cover that perpetually veiled the mountains of northern Laos, since that was something all the pilots had long been resigned to, but the images were made even more hopeless by a frantic blur, caused by the erratic maneuvering of the RF-101 Pathfinder that had taken the snaps, and which was desperately evading a hell of a lot of unexpected flak at the time. The recon mission had to be aborted, and the location of the anti-aircraft artillery couldn't be adequately resolved solely from the recollections of the pilot. Therefore, the only logical recourse they had to protect the bombers, as outlined by the flight commander, was to use bait to make the enemy show themselves. The F-105 Wild Weasel, the plane that Kozeny was assigned to fly, had electronic sensors to detect the radar that the AA guns used for tracking hostile aircraft, and thus it was the typical lure to expose the enemy's defenses, although a heavily armed one: the bomb racks under the wings held twelve 750-lb. bombs, as well as a couple of 2.75-inch rockets, and two CBU-2A cluster bombs. Kozeny's part of this mission, along with his Electronics Warfare Officer and three other F-105 crews, was to get the bearing and range of the enemy radar, and knock out the gun emplacements so that the next six flights of bombers could come in without risk.

This wasn't the first time Kozeny had flown flak suppression in a Wild Weasel, although the missions he had flown over North Vietnam were tempered by better intelligence and more discernible targets; not such a blind run as this one. But that wasn't the only thing stirring his doubt.

Actually, the thing that was gnawing inside him was a facet of the mission that had little to do with his own tactical responsibilities: the bombing targets, if there were really any to speak of, were poorly defined.

The exercise was part of 'Operation Rain Dance' with the objective of retaking the Plain of Jars, this particular mission being a retaliatory strike near Ban Ban. The 7/13 Air Force at Udon was busier than hell, especially the Tactical Fighter Squadrons with over three hundred sorties a day. The Intelligence and Operations briefing had told of a general concentration of troops in the target area, and the bombers would be flying a free-strike zone, loosely guided by the Airborne Command and Control plane circling high above them at 35,000 feet. At other times, release would be at the discretion of each individual Weapons Officer. In plain and simple terms, the idea was to pulverize the area, so that the Special Guerilla Units of General Vang Pao could come in and clear it on the ground.

The only features that Kozeny could clearly make out on the recon photos were the huts of a couple of small villages, and a structure he guessed to be a makeshift temple. But he knew that even if nothing of worth was visible, the bombers had to drop their munitions somewhere, and it bothered him that there was no predetermined fixed target for unused ordnance at the end of a sweep. There was no way that a plane would risk landing with armed weapons—they had to dump them. "What about civilians?" someone had asked. "No problem," was the response, which could be interpreted to mean that they were the same as the enemy.

This aspect of the mission disturbed him, prodding him uncomfortably with a reminder of the letter he had just received from Cynthia, a letter that couldn't have come at a worse moment. Then again, if only he had never decided upon this second tour, maybe he wouldn't have lost her.

If only...

If only he knew what would be happening on the ground in the little village that lay in the middle of the target area, just as the planes would be nearing their specified coordinates. Old Man Souvanna would be at the market shopping around for high quality areca nuts, spending endless amounts of time inspecting them before committing to purchase. Young Keo, with a bamboo switch in his hand, would be taking the buffaloes to pasture alongside his father. Boon-mee would be heading home after fetching water, the large earthen pot on her head threatening to topple her frail, diminutive body. And 19-year-old Jita would be skipping through the fields with thoughts of romance in her head, ecstatic over the hibiscus flower that her beau had just given her.

If only...

But it was too late—he was airborne, gazing at the gray, cloud-filled horizon ahead of him. He looked down below at a hazy patchwork of forested mountains and bare vertical cliffs that flaunted an unspoken menace. Kozeny then put his mind on the mission, alternately glancing out of the cockpit to key on his flight leader, ahead and to his left, and then at his Heads Up Display, the HUD, a hologram beamed into the air to his right reflecting his most salient meters and gauges. With this projected image, the pilot averted the need to look down at the actual dials—looking inside the cockpit could induce vertigo and cause a fatal collision.

Airspeed 650 knots, altitude 14,000 ft...looking out, sighting the leader, then glimpsing right at the HUD; leader, HUD, leader, HUD, all the while intuitively perceiving and adjusting the proper motions of his aircraft.

There was an orange haze, eerily beautiful, as the sun came up in a mist, shooting its rays to the heavens...

"Whoa! Oyster 2, got a beep!" called out his backseater, Lt. David Lewis, the Electronic Weapons Officer. "Triple A frequency, bearing zero-one-zero, range 7000!" His voice betrayed a buoyant excitement. Kozeny as well experienced a giddy rush of adrenaline, since the both of them had expected the typical North Vietnamese maneuver of turning on the artillery radar at the last minute, too late for the electronic countermeasures of the Weasels to be effective, and which would have left their asses wide open.

"Jamming pod formation," cackled the radio. The leader of Oyster Flight was ordering them to switch on their jamming pods, and to fly abreast with a staggered separation, to confuse the enemy radar into reading one huge blip, rather than four individual targets.

"Oyster-1, going in, engaging afterburners, on the nose twelve miles, fifteen high…maintain position on Oyster-1…"

Although the flight leader shoulders a greater responsibility, it was actually harder to fly wing because one had to maintain position. To Andrew, this part of flying summoned in him an indescribable sense of balance and timing, and the high-tech choreography that ensued gave him an unequalled thrill.

At supersonic speed with the afterburner thrust, the hillsides melted into a greenish blur. Kozeny released the radar chaff, strips of aluminum that fluttered to the ground, to further confound the enemy radar. He flipped on the switches arming his ordnance, and checked his angle-of-attack indicator. "Reversing right and level, ready to pickle…"

"HOLY FUCK!" Dave screamed.

All around them, the colorful lines of tracer crisscrossed the sky, dotted by the puffs from exploding shells. The bursts of smoke were blue in color, telling them they were 57mm, and they were coming from somewhere other than their original target. The baiters had been baited, drawn in by one AA battery, while the other with its radar off silently waited for the kill.

"CHECK YOUR SIX! CHECK YOUR SIX!" Andrew yelled into the radio, alerting the others to watch their behind. He followed his lead down the chute, released the Shrike missile which would at least home in on the radar of the first AA unit, then banked left and pulled up, but not before his right wing was hit. "OYSTER 2 WE'RE HIT!"

Andrew rolled right now, banking and yawing, his pressurized suit nearly suffocating him as it inflated in response to the high-G maneuvers. If not for the suit, the acceleration would force blood out of his brain and into his extremities, causing him to black out….

He was losing altitude, getting too low. Then, machine guns, Kalashnikovs in automatic mode, unleashed a barrage of fire that penetrated the aircraft. Kozeny was scared, even more so when he realized that Dave's body had just been riddled apart. Covered with spatters of blood and flesh from his ex-backseater, Andrew struggled to control the aircraft, the jet now screaming and whining as if in great pain, and violently hurtling itself at 1000 miles per hour, one and an half times the speed of sound, but despite all his efforts he could not bring her up. He dropped his entire payload to gain altitude but it was not enough to pull clear of the mountains ahead of him. His frantic hands manipulated the controls to ascend, while his mind raced through emergency procedures. The plane initially shot up into the sky, giving him some hope of regaining her, but then lurched and rocked, lost airspeed, and started to nose down.

For Lt. Andrew Kozeny, the journey leading to that flash of a moment was about to begin.

BOOK 1

DOROTHY'S SEARCH

Chapter I

Ohio 1989

"...Defense Department Policy for response on U.S. operations in Laos still applies and is quoted as follows: Quote. The preferable response to questions about air operations in Laos is 'no comment'."
Instructions from the Commander of the Pacific Air Forces sent to U.S. Air Force commanders in Thailand, February 1969

Dorothy Kozeny was merely going through the motions; trying to stick to the same routines she had followed each day for more years than she cared to remember. She had made her bed, replacing her paisley bedcover. She had washed the clothes, hung them to dry, ironed and folded them, all with an automaton-like indifference. But no matter how hard she tried to believe otherwise, today, what seemed a boringly ordinary autumn day, threatened to be different. Without any warning, her chores lost that familiar character of regularity she had been carefully cultivating over the years. She brewed herself coffee, fed the cat, and washed the dishes, not out of years of habit, but with a strained and willful tenacity, refusing to admit the possibility that things were indeed different than they were before this morning. Even watering her garden, her lovely crocuses and bougainvillea, was devoid of the usual pleasure.

It was hard to find a word for what some person who didn't even have the courage to leave a name had done to her, just as she started her day. Despicable maybe, contemptuous perhaps, cruel certainly, considering the painstaking effort she had made to build all those protective layers around her heart, a mother's heart, just to have them shattered, to be taunted twenty years later with the loss of her only child.

Whose ashes did you get?

Weary after a whole day of fighting off her distress, she plopped herself down at the dining room table and cradled her head in her hands.

It was nearly the end of October, so it was already dark at five-thirty. Now that they had set the clocks back the days seemed to end prematurely. She sat in the gathering gloom, oblivious to the passing of time, the progress of which was nonetheless marked by the emphatic tick-tock of the grandfather clock on the opposite side of the room, its persistent stroke piercing the funereal silence.

The year was 1989. The twentieth anniversary of that horrible day had only just passed.

She was alone, and had been so ever since her husband Bill had died of a stroke seven years before. Was it only seven years ago, or did her husband die before that, the day the news came from the Air Force Casualty Office? To be given a lump of ashes and charred bone fragments, and to be told that this was all that remained of your son, your future hopes, was something that could make you resign from living. And so, understandably, William Kozeny began to shrivel up inside. For Dorothy, however, tending to her husband's grief, in some ways, had made it easier to deal with her own. Together, the both of them had gone through all the stages, from horrific shock to searing pain, to the endless chronic ache of sorrow. Until the rent in their souls could at least heal to a malformed scar. And now, to go through all that again, alone...*Whose ashes did you get?*

No longer able to contain her emotions, she sobbed aloud, her doleful moaning filling the darkness and echoing off the oak-paneled walls. It took a few minutes before she managed to restrain herself, sniffling her way back to self-control.

It had come that morning, in the mail, inside a plain white envelope with no return address, but with a faint postmark she made out to be Rockland, Maine. Was it a hoax, a malicious prank, or was there some substance behind it? On an A4 sheet of paper, in what appeared to be a demonic, handwritten scrawl, only the words: '*Whose ashes did you get?*'

The clanging of her baking timer startled her. Good, she thought.

Movement. Get up and move; movement will keep the brooding at bay. So, in an over-affected manner, she forced herself out of her chair and walked into the kitchen, which, in contrast to the darkened dining room, was blazingly lit by a circular tube of fluorescent light set in the ceiling. She opened the oven door to check on the rhubarb pie that she was baking for the bridge party. If she kept herself busy, maybe she could forget about this asinine letter. Inserting her hands into the oven, she noticed they were shaking...she would go to the Jack La Lane's Spa first, she told herself in her head, and go to Elizabeth's house directly from there...rhubarb pie, bridge party, Jack La Lane's....

Not paying attention to what she was doing, she burned her hand on the hot insides of the oven, causing her to drop the pie on the floor, the pie dish making an awful clatter as it rolled around, the filling splattered onto the tiles like blood from a wounded creature. She covered her face and burst into tears again.

Whose ashes did you get?

Feeling faint, Dorothy quickly sought a kitchen chair to sit down in. Her pulse started to race, her heart thumping heavily. It had been so long since she'd had a panic attack; she wondered if the Xanax in the medicine cabinet was still good. She jumped up to go into the bathroom, turned on the light, flung open the mirrored door of the medicine cabinet, and retrieved the orange plastic vial. Two tablets later, sitting on her bed and taking slow, deep breaths, she waited for their calming effect. Once her anxiety was under control, she stood up and challenged herself to open that drawer of her dresser, the one that had been safely closed for years, the one with the photo album and the framed pictures that had once hung on the wall and kept her company on the night table.

By the dull glow of an ornamental lamp with a shade made of clamshells, a souvenir from their trip to Bermuda, she went through the photographs one by one, trying to picture her son's face before her, evoking memories. There was the one with a little boy, a towel tied around his neck to serve as his Superman cape, on top of a chair, ready to jump off. Even then, he was fascinated with flying, incessantly jumping off things until she and Bill had to put a stop to it when the stove came crashing down one morning while they were still snoozing in bed. She smiled wistfully at this recollection. In another photo, he wore a mixing bowl on his head, and using a ruler for a microphone, sang *Pennies from Heaven* to a Tony Bennett record. This snapshot broke her short-lived composure and elicited a further bout of weeping, but she managed to carry on to the next photograph, a little Andrew sitting amidst a pile of toys under the Christmas tree...there he was again, wearing a cake-icing mustache at his sixth birthday party... posing in a kid-sized blue suit for his Communion at eight years old...and in a red robe for his Confirmation four years later...

He was a good boy, who went to church every Sunday, without any pressure from her or Bill, who were only intermittent churchgoers. Only after Andrew had died did she go weekly to light a candle for him.

Flipping through the photo album, the pictures traced his life to young adulthood—at the wheel of his first car, a '58 Rambler; posing with his medal for the state cross-country championship; then, some time after, standing by the Piper Cub he flew for his flying lessons...

He was such a handsome boy: tawny blond hair, long-lashed, sky-blue eyes, and a charming smile; she could only find fault with the slightly pug nose. Probably got that from his grandfather—her father—she mused to herself.

She touched the photos imploringly as she gazed at them, as if they were privy to the knowledge concerning her son's fate, hoping to extract answers from an unlikely inspirational connection.

...*Whose ashes did you get?*

"Oh Dear God, why?" she cried out to an empty house. "Why, Lord, did you make me bring him into this world...then take him away so violently...without the dignity of a normal burial? WHY!" she screamed.

Her bitterness vented, she continued looking through the album, her eyes brimming. In the last batch of pictures, Cynthia, Andrew's ex-steady, now appeared together with her son.

Outside of his parents, Andrew had two great loves in his youth. One was flying. He had worked his whole adolescence saving up money for his flying lessons. Both she and Bill were so proud of him when he finally got his license. Dorothy, now on an emotional see-saw, grinned widely, recalling the time Andy took his father up in the rented Piper. Poor Bill, who felt uncomfortable in a mere elevator, had been paralyzed with terror, but, as he confessed later, there was something wonderfully intimate in putting his life in his son's hands. The next autumn, Andrew was on cloud nine after he was accepted at the Air Force Academy in Colorado Springs—for him it was a dream come true. That was back in 1963, when the Vietnam War was only a faint rumbling in the distance.

Her son's other great love was Cynthia. Golden-haired and athletic, she had the poise and self-assurance of a beauty queen, though she was, paradoxically, more of an unaffected nature girl …what was it that Bill called her? Earth Child, wasn't it? She was always dragging Andrew off hiking and fishing, and she seemed to be forever wearing those cutoff shorts. When Andrew attended the Air Force Academy, she followed him a year later, enrolling as a student at the University of Colorado in Boulder. For eight years, from high school sophomore, to his assignment in Southeast Asia, Cynthia was Andrew's devoted sweetheart. Perhaps what made their intimacy more intense was that they both lacked any siblings, each an only child.

Yet Dorothy knew all too well that, even in the most favorable of times, young love is tested by the changes that usher kids into adolescence. Goodness, on how many occasions did she and Bill split up? The 1960s were exceptionally volatile, a period when values were being questioned, old standards were being discarded, and new fads were being adopted with each and every Beatles album. In 1969, America's eminent triumph in landing men on the moon was tainted by the protests and demonstrations of her youth that disclaimed her. To be patriotic was no longer fashionable, and war was seen as murderous, not glorious.

1969 was a bad year. In 1969, the Kozeny's lost their son. A son Dorothy had fed with her breasts, carried in her arms, and consoled when he was hurt.

Why, she found herself wondering, couldn't they have had other children? It would have made his loss so much easier to bear. She immediately felt guilty at that last thought, which led her to cry again, a soft, whimpering cadence of self-pity. She removed her reading glasses and rubbed her eyes before resuming her despondent journey down memory lane.

Cynthia. It had been so long ago.

Andrew's decision to go back to a second tour had angered Cynthia, and aggravated an ever-widening rift between the couple. It was unfortunate, for Dorothy had quite naturally assumed that they would soon get married. But Cynthia had joined the peace movement and became an active antiwar protestor, a transformation that was discordant with Andrew's military career. When he went back to the war a second time, she told him she didn't want to have anything to do with him. Or so Dorothy had heard, for neither one of them got the chance to explain to her just what the problem was. Regrettably, the breach in Cynthia's relationship with Andrew had also estranged her from the rest of the Kozenys, and contact between them soon ended.

Could it be her…after all these years…would she…no, not in such a grisly way…she would never do a thing like that. Still, she might have an idea; she was an investigative reporter now or something similar. Dorothy of course, had heard about the tragic highway accident in which both her parents had been killed. She had also heard through the grapevine that afterwards Cynthia had refused to sell the family house, and didn't even rent it out, preferring to use it herself for periodic retreats from her hectic life in LA or New York or wherever. Though Cynthia resided in Camden for only a few months of the year, lessening the likelihood that she was in, Dorothy's urge to call her was irrepressible.

She went into the living room, flipping on the lights along the way, and sought out the telephone notebook that she kept in the drawer under where the telephone sat. Paging through it, she belatedly realized that the number wasn't in there; it's in the old notebook, the one in the shoebox in the closet.

She dived into the closet and dug her way through until she found the shoebox, then carried it to the living room to the end table with the telephone. She threw open the lid, recovered the faded green notebook, and with trembling fingers paged to S for Soronson.

With her fingers still quaking, she dialed the number. She put the receiver to her ear, then quickly pressed the button on the cradle to disconnect. She slowly put down the receiver and took a deep breath. She picked up the receiver again, then put it down again, but keeping her hand on it. Summoning her resolution, she picked up the receiver for the third time, dialed once more and braced herself.

The distant ring on the other end heightened her anticipation.

"Uh, hello?" came a voice from the past.

"Cynthia?" she blurted, suddenly petrified. What should she say? "Is that you? This is Dorothy, Dorothy Kozeny."

"Dot?"

Being called Dot, the affectionate name that Bill had always used, nearly broke her voice.

"Yes, Cindy, it's me."

"Well, hello, how are you?"

"I'm fine, just fine...it's just that it's been so long and I thought...well, really, I was fine, but now, I'm not so sure, I...I just thought...Well, I have to...I need to... talk to you..."

"Yes, of course, I'm..." There was a slight pause on the line. "I'm sorry that I've been out of touch. I didn't mean anything by it, it's just...you know..."

"Yes."

Another pause.

"Dot?"

"Yes?"

"Is everything okay?"

"No!" she whined, and the floodgates damming her emotions opened.

Camden, Ohio had grown larger over the past twenty years, so by now it was a mini-city replete with office blocks and mega-malls, but there were a few persistent landmarks that still imbued a small town atmosphere. Rosie's C'mon Inn, where all the kids a generation ago used to hang out, attracted by its wide, discreetly shaded parking area, not to mention those famous Chili Burgers, was one such place.

After Dorothy had related to Cynthia the story about the puzzling anonymous message, a lengthy discussion had ensued on the telephone, including the exchange of apologies, and promises not to let such a long lull happen again. There followed a quick review of what had taken place in their lives since their last contact. When Cynthia told her that she hadn't married anyone yet, Dorothy had noted it with some significance. Their conversation finally culminated in a plan to meet face-to-face. Rosie's C'mon Inn was the first place that had popped into Dorothy's head, unconsciously associating it with the bygone courtship between Cynthia and her son.

Before leaving the house, Dorothy had studied herself in the mirror, wondering how Cynthia would perceive the changes in her. She debated whether her beige pants suit was appropriate or whether it was it too formal and cold. Beyond the immediate issue of her attire, she pondered the years that had passed. Her streaky, silver-gray hair was now worn in a pageboy with bangs, and crow's feet had sprouted from the corners of her pale blue eyes. Her skin was peppered with orange age-spots, and a pair of faint lines on each side of her face demarcated her cheeks. Around her midsection, a girth had developed, but despite her sixty-four years of age, her body was still surprisingly athletic-looking (Jack La Lane's Fitness

Center had been a worthwhile endeavor, she concluded to herself).

When she arrived at the diner, it was fairly quiet, the only other customer being a rotund, bald-headed man sitting at the counter busy shoveling his eggs onto a piece of toast. Waiting in the corner booth, Dorothy nervously rummaged through the contents of her pocketbook: removing the old orphaned sheets of Kleenex, rearranging her vial of Tylenol, putting the lipstick back in her cosmetic case, taking out the money from her purse and sorting it …and then she saw her, walking through the swing door. It had to be her, but yet it wasn't. Dressed in a denim shirt and a pair of tight jeans that advertised her shapely hips, her hair in a wild, honey-brown mane, she strode in with a brashness that Dorothy couldn't recall Cynthia ever having previously possessed. God, she looked older, but of course she was older, must be nearly forty by now. Her hair was darker, her body heavier, and the soft curves of her face had hardened into angular edges. Despite a slight puffiness around her eyes, she was still quite good-looking, and her beautiful smile was much the same as ever, one forming now as she recognized Dorothy immediately and approached.

Dorothy stood up to hug her and couldn't stop her eyes from watering. She had underestimated just how emotional it would be to see her. "Cynthia!"

"Oh Dot, I'm so sorry," she consoled, squeezing her affectionately.

The two of them ended their embrace and, linking their hands, stood back to take stock of each other.

"Dot, you look great!" Cynthia said, the sparkle in her eyes showing the sincerity behind the cliché. "You really do. You haven't aged a day!"

Dorothy forced an abashed smile. "Thank you. And you, you still look like the 'Earth Child'."

Cynthia simpered self-consciously. "No, I doubt it. Maybe more of a 'Globetrotting Mama'…let's sit down for God's sake!" Slipping into the booth, she resumed with her consolations. "Dot, I'm sorry about Bill. I wanted to come to the funeral, but I was in Chile at the time."

Dorothy released a pensive sigh. "Oh, that's all right. I understand. I try to convince myself it was for the best, you know, he was never the same after...well, you know...I think that's what really killed him."

"Well, none of us are the same, are we? I'm sorry about everything else too."

"No, please Cynthia, don't feel bad. What's past is past."

Dorothy wanted to steer the conversation off this melancholic track. She remembered that Cynthia had told her that she was a freelance journalist, writing for various publications ranging from *National Geographic* to *Ramparts.* "How is your work going, I mean, I hope I'm not keeping you..."

"Don't be silly. I'm glad we're finally getting together. We should have never lost contact." Cynthia raised her arm, signaling a waitress. "Are you hungry?" she asked Dorothy.

"No, I really don't want anything."

"Coffee?"

"Yes, that would be fine."

"Two coffee's and one plate of quiche, please," she told the waitress. Then, to Dorothy, "I can imagine how upset you must be over that note you got. I don't know what to say, it's really bizarre. I've been digging up some background stuff since you called, and, strange as it seems, there might be something to it."

"Something to it?"

"Yes, well, I mean, it might be more than just a nasty joke. But who the hell would send a message like that in such a cryptic manner is beyond me."

At this point, she stopped her dialogue to dig into her buckskin pocketbook, coming out with a pack of cigarettes.

Cynthia smoked now?

She lit her cigarette with a Zippo, clicking it shut with an aggressive mannerism that seemed masculine, followed by frantically waving the smoke away with her arm. This image of Cynthia conflicted with Dorothy's vision of the sweet, polite girl she had kept in her memories.

After exhaling a puff of smoke, Cynthia continued her explanation. "You know, a few years ago, they excavated the crash site of a C-130, that's a type of cargo plane..." She paused to take in another drag, "...at Pakse, a small town in Laos. It was carrying munitions and thirteen men."

"Where?"

"In Laos. It went down..."

"I'm sorry, but just where is 'Louse'?"

"It's the country next door to Vietnam," Cynthia answered with her eyebrows faintly raised, surprised that Dorothy didn't know. "The plane was on its way back to Thailand when it went down in a fireball. The remains of those on board ended up as thousands of burned bone shards, but they claimed they had positively identified which pieces belonged to all thirteen men. The wife of one of the men, Anne Hart, refused to accept her husband's remains without an independent expert to examine them. But the Navy was having none of her bullshit..."

Dorothy winced. She couldn't picture the other, younger Cynthia using such words.

"... and they tried to force her to accept what they were offering. She refused, and sued them, got a court order to allow a private forensic expert to make an examination, and guess what? —it wasn't her husband. The dog tag they gave her burned at a different time and temperature than the bone shards. In fact, the expert said that with the discredited methods they were using, it was tantamount to fraud to claim that any of the ashes and bone fragments could be identified as anyone. Well this just about opened up Pandora's Box. The relatives of the other C-130 crewmembers, as well as families of all the other pilots that were incinerated before that, began exhuming the remains of their loved ones and having them tested, and it was much the same. It blew up into a big scandal. It seems the military just wanted to provide anything to shut people up, to prevent any widening of the MIA issue, especially since what they were doing in Laos was supposed to be a secret."

"Are you saying that...?"

"Maybe, Dot, I don't know," Cindy said cautiously, "maybe..."

Dorothy suddenly felt as if she were in an elevator dropping twenty stories. She felt her stomach trying to come out of her mouth, and knowing she would never make it to the ladies room, instinctively grabbed the linen napkin that was set on the table and heaved up into it. Luckily she hadn't yet eaten anything that morning and it was only mucous. Cynthia jumped over to her side of the booth and gave her a quick hug. "I'm sorry, Dot."

"I'll be okay," she stated in a cracked voice.

Now that the suspicion had suddenly become a tangible possibility that Andrew had never come home in any form, not even in ashes, a whole plethora of scenarios crossed her mind, dominated by the flimsy hope that he could still be alive. However improbable, it was nevertheless a mother's natural faith, which could only be quelled by seeing the body, even one that was, as much as it hurt to see it, seared to cinders.

An embarrassing moment as the waitress came over with the coffees and quiche. "There you go," she smiled, and began to tactfully walk away.

"Can you take this please?" Cindy requested, handing the waitress the soiled napkin. The waitress made a face as she picked it up and deposited it on her serving tray, then curtly withdrew. Once she was out of earshot, Cynthia turned to Dorothy and said, "Listen, Dot, this is what we're going to do. Step by step. First, if you want, I can help you get a court order to exhume, and arrange a forensic specialist to do the examination. If you want."

"Yes."

"If it's not Andrew's remains that you got, we'll have to get his status changed from Killed In Action to Killed In Action Body Not Recovered. That's not just semantics. Without a body, it makes Andy automatically Missing In Action, according to a court ruling in 1979."

Cindy hoped that by mentioning all this technical detail, Dorothy would be too preoccupied trying to concentrate, thus forestalling any slide back into an emotional muddle.

"All this has to be done in the POW section of the Defense Intelligence Agency, but rather than do that directly, we'll try to get a special volunteer group to do that on our behalf. There is an organization called the 'National League of Families of American Prisoners and Missing in Southeast Asia'. They have some pull with the DIA, and that gives them a better position. It's going to be tough, the whole MIA thing has become very politicized, and even the League may not help us. But if we succeed, the DIA will be forced to open a file on Andy and investigate what happened to him. You understand what I've said so far?"

"Some of it... I think."

"Well, don't worry about all the details for now. Just realize that there is a way to go about this. I'll run it by you again when the time comes. Now don't get any false hopes, Andy's...well...let's be realistic, none of this is any proof that he's still alive."

Dorothy sniffled acquiescently. "I know."

"The other thing we have to do is to find out who sent you that message. Leave that to me. I'm a professional snoop. I already have a plan to bait this mysterious messenger. You have the letter?"

Dorothy retrieved it from her pocketbook and handed it over.

Cynthia pulled out the sheet of paper and examined it briefly with a pondering frown. "Don't worry, Dot. I'll be with you all the way through this." She put the letter back in the envelope, which she put it in her bag, before pulling the plate of quiche closer to her.

Dorothy sat quietly for a few seconds before contemplating what she would say next. "Cynthia?"

She was now in the middle of devouring her quiche. "Yes?" she said after swallowing hastily.

"I don't mean to pry, but I just have to ask. How come you never got married?"

"Ah." Cynthia put down her fork, swallowed again, this time a bit too hard, and thought awhile before she spoke. "Well, I have love affairs, but in the end I always seem to be disappointed. Nothing is quite like the first time. And then again, my work keeps me busy, always hopping around here and there."

"I'm sorry."

"About what? About me and Andy? Don't get mushy, Dot. It wouldn't have worked out between us. It was bound to end anyway."

Dorothy sat back in her chair and looked away pensively. Fitting, she thought, that there should be such doubt. Genuine or not, ashes aren't a person. He never came home, that was the point. And their lives had never continued, their plans had never culminated, and their past would never be sealed.

"What are you thinking about?" Cynthia asked, looking up from her plate.

"Nothing," Dorothy said with a waxen smile.

Cynthia Soronson hadn't been entirely open nor forthcoming in her encounter with Dorothy Kozeny. She hadn't mentioned anything about the correspondences she had had with Andrew while he was overseas—those letters of condemnation she had sent to him. She hadn't mentioned the harassment by the FBI and the IRS that had started soon after Andy had died: her arrest, the wiretapping, the financial audits…nor had she said anything about Mitch, her lover at Berkeley. She had her own ghosts of the past to grapple with. It was too soon, too soon to tell all. She was proud of herself though, feeling her performance in Dot's presence was laudable, her staged self-composure worthy of an Oscar. She had to be strong for Dot, for the both of them. But now, alone in her apartment, she could afford to release the reins that had been cramping her insides with emotion.

In her bedroom, she flung her buckskin pocketbook on the bed. One arm went up to cradle her bowed head; her elbow supported with her other hand. She shifted her weight left and right, rocking her body back and forth, left and right, back and forth. "Shit!" she swore to herself. She had thought that that particular segment of her life was over with, filed away somewhere safe. Why the hell did she agree to meet at Rosie's of all places?

She stopped her rocking. Stifled sobs welled up in spurts. One, and then another, and then another. It felt good after such a long time, like vomiting after a prolonged night with a stomachache.

"I'm sorry, Andy," she cried. "Sorry for being such a bitch." Talking aloud like that made her feel stupid enough to stop weeping. She lay down on the bed, while her thoughts roamed back.

Their teenage romance began at Rosie's. She was sitting in a booth with Carol and Ann-Marie, two of her friends that, because of the way she attracted boys, probably thought it was to their benefit to hang out with her. But Cindy had little interest in any of the boys, except for Andy. He had walked in that day, and all three girls thought he was so cute, with his shy, sweet smile. Ann-Marie, just moments before, waving her arms to tell a story in her usual colorful way, had spilt her soda pop, creating a mess on the floor. When Andy walked by, he slipped on the wet spot and went down headfirst, flinging his milkshake in Cynthia's face and banging his head on their table in the process. What a riot, everyone screaming in laughter. But Cynthia got down to rescue him, taking the ice cubes from her soda pop and putting them in a linen napkin, which she pressed to the bump on his head. For a 14-year-old girl in a small Midwestern town, it's hard to imagine anything more romantic.

Two years later. Again, they were sitting in a booth at Rosie's. She was sixteen, a junior in high school.

"Hey, maybe we could fly there," he proposed.

She knew he was trying his best to lighten the pain of their discussion, a discussion that concerned their inevitable separation.

"I could rent a Cessna, and we'll see the country from a bird's-eye view. How's that sound?"

Cindy responded merely with a pout.

"Then after my orientation we could fly up to Boulder, and you can check out the University there. Whaddaya say?" He playfully shook her shoulder in a futile attempt to lift her spirits.

"Andy, I still have a year to go," she complained in a nasally whine, emphasizing her resentment of the situation.

"I guess, that's why they say, 'this is when life begins'," he said wistfully. "The choices, decisions…"

She looked deep into his sea-blue eyes. "I love you, Andrew Kozeny. That's where my life begins… and ends."

40-year-old Cynthia, lying on her bed, nearly cringed at the recollection of such a hackneyed line, but it hadn't sounded so corny at the time. Her teenage mind had considered it poetic. In any case, what was really important was that it expressed her genuine feelings.

What happened after that? Oh, yes…with bittersweet timing, their song began to play on the jukebox, *Smoke Gets in Your Eyes*.

"I love you too, Cindy," he had said.

They were sitting silently, listening to the music.

"So we really shouldn't worry, not if our love is true," he had teasingly assured, mimicking the lyrics of the song. There was just a hint of faltering in his false bravado.

Their song soon finished.

On the night of Andy's high school prom, they had lost their virginity to each other. That only made the next year apart even worse. Now, reminiscing in her bed, she could almost taste that aching, that longing of first love.

When she finally made it to Boulder, life was great. He would fly in on a rented plane every weekend. She loved flying with him, how he did it so effortlessly, so naturally, like a bird in flight. They cycled the Rocky Mountains in the summer, and skied them in the winter. Those three years were the happiest of her life.

Later on he was assigned to McConnell Air Force Base in Kansas. He had already asked her to marry him, but she wanted to go to graduate school first. Another two years, she told him, and she'd be ready to have lots of babies with him. She enrolled at the University of California at Berkeley. After that, they saw each other less.

That was in 1967. In 1967, 50,000 demonstrators, including some celebrities, marched in protest outside the Pentagon. In November of that year, peace activists, led by Bertrand Russell, held a mock tribunal of International War Crimes against the US. In the same month, a state of the art navigational beacon was installed on Pu Pa Ti Mountain in Laos to allow all-weather, twenty-four-hour bombing of North Vietnam.

When he was transferred to Nellis Air Force Base in Nevada, she wasn't allowed to visit him. He was learning secret electronic warfare stuff, he had told her, and access to the base was limited. And when he underwent a three-month language-training course at a Defense Department Institute, to learn Thai and Lao, she asked him why, fearing the worst—a posting in Indochina. Somehow, things were deviating from their plans, and Cindy was finding it more and more difficult to justify his Air Force activities to the new set of friends she had made at Berkeley.

A year later, again at Rosie's C'mon Inn. They had both come home, she, for summer vacation, he, on a short furlough. She remembered the anger that had been grasping at her while she listened to him.

"Look," he said, "they told me I wouldn't be seeing much action this time around. And if I do it now, it's over with. If I don't, they might call me to do another tour again next year."

"Next year the war might be over."

"All the better. But maybe it'll get bigger. Let's be realistic, they own my ass for four years. And I'm getting a lot of pressure."

"Fuck them. Quit."

"I can't just quit. I have to do the four years. I don't think you know what it means to be in the Air Force."

"It's you who doesn't know what that means. It means you'll do as they say whether it it's wrong or right. And the war is wrong, Andrew."

"But it's not like I'm killing anyone. I'm just hitting bridges…"

"And planes, with a pilot inside…" She was referring to the MIG he shot down over Haiphong, the one that had earned him the Distinguished Flying Cross.

"Well hell, he wouldn't have thought twice to have shot me down."

"That's just it, you stupid ass!" she cried. Men were so thick, she thought. "Do you know what you're fighting for? I bet he did."

"Look, he bailed out, I saw him."

"That's not the point. The war is wrong. You just enjoy playing the hero. Do you think that impresses me, do you, that medal you got, huh, do you?"

His voice became louder, betraying his frustration. "You don't know what you're talking about."

"Maybe I don't. But it's easier to take back what I say than to undo what I've done."

"Cindy, I…" he paused to search for words. He couldn't confess to her that flying a jet fighter gave him a rush better than sex. No, that would surely finish it between them. But she knew anyway, knew that her rival mistress took the form of an airplane. Changing tack, he asked, "You don't want me to be a pilot?"

"You don't need the Air Force to be a civilian pilot."

"You know what I mean, an airline pilot."

"It wouldn't matter to me if you were a crop duster, or a janitor for that matter. Better than a killer."

Andrew turned silent. This was his way of signaling the end of the discussion. It was annoying to her, the way he always let her have the last word. What made it more annoying was that it worked. His silence eventually made her give in. Despite everything—her new friends, her new politics, her new lover—she couldn't just flick a switch and stop loving Andrew Kozeny. It just wasn't that simple.

Ah, regrets! No matter how carefully one tries to tread through life, one just keeps stumbling right into them. Each time, you think you know better, until later, the cold judgment of hindsight condemns you as a fool.

But if only she hadn't been so harsh in her last letter, if only she had known she would never see him again. If only....

Chapter 2

Ohio 1989

"If we are given the right to use nuclear weapons, we can guarantee victory."
General Lemnitzer, of the National Security Council, 1961

It took six weeks to get the court order. During that time, Dorothy had tried to occupy herself with mundane chores, sometimes even making the effort of creating lists to find things to do. Her workouts at Jack La Lane and her garden were the only effective outlets of relief, for she couldn't bear to go out and socialize with her friends, to whom she hadn't mentioned anything of these recent events. She made excuses for missing their Saturday night bridge parties, and did her shopping early in the morning to lessen the risk of bumping into someone. What made things worse was that it was the holiday season, which not only slowed down the legal process for the exhumation request, but also placed Dorothy in a deep rut of melancholy, as she passed Christmas and New Year alone. Cynthia had gone to Sweden to spend the holidays with some journalist friends, but before she left she had managed to get hold of a forensic specialist, a lecturer at John Jay Criminal College in NY, whom she said would make the examination free of charge. He and his colleagues were to use a relatively new technique that looked at the DNA, provided that the bone fragments weren't too badly damaged by fire. In that case, Dorothy was to provide a sample of her own blood for comparison.

As it turned out, all this sophistication was unnecessary. The bone pieces weren't even human. Probably cattle bones, the specialist had said.

Dorothy emotionally collapsed at the findings. Her doctor subsequently decided on something stronger than her Xanax; he prescribed Valium for her. A dull, cold pain inside her characterized the time that followed, and she moved about like a zombie, trapped in some horrible, grotesque dream. Sleep was her only solace.

What had happened to her son? How could the Air Force, the US government, make such a loathsome mistake? They couldn't have made such a mistake, no, not possible. But there is a big difference between a man and a cow. Or is there? How could you tell from little pieces of bone? Maybe there was a cow standing right where the plane crashed, and all their shattered remains got mixed up in the wreckage. How can the scientists tell the difference? They do chemical tests, don't they? Maybe they got the results mixed up from another sample? Yes, that's it! Or is it…?

She suddenly found herself with nothing to do but think, and more than enough time to do it in. It was only through Cynthia's assiduous support that she managed to carry out the next step, contacting the National League of Families of American Prisoners and Missing in SE Asia.

They checked her son's name against a recently declassified MIA list. They told her that he wasn't on it, and therefore they couldn't provide any information, a file had to be opened with the Defense Intelligence Agency first, they said. She told them, with a weary patience that sapped her strength, that yes, she understood that, but she was asking for their help to change his status so that such a file could be opened. With renewed exasperation, she described the exhumation and the results of the forensic exam, and she also informed them that she had never received his dog tag. Neither was she given his Air Force nor his Geneva Convention identification cards (it was a clearheaded Cynthia who reminded her of this fact). They took down her particulars, including those of Andrew's posting at the 8th Tactical Fighter Wing, 430th Tactical Fighter Squadron in Udon, Thailand, and said they would get back to her.

They indeed got back to her, surprisingly fast, in just a little over a week. But the response she received in the mail wasn't the one she had expected. It merely stated, in a cold and terse manner, that the

POW/MIA Office in the Defense Intelligence Agency had insisted, whether the body was deemed recovered or not, that the case of Lt. Kozeny was closed. There was overwhelming circumstantial evidence to keep his status classed under 'Presumed Findings Of Death', and therefore a change of status wasn't possible.

Cynthia, once Dorothy had told her of this disappointing reply over the phone, rushed over to Dorothy's house that very evening.

They sat drinking tea in the living room of the two story Four Square Colonial house, the one that Bill had bought just after he'd got his job as an insurance salesman, when Andrew was still an infant. In fact, it was in Bill's favorite armchair where Cynthia was now sitting. After reading the letter, she put her cup down, fumbled about in her buckskin handbag, and opened a new pack of cigarettes. They must be menthol, Dorothy noted, because the pack was bright green.

"There's definitely something not kosher here," Cynthia commented, before proceeding to light her cigarette with overstated deliberation. "We could go to court over this, but it'd be a long drawn out affair, and might attract nationwide publicity. In fact, we would need the pressure of publicity in order to win."

"No, please, no more litigation."

"I'm of the same opinion. We're not ready do battle with the DIA, especially since it looks like they're stonewalling the League, which is a bad sign."

"Why should they do that?"

"Sorry, Dot, I don't have all the answers."

Dorothy sighed dramatically. "Maybe not, but you've impressed me so far. Honestly, I don't know what I would have done without you, Cynthia. It's all so complicated. I probably would have given up already. But then I would have been haunted for the rest of my life. I'm really grateful for all the assistance you've given me. Thank you, Cynthia."

Cynthia then did something very strange—she turned and looked away from Dorothy, a sour look on her face, an expression marked by a tinge of remorse.

The time had come. She stubbed her cigarette out in the ashtray with undue commotion, practically breaking it into shreds. "I haven't been totally open with you, Dot," she confessed. She returned her face to look once again at Dorothy. "I thought it best if you took things a little at a time."

"What? What's that supposed to mean?"

"Do you know where Andy was shot down?"

"They just said Southeast Asia. I naturally thought it was Vietnam..."

"That's bullshit. Andy was shot over Laos."

"Laos? You mean the same country where the other plane burned up with all those men? What is this Laos? Was there a war there too?"

"Yes, a secret war. Do you know what Andy was doing when he was shot down?"

"They said it was a reconnaissance mission."

"More bullshit. He was dropping bombs on villages."

"In Laos?"

"Yes."

"I don't understand."

Cindy decided to bring up the real issue that was on her mind. "I never got all my letters back."

"What?" Dorothy exclaimed, befuddled at the turn this conversation was taking. "I gave you all the letters I had, all the ones they gave me when they handed over his things."

"Precisely. All the ones they gave you. But they weren't all of them. For example, I didn't get the last letter I wrote Andy. A letter that, believe me, I would have recognized if I had read it."

"Are you saying the Air Force lost some of Andrew's belongings?"

"Lost? No, I'm not saying that."

"Then, what are you saying? The Air Force kept your letters? Why on earth would they keep your letters?"

"Because we were discussing the bombing in Laos, and nobody was supposed to know. The pilots were told not to write about it or mention it to anyone."

"Why did Andrew tell you about that, and not us?"

Cindy felt a bit guilty over this issue. How could she explain it? "He was flying missions in Laos for only a month or so, and it was disturbing him, or maybe it was me who was disturbing him...you see, I knew about the bombing in Laos because of my involvement in the antiwar movement. Even though the war was secret, things leaked out, and well, I confronted Andy, especially in that last letter."

Dorothy was becoming overwhelmed at how the past didn't go away, but lay hidden, ready at any time to ambush the present. Not the past that she had remembered, a new past that had treacherously concealed itself all this time.

Both women sat in melancholy reflection.

"This is what I suggest," Cindy broke in, wishing to dispel the lugubrious silence. "We can make a 'Freedom of Information Act Request' to gain access to documents relating to Andy's case. Hey, now that I think about this, I know someone who knows someone inside the DIA. Nobody big, just a clerk. But even that would make things much easier. If we could get a look at these documents, we could examine this so-called 'overwhelming circumstantial evidence'."

"If that's what you think we should do." Dorothy felt drained, willing to accede to anything.

"Yes, it is. The both of us have been too complacent about this for far too long, me in particular."

"Please stop, Cindy. No more blaming yourself."

Cindy tactfully changed the subject. "Now, about that mysterious message. I put a notice last week in all the local newspapers in Rockland, and even in the Veterans of Foreign Wars newsletter of the Rockland chapter. Maybe that'll draw this character out and solicit a response. But we have to be cautious."

"I don't know how I should feel toward this, this," Dorothy stammered, "... I hate the person, but I'm indebted, aren't I? In a way, I guess, to whoever it is." Her face put on a severe frown. "But why stay silent all these years?"

"Any number of reasons. Out of fear, maybe. Or maybe they didn't know before. We'll have to wait and see. Now, I think that's enough for one day. Let's have a walk in the garden and take a look at your crocuses."

A few days after that, Dorothy received a phone call.

"Hello? Mrs. Kozeny?"

"Yes?"

"Hi, I'm Jack Shilby. I'm a consultant to Congressman Stephen Ames of Minnesota."

"Yes?"

"I'm calling you about that notice you placed in the Veterans of Foreign Wars newsletter, the one in Rockland, and I just wanted to introduce myself. Perhaps I can be of some assistance."

Dorothy's interest was piqued. "Assistance? How can you help me?"

The man on the other end coughed stiffly, signaling the beginning of his pitch. "Well, as a consultant on POW/MIA cases for the Congressman, and for others like yourself, I am in a unique position to investigate such matters. I can get my hands on documents you might not even know exist. I'm also in frequent contact with a group of ex-military people, who, out of frustration with the government's incompetence at solving the MIA problem, run their own intelligence gathering operation out of Thailand and Laos. I'm sure that together with them, we could find out what happened to your son, even recover his remains, or just maybe, if he's still alive, which, believe me, there have been known to be such cases, we could get him out."

"Get him out of where?"

"A POW camp. Many of our boys are still being held, didn't you know that?"

"Well, there was some talk of that, but I thought they were just rumors. They said there was no proof…"

"That's what they want you to think. The past few administrations have been more worried about diplomatic implications than they are about rescuing our brave soldiers who risked their lives for their country. In fact, Mrs. Kozeny, I have already begun making inquiries, and this may be true of your son. I haven't confirmed anything yet, but we're working on it."

Dorothy's excitement rose. "Are you trying to tell me my son is alive in a prison camp? Oh Lord, where, where for God's sake?"

"Actually, it's best not to talk about it over the phone," the man cautioned in a surreptitious tone, "so what I'll do is leave you my number and if you want, I could come down to discuss this with you."

Shilby then gave her his number, a toll-free number, and asked her to seriously consider what he had said and not to talk to anyone about it.

Dorothy hung up the receiver in a mood of elation. Finally! They were getting somewhere! And he said that Andrew could be alive in a POW camp, but the government was too embarrassed to admit such a grave mistake!

She called Cynthia immediately.

"Cynthia, that idea of yours, posting that advert, it really worked!"

"What are you saying?"

Dorothy told her about the phone call, and the possibility that Andrew was still alive.

"What was the name of that guy who called?"

Dorothy nudged her reading glasses up her nose and read from the slip of paper she had scribbled on. "Shilby. Jack Shilby."

"Oh no! It's all my fault. I should have thought about this more carefully. I should have put my phone number in the ad, that way I could have fielded the calls myself and screened them."

"What do you mean, screen them?"

"The man's a scam artist."

"How do you know that?"

"Believe me, I know."

Cynthia went on to explain that the POW/MIA issue had become a cult thing, just like UFO's and the Second Coming of Elvis. Worse still, it had become a source of income and a good business for some, and a political platform for others, including Ames and a couple of other Congressmen.

"How did he know of our advert?" Dorothy wanted to know.

"These vultures engage clipping services who scan all sorts of things, magazines, newspapers, wire services, and who look for information which might be relevant to their clients."

Cynthia expanded on the problem. There were those like Shilby, slick salesman who sold false hopes, and then there were others, wannabe Rambos who stage amateurish adventures into Laos, get into trouble, and embarrass the US. These cowboys, who often were nothing more than avid readers of Soldier of Fortune magazine, even managed to hoodwink many prominently rich businessmen who subsequently doled out huge sums. Those mercenaries that were indeed genuine ex-military men, also had a poor track record of clownish attempts, and no such operation, despite being very expensive to fund, had ever come close to succeeding. In the most unscrupulous cases, they would return animal bones and claim that they had found the lost loved one they were paid to find.

Needless to say, this all but crushed poor Dorothy. Whenever someone called, she now referred him or her to Cynthia. All the calls were bogus. Letters came as well, and she handed them over to Cynthia without opening them, also all bogus. The whole thing was beginning to make her sick to her stomach.

As for the Freedom of Information Act request which they had made, it was granted quickly, perhaps due to Cynthia's contact who in turn had a contact at the DIA. Dorothy was given a choice of going down to Washington to pick them up, or paying an extra charge of having them hand delivered by courier—they wouldn't send them through the mail. She chose the courier.

When the papers arrived, she and Cynthia went over them together. Portions were blacked out, or rather, 'redacted', the word Cynthia used, because they concerned things that were still considered classified. Other than that, they were mundane records describing the same story, except in more boring detail, about the reconnaissance mission near the border of South Vietnam.

A month had passed and Dorothy was now contemplating giving up. Their efforts were producing nothing more than a morbid disruption of her life. She wanted her old existence back, when Andrew was peacefully buried. It was in such a state of resignation that she answered the doorbell.

Cindy stood in the doorway. "There's something you should see," she gravely stated as she walked in.

It was a large manila envelope that had come in last week's mail, and which she had dutifully handed over to Cynthia just the other day.

"You better sit down first," Cynthia warned, handing her the papers that were inside.

Dorothy went for her reading glasses and put them on, then took a seat at the dining room table.

Dear Mrs. Kozeny

I was going through my son's papers the other day, and in his drawer I found several clippings of your advertisement from the newspapers and the VFW gazette, the one describing the terrible situation about your son's remains and the letter someone had sent you in the mail. I suspect it was my son who sent you that message.

Since he came home from the war, he had not been a whole human being. They took his soul from him, and perhaps he never came back to me at all. He has been in and out of jail, alcohol rehab, and even mental hospitals. He became a stranger to his wife and children, who eventually left, and even to me, his mother. I know the suffering you must feel as a mother, because I have also suffered. Perhaps you were lucky to be spared what I have gone through.

It was only a month ago that my son put a gun in his mouth and took his life. That would be just about a week after you posted your advert. I think that maybe my son was trying to set things right in his own crude way before departing this earth.

Enclosed is his diary of sorts, sheets of paper on which he wrote his thoughts. Some of it is not easily understandable, disturbed you might say, but there are other parts that appear to make sense. I tried to read through it all, but it was much too painful for me. I have sent it to you in the hope you might learn about what happened to your son. Please don't think ill of me, or of my son, whatever you find out.

I am sorry I cannot offer you more than that, except my humble sympathies.

Yours Truly

Alberta Anatoly

"It was a good idea about me screening these correspondences," Cynthia said, standing behind her. "I took the liberty of extracting only what is relevant to our situation. Some of the other stuff is a bit weird, sort of a bloody stream of consciousness. This guy was really fucked up, pardon my French." Cynthia handed her more sheets of paper, which Dorothy, now thoroughly baffled, accepted.

Cynthia sympathetically put her hand on Dorothy's shoulder. "I'll be in the kitchen, putting on some tea."

The Destruction of the Innocents

The Confessions of Stephen Anatoly

First of all, I would like to say that it wasn't my fault. Not mine, and not any of us other guys that you MOTHERFUCKERS SENT! We thought that what we were doing was right. You look to your elders, the ones who sent you, and you believe in them. And they fucking know that! That's why they take us when we're young and innocent – fresh meat – so they have a clean slate to brainwash. They set us up, and no way were we prepared for the reality that followed. Why??

Who were those villagers to me? What did they do to me? You slimy scheming filthy fucking politicians playing little fucking chess games with our lives...

Dorothy looked away from the papers and took in a deep breath. She wasn't quite prepared for such a depraved narrative. Reluctantly, she resumed her reading.

I wasn't just a Marine. I was in First Force Recon. First Force makes the Green Berets look like a bunch of soft wet plushy pussys. I was given extensive training in hand-to-hand combat, sniping, parachuting and demolition as well as advanced tracking and camouflage techniques. I was made familiar with Soviet and Chinese weapons. They sent me to Okinawa, like the other Marines, as a mechanic of all fucking things. Mechanic my ass, mechanic like the Charles Bronson movie. Then they sent me to Saigon, but not directly. First I got on a fishing boat that took me to Subic Bay Naval Base in the Philippines, then on a Navy boat to Bangkok. From there I had to take a domestic flight to Udon and then got on an Air America flight (that's CIA if you don't know) to Saigon. They did this because they had to have my records 'sheep-dipped'. I was assigned to Command & Control North, Da Nang, which was under the SOG, which was supposed to mean the Studies and Observation Group, but more like the Special Operations Group. The SOG was an independent organization that answered directly to a top-secret section of the Joint Chiefs of Staff. These fuckers issued directives to be carried out by special teams whose members could come from all branches of the armed forces and the CIA, and could work 'over the fence', which was their fucking term for cross-border into Laos. I particuipated in the Phoenix program – to identify the VC infrastructure, and neutralize those considered key members. Neutralize means assassinate if you haven't guessed. This thing was so fucked up, I mean you had South Vietnamese generals and politicians branding people who owed them money, or who ran rival businesses, or whose wife they wanted, or anyone they had a personal grudge against, as Viet Cong, and we would go out and kill them.

What did I know? I was ignorant then. Until that day I had to get some guy in the village who was supposedly hiding a 105-mm for Charley. I had to kill his family to make it look like the Viet Cong. Slit a ten-year-old girl's throat and disembowel both the guy and his wife, 'cause that's what the commies did if you were a traitor. I had to practice on dummies, but it wasn't the same as when you feel their hot wet guts pouring over your hand...

"Oh Dear Lord!" Dot exclaimed, horrified at Anatoly's graphic descriptions.

...After that I was no longer an innocent. Then they gave me an assignment about some Bennie, that means Benedict Arnold, a traitor, some fucking pilot, they wouldn't tell me his name, but I found out who it was, and it ain't no one's business, except maybe his parents. I was part of a hunter-killer squad with a CIA guy, a wacko named Botkin, and a group of tribesmen. So now I was supposed to kill other Americans. Was I a soldier, or did they turn me into a murderer? I fucking showed them.

Botkin got weird on me, and so I had to carry out that mission in my own way...

The rest of the writing rambled on about other escapades that enraged Anatoly, and told of his crack up when he held an SOG Colonel hostage with a knife at his throat, demanding to be discharged from the military.

Dorothy remained in her chair and stared into space, numbed. Her son was assassinated for being a traitor? Things were getting stranger and stranger, and she was aghast at the can of worms she was opening. She couldn't swallow this. Still, it troubled her; the reticence of the Air Force authorities, the crank calls and letters, and now this vile insinuation.

She rose from her chair as if in a trance.

"What does 'sheep-dipped' mean?" she asked, walking into the kitchen, where she found Cynthia drinking tea.

"Ah, good question. It means that the documentation of who he was, where he was, and what he did, should be made nonexistent. I asked my friend to ask his friend at the DIA to check out the records of Anatoly, and sure as the Pope is Catholic, Anatoly was listed as a mechanic in the motor pool at Okinawa and remained there until his discharge. According to the Military, he was never in Vietnam or Laos."

"And what about this other man, Botkin?"

"Another mystery. Robert Botkin, a real nutjob. Went around with a shaven head. He was famous for cutting off the ears of his enemies. Supposedly went missing in Laos in 1970 and presumed dead. Never found his body. At least that's what the records show."

"What do you think Anatoly means by," Dorothy positioned her reading glasses and read from the paper, "'Botkin got weird on me, and so I had to carry out that mission in my own way'?"

"I don't know, Dot. I have no idea what he was talking about. I'm sorry."

Dorothy sat down and had a quiet cup of tea. "I think I want to be alone now," she suddenly said.

"Sure, of course." Cynthia gathered up her coat, and gave Dot a peck on the cheek. "I'll call you later."

Dorothy began to take the Jack La Lane fitness spa more seriously now. She went every day. Thirty lengths of the pool, a half hour lifting weights—doing her legs as well as her arms—not to mention the twenty minutes each on the bicycle, stair-stepping machine, and treadmill. She ached for the first two days, but the stiffness soon subsided and she felt her body growing harder and firmer along with her resolve. At home, she ate rice, raw vegetables, beans, fish, and more rice. She learned Thai recipes and tried to cook them. As for health and first aid, she had no worries there. Dorothy had been a nurse for seven years before Andrew was born, and continued later on for a few years until Bill got sick. She could look out for herself in that department, no problem. She would get the necessary shots and get a prescription for a malarial prophylactic.

Tired of being in the dark, and to ensure that no one would again take her as a fool, she went to the library in the afternoons and took out books on the MIA issue, Southeast Asian culture, the history of the war in Laos, and American foreign policy in Indochina. She decided to review her French as well, just in case she needed it.

She was preparing herself. Her goal was that she should be ready in three months. What had started as an embryonic stirring, rapidly developed into a decision so right, so obvious and clear, so inescapable.

She was going to Laos to find out the truth about what happened to her son.

At first Cynthia was incredulous. Once again, they were sitting in the Kozeny living room when Dorothy made her announcement.

"Are you serious?" Cindy gasped out, nearly spilling her coffee.

"I've never been more serious in my life."

"Hurray for you!" Cindy cheered. "It's been done before. By 1973 at least three wives of MIA pilots had gone to Laos in search of their husbands, and that was just after the war."

She then related the story of the undaunted Marian Shelton, who, being denied an entry permit, bribed a boatman to take her across the Mekong and stayed in Laos for nearly two months looking for her husband.

"There have been many more since. None of them were ever successful though. But that's no reason to be dismayed. I'll go with you."

"No," Dorothy refused. "It would be easier to keep a low profile if only one person went." For some reason, call it instinct, or a keen sense of judgment, Dorothy couldn't trust Cynthia to remain low-keyed on this assignment. Her job and her personality were just too extraverted for her to remain hushed about it all. "Since it's my decision," she tried to justify, "I should be the one to go."

Cynthia reluctantly agreed, and then informed Dot of yet another layer in the quagmire of military bureaucracy called the Joint Casualty Resolution Center. The DIA, she said, were only analysts who processed and managed information on behalf of the JCRC, whom they had to answer to. In other words, the JCRC were the real implementers of any action to be taken. Dorothy could go over the heads of the DIA and approach their boss, the JCRC, who had a branch office in Bangkok, under the name 'stony Beach Unit'. They should be the first people she should contact before doing anything else. There was an outside chance, albeit unlikely, that they would assist her.

Cynthia went on to proffer more advice. There was an American embassy in Vientiane, the Lao capital, but it was staffed only at the chargé d'affaires level. There had been no ambassador since 1975. Cynthia cautioned that the Lao Government, after the communists took over, became an authoritarian regime, overzealous after their victory, and that there was trouble with the Hmong hill tribe and other rightists that had fought against them. Even at present, 1990, incidents still occur, now reported as banditry.

"Since 1986 there's been considerable moderation," she continued, "and I hear it's generally peaceful. But Laos is still a closed and secretive country. Tourist visas are possible to get, but not an easy process. They take a long time and allow only a limited stay. What I suggest is that you make contact with someone in Bangkok."

"Can I not get a visa here, before I go?"

"Well, if you want to do it the official way, it might take forever, or may even be denied. Believe me, I know how these things work. You need local help. Besides, you have to go to Bangkok anyway. As of yet, there are no commercial flights from here to Vientiane, the Laotian capital. Hell, I don't think they have an international airport that can land a big jet like a 747, or even a DC10."

"So I go to Thailand first?"

"Yes. When you get there, arrange a way for us to communicate, either through fax or telephone. I'll also try to prepare some info on US plane crashes in Laos before you go. Don't worry, you'll make out okay."

Dorothy made an airline booking to Bangkok through a travel agent recommended by Cynthia. She was to travel on Northwest Airlines, stopping in Tokyo in five weeks time. In the meantime, she continued with her groundwork.

What she found the most difficult to deal with was learning about the history of events leading to the war that claimed her son. At first she was flabbergasted to discover that the US involvement in Southeast Asia actually began in Laos, nearly a decade before the Vietnam War, with very few Americans aware of what was going on. Worse still, the events that followed were incredibly confusing and irrational: a political soap opera, which, in large part, was fomented by bitter rivalries among the various branches of the US government. At times she actually became infuriated during the course of her research.

And of course she had to affirm everything through more conversations with Cynthia. There was mention of the Domino Theory, and the backing of competing political leaders by the Defense Department, the CIA and the State Department, each agency supporting their own candidate, which made Cynthia equate US foreign policy to a football pool. There were two conventions held in Geneva, where everyone agreed on things, but went on doing what they wanted anyway, namely fighting. But as confusing as the unfolding chronicle was, the end result was clear.

After nine years, seven billion dollars, three and a half million tons of bombs, a half million dead, and 750,000 homeless, the US had failed to achieve any of the objectives it had aimed for.

Politics, War, Football, or Dominoes, it was all the same to Dorothy.

Andrew had died for nothing.

Chapter 3

Laos 1969

"Why? Why? I don't even know where America is!"
Lao peasant woman who lost her family and home in the
bombing of the Plain of Jars, 1969

The goddamn parachute would not do what he wanted it to do. The
downdraft was too strong, blowing him across the valley, despite his
desperate, feverish efforts to fight against it. He continued to
struggle, knowing that he needed to land near the mountains. From
the air he had seen the strobe lights at the top of the peaks, flashing
signals that the Special Guerilla Units used to identify their
positions so that they could be recognized by the bombers and not
have the shit bombed out of them, and that's where he wanted to go,
to land amongst the 'friendlies' in the hills. However, the wind was
sending him in the opposite direction.

Wafting along on a hurried breeze, he found himself admiring
the lush valley without consciously intending to. In a short while
that beauty would be bombarded, and he himself needed to get out
of the way of the 'party', but that was not to be.

He had seen his plane crash into the hillside, and now to the
south he saw the last outburst from the ordnance delivered by the
other 105s and heard the delayed, detached sounds of their blasts.
The AA guns must be wiped out by now he figured, and the
bombing squads would be cleared to follow. It would all begin in a
matter of seconds. He hoped to God someone had seen his chute.

As the ground rushed up to meet him, he noticed that the area he
was about to land in was considerably populated, adding to his
already profound consternation. He looked down upon people
tearing out of their huts and houses, while others were running from
their fields, scrambling from all directions. It was obvious they

knew what was about to take place.

The wind let up, allowing him to drop more swiftly. After making some last-minute corrections to avoid a stand of trees, he came down with a thump in the midst of a raucous, fleeing mob. He struggled frantically with his chute, disentangling himself from the harness, but the villagers were too busy gathering up their children and coaxing the elderly to give him any notice. For lack of a better plan, he ran with them in the same direction.

It was only seconds later that the maddening chaos began. The first planes streaked in with piercing wails and dropped their CBUs—cluster bombs that opened a short distance above the ground and released hundreds of bomblets that fragmented like grenades. Andrew dove to the ground as the air filled with whizzing pieces of sharp metal, ruthlessly ripping through anything in their path. He heard shrieking, howling, and yelling, a continuous clamoring everywhere. But the most strident, dreadful sound was the screaming of the children.

Scores of people were cut down, riddled by the flying steel splinters. Some of the bomblets didn't explode right away and lay on the ground like brightly colored tennis balls, waiting to be touched. Andrew, quickly picking himself up, had to look carefully down at the ground as he resumed his running, while some of the fleeing were, unfortunately, not so attentive, and ended up as legless torsos catapulting into the air, driven by the upward force of shrapnel.

For a split second he could pick out the roar of more jets, then, an instant later, thunderous explosions shattered the air—they were going in now with the 750 pounders to destroy the village.

All hell broke loose. His head rang from the earsplitting concussions, until he completely lost all sense of hearing. Without the background of sound, everything before him appeared as absurd hallucinatory images, all moving in slow motion; human forms running helter-skelter, frenzied shadows stamping about, while all around them were bright orange flames and billowing black smoke. "Oh dear Jesus! Oh dear God!" he found himself crying as he ran, while terror made his bladder empty uncontrollably.

Running with the crowd, he now saw the destination everyone was heading for—dugout holes in the forest at the edge of the village. In the midst of his flight, crossing the path in front of him was a little girl, seven or eight years old, who ran about haphazardly, screaming hysterically for her mother. Andrew quickly snatched her up, glancing desperately for the nearest hole. The pits were funnel-shaped and lead into man-made caverns carved out of the earth. He headed towards one, clutching the girl firmly like a frightened kid clinging to a rag doll, then broke in mid-stride as he saw the searing white flash of a phosphorous bomb streaking towards them. He could feel the heat of its flames as he swiftly reversed his direction, hearing a whoomph behind him as the incendiary bomb took the oxygen out of the air. The napalm let loose a sea of fire which encircled them, spreading like the fires of hell, cutting off the village flanks and enveloping a hapless few in a fatal, torrid inferno. Clothes caught on fire and burned on their bodies as Andrew slung the bewildered girl over his shoulder and ran deeper into the forest, where the napalm canisters would get caught in the trees and merely burn the canopy. Finding another hole, he crawled frenetically on his knees, wriggling himself and the girl inside with an urgency summoned by self-preservation. The hole was already full of people, six or seven of them, huddled in submissive fright at the walloping sounds of destruction above them.

Inside the underground shelter, a murky glow illuminated the face of a wailing woman, her eyes compressed shut, her mouth blubbering tearful prayers, the bloody body of a boy in her arms. The kid's leg had been blown off below the knee, the remaining stump hastily tied up with what must have been his shirt. The boy gave out little moans as she rocked him back and forth. The rest of them stared at Andrew in shocked silence, while the little girl hung onto him tenaciously, her nails piercing his skin, as she continued her ranting. A woman offered out her arms to take her and Andrew dutifully handed the child over, and to his relief, this mollified her howling, which to him was even more terrifying than the booming of the bombs.

In the endless moments that followed, cowering in this dark, damp pit with these simple peasants, he felt a crushing shame clenching him, mortified that he was actually a part of what was happening to them. Though their faces showed no rancor, only fright, he couldn't bear to look at them. The woman continued to sob over her son, as Andrew cradled his head in his arms, smelling the stench of his own piss that had wet his pants.

The bombing was over in fifteen minutes, but it could as well have been an eternity. After waiting what seemed to be a prudent interval of unnatural calm, one of the old men crawled out, followed by the others. An elderly woman turned to Andrew and told him, "*Bai, bai*! Go!" Although he couldn't hear her voice, he understood enough to leave the hole.

Outside, the destruction of the village was total. The timber and bamboo houses were burnt and smoldering; the brick houses were empty shells, ghostly and roofless. The villagers looked at what were once their homes, and cried. Others called desperately for missing loved ones. Andrew stumbled around aimlessly, until, out of a morbid curiosity, he peeked in the hole that he had originally wanted to enter. The hole stank of cooked meat; the smoking bodies were piled on top of each other. They had, in all probability, had the air sucked out of them and died of asphyxiation before the heat of the napalm had baked their corpses.

He continued to walk around in a daze amidst the smoke of the devastation, which clung low to the ground like a fog of death. The air was filled with the acrid smells of charred flesh and vegetation, and a scene of surreal horror prevailed. Bomb craters, twenty feet wide and six feet deep, with dirt heaped up along the rims, pockmarked the scorched earth, still steaming from the heat of the blasts. Bodies were strewn here and there, reduced to barely recognizable pieces of debris.

Until that moment, the only dead body Andrew had ever seen

was the corpse of his grandfather, lying like a wax dummy in artificial repose in an ornate coffin.

He halted his groggy ambling, abruptly horrified. On the ground in front of him, a beautiful girl, the hibiscus flower pinned in her hair the same color as her blood, lay torn apart with her exposed entrails giving off little vapors of steam, and upon which a swarming black mass of flies had already gathered to feast. She was still alive, her eyes bulging with terror, and panting heavily in short, quick breaths: frantic, desperate breaths of the dying. Then, all at once, her rapid heaving ceased and her eyes glazed. Andrew, numb with shock at this sight, crouched down and, without knowing why, carefully removed the flower from her hair and held it in front of him. Gazing at it catatonically, he dropped to his haunches and sat on the ground, stupefied. He covered his face and began to sob.

He couldn't recall how long he had been sitting this way, with his hands covering his face, still holding the flower between his fingers, rocking himself and crying like a baby, wishing it wasn't happening, wishing it had never happened, that it was only a terrible dream that would go away, when he was prodded urgently from behind with a rifle butt. Looking up, he saw short thickset soldiers in camouflage khakis and green berets surrounding him.

"Tahaan Vang Pao! Vang Pao's army!" one of them shouted in the Lao language. To Andrew, his voice sounded like it came from very far away. Two of the others lifted him up by the armpits. *"Bai! Bai!"*

As Andrew got to his feet, he saw that the suffering wasn't yet over for the villagers. These soldiers were the Special Guerilla Units, the Hmong army formed by the CIA, who had come in to mop up, and as they rounded up the lowland Lao, there was a great deal of kicking and beating, women screaming and men yelling. Most of the confrontations revolved around the soldiers pillaging what little remained of the victim's personal possessions, with those protesting being severely dealt with. Some young girls were dragged off crying; for an intention that was all too obvious. All the rest were being herded together at gunpoint, being readied for a forced evacuation. The madness he had experienced wasn't finished, only taking on a new form.

These armed men were the 'friendlies' and were there to rescue him, yet why did he feel like a traitor, as if he were abandoning the mass of people who were now being pushed and shoved into orderly groups? Were they the enemy?

There was no enemy here. Maybe five miles south, where those guns were. Or were the guns here merely to protect the village? If there had been any troops in the vicinity, they would have fled deep inside the forest long before the attack. Of course, the mission planners knew that, didn't they? This was just punishment. A lesson to be taught. Leave your homes now, or else. Abandon the only lives you ever knew, or suffer the consequences.

Cindy, thousands of miles away, had known more than he had, despite the fact that he was right in the middle of it, helping to make it happen.

His rescuers urged him on. "*Bai, Bai,*" said the same guy as before. Then he said, "too many danger," an attempt at English, to drive home the gravity of Andrew's predicament. It was almost a certainty that the enemy had seen him bailing out, and despite the bombing, this was still a contested area not yet securely held by either side. The CIA army had orders to get pilots out of the area as fast as possible. Meanwhile, Andrew instinctively grabbed for his portable radio-beeper, and noticed it was gone, dropped somewhere in the debris of the wrecked village. Without these Hmong soldiers, he would have been up shit's creek without a paddle.

They struck out in a northerly direction, while the villagers, in the company of the majority of the other soldiers, were being led south, presumably to a refugee camp at Sam Thong, or Long Chieng, in areas controlled by US-backed forces.

There were eight of them escorting him, leading him toward the mountains that he had originally wanted to get to when he was drifting with his parachute. Three of the eight were only boys, barely ten or eleven years old. He had heard about the child soldiers in Vang Pao's army, and now he was seeing it with his own eyes. The ridiculously oversized uniforms hung loosely over their small bodies like flowing robes, practically hiding their hands and feet, while the butts of their M-1 Carbines, slung casually over their shoulders, nearly scraped the ground as they walked.

The guy who had first spoken to Andrew, and who seemed to know a bit of Lao and English, carried a PRC-25 radio in a pack on his back. He, along with the rest, set a fast pace, for the Hmong knew the jungle, how to avoid the enemy, and exactly which way was safe.

Over creeks and through the forest, they were making for the broad shelf that skirted the peaks, walking for nearly two hours. In the jungle, the trees were huge fluted columns, barren of branches, rising to a roof of foliage, a canopy that exploded into a vast layer of leaves that blocked the sun, only permitting a soft green light to filter through.

They were advancing straight up towards the peak, not deviating to follow the contours, but choosing the path of least distance rather than least resistance. As they got higher, they began climbing along flinty paths, stumbling over stones and tree roots, then picking themselves up again. Soon they were traversing an even trail, and the only sound in the silence of the mountain jungle was the crunching of their footsteps on the thick gravel.

Andrew was finding it harder and harder to keep up. He wasn't paying enough attention to where he was walking, causing the man behind to continually bump into him. Although he had recovered emotionally, his mind was still fixated on the horrors of the bombing he had just witnessed: the scenes of anguish in the hole with the villagers, and outside as they lamented their loss. He could still see the girl with the hibiscus flower in her hair and the pile of cooked bodies. He could still hear the children screaming.

He did that. He and his fellow pilots. But he had never considered himself, nor his fellow pilots, capable of unleashing such terrible suffering; all the guys in the squadron were ordinary, good-natured, conscientious young men, not sadistic butchers who relished bloodshed. For all of them, waging battle involved controlling an incredibly sophisticated aircraft, pushing buttons and pulling levers to release ordnance on people that they didn't have to see, making war a cold and distant technical undertaking, divorced from the consequences of their actions, stripped of malevolence or hostility, with no subsequent pricks of guilt. But today, by a freakish twist of fate, he himself had experienced it from below, looked upon the victims, and witnessed the result.

When the troupe got to a flat clearing on top of one of the smaller hills, the soldier with the radio powered it on and began talking in Hmong language, jolting Andrew from his pensiveness. He was communicating with a 'Raven', a low altitude Forward Air Controller. There was typically a Hmong in the back seat of the FAC who could interpret the messages from the ground patrols to the American pilots flying these small planes. Sure enough, within minutes, a single engine Cessna buzzed overhead, appearing in a daringly low run just above the trees, and then came back again and dipped his wing in a sign of recognition. The Raven had pinpointed them, and ten minutes later the FAC was guiding in a chopper, an H-134, a Jolly Green Giant, which waddled in like a flying hippo, its rotor making loud whopping noises and blowing dry air in their faces. As the thing landed, the Hmong helped Andrew in, and the helicopter took off as abruptly as it had come down. By calling in the chopper, these diminutive mountain men had just risked their own lives to rescue him, for the North Vietnamese troops and the Pathet Lao now knew their location, and the Hmong would have to hightail it out of there to avoid a firefight. Somehow, still reeling from what happened down on the plain, Andrew could not manage to feel grateful.

The chopper pilot turned around to Andrew, who was squatting on the floor, as there were no seats in this rig. "MAN, YOU SURE ARE

LUCKY!" he shouted to him.

"WHERE'RE WE HEADING?" Andrew shouted back over the loud throbbing of the rotors. His hearing had returned almost to normal, except for a persistent ringing.

"Lima 32! Bouam Loung!"

"We're heading north, behind enemy lines!" Andrew hollered.

"That's right!" the pilot yelled back, craning his neck to half face Andrew. "Lima 32 is currently our northernmost position. It's where we conduct search and rescue operations, ever since we lost Na Khang. There it is, right there," he pointed.

They were coming into a five-thousand-foot high, bowl-like valley wedged among a ring of peaks, with small lakes near the edges. It was odd, the lakes, considering the rainy season hadn't yet gotten underway, so there had to be springs. On some of the passes between the peaks at the edge of the bowl, Andrew could make out heavily fortified positions, complete with sandbags and trenches. Near the camp was a landing strip with two more choppers and a Helio Courier airplane parked at one end.

The helicopter landed in a swirl of dust. A tall, lanky young man, presumably another American, and about the same age as Andrew, ran gawkily out to greet them, his left hand occupied in holding down the large cowboy hat on his head so that it wouldn't blow off. He was sporting a flowery Hawaiian shirt and pre-bleached hippy style dungarees, attire that seemed to flout the dire reality of the war that raged around them.

"Welcome to the 'Fortress'!" he hailed. "I'm Mr. Magoo." He tipped his hat in a pretentious imitation of a cowboy.

He was a red-haired fellow, with a reddish beard that matched his hair and a pink skin dotted faintly with freckles, his blue eyes sparkling with excitement, giving his face a bright and cheery demeanor. Consistent with this, his mannerisms reflected an overabundance of enthusiasm.

Mr. Magoo, what childishness! A spook, Andrew realized. A CIA paramilitary advisor; 'Sky Men', as they were known to the Hmong.

And the chopper belonged to Air America.

Andrew felt like giving him some stupid codename back, just to be sarcastic, but it was not in his nature. "Andy," he said, accepting the CIA man's handshake, and noticing his Seiko watch. In Laos, all Americans working in covert operations, particularly SKY advisors, wore expensive Seiko's. "you're CIA, right?"

"I'm with CAS," the American corrected. CAS stood for Controlled American Source, whatever that meant, and it was the cover name for the CIA in Laos. More infantile charades, thought Andrew, as if nobody knew who they were.

"Let's go!"

Following his host, he noted the collection of prefabricated metal Quonset huts, arranged around a towering antenna. What the hell was such a big antenna doing here? This place had to be more than a staging area for Aerial Re-Supply and Search and Rescue. It must be a communications center. A listening post?

In fact, Buoam Loung was an intercept facility, monitoring broadcasts from Hanoi and beaming them via a National Security Agency satellite hookup to Washington.

"How do you like our little Meos?" Mr. Magoo cajoled. Meo was a derogatory Chinese name for the Hmong, which their leader, Vang Pao, had repeatedly requested to the CIA that they not be addressed as.

Andrew gave no answer.

"Saved your ass pronto, before anyone knew you were gone. Not even half a day." Magoo seemed determined to elicit a word of praise from the rescued airman.

"Got here in about three hours," Andrew confirmed laconically as they stopped outside one of the huts.

"Hey, you hungry? I could boil up a few hot dogs. We got some time while the chopper refuels," he suggested, removing his hat and slouching his way into the hut.

"Yeah, sure," Andrew replied atonally. But food was the last thing on his mind. He as yet couldn't wrench his thoughts away from the slaughter in the valley.

They sat inside the airless metal hut on a mat laid on the earthen floor, Mr. Magoo chomping on hot dogs and washing it down with beer, while Andrew listened with disinterest to his life story.

"My real name is Arthur Jinkweiler, and I was a smoke-jumper for the Forest Service when the CIA recruited me as a 'kicker' for Air America. You know what a 'kicker' is?"

"I've heard the term before."

"A kicker shoves cargo out of an airborne plane. You have to wear a harness so you don't fall out along with the load. After two years of that, they picked me to attend paramilitary training and counterinsurgency school on the 'Farm' in Virginia. Got reassigned here to Lima Site 32. And here I am."

Andrew didn't touch his hot dog. "You sound like you're happy to be here."

"Shit, yeah, what a fucking adventure. What some people always dream of."

Dream of? Who the hell dreams of death and destruction?

"Not like you flyboys," Jinkweiler continued, "who hot-rod in the air for an hour or so and then back to base. No offense," he apologized belatedly, awkwardly remembering that Andrew had just been shot out of the sky. "I know it can get hairy with those AA guns and SAMS. But down here on the ground you really get to see what the war is all about, ringside seats. And the Meos, they fucking worship us. They love Americans. You really see what it's all about," he repeated.

"And what then, is this war all about?"

Jinkweiler took that question as it was, rhetorical and confrontational, and responded with equal derision. "Well, if you don't know Andy, maybe you better head off to the library and take out a few books."

Ignoring that, Andrew answered his own question. "Strategically speaking, our goal is to drive out the North Vietnamese army and the Lao communists. But I've just come out of a village that was bombed to smithereens and there was no sign of any enemy troops."

"They hide and use the villagers as cover. And the villagers support them. No villagers, no cover, no support. Simple as that."

Andrew wondered if Jinkweiler would have still taken that view, had he seen what he himself had just witnessed. Perhaps he would have, perhaps he would have still insisted on the legitimacy of such cold, hard, military reasoning. Perhaps it really was different on the ground, easier to lose one's humanity.

"What's up with you anyway? Found a Lao girlfriend while you were down there?" he quipped, pointing to the hibiscus flower in the breast pocket of Andrew's flight suit.

Andrew felt like telling him to fuck off, but at that moment their attention was diverted by the sound of an aircraft approaching.

"Hey, just in time for the show." Mr. Magoo jumped up and exited the Quonset, striding briskly towards the C-47 that had just rolled in on the dirt strip. Andrew had emerged along with him, but chose to remain close to the hut. The plane taxied a short way and came to a halt, after which the cabin door swung open and the pilot, also dressed in 'civvies', jumped sprightly down on the ground. Magoo greeted the pilot with an overindulging eagerness as a group of Hmong set about busily loading pallets of cargo through the plane's rear end, the engines still idling.

Fifteen minutes later, as the plane was taking off, Magoo came back with a pair of binoculars hanging from his neck.

"See that ridge out there?" he indicated, pointing to a long massif of rounded, lavender peaks that formed the skyline. "That's Pu San. We've got four firebases there with 105-mm cannons. Gonna make an air drop of ammo."

Magoo stood with the binoculars fixed into his face, apparently delighting in this activity. It seemed to be just a game to him. A short time passed as they stood in the sun. When the plane reached the ridge, it dropped parcels attached to parachutes that opened out like flowers.

"Right on target," Magoo said, looking through the binoculars, a big grin stretching across his face.

The helicopter pilot called, signaling it was time to go. Much to his disappointment, however, Andrew was informed that he would be dropped off at Long Chieng, where he would catch an Air America flight back to Udon.

Long Chieng. Shit! The last thing he needed right now was to be around more CIA cowboys.

Nestled in the clouds, nearly a mile high, smack dab in the middle of the Laotian jungle, was Long Chieng. Surrounded by formidable mountains, the settlement itself was dotted with one-story buildings and indistinguishable shacks. The most prominent feature was a runway, almost a mile long, forming a central artery to which every-thing else was built around. It terminated abruptly at the foot of an immense wall of limestone. A serrated ridge to the east formed a natural fortification.

Long Chieng was the forward staging area for the CIA's 'secret war' and it bustled with military activity. The CIA section of town, a jumbled collection of cabins and sheds, was marked by a forest of aerials and antennae. The town's population, in 1969 estimated to be over 40,000, was nearly all comprised of refugees. They lived in shacks hastily fabricated from flattened fuel drums and burlap sacks that once held USAID supplied rice. All of the occupants bore the faces of war, and among them were amputees hobbling about on the tree branches they used for crutches. Others were housed in tin barracks, the insides of which were filled with a double row of beds placed head to head down the center, leaving a narrow aisle down each side. The refugees strung the little baggage they had over their beds with the mosquito netting. They had to cook where they slept, so everything was darkened with charcoal smoke. There were no toilets.

These were the things that fate had Andrew see as he walked around waiting for his plane ride back to his base in Thailand. He saw war. He didn't see glory, or honor, only depravation. Images so graphic they seemed to belie reality, not the least of which were the scores of small children with vacant eyes caked with pus, too weak to utter anything other than muffled moans. A mother, whose teats hung like empty leather sacks, could not pacify her infant daughter, a wraithlike creature posing as a symbol of starvation. An ambiance of apocalyptic gloom, miserable and debased, bore down on all the hapless wretches who had been brought here.

He wondered when those people in the village that had just been bombed would arrive to join this multitude of human suffering. The boy that had gotten his leg blown off, if he was fortunate enough, would probably die before then.

All of this was a bit too much for Andrew to take, and it only served to hasten the psychological and emotional transformation that was already taking place. At 1800 hrs, he finally climbed aboard his Air America flight and left Long Chieng. He reached Udon Thani Royal Thai Air Force Base in the early evening. Fifteen hours had elapsed since he had taken off from there that dawn.

Fifteen hours that had changed his life forever.

Chapter 4

Thailand 1990

"Risk! Risk anything! Care no more for the opinions of others, for those voices. Do the hardest thing on earth for you. Act for yourself. Face the truth."

Katherine Mansfield, author, 1927

There had been only two occasions in her life when Dorothy Kozeny had dared to venture out of the familiar bounds of Ohio. The first time was when she and Bill went to California to treat their son Andrew, then eight years old, to a trip to Disneyland. The other outing was to celebrate their second honeymoon—their 25th anniversary—when they had taken a cruise to Bermuda.

However, this time was entirely different. She was alone, crossing the ocean to a foreign country, and she wasn't going for a holiday. Nor was she traveling on business. Once she found herself actually on her way, the determination that had previously driven her began to wither. In fact, she didn't really understand why she was going at all, quibbling to herself that this was a trip that had no rational basis; nothing more than an inane act of impulse, and it would end up producing nothing but heartache.

Throughout the twenty odd hours in the air and including the one-hour wait at Chicago, the two-hour wait at LA, the four-hour wait at Tokyo Airport, and up to the five-hour flight to her final destination, she struggled to numb her mind and quell her uncertainty. During her weakest moments of self-doubt she had read her notes and Andrew's letters that Cynthia had given back to her. Now, at 4:30 in the morning at Don Muang Airport, Bangkok, she was nervous as she stood in the queue for immigration control. The arrival terminal was ultramodern and affluent, yet it intimidated her: a series of capacious corridors, with acoustics that smothered the harshest outburst to a distant whisper, and with a surreal aura that seemed designed to swallow up its occupants. She lined up waiting her turn in the silent, neon-lit expanse, fearing all sorts of questions. When it came time for her to face the man in the booth, she found that, to her pleasant surprise, the process was quick and efficient: as she was an American, she didn't require a visa. Her spirits immediately lightened as he stamped her passport with a perfunctory air. She proceeded blithely to the baggage claim and discovered her backpack and duffel bag already circulating on the conveyor belt, waiting for her to retrieve them. Within ten minutes, she found herself out of the domain of an aloof customs officer and through the exit doors to the terminal lobby.

It was all happening so fast. She was half a world away from home, in Thailand! A few months ago she never would have believed it.

She approached the Tourist Service desk in the airport lobby exactly as the travel agency had instructed her to do. At the fluorescently bright tourist office, the young oriental man behind the counter was all smiles. "Wercome to Thairand. You want hoten?"

"I have a reservation, they told me Park Hotel?"

"Name, madam?"

"Maybe I better write it out," she suggested. With pen and paper given to her, she proceeded to do just that.

The young man's lustrous black hair gleamed in the artificial light as he bent his head behind the counter trying to find her reservation documents.

"Oh yes, Mrs. Gosini," the clerk announced. "Here you are," he said, handing her an envelope with a ticket in it. "And tomorrow you have a car the whole morning with pretty girl travel guide."

A man from out of nowhere suddenly appeared at her side, and Dorothy was urged by the clerk to follow him. She was led to the bureau de change and promptly changed $300, and was then spirited outside into pre-dawn darkness, where she was bluntly assailed by a dense and sticky heat. The warm, humid, thickly scented air reaffirmed that she was indeed in a tropical country, twelve time zones away from Camden, Ohio.

Before she knew it, she was in a taxi on a six-lane expressway. The driver was silent the whole trip, and Dorothy mistook his reticence as oriental propriety, but the fact was, the driver knew very little English. Once off the expressway, it seemed like ages traveling through dark and narrow back streets, although some of the places they passed were brightly lit with what appeared to be flashing Christmas type lights.

When she finally arrived at the hotel, she struggled through her fatigue to fill out the registration card, then followed the bellboy to her room, fumbled for a tip, hurriedly undressed, and after a brief phone call to Cynthia to say she had arrived safely, collapsed on the bed totally drained.

At 7:30 in the morning, after only two hours of sleep, the phone rang in her hotel room and woke her up. She grabbed the phone out of an instinctive impulse to stop the maddening tinkle, and holding the receiver, pondered on where she was. "Hel...hello?"

"Your car is leddy, madam."

"Car?" she mumbled. Dorothy was still bewildered. "Well, I'm afraid they'll have to wait, I just woke up," she complained in a cracked and hoarse voice.

"No plobrem, they wait you."

In spite of her grogginess, she got up and forced herself to take a cold shower, which was refreshing enough, but after that her crisis started. What to wear? She knew that she had to be well presented for her meeting today, yet she also knew the climate was against her. In the end, she opted for a floral summer dress she used to wear at the barbeques Bill's company hosted every July 4th. After having a quick to-do with her makeup, she made sure she had her keys, wallet and pocketbook, then quickly exited the room and caught the elevator.

Downstairs in the lobby, a dainty girl bedecked with a chaotic swab of perm-curled, auburn hair, posed as if she were waiting for someone. She had on a prim white blouse and fashionable black slacks. Spotting Dorothy emerging from the elevator, she moved away from the reception counter. Must be the guide, Dorothy presumed. As the girl drew closer, Dorothy took quick note of her wide, agreeable mouth, embellished with a flaming red lipstick that clashed against the dark, tawny-bronze complexion of her face. Only her high cheekbones indicated an Oriental origin. Notwithstanding the copper-colored, wavy hair, she more-or-less resembled a fashion-conscious Cherokee squaw wearing an expensive wig. Not at all what she expected a Thai girl to look like. She was short, yet, in contrast to her diminutive size, she was carrying a rather large leather handbag that hung from her shoulders and seemed to contain everything but the kitchen sink.

"Mrs. Ko-zany?"

Dorothy was surprised at how close the girl was to correctly pronouncing her name. "Yes, that's me."

"Welcome to Thailand." She then made a gesture that involved bowing her head and putting her palms together as if in a graceful motion of prayer. "Have you had breakfast?" she asked, looking back up at Dorothy.

"No, I haven't had time, but it's okay. I'm not hungry just yet."

"Okay, we can go then." Her English, barring a bouncy lilting accent, appeared rather good. Dorothy followed her outside.

It was already hot and muggy at 8:00 in the morning; the side street in front of the hotel was aglow with flaxen sunshine. As they got into the car, the girl guide in the front, she in the back, Dorothy announced, "American Embassy, please."

"You're very funny," the girl commented rather directly. "Typical American. You just got here and want to go right away to your Embassy. you're not interested in the tour?"

"Ah yes, I'm..." Dorothy stuttered. She didn't recall anything about a tour. She thought she could go wherever she wanted, and she wanted to go to the Embassy. "I have business at the Embassy," she explained succinctly. "I was to contact them when I arrived."

That seemed to pacify the pretty guide somewhat, though not completely. "*San-tan-toot amerika,*" she tersely announced to the driver.

Dorothy was stupefied at the frenzied vitality of the city, not only the hustle and bustle going on around her at street level, but at the hubbub emanating from the concrete elevated highways, supported by great pillars, and which blocked out the sky above them.

The taxi was soon swept up into a rabble of countless cars, and an even greater number of motorcycles of all types from Harleys to Hondas, which made a racket that sounded like a swarm of angry wasps. As the traffic came to a standstill, the first of many bottlenecks they were to encounter, the motorcycles would weave in and out between the immobile cars.

When the traffic began to flow again, the taxi driver bullied his way through the maelstrom, causing Dorothy to catch her breath as he fought to carve a space for himself, alert to any opportunity and ready to do battle over the minutest measure of headway. It was apparent that cutting people off wasn't merely expected behavior, but was an obligatory rule of the game. Dorothy took to staring out the side window to calm her jumpiness.

As she looked at the signs and the marquees of the shops, she remarked to the guide about something that she had noticed as soon as she had arrived at the airport the night before. "Thai writing looks like Arabic, or Indian."

"Yes, it comes from Sanskrit," the guide replied, thinking her answer was adequate.

"Is that Arabic or Indian?" Dorothy wasn't sure.

"Indian."

An advertising board on the side of a red city bus struck Dorothy's attention, probably because there were actually some words written in English. It promoted a deodorant for motorcycle helmets. 'HELMET FRESHENER, THE SPRAY THAT REMOVES STINKs'.

Soon, they ended up cruising along one of the elevated highways, where the view was a vista of high-rise buildings of striking contemporary architecture, their tinted glass beaming in the morning sun. They didn't form anything at all like a skyline; rather they were dispersed, clustered here and there without rhyme or reason, like isolated icebergs in a frozen seascape. A number of them were still undergoing construction, distinguished by naked girders and columns and mounted with huge derricks.

Dorothy was ignored for the time being and it wasn't until they were cruising along Wireless Road that the driver said something to the girl that involved their foreign passenger. Turning, she addressed Dorothy. "Which side?"

"Huh?"

"There are three parts of the embassy; one is on the opposite side of the road."

The 'road' was actually a four-lane avenue with an impassable concrete barrier dividing the comings and goings.

"I don't know. I've never been here before."

Luckily, they made the correct choice of the biggest building of the three. Dorothy alighted from the car and went through a security check at a concrete booth by the gate, where they confirmed her appointment with a Major Hackwell via an interoffice telephone. They gave her a visitor's badge, and told her to fill in the details of her appointment in a ledger-type book, before proceeding to the main building.

Entering the office block, she found herself in a tiny lobby where a Marine behind bulletproof glass asked her what she wanted.

"I have an appointment with Major Hackwell of the Stony Beach Unit."

Two other marines searched her and her bag, then made her walk through a metal detector before she was allowed into a small, clinical-looking waiting room.

Dorothy was flipping through a TIME magazine when Major Hackwell came to receive her. Despite his title of Major, he was dressed as a civilian in a dark blue suit. Medium height and well-built, with salt-and-pepper hair, he was a handsome man, around the same age Andy would have been. She wondered if he had served in the Vietnam War. His eyes were cold, however, and his features too severely square-set for her liking.

"Pleasant flight?" he asked her perfunctorily.

"Yes, considering I slept on the plane. It was a long trip."

Hackwell didn't acknowledge her reply. When both were alone in the elevator, he stood with an unfocused gaze at the elevator doors without anything else to say. His offhand manner bordered on premeditated rudeness, making Dorothy nervous. She had gone over her notes time and time again, and now she was hoping she was at last ready to confront government officials without looking like an idiot.

Once in the office, a red carpeted room with the antiseptic décor typical of bureaucracy, she was led to a plush black leather couch, as Hackwell took his seat in a similar chair on the other side of a plain coffee table made of metal and glass. Dorothy accepted the ritual offer of coffee, then fumbled in her pocketbook for her reading glasses and her papers. She perched the tortoiseshell spectacles on her nose whilst she was being lectured to.

"We don't encourage people to come out here looking for their lost loved ones. The government and the military are fully aware of the problem, and we have committed the resources to address it," he preached in the didactic tone of an embassy official. "If you've been reading the newspapers and following the news, you should know the effort we are putting into recovering all relevant information concerning our MIAs. But don't believe any of that nonsense about POW camps still operating in Laos. We have absolutely no indication, not even one tiny shred of evidence. Our intelligence out here is excellent, and you should also realize that we have satellites that can…"

"Yes, I know—that can 'determine the color of a dog's droppings'—Ray Mitzner, Warfare Technology, November 1989,"

Dorothy cited, reading from a slip of paper.

"Excuse me?"

Looking up, she told him, "But I am not expecting to find my son alive in an imagined POW camp. However, I do have the right to know the truth about what happened to him, and no one seems to want to tell me."

"Ah, yes," Hackwell said, recovering after being somewhat disoriented by Dorothy's style. "As for your son, we contacted the Defense Intelligence Agency and they say your son was killed, and that you were given documents that testify to those findings. I realize there was a mix-up concerning his remains..."

"Is that what you consider it, a mix-up?"

"I'm sorry, I don't mean to be so cold. But you have to understand, there were 8,000 unaccounted-for US soldiers in the Korean War, 80,000 in World War II, and in the Indochina theater itself, 300,000 Vietnamese are still missing compared to only 2000 or so of our boys."

The military usage of the word 'theater' didn't slip by Dorothy unnoticed, as if war was a play, a film, an entertaining show put on for military leaders. All in all, it sounded like a rehearsed spiel.

"I do understand, Major Hackwell," she assured him, "but I am afraid I disagree with the findings, particularly the location of where my son was shot down. Andrew wrote to me about the bombing he was doing in northern Laos," she lied.

Hackwell brought his arms against his chest, and clasped his hands to support his chin in a deprecatory manner. "Well, even if you assume that he went down over Laos, you would then have to consider the immensity of the problem. Laos was in chaos at that time, and even at present, there are still no centralized records. The Pathet Lao never publicized names, and they gave out contradictory information. To make matters worse, we don't have any political or economic avenues to exert pressure on their government. You also have to understand that Laos is a rather remote place full of inhospitable terrain, and that during the war there were very few people living in those places where neither side controlled."

Yes, Dorothy thought sarcastically, they were all in refugee camps.

"Many other complications as well," continued Hackwell, now releasing his arms to stretch them to the coffee table. Despite his affected posture, he seemed nervous. "I'm sure that quite a few of the downed pilots died of injuries while lost somewhere out there. Also, there were hardships encountered in moving POWs through rough country to the Pathet Lao central control area in Sam Neua. It's very likely that some died along the way. There have also been cases where undisciplined PL troops may have executed their prisoners because they didn't want the political and logistical burden of bringing them there. Bombing as well probably destroyed many gravesites."

"Let's not forget the nature of the secret war," Dorothy put in, "which hamstrung the possible efforts at rescuing our boys. Search and Rescue was politically risky. To admit the loss of American military personnel would have exposed flagrant violations of the 1962 Geneva Accords, and make the US look culpable."

This articulate monologue she had copied directly out of a book and had subsequently memorized. She had liked the way it sounded. Now that she had delivered it, she was hoping that Hackwell would be impressed, but he wasn't.

"Huh?"

So she tried again.

"Do you believe there are some POWs still being held for intelligence reasons, that is, they possess information so valuable, like secret weapons or new technology, so that the other side didn't want to release them?"

She did better with this approach, because he gave it an answer.

"There is some speculation," he said, "that several pilots were taken to the Soviet Union, but nothing has come of it yet. As for there being POW camps still operational in Laos, that's just pure fantasy," he repeated, still suspecting that Dorothy had such a belief.

"But there were others..." he hesitated, as if unsure to continue, "who were deserters and defectors, and who have remained voluntarily."

"Is it true that hundreds of Americans were," she paused to emphasize the crude idiom, "'taken out'? So-called 'Bennies'?"

"I'm sorry but I never heard of anything like that." He was starting to get irritated, because she was being provocative now, and he didn't feel like being on the receiving end of someone else's bitterness that morning. But that wasn't the only thing that irked him. He actually sympathized with this woman, and was really annoyed at his own inability to help her. Still, he felt on the defensive. "But if any of them were a traitor, it would serve them right," he opined.

That comment had a less than calming effect on Dorothy. "Are you going to help me in getting information about what happened to my son?" she asked him directly.

"I'm afraid it's not that simple. We're a bureaucratic machine; we're not designed to respond to individual requests. I apologize for the cliché, but actually, everything does have to go through the proper channels."

Dorothy rarely got angry. She hardly ever thought swear words in her head, leave alone speak them aloud. Phony bastard, she thought, like all the others in Washington. "Our fighting boys must behave with honor, and pride, and unwavering loyalty, but apparently that requirement doesn't hold with our leaders."

"I'm sorry, Mrs. Kozeny, but I don't understand what you're talking about." For Hackwell, irritation was growing into anger. "Mrs. Kozeny, I'm very busy, so if you don't mind..."

She jumped to her feet, her glasses sliding down the bridge of her nose, threatening to fall off her face. "They gave me a cow's bones and called it my son!"

Hackwell countered her by also standing up. He didn't like anyone standing over him, much less a hysterical woman, even if she did remind him of his mother. Of course she had a right to be upset.

But his office was, nonetheless, no place for histrionics.

"I'm afraid that I have to ask you to leave this office right now."

She took off her glasses and put them back in their case. Then she took her papers and her pocket book and turned to leave.

"Oh, and Mrs. Kozeny, before you go, I must tell you that we are not in favor of any American traveling to Lao PDR looking for MIAs. We're still in the process of negotiating agreements on these things and you would not be welcome in that regard. You won't get a visa, I can assure you. Please, I'm telling you for your own good, go back home."

"Thank you, Mr. Hackwell, for your support," Dorothy said sardonically and abruptly left the room.

In the elevator, she continued fuming over the intractability of government bureaucrats. But in reality she was angry with herself. She had overdone it, trying too hard to sound like a sophisticated political analyst, trying to be like Cynthia, which she obviously was nowhere near. Maybe he would have offered some advice, or even helped her, if she hadn't acted like a nitwit. He probably was a decent man who was merely frustrated at the very bureaucracy he was a part of. It was her own fear of rejection and ridicule that had sabotaged the entire effort.

Walking out through the Embassy waiting room and into the street, she was still flustered.

"Your meeting finished already?" the guide asked, as Dorothy opened the car door and gently eased herself in, not answering.

"We still have time for the tour," the girl insisted. "It's too early now for the afternoon tour of the Grand Palace. But maybe we can first go to the Marble Temple?"

"Well, I'm really not in the mood and I'm very tired." She saw that this response was taken as an affront, so she promptly reconsidered and gave in. "Marble Temple? Sounds fine, let's go," she acceded half-heartedly. The tour would at least provide diversion enough for her to forget the embarrassing scene in the Stony Beach office.

It worked. Dorothy was fascinated as the young girl explained the origins of the Marble temple, and how the original Buddha image was brought on a large raft on the river from some place called Pitsanaloke. However, the Pitsanaloke people demanded it back, so they had to make a replica of it to put in this temple. She then went on to describe the statues which lined the halls of the colonnade, as well as expounding on the tenets of Buddhism, the history of Thailand, and the present state of the economy, all in exuberant narrative. Dorothy found herself growing fond of her, and not only that, but she was also genuinely impressed at the towering gilt of the temple itself. It had a stack of flamboyant roofs, each one resting on top of another, getting progressively smaller towards the top, all sloped at high angles and trimmed with rhythmic curves. The diminutive top roof, straddling the middle, spawned a slender, shimmering gold spire that seemed to reach for the sky. Below, she walked through large fluted teak doors, guarded by two green-colored creatures with large garish teeth. Gloriously bright colors adorned the walls of the temple, which were painted with cryptic religious scenes, and watching over all was the ornate Buddha calmly squatting inside.

"You seem to be very knowledgeable," she finally told the guide. "Tell me, how can I get ..." Dorothy realized she didn't know the girl's name. "I'm sorry, but I didn't get your name?"

"In Thai, my nickname is May-oh. It means cat, you know, the pet? 'K', 'A', 'T'," she spelled out, "Kat."

"You can call me Dot."

"Dot..., yes, it sounds almost Thai."

"Listen, Kat, what I wanted to ask you is...I have to go to Laos. Do I need a visa or something?"

"Of course. Laos is not like Thailand. Here, everyone is welcome." Composing herself into a more serious posture, she added, "You are an American. Might be a problem. The visa will take a long time. But I know someone who can fix it fast. Give me your passport when we return to the hotel."

Dorothy briefly debated to herself whether giving Kat her passport was a sound idea. She had heard stories about selling American passports on the black market. But such thoughts departed as fast they came. Kat seemed to display her heart rather openly, and it was plain to see that it was a good one.

Back inside the car, Kat still chatted away. During the short pauses of her flowing prose, Dorothy could manage a glance out the window at the strange blend of wide, car-choked avenues branching off into picturesque side streets full of food stalls and little shops, a juxtaposition of East and West. In such streets, vendors trundled various wagons dangling with assorted items, most of them victuals of a nature she couldn't make out. But on one cart that a young man happened to be pedaling by them, was a tray full of what unmistakably looked like insects—giant orange-colored grasshoppers.

"My goodness," she cried out, "do people eat those?"

"Oh yes. Very delicious, but very fattening. I love them, but…" Kat patted her midriff "…I have to watch my figure."

Along with the cars and motorcycles, were gaily decorated, but raucously noisy, three-wheeled, motorized rickshaws, which she later found out were called tuk tuks. At several points during their drive around the city, the taxi traversed arching overpasses suspended above fetid-smelling canals that gave off odors reminding her of rotten eggs. Even these canals were busy thoroughfares, their leaden gray surfaces plied by water taxis crammed with commuters.

When they got to the hotel, she did give Kat her passport. Kat, in turn, offered her business card.

"I will meet with you in the evening," she said, "to tell you how long you have to wait for the visa. Call me if you need anything." And with that, she wheeled around and left the hotel lobby.

Dorothy was exhausted, but she managed a western-style lunch of a club sandwich and salad in the hotel restaurant before going to her room. She noticed that whenever any of the hotel staff came near to her, they made that same motion that Kat had performed, bowing their heads and putting their palms together. It was pleasantly sweet-tempered, but somehow it made her feel awkward. Apparently, she would need some time before adjusting to the delicate manners of the Far East.

Shortly after five, the phone rang—it was Kat the tour guide, who, having dialed from the reception desk, was waiting in the lobby downstairs.

"I'm afraid I have some bad news for you," she said as Dorothy met her sitting in the lounge. "No visas for individual travelers. You have to be part of a tour group."

"Oh, darn. That's not what I intended to do." Dorothy settled slowly into the plush leather chair, thinking of what to do next.

"What would you like to see in Laos? I can suggest some tour operators with popular itineraries."

Dorothy just sat there, with a face full of dismay.

"You're not interested in sightseeing, are you?"

"I didn't come for that."

"So? Why are you here?"

Dorothy put her elbows on her knees and rested her chin on her hands. What the heck, she didn't see any other option but to take the risk. "I'm trying to find out what happened to my son."

Kat grew more attentive.

"My son was a pilot in the war in Laos. They say he died, but they never found his body or dog tag."

"Is that why you are here? Is that why you wanted to go to the Embassy?"

"Yes."

Kat put her finger in her mouth, pensively, then removed it. She leaned over. "Let me try one more time. I make no promise, so we will just have to wait and see. I will inform a friend of mine. Give it two or three days."

For Dorothy, the next three days were a matter of waiting. One of the first things she did was to get her hair cut short in a pixie, at the hair salon in the hotel lobby. It would give her less bother while traveling in this hot climate, she reasoned. Other than that, she only went out twice, reluctantly, once to change her hotel on Kat's advice to a place that was one third the price. The other time was to find a bookstore for reading material. The heat and the car fumes, together with the manic bustle of Bangkok, didn't appeal to her.

Despite the fact that very few people knew English, Americana was everywhere. Kentucky Fried Chicken, McDonald's, Pizza Hut, and even 7-Elevens were all conveniently located. In one shopping mall, an ebullient plaster of Paris Colonel Sanders bid a cordial greeting to a jolly plaster of Paris Ronald McDonald waving back across the way.

From the bookstore, she had bought maps of Thailand and Laos, as well as a few light-reading novels. She studied the maps, marking out Udon Thaani, where her son had been stationed and noted that Nong Khai, only forty miles away from the airbase, was to be her crossing point on the Mekong, the border with Laos.

In between reading, she switched from dubbed American movies to Thai soap operas and game shows on the TV. By the third day she was bored, and worse still, doubts and misgivings about her presence here in Southeast Asia still pestered her mind. She had to find things to do.

Kat called to tell her that the visa wasn't yet ready and would take a bit longer. Something in the girl's tone sounded grave. Although Dorothy realized that it wasn't a fast process, it seemed to be taking an inordinate amount of time.

The next day, after the one time Dorothy had ventured out for a walk, she was given a message, left by Kat at the reception desk. It said that her friend had been successful in getting Dorothy the visa, and he wanted to return the passport to her personally. She should meet them at a restaurant on the corner of Sutthisan and Soi 28, at six o'clock. Just tell the taxi driver the street names; he'll know how to find it.

Apparently it was an easy place to get to. The taxi driver merely nodded his head when she gave him the address, not requiring any further instructions, and dropped her off at the exact spot. The restaurant was indeed right on the corner, with ornamental tables arranged outside, and there was Kat, in a gaudily patterned dress, with her associate sitting at one of them. Beside the table, which was laid out with various dishes, there was a side cart with a bottle of Johnny Walker and a bucket of ice, as well as bottles of soda water.

The name of Kat's friend, as she was to find out, was Prasert, a good-looking man, with short and neat, silver-gray hair handsomely capping his streamlined head. He was in his early fifties, Dorothy guessed, and with a blue long-sleeved shirt rolled up to his elbows, he looked like an executive working past office hours. His face was affable and engaging, an amalgam of the many races of Asia, though his nose was slightly larger than that of a typical Oriental. The most striking features were his large elliptical eyes, which shone with crystal clear perceptiveness. In between his slender, well-manicured fingers, was an amber-colored cigarette holder with a lit cigarette, which he seemed to be sipping rather than smoking. He carried an air of cosmopolitan civility as he stood up to greet her, as well as a candid, obliging kindness. Refined was the word Dorothy would use to sum him up.

"Welcome, welcome, madam. I hope you are having a pleasant stay in our country." He was beaming a large smile, and Dorothy got the distinct impression that this stranger had already decided to like her. He put his hands together in that submissive praying gesture and bowed his head.

Dorothy looked at her hosts. "Is that how people greet each other here?"

"Excuse?" Kat asked awkwardly, leaving out the 'me'.

"You know, the hands thing…" Dorothy performed a clumsy imitation with her own hands.

"Yes," Kat answered, "It is called *wai*." She pronounced it like 'why'.

"It's very elegant."

Dorothy made an awkward attempt to 'wai' back. Awkward as it was, it was appreciated, for the man reciprocated with the gesticulation again.

"I am proud to meet a woman on so noble a journey," he said as they sat down. His English was impeccable.

"Oooh, I like your new hairstyle," Kat purred. "It makes you look young and sexy."

"Why, thank you, Kat."

"Kat has told me about you," Prasert resumed, "and your wish to find out about what became of your son. Please be careful and don't disclose that to anyone else. There are many people selling MIA items and false information—dog tags, letters, doctored photos—with promises to deliver POWs. At one time, almost every taxicab driver and street vendor was running a sideline on POWs."

This brought to mind the phone call from Jack Shilby. "Yes, there seems to be the very same problem in the US."

A waiter, who had been hovering by the table, took a glass and dumped ice in it, poured a modest amount of scotch, then topped it up with club soda before placing it in front of Dorothy. He then proceeded to do the same for Kat.

"Therefore," Prasert continued, "I advise you to tell no one of your intentions, especially in Laos. Oh, before I forget…" he reached down for a flat, leather satchel, the type used for holding papers. He unzipped it and produced her passport, which he handed over. "I managed to get you a special type of visa. You can stay in Laos for forty-five days. Longer than that is not possible; a typical tourist visa is only fourteen days, and even those are not granted to individuals, as Kat may have told you already. Visitors normally must come with a tour group booked by a company allowed to operate in Laos. I had to arrange a story that you were a travel author writing a book on the attractions of the country, so please maintain that guise."

"I don't know how to thank you. How much do I owe you?"

"Please," he said, "it is my pleasure."

"We feel it is our duty," Kat tried to explain.

"No, really, I must compensate you for your efforts," insisted Dorothy

Prasert put his hand up in mild protest. "No, no, no. You are embarking on a journey where there are many risks, and you are alone. You need friends to support you." He reached into the breast pocket of his shirt. "Here, this is my card," he said, handing the card over. "They know me at the hotel where you will be staying in Vientiane. If you need to get in touch, the number of my phone and fax is written there."

"Thank you very much, Mr. Prasert. In fact, here is a number in the United States which I may need to contact from time to time." She gave him in turn a slip of paper with Cynthia's name as well as her phone and fax number. "Would you be able to contact her on my behalf if such an occasion comes up? I am ready to reimburse you for the overseas calls."

"Don't worry about that. No problem whatsoever," Prasert assured. "I have also taken the liberty of notifying an acquaintance of mine to receive you in Vientiane. He will assist you in any matter you may require, including accompanying you in your travels upcountry."

"I don't know what to say, you are too kind." Dorothy privately questioned her own good fortune. "You don't know me, we've never even met. Yet you have truly helped me."

"I am being practical. It is not something you should do by yourself; you could get into much trouble. Laos is very different from Thailand. It is very underdeveloped, there are no good roads, traveling is restricted, and many amenities are lacking. People are not as accustomed to visitors as people are here. And you do not know the language."

"Also," Kat broke in, "be careful of Lao people. They are liars, cheats, and crooks."

"Is that true?" Dorothy asked, dismayed.

Prasert laughed heartily. "When you go to Laos, you just might find someone over there saying the same things about us Thai. But don't worry; my friend in Vientiane will help you."

"How could I have known that I would meet such lovely people?" Dorothy remarked in gratitude. "I'm so lucky."

"Please," he said, passing his hand over the delicacies on the table, beckoning her to partake.

Thai food was an adventure. Much of it was spicy hot with various chilies, but the delicate tastes of ginger, coriander, and lemongrass combined to create wonderfully unique sensations in her mouth. The tom yam, bubbling over a candle flame, was especially delicious.

Dorothy had a question on her mind. "On the few times that I've gone out, I noticed that people referred to me as 'farang'. Is that the term for a Caucasian?"

"Yes. The first Europeans to come in large numbers to Southeast Asia were the French, who called themselves Farancais, which was pronounced *farang-set* by the local people. So that is the word for Frenchmen. Farang for short. Later it became the word for all Westerners."

Inevitably, the conversation turned towards the war that had passed in Indochina.

Prasert discerned her bitterness and perplexity, and attempted to balance her arguments so that she could make sense of what had taken place during those times.

"Yes, I was involved in it myself. Very bad times, very bad. The war in Laos was just as much a Thai war as an American one. Many Thais fought in that war, especially as pilots and artillery units. Even if the US had no political agenda of its own, it still would have had to intervene militarily at our request. The US would have had to help us if they wanted to remain our friends."

"You mean we were protecting Thailand?"

"Thailand, Burma, Malaysia, even Indonesia and the Philippines. That was what was meant by the 'free world'. The Communists were sponsoring movements to overthrow the governments in all those countries. Even here in Thailand, both the Chinese and Vietnamese, as soon as the US pulled out of Indochina in the mid-seventies, began giving arms and support to guerillas in the mountains. We had our own minor war here. While it may be said that communism helped to save and unify the countries of China, Vietnam, and Laos, it would have meant disaster here. We would have died before surrendering."

"Did that justify the bombing of innocent people?"

"Are you referring to the Plain of Jars?"

"Well, yes, I've done some reading and..."

"Like the center of a chessboard," Prasert responded abruptly, "the Plain of Jars was the tactical key in controlling northern Laos. The Chinese and Vietnamese were afraid that the US could use it as a staging area for the invasion of either or both those countries, so they could not allow it to fall into hands other than their own. Of course, we felt the same way, because it gives access to the Mekong valley, and to Thailand..." he again paused to sip his whiskey and soda "... but justify? That is a strong word. The fate of human beings is often not immediately explainable. What is considered 'just' depends on which perspective you are viewing...tangled up in an endless cycle of action and reaction. Let us simply call it Karma, for lack of a better explanation."

"Is it Karma that my son died?"

"Yes," Prasert answered, with unquestionable conviction.

Silence followed.

"These events are of the unchangeable past; we shouldn't dwell on them too much" he continued. "The important thing now is your journey to find out what happened to your son. We Buddhists believe the truth can be found inside ourselves. Look to yourself and use your third eye, your sixth sense, and you will arrive at your destination."

"I will go to the temple," Kat offered, "and ask the Lord Buddha to help you."

"Thank you, the both of you."

After that, they discussed topics of a less serious nature. They were curious about life in Ohio, and even more curious about Dorothy's life in particular. In turn, Prasert and Kat offered brief descriptions of their own lives. Prasert's was particularly interesting, from his early days as a teacher in Burma, to the time he was an interpreter for Air America. At present, he was the General Manager of one of the largest Thai-owned tour companies. They ended up talking for two more hours.

"Now, I regret that it is time for me to leave," Prasert announced. "I really enjoyed talking with you Miss Dorothy."

"And I also, very much."

"I do hope to meet you again, but if not..."

"That's Karma," Dorothy interjected.

"Yes," Kat giggled in the background.

Prasert took Dorothy's hand in his, placing his other hand warmly on top. "I wish you all possible success on your journey."

Not since Bill died had she ever got the urge to kiss a man, not even on the cheek. Of course she couldn't risk being so forward. Instead, when he let go of her hand, they wai-ed each other good-bye.

"I'll go with you to your hotel," said Kat. "It's on my way."

Chapter 5

Thailand 1969

"Well, we had all those planes sitting around and couldn't just let them stay there with nothing to do."
U.S. Deputy Chief of Mission, U.S. Embassy, Vientiane 1969, commenting on the bombing of the Plain of Jars

Andrew Kozeny remained deeply disturbed by what he had witnessed after parachuting into that village. The memory of that experience had been branded irrevocably in his brain, rewinding and replaying over and over again in an unremitting sequence, a relentless echo bouncing off the walls of his conscience. He was so distraught, he couldn't write home to tell anyone of the incident, not even Cynthia. His sullenness hadn't gone unnoticed back at the base. His Squadron Operations Officer, Colonel Fark, suspecting it was due to being shot down and losing his Weapons Officer, suggested an immediate week's worth of R&R in Bangkok so that the young pilot could drink it and fuck it out of his system. Andrew had gone, but he had kept himself apart from the other two pilots that had gone along with him, and once in Bangkok he had set out on his own for a four-day drinking binge in Pat Pong. Of course, this didn't rid him of the malignant disquiet that continually tortured him any more than morphine could cure cancer. It persisted unabated, like a chronic ache from a wound that had only partly healed.

So, when Andrew returned to the base with his disposition unchanged, Colonel Fark was naturally concerned. That was one of the reasons why he had called him into his office.

Andrew, fretful at being summoned, meekly entered.

"Sit down, Lieutenant."

Dutifully, he sat down in the chair facing Fark's desk. The office was typically military, soaked in the white glow of buzzing strip lights. Behind the desk was a big-blown up map of Laos. The left side of the room was wall-to-wall window, discreetly guarded by half-closed Venetian blinds, while the other wall hosted an ample-sized bulletin board covered with frag orders and memoranda, illuminated by a little white tube-light fastened to the top.

Fark, as well, displayed a regimental appearance. The hairline of his crewcut receded in the wake of an expansive brow, making his thick, gray eyebrows stand out, which in turn emphasized the uncompromising glare in his eyes. His rectangular face and jutting jaw formed a countenance of authority.

"I know you're upset about losing Lewis. And being shot down is a traumatic experience," Fark consoled. "These things happen—we're in a war. If it makes you feel better, you might be happy to hear that you are seriously being considered for both the Purple Heart and the Air Medal, and a promotion to Captain. To level with you, this waiting period is only a formality. I can tell you confidentially that it's in the bag. You deserve it Kozeny, you're really one hell of a flyboy."

"Thank you, sir."

Once this opening nicety was finished, Fark got immediately to the point. "Things are at a peak now. The communist forces have hit us hard in their last dry season offensive." He turned around to point mechanically at the map behind him. "They've taken Muong Soui, and driven all the Meo out of Sam Neua." He returned his face to look at Andrew. "Operation About Face is ready to commence. We need all our resources. Not just the planes, we need everyone at their fullest, from maintenance to pilots. From the guy who scrubs the 'can' to old fart-asses like me. From tomorrow, you'll be back on the active roster. Expect another mission within thirty-six hours."

"Yes sir."

Andrew, who once viewed the man in front of him as a father figure, now found himself put off by the sight of Colonel Fark, by his face, his uniform, and what he stood for. Ever since he had been shot down, things had taken on a different aspect, as if he had shifted to the other side of the room, so to speak, to stand in the same corner with Cindy. This new angle of perspective was like a photographic negative, reversing the meaning of right and wrong, and exposing unsightly deformities previously hidden.

He struggled to hide his inner turmoil from the Colonel, a man who unquestioningly upheld the virtues of military honor, steadfast obedience, and sacrosanct duty. If Andrew were to tell him about the flower he had picked from a dead girl's hair and kept in a jar of water in his quarters, Fark would only think him weak. No, he dare not tell him that he was actually afraid to go to sleep, that sometimes he would wake up on the floor crying, shivering in fear. He wouldn't be able to explain that even pills and alcohol couldn't repress the poisonous nightmares. Night after night they came back, filled with the images that badgered him, the tortured souls entering into his sleep, surrounding him like a jury of reproachful phantoms. Certainly, if he had told him what had happened to him that last night in Bangkok, Fark would have been appalled. The night he dreamt of the girl with the hibiscus flower in her hair.

She had come to him like an apparition, floating, with her body still split open, her bloody viscera streaming down, her soft, pretty face grimaced by her pitiful sobbing, begging to know why, why, why did he do that to her. In his confused dream state, she was also Cynthia, and he was overwhelmed by feelings of deep love and burning regret that tore him apart, a stinging sensation of grief that cut him like a knife and made him wake up in a cold sweat. He had then bolted up in the bed, and when he saw a young girl lying beside him, he couldn't help screaming, "Aahhhh!"

Susie, the bargirl, had jumped up in fright. "Wuh, wuh you doin'?" she had exclaimed, wide-eyed and confused. When he told her about the dream and the bombing of the village she had screamed "*Pii! Pii!* Ghost!" The picture of the girl he described had reminded Susie of *pii dai hong*, 'a spirit that died wrongly'—a spirit capable of murderous revenge. She then grabbed her clothes and dressed so hurriedly before scramming out the door that Andrew later found her panties on the floor when he was checking out of the room.

It was a common belief throughout all of Southeast Asia: for those who die in violence, the soul remains attached to this world to haunt the ones who caused their death. Could tormented spirits be the source of his emotional suffering? he wondered. He was considering this when he realized that Fark was still talking to him.

"The new F-one-elevens have been delivered and we're anxious to see what they can do. As someone who has participated in Harvest Reaper, naturally we're going to assign you to the Combat Lancer program. You should consider this an exciting and enviable challenge."

The F-111 was one of the most controversial aircraft that ever flew. The Harvest Reaper program of June 1967, in which Andrew had been a part of at Nellis Air Force base, was intended to identify unknown flaws and to prepare the aircraft for combat. Combat Lancer was the proving ground so to speak, i.e. actual combat in Southeast Asia.

"Yes, sir."

Fark sensed that Kozeny remained somewhat detached, and it was more than just a matter of discipline and soldierly respect. Something was troubling this boy. "Am I getting through to you, son?"

"Yes, sir."

"Somehow, I get the feeling that I'm not. Are you still disturbed by being shot down and losing Lewis?"

"No, sir. I'm over that part."

"Is there something else, trouble at home maybe?"

Andrew didn't answer.

The Colonel realized that there were limits to how personal a superior office could be with a subordinate. There were too many other things he had to think about, and too many other pilots under his command. And of course there was his own private rule—never get too close. That way it wouldn't hurt so badly when one of his boys didn't make it back. "Perhaps you better see the chaplain. Consider that an order. Dismissed."

Andrew stood up, saluted, about-faced, and exited.

He went to see the Catholic chaplain, not only because it was an order, but also because he agreed with Fark that it might help him. He had been raised a Catholic, and despite the fact that his parents attended church only on holy days, he himself submitted willingly to the ideas of right and wrong that the nuns had taught him, and as a kid, he would enter the confessional weekly to purge himself of all the venial sins he had committed. However, this visit was to be a disappointment. The room that served as the chapel was dark and somber; the outline of the crucifix hanging over the little altar was draped in a dreary shadow. The chaplain, whose name was Callahan, was equally morose-looking: a thin man with stringy gray hair and a face that seemed etched from stone. Sitting next to Andrew in the front pew, one hand supporting the side of his face in stern contemplation, his legs crossed in a manner of paternal sagacity, he began by giving a well-prepared oration on the imperfections of mankind, and how these imperfections sometimes made war unavoidable.

Andrew wasn't interested in a canned speech. "Father, did you ever consider that you serve two masters, God, and the Air Force?"

It was a confrontational question, intended to needle him, but a good one nevertheless, acknowledged the priest. "God is my ultimate boss, and if there were ever a conflict of interests, there would be no doubt in my mind as to which one I would choose. But it is Satan who is usually behind these wars, who takes delight in hatred and brutality."

"So was God behind Custer at his last stand, and Satan with the Indians, or was it the other way around?" Andrew challenged acerbically.

Father Callahan noted the anger of this young man, and wasn't offended. Uncrossing his legs and leaning forward, he answered with a judicious patience he had learned to develop in his many years as a chaplain.

"No, I was thinking more in terms of World War II, which I fought in, and of Hitler, whose demonic behavior was responsible for the deaths of millions and millions of innocent people. And the communists of today, they too are threatening the world; they want to take it over with their godless, inhuman ideologies designed for mass enslavement. Their goal is nothing less than to eliminate God from this earth, and it is our duty to root them out and destroy them."

He went on to list the atrocities of the Viet Cong—the disembowelment of pregnant women, smashing babies' skulls against rocks, the barbaric beatings and torture of those that disagreed with their blasphemy.

Andrew felt this was a characteristic ruse used on the gullible to make them fight. The enemy has to be mystified into a paradigm of evil, to be dehumanized, in order to justify killing another human being. And it would have worked on him; except for the fact that he had seen his targets close up, and the villagers who ran for their lives during the bombing didn't look like devils to him.

"I'm sorry, Father, but I disagree. I feel that what we're doing is wrong." Andrew then went on to tell him of his horrible experience during the bombing raid, the kid whose leg was blown off, and the young girl with the flower in her hair, gasping her last breaths with her entrails splayed out on the ground.

"Hmmm." There was a slight pause as the priest considered what he was about to say. "Perhaps, you've had an emotional shock. I think it might help you if you could see someone who would be more suitable to your situation, a professional."

"You mean a shrink, don't you?"

"Well, a psychiatrist, yes. Of course we don't have any at the moment here in Udon, but I could ask Colonel Fark to request…"

"That won't be necessary, Father. I did consider this a spiritual, or at least, a moral matter. Thanks for your time, anyway." He politely thanked the priest, promising him that he would think about what they had discussed.

So now, Andrew could look only to himself to find the answers. He had to question why he had joined the Air Force, and why he had signed on for a second tour. He understood that his love of flying had led him into his current predicament. Perhaps that had always been an escape, his way of getting high; his version of a drug experience. The weapons training was just an academic exercise to him, even fun. He hadn't considered ever using what he learned on real people. When he had joined up in the early sixties, there was no Vietnam War.

How was he to know that President Johnson would pick a fight with the North Vietnamese—like a schoolyard bully that snatches your lunch and orders you to take it back, and then wallops you good when you do. That was the Gulf of Tonkin incident. Communications ships just beyond the coast intercepting Hanoi's transmissions, taunting North Vietnamese torpedo boats. To this day it is doubtful that any US ships were ever attacked, despite the claims made at that time. However, it was excuse enough for a retaliatory bombing and a resolution to be passed that gave Johnson virtually unlimited powers to wage war without having it declared.

So why then, Andrew asked himself, did he continue with a second tour?

He had an answer for that too. The bombing campaign in North Vietnam, Operation Rolling Thunder, had strict rules of engagement—Johnson wanted to avoid civilian casualties at all costs, so much so that the President deemed it necessary to review the missions and approve their targets himself, which really irked the military strategists trying to fight the war. It was in this campaign that Andrew got his first taste of combat flying, but the targets were all tactical ones: steel mills, bridges, supply depots. It was a high-stakes game that challenged his technical skill without him having to ponder about the ethical implications of what he was doing. He became a hero; some said the greatest flyer they had ever seen. He admittedly enjoyed all this praise lavished upon him by his superiors, and readily succumbed to their urgings to sign up again.

They would switch him to combat patrol and he would fly an F-4.

How was he to know that Pu Pa Ti was to fall to the communist forces?

Pu Pa Ti was a mountain in Laos close to the North Vietnamese border, where the Air Force had installed a navigational beacon with advanced capabilities, a technology called TSQ-81 that allowed the precise pinpointing of targets, day or night, in all kinds of weather. After it fell to the enemy in February 1968, 'surgical bombing' was no longer possible, and neither was the ability to ensure that no US aircraft would violate Chinese airspace, another of Johnson's big worries. It wasn't surprising then, that a short time after the TSQ-81 beacon had been knocked out, Johnson had ordered a halt to the bombing of North Vietnam. And that's when the air war shifted to Laos, and when the bombing on the Plain of Jars intensified.

In Laos, there was no enemy air force, therefore air superiority was irrelevant, and so combat patrol in an F-4 for Andrew had to be put on the shelf. In Laos, there weren't many strategic targets, other than the inhabitants themselves. In Vietnam, such tactics were unthinkable, because the eyes of the world were intently watching, but in Laos the war was a secret, and the bombing of civilians was a feasible option.

This turn of events may not have posed a moral dilemma in itself, if it weren't set against the backdrop of Cynthia's last letter:

...Today, an ex-International Volunteer Services worker came to speak about the bombing in northern Laos...kept secret from the American public and the rest of the world...pilots instructed to deny the bombing of the Plain of Jars...a war where machines obliterated people...the strategy of population removal and to intentionally create refugees...

...people first escaped to the outskirts, then deeper and deeper into the forest...CIA guerilla units force them into CIA camps where their movements are restricted and they can be controlled...the bombing is directed specifically against the poor peasants...meant to create so much misery they would have to leave or be bombed to jelly...people

have lived in holes for two years...when the military found out people came out at night to farm, they used flares to bomb at night as well... we saw pictures that were so graphic...jets come several times a day and destroy everything, even temples and schools with nothing left standing ...Andrew, how can you allow yourself to be so inhuman as to participate in this massacre...how do you sleep...how can I sleep, knowing that you're doing this? How can I love a man who EXTERMI-NATES DEFENSELESS WOMEN AND CHILDREN...INCIN-ERATES THEM WITH PHOSPHOROUS AND NAPALM...how can I even allow him to love me?...after much painful thought, it has become obvious to me that this is where we must part our ways...it's over between us Andy...FINISHED!

At the Intelligence and Operations briefing the evening before his next, and what would turn out to be, his fateful last mission, he sat listening to the Air Force Intelligence Officer, who almost echoed Cynthia's words verbatim...

"...Pinpointing of military targets is not the issue here, and random strikes are a waste of ordnance, which makes our operation one of carpet bombing...our objective, gentlemen, is nothing less than population removal, to destroy the Pathet Lao economy and social fabric, to deprive them of food sources and labor for transport. Remember, the communists are fighting a people's war, something that is difficult to do when there are no people...

"...I need not remind you that you should refrain from mentioning any of our activities in Laos in your correspondences stateside, not even to loved ones..."

It had also become clear that on this mission, due to the stealth and firepower of the F-111, Andrew wouldn't be flying to simply weed out and destroy AA guns, but would be actively participating in the bombing of civilians.

Racked with uncertainty, wondering how to get out of his quandary, he went over to the mess hall and sat mindlessly nursing a cup of coffee. When he saw Wallace, a young pilot from Maine, wandering over to his table, he brusquely stood up to go.

"Hey, Andy, what's up?"

Andrew clutched his stomach, pretending discomfort. "Bad stomach."

"Yeah, I hear ya. Butterflies before a mission. Trick is not to eat them greasy eggs. Try oatmeal or cornflakes next time. That's what I do."

"Right."

The logical place to go to make his act convincing was the 'john'. At least there he could be alone. He locked himself in one of the stalls, loosened his trousers, and sat on the bowl.

He felt he had been cheated; lied to. Yes, Father, Satan does delight in bloody conflicts. Except we're the Nazis in this one.

He had wanted to fly so badly that he had sold his soul to the devil and lost everything. He had lost Cynthia.

That's it. He couldn't go; he wouldn't go, plain and simple. He did up his pants and left the toilet. There was no other way out but to see Colonel Fark.

The office door was ajar. He pushed it open and saw Fark, standing by the frag order board, along with his adjutant.

He saluted. "Sir, I need to talk to you. In private."

Fark turned toward his aid. "Would you excuse us for a minute."

The adjutant left, brushing past Andrew in the doorway without so much as a glance. Andrew feebly advanced into the room.

"This better be important, Kozeny, I gotta a lot of prepping to do."

"I can't go on this mission, sir."

Fark looked at him, his square jaw twitching. He wondered what in tarnation was wrong with this boy. He knew that Kozeny wasn't a coward—he had already proven himself in battle. In his judgment, the boy had just lost confidence and was haunted by guilt over the death of his backseater. He had seen this sort of thing before, and he knew the remedy. A good, swift kick in the backside to straighten him out. He would scare the living daylights out of him; wake him up with a cold, hard slap.

"Listen, son, the Special Review of the F-111 Operational Procedures is at 2100 hrs. That's in fifteen minutes, so get ready. We launch at 0430, less than eight hours from now. All pilots capable of flying this machine have been already assigned, including you. There are no alternates available…" a purposeful pause "…By God, if you don't pull your finger out of your ass and get into this mission, mind, body, heart, and soul, I'll have you charged with insubordination in the face of a military engagement, have you court-martialed, and see to it personally that you do time in Leavenworth. Am I making myself perfectly clear?"

"Yes, sir."

"And I'll also make sure you never fly so much as a kite for the rest of your life. DO YOU UNDERSTAND ME?"

"YES, SIR."

"Dismissed."

Since that approach didn't work, he went to see the priest, who was in his quarters. Father Callahan advised him to heed the Colonel's words, to have faith, that God would protect him. Even Our Lord Jesus had his doubts and was tested by Satan in the desert. When the time came, God would be there with him. God would know what to do.

Andrew hoped so, because he sure as hell didn't.

In the late 1950s, Secretary of Defense Robert McNamara directed that the Armed Services study the development of a single aircraft that would satisfy both the requirements of the Air Force and Navy, an aircraft capable of low-altitude operations and supersonic dash performance. The Navy also insisted that the cockpit be capable of doubling as an escape capsule for the crew, which could be blown free from the aircraft in the case of an emergency.

It was in this background that the F-111 was born, a fighter jet that turned out to be one of the most effective all-weather interdiction aircraft in the world. The Air Force version was appropriately designated the F-111-A, and because of its long snout, tilting downward at an angle, it soon acquired the nickname Aardvark. The Navy version had a much shorter nose so that it could fit in a carrier elevator, and was called the Switchblade.

But the aircraft took a long time to perfect for several reasons. First there were the usual problems of defense contracts—contractor duplicity in cutting costs resulted in shoddy work, notably the welding. Secondly, because the aircraft had so many advanced features it became a case of having too many pots on the stove. Thirdly, there was a rush to get it to see action, to test it in actual combat. The developers were lucky enough to have a war currently going on in Southeast Asia, but they didn't know how long it would last. Get into it now while it was hot—it was a perfect testing ground.

By the time Andrew's last mission was being planned, most of the imperfections had been ironed out, and the plane was ready for a secretive unveiling.

The F-111 was the world's first 'smart' jet fighter. Air war had been progressing along the lines of dumb planes with smart bombs, that is, bombs that could find their targets through computer calculations, radar attraction, or heat sensing. Here was a plane that, with dumb bombs, could accomplish missions that formerly required scores of planes with smart bombs. Computer technology allowed for deep strikes into well-defended territory without a host of escorts. The aircraft was equally good at flak suppression, precision bombing, or air combat. It could cruise long distances below radar coverage, a mere 300-400 feet above ground through dense turbulent air 'that could shake your eyeballs out'. The state-of-the-art terrain-following radar was the key to this ability. It analyzed data from an antenna scanning the landscape, and the plane responded in millionths of a second—rising, descending, turning. Whether uneven terrain (like the mountains of Laos), poor weather (like the monsoons of Laos), dwindling daylight, or dangerous conditions, the F-111 automatically followed the contours of the land. All of this new flight technology, especially the new terrain-hugging radar, would enable Air Force planes to easily penetrate Soviet air defenses in case of a US-USSR war. Since the North Vietnamese and Pathet Lao's air defenses were exact duplicates of Russia's own systems, the Air Force was using the Indochina war as a test track for their penetration strategy against the Soviets.

For Andrew, this had all been exciting fun when he was back at Nellis. However, on the night before the mission in Laos, he wished he weren't flying this plane. In particular, the cockpit setup bothered him. Most pilots would share this negative feeling, but for different reasons. The side-by-side seating meant that a pilot couldn't look out to his right, but depended on his navigation and weapons officer, which meant you had to depend on someone other than yourself. What if the guy took a hit, or had a heart attack or something? That wasn't Andrew's concern, however. It was the ejection feature that troubled him. The fact that it was a capsule meant the two crew members went out together in a specialized escape pod, which ordinarily was a good idea—they could help and support each other once they were on the ground. Though in Andrew's case, he subconsciously loathed the fact that his fate would be bound up with another. He wanted to be alone.

Poor Lieutenant Withers. He was the one whose fate would be bound together with Andrew. Of course, that was his own Karma, wasn't it? In any case, when he saw Andrew at the flight briefing, he realized that Kozeny was bothered by something. He made the obligatory condolences.

"Sorry about Dave. That was a tough one."

"Yeah."

"Anyway, at least you got out okay." Then, thinking that perhaps that was the wrong thing to say, he corrected himself. "I mean, we're glad we didn't lose both of ya."

"I don't know, Jerry, maybe you have...lost the both...of us," Kozeny retorted, walking away with an inert face.

That's when Lt. Jerry Withers began to have bad feelings about this one.

At the pre-flight briefing, when the flight leader announced that the flights would be named after American Pies: Apple, Pumpkin, Blueberry...

"Hey, and Arnie dunce-head wants Beef-Pot!" someone broke in.

This elicited a roar of laughter from the pilots, except for Andrew, who, with a dour face, murmured mockingly, "Ha, Ha, Ha. Asshole."

Withers, seated to his side, turned and looked at him, with some qualms.

"All right, listen up," the flight commander ordered. "We'll be going in with two flights, Apple and Pumpkin." With the hint of a smile on his face, he looked over to one side of the room at one particular pilot. "Beef-Pot," he rebuffed in a low dismissive tone, shaking his head. This caused more laughter and chuckles. Then, the flight commander abruptly regained his serious tone. "Because we'll be flying Aardvarks, we won't be going in with any escorts for barrier patrol. Apple will be first flight, Pumpkin behind and above, five and two. We'll clear the area first with CBU's, then three more passes to expend the rest of the mixed ordnance. The AB triple C guiding us in will be Cricket."

AB triple C—Airborne Command and Control Center aircraft— were present twenty-four hours a day, continually circling the skies of Northern Laos to coordinate air strikes. The daytime shift was called Cricket. At night, it was Alley Cat.

"Then we'll refuel with a KC-135 tanker over Chieng Khong at Victor Hotel one-two-seven-seven. We re-arm here, then we go back for more."

"Yeah," Andrew shouted out, "vaporize everything down to the last chicken."

Some embarrassed snickers followed, then an awkward silence before the flight commander continued.

Throughout the rest of the flight briefing, Andrew was rather laconic, and when he had to say something or answer a question, he responded rather dryly, in as few words as possible. This too, distressed Withers, but in the end he rationalized that Kozeny was one of the best, and when it came down to the crunch, he was probably lucky to be flying with him.

But in the early hours, during their launch routine, it was the same, and Withers was honestly starting to get nervous. At first, he tried to be casual. He let forth with a good-natured chuckle. "Did you get your morning fix?"

Withers was referring to the vitamin B12 shot that the Air Force doctors regularly gave the pilots. B12 immediately cleared up all the symptoms of a hangover.

Kozeny kept absolutely quiet.

Withers had no choice but to say what was on his mind.

"Look, Andy, if something's bothering you, you know, just come out and say it."

"Nothing's bothering me, Jerry," he lied.

"I know you were used to flying with Dave, but I've had some seasoned flying time myself and I'm not a cut up. So if that's what you're worried about…"

"No, that hasn't anything to do with it."

"Is it the bird? The fact it's got a bad track record out here?"

"No, it's a fine plane."

"Well, I was just wondering, 'cause…"

"Hey, Jerry, do you realize that we're about to go out and kill people?"

"Kill? We're just doing our job…"

"Forget it. Let's get mounted."

Oh shit, maybe this really is going to be a rough one, thought Withers.

Andrew studied the lines of the airplane with concealed pleasure. She was sleek and beautiful, despite having been dressed for war, painted up with patches of green and brown camouflage. With her nose long and bent, she actually did look like an aardvark. The real pleasure of flying her was that you didn't need to wear a pressure suit that squeezed the life out of you, or a parachute that restricted your movements. It was like the difference between skinny-dipping and wearing a bathing suit, or between having sex with and without a condom. The cockpit, because it served as an escape capsule, was pressurized and temperature controlled, so you could fly it in your shirtsleeves. Its performance envelope allowed you to do things in the air that you couldn't do with other aircraft. To the Laotians on the Plain of Jars, it was known as the 'Whispering Death'. To Andrew, it was the ultimate flying machine. It's a pity, he thought, that he would have to put her down.

He went into his pocket and took out a laminated index card, upon which he had pasted the faded red hibiscus petals. The flower he had been keeping in the jar had wilted and he thought to preserve the petals by pressing them in a book. Then he made this card, writing the words 'I'll always remember' on the back, and sealed it in cellophane wrapping. He quickly put the card back in his pocket as Withers approached him.

"What's in the bag?" Withers asked, pointing to the loosely packed duffel bag Kozeny was carrying.

"Lunch, in case we decide to stop for a picnic," he answered sarcastically.

Withers had never gotten to know Kozeny well, but he was always under the impression that he was a shy, quiet, polite kid. Perhaps this dry sarcasm was actually a part of his nature that had been kept hidden from him.

The two men climbed into the aircraft, Kozeny placing the half-packed bag behind his seat. They conducted the pre-flight checks and prepared for takeoff, with only the words necessary to carry out their duties. Ignition, revving the turbines, two-minute warm-up, taxiing to takeoff position...

Seconds after their flight leader lifted off, they too, roared down the runway feeling that familiar acceleration, streaking low across the horizon, heaving a din of thunder behind them.

They joined up in formation and inside of four minutes they were over Vientiane, the Mekong, a tawny serpent below them slithering its way south. Withers was spooked by the distant expression on Kozeny's face. It was too tight, too rigid. It wasn't typical. Pilots invariably tried to be loose, to relax themselves with morale-boosting banter before the engagement.

"Are you okay, Andy?"

"I'm fine, Jerry." His voice carried an eerie tone. Although he appeared unperturbed, he was actually writhing inside with a multitude of emotions. Fear, loathing, sorrow, even a euphoric relief, all jostling for space inside his soul as he verged closer toward that flash of a moment that was waiting ahead of him.

They crossed the Mekong floodplain to enter the mountains, flying over Vang Vieng, and were soon heading into a blanket of cloud with the mountain peaks knifing through, standing like black islands in a white sea. Kozeny seemed to be in perfect control, but he was far away, not participating in the usual way to the radio chatter that everyone else was engaging in, except to make the required check-ins. Over Long Chieng now, and through a large gap in the clouds, the Plain of Jars came into sight, still in the distance, a yellow patch in the landscape of jagged ridges. It was in the shape of a distorted diamond, like a sheet stretched taut and pegged along its perimeter by the surrounding mountains. Drawing nearer, they could make out the ribbon of Route 7, and even the dots that were the huge, mysterious stone jars that the area was named after, the remains of a forgotten epoch.

Time was up. That flash of a moment had arrived, and Andrew entered into it as if sucked up in a vortex.

"Now let's see what this baby can do," Kozeny said with a demented smile. He abruptly broke formation and veered. Engaging the afterburners, he swung into an echelon right and peeled into a forty-five-degree dive. Withers heaved up his breakfast as the aircraft made the high altitude to low-level transition, and the aileron rolls on the way down intensified his nausea.

"ARE YOU CRAZY, WHAT ARE YOU DOING?" Withers screamed.

"Apple-2, get back in formation, repeat, get back in formation and maintain position," the radio ordered. Andrew shut off the radio.

"Andy, tell me what the hell is going on!" Withers pleaded desperately.

Kozeny knew that this was to be the last time he would ever fly an airplane, and he wanted to make it good, to pull out all the stops. At his command, the plane dashed inside the mountain valleys at nine hundred miles per hour, and the baby responded to its terrain-following radar true to form—the ultimate rollercoaster ride—up, down, and around at breakneck speed. Then Andrew shot the bird back up, the negative g-forces slamming the both of them against the backs of their seats.

One final move to make before they had to egress. At 20,000 feet he nosed her down. "This is where we get off," Kozeny announced. "I'm ditching her!"

He grabbed the ejection initiator, a D-shaped handle near his knee that, when gripped, acted as a three-way switch—he squeezed the grip, pushed it down to release the locking pin, then pulled it up hard to start the ejection sequence. The only way to stop it was to engage the mechanical-explosive interrupt. Anticipating that Withers would go for it, Kozeny grabbed his wrist. Withers, in his panic, didn't realize that Kozeny had switched off the terrain-following radar, and they were heading straight for a mountainside. If they didn't leave the aircraft, they would end their existence as a smoking hole in the ground.

The restraint harnesses abruptly seized the both of them, pinning them forcefully in their seats as the detonating cord wired into the compartment set off a rapid series of small explosions that shook the cockpit, triggering the hidden guillotines that severed cable connections and the primary oxygen hose. Emergency oxygen came on, giving a ten-minute supply. The capsule blew, along with a section of the fuselage behind it, tearing itself violently away from the diving plane; at the same time, the rocket motor ignited to send them hurtling upwards with a thirty thousand pound thrust, propelling the two men to the limits of human sensation.

They cleared the aircraft. A bang was heard as the brake parachute catapulted open, and, together with the stabilizing glove, the piece of fuselage that had come away with them, helped to stop the downward tumbling of the module as the rocket cut off. Falling downwards, the two men clutched at their seats, their minds reeling. Again a blast, spewing radar chaff which showered down to the ground to confuse enemy radar. At 16,000 feet of altitude, another explosion and the main parachute opened, giving them a jolt. A second jolt followed as the reefing lines were cut, allowing the parachute to blossom to its full extent. The escape pod started to level out once the bridle lines were deployed. Three seconds later, another loud pop signified the bursting of the nitrogen bottles, filling the impact attenuation bags on the bottom which would cushion their landing. The final sound was the actuator firing to extend the emergency UHF antenna.

They were wafting gently downwards, slow and steady, when, without warning, their fall was stopped, and the capsule and the men inside it jerked abruptly like a yo-yo on a string. The capsule was designed for almost all contingencies that the planners could think of. On land the cushion bags had blowout plugs so that they would deflate upon impact, reducing the shock to the crewmembers. It was watertight and had flotation bags so that if it landed in water, it would float up and right itself, and the parachute automatically detached so it wouldn't fill with water and drag them under. It even had a bilge pump.

But the one thing the designers hadn't thought of was coming down through a thick tropical rainforest. The capsule, with its parachute entangled in a maze of branches, rocked like a seat on top of a stopped Ferris wheel, a good fifty feet above the ground.

Both men were quiet for several seconds, attempting to recover from the physical trauma they had just been through.

"You okay, Jerry?"

"Okay? Okay? What stunt are you trying to pull off, Kozeny? How are we gonna get outta here?"

Kozeny carefully reached for the bag behind his seat. He opened it and slowly pulled out a three-quarter-inch nylon rope with a 'spie' harness attached. At least he had thought of the possibility of getting hung in the trees. "I'm going to go first. Then I'm taking off."

"Whadda ya mean 'taking off'? you're just gonna leave me here?"

"I don't see the point of waiting around. We're not going in the same direction. When I reach the ground, pull the harness back up," he told Withers, tying a double hitch around the base of his seat. "You got your beeper?"

"Yes."

"Here," Kozeny said, handing him a canteen of water. "Head west towards the mountains, that's your best bet."

"Hey, where're you going?"

"I'm sorry I had to involve you in my decision, Jerry."

"Hey, wait a minute."

Kozeny descended down the rope, rappelling against the tree that the capsule was stuck on.

"Kozeny, where you going?" Withers repeated in a shout, craning his neck to see what his comrade was up to.

When Andrew got to the ground, he undid the harness and slipped into the undergrowth.

"Hey, WAIT!" heard Andrew as he ran deeper into the forest.

Chapter 6

Lao PDR 1990

"Laos can't be saved, I know. How can you save a nation which doesn't exist, a people that won't fight...?"
The words of Francois Ricq, in the Bronze Drum by Jean Larteguy
1960

Twenty-one years after her son's fateful flight with the F-111, Dorothy Kozeny stood on the Thai side of the Mekong, gazing at the vegetable gardens and riverine growth on the far bank that belonged to Laos, the brown and green colors crisp and clear in the freshness of the morning sun. It was quiet, save for the parakeets and turtledoves, fluttering and twittering among the flamboyants and frangipani trees that bordered the river. Long, narrow, teak canoes, in soundless motion, spawned ripples in the calm brown water that flowed lazily before her. Despite the placidness of the scene, wave after wave of apprehension washed over her as she stared at the Lao immigration post across the way. She was about to enter the black hole that had swallowed up her son, purposefully going into an anti-American communist country that had virtually been closed to the outside world for fourteen years. Panic gripped her, panic at the unfamiliar. Her discomfiture wasn't unexpected, for she had been dreading this moment for the past few days.

The evening before, she had embarked on the night train to Nong Khai, deciding not to stop at the air base at Udon Thani. For most of the journey, she had lain sleeping in a second-class bunk bed, so she didn't get to see much of the beautiful paddy country of northeast Thailand. After arriving in the morning, she had summoned an upcountry version of a tuk tuk, which seemed nothing more than a motorcycle with a brightly colored cart fixed over its rear portion. This dilapidated conveyance had taken her to the official crossing point of the river, where she had her exit out of Thailand officially stamped in her passport, and where she was now standing, waiting in a state of almost paralyzing trepidation.

There was some talk that the Australians would soon build a bridge here, linking the two countries, and signifying a new era of cordial relations between Lao and Thailand, two nations where the people shared the same language and cultural identity, but were divided by Cold War ideologies. Everyone agreed it would be a profound turn of events, considering that just two years ago they were almost at war, with armed patrol boats cruising up and down the Mekong. A major dispute had arisen in 1987 over territory claimed by both sides, and the fighting that had ensued claimed more than a thousand lives before a ceasefire was declared in February 1988.

"You cross now, that boat take you," said the Thai immigration officer standing next to her. He was pointing to a boat that looked like the others, except it had a small shelter at the end of it and a long iron rod twenty feet or so long that dipped into the water at an angle, presumably attached to some sort of motor and propeller.

She walked down the concrete steps built into the riverbank and, while avoiding the water calmly lapping the shore before her feet, stepped gingerly into the unsteady boat, a maneuver that was more difficult for her than for most people, she not being very adept at anything that required balance, then nervously tucked her long skirt under her as she sat down. The old man piloting the craft beamed an amused smile. He started the motor, and then turned around with his hand resting on the end of the iron rod, using it as a tiller to shift the angle of the prop. The buzz of the engine was only a slight disturbance to the tranquility that pervaded the midmorning hour. The sun was shining, but not too fiercely, just enough to douse the tropical scenery with a mellow radiance. Even the clouds appeared unperturbed; frothy cotton balls suspended idly in the sky. She gazed at them hoping to draw some of their sweet languor. As the boat drew nearer and nearer to the opposite bank, deviating this way and that to avoid the shoals, her pulse quickened. It didn't take long to cross; it was less than two city blocks in Dorothy's estimation. The old man switched off the engine as the boat pulled up to a concrete ramp on the Lao side and Dorothy got out, almost reluctantly, paying the boat owner his ten *baht*.

Well, here goes, she thought to herself.

She found herself looking up at a man who stood before her, his arms folded across his chest. His dark brown skin, jet-black greasy hair, and his short but large-boned physique presented a portrait of an indigenous Indochinese. Despite the lack of gray in his hair, deep creases in his face indicated he was in his fifties, perhaps the same age as Prasert, the generation between herself and her son. Dressed in black sweatpants and a red T-shirt that exposed his bulging biceps, he seemed intimidating. Thick fleshy lips, an expansive forehead with prominent brow, and high cheekbones set in a gaunt face, made him look a bit Neanderthal.

"Miss Doro-tee?"

"Yes?"

"I am Kampeng. Friend of *Ai* Prasert."

She noticed he had several bright white cotton strings bound around his left wrist, striking against his dark skin, and wondered if he had tied them on to remind him of something he had to do. "I am very pleased to meet you. Mr. Kampeng, is it?"

"Yes. Come with me. No worry, everything okay."

Notwithstanding Kampeng's appearance, she was comforted by the fact that a Laotian would see her through the entry procedures, and true to his words there was nothing to worry about. Soldiers in ill-fitting, somber green uniforms, who sat slothfully on the steps with large guns slung over their shoulders, appeared less intimidating with Kampeng at her side. She herself didn't seem to warrant their attention; they continued their indolent chitchat without so much as a glance at her. Once at the counter at the side of a plain, weather-stained brick building, the uniformed officer behind the window looked briefly at the visa in her passport, stamped it, and gave it back to her with a shy smile. He then handed her a form written in Lao script, which Kampeng helped her to fill out. The officer stamped that too, before waving her off in a friendly manner, indicating that she was free to go on ahead.

"We have taxi waiting. It is twenty kilo to Vieng Chan," Kampeng announced, using the original name of the town, rather than the French derivative. Dorothy assumed 'kilo' meant kilometer.

"Yes, I saw on the map that Vientiane is still upstream from here. What is this sheet of paper? The one I got back with my passport?"

"That is *laissez passer*, you know? You need that for go outside Vieng Chan." He strode with a bouncy, loping gait and led her to a barren clearing where an ancient white Renault sat parked.

"Sabai dee!" A stout, swarthy driver, with a wide grin that lacked a few teeth here and there, opened a creaking door for them to sit in the back before getting in himself. Following that were several vain attempts with the ignition key that gave out an awful screeching sound, until he finally started the car and they were off, bumping down a wide, rutted, dirt road.

Dorothy couldn't help being struck by the difference between the Thai side and this side of the river she was now on. She found herself in a place that was imprinted with a decidedly lethargic laxity. Yet, the waterway presented no more than a few hundred feet of geographical separation between the two countries. Hardly any sort of a physical barrier. Rather, it was more like a temporal dislocation, as if the Mekong were a portal through which she had been transported back in time. There was no one else on the road, except for a few bicycles and a couple of small motorbikes. The sides of the road were quite bushy, which broke clear from time to time, revealing extensive tracts of irrigated rice paddies. As the old car bumped and jerked its way forward, a few large, ugly warehouses, factories, and lumber yards flanked the road; their appearance suggested they were holdovers from the colonial days of the French. The sense of listlessness was quite a contrast to the busy roadside views of Thailand, which had neatly paved thoroughfares lined with concrete storefronts, and which were perpetually teeming with activity.

"You are American," Kampeng stated, rather than inquired.

"Yes."

"I like American. America good."

"Really?" She was genuinely surprised. His remark was contrary to her expectations.

"During the war, I fight in American army, you know? Then communists and Vietnamese take my country. No good. Americans go away."

She wondered if it was safe for him to talk this way. After all, Laos was supposed to have a repressive, authoritarian government, yet he made no attempt to conceal his voice to the taxi driver. Maybe it was because Kampeng knew the driver didn't understand English, or maybe he just didn't care who heard him.

"That is when I meet *Ai* Prasert. During war."

"He's a very nice man, Mr. Prasert."

"Yes, not like other Thai. They lie and cheat."

That line sounded familiar to Dorothy.

The car hit a pothole and Dorothy bounced up and banged her head on the roof. "Ouch!"

"You see? Government cannot fix road. When Americans here, you know, all road good."

After that, the car went only a little way before it conked out. The driver turned to Dorothy and once more gave out his gap-filled grin. *"Bo pen yang,"* he told her, which literally meant 'it isn't anything'.

"Never mind," Kampeng loosely translated.

The driver got out and opened the hood. Kampeng also exited the car, and Dorothy, out of curiosity, did so too. The driver looked at the engine while engaging in a short conversation with Kampeng, then leaned over the air filter until his short legs left the ground and his butt, clad in white shorts, stuck up in the air, causing the upper part of his body to disappear in the murkiness of the car's innards. Following a few minutes of fiddling in this position, he emerged and banged down the hood. *"Bo pen yang,"* he repeated.

Only after the engine finally turned over did Dorothy and Kampeng get back in the old sedan.

"Prasert, he tell me that your son was pilot shot down in Lao."

"Yes. I am here to find out what happened to him. They never recovered his body, at least not to my knowledge."

"Kampeng can help *Oo-way* Doro-tee. Go many places in Lao, you know? Kampeng from the south, but travel all over, to Luang Prabang, Long Chieng, Nam Bac, Phongsaly...everywhere."

She surmised that 'Oo-way' was a Laotian title for a woman, Miss or Mrs., but she was a bit perplexed at his use of the third person when referring to her or even himself. It was a speech pattern she would soon get used to. In Southeast Asia, such a manner of speaking was considered formal and polite.

"Well I trust Mr. Prasert made a good choice in choosing you as my guide. I also have some information with me that could narrow our search."

"First, *Oo-way* Doro-tee go by airplane to Xieng Khouang. There, we have car. Don't worry, *Ai* Kampeng very good driver."

'Ai' must mean Mr., she thought to herself. "Well, of course, why shouldn't you be?"

By this time, she had already glimpsed a few of the road signs, and, after double-checking her *laissez passer*, observed that the Laotian script looked a lot like Thai writing.

"Is the Lao alphabet the same as Thai?" she asked him.

"Yes, same, same, but different."

A giant billboard flanking the road grabbed her attention. It was extremely colorful, with two large flags painted on it, one of them red with that awful hammer and sickle emblem of the socialists. Underneath the flags was a scene filled with a multitude of figures, from school children in uniforms to hard-hat construction workers, village farmers, and traditionally dressed Laotian peasants raising their fists provocatively and carrying placards. It was, without a doubt, a portrait of communist propaganda, which appalled her; she almost heard the painted figures shouting out hatred for anything American. But the most striking thing was 'Pepsi Cola' written in English below the Lao script, complete with the red, white, and blue bottle-cap logo.

"What does that sign say?"

Kampeng squinted at the billboard. "My English not so good, but it say something like 'People's Party good, ten years of Revolution bring us good things.'"

(Actually, the sign said, 'Pepsi Cola celebrates the tenth anniversary of the Revolutionary Victory, the Leadership of the Party is the Way to Prosperity').

This bewildered Dorothy. Pepsi Cola, one of the bulwarks of capitalism, saluting the communists. It made her angry, and only reaffirmed to her that her son was duped into sacrificing his life for a group of self-interested people who would sell their own mother for a buck. The only thing that impressed her was the fact that Pepsi got their foot in the door before Coke.

There was a short pause before she asked him, "Tell me, since you were in that war twenty years ago, how do you feel about it?"

"During war, many American here, you know? Help us fight North Vietnamese."

"They dropped a lot of bombs too."

"Yes, many many bombs."

"And killed a lot of innocent people."

"Eee-no-sent? What mean?"

"You know, women and children for instance, not enemy troops."

"Ah. You don't know, you don't know."

She wasn't sure what that last statement was supposed to mean, but it somehow terminated the conversation.

As they got closer to Vientiane, the traffic and activity increased, and so did the dust, which billowed up in miniature clouds all around them. Peering through the dusty haze, Dorothy saw modestly constructed shacks on each side of the road — crude roadside cafés and grocery stores. Dark-red clapboard houses on stilts, with the natural look of unfinished teak, began to line both sides of the road. Around them were children playing, babes-in-arms crying, and plainly dressed men walking on the curbsides. All the women wore sleeveless, lace-trimmed blouses, together with sarongs wrapped around their midriff, which Kampeng told her were called *paa-sins*.

On the backs of the bicycles and motorbikes, these women passengers were obliged to sit sideways, their sarong-covered legs dangling over one side, which was more modest than straddling their legs over the seat. Elegantly balanced and unruffled, some of them were even holding vividly decorated parasols to shade them from the sun.

When she started to see small, three- to four-story buildings of French colonial architecture, Dorothy realized she was finally in Vientiane. In fact, she had already passed the airport without even noticing it. It wasn't what she had anticipated. She had expected a capital city. Instead, it was a dusty, desultory town, abandoned in a bygone era, where even the main streets were dirt roads or rotting asphalt laid down long ago in a distant past. But, in spite of that, she liked it. It seemed peaceful and quaint. It was hard to believe that three hundred years ago Vientiane was an impressive capital, renowned for its art and architecture, its literature and learning.

The road began to widen, and soon the two lanes of opposite traffic became separated by a grassy barrier. As the road curved left into the main part of the town, the Renault itself made a right turn at the corner of a temple, following a sandy road pockmarked with water-filled potholes down to the end, finally stopping at a small box-like building.

"Riverview Hoten," announced Kampeng. "Ai Prasert make booking and pay for two nights."

It was an old hotel, less than fifty meters from the banks of the Mekong. Inside, the lobby was charmingly decorated with giant hand-painted folding fans, as well as various drawings of rural scenes on the walls, some etched on silver and gold mirrors. In various places were showcases filled with ceramic and bronze vessels and elegant glass sculptures. There was bric-a-brac everywhere, tastefully arranged.

"Sabai dee!" greeted a young man behind the counter, neatly attired in a white shirt and a black necktie.

"It mean 'hello, how are you'," Kampeng translated.

The boy put his palms together and brought them to his nose.

"So they *wai* here as well," Dorothy observed.

"Yes," Kampeng said. "But here in Lao we call it *nop*."

"Two nights pay already," the smiling concierge informed. "Room one, tree, four."

"How do you say 'thank you'?" she asked Kampeng.

"Kopjai. Kopjai lai lai."

"Kopjai lai lai," she repeated to the concierge.

With the help of the concierge, she filled in the registration form, blissfully unaware that her name, along with those of the other hotel guests, would be routinely submitted to the local police station that night.

Kampeng announced he was leaving. "You rest now, I come in evening, about six o'crock," he told her.

"Wait, what about money? I need to change some."

"If you have Thai baht, can use baht. Ten *kip* to one baht."

"Kip?"

"Yes, Lao money."

"I have dollars."

"You can change here at hotel, but rate no good. Give to me, I change for you."

Dorothy rationalized that she would have to trust him sooner or later. She gave him an amount she felt was appropriate to her needs.

He took the money and put it in his shirt pocket.

"I need to call Mr. Prasert's office."

"Yes, they help you," Kampeng said, indicating the staff behind the counter. "I see you in evening. Have good rest." He exited, leaving her to her own devices.

"I need to make a phone call," she said to the handsome boy behind the desk. He was very young, barely a teenager.

"Telephone? What number, preese?"

She recited the number, while he faithfully wrote it on a slip of paper. It took a few minutes to get through, but Prasert wasn't there. So, she left a message with a secretary, requesting Mr. Prasert to contact Cynthia and inform her of her safe arrival in Vientiane.

"Go to room now?" asked another young lad, picking up her luggage, a duffel bag and a backpack.

There was no elevator. Dorothy followed the boy carrying her bags up a very wide staircase brightly lit by sunshine radiating through stained-glass windows. The inside of her room wasn't as pleasant as the lobby or as bright as the staircase, but it looked comfortable enough. As long as everything functions, she thought to herself. She tried the faucets and was relieved that water came out, flushed the toilet and noted it worked. She was doubtful about the old Russian water heater though. That would have been the last of her worries, until she saw a huge cockroach scuttle away down the shower drain. It was so big that she gasped in fear and loathing of the hideous thing. If such a creature frequented modest hotel rooms in the capital city, what was awaiting her upcountry?

Putting her minor trauma behind her, Dorothy set about organizing her things. She had come well-prepared: insect repellant, wide-brimmed hat, sunscreen, water purification tablets, flashlight, and a first aid kit that contained Band Aids of all shapes and sizes as well as antiseptic cream. There were medications for every type of tropical ailment she could think of, not to mention antacid tablets and Tylenol. There was also, just in case, a bottle of Xanax; and of course, toilet paper and tissues, lots of it. In some ways, she thought amusingly, her age was of some benefit on this journey. At least she didn't have to worry about bringing tampons.

With that done, she sat idly on the bed, and almost immediately a surge of anxiety engulfed her. She was scared. Scared to be in this strange place, and scared of the likely failure of her mission. Don't falter now, she told herself, you knew this would happen when you first arrived. It's only natural. Even Cynthia had told her it would happen. Pull your socks up and keep your mind on what needs to be done.

She stood up with disciplined resolution. Searching amongst her myriad of belongings, she eventually took out two maps which she spread out on one of the twin beds.

Cynthia had proven to be invaluable once again. The maps were prepared by her friend of a friend at the DIA. The preparation of one of them was ingenious, and it made Dorothy finally appreciate computers. The first thing they had done, Cynthia had explained, was to inquire a database on all known crashes in Laos, then filter that information for crashes that occurred in 1969, where the type of aircraft was an F-105, the type that Andrew had supposedly been flying. Using the coordinates that were listed as part of the records, and special software Cynthia had called a Geographical Information System, they plotted symbols marking the sites on a one to one hundred thousand topographical map, along with the roads rivers, and towns. The other map included every crash known to occur, regardless of the date or type of aircraft, and it was a jumble of symbols.

Unfortunately, neither of the maps had the names of pilots associated with the crashes. The names of pilots assigned to the missions in Laos were still classified information, except for those considered Missing In Action. Since Andrew's remains had been officially handed over, he wasn't an MIA, and his name wasn't on that list. However, Cynthia's friend of a friend said he might be able to access the linked database that had the pilot's names, but it would take some time and finagling.

It was reasoned that Andrew must have been shot down between March and August of '69, when the bombing was the most intensive. During that period there were two major operations carried out by the Air Force, Operation Rain-dance, followed by Operation About Face. The Plain of Jars had been in and out of each side's hands like a hot potato. US-backed Royalists and Hmong would take large portions of the area under cover of US airstrikes, then hold ground only for a few weeks, until a Pathet Lao counteroffensive took it back, after which there were additional air strikes of a retaliatory nature. All this air activity covered a fairly large amount of ground, but there were only two sites that related to F-105s going down in 1969, and although they were spread out and isolated, forty-five days seemed more than enough time to check these places out. In each area of a crash, she would seek out the old people, who might have some knowledge of the incident, and in addition, could perhaps speak some French, or so she hoped. With French she would be able to communicate directly without requiring an interpreter.

The telephone rang.

"Mr. Kampeng here to see you."

"It's six o'clock already?" she asked aloud to herself.

She was just about to tell him to come up, when she thought that it might be construed as inappropriate. "Tell him I'll be right down."

She came down with the maps and Kampeng was immediately interested.

"These very good maps, where you get them?"

"Believe me, it wasn't easy. This old one here," she showed him, "cost me over $100 to duplicate. And this one was prepared by someone in the US Defense Intelligence Agency," she said, handing that map over for his perusal.

While holding the map in front of him, he walked over to the small dining area that was set in one corner of the lobby. He spread the map out on one of the tables and mulled over it, resting his chin in his hand.

Dorothy followed him. "These maps are confusing," she said over his shoulder. "Some towns and villages exist on some maps but not on others. And to make it more confusing, sometimes the same town has a different name on each map."

"Yes, after war some villages no more," he replied, still studying the lines and names.

"You mean literally wiped off the map?"

"Yes, you know, no more. Then after war there are new villages."

She laid out the other map on the opposite side of the table, the map that had the sites for the F-105s. "You see these two little stars?" she asked him. "They represent a crash site of an F-105 jet that was lost during 1969. That's where we should look first."

"Airplanes, ah, yes. I remember, something I must to tell you." He straightened up to face her. "All flights to Ponsavan cancel. We must to wait."

"I thought we were going to Sieng Khouang?"

"Yes. Xieng Khouang province, but town near airport call Ponsavan."

"I don't see it on this map," she decried, pointing to the DIA map of crash sites.

"It has other name, Muang Bek," he explained.

"Oh, I see. So what are we going to do about getting there, whatever it's called?"

"Sometimes can fly to Luang Prabang. Then other plane from there go to Ponsavan."

"We'll do that then."

"No, we can't do. Because of flights cancel to Ponsavan, flight to Luang Prabang full for next two weeks."

"Two weeks? That's fourteen days. I can't afford to just sit here all that time." She knew that staying around Vientiane with nothing to do would seriously jeopardize her morale. "We'll have to go by road."

"No, no, can't go by road. Very difficult, you know?"

"It doesn't seem too difficult. We take this road here," she argued, studying the map, "number thirteen, up to this place called Sala Pu Koun, and then take number seven. They are both major roads."

Route 13 was the main road of all Laos. It ran north-to-south from China to Cambodia, paralleling the Mekong for most of its way. About fifty miles south of Luang Prabang, there was a junction where Route Seven branched off and headed east, through the Plain of Jars and on into Vietnam, connecting to the road to Vinh.

"No bus on Route Seven," he warned. "Very dangerous, you know?"

"Dangerous? How?"

"Road very bad, on mountain. Also many Chao Fa."

"Chowfa? What?"

"Chao Fa, Chao Fa," he repeated, as if she should know. "Hmong rebel. Kill people."

"Why?"

"They fight government."

"What does that have to do with us? We're not the government."

"It no matter," he told her. "They see me, they kill me. They see you, they kill you. They kill farang before. You know?"

"Why kill ordinary people?"

"They kill, then government see, say 'oh, Chao Fa killing people, oh, Chao Fa give problem'."

"So they are just terrorists then?"

"Maybe," he concurred, trying to be agreeable, and without knowing the word 'terrorists'.

"Everyone would be better off if they stopped their violence."

"Ah, you don't know. Everyone different. They hungry. No job, no money, no food. Chao Fa don't like Communists. You don't know."

As soon as she heard the 'You don't know', she sensed that further discussion of the topic would be feckless. She got back to the business at hand. "If buses don't travel on Road Seven, are there any other vehicles which go that way?"

"Yes, big ones with soldiers."

"Trucks?"

"Yes, big trucks."

"Is it possible to get a ride from them?" she asked, a question fringed with hope.

"Yes, they help people go."

"Good. That is how we will go. We'll take a bus to Route 7 and hitch a ride from there."

"No, not good. You don't know."

"Mr. Kampeng, I will wait for two days while you try to get seats on the airplane. If by that time we cannot get a flight, I shall travel by road with or without your company."

"Okay, two days. I get seats. *Bo ben yang.* Never mind." Then, after an awkward pause, "Oh, here your money." He handed her a large plastic bag full of greenish looking notes.

"I can't believe all this money. I just asked to change one hundred dollars."

"Yes, fifty thousand kip."

"How am I supposed to carry all this?"

"Put in your bag."

Dorothy raised the plastic bag, inspecting it, still astonished.

"You hungry? Would you like go eat?"

"No, I'm not hungry just yet. I might have something small later in the hotel. I'm rather tired."

"You don't want go out and see town?"

"No, I think I'll just stay in for the evening."

"Okay, no probrem. I see you tomorrow morning."

In her room, she eventually fell asleep, but woke up at five in the morning to the mystical sound of gongs, which she realized, after a few minutes, were coming from a nearby temple. She remembered that Kat had mentioned something about monks getting up very early for prayers, before they went on their morning rounds to accept food from the devout.

After a session in the bathroom, which included a shower, she was still restless, and with her fears about being in Laos gradually subsiding, she chose to get dressed and embark upon an early morning walk. At a quarter to six the day was breaking. Birds chimed a dulcet dawn chorus as Dorothy sauntered down the riverside road that ran alongside the hotel. Gliding past her were troupes of schoolchildren dressed in black and white uniforms already proceeding to school on their bicycles, while the sound of gongs and bells continued to resonate from the many temples. Magnificent trees, crowned with profuse greenery, showered the little lane with a lush opulence. Vegetable gardens covered the river-banks, and she could see women, wrapped in sarongs, washing themselves at the water's edge. Farther offshore, boats with square prows were setting their fishing nets.

Her attention returned ahead to a scene on the road, where a procession of shaven-headed monks in orange-colored, toga-like robes walked in single file holding out their begging bowls to people kneeling on the ground, who piously deposited rice and other food as the holy men shuffled past them. She stood and watched this ceremony for a few minutes, awed by the sincere devotion of the act.

Back at the hotel, she found Kampeng waiting for her.

"Ah, yes, good morning," he greeted. "Sleep well?"

"Yes, actually I did. I woke up early so I went out for a walk. Goodness, it's eight o'clock already."

"Yes. You hungry—want eat breakfast?"

"I was about to suggest that myself."

After breakfast, Kampeng offered to show Dorothy around the town. There were a couple of main streets, but they were too small to hold the increasing amount of two-way traffic, so each had become a one-way thoroughfare. The back roads weren't much more than large alleyways, on the sides of which were women selling meat skewed on sticks and grilled over a charcoal brazier. A man rode by on a bicycle-driven cart selling French bread, pedaling past old buildings stained dirty gray from years of soot. Temples appeared on every block. They were simpler and smaller than the ones she saw in Bangkok, but just as beautiful—resplendently oriental buildings with steep-curved red roofs, surrounded by feathery rain trees.

They walked down a tiny street and made a left down another. Without any advance notice, the small road suddenly brought them to an expansive six-lane boulevard, which seemed to come right out of nowhere and was totally incongruous with the rest of the town.

"Lane Xang Avenue," Kampeng announced. "This our main street."

"Well yes, I can see that. Oh my goodness! What is that over there?"

It was a colossal monumental arch, fashioned like the Arc De Triomphe, but with ancient oriental motifs. On its flat top, four watchtowers gave it a menacing look, like a Chinese fortress.

"*Patusai, annoo-sa-waree*. Patusai Monument. Built with American aid, ha, ha!" he covered his mouth as he laughed.

"Why is that something to laugh at?"

"Ah, you know, Lao people very funny. In 1957, America give many ton of concrete to rebuild airport. Lao leaders build this instead."

They ended up ascending to the top of the monument (there was a staircase inside), to get a bird's-eye view of the town. After that, he had to take her to Tat Luang, the great sacred stupa. In fact, he had insisted, since it was the national symbol of Lao. It was the most amazing architecture she had ever seen. Protected by an ornate, golden-painted wall, rising out of what seemed to be a huge concrete egg, the stupa rose to over one hundred and fifty feet, its curved lines echoing the form of an elongated lotus bud. The golden pagoda was intensely bright in the midday sun, and it almost hurt her eyes to look at it.

"How are we progressing along the lines of plane tickets?" Dorothy asked as they were leaving.

"I have friends at Lao Aviation. We get seats tomorrow. Bo ben yang. Never mind."

Kampeng had informed her that, unfortunately, he wouldn't be able to meet her in the evening as some private business required him to go out of town. Not far, he assured her; he would come back tomorrow morning. By then, the plane tickets should be ready, or so he had promised. He suggested that if she was bored and lonely, she might want to stop at the Nam Pu, a watering hole frequented by many European expatriates.

The Nam Pu Bar & Restaurant was located in an open area in the middle of a quiescent plaza, surrounded by various shops and eateries catering to European tastes. The place itself was an outdoor bar in the center of this plaza, with tables arranged in a circle around a giant central fountain. In fact, *nam pu* in Lao means 'water fountain', and this one was particularly ornate: an enormous stone pool, in the middle of which was a huge sculpture of a lotus flower that shot jets of water in the air and was colored by red and green spotlights. Water dripped off the petals of the flower statue, creating pleasant cascading sounds.

All the tables were occupied. Dorothy wandered around until she spotted a table where a lone Caucasian man was sitting. He seemed to be writing something in a book, engrossed in what he was doing.

"Excuse me," she interrupted, "may I sit here? I promise I won't disturb you."

The man looked up from his labors. "Oh yes, of course, go right ahead."

Dorothy took her seat.

"Cheers," the man said. He was British, in his late forties perhaps, and quite good-looking. His hair was a silver-gray, the front locks of which hung boyishly across his wide, polished forehead. His aquiline nose jutted out between bright blue eyes.

"If you drink beer, I suggest the lager on tap," he commented. "It's a bit lighter than the bottled brew."

"Yes, that sounds nice."

"Good. I'll order what the staff here calls a jug. I was fancying a pint or two myself right now." He signaled a waitress, a beautiful young Lao girl in a sarong, and made the order. Then he extended his hand to Dorothy. "Nigel Coddington."

"Dorothy Kozeny."

"American, are you?"

"Yes. And you yourself must be from England."

"Quite right. Cornwall, a beautiful place in the southwest. Have you ever been to Britain?"

"No, I've never had the chance."

"Well, I guess we're even on that score. I've never been to the States."

The jug was brought with two glasses, and Coddington did the honors. "Cheers," he said, raising his glass.

"Cheers."

"So, how long have you been in the country?" he inquired. "I must admit I've never seen you before. Odd, considering that there aren't many Westerners here at the moment."

"Just a few days. I'm only a tourist."

"Oh, I dare say there aren't many of your sort around. I suppose they shall be coming in increasing numbers now that the country has opened up a bit."

"I assume you work here?" Dorothy asked in a half interrogative tone.

"Some of the time. I'm in and out. Sometimes here, sometimes in Cambodia, Vietnam, even Afghanistan."

"What do you do?"

"I'm in the UXO line of work."

"Excuse me?"

"I'm sorry. Unexploded Ordnance. Unexploded bombs," he clarified.

"You defuse bombs?"

"No, not really. In these situations, we usually blow in place. Attach charges, or some other method to make them go off. Once they go off, they're no longer dangerous. The hard part is finding them."

"Are there many unexploded bombs here in Laos?"

"Oh goodness yes. The worst are the 'bombies', cluster bomb units. Little grenade-type things with an anti-disturbance fuse, about the size of a child's ball. Must be several million live ones lying around."

"Millions?" she asked incredulously.

"Oh easily." He then embarked upon a benignly patronizing speech. "Without a formal declaration of war, this country became the most heavily bombed country of all time. Between 1964 and 1973, the US dropped on Laos the equivalent of one B-52 payload of ordnance every eight minutes for nine years. you're an American, you should be aware of these things."

She became uneasy at his affected tone of disapproval. She felt like telling him that England was fully aware of what was going on: yet his own country didn't voice any objections. "Yes, well, I know about the bombing, I just didn't realize that a lot of it never went off and is still a danger," she remarked, indulging him.

"Oh yes. I estimate there was as high as a twenty-five percent failure rate." He paused. "Most people think that the war is over when the treaty is signed. But that's not quite true. It's only when people like me...no, I shouldn't say like me...the people who go in the field rather, and risk their lives until the land is cleared of bombs...that's when it's over."

Dorothy was silent.

Coddington, seemingly absorbed in thought, suddenly spurted, "Your country can be a damn nuisance sometimes. Like the blueprints we need for render-safe procedures. They won't release that information, even though these weapons are thirty years old and no longer used by the US Military. As long as they have allies who have the particular weapon stockpiled, they won't declassify anything that deals with fuses and internal workings. So now our staff sometimes have to risk their lives unnecessarily."

She continued to humor him, hoping his snobbishness would ease up. "Yes, I'm sure it's dangerous work. Interesting though, and worthwhile."

"Oh, not all the time. Much of the time it's merely paperwork and logistics. Right now, I'm putting a detection and disposal plan together for the United Nations. Cheers," he said again, raising his glass in another toast.

The waitress came over to their table. "Mitter Codd-ton, telephone."

"Excuse me," he said to Dorothy as he got up.

She fidgeted about uneasily, while waiting for him to come back.

"Sorry about that," he said returning to his seat. "I will have to leave in a few minutes." He sat quietly for a few moments, with his face resting in his palm. Suddenly, he perked up.

"Ah yes, now here is a story which might be interesting to you. Although to me, it's yet another bother I have to contend with. Actually, I wouldn't say this to anyone, but it's just been bothering me, and I need to get it off my chest. And since you're only a tourist, I guess there's no harm." He paused again. "It appears there is someone here doing this work on his own, someone who apparently has been here in Laos for many years. The Laotian government wants me to work with him."

"Why is that a bother?"

"This is what you might find fascinating. Quite a colorful chap, a veritable eccentric. He's an American, or so they tell me, but has a completely shaven head, like these Buddhist monks you see around. In fact, I do believe he actually is a monk. Goes around dressed in a robe and his body is covered in tattoos. Wears dark sunglasses, and to top it all off, rides an elephant!" He began to guffaw heartily, all the while covering his mouth in awkwardness.

"That's wild!" Dorothy agreed.

"Yes it is! He even claims his trusted pachyderm can sniff out the bombs." He snickered and snorted for a few seconds, before regaining self-control. "Name's Johnson, or some-other. And he's had some success they tell me, so he might be daft, but no fool. He must know something about munitions. Actually, with his knowledge of explosives, and the fact that he's been here since the war, makes me think he's some sort of rogue operative leftover from the CIA. That might explain the odd guise, perhaps a form of psychological warfare, you know, to make the locals fear him. And he seems to have some power over the Chao Fa. He's about the only outsider that can enter their territory at will. All the more reason to suspect he's an ex-CIA fellow. You've heard of the Chao Fa, I presume?"

"Yes, I've heard of them."

"This fellow has managed to create a myth around himself," Coddington continued. "The people of the area claim he has super-natural powers and is invincible—can't be killed."

What an intriguing story, Dorothy thought. Ex-CIA? If that were true, then anything could be possible, maybe Andrew was also still around…

"I'm sorry, I have to leave in a rush," Coddington said hurriedly looking at his watch. "I must meet with someone related to work. He's leaving very early tomorrow morning, so I better see him now. I've paid the bill. It was nice meeting you, Dorothy, I do hope we meet again."

"Likewise."

She took a tuk-tuk home. But instead of returning relaxed as per her intention, she was a bit disturbed, and slept fitfully, although in the morning she could not recall the bad dreams that ruined her sleep.

The next morning was the departure time for the flight to Luang Prabang. On the way to the airport, Kampeng assured her that there was nothing to worry about. Never mind, Bo ben yang, he told her for the third time.

At the airport it was chaos. There were obviously more potential passengers than the twenty-one seat Chinese aircraft could carry. Kampeng was confronting someone in a Lao Aviation uniform, with heated, convulsive Lao words leaping from his mouth. But it was to no avail. In the end they were compelled to return to town.

Dorothy sat rigid in the taxi on the way back. "That leaves us no choice but the bus."

Despite the early hour, the Morning Market was a bustle of

activity. Crowds of people were milling around, while vendors, wearing cone-shaped hats, hawked their wares in a persistent chime. Others, balancing long shoulder poles with heavily laden baskets hanging pendulously from each end, walked with strained and hurried steps under the weight of their burdens. And of course there were hundreds of bicycles, motorcycles, and tuk tuks. The section at the end of the market where the upcountry vehicles were stationed was no less hectic.

Dorothy, sauntering behind in her floppy safari hat, flowery Bermuda shirt, and pink baggy culottes, couldn't believe that what Kampeng directed them towards was a bus. It was an Isuzu truck with a wooden roof supported by poles attached to the bed. Inside it were wooden benches. Like everything else in Southeast Asia, it was ornamental, painted in happy colors of red, white, blue and yellow. A little ladder made of branches facilitated climbing inside. Dorothy, with the help of Kampeng, dumped their luggage in the back and secured a side seat so that she could look out.

The 'bus' left exactly on time, except it didn't actually go anywhere. It roamed the side streets of Vientiane looking for more travelers. Even when it was finally proceeding on Route 13, it still stopped every minute or so to pick up people waiting by the roadside, and before long it was packed. Besides the human cargo, there were sacks of rice as well, stuffed under the benches along with the live chickens. The passengers were chattering away, and the noise level soon rose to a hubbub.

As the bus got farther and farther away from Vientiane, it stopped less often. Traversing the Mekong floodplain, they passed a verdant flatland of paddy fields that stretched out as far as the eye could see, broken only by isolated thickets of bamboo. Pretty timber houses on stilts, festooned with plants and flowers, stood amidst green-colored ponds, some of them marked with floating pink lotus blossoms. It was a bus ride the likes of which Dorothy had never imagined.

On the bus were old people, cheerfully exchanging jokes and

stories, smoking hand-rolled tobacco and chewing betel nut. Their happy vitality belied their aged, weather-beaten visages, which otherwise attested to a life of toil. There were also a few young mothers and their children, the little darlings looking up from the green fruits they were nibbling at to stare at Dorothy with wide, liquid eyes, and she felt her heart warming to their adorable caramel-colored faces. Shrill sounding music eked out from little speakers set in the wooden roof, playing strange songs that Kampeng described to her as *mawlam*. There seemed to be two types of this mawlam—a slow, sad sounding lament, and one with a driving rhythm that made one want to get up and dance. Animated conversation from the passengers competed with the music.

Although Dorothy herself stuck out like a sore thumb, she felt totally relaxed in the company of these Lao common folk, none of whom seemed to be particularly concerned about her presence.

Up ahead, she saw a wall of foothills that extended along the horizon. The bus was about to leave the floodplain and enter the mountainous country that covered more than half of Lao. From this point on, it would be up and up and up. In accordance with the terrain, the Isuzu shifted into a lower gear and reduced its speed. They climbed for about an hour through sloping, open woodland, passing a few small settlements, until the land leveled out over a wide limestone valley: a landscape of karsted, water, sculpted-peaks of various globular shapes and sizes. Dorothy was agog at the beauty of these limestone towers, nature's art forms, rising in shapely, green-covered whorls touching a royal blue sky.

"Vang Vieng," Kampeng informed her, referring to their current location.

"It's beautiful."

"Yes, and much water. The River Song never dry up, and there is much springs."

They continued to follow the valley until they stopped at a place called Kasi for a lunch break, six hours after leaving Vientiane. It was a good thing too, since Dorothy was suffering a severe pain in her buttocks as well as muscle cramps in her legs from sitting for so long on the hard, crowded bench.

At the little roadside restaurant, Dorothy opted for the familiar noodle soup. After that was the opportunity to go to the toilet. She was directed towards the rear of the restaurant, where a door opened up into a small room barely bigger than a closet. The toilet itself was an elliptical porcelain bowl set into the floor, forcing her to squat rather inelegantly. The bowl was flushed by manually pouring water down it, the water being provided by an earthen vessel with a plastic mug floating on the surface.

All their immediate needs fulfilled, the passengers re-boarded and the Isuzu was on its way. Not long after, they came by a police checkpoint. The police were especially interested in Dorothy. She had to get off the bus with Kampeng, who did all the talking. Dorothy heard frequent mention of Luang Prabang during the fifteen-minute discussion, so when the police finally stamped her *laissez passer* and let the pair back on the bus, she asked Kampeng what he told the them.

"I tell them we go Luang Prabang. You write for travel guide. Luang Prabang is famous place for visit."

"But we're getting off at Sala Pu Koun."

"Yes, but say Luang Prabang. Easy, no problems. Bo ben yang."

The ascent into the highlands grew steeper, and the mountain scenery became spectacular. The earth seemed to fall away from them, as they looked down at tree-covered rock pillars and fertile valleys. Great walls of limestone stood defiantly to the sky, draped with mantles of thick forest. Dust-covered timber houses hung precariously on the edge of the cliffs that bounded the road, where the local denizens loitered around outside, somnolently staring. The children, on the other hand, were quite exuberant, running, cheering, and waving; a vehicle passing through their quiet habitat was an exciting event for them on a road where only a small number of vehicles passed each day.

Up and down the ridges they went, climbing steep gradients and flying downhill around hairpin turns. Some of the passengers, Dorothy was surprised to observe, were struck by motion sickness, and were vomiting out the windows.

Hours went by in this fashion, the truck-bus weaving along the circuitous mountain road past spectacular scenery, but soon even the beauty of the land couldn't quell the aches she got from sitting for so long in one position.

It was early evening when they arrived at Sala Pu Koun: a diminutive settlement fearlessly perched on top of interconnected peaks. It was to be Dorothy's first taste of upcountry Laos. Although at first, she was relieved that her jarring, jolting ride was over, she subsequently looked dubiously around her, eyeing her surroundings with the wonder of an astronaut who had just landed on Mars. This feeling was reciprocated by the residents of this place, who, in the course of their myriad activities, would stare back at her as if she were the Martian. Children would stop to point, and then scream out "Farang!" before running away in a fun-filled panic.

The isolated hamlet was like a frontier town, and it was laid out in a novel fashion. Since it was at the top of a mountain, there was really no place to build except along the same parallel ridges that determined the course of the road. Whereas most of the settlement was visible from each ridge, the deep ravines prevented any straight-line traverse, so you could only walk from one place to another via the winding road. The center of Sala Pu Koun was a local depression where Route Number Seven branched off to the mountains of the east.

There was only one guesthouse in the place, which, to Dorothy's dismay, was simply a long barracks-looking timber shack. It had three crude sleeping areas meant to cater for Laotians who got stuck waiting for a ride. Each individual accommodation consisted of a blanket on the floor of a 'room' partitioned off by pressed fiber-board. There was no water for bathing.

Well, it's only for one night, she thought. In truth, as she settled into her bedding on the floor, she felt an excitement similar to the time she had camped out in the backyard when she was a little girl. This, however, was certainly different than anything she'd ever done, and together with the bus trip, reinforced the idea that she was on an adventure.

That was fine enough for Dorothy except for two things. For one, since all the dwellings were along a mountain road, the outhouse behind the lodging was positioned on the side of a cliff. This required extra caution in the middle of the night. She thought about this situation, and of the other mountain villages they passed on the way, and wondered how many children they lost per year.

The other thing was the presence of the rats. She knew they were rats because after hearing a ruckus and going out to investigate, she saw one scurry away. And she was sleeping on the floor! After that, she spent an hour sitting up with her flashlight and scanning the environs of her sleeping place until she grew weary. But despite these trivial dangers, she made it through the rest of the night without incident.

The next day was the hard part—waiting for the ride. It seemed that no one was going that way, at least not all the way to Ponsavan. Kampeng tried to keep her amused by showing her the salient features of whatever there was of the 'town'. Motor scooters scurried here and there, and people pushing carts full of makeshift water containers traveled back and forth, to and from a piped spring about a mile up the road. Every so often, a strange vehicle of local style would pass by—a cart hitched up to what looked like a miniature tractor with two long handles, which reminded her of a handheld plow, and which the driver used to steer.

"*Rot dok-dok,*" he told her, pointing to the contraption.

Kampeng pointed out the Hmong to her, the women selling the vegetables by the side of the road. They wore clothing of heavy, black, homespun cloth, enriched with elaborate designs of colorful patchwork and embellished with ornaments of old silver coins. Many of them wore headdresses that reminded Dorothy of Russian pillboxes. In any case, they looked discernibly different from the lowland Lao women in their sarongs.

On the whole, the little town only fortified her sensation of traveling back in time. Barring the motor scooters, there were very few things that acknowledged the existence of the outside world in which she herself spent her life. The place was an alien throwback, hidden and secluded within its own remoteness.

By noon, she was desperately anxious. She couldn't bear the thought of being marooned here, to wallow in endless nights and days in existential limbo, despite the town's unique and colorful character. For Dorothy, the paramount quality of the place was the remarkable awe-inspiring view. Having nothing else better to do, she walked over to her favorite spot.

It was an incredible scene of the landscape that she would soon enter. The peaks, the summits, and the ridges were like frozen waves of earth, ripples in an ocean of mountains. So deep, so vast. So pitiless. Her elation was replaced by a pensive sadness, thinking of Andrew, how he might have been alone in those mountains, alone with no one to comfort him. Did he really die instantly, in a flash, or was he hurt and scared, waiting for the end? Oh dear God, did he cry out to me? At that thought, she put her hand to her mouth and broke into tears.

"Miss Dorotee!" Kampeng yelled out, panting heavily as he ran towards her. "We get vehicle, this one here!" he pointed.

Dorothy quickly dried her eyes and gazed in astonishment at the ten-ton truck loaded up to the hilt with cargo. Even at that early juncture, something told her that she was about to embark upon the ride of her life.

Chapter 7

Laos 1969

"Morality is contraband in war"
Mohandas K. Gandhi, Indian political and spiritual leader, 1942

The whole of the morning was torn apart by the bombardment of the adjacent valley, the reverberations ricocheting off the mountains like high-velocity balls of thunder and shattering what little remained of his nerves. But all he could think about was running, running as fast as he could to get as far as he could in the shortest amount of time. That's why he chose to stick to the valley, where the going was easiest, not concerned that he was leaving signs of his passage. It was okay for now, although, sooner or later, he would have to change this tactic and get to higher ground, as his trail here in the lowlands would be too easy to pick up. He assumed that the Hmong CIA army wouldn't track him until they were explicitly ordered to do so. That might give him a day or two, even if Withers was picked up fairly soon. He didn't dwell on the possibility that Withers might not be rescued. He had worries of his own, concerned with fighting his way through tall tropical trees tangled up with vines and creepers and watching out for anyone crossing his path. Of course, if he spotted someone, it would be too late to avoid them, since many of the trees had huge leaves that hung down and blocked the view ahead, and the racket he was making smacking them out of the way would give his position away long before being seen.

When he calmed down, he checked his pace and tried to keep to a rhythm, a slow but steady trot, without any lagging or acceleration that would increase his exertion, summoning his former skills as a cross-country runner. To accomplish this, he had to study his immediate surroundings on the fly, taking note of the bushes and rocks, so that he could plan his move as he got there to minimize any hesitation. But the density of all the jungle obstacles required an intense concentration that eventually drained him, and he frequently tripped and fell headlong over the boulders, roots and ensnaring trailer stems, so that, before long, he became considerably bruised. After several hours of this steady tramping, he slowed down and took frequent pauses to catch his breath. By that time, the humidity had already begun to stifle him.

It was about ten o'clock in the morning when, panting heavily and soaked with sweat, he took his first break. As he sat hidden in a thicket, tiny gnats bit into his scalp underneath his damp hair, adding to his discomfort. That was the least of his problems, however, for he had finally run out of water, and he knew that he wouldn't be able to keep this hurried pace as the day grew hotter. Then there was the issue of food. He ate the last of the boiled corn, woefully aware that it might be some time before he would again be able to consume enough roughage to stimulate his bowels. At least he had stuffed his face full of carbohydrates just before the mission, including three large plates of spaghetti.

But time was already working against him, bringing him inexorably closer to starvation, and so he had to spend it wisely. Running helter-skelter through the jungle wasn't good enough; he had to figure out just where he was going, and to that purpose he searched his small duffel bag for his compass. Holding it unsteadily in his hand, he took his bearings as best he could against a dim sun veiled behind a curtain of clouds. Heading due north at this juncture was probably his best bet, as neither the enemy nor the Air Force would immediately expect him to go that way. Furthermore, he would now proceed in a more surreptitious manner, repositioning disturbed vegetation, and advancing against the contours, a technique known as cross-graining. With a vague idea of his location, he rose to his feet, slung the bag over his shoulder and continued on, albeit at a slower gait.

It wasn't long after, when he came upon a large expanse of elephant grass, taller than a man's head, in a field that went all the way down to the stream in the middle of the valley. Andrew was pleased, for he felt he could mix up his trail in there. He headed towards the stream, where they would expect him to go, deliberately leaving clues concerning his route, and then doubled back and climbed up until he was out of the grass and into a dense understory. While inside this patch of jungle, the sound of helicopters verged upon the mountainside, filling him with overwhelming alarm. No doubt they were patrolling the area with the hell-bent objective of searching for their recreant pilot. A panic well-known to the hunted made his heart contract forcefully. Crouching low, breathing hard to sustain the demands of his fear, he waited until the pulsing beat of their blades was no longer audible.

Mindful of the need to be vigilant, he struggled through the bushes and brambles, now following the contours, keeping the pace up for nearly two hours, until a rock-filled brook crossed his path. As well as providing his urgent requirement of water, he saw here another favorable opportunity to further confuse any potential pursuers. After imbibing his fill and topping up his water container, he followed the stream up the hill towards its source, stepping only in the water, carefully avoiding any exposed rocks, which might retain a print. He splashed his way over the cobbles, not happy about the prospect of having waterlogged boots, and when he felt he was high enough, he re-entered the jungle on the opposite side.

The daylight itself was growing dimmer, and Andrew's energy waned proportionately. The muscles in his buttocks, his hamstrings, and his knees ached intensely, yet since the time he had been fighting his way through the thick undergrowth, he knew he had hardly made any headway. He was out of water once again, and he wasn't sure if and when he would be able to get any more.

Electing to abandon the jungle terrain that was retarding his progress, he followed a small ravine up the hill, scrambling over rocks and uneven ground, where fortune smiled upon him in the form of a spring, probably the source of the stream he had encountered below. He guzzled canteen after canteen and hurriedly ate the concentrated protein bars he had brought with him. Risking the chance of being seen, he climbed up until he reached the top of the ridge and hiked along in open view. The sun set but he didn't stop.

The extent of the ridge was broad and flat, covered with wild grass and ferns with newly sprouted fronds. This was the easiest walking he had done so far, but even this minor relief was short-lived, for not long after, the flat stretch of the ridge gradually narrowed into a clearly defined crest, where a huge wild rubber tree stood silhouetted against the fading glow of the sky. He carried on down the other side into a northward-facing valley, which was more overgrown and more rugged as well, as evidenced by furrowed depressions which grew into deep ravines farther down the slope. Twilight set in, cueing the crickets to begin their shrill cadence. Still, Andrew kept rambling ahead.

Fighting the bracken and the underbrush during the next few hours was exhausting; he had to deaden his mind and make his body move in a debilitated, involuntary mode. He looked at his watch. Two-thirty in the morning, almost twenty-four hours without sleep. He couldn't go on any further, he told himself, and duly collapsed on the ground. Using the last of his strength, he cleared the spot and removed the larger rocks.

Andrew lay curled up in his self-made hollow, warily listening to the night sounds of the forest. Save for the occasional cries of distant nocturnal birds and animals, it was quiet. God, it felt so good, just to rest. If only he had something to eat.

Tomorrow, he would begin his dependence on the wild foods of the forest. His tentative objective was to head to the northwest corner of the country, and slip into Burma. The war was much quieter in that region, and although the odds were against him, it was the best option he had at the moment.

For now, his immediate plan was to avoid the lowlands, which he knew would be continually bombed in an attempt to drive out the Pathet Lao from the Plain of Jars. The lowlands were also bad from the point of view of being discovered. If anyone were to spot him, the Pathet Lao would surely be alerted and would doggedly pursue him, and more than likely, he would be captured. On the other hand, he had to be careful of the hills as well, watching out for both friendlies and the enemy. His strategy, therefore, was to avoid following any semblance of a trail, which usually meant some degree of habitation, and even in the forest he would only travel at night. At night, both lowlanders and hill people shunned the forests for fear of the spirits that inhabited them, and he could travel undetected. He would minimize the use of his flashlight, and try to make maximum use of the waxing moon over the next ten days. In the daytime, he would hide himself and hope that he wouldn't be stumbled upon. Today he had been lucky.

And luckier still, judging by the soil condition, the past few nights had been dry, but he couldn't expect the weather to remain that way. It was August; the middle of the monsoon season, and traveling would be rough, if not outright dangerous. With this in mind, he pulled out his poncho from his duffel bag, put it on and slipped the Colt pistol into a side pocket. He would use the gun only if he had to, for protection against aggressive animals and, if it came to it, humans.

He probably wouldn't make as good progress as he had done this first day. He would eventually grow weaker, and of course, death was an odds-on possibility. If he could get out of the thick of the fighting, he would continue his journey through the riverine valleys already abandoned from the depopulation tactics that were being used, and after that, perhaps he could find intact villages where the populace could help him. Or maybe, seek refuge in temples along the way.

Andrew, huddled on the ground, shivered at the enormity of his plight. It was hopeless, he thought; he would probably die of starvation, alone and miserable in this wretched triple-canopy jungle.

Was it a death wish that led him into this crazy predicament? Maybe he just should have been a good soldier and carried out his orders. But by then he was already dead, stripped of all that he had been, robbed of everything that was dearest to him, including Cindy. This was the noblest thing he could do. At least this way, he didn't take anybody else down with him.

Of course Cindy was right. She always saw things for what they were. The war in the air was nothing less than a ruthless, inhuman obliteration of life. And if he refused to participate in such an act, it was made perfectly clear that they would punish him and brand him with disgrace and humiliation, just as Fark had threatened.

Alone, lying desperately in the moist earth, all those things he had once thought important and achievable became pointless and beyond his reach.

There was no way he could have faced trial in a military tribunal, a court-martial and dishonorable discharge; no way could he have endured serving time in a military prison. Better to die here alone. A crushing anguish engulfed him, thinking of his parents, knowing the pain they would undergo, and that he would never be able to see them again. He began to cry, muffled and sniveling, whimpering like a baby. "Mama," he moaned, a cry in the dark.

He couldn't do it, couldn't drag them down with the notoriety that he would bring, and that he alone was responsible for. It would certainly have been a major news item, and the stigma of national publicity would have destroyed the quiet lives his parents led in such a small town as Camden. How many pilots purposely crashed their jet fighter to avoid a combat engagement? The ignominy would be unbearable. It was better to die here alone, he kept telling himself. He knew the military well enough to figure out what the official report would be. They would tell his family that he had died a hero. He himself would suffer the consequences. For it was he who had wanted to join the Air Force, he, who, duped by his own vanity, had signed up for a second tour, and it was he who had decided to crash a twenty-million-dollar airplane and desert during a time of war.

He had once been proud to be in the Air Force, but it was a shallow pride, a pride that Cynthia easily shattered, like that time in

Rosie's diner, on leave after his first tour. She had been picking at his conscious until, after her last letter, his pride had turned to shame.

Even in his fatigue, his thoughts kept on tormenting him.

Cindy.

Their love had been so natural, so candid, so nurturing, they hadn't needed anyone else. Until now, that is, for he knew in his heart that she had found someone else to give herself to. He felt he had abandoned her, taking her love for granted and practically throwing her into the arms of another man. Thinking about her, conjuring up her beautiful image, he trembled with a feeling of desolation, starving for her love, thirsty for her affection, all of which he was to never have again.

A hot rush of self-pity overcame him and a choking sensation blocked his throat. The life he had led up to now, all he had known was a closed chapter, abruptly concluded. The aura of hope that had framed his youth had dissipated with one bold, impetuous act. As he lay in the moist earth, a sad gust of nostalgia blew through his soul, mournfully decrying the death of a comfortable and familiar past.

In his distress, he pulled at his hair and yanked it, and began weeping once again. God would be there with him, the chaplain had said. God would know what to do.

"Help me God," he whimpered.

He was awake at first light only a few hours later, a baleful haze in the air, a sensation of unreality closing in on him. His face was practically swollen from mosquito and ant bites, and his whole body itched so bad it burned. As he got up, he was greeted with extreme muscle spasms in his legs and back, and felt thoroughly bruised, as if he had been beaten with a baseball bat. He took a pee, after which he set about trying to make his makeshift bed more comfortable. Then he lay back down in it, intending to rest for the remainder of the day, too tired to do anything. He decided he would forage for food towards dusk, before embarking again. Water was the main problem, however, and he would have to find some, as his canteen was now nearly empty. The dilemma that water presented was that everybody else wanted it too, and the chance of meeting someone drawing it, someone who wasn't afraid of the jungle spirits of the night, a hunter maybe, could prove to be an obstacle. If the break in the monsoon ended, and it started raining again, his problem would be too much water. While weighing these issues over in his mind, he fell asleep once more.

It was a wet patting on his face that woke him up. The weather had noticeably changed to damper and cooler. At this point, the rain was merely a gentle shower, and he wondered whether it would remain that way to give him enough time to gather some wild foods. He checked his watch—relieved to see it was still working—a bit past five in the evening. Somehow, knowing the time gave him a tenuous sense of security, an illusion that made him feel he was still tied to a routine existence. He raised himself up, battling his body's reluctance, and did some stretching exercises to rid him of his stiffness.

While Andrew was stationed at Udon, he had had the foresight to take advantage of the many opportunities to go hiking in the mountains in Northern Thailand with locals. What he learned on those trips about the naturally growing greens and wild foods of the forest was more valuable than any survival training they had taught stateside or even in the Philippines. What Cindy had taught him from their hiking days in the Rockies could as well prove to be handy. She had taught him how to taste a leaf and recognize the types of bitterness to tell poison from healthful herbs.

He put on his poncho hurriedly and set about searching the ground for mushrooms and fallen wild olives. He kept his eyes open for lizards as well.

He saw a tree that looked like the *sadao* tree he had seen in northeast Thailand. It was an important find. Its leaves weren't only nourishing, but served as a general antibiotic as well, and he practically stripped the lower branches bare, stuffing some of the leaves into his mouth and the rest into the pockets of his poncho.

Soon, the rain began to pummel down, and the evening got dark and dismal. The wind picked up, accompanied by an intimidating barrage of thunder and lightning. The vegetation itself seemed to come alive, as leaves shook and branches swayed under the fury of the oncoming storm. Not long after, sheets of water smacked the trees, making a noise that sounded like cracking glass, and created a blurry curtain. His attempt at scavenging was now hopeless. He sat down under a tree watching the thick turbid flows of topsoil and leaves spill past him and worried about the night's journey.

The rain lasted a little over an hour. Gradually the storm moved on, and the pattering of dripping leaves was a soothing euphony. Andrew resumed searching for food, but by the time night had fallen, he found himself in terrain that seemed to be smothered in bushes. He spent much of his time trying to extricate himself from all this wild growth, and ultimately decided that he would have to get lower down if he was going to get anywhere tonight. In the dark, he picked his way slowly, looking for opportune places to move downward.

Then it started to rain again. In the pitch black, the forest floor was muddy and littered with watery mulch. Andrew grunted with exertion as the liquid soil sucked at his boots. The rain came down harder in another deluge that battered him; lightning sparked the air, photographing the jungle every few moments. Clambering down the squishy, slippery slope made him lose his footing and stumble, and he had to grab at tree trunks and branches to recover his balance. He dreaded the idea of having it rain the whole night, though he knew such long-lasting rain wasn't uncommon for this time of the year.

It was an hour later when he arrived at a thick bamboo grove. The cloudburst finally reduced its vehemence, but remained at a steady enduring pitch that sounded bleak and atonal, as the night turned dank and icy cold. Andrew realized that the bamboo jungle he was in was worse than the bushes he had originally evaded. One could easily get lost, and he already didn't have any idea of where he was.

He decided to make notches in the bamboo stems with his survival knife as he went along.

In all directions was an impervious blackness, and without his flashlight, any forward advance would have been impossible. The rain increased its intensity once more and didn't let up throughout the night. Andrew was fatigued to the point of delirium, stumbling in the wet cold darkness, smacking at the plethora of growth that blocked his way. When, after hours of this wearisome activity, he noticed a notch cut into a bamboo stem, a notch that he himself had made hours before, he slumped to the ground and broke down crying in despair, the tears on his face mingling with the drops dripping off the hood of his poncho. He had walked for most of the night only to go around in a big circle.

"God, help me," he sobbed. "Help me. What have I done? I don't know…I don't know what I'm doing…what's going to happen to me…?"

He took out the laminated card with the hibiscus petals, which he had been keeping in the breast pocket of his shirt. Sitting, sopping wet in the pelting rain, he gazed at the petals, shivering from his sobbing as well as the cold, and contemplated the mess he was in. The pieces of flower reminded him of why he was here, and the alternative that he had rejected. Intense emotions drained out of him, leaving him empty.

The brief breakdown was like a purge of his doubts and apprehension, for he stood up, ready to continue and face whatever was ahead, without any expectations, hope, or even fear.

Four-thirty in the morning. The valley Andrew was skirting became enveloped in a thick fog. The fog grew thicker until it became a soup, and he had no choice but to climb back up and try to get out of it. He knew that the cooling air at night slunk into the valleys and caused this condensation, and perhaps it would be clearer up top.

Ascending the wet slope was considerably easier than going down had been. But the fog only became denser, and it was obvious that to continue would be a pointless waste of energy; thus, he chose to stop where he was.

On the ground, with his knees drawn up to his face, he sat wet and trembling, persevering through a night that had become a frigid, endless torment.

When dawn finally arrived in a silvery glow, his spirits lifted. He consumed as many of the *sadao* leaves as he could, washed them down with the last of his water, and rose to his feet to continue his trek. Nearing the top of the ridge, he stopped and looked around at a vista of misty mountains, and the blanket of opalescent clouds that scraped past their peaks. He turned around and, with stoic determination, forged ahead, trudging into the grayness.

In the Plain of Jars and the surrounding mountains, the battle lines were always changing, and there was no way for Andrew to know that he was about to enter enemy territory.

By this time, Andrew's situation had finally been brought to the attention of the Studies and Observation Group. The Studies and Observation Group, the SOG, was established in 1964 when President Johnson authorized covert missions and allowed cross-border operations. Every month or so, the CIA and the SOG held regularly scheduled coordination meetings at the CIA office in Udon, Thailand. Frequently, the attendees at these monthly meetings discussed the placement of teams into Laos, but this is only speculation, since the records of such meetings have never been declassified. However, this particular meeting wasn't typical. It was called on short notice to decide on a matter that was considered urgent—Priority One.

The meeting was held in a two-story, whitewashed, windowless building nicknamed the Taj Mahal, located in the southeast corner of the Royal Thai Airbase at Udon Thani, in a room that was painted in a cold casting of austere gray. Those in attendance were the usual members: a Colonel from SOG High Command, and a Major from Marine Counter-intelligence representing the First Force

Reconnaissance Unit at Command and Control North in Da Nang. Of course, the resident CIA man at Udon, discreetly called the 'Special Assistant', was also present, as well as the CAS (Controlled American Source) man that was the assistant to the CIA Station Chief at the Embassy in Vientiane. There were two others in addition to this customary gathering: a General from the Air Force Office of Special Investigations, and Colonel Lawrence Fark, Squadron Operations Officer for the 432nd Tactical Fighter Squadron, Eighth Tactical Wing, Udon Thani Airbase. The CIA 'special Assistant', with meticulously combed hair and wire-rimmed spectacles, was dressed in an AberCrombie & Fitch safari jacket; the CAS operative from the Vientiane Embassy, an ugly man—short, stodgy, and whose face was conspicuously marked with liver spots—wore a white tropical leisure suit. The rest of the men were in their respective military uniforms, exhibiting an almost Puritanical neatness. These men were seated, arranged in no particular hierarchy, around a long rectangular Formica table, their faces chalky white in the glow of fluorescent ceiling lights that emitted a faintly audible background buzz.

The SOG Colonel, the unofficial chairman, anxiety evident in his ruffled middle-aged face, opened the meeting. "Gentlemen, we've called this meeting on short notice to discuss a matter which not only threatens our war effort here in Indochina, but may also pose a risk to the security of the United States in the global context. As a consequence, this matter has been given a Q-clearance classification."

Q clearance was even more secret than Top Secret.

"I would first like to introduce you to General Cassius Wheeler, from the Air Force Office of Special Investigations, and Colonel Lawrence Fark, from the 432nd TFS, 8th TFW, here at Udon, who will now brief us on this emergency. Colonel, if you will..."

Fark performed the customary protocol of clearing his throat. "Good afternoon, gentlemen. Three days ago, two flights of F-111-A's took off at 0436 local from Udon to assist in air support of

Operation About Face on the PDJ..."

PDJ stood for the French name Plaines des Jarres. The military and intelligence communities seem to love acronyms, perhaps because they find their own jargon so difficult to use in speech.

Fark continued his narrative, embellished with much of this jargon. "One aircraft, from the second flight, piloted by Lt. Andrew James Kozeny, went down after HF check in to AB triple C 'Cricket' at 0452, fifty nautical miles southwest of 'invert'. Invert painted a good ID. Aircraft passed 'invert' four nautical miles southeast at 0457, on a heading of 085 degrees at 10,000 feet AGL. Aircraft then broke formation without explanation, on heading 342, and dropped altitude. At about the same time radio contact was lost, and at first, we were not sure if it was due to intervening terrain, or, for some strange reason, that the pilot had switched the radio off. Last radar paint was at 0503 local, 190 degrees true, approximately twenty miles from 'invert'. No enemy activity was noted in the area. Two other pilots from the same flight reported seeing the aircraft emerge from a canyon and entering a seventy-degree climb, before leveling off and then diving, making a controlled flight into terrain. Last known coordinates at North 19 32 00, East 102 29 00."

"Excuse me," the AFOSI guy, General Wheeler, broke in. He was a big man, with the massive facial features of a Viking, his hair cropped to a colorless stubble. "Did you say 'controlled flight into terrain'? You mean he crashed the plane intentionally?"

"That's correct," Fark confirmed. "This was not, I repeat, not a case of target fixation or negative–g blackout. Yesterday, SAR helicopters called in by Cricket and guided in by a local Raven, picked up the navigational and weapons officer, Lt. Gerald Withers, who claims that Kozeny went nuts, ditched the plane and forced them to egress. Said that Kozeny ran off into the jungle, he doesn't remember which direction. Hmong Special Guerilla Units sighted the escape pod approximately four miles due east from where Withers was picked up."

The CAS man spoke up. "Will there be a need to go in and

sanitize the wreckage?"

Fark answered him. "The aircraft was seen going down in a fireball. Apparently, Kozeny armed all his weapons before egressing. But the escape module is hanging in a tree somewhere. Its destruction would be desirable, if at all possible."

"The main threat," announced the Special Assistant, adjusting his glasses as he looked down and opened a manila folder, "is the pilot." With the papers in the file now accessible, he looked up to address his associates. "Not only is he intimate with the F-111, but he was flying ECM before, was he not?"

"Kozeny was flying Wild Weasels using our latest Electronic Counter Measure technology," Fark confirmed. "If the enemy can figure out our radar detection and jamming tools, our aircraft will be sitting ducks to their AA guns and SAMs."

"He's also seen our communications setup at Bouam Luong," the CAS man added. "This kid's a real intelligence liability."

"Before we go into the pilot's background," interrupted the SOG Colonel, "we would like to know, Colonel Fark, if you noticed Kozeny exhibiting any unusual behavior before the mission."

Now Fark was on the defensive. "He did seem a bit disturbed since he was shot down and lost his back-seater a few weeks ago. I gave him a week's leave to go to Bangkok and put it behind him. I don't think he fully got it out of his system. He came to me the day before the mission and told me he couldn't fly it. I didn't think much of this at the time, because I knew his ability and his moral fortitude... hell, he was a hero already. So I basically told him to straighten out and pull his socks up. It was only after the incident that the Catholic chaplain came to me, and told me that Kozeny was bothered about something, and that he was having some psychological crisis, but of course by then it was too late..."

"Distinguished Flying Cross," the Special Assistant stated, reading from his dossier. "Shot down a MIG, in Pack Six."

North Vietnam airspace had been divided, in the context of tactical air battles, into several corridors, called Route Packages, and

Route Package Six over Hanoi and Haiphong, called Pack Six for short, was only given to pilots who were the cream of the crop.

"For us flyers," Fark informed him, "that doesn't say enough. Kozeny was flying barrier patrol, then, noticing our Phantoms were outnumbered, pulled up and lured three MIGs, one of which he shot down. Now the F-105 is not an air superiority fighter, and a MIG can outmaneuver it any day with only minimum effort. But Kozeny knew the flight envelope of his aircraft, knew that the 105 could outrun a MIG, so he dived down and did just that before turning around and shooting one of those bastards out of the sky." He added a finishing statement, happy for the chance to exonerate himself. "That kid could really fly. He was a natural."

"Andrew James Kozeny," said the Special Assistant, again reading from his dossier, "born to Dorothy Walsena and William Stanislaus Kozeny, 1945. Apparently a furlough baby, since the elder Kozeny was in the infantry at the time, US Army 101st. Interestingly enough, William Kozeny was in the Battle of the Bulge where he went missing, and was found two days later wandering in the Black Forest. Was put in the brig and charges of desertion were brought against him, then dropped. Became an insurance salesman, worked his way up to Sales Manager, no apparent hobbies, and the only affiliation we found is with the Polish-American Union of Camden, Ohio. Mother, Dorothy, also a member of same union, is a registered nurse in the state of Ohio, where she worked for seven years at St. Boniface Hospital in Camden before giving birth to her son, and started work again at same hospital five years ago until present. Both Catholics, at least outwardly practicing, since their son received both his Communion and Confirmation. No evidence of contact with any communist organizations, and finances show nothing out of the ordinary."

"Any living relatives in Poland?" the CAS man queried, leaving no stone unturned. Poland was, after all, an Eastern Bloc member.

"None close enough for them to maintain contact with. 'Cousin' in Warsaw," the Special Assistant explained, 'Cousin' referring to the

US Embassy, "has already investigated that angle." He took off his glasses and chewed pensively at the end of its ear clasp before looking back down at his papers and continuing.

"Andrew Kozeny, attended Roosevelt Public High School 44 in Camden, and, what might be of some relevance, was Ohio High School State Cross-Country Champion. Accepted at the Air Force Academy in Colorado Springs, where he also won a few more medals in the same sport. He spent four years at the Academy, then assigned to the 480th at McConnel AFB in Kansas, after which he was transferred to Nellis 428th TFS in June 1967, where he was taught advanced electronic countermeasures, and later participated in the Harvest Reaper program for developing the F-111. Attended the Defense Department's language school in Monterey, California, where he excelled in Thai and Lao. As well as instruction in Escape and Evasion tactics at Udon, he also had survival training at Clark AFB, Philippines. Medically fit, no previous history of any mental or emotional breakdown. Promotion to Captain had already been confirmed, and currently being reviewed for the Purple Heart and Air Medal. Three months left on current tour."

"I'm not sure I'm getting this," said the SOG Colonel. "From our experience we found that most deserters are white-trash dopers who didn't want any more combat and hung out in the villages with their whores, and figured they could stay put getting high until their tour was over. And as for defectors, this guy doesn't fit that 'psy' profile either. Since we've been in this war we've had over one thousand cases of mutiny and defection, and the common psycho-social profile is typically that of enlisted men with the lowest military paygrades, and just about all of them show troubled backgrounds or extreme poverty."

Fark made a small confession. "Well, Kozeny was a bit out of the ordinary. He had a kind of humility you don't normally find in pilots. A quiet kid, didn't say much, and so he was often outside the group, you might say. That made some of the pilots a bit uncomfortable around him, but because he could fly so well and didn't lord it over them, they overlooked his peculiarities."

"Since his disappearance," resumed the Special Assistant, "we have opened his footlocker and have produced a detailed three page inventory of contents, looking for diaries, any significant magazine or news clippings, noting book titles of any books etc. etc. There was also one roll of film, which CIA Udon developed, with frame-by-frame descriptions. All of that revealed very little. Except for the mail. This one particular letter we found notable, and we have photocopies so you can read for yourselves." He passed around photocopies of Cynthia's last letter to Andrew, as well as a snapshot Andy had kept of her, posing in a bikini.

The CAS man from Vientiane, after reading the letter, picked up the photo and spoke first. "So this bitch is the reason why we're all here. He must have had a happy time humping her." He gave out an ironic snort. "US security threatened by a blonde-haired twat."

The Special Assistant proceeded, ignoring the rude remarks. "Cynthia Soronson, childhood sweetheart, went to the same high school as Kozeny, then followed him to Colorado, majoring in English Literature at the University of Colorado in Boulder. After graduating, she went on to graduate school at the University of California at Berkeley to study journalism, and that's when all the trouble began. Started sleeping with a professor in the Political Science department, a leftist called Mitchell Talbot, and has subsequently joined several subversive antiwar organizations. Member of the Berkeley May Day Committee, Students and Teachers Against the War, and Science for the People." The Special Assistant stopped his narrative and looked up at the men around the table. "Langley has given this a full-facility grading. We've already contacted the FBI, and they've called her in for questioning, as well as putting a tap on her phone. So far, they have her on possession of marijuana, and her movements are being monitored. The IRS, with our cooperation, is doing a full audit of her finances. The usual procedures. The same goes for Talbot, the professor she's having an affair with, and he's been arrested on drug charges as well. We're also applying pressure for the University to dismiss him, so it's likely that Mr. Talbot will be out of a job in the very foreseeable future."

"Serves the bastard right," said the CAS man. "He'll no longer be in a position to corrupt our nation's youth."

General Wheeler was growing impatient. "None of that is directly solving our problem here. The F-111 is our secret weapon, our ace up the sleeve against the Russkies. Hell, one F-111 has the fighting power of five F-4s. We can't afford any exposure of this technology; it would set us back six years and billions of dollars, not to mention all the security and political implications, and all because of a love-struck, pussy-whipped pilot who gets a Dear John letter. So what are we going to do about Kozeny?"

The Marine Counter-Intelligence guy, who had been quiet up to now, determined it was finally time to make his offering. His looks were stolid, devoid of emotion, and could have very well belonged to a department store mannequin. "I don't think we have any choice but to insert a hunter-killer team. Cross-country champion or not, my bet he hasn't gotten very far. The Laotian jungle is quite a different kettle of fish than the woods of Ohio. I can have a First Force Recon team ready in less than twenty-four hours. They could come in 'on strings', on the coordinates of the capsule sighting, BMNT tomorrow."

BMNT stood for 'Before Morning Nautical Twilight'. It was a good time for a helicopter insertion—enough light for ground activities but not enough to see the helicopter from a distance. 'Coming in on strings' meant the team would rappel down ropes dropped from the chopper.

"We agree," commented the Special Assistant, "however, we feel that as few Americans as possible should be involved in this exercise. This facilitates in making the matter plausibly deniable. We suggest that you offer only one of your personnel to lead the killer part of the team. Since our assets in Laos include the Special Guerilla Units, who already possess excellent intelligence of the area, we can use them to track Kozeny. We will provide one of our paramilitaries who has experience in working with the SGUs to be the lead hunter."

"Fine," said the Marine CI Officer. "We'll give you one of our top guys. Sgt. Stephen Anatoly. A real hotshot, but very serious about his work. He's been on seven missions in Laos, and he's never let us down."

"What about Withers?" Fark asked. "And the team that debriefed him, including myself?"

"Okay," said the AFOSI General, "the official story is that a malfunction of the aircraft's tail servo actuator caused a sudden and uncontrollable pitch-up and roll. This failure in the flying controls system caused the aircraft to break up in flight. I've written a classified memorandum to this effect," he said, handing Fark a sheet of paper. "In other words, a freak accident that could render the aircraft uncontrollable in rare circumstances. Given Kozeny's record, pilot error would be less believable. Withers should report that Kozeny fell to his death when he tried to depart the capsule." General Wheeler paused. "Because of this incident, we are considering dropping the Combat Lancer program and grounding the F-111s. There's too much risk."

"As for the parents," the SOG Colonel brought up, "can we have the Air Force Casualty Office contact them? To inform them that their son went down in a recon mission in Southeast Asia. Hit by a SAM and the plane went down in a fireball. We'll create the documentation, and provide some ashes." He paused to look around the table. "Is there anything else gentlemen?"

All murmured in agreement that the meeting was over.

The SOG Colonel placed both his hands firmly on the table in a gesture of conclusion. "Good, then we will leave it in the hands of our Intelligence people."

As the meeting broke up, the CAS man leaned over to the Special Assistant. "I have Botkin waiting for us in Briefing Room 004. I think that Major Barwood should accompany us," he said, turning around to look at the Marine Counter Intelligence Officer. "Major," he called, "perhaps you should come with us, we have the paramilitary officer who will be leading this mission in a briefing room down the hall." Major Barwood closed his notebook and looked up. "Fine."

The three men exited together and marched down the corridor, which, similar to their meeting room, was pallidly lit by neon strip lighting.

"We have to be a bit careful with Botkin," announced the CAS man as they were walking, "he's a bit of a live wire. We had him in the center of things, as an advisor to some of Vang Pao's units, but he repeatedly disregarded orders, which forbade directly engaging in combat. Also a bit unstable. Some of his missions were unauthorized. We gave him some work in the quieter areas in the northwest, to work with the Yao, another hill tribe. Keep him out of trouble so to speak. Still, I think he's the best for the job, considering the nature of this mission"

The Special Assistant opened the door of the designated room. Inside, sitting at yet another rectangular Formica table, dressed in camouflage fatigues, was Robert Botkin, code name, Mr. Sheen.

Like the character on the bottle of the household cleaner known as Mr. Clean, he had a totally shaven head, before such head-styles had become fashionable. Indeed, he had originally intended to adopt that appellation, Mr. Clean, but to his dismay he had discovered that it had already been taken by another shaven-headed operative, and so, recalling the jingle, 'Mr. Clean leaves a sheen where he cleans', he had to settle for Sheen. His oval face was dominated by distinctly prominent cheekbones, which jutted out like a pair of ridges, guarding his cold, steel-gray eyes. His expression was humorless, reflecting his attitude that this war, and the world in general, was a mess because it was run by suit-wearing, paper-pushing men who had no balls.

Robert Botkin, also known as 'Bobby Bo', was over thirty years of age, but still fit and strong, though considered by many to be a braggart and a bully, as well as an obnoxious drunkard and 'sick fuck' to boot. As part of his training for the Special Forces, he was dropped in the jungles of Panama with a knife and a compass, and was told to find his way out, which he did, but, as rumor has it, not before killing a few Indians he had found along his way, just to simulate the real thing. He had been deployed in covert action in Korea, then Burma. As a paramilitary advisor in Laos, he took pride in making crude claymore mines with nails and plastic explosive, and homemade napalm with detergent and gasoline stirred over heat, hobbies he indulged in mainly out of boredom whenever there was a lull in the fighting. He liked putting live hand grenades in jars and throwing them out of an airplane when traveling with an Air America Cargo flight. He habitually wore dark-tinted, wire-rimmed sunglasses, even when there was no bright sun.

"Hello Bobby," greeted the CAS man. "I think you know Carling, our Special Assistant here in Udorn."

Botkin removed the sunglasses from his face, stood up and offered his hand. "Yeah right, how ya doin'?"

"And this is Major Barwood, Marine CI and head of Control and Command North, Da Nang."

"Pleased to meet ya, Major." Botkin shook his hand as well. Botkin felt that because he was working for the CIA, there was no need to salute.

"Botkin," addressed Carling, "we have something for you that we think would be interesting from your point of view. We want you to lead the hunter part of a hunter/killer operation in Laos. Target is a 'Benny.' Someone who's in possession of important intel."

"Bobby," the CAS man joined in, "the guy's a pilot who is familiar with airborne ECM and our latest aircraft, the F-111. We have overwhelming evidence that this guy flipped somehow and ditched his aircraft on purpose. We have no fucking idea what his plans are, or where he's going."

All four men sat down at the table. Carling, the Special Assistant, reached into his folder of papers and produced a military personnel photograph of Andrew, handing it to Botkin. "His name is Andrew Kozeny. I'm telling you his name, but his identity is not to be revealed to anyone else except on a need-to-know basis. He was shot down in a previous incident, and was rescued by some Hmong SGUs. We're currently in the process of acquiring those same guerillas for the operation, and they will accompany you, to make the ID easier. We want you to command the operation. A First Force Recon Marine will be coming from Da Nang to assist you. His job is to bag the target. Yours is intel, is that understood?"

"Right," Botkin replied dryly.

Barwood spoke. "We'll get Anatoly here this evening, and have an official briefing at 1800 hrs."

Botkin looked reflectively up at the ceiling, putting his index finger to his chin. "Wait a minute, isn't this the guy that Mr. Magoo picked up?"

"That's right," answered the CAS man.

"So this scumbag," he gave a conciliatory glance to Barwood, "excuse my terminology…" then, turning back to the CAS man, "he also knows about our setup at Bouam Luong?" Bouam Loung was one of Botkin's previous assignments.

"That's correct," replied the Special Assistant. "We'll go over all the details this evening, at the briefing."

"I'll have to go to Vientiane first and come back," informed the CAS man. "I'll have to inform the ambassador. Oh, and by the way, Bobby, would you tell the guys you left in Military Region II to stop sending the ears? They're upsetting the secretaries at the Embassy."

When Botkin was working with the Hmong, he was paying a bounty of one dollar for a human ear, supposedly from an enemy's head. The Hmong would send them to Vientiane so that payment could be confirmed, and the secretaries often opened these parcels and screamed at the contents.

"Yeah, okay. But I still think it was a good idea, although some of them maybe got carried away." Botkin was probably alluding to the father who cut off the ears of his own son to collect the reward money. He turned to Major Barwood. "Sometimes we would nail 'em on the door of the village headman's house, to let them know we were listening. You know, psychological operations."

The CAS man did indeed return to Vientiane, where he briefed his boss, the CIA station chief. The two of them then went to see the Ambassador, who suggested they retire to the special soundproof, bug-proof chamber, nicknamed 'the bubble', a neon-lighted, transparent plastic cubicle which had been installed in one of the so-called libraries in the Embassy. The library itself was a decorously plush room paneled in mahogany, with electric candles on the walls and furnished with baldachin sofas. The bizarre booth, with a more austere table and smaller chairs inside it, floated surreally against the backdrop of its elegant surroundings. Once seated inside, the CIA men informed the Ambassador of their intent to place a hunter-killer patrol on Laotian soil in order to neutralize a defector who possessed sensitive intelligence that could compromise US security in the region and elsewhere. They told him that the target was a highly placed South Vietnamese officer, not an American pilot. After all, that information was on a need-to-know-basis, and since what was required of them was merely to announce to the Ambassador the presence of the covert team on his turf, he didn't need to be told about that immaterial detail.

Chapter 8

Laos 1990

"Travel, in the younger sort, is a part of education; in the elder, a part of experience."
Francis Bacon, Essays, 'Of Travel'

It looked like a Russian troop carrier. The troubling thing about it was that it was very high. The first issue Dorothy had to reckon with was to figure out how to get up there—the railing she had to get over was at least ten feet off the ground. After circling to the back of the truck, she was dismayed to find that it would be a lot more difficult that way than climbing up the side. But the side didn't look much easier, despite the fact that Kampeng had leapt up and over it like Spiderman scaling a building and just as deftly wheeled around extending his hands to receive her bags. While handing him her knapsack and duffel bag, she deduced well enough that she had to use the tire as her first foothold, but after that, she wasn't sure. To make it worse, she felt everyone was looking at her. With a frail dignity, she hitched up her culottes, then scrambled up and struggled to the rail, her white, blue-veined legs flailing anxiously, her feet direly searching for support, and eventually got to the top, red-faced and panting with fright as Kampeng assisted her over. An old man in the corner clapped his hands in genuine applause, while the others cheered and chuckled.

Now that she was up there, it struck her that she would have to deal with finding a way down.

There was the old man and an old woman next to him, as well as a young mother with two children—a boy about five and a girl about three—and two other men passengers. There were also four military men in camouflage fatigues with expressionless faces holding automatic weapons. The unseen freight piled up in the truck was covered with a heavy canvas, but there were a few things that lay about on top, outside of this protective covering, including a spare tire, some sacks of rice, lots of loose coconuts, several big baskets of live chickens and one rather large pig.

The huge vehicle jerked forward, and Dorothy, unprepared, fell over on her face. She didn't realize how much the trailer body would rock and sway—it was like being on a boat in rough water. She clung frantically at a fold in the canvas, and kept her body low. Everyone else seemed as nonchalant as could be, indicating that this sort of travel arrangement was fairly commonplace. The young men lit up cigarettes, while the old man prattled away, offering the pearls of wisdom he had gathered over the years. The old woman, evidently his wife, would also contribute to the animated conversation they were having with one of the guys with the guns. Even the children were unperturbed; comparing the little cakes each was eating. Kampeng looked at Dorothy and patted his hand on a depression in the canvas next to him, suggesting she sit there. It was a good spot— in the middle, exactly where she wanted to be. Dorothy crawled over, and as the truck yawed abruptly to the right, her body froze up in fright.

"Don't be afraid, you no fall," Kampeng assured her.

After the vehicle sluggishly rumbled round a bend, Sala Pu Koun disappeared behind them with only a few remnant huts straddling the road. The scenery opened up into a breathtaking view, much like what she had been looking at before she boarded, but more expansive. Billowing mountaintops all around them, purple and brown, did indeed give her the sensation that the huge truck was a ship plowing through a sea of mountains, rising and falling with the crests of the terrain. But she was too nervous to relish it.

From her vantage point, when the truck climbed up a hill, it pitched backward at a frightening angle. On the other hand, when going down an incline, she felt she had to stop herself from rolling forward. The unevenness of the road surface made the truck lean over, left and right, and Dorothy was sure it was just about to tip over. On one occasion, she grabbed for Kampeng, painfully embarrassed.

Despite these alarming motions, the vehicle was proceeding rather slowly. In fact, it was difficult to describe just how slow this truck was moving. Dorothy felt she could have gotten down, run far enough ahead to file at least one hand's worth of nails, and reboarded when the truck caught up. It strained to surge ahead as if it were a living animal, goaded and beaten to drag its load over the rough track. Pretty soon, she realized that, despite its designation as a major artery, Route Seven wasn't a route, not even a road, but little more than a wide trail. She attempted to estimate their time of arrival based on their current speed. It was approximately a hundred and thirty kilometers to Ponsavan, which was equal to about eighty miles, and she judged they were doing around ten miles an hour, so that meant a journey of eight hours. Goodness, it was four o'clock now—they would travel a great deal through the night.

"Isn't it dangerous, because of the Chao Fa, to travel at night?" she asked Kampeng.

"No, it better. Chao Fa no attack at night."

"Why not, I thought that would be the ideal time?"

"Their gods sleep at night, no protect them. Only in daytime when their gods awake."

"Is that the real reason?"

"Also in dark they cannot see truck. Think maybe army, with many guns. They don't know. Afraid to attack."

With that point cleared up, she divulged the results of her calculations. "We should arrive around midnight," she told him.

"Maybe before. Maybe around three in afternoon."

"Three in the afternoon? It's four o'clock now!"

"Yes, three in afternoon tomorrow."

"It can't possibly take that long. It's only a hundred and thirty kilometers!"

"Road very bad up ahead. You don't know, you don't know."

Dorothy was seized with a sinking feeling in her stomach. Not only at Kampeng's pronouncement, but she could also feel that familiar urge to pee. She regretted not thinking of that before she left. She silently suffered for about an hour, her diaphragm stinging with aches before she asked Kampeng when they would stop for a break.

"Soon, we stop," he told her.

Uncannily, less than five minutes later, the truck halted and the driver cut the motor. Everyone must have had the same idea, for they all disembarked, including the two little kids, who were handed down like floppy baggage by their mother to the soldiers who had already alighted. Even the old couple got off, shaming Dorothy with their slow, yet unfaltering sprightliness as they clambered down. Dorothy, the last one remaining, decided she would exit via the back, which lacked a railing and was thus closer to the ground. Because there was no foothold, she climbed over and hung from the tailgate, then let go to drop to the ground. While the men conveniently urinated close to the road, Dorothy followed the other women deeper into the bush to relieve herself. And it certainly was relief, psychologically as well as physically. The price, however, was a repeat performance of her frantic struggle to get back in the truck.

The road hugged a mountainside with a panoramic view to the left, and as the sun sank lower and lower into the sky, the roughcast land became covered in an orange light. She had to admit it was enthralling, sitting up high on top of the lorry. The old man was asking Kampeng a lot of questions, presumably about Dorothy, who on her part, not knowing Lao, could only smile back in ignorance of what was being said. The old woman became involved, and so did the young mother.

"They think it strange, they never see farang travel this way," Kampeng said.

"Well, I think it's strange too. Honestly, I never thought I would be doing this. But I have to get to Ponsavan, one way or another."

"They want know why you go to Ponsavan, and if you ever go

before."

Dorothy looked at their smiling faces. "*Sabai dee*," the young mother said, followed by choruses of the same greeting from the old couple, all of them putting their palms together and placing them to their foreheads, gestures imbued with grace, distinction, and guiless inhibition.

"Sabai dee," Dorothy answered, one of the few words in Lao she had managed to learn so far. She didn't bother to put her palms together for fear of losing her balance. "So what did you tell them about me going to Ponsavan?" she asked Kampeng.

"I told them you with Mennonites. A doctor."

"But that's not true!"

"Well, they no understand 'travel guide'. I tell them what they understand."

One of the uniformed men said something to Kampeng.

"The soldiers say no foreigner allowed to travel on this road. They say you get stopped at Nam Chat, on way to Ponsavan. All farang, even Mennonites."

"What will we do?"

"Bo ben yang, don't worry. Kampeng is here."

She wasn't at all assured by Kampeng's optimism, recalling the issue of the airplane tickets.

The light of day imperceptibly dimmed until it expired completely. Night eventually came, a night ruled over by a three-quarter silver moon which imparted an ethereal glow to the landscape. The silver moonlight was surprisingly clear, and she could even see details that were ordinarily hidden by the glare of the daytime sun. Ghostly radiant, the landforms took on a regal beauty, and gave the trek the quality of a solemn drama. A feeling of reverence overwhelmed Dorothy.

They traveled through the lunar-lit night for another hour before they stopped at a village that appeared to be on the edge of the world.

"Is this Nam Chat?" Dorothy asked.

"No, this Pu Viang. Nam Chat still far."

"How many kilometers have we traveled already?"

"Twenty kilo."

Almost four hours and only twelve miles!

"We make good time. Very fast," Kampeng noted. "*Ooh-way* Doro-tee pick good time to come to Lao. Dry season. In rainy season cannot travel by road. Very difficult."

Several more people got on: another youth and another woman, the latter middle-aged, with many sacks of rice, apparently a trader. Inevitably, there was a lot of chitchat between the newcomers and those already on board, and Dorothy, the novelty, was forgotten for the time being.

There were quite a few villages after Pu Viang, where the truck would stop and some of the youths would get off and other people get on. The pig was still with them, as was the owner, who had given it a few swift kicks when it tried to get up and roam around. But soon, only Dorothy and Kampeng, the old couple, and the young mother were left with the soldiers. The pig had already departed, squealing as it was thrown off the back. It was nearing midnight Dorothy estimated, and Nam Chat was nowhere in sight. She was beginning to have grave misgivings about this trip.

As it became colder the Lao passengers wrapped shawls, put on jackets, and covered themselves with blankets. Dorothy also felt a bit nippy, especially around her exposed legs, but so far, she thought it was rather refreshing.

The road got tighter as the vegetation on both sides closed in. Soon, it was like a tunnel through the forest, a scary mysterious forest made more phantasmagoric by the eerie moonlight. As the way got narrower, the overhanging growth made Dorothy claustrophobic. A new danger appeared, as branches and vines would sweep across the top of the truck, violently slapping anyone not wary. Pretty soon, everyone was lying down to avoid the evil arms of the enveloping horde of trees and rattan.

The hours passed and the moon slowly crossed to the other

horizon, and still they hadn't arrived at Nam Chat, which Kampeng had explained was the halfway point. Dorothy, lying on her back, could now see stars passing through the breaks in the tree cover, traveling along with the truck, keeping pace to accompany them through the night. The forest gave way and the sky expanded, unfolding into a mosaic of constellations. She recognized Orion in the middle of the sky, and the Big Dipper above the eastern horizon, both crystal clear in the indigo night. The intense brightness of the stars made them appear so close she could reach out and touch them, their fervent glimmering animating them, as if they were burning with lives of their own.

The overburdened truck cautiously negotiated a descent full of rocks and ruts, leaning left, then right, and crawled into the settlement of Nam Chat. The driver parked the truck on the side and everyone got up to stretch their legs.

"Nam Chat. We rest here."

That meant getting off again.

Once on the ground, Dorothy looked around. On all sides were the shadows of peaks, silhouetted against the star-studded sky. They were in a place that was cozily snuggled in the encircling mountains. The settlement itself had many timber structures along the road, some lit inside by kerosene lamps. It was a bit surreal, this human habitation amidst the wilderness, in the dark of deepest night.

A bicycle glided past them, the woman sitting on the back holding a sputtering flashlight to see the way.

"We have to report to military," Kampeng said. "We get permission to travel."

This was easier said than done. Inside a nondescript shed illuminated by a candle, a long palaver ensued. There was no way the young officer in charge was going to let Dorothy proceed, whether as travel guide, Mennonite doctor, or Mother Theresa. The fear of his punishment for allowing her passage weighed greater influence than any case Kampeng could present. The officer was worried about what would become of him if the elderly farang woman, an

American, should get into any problems. It was for her own good that she should be prevented from traveling further. Kampeng kept showing him the visa, trying to convince the army guy that it was a special visa that could only be granted by higher authorities to special people. Much to Dorothy's surprise, it was Kampeng's doggedness that won in the end, for the officer gave her back the stamped piece of paper and she was allowed to continue her voyage.

Back on top of the truck, everyone brought out their *kow nee-oh*, or sticky rice: waxy, glutinous grains all stuck together and eaten in much the same way that a European would eat bread, of which Dorothy was invited to partake. Kampeng had the foresight to have brought some of their own, as well as buying some fried beef here in Nam Chat. All the food was arranged centrally on the canvas in front of them for everyone to share. There was the ubiquitous *tam som*, unripe papaya salad, and a little bag of chili sauce they called *cheo*.

"*Kin ben?*" the old woman asked.

"*Ben, ben,*" Kampeng answered on Dorothy's behalf, and then explained, "She want to know you eat Lao food. I say you eat, no plobrem."

"Ben," Dorothy asserted, facing the couple while imitating Kampeng's response. She dipped a hefty ball of the glutinous rice in the chili sauce and placed it in her mouth. "'Ben', does that mean I can?"

"Yes."

"*Geng,*" the old man abruptly said.

"He say you expert at eating *kow nee-oh*."

The old man was patronizing her good-naturedly, she knew, like a parent praising a child. "Well there isn't much to it, is there?" she remarked rhetorically.

The young mother woke her two sleeping children and made them eat. They sat up, eyes half-closed, slump-shouldered from sleep, and took their sticky rice half-heartedly. The old couple continued talking jovially to Kampeng in happy carefree voices which amazed Dorothy, considering the arduous conditions they were under. She, being a fellow senior citizen, was touched by this gaiety of the elderly.

The soldiers got back on, and the truck set out once more into the obscurity of a gloomy wilderness fluorescent under the blue glow of starlight. Ahead of them, the headlights illuminated the overhanging limbs and creepers and cast shadows that exaggerated the bumps and dents of the road, a road that, to Dorothy's astonishment, seemed to be getting narrower, something that she didn't think was possible—a wall of undergrowth to their right, and on their left, a steep drop into bushes and trees. Making it even more hair-raising were the unstable patches where springs and waterfalls crossed a low part of the road, rendering it a waterlogged, churned up, jumble of mud. There were a couple of instances when she sucked in her breath in trepidation, doubtful that the truck could make it through the watery mess judging by the way it was slipping and sliding, and, at least from her perspective, almost skidding off the edge.

Then of course, the inevitable happened: the headlights of an oncoming truck blinded them as it came around a bend, blocking the way with its bulkiness. Now what? There was no way either could pass. Somehow an unspoken communication had taken place between the drivers of the two trucks, and the one Dorothy was on seemed to get the short straw, for the driver attempted to pass around the outside of the other, negotiating the scant space available. The left tires treaded on the very limit of the road on the edge of the cliff, and the truck listed over at an alarming angle as Dorothy's heart pumped frenetically at the prospect of tumbling down the mountain. An endless series of moments passed before the two lumbering behemoths were clear of each other.

Throughout the night, there were several of these fragile encounters with opposing trucks, which added to the other horrors of the ride. Like the cold for instance. The deeper they traveled into the night, the colder it got. Despite the rig's slothful speed, it was enough to generate a chilly breeze that froze her bare arms and legs.

She had to rummage through her bag in the dark, on top of the moving truck, to get out her pullover and sweatpants. She tied a kerchief on her head and put her safari hat on as well. But the draughts pierced through these defenses and she ended up shivering.

All these things, together with the unpleasant lurching of the lorry, made it impossible for Dorothy to sleep in spite of her intense fatigue. Worst of all, she had to go to the toilet again! Fortunately they did eventually stop, but it was a torture getting down and back up again in her enfeebled state.

After that, they continued to trudge on with a tortoise-like advance. The chattering of the Laotians had long since faded, overpowered by the bewailing roar of the engine. She was hoping that this seemingly endless night would end, and that the morning would come to lift her spirits. As if in deliverance, a faint glow on the horizon nibbled away at the darkness of the sky and revealed an outline of jagged ridges. And as the day grew brighter, so did Dorothy's frame of mind.

Standing in all directions were range upon range of lofty peaks and rows of mountains, one behind another, successively overlapping into the distance. They passed valleys where shreds of cloud hid hovering over emerald forests, trapped in by walls of limestone. Villages started to appear again, separated by kilometers of wilderness. They were pretty, pastoral scenes, with houses built on the edges of cultivated valleys and terraced rice paddies with a mosaic of dikes.

Soon, the truck slowed to a halt in another undistinguished village.

"We eat lunch now."

Lunch took place in a shack, and consisted of cold, deep-fried fish and sticky rice. The fish were puny, the size of which would impel a fisherman in Ohio to throw them back. The little bones inevitably got stuck in her teeth, and Dorothy found this unpalatable. She just ate portions of the rice.

After lunch, it was back on the road, but before reaching the end of the village, there was another police check. Due to the stamp she got at the first one during the night, this officer required less convincing on Kampeng's part to give out another stamp and let her through. She wondered if she was still a Mennonite doctor.

The road became one of sand and powdery mud, and dust now became the main nuisance. Everyone was soon covering their mouths and wrapping their heads with anything that could be used as a makeshift turban. The dust made their skin dry and itchy and parched their throats. The heat from the hot afternoon sun added another unbearable discomfort, and despite her frequent gulps of water, Dorothy felt she was becoming dehydrated.

The truck trudged on with a grinding pace, the tires laboring against the resisting earth, while a monotonous chorus of gears—first gear, then second, then first again—caterwauled over and over again until they became a dismal, perpetual sound. There was yet another police check, and as Dorothy accumulated stamps on her special piece of paper, the procedure became more routine. Then onward again through more dense forest and the welcome relief of cool shade, as well as more climbing. Dorothy by now was feeling weak and nauseous, with a headache that persisted in spite of the three Tylenol's she had taken. She now understood Kampeng's reluctance to make this trip by road, and she herself was regretting it.

The day grew paler and darkness wasn't far off.

"Are we close to Ponsavan yet?"

"Yes," Kampeng replied, "another six hours."

But that wasn't close enough for Dorothy. Now she began to dread those same terrible afflictions that had plagued her the night before, and the torment of sleeplessness. This was a punishment equaling anything that hell would have to offer, riding on top of this darned truck for eternity. It already seemed like an eternity—what a horrid journey!

With the night came a new development. The truck broke down.

It was the transmission.

So there they were, in the middle of nowhere, with the transmission splayed open in front of the light of the campfire. The men were taking turns banging at something which they passed around. Everyone else was babbling. It went on like this for an hour or so, banging and babbling, and just when Dorothy was giving up hope of ever getting out of there, they set about putting the transmission back together.

The night was extraordinarily still, except for the shrill chirping of the crickets, a sound that seemed to come out of everywhere. The driver and his assistant, along with the soldiers, were under the truck mounting the transmission; their voices clear yet muted in the immensity of the highland wilderness, the moving halo of their flashlights uncanny in the darkness. Suddenly, from somewhere in the depths of the jungle, a hideous scream echoed out.

"What is that?" Dorothy asked in a panic.

"*Gra-tair.*"

"Gra-tair? What's that?"

"It live in trees."

"Is it dangerous?" Dorothy didn't realize that *Gratair* was a tree shrew, a rodent about the size of a mouse.

"Not dangerous."

The men clambered out from under the truck and indicated to everyone to get back on, and within minutes they were continuing into the night. Before long however, their progress was considerably retarded by a fog that grew denser by the moment. In due time, it was so thick she literally couldn't see two feet in front of her; maybe a foot, a foot and a half at most. It was too dangerous to drive any faster than walking speed, as each curve and bend revealed itself only at the last moment. Oh great, Dorothy bemoaned to herself, what a way to go, driving off the edge of a cliff.

No one was sleeping. All were awake and staring wide-eyed in silent suspense into the silver-gray curtain that hid the world. This went on for nearly an hour before they could get out of the clouds, and it seemed to mark a turning point, for not only did it become clearer, but the road got wider and the thick forest became sparser.

As if in celebration, the old man, with an impish grin on his face, brought out a plastic bag, just as one would present a surprise gift, and emptied its contents into a tin bowl.

"Pla dek," Kampeng told her.

It stank to high heaven.

"What's that?" Dorothy asked, holding her nose.

"Fish, but very old."

Fermented, she realized.

Baskets of sticky rice were produced and Dorothy was compelled to partake. Even with the foul smell, it didn't taste too bad, a bit sour and salty, and very fishy. The fact that she was famished made it easier to swallow it down.

Soon after they finished their meal they passed human dwellings, spectral shadows of villages sleeping in the dead of night. One was Muong Soui, where the old couple disembarked quietly. After that, Dorothy finally fell asleep.

She awoke to a wondrous sight. The Dance of the Mists she would refer to it afterwards. They were coming off the mountains, approaching the Plain of Jars, the western portion of which was now in view, bathed in the newborn light of dawn. Among the small, brown hills of the undulating plain below them, nature was staging an enchanting show, a primordial choreography, with mists streaking across and connecting the tops of zigzagged lines of trees; other wisps steamed up out of small hollows, spiraling gracefully like slow motion geysers. A white and silver band of cloud cut across the base of distant mountains, making them appear as if they were floating in the air. The early morning had created this marvelous display for her, causing her to forget the traumas of her trip and making her arrival magical. She felt like that other, younger Dorothy in the Wizard of Oz, who, after going through the forest, first set her eyes on the Emerald City.

"Tung Hai Hin," Kampeng confirmed. "The Plain of Jars."

Chapter 9

Laos 1990

"Bombs like streams of devils
Bursting clouds of flames,
Blowing villages into the sky,
Turning all into dust"
Old Laotian man recalling the bombing of the Plain of Jars, from
Voices from the Plain of Jars

The Plain of Jars presented a striking contrast to the rugged terrain
Dorothy had traveled through to get there. An elevated plateau of
friable, chalky limestone, washed out from the surrounding harder
rocks by a million years of rain, it offered a welcome relief to the
harsh land around it. The Laotians call the place Tung Hai Hin, while
the Vietnamese still refer to it as the Tran Ninh Plateau. From above,
it is an abruptly conspicuous feature, occupying an area of one
thousand square kilometers, sitting more than three thousand feet
above sea level. The Plain, contrary to its name, is not monotonously
flat, but undulating—a rolling meadowland with softly curved,
breast-like hills, changing colors with the seasons, remaining a vivid
green after the monsoon rains, until the sun sears it pale yellow
during the hot, dry, tropical summer. Long broad valleys of rich,
moist soil separate scattered masses of solitary mountains which
stand like lonely leviathans, stark and lost in the midst of their puny
surroundings, inexplicably cut off from the herd of great ranges
beyond.

In the past, a crude network of roads had made Tung Hai Hin a
commercial entrepot, and merchandise such as opium, cloth, salt,
and silk, had passed for centuries through the province to cities
throughout Southeast Asia. This thriving trade financed the building
of splendid cities with hundreds of golden, bejeweled pagodas. But

it was also a place plagued by tragedy. For seven hundred years, up to the time of the Indochina war, one group after another would war on the area, hold sway for a number of years, then give way to a new set of conquerors—the Burmese, Siamese, Vietnamese, the Haws, and the French. The tiny Kingdom of Xieng Khouang, established by indigenous Lao who called themselves Puan, was constantly threatened with foreign subjugation and often had to politically maneuver its alliances to pit one rival against another, seeking protection from whoever was more powerful at the time.

In 1826, thinking the British would support him, Chou Anou of the Kingdom of Vieng Chan, encouraged by the Vietnamese, foolishly attacked Siam and marched towards Bangkok. His armies were routed long before he got anywhere close to the Siamese capital, and Chou retreated hastily to the Kingdom of Xieng Khouang, which offered him sanctuary. The Siamese army pursued him, right up to the Plain of Jars, punishing Xieng Khouang by depopulating the area, forcibly evacuating the populace, while Chou himself ran away to Vietnam.

Then, fifty years later, the Haw came.

Known to Western Historians as the Black Flag, they were ruthless marauders that swept down from China with unmitigated brutality. They pillaged, plundered, murdered, and raped, compelling the Puan to flee the area. Those escaping the havoc ran right into the arms of an advancing Thai army sent to confront the Haw. The Thai army captured the hapless refugees and drove them on a forced march full of suffering and death all the way to Bangkok, where they became slaves of the Siamese nobility.

Less than a century later, the peoples of Xieng Khouang would suffer once more under the strategy of depopulation, abandoning their homeland in the terror of the most intensive aerial bombardment ever conducted in the annals of war.

Was this a curse, for people to be driven out of the Plain of Jars, or did the US military get the idea from history, Dorothy mused, sitting atop the truck as it staggered into Ponsavan.

Although a fairly recent town, having been reconstructed after the chaos of the war, Ponsavan seemed nothing more than a sprawling, dilapidated place, with a grid of dirt roads flanked by drab-colored, cubicle buildings rarely larger than two stories high. The streets, bare and featureless, were disproportionately wider than the traffic they accommodated, which for the most part consisted of motorbikes and a few rumbling trucks. Everything within the town was covered with a thin veneer of dust. There was nothing aesthetic about the place, nor was there anything even remotely modern about it. Dorothy was slightly taken aback at the numerous Russian vehicles traveling about, all military green in color.

"So many military jeeps and trucks! Do they belong to the army?" she asked Kampeng.

"No, they private. People buy them. Very old, thirty years. From war. But they are strong, still go good."

"From the war?"

Kampeng abruptly leaned forward and banged on the cab of the truck. *"Jawt yuu nii!"* To Dorothy, he turned and said, "We get off here."

The truck stopped and left them off at the market in front of a fleet of motorcycle tuk-tuks, one of which they boarded. On Kampeng's instructions, the tuk-tuk driver took them to Pantivong Guest House, located at the end of a back street choked with fruit trees and dreary tangles of bushes. By the looks of it, the guesthouse made no pretense as to the standards of accommodation it offered. Dorothy stood outside in the morning sun, trying her best to hide her disappointment as she cursorily inspected the primitive looking concrete block, which was painted a faded powder blue and marked by black smudges of unknown origins. A yellow sign, embellished with red flowing Laotian script, hung lopsided over the entrance.

"This best guest house in Ponsavan," Kampeng declared.

"I wouldn't want to see the worst," she retorted under her breath.

Glumly, she entered and climbed up a dark staircase fashioned out of concrete and was shown her room. It was bare, save for a low-standing queen-size bed made from wooden planks, and a small, crudely fashioned night table. In the adjoining bathroom sat a large water pot with a plastic ladle for bathing purposes, and the toilet was like the one at Kasi, a long oval-shaped porcelain bowl set in the floor, which one flushed by pouring water in it. In the corner, leaning against the wall, was a large broken piece of mirror. The paint was peeling off the walls, but at least the floor was brightly tiled with a flowered motif.

"You stay here, rest. I go get car," Kampeng said, after showing her the room.

Dorothy's first priority was to get the coating of soil and sweat off her skin. The splash bath turned out to be delightful, regardless of the chill of the water. After that, she fell into a wonderful sleep on a bed that was the hardest she had ever lain in, but nevertheless, a bed infinitely better than a sack of rice on top of a truck.

She awoke a few hours later to the sound of banging on the door. To her consternation, the room was now pitch black. "Who is it?" she cried out in the darkness.

"Kampeng," came the reply from the other side of the door. "You hungry, want eat?"

"Yes, just a minute, let me get dressed." She got up and groped along the wall until she found the light switch. She flicked it but nothing happened. Oh great. No lights. Standing helplessly in her night frock, she puzzled over how she would go through her clothes and get dressed without being able to see a thing. "There's no lights," she proclaimed.

Kampeng, outside the door, explained, "Yes. Go on at six o'crock, but today I don't know plobrem. Here, take candle."

She opened the door and accepted the candlestick. The timid flame gave out a feeble, but sufficient glow, enough for her to accomplish her tasks. She rummaged around in her duffel bag until she found her cotton summer frock, ultimately resigned to doing without the amenities she was so used to back home in Camden. She was also starting to get homesick. She longed for her cozy bedroom, and she missed Felix, her cat, whom she had given to Elizabeth to take care of. Her garden, the bridge club, Jack La Lanne's, and Wal-Mart's at the Livingston Mall, all seemed so far away.

Yet she wasn't entirely downhearted, since she also experienced a sense of accomplishment, as well as excitement, being as she was one step closer to her objectives. On top of that, she considered her journey to Ponsavan as a baptism of fire, which would make the rest of her encounters seem easier by comparison. Things were progressing rather well, she concluded. By the time she was putting on her socks, she was humming to herself.

Once dressed, she blew out the candle and walked out of her room, where she found Kampeng waiting for her in the crypt-like murkiness of the hall. The place was gloomily silent; they were apparently the only lodgers in the little establishment.

"Is there a place where I can make a phone call?" she asked him, as they cautiously descended the uneven concrete steps of the staircase, guided by the wide beam of Kampeng's flashlight.

"Yes, in owner's house. Who you want to call?"

"I would like to leave a message with Mr. Prasert, to say that I have arrived in the Plain of Jars."

They entered the 'lobby', a vault-like room whose grimy plaster walls were faintly lit by more candles on a low table in the corner.

"Okay, you stay here, I do for you. I call Riverview Hoten, I tell them to call Ai Prasert in Bangkok."

"Yes, and he is to fax the message to Cynthia Soronson."

"Who?"

"Mr. Prasert knows this already."

While waiting, she put on her reading glasses and tried to study an old map on the wall, but the dim light made it difficult to read, and it took her several minutes to discover that the names of places were labeled in Laotian letters, which were meaningless to her.

Kampeng returned shortly. "Okay, I leave message, now we go."

Exiting the guesthouse, Dorothy was introduced to their mode of transport, unsurprisingly, a Russian army jeep. It was rather loud and bumpy as they rattled off down the sandy main street to a Laotian café, where Kampeng had apparently decided they would dine. The premises of this restaurant were outlandishly done up, with sundry bomb casings and mortar shells functioning as aberrant decorations. Some of the spent projectiles were used as flowerpots; others had the words 'bomb' and 'USA' written on them in white chalk, a macabre and vulgar display that made Dorothy just a bit uncomfortable. Because the town's electricity hadn't yet been turned on, the tables inside were lit with candles. The sallow light couldn't conceal the shabbiness of the décor—whitewashed walls, a leaden-colored concrete floor, and plain wooden tables complimented with curved plastic chairs in assorted tawdry colors. They took seats opposite each other at a table by the wall.

"They have tourist food here," Kampeng stated, as he picked up the menu.

"I suppose this is the best restaurant in Ponsavan."

As Kampeng didn't answer her, she perused the menu, where the bill of fare was graciously translated into misspelled English underneath the Laotian descriptions. The tourist food was a choice of either 'water-bufelow steek' with French 'flies', or 'flied' rice, or 'flied' noodles. After living for days on sticky rice, papaya salad, rotten fish, and assorted alien vegetables, she unhesitatingly opted for the steak.

A conversation developed concerning their plan of action.

"Today," Kampeng announced, "I ask if any Chao Fa on road to Muang Kham. The road is safe, so we go there first."

"Muang Kam used to be called Ban Ban, yes?"

"Yes. It eastern end of Xieng Khouang. Sixty kilos away."

A middle-aged waitress in a headscarf fussed around their table unloading their food

"Do you think we could find anyone who saw something, maybe who can lead us to the crash site?" she asked, while attempting to cut her steak.

She didn't look at him as she asked this, preoccupied as she was with getting the knife to penetrate the rubbery piece of meat on her plate.

"Maybe. After war, some people no go back, they stay in Vieng Chan, but many people return to their villages."

"Well, since it's our farthest site, perhaps it's best we should make it our first stop."

Dorothy gave up wrestling with her steak and studied the soupy stew Kampeng was eating. "What's that?" she inquired, pointing at his bowl.

"*Geng Om,*" he replied. "Lao specialty."

"Could you order one for me?"

As Kampeng turned to call the waitress over, the lights came on.

"Hurray!" Dorothy cheered.

It was a radiantly clear morning, and Dorothy was energized by a certain thrill, eager to begin her fact-finding mission, a journey she hoped would lead her back to the end of her son's life. They were in the jeep, and the road they were following was part of the same Route Seven that they had traveled on during their horrendous ride to get here. However, this portion of the route was a bit more bearable, though in a terrible enough condition as to compel them to travel along at a moderately slow speed. It took them on a meandering path over the rim of the Plain of Jars, continuing to the east through dusty reddish brown hills, passing small unremarkable settlements until they reached Khang Khay, where, Dorothy had once read, Souvanna Pouma had vainly tried to set up a neutralist base. It was a letdown. Besides a few leftover concrete buildings, there was nothing left of the place. After that, the countryside retained a tinge of desolation. In most of the valleys between the red ridges lay dry, dull-colored paddies bordered by dikes, and which were filled with the yellow stubble from last year's harvest. In some of the other lowlands sat small, dark-colored lakes, which, Kampeng pointed out, were fed by groundwater seeps. Dorothy was relieved when they at last came upon some small villages, pretty pastoral scenes arrayed with large-leafed banana and palm trees, alive with peasants in grass hats. Along the way, they jostled past lumbering water buffaloes with swaying white underbellies, and barefooted monks shading themselves with orange parasols the same color as their robes. Occasionally, groups of children could be seen walking and cycling on the road, the little girls in their diminutive-sized sarongs and schoolboys in white shirts and black shorts. It was at this point that Dorothy began to notice all the bomb craters set in the landscape, and reflected on how the serene setting before her was once a place of hellish destruction.

According to Dorothy's map of crash sites, the location they were interested in was somewhere between Nong Pet and Muang Kham, the latter written on her map as Ban Ban. Inside an hour and a half, they arrived at Nong Pet, a large village at a junction, where they stopped.

"Do we turn off here?" Dorothy wanted to know.

"No, we stay on Route 7."

"Where does that road go?" she inquired, pointing to the track that headed in a northward direction.

"That go to Lat Buak."

Once outside the vehicle, Kampeng, without delay, proceeded to make numerous inquiries among the locals, while Dorothy amused a small crowd merely by standing in front of a large wooden shack that served as a shop, drinking a Pepsi, smiling and responding with a Sabai dee to everyone, regardless of what they said to her. The bright-eyed little kids were especially enjoying it, tirelessly echoing her greetings back to her. She noticed one young boy standing alone at the corner of the wooden shop, both his arms covered in bandages, and there was another large bandage on the left side of his face as well.

Kampeng, apparently armed with sufficient information, informed Dorothy that they were to proceed to Muang Kham. "We will speak to District chairman. People say that he know story of pilot."

"That's excellent." She finished her Pepsi and paid for it. "Mr. Kampeng, can you find out what happened to that little boy over there, the one all bandaged up?"

"Ah yes. This morning six child get injured when they find bombi. They look like little color balls, so child, see them, want to play with them."

"Bombi?" she asked.

"Yes, see-bee-yoo."

"CBU?"

Kampeng turned towards the children and precipitated an animated discussion with the youngsters—over ten of them by now had gathered around Dorothy.

"Oh, I sorry, seven child get injured. One boy lose leg."

"Terrible, terrible!" She was perturbed by the ostensible casualness they all seemed to have regarding the incident. Some of the kids were smiling, pleased at all this attention they were getting.

One little girl broke into a song, and the rest of them joined in. It was a bouncy, lilting melody, similar to the songs she had listened to while on the bus to Sala Phou Koun.

"They sing song about the *luk labert*, the baby bombs. No play with them. They learn in school," Kampeng remarked.

When their song was over, Dorothy treated them all to sweets before she and Kampeng got back in the jeep.

The ridges grew higher, dominating the lowlands between them, as the jeep ambled past dreary, isolated villages of the Hmong and Black Thai forlornly perched on the slopes. They passed by fishponds and small dams, and hillsides cleared by swidden farm plots. Within a short time the road gradually spilled onto a broad stretch of country bordered by mountains—a valley dappled with hundreds of comely, compact dwellings that made up the town of Muang Kham.

"It's very pretty here," commented Dorothy.

"Yes, and land very good. People here are rich. Have much rice and animals."

Neat rows of traditional houses, arranged along narrow dirt lanes that were lined with flowery trees, designated Muang Kham as a quaint settlement rather than anything Dorothy would classify as a town. They took one of the side tracks, where Kampeng decided to halt and ask a few strolling passersby for directions. A right turn down another lane and they soon slowed to a stop outside a bamboo fence, in front of which was a rather large tree. There, a group of children had congregated, some throwing stones up at the branches and others poking into the tree crown with long staves of bamboo, diligently engaged in knocking fruits off the boughs. Within the compound of the homestead, stood a large teak house on stilts, the shutters open wide to let in the light. In the dark recesses beneath the elevated house, were a couple of big, hairy, gray pigs snuffling about for food scraps, and to the side, in its lee of shade, were two youths who sat sedulously lashing grass fronds onto branches, presumably making new thatching for the roof. Talking to the boys was a one-legged man standing on crutches.

The man's deformity was rather obvious, since he was wearing shorts and there was nothing but air outside one leg of his shorts. He also wore a khaki-colored shirt with epaulettes, ostensibly to denote his administrative position as district chairman.

The couple alighted from the jeep, Dorothy self-consciously smoothing her pleated skirt, while Kampeng made elaborate acknowledgements to the lame man, which included repeated nops, before introducing him to Dorothy. "This is district chairman. He name Keo."

He was light complexioned, capped by a nice head of black hair parted to one side. His eyes were large and luminous, and although he was perhaps in his mid-thirties, he seemed to have preserved his youth by virtue of a bright, friendly face. He perambulated towards Dorothy with the help of his crutches. "Sabai dee!" he exclaimed, grinning profusely, and, supported by his crutches, held out his hand to greet her in the Western way.

"Sabai dee," she returned, taking it.

They were invited to enter the timber house, which one did by way of a ladder propped against the raised veranda. Dorothy felt rather discomfited when the crippled man flung his crutches to the porch above and crawled up the rungs on his three remaining limbs. Once up on top, he recovered the crutches and struggled back up on his only leg.

The interior of the house was spacious and airy, but dark, and bare as well, lacking any furniture except for a bureau and a couple of beds at the far end. The disabled man eased himself down on a straight-back chair against the wall. They themselves sat on a woven mat laid out on the wooden floor, and it was seconds later that Dorothy realized how the man's handicap prevented him from joining them. They were soon attended to by a young girl in her *paasin* sarong, a dainty creature with bashful eyes and a timid smile, her hair bound up in a pretty clip. As she approached them she walked with her back bent, which Dorothy supposed was some sort of subservient gesture of respect, and, still in this stooped position, unloaded three glasses and a porcelain kettle from a tray before diffidently departing. Kampeng conversed with the chairman as they indulged in Chinese tea, a beverage that was brown in color and insipid in taste, brewed from green leaves. A quarter of an hour later, Kampeng finally put into English what the chairman had disclosed to him.

"Chairman say he from small village north of here, it called Ban Khoum. When Americans bomb, the people hide in holes in ground. During bombing he boy, and he very much injured, so he no remember much, but people say American pilot hiding in same hole that he in. After bombing, chairman go with everybody to Long Tieng where doctor treat him. But pilot not go there."

"Is that how he lost his leg?"

"Yes, bombi. He step on one. He say he lucky. He take buffalo out to eat with his father. Father get killed."

"What happened to the pilot?"

The chairman was now beaming an eager smile at Dorothy. There was no trace of bitterness in his demeanor. Then he thoughtfully spoke after Kampeng translated the question.

"He say he don't know, but another woman from Ban Khoum come here after war, maybe she know."

Their host yelled out to one of the boys outside.

"He tell boy go call her," Kampeng informed.

The two men continued their dialogue in Lao, even as the young hostess came back to set out bowls of food in front of them, with the girl making a conscious effort to keep her head low. An older, brown-colored woman, with a portly figure and her hair bound in a kerchief came behind the girl holding a basket of sticky rice, saying something to Kampeng as she placed it on the mat. She gave Dorothy a smiling Sabai dee as she shyly retreated.

"Chairman's wife want to know you eat spicy food?"

Dorothy found another occasion to use one of the few other words she had learned in Lao. "*Noy-nung*. A little bit."

The chairman laughed and made a comment.

Kampeng translated. "He say you speak Lao very well."

"*Lop plaa*," the chairman said to her, pointing at one of the bowls.

"Fish lop, is Lao food," Kampeng clarified.

It was ground up fish, raw, like a paste, but it was tasty, though a bit strong with all the chilies and lemon grass. It was eaten by dipping balls of sticky rice into it.

Throughout the meal there was more conversation, unintelligible to Dorothy. When they had finished eating, their host offered Kampeng a cigarette and held out the pack to Dorothy as well, who refused with a smile and a shake of her head. Not long after that, an attractive woman in her late twenties, wearing a pretty frock, came to the door, demurely asking permission to enter. Greetings were exchanged all around, and it was understood by Dorothy that this was the woman that was sent for. The woman squatted on her haunches as she listened to Kampeng and the chairman explain the situation, to which she responded by repeatedly making utterances that sounded like 'err, err'. Despite Dorothy's eagerness to hear what she had to say, it took a while to get to the issue. Understandably, the woman herself had a great deal of questions concerning Dorothy, which Kampeng answered, before she resolved to relate her recollections of the bombing incident.

"Her name Boon-mee. She say she little girl, she bring water when the bombs come, and her mother is killed, and she very afraid. She very afraid, lots of noise and smoke. Then big man, farang, take her and carry her in hole. They all in same hole with chairman."

"Does she remember what happened to the farang?"

More words in Lao were exchanged.

"No, she no remember, but she have grandmother, and grandmother say he come out of hole, then sit on ground and cry many tears. After, Hmong come and take all of them away. Hmong also take farang, but go in different direction."

Dorothy took out Andrew's photo from her bag. "Ask her if this was the farang."

The woman accepted the photo, and duly commented.

"She say it look like him, but she young child and very afraid and no remember well. She also say that all farang look same to her."

"Is her grandmother alive? Maybe I should talk to her."

"No, grandmother, she die many years ago. But I not think this man Dorotee's son. Hmong rescue this pilot. He not your son."

"Maybe. Maybe not. Maybe something happened to them before a rescue helicopter could reach them. Is it possible to go to Ban Khoum?"

"No more Ban Khoum. Get destroy."

Darn it, she thought, if only she could have gotten the pilot's names.

Although lively sounding comments continued to be exchanged between the three Laotians, no further information was forthcoming. Dorothy waited impatiently until the lame man signaled their imminent departure by raising himself out of his chair. He accompanied them to the porch, where he and his family remained standing, waving goodbye as Dorothy and Kampeng re-boarded their vehicle.

"Chairman say I take you to see Tam Piu. It not far," said Kampeng, once they were back in the jeep.

Dorothy, remembering Kampeng's progress reports during their odyssey aboard the truck, wondered how short a distance qualified as 'not far'. "What's at Tam Pui?" she asked.

"Tam Piu is cave. People hide from bombs. Get killed."

Actually, the drive didn't take too long. Fifteen minutes out of Muang Kham, they came to a wooden shed where an opulent woman and two children stood outside. The woman, dressed in a baggy blouse and a large-sized sarong, holding a small ticket book, approached Kampeng's side of the vehicle. They had to buy a ticket for one thousand kip, equivalent to fifty American cents. Close by the entrance, serving as a memorial, was a white-washed slab enclosed by a chain link fence, and past that were steps that went up the side of the cliff and led to a huge opening in the rock face, about a quarter of the way up.

"Rocket go inside cave. Everyone die."

"My goodness! How many people?"

"Four hundred. Maybe more."

"Oh dear Lord!"

"You go see cave first. I wait here."

Dorothy alighted from the vehicle and began her ascent up the steps. It was rather steep, obliging her to pause for a few breaths before she entered the mouth of the cave. The rock chamber was fairly wide, and the roof was very high. Because of the huge entrance, and the position of the afternoon sun, it was well lit inside for several hundred feet. Beyond that, the floor of the cave dropped off into a creepy darkness. She could easily imagine how it could hold four hundred people. The ground was littered with cobbles, and she had to walk carefully. Among the rock rubble, she noticed something that gave out a tiny reflection, and upon closer inspection, saw that it was a small silver earring, sadly conjuring up images of a once human presence and making the calamity much more real. How horrible, she thought. Just the shock wave from the explosion inside the cave would be enough to shatter a person to death, leave alone the blast, the heat and the shrapnel.

Leaving the cave, she was confronted with a gorgeous view of Muang Kham and the lovely valley that contained it, all the trees and bushes resplendently green in the sunshine. Again, she found it hard to imagine what it was like during the air attacks, a whole other nightmarish world.

She met Kampeng inside the fenced area enclosing the memorial. "So where were the armies of the Vietnamese and Pathet Lao? Were they inside too?"

"No, too big, see easily. Only villagers, many women and children. Communist army hide in jungle far away."

Insane, she thought. She could just picture everyone on the American side whooping congratulatory hurrahs for such a good hit on the target, like scoring points in a Nintendo game. She stood and read the plaque on the memorial:

DEPLORING TO THE SPIRIT OF VILLAGERS, WHO GOT IL BY ROCKET ON 24/11/68 FROM AMERICAN'S IMPERIALIST

The dreadful English seemed to express a childlike innocence of the Laotians, which made the tragedy even more poignant.

As they left, the woman gatekeeper, joined by her two gleeful children, a little boy and a girl barely ten, waved fervently. "Bye-bye! Bye-bye!" the kids shouted mirthfully, the only English they knew, jumping up and down in artless excitement. Twenty-two years ago, there were children like that in the cave when the rocket hit, Dorothy thought to herself.

Dorothy covered her face and cried quietly. Graciously enough, Kampeng didn't say a word; he too seemed to be in a somber mood.

Please Dear Jesus, she silently prayed, Lord of Compassion and Mercy, no matter what happened to Andrew, all I ask of you, whatever I find out or don't find out, please let it not be so, that my son was ever involved in such a massacre. Then oddly enough, as if in response to her plea, a faint voice from somewhere inside her soul confided in her. The pilot who carried the little girl to safety, who hid in the hole with the chairman and the other villagers, and who sat down and cried in front of them, was none other than her own child, Andrew.

"That pilot in Ban Khoum was my son!" she tearfully declared to Kampeng.

He drove on looking straight ahead, stone-faced, not knowing how to react.

Throughout the evening and the night, and even the next morning when she awoke, Dorothy felt burdened by a weighty depression. The enthusiasm of the day before was gone, and she found herself wishing for the day when she could return home. It was in this spirit that they set out for the second crash site at a small village near the market of Lat Huong. The going was a bit easier here since they were traversing the milder terrain in the middle of the plateau. The smooth curves of the land offered pretty scenery, and reminded her of the rolling farmland in the Ohio River valley, except here, the hillocks were bare and brown, pockmarked by garish white bomb craters that uncovered the underlying chalky soil. Overall, it was very open country lying under the full expanse of the sky, with little in the way of shade and much exposed to the harsh rays of the sun.

The closest location on her old war map was called Ban Si, but of course that didn't exist anymore, so they were going to somewhere called Ban Kam Nyao. Fitting in with her mood, it seemed a lonely place, with few houses sparsely scattered among newly planted teak and eucalyptus trees.

They disembarked from the jeep and walked. They passed a house where two young women were hulling rice in a hollowed out tree stump using long poles as pestles. As one woman brought up her stick, the other would bang down, resulting in a pounding sound that alternately rose and fell. Other than that, it was quiet. There seemed to be no one else about, not even the usually ubiquitous children.

Continuing their stroll, they eventually did come upon some inhabitants, two old geezers playing checkers on the veranda of one of the houses. Obligatory greetings having been made, the couple approached them and permission was offhandedly granted to climb up. Dorothy followed Kampeng up the ladder to the wooden porch that was enclosed with a shoddy bamboo railing. The checker players were sitting on what could loosely be described as stools but were actually small rectangular slabs of wood nailed together, and which stood only a few inches high. None of the men regarded them further, being grossly engaged in their game. Even Kampeng looked on with bona fide interest. The board they were playing on was homemade, painted by hand, and they used bottle caps for the pieces. One of the players, a wiry little man, without bothering to look up, initiated a conversation with Kampeng in the Laotian tongue. Breaking away from the game, the old man cocked his head at Dorothy and his weathered rawhide face folded into a thousand creases as he smiled, exposing a mouthful of small yellow teeth. *"Parlez vous francaise? Comment ca va?"*

Dorothy was elated at the chance of speaking directly with someone. *"Oui, oui, ca va bien! Et vous, ca va bien?"*

"Oui, oui. Je m'appele Vintong. Et vous?"

"Je m'appele Dorothy. Where did you learn French?" she continued in French.

"My uncle, he married my father's sister. He was a schoolteacher in Luang Prabang. When he visited home, he liked to teach us French, and his son, my cousin, would stay here also and we played together and speak French."

"Vous pouvez se souvenir de la guerre? Are you able to remember the war?"

"Oh yes, of course, I was here since I was a boy. You see the hills and the fields, they are so beautiful, and we lived never wanting for anything. It was a happy life, until the war. Is it like this in America?" His French was a bit ungrammatical, but clear and understandable.

"Yes, in some places, not everywhere."

"Is it cold where you come from?"

Dorothy became anxiously aware that the conversation was in danger of straying off the course she wanted it to follow.

"Yes, sometimes. It depends on the time of year. Can you tell me how it was during the war here? I would like to know," she interjected, attempting to rein things in.

"At first it was just the big guns, but they were in the mountains and shot over our heads. Then later airplanes came, but they only bombed the roads and sometimes bridges if they saw any. We would hide behind the paddy dikes. We were afraid, but we could still farm. After that, they started to bomb in the villages."

His partner indicated that it was his move, so Vintong took his gaze off Dorothy to study the board. She had ascertained by now that the man had something wrong in one eye, because whenever he needed to look at something he made jerky movements with his head. He jumped his opponent, who responded with a double jump of his own, after which Vintong issued forth a mild protest.

"What did you do when the planes started to bomb the villages?" Dorothy horned in, undaunted.

He jerked his head with a bird-like movement. "We made holes in the ground, very deep and very big, so we could hide in them. But we couldn't do anything in the day, not even cook, for if the planes saw the smoke, they would drop bombs. So, we would come out at night to farm…"

Though the man's French would have driven a Parisian mad, his words ran at a pace that required all of her concentration to take them in.

"…But then the planes would come at night and drop powerful lights, called *falair*, that would turn night into day, and if they saw anyone they would shoot at them and drop more bombs. After that we moved into the forest and lived in caves. But the forest was also dangerous because they dropped the little bombi, and we had to stay on a very narrow path because a lot of them would still be on the ground. They explode if you step on them."

The checkers game was abandoned, as Kampeng began a parallel discussion in Lao with the other old man.

"...And they also dropped poison," Vintong continued to Dorothy, "which made cows and buffaloes die after they eat the poisoned grass. Sometimes, we saw it drop into the water or on the rice fields. Pigs, ducks and chickens also would die because of it. And all the plants die, and our rice too."

Defoliant? Dorothy wondered. Agent Orange? Whatever it was, she decided she had better get to the point. "Do you remember a plane that crashed near here?"

"Oh, yes, over there," he said, pointing to the hills in the east.

Meanwhile, the other man, in the midst of his discussion with Kampeng, also pointed, but he pointed south.

"Did you see a parachute? Did the pilot get out?"

"No, the plane burned up in the air, pilot didn't get out."

"Excuse please, Miss Dorotee," Kampeng broke in excitedly, "this man say that a plane get hit by gun and fall over there." Kampeng pointed to the south. "Man jump out with parachute, but he wounded, then die. The people bury him, not far from here."

"Mr. Kampeng, this man says the plane crashed over there," Dorothy argued, her arm indicating the hills to the east, "...and he didn't see any parachute."

Kampeng addressed the two men, after which the three of them began a volatile debate in Lao. French or no French, it seemed that once again Dorothy wasn't to have an unmediated discussion. She stood impatiently in the breezeless heat of the veranda, fanning herself with her floppy bush hat.

"Ask them what type of plane it was," she instructed Kampeng.

More quibbling followed.

"Your man say it was small plane that make noise like bee, one that look for people, and this man say it was eff four type that drop bombs."

There must have been two planes that went down here, one was a spotter, and the other, while the man may have misidentified it as an F-4, was at least a jet bomber.

Kampeng's man made a funny, whining sound.

"He say eff four scream like angry spirit."

Dorothy took out the maps from her bag, choosing the one that marked all the crashes of all planes during the entire period of the war. Sure enough, both an L-19 and an F-105 crashed in the general area, only a few miles from each other.

"Ask them in what year did these planes crash," she told Kampeng.

He did so, then came back to her with their reply.

"This man say Horse, the other say Chicken."

"What?"

The traditional way of reckoning years was virtually the same as the Chinese calendar, and followed a twelve-year cycle, with each year represented by a different animal. Only twelve animals were used for this purpose, so the thirteenth year began with the first animal all over again.

Kampeng made some quick calculations in his head. "Small plane crash in 1966. Eff four crash in 1969."

"And they buried the pilot of the jet, the F-4 or whatever?"

"Yes."

Dorothy pulled out Andrew's photo. "Was this the pilot?"

Kampeng gave the photo to the man, and he and his one-eyed companion huddled over it, talking excitingly.

"He say that him," Kampeng reported, "The pilot they bury."

"Is he sure?" Half of Dorothy hoped that he was wrong.

"He say he sure."

"Can we visit the gravesite?"

The three Lao men discussed this matter.

"Yes, we can go now if you want," Kampeng informed her.

Dorothy, trying to get back into a more active role, used her French again to ask the man with the bad eye how far the grave was.

"The time it takes to boil two pots of rice," he answered.

Apparently, it required roughly an hour to cook up two pots of rice, since that was the time it took to reach the location. The campestral, steppe-like terrain had very few trees for shade, and it was scorching to be so exposed to the sun. The man leading the way, the one proffering the parachute story, held a small black umbrella to shade himself. He kindly offered it to Dorothy, who politely declined; she felt her droopy broad-brimmed hat was sufficient protection. After climbing a small knoll, the umbrella man pointed to the ground. It was rather anticlimactic. There was nothing to indicate that anything had been buried, save for the fact that the spot was devoid of the brown stubble of dead grass that covered everywhere else.

"Would we be able to dig up the body, I mean, do we need permission or something?" Dorothy asked Kampeng.

"No body here," he answered.

"But isn't this the place where he was buried?"

"Yes, but the man tell me that Americans come here three years ago and take body. So it not your son."

So why on earth did we gallivant all this way, she complained silently to herself. Still, she refused to accept this setback. "But he also identified the pilot as Andrew," she protested. "He said it was the same man as the one in the photograph."

"Yes, but Lao peoples very funny. Say anything. Want to make you happy, want to help."

"Maybe it was my son. Maybe they took his body and they didn't tell me."

"Why would American government do that?"

"I don't know. Why would the American government send me the bones of a cow and tell me that it was Andrew?" And without waiting for an answer to her rhetorical question, she started off by herself, trudging back, tired and defeated.

She didn't say a word the whole ride back. Once in Ponsavan, she went straight to her room, and later on in the evening when Kampeng came by to ask her to come along for a walk and perhaps get something to eat, nothing he could say or do would get her to come out.

It wasn't until the morning that she left her room. Kampeng found her sitting on the veranda of the guesthouse with all her maps in front of her.

"Sabai dee."

"Sabai dee."

"You feel okay this morning?" he asked her.

"To be truthful, I'm a bit disillusioned, Mr. Kampeng."

"*Disloosend*. Is that good?"

"No, it means I'm disappointed."

"Oh, you are sad."

"Yes."

"I must remember that word, *disloosend*. I sorry my English not good. I not speak much after war. I also sorry you are disloosend."

Dorothy gazed at Kampeng, with his jet-black hair hanging haphazardly over his high forehead, the creases in his dark face indicating a hard life. She realized she was being unfair, and her dismal mood wasn't helping anyone. "No, Kampeng, I am the one to apologize. I'm sorry for being ungrateful. you've helped me a great deal. And I thank you."

"Bo ben yang," he said smiling, glad to see she was feeling better.

Dorothy gave him a warm smile back.

"You see anything more on maps?" he asked, pointing to the sheets piled up in front of her.

"Well, there are a lot of small planes and some jets, but they were shot down after Andrew died. I really don't know where to go from here." She looked down at the maps again. "Today is my birthday," she suddenly said.

"Oh, happy birthday! Kampeng not know, I no have any gift."

"That's alright, Kampeng."

"How old you now?"

"I am a golden sixty-five."

"Ah, I think forty-five. Anyway, still young."

Dorothy beamed at his sweetness, not to mention his shrewd manner of cheering her up. "Thanks, Kampeng."

"I put diesel in car. We go for drive. Forget problems. I show you Tung Hai Hin."

"Show me what?"

"Stone jars."

It was another bright, sunshiny day as they went down the same dusty main road as yesterday, called Route 4, for about twenty kilometers, where they then branched off onto a smaller road, bringing them into a country of pretty hills and wide pasturelands. Kampeng stopped the jeep as they passed a village and pointed out of Dorothy's side.

"See? Russian Tank."

There it was, lying on a small slope below the road, a pale green hulk that reminded Dorothy of the Merrimac and that other crude iron warship used in the American Civil War. They got out to have a closer look. The tank's treads were gone, as well as the gun barrel, and the turret had been separated somehow, lying farther down, practically in someone's back yard behind a Lao house. The insides of the tank were stripped bare.

"Soviet PT-76, Vietnamese army," he disclosed. "A bomb hit it up there," he said, pointing up on the other side of the road, "and it roll down here."

"Was that part of the Soviet airlift?"

"No, no, much after. From Vietnam. Vietnamese drive them to Nong Het on border, then from there, push them to Plain of Jars."

"Pushed them? Over fifty miles?"

"Yes, that way no one hear them. No one know they come."

She shook her head, refusing to believe this.

Back in the jeep, they resumed their drive until they reached an attractive village, where neat fences surrounded well-kept houses garnished with flowers. She noticed that many of the fence posts were bomb casings from the cluster bomb dispensers. Among the dwellings was an abundance of delightful dark green trees that opened up like umbrellas. A small temple, angelic in its simplicity, was located in the middle of this rural community.

"Ban Sieng Di," Kampeng announced.

At the end of the village, they parked the vehicle by a tree, where they bought tickets from a man sitting at a table in the shade, again for one thousand kip apiece. They walked along a path, across a small footbridge, and up a little hill. At the top, standing and lying in all sorts of random positions, were the stone jars, giving the site a prehistoric, Stonehenge type quality.

The stone jars, thousands of years old, are among the wonders of the world, yet they are relatively unknown outside of Laos. Their creation was attributed to a race of the Mon-Khmer people, the original inhabitants of Laos, collectively called the Lao Toong by present day Laotians, and whose descendants now inhabited the hill slopes.

"They make from different rock than here," Kampeng informed her.

"Which means they were brought from somewhere else. I don't see how. They must weigh several tons."

"People believe they wine jars from big party after they defeat evil king."

"I heard they were used as burial urns."

"Yeah, that too."

Dorothy was amazed at how perfectly round the insides were. What tools did they use to carve such hard rock? Some of them even had lids lying on the side. Ironically enough, there was a huge bomb crater adjacent to the site, in which a grove of trees had taken root and flourished.

"It was lucky that none of the bombs destroyed any of these wonderful jars."

"Yes," Kampeng agreed. "Very lucky for Pathet Lao. They used to hide in them, but the planes never saw them."

The view from the hill was striking: the village sitting placidly below them, and beyond, the breathtaking expanse of the Plain. In back of them, to the south, were forest-covered mountains, gashed by tree-covered ravines that cast oblique shadows, the mountains forming part of a range that trended in an east-west direction. There were four peaks, and the most easterly, the highest, looked like a round head on broad shoulders.

"What mountain is that, the tallest, with the round peak like a head?"

"Pu Khe," Kampeng answered.

They became silent as they surveyed the land, relishing the exhilarating scenery.

"You see houses over there," Kampeng asked, pointing with an outstretched arm.

Actually, they weren't houses, just frames of branches covered with grass thatch. "That is where they keep buffaloes for sleep."

"Corrals," Dorothy said.

"Yes...what is word...Kor-als?"

"That's right. Where you keep animals penned in."

"Yes, Kor-als." Kampeng almost forgot what he wanted to say. "Yes, and there," he continued, pointing to an adjacent rice field, "old village before war. It called Ban Na before."

"Ban Na?"

"Yes. During war it get destroyed and all people move out. In 1975, they come back and build this village, Ban Sieng Di."

The distance between the old Ban Na and the new Ban Sieng Di was less than a few city blocks.

"They built a very beautiful village," Dorothy commended.

"We go down and take walk?"

"Good idea."

They descended the same way they had come up, and then, after passing their jeep, took a footpath into the village. It didn't take them long before they found out that there was a party going on somewhere. Maw lam music, loud laughter, and women yelling out woo-a-woo hay-haaay sounds, verified its location.

"Lao wedding. Much fun," Kampeng told her.

They were welcomed into a large fenced compound enclosing several houses, where a mob of people in different groups were strewn here and there, each engaged in various activities. An atmosphere of industrious fervor prevailed, along with the unadulterated merriment. Dorothy and Kampeng wandered amidst the crowd while the music blared from huge loudspeakers. There were clusters of woman cooking various foods, and others that appeared to be involved in making elegant decorations. In the corner of the large yard, men were preparing to slaughter a water buffalo, and Dorothy hurried along not wishing to witness that part of the ceremonies, but had to step gingerly as she approached a throng of old women sitting merrily pounding betal nut in little wooden mortars. Throughout the throng, children played and gamboled amongst the busy adults.

A small gathering of joyful Laotians, sitting in a leisurely way on a bamboo mat spread on the ground, invited the newly arrived couple to join them and commenced shifting themselves to make more space. The women wore paa-sins and faded, dull-colored, sleeveless blouses; the men were dressed in tattered shirts and threadbare polyester pants. Together, they posed a typical portrait of third world peasants, the type Dorothy would see in ads for charitable organizations like Save the Children, or CARE. She and Kampeng consented to sit down on the mat, and Dorothy, in the same pleated skirt she wore yesterday, attempted to sit cross-legged like everyone else, though she knew this wouldn't be appreciated by her less than pliant knees.

The group had been sharing a bottle of clear liquid, pouring a little bit in a single glass and passing it around in turn. Kampeng accepted the traveling glass from a middle-aged matron in a colorful paa-sin, swallowed its contents and then handed the glass back to her. It was refilled and given to Dorothy.

"*Lao-kao*. Rice whiskey," Kampeng told her.

Dorothy looked at the glass. There was only a small amount of the stuff, so she figured that if she took a quick swig it would be relatively painless. It burned the back of her throat as she gulped it, then lit a minor fire in her belly.

"Haaay-haaay!" they all cheered in approval.

She gave back the glass, and it found its way to one of the men, who looked at everybody and said *"Soke dee!"* before slugging it back. The glass went around and everybody did pretty much the same. Soon it was Dorothy's turn again.

"What is it that you say before drinking it?" she asked Kampeng.

"Soke dee, it means 'good luck'. Also is our custom to look at everyone and raise glass before drinking."

Dorothy did so just before crying out 'soke dee' and downing the liquid fire once more.

The men laughed, and the women shouted, "woo-a-woo hay-haaay!"

The man sitting next to her gazed at her for an unduly long time. His face was fat, feline-like, brown as chocolate and round as the moon. He had a tantalizing smile. "What... is... your... name?" he asked, in a slow, almost rehearsed manner.

"You speak English!" Dorothy exclaimed.

"I...speak... good...inglit."

Guffaws from the crowd, and another "woo-a-woo hay-haaay!" from the women.

"My name is Dorothy."

"Doro-tee."

"Yes. What is your name?"

"Yes. My name Sita. What are you come from?"

Again, everyone roared heartily in amazement at Sita's proficiency of English.

She hesitated, wondering how the Laotians would react to the fact that she was from the country that had once rained bombs down on them.

"United States of America."

Everyone's eyes were on her, but their wide grins and jovial faces showed no sign of any enmity. "Oh, Ameri-ka, very good."

More laughter followed and children started to gather around, their eyes wide with curiosity, watching what had now become the Dorothy and Sita show.

Another drink for Dorothy. She realized that she was starting to feel very happy from the lao-kao.

"How long stay in Lao?"

"Two weeks."

"You like Lao, very beautiful, yes?"

"Yes, I like Lao, it is a beautiful country, and the people are beautiful too."

The man laughed heartily, then translated to the crowd.

"Woo-a-woo hay-haaay!"

Kampeng turned to Dorothy. "Having nice birthday?" he asked her.

"I think it will turn out to be quite memorable," she replied with a wide, slightly inebriated grin.

He assumed she meant 'yes'.

Within a short while, everyone rose to their feet to watch the young bride and groom as they came into view on the veranda of the main house, the both of them decked out in colorful, elaborate costumes, particularly the young girl, who was done up like a lovely princess. Through the blurry haze of alcohol, Dorothy saw a series of images: simple cotton strings were being tied onto their wrists by an old man, the bridal couple kneeling in obeisance in front of a line of robed monks who were chanting an atonal plainsong, the bride and groom jointly holding a big spoon putting food in bowls placed in front of each monk...To Dorothy's surprise, many in the audience soon followed suit, streaming on to the veranda to offer the holy men food. Even Kampeng participated in this ritual.

After the monks had eaten, the newlyweds prostrated themselves again, and each priest in turn would splash them with water using small tree branches. The water was probably some sort of holy water, Dorothy assumed.

When the formalities were concluded, everyone, including Dorothy, who at first couldn't help feeling ridiculous, danced the lamvong. Her bashfulness at appearing silly was soon extinguished as the rice liquor took hold. In contrast to the wild exuberance of the participants, the dance itself was composed of delicate, restrained motions. They walked in a circle, couples astride in pairs, taking a few steps at a time while making elaborate and subtle, typically oriental movements of the arms, hands, and fingers. Kampeng, Dorothy's partner, was intensely absorbed, his arms flowing gracefully with his eyes closed and a contented smile on his face. He was also very drunk.

During the festivities, groups of people would come up to her, saying words she couldn't recognize, but which she repeated mindlessly, like a parrot. At other times she would communicate with them using hands and gestures, and there was much laughing at her awkward attempts to converse.

Without noticing the passage of time, night set in, but the party continued with more dancing and more drinking. Through the loudspeakers came that other type of mawlam, the one with the throbbing beat, and accordingly, the tempo of the party picked up. However, the lao-kao eventually became too much for Dorothy. She vaguely recalled running to the bushes to vomit.

She never did remember how she got to bed, although she really wasn't on a bed, but on a quilt that had been laid out on the floor. She was inside someone's wooden house. She sat up, running her fingers through her now greasy hair, feeling seriously groggy and with a pounding headache. There were a few other people lying on the floor alongside her.

An older woman appeared, offering her a glass of green tea. One side of her face was severely scarred, to the extent that the left side of her mouth was grossly misshapen and there was no skin under her left eye, an unsightly deformity that made the eye look as if it had popped out of its socket. The woman was about the same age as herself, Dorothy reckoned, breaking her stare and trying to act casual.

"I could really use a cup of coffee," Dorothy said aloud, but to herself.

"*Gafay? Gafay nom?*"

"Yes, gafay." It sounded close enough.

The woman came back with a milky coffee in a glass.

"Thank you. Kopjai," said Dorothy.

Kampeng wandered in. "Sabai dee?"

"I'm not sure," Dorothy replied. "I think I have a hangover." She nursed her coffee while remaining in her makeshift bed. The coffee was sickly sweet and very hot, so she could only take it in small sips.

"Hangover?" Kampeng seemed to know this word. "If you take bath, feel better. We go to river."

"A bath in the river? Isn't there a place here where I can bathe?"

"Yes, but river more interesting. Not far."

"Not far? How many pots of rice?"

Kampeng, oblivious to her sarcasm, said something to the woman who had given Dorothy her morning beverages. She came over with a long, green, cotton paa-sin.

Kampeng handed it to Dorothy. "Here, go take off clothes and wear this."

It was a bit of a walk, almost a pot of rice she figured. But it was worth it. Not only was the morning air cool and refreshing, but the sun's gentle early rays felt good on her skin as well. The riverside was a beautiful, hilly bank covered with an opulence of trees and orchids, and the river was already alive with frisky children cavorting excitedly in its crystal waters. Kampeng gave his hand out to help Dorothy down the slippery bank.

"Where can I go to have a bit of privacy?"

"River not private. Many people here."

"Well I can't bathe in front of everyone!"

"Why?"

"What do you mean, why?"

"Everybody else do."

Dorothy looked at the human forms in the river. The younger kids were all naked, but the older girls and women were washing themselves underneath their paa-sins, which stayed in place to conceal their bodies. The few men present were in their underpants.

"I don't take off?" she asked, tugging at her paa-sin.

"No take off."

Dorothy gave herself a quick, but insufficient, washing with soap. How could she do it properly with all those kids flocking on the shore to stare at her? At first she was quite exasperated, but eventually they won her over. It started with a bit of splashing water at them, more out of angry frustration on her part rather than a desire to play. Soon, Dorothy and the kids were romping around the water chasing each other with screams and shouts. Kampeng himself had stripped down to his underwear and was jumping off a big rock with the other kids. The women who were standing on a sandbar washing clothes broke into peals of amused laughter, and an old man on the shore raised his hands and clapped continuously. Dorothy sat down in the clear flowing water, watching the frolicking children, looking at their saucy, lively brown faces, listening to their artless shrill cries. If you could bottle their joy, you could sell it as an elixir, she imagined. She really meant what she had said to the man at the wedding party. Lao was indeed a wonderful country, a modern-day Garden of Eden, where the people were as beautiful as the land they lived in.

"This is truly paradise," she said to Kampeng as he walked past her to the shore.

"I remember when I young, jumping off rock like that in river in my village," he reflected, throwing on his shirt.

"You don't know how lucky you are."

They returned to the house at noon. It was the longest bath Dorothy had ever taken.

Of course, they had to eat lunch before they departed. So Dorothy waited another half-hour after getting dressed while Lao conversations went on between Kampeng and the people of the household. The talking went on even throughout the meal, the latter consisting of, among other things, that stinky fermented fish, the pla dek. It wasn't until after they had finished eating that Kampeng finally spoke to her.

"This is grandfather and grandmother of bride." He introduced an old man, and the 60-year-old disfigured woman whom she had met in the morning. "This their house."

Sabai dee's were exchanged.

"I tell Grandmother why you come to Lao. She tell me now very interesting story. She say that during war, Pathet Lao bring prisoner here, when village has name Ban Na. They show prisoner to people. He American pilot. She say he have kind face. His feet have bad wounds. She clean his feet. Then bombs come and they hide in caves, in mountains you see yesterday. After that Pathet Lao leave and take pilot with them, and she go with them also, to carry food. She say there is much fighting and pilot want to escape. She say she save his life when a Vietnamese want to shoot him. She hit Vietnamese on head with big basket, and knock him down. Pilot run away. Then she run back to caves in village. She not know about pilot, maybe get killed because there is much fighting and big guns."

To Dorothy, the story sounded utterly ridiculous.

The old woman said something to Kampeng, then abruptly got up. Kampeng looked in her direction as she disappeared in a side room. She came out about a minute later and held something in her hand which she offered to Dorothy.

"She say he give her that."

It was like an index card, but unlined, sealed in cellophane, with ugly spots on one side. On the other side was some writing, but the ink had faded. She could barely make out the word 'remember'. She knew it was probably wishful thinking, but the little handwriting that was visible reminded her of Andrew's style of script.

"She say there was flower inside. But now gone, dry up."

Dorothy sat looking at this card. "In which direction were the Pathet Lao and the American pilot going when they left here?"

After Kampeng translated this, the old woman went to the door and Dorothy jumped up to follow. And although she didn't know much Lao, she distinctly heard the words 'Pu Khe'. Sure enough, the woman was pointing at the mountain that had a head on its shoulders.

Chapter 10

Laos 1969

"… the Pathet Lao are running the show from caves in Sam Neua, like rats in a hole…They are not to be admired, they are the enemy, they are to be destroyed…"
Anonymous Air Force Intelligence Officer, 1969

A sinister, throbbing drone, like a giant insect beating its wings, disrupted the quiet of the forest. All at once the helicopter instantly materialized out of a fog bank. The pervading mist had made the descent perilous for those on board, but the milky shroud covering the ground promptly yielded in the windy advance of the UH-1 chopper. The downwash of the whirling rotors shoved the mist away and flattened the elephant grass as nine figures popped out of the doorway one by one in rapid sequence, and within seconds after touchdown, the entire team was running through the grass to get to the shelter of the adjoining trees. They dived on the ground while the UH-1 took off, and remained motionless until the helicopter could no longer be heard.

The Hmong soldiers moved out, first in an inverted 'V' formation, shielding Botkin and Anatoly, who were behind them. Once confident that there were no booby traps, they changed into an advancing crescent to form an enveloping movement. They proceeded slowly through the misty jungle, like wraiths, soundless, cautious, and deliberate, looking, listening, even smelling for the presence of anyone else in the dim, steamy forest. The trees were tall, their trunks disappearing into an opaque grayness above. Stalks and vines hung down like tentacles of a great sea beast. Everything was dripping.

After an hour of walking in their semi-circular formation, Botkin made a birdcall type of noise and they regrouped to march in single file. Each man had two pieces of tape on his back. The rule was that when walking behind someone, if you saw that the two pieces merged, you were too far behind. They snaked their way through the dense tropical growth for most of the morning before stopping to rest at the verge of a small patch of scrub.

"We were supposed to come in on strings on the original coordinates," Anatoly complained as soon as they had halted. "You exposed the helicopter to unnecessary risk in that open clearing."

Botkin took a swig out of his canteen. He replaced the cap before making an affected and pointless gesture of looking at his Seiko wristwatch, openly ignoring Anatoly's comment, then raised his head to gaze off into the distance, his dark-tinted, wire-rimmed sunglasses reflecting the scenery and giving his face a callous, inhuman look of stone. Without bothering to face Anatoly, still looking off at nothing, he said, "Okay Anatoly, listen up. First, a little lesson in warfare, especially in a place like this. Cloud cover can either fuck you or help you. You just gotta know how to exploit it. I know the area, and I know this spot, and that's where I wanted to go, fuck your Major Barwood. Secondly, I lead the hunter part of this mission, and so I'm in charge of finding our boy. When we find him, you take him out, but until then, I give the orders." He turned around to glare at the young soldier. "Is that clear, Marine?"

"Very clear...Sir."

Anatoly didn't like the fact that Botkin didn't follow the orders of Major Barwood, who was not only Anatoly's commanding officer, but also a Marine, nor did he appreciate the rude, disrespectful expression that he had used in referring to him. It was an insult, telling him to fuck his CO, who was a decorated Korean War veteran who had earned the Purple Heart because he had risked his life to save fellow Marines.

"Now this guy might be a screwball, but he's not stupid," Botkin continued. "If he was stupid, he'd head dead west into Thailand, but the Thais would eventually catch up with him and hand him over to us nicely gift-wrapped." He opened his canteen again and took another pull. "Na, na, this guy had a plan, a shitty one maybe, but all the same he thought a little about it. Now, if he was a true defector, he would head northeast until he ran smack into the Pathet Lao. But we know he's not a genuine defector, just some fucking, confused soul who gets a letter from his hippy girlfriend and decides he's doing a bad thing. The place where he ditched the plane was a place that was cleared out, everybody shifted east from there. So what I think he's gonna do, is to try and slip through the narrow alley between Luang Prabang and Nam Tha where there's less action going on. He'll try to hit the Golden Triangle and slip into Burma. That's his only option, even though it's a long shot. And remember, this guy can run long distances if he has to. Now, if we were to land at our original designated insertion point, I figure we'd have lost a day. By landing here, we got a slight jump on him. Understood?"

"Understood."

"And another thing…there's no way I'm gonna come down a rope in a fog like this in the middle of the fucking trees. But that's neither here nor there, 'cause now, we're on the ground already, so let's fucking get moving."

They crawled through the scrubland on their bellies for only a hundred yards or so until they reached another stand of elephant grass that was on the other side. There they got up on their feet again, walking through the high grass. They were looking for signs, not only footprints, but above ground evidence: leaves of plants showing their undersides, and the presence and absence of cobwebs. The lead Hmong abruptly stopped and waved his hand, motioning for Botkin to come.

To a trained eye, the grass was slightly bent and had been disturbed. The Hmong tracker pointed to the ground.

"Well, that certainly don't look like a fucking sandal to me," Botkin surmised aloud.

It was a boot print.

Anatoly bent down to have a closer look. "It's not Air Force standard issue. The soles look like they were made in Italy, but could be an American brand of hiking boots, certainly not something you'd expect an NVA regular to wear," he added.

"What did I tell you?"

"I wouldn't be too overoptimistic...Sir. The Pathet Lao rummage anything they can get, even off corpses, so I recommend we keep our eyes open and expect anything."

"Noted...Marine."

They moved onward into a dense stand of bamboo, fighting their way through. The effort they made to try and minimize the noise of their movements forced them to advance at a slow rate. In any case, they were not in a hurry, methodically searching for signs of human passage. Evidently, they finally found one, as the tracker again signaled.

Botkin and Anatoly approached him. The tracker was pointing to a notch, made by a knife, cut into one of the bamboo stalks.

"Now," Botkin snidely asked Anatoly, "do you think a Pathet Lao or Vietnamese regular would make something so stupidly obvious as that?"

Anatoly shook his head in negative agreement.

"Excellent. That could very well be our boy," Botkin commented.

The sky and ground were no longer separate, having been woven into a seamless, wooly cloak of gray; a bleak, cloud-covered day of a tropical monsoon. Throughout the morning, the rain had been soft and steady, broken only by short periods of heavy overcast. Dismal, drab-colored billows swirled down to engulf the world with a dreariness that mirrored Andrew's predicament. Pressing forward through this forlorn scenery, he didn't stop, concerned about making up for the debacle of the previous night when he had wandered about without direction. By midday, the sun had radiated the cloud cover to a blinding whiteness. Physically drained, suffering from hunger cramps, he picked a spot at random to finally rest. He fished in his pockets and ate more of the sadao leaves. Within minutes, he fell asleep.

A few hours later he awoke hungrier than he had ever been in his life. Obligingly enough, it appeared as if the weather was clearing up, and the sun managed to burn its way through the cover of clouds. He raised his torso, and drawing up his knees, stared at a landscape covered in green, ornamented with fog-filled valleys. Around him were beautiful trees and wild white orchids. He remained sitting, fighting to fend off the hunger pangs, trying to figure out his next move. Apart from leaving the immediate area, he had no other timetable, no other plans, outside of staying alive.

He knew very well that even in this seemingly uninhabited place the war penetrated every corner, with planes in the sky and guerilla soldiers on the ground; the latter, he was almost certain, had to be somewhere out there in the jungle. But thoughts of food and eating overwhelmed him, and he contemplated the fresh bamboo shoots he could find lower in the valley. He was also out of water. The prospect of a bath similarly tempted him, and all these things combined, led to a decision to go down again. Better to take the chance here and now, he rationalized, before he found himself in a more populous place that would prevent access to such luxuries.

After destroying his crude shelter of foliage and repacking his duffel bag, he proceeded down the slope at an acute angle. He crossed into more elephant grass, which made him feel safe inside its protective cover. An hour or so later, the grass ended in a woody clearing. It had a blackened appearance, denoting a burned out area, perhaps as recent as this year, and Andrew now questioned his decision to leave the higher ground. When he arrived at a section of cut forest studded with five-foot-high tree stumps and discovered a trail which led directly to it, he knew he had made a mistake. This area was probably abandoned, but only recently, and he was pressing his luck being down here. While there might not be any villagers around after the bombing, it was quite conceivable that the Pathet Lao were still hiding in these very same hill slopes. He turned around to go up and after a few steps he stopped to listen.

All was quiet except for the intermittent whirring of cicadas. Yet, he thought he had heard something else. Perhaps it was a wild boar. He began to take slow, deliberate steps forward, while fantasies of roasted pork danced in his head, intoxicating him to such an extent that he didn't realize anyone was drawing near until a shout made him stop dead in his tracks.

"*Yut! Yut!* Stop!"

Someone was approaching from behind. Andrew stood frozen, not daring to make the slightest move. The man who had shouted came around to confront him. His face was brown, heavily scarred and pitted, with squinty eyes and small lips. His greasy hair was unkempt. He was comically dressed in a woman's style low-cut sweater, flamboyantly colored boxer shorts, and bright red sneakers, and was holding an M-1 carbine. As he gave a shout into the air, the bushes came alive with peasant soldiers, most of them donning torn T-shirts, and pakimas, a striped length of cloth that was the male version of a Laotian sarong. Each of them had a rope tied around their waist that held up a sheathed machete, and a miniature basket where they kept their sticky rice.

A couple of them shoved Andrew to the ground, and he could feel the muzzle of the M-1 pressed against the back of his head as they took his duffel bag and searched his person. After emptying his pockets they forced him to his feet, handing their findings over to the man with the carbine. Everyone else was looking around impatiently, nervous and expectant, very much like pursued quarry. Then the two guys who had searched him tied one of his wrists, looped the rope across his throat, and tied the other wrist. They wrapped the rope once around his waist to bring it forward, and thenceforth used it as a leash.

"*Bai, bai!*" barked the man with the carbine.

They all began to run in single file, about three in front of him, four or five in back of him, towards the direction Andrew had just come from, but along an overgrown trail that was lower down the slope. They got to the elephant grass that Andrew had already been through and stayed with it as long as they could. Sharp pains stabbed at Andrew's insides from all the running. Their no-nonsense pace mocked his own previous efforts at moving through the terrain, and their stamina humbled him. Pretty soon, the pangs of physical distress made him groan aloud. Still, there was no letting up, running, running, running.

There were a few merciful moments of rest, however. Whenever they came to a clearing, they would all stop, quietly inspecting the sky and listening for any spotter planes, before making a mad dash across.

When the sun was beginning to set, they slowed to a walk, entering thick forest. The relief he felt from this more leisurely speed almost made him forget the thirst that was constricting his throat. He persisted in trying to swallow as much of his saliva as he could, even though swallowing soon became painful. He wondered when his captors would also experience the need for water.

The trail became rank with vegetation for several kilometers, before reaching a place where the undergrowth distinctly thinned out, apparently due to human effort. The ground was cleared of bushes, but there still remained a thick cover of tall trees. Holes and trenches had been dug throughout the site and empty ammunition shells littered the ground. The place seemed to be a temporary forward striking camp. It was here where another group of Pathet Lao greeted them.

The man with the carbine addressed the boss of the outfit stationed here, who was easily identifiable by the olive brown uniform and the belt with a red star emblazoned on the buckle. He wore a soft round peaked cap, similar to the ones Chinese soldiers wear. Even as he drew near to question him, Andrew couldn't make out his face in the gloom of a thick dusk.

"*Vao pasa Lao ben bo?* You speak Lao?" this soldier asked him.

"Yes."

He looked over Andrew's identity cards, then asked "What is this?" He held out the laminated index card with the pressed flower petals.

"It is to remind me of someone."

The officer stuffed it roughly into Andrew's shirt pocket.

"Where did you crash?"

Andrew, still bound, turned his body and nodded his head in an arbitrary direction, by now truly not able to discern where he had ditched the plane.

"Perhaps over there?" the Pathet Lao officer proposed, pointing to the northwest.

"Maybe. I can't tell, I've been walking for days."

"What type of airplane were you flying?"

"F-105."

"I think you fly new type of airplane, 'Whispering Death'. Seven of them bomb villages near here three days ago."

Andrew didn't answer. The officer called over a couple of soldiers, who bound him to a tree. One of them offered Andrew a cigarette rolled with a banana leaf, attempting to place it in his mouth, which Andrew declined by shaking his head. He was finally given water, administered from a glass bottle held to his mouth. He drank so frantically that he nearly choked. Not long after, he received a large portion of sticky rice, which he had to eat by bending down and dipping his face into the bowl. He finished by licking the bottom clean, very much like a dog.

That night Andrew remained tied to the tree, with two guards watching over him, the glow of their bamboo pipes casting a gentle radiance on their rough faces.

They heard bombing throughout the night, but it was far enough away from them that they didn't bother to sleep in the holes and trenches, nor did they care to untie Andrew from his tree, even after it had started raining. In the beginning, he had found it difficult to sleep, his body soaking wet and with his arms aching in that position, but weariness eventually vanquished his pain and discomfort, and he fell into a deep slumber, although this soothing respite didn't last for more than an hour. After that he fell in and out of consciousness several times, sleeping fitfully. In the morning it was no surprise that his arms were totally numb.

They untied him, so they must have figured he was too weak and groggy to run away, and it would have been foolish in any case, considering how well-armed they were, as most of the group here had Soviet-made automatic weapons, probably left over from the Kong Le airlift in '61. He was given more sticky rice; this time with fermented fish and chilies to dip it in, and was allowed another drink. Thereupon, it was an early start, which included the PL patrol they had met here as well as the scouts who had initially encountered him, so their number swelled to about twenty. They walked quickly—but they didn't run—in a line strung out like a caravan. It was very foggy, and one could only see one's immediate surroundings. When they got to a stream, they all had a quick bath—even Andrew was permitted to wash himself under the escort of two guards. They resumed their trek by walking in the shallow flowing water of the streambed and then picked up the trail again where it emerged further down. It was a similar tactic to the one Andrew had used on his first day in the forest. After that, they bound him once again in the same fashion as they had yesterday.

At this point the pace was less hectic, and as he recovered from his exhaustion, he found the mental resources to think, or rather worry, about what they were going to do to him. Even though, from the very outset of his ridiculous plan, he had been cognizant of the possibility of capture, he had refused to dwell on it before, convincing himself that he would face that predicament if and when it arose. Now that he was a prisoner, he could only wonder about his fate, helpless to do anything else about it. Would they kill him?

No, killing him wasn't likely, he being a pilot. He theorized on where they could be taking him. To Sam Neua? Or all the way to Hanoi? In any case he mustn't let them suspect that he possessed important intelligence—information that would interest the Soviets as well as the Vietnamese. He had to look for a chance to escape.

Instead of the day clearing, the visibility became worse. They stopped for several minutes, while a passionate and boisterous polemic took its course. The heated arguments were evidently concerned with taking advantage of the cloud cover. There were some that were in favor of crossing the flat cultivated valleys, given the foggy nature of the morning. Normally, this type of weather ruled out bombing raids, but with the tactic of carpet-bombing in a free-strike zone, and with the F-111 capability, weather became an irrelevant factor. The PL guerillas, regardless, decided upon hiking across the rice paddies in the middle of the valley.

They had to travel on top of the bunds, or dikes, which bordered each paddy basin. The troupe snaked along a zigzagging course making many ninety-degree turns at the intersections of adjoining walls. They were resolute about not going through the ponds and stepping on the young rice. The slippery mud surface on top of the narrow dikes was difficult to tread, and the deep indentations from the hoof marks of water buffaloes made it even more onerous to walk upon. Andrew found it difficult to keep his balance with his hands tied behind his back, slipping, sliding, and even falling on his face a few times, which made everyone laugh, giggle and guffaw. Andrew felt that his role, as well as being a prized captive, was to play the clown to lift their spirits.

They didn't have much else to enjoy, he reasoned. These guys were constantly on the move without respite, continually marching and fighting, under a sky full of planes dropping napalm and cluster bombs. There was no helicopter to evacuate them if they got wounded. There was no time off in a well-laid-out base camp with cushy bunk beds, commissaries, or USO shows; the forest was their permanent base. It was an inscrutable fact that they were out here at all.

After crossing the farm valley, they entered a swampy area. They plodded through the muck of the marsh and sloshed through the flooded depressions with a renewed reticence, an unspoken silence that seemed to vaunt their resolve. The ground was soft, wet, and treacherous, covered with ensnaring spreads of ferns and club mosses. Pools of mud, hidden in the crowded scions of underbrush, grabbed at their feet. As they came up out onto drier land, they all stopped and pulled up their pakimas and trousers. Someone motioned for Andrew to do the same. Scores of leeches were affixed to his ankles, with little streams of blood running down. The sight revolted him, and two of his captors came over and gave him the same treatment that everyone else was applying to their own legs. They put tobacco in their mouths and chewed on it for a few seconds, spitting out the juice, then smeared it on the little slimy bastards. Most of them dropped off immediately, and the rest they scraped off with a stick. Leeches secrete a substance that prevents the blood from coagulating, so it took a long time for the bleeding to stop. After that, they all had bleeding legs.

On their way once more, they went up a ridge and down it as well, where they stopped for lunch midway downhill. Andrew was starving, and when he asked for seconds, they gave it, so he asked for thirds and they gave that too. Apparently, for whatever reason, they did show some concern for his welfare, and the lecture he got in Udon about the PL guerillas not taking prisoners no longer proved to be relevant.

By this time the clouds had broken, so they couldn't walk conspicuously in the valley among the open rice fields, or on top of the more exposed ridges, but had to remain within the forest cover. Sure enough, shortly after the sky had cleared, the bombing raids began again. The blasts seemed to be everywhere, a terrible resonance that penetrated throughout the jungle, the horrendous booms and rumbles quivering land and vegetation alike.

In the face of this aerial barrage they continued hiking, keeping close to the base of a ridge, skirting the valley, and soon they came upon abandoned villages, many of them bombed out. Craters were everywhere, like giant, ghoulish mouths gaping in the afternoon sun. There was a lull in the bombing while they passed through this ghostly scene, the thundering replaced by a deathly stillness; not even the sounds of birds could be heard. Andrew wondered who was tending the rice fields they had passed.

Abruptly, the guy in front of him yanked at his leash and they all started to run like mad, the way they had done yesterday. The ground was a jumble of craters and mounds, making the going rough, but they moved as fast as they could; what they were fearing were possible delayed-fuse bombs, dropped days before, but which could go off at any time. Just then, more jets came screaming in, but this time they homed in on the trail that the guerillas were using, forcing them to flee for cover.

The Pathet Lao seemed to have been prepared for this eventuality. Andrew followed them as they scrambled up the hill, and within minutes, they were inside a well-concealed cave. They all huddled for a few minutes at the mouth, looking out at the jets tearing through the valley.

Several of the men ran outside, quickly gathering up leaves and putting them in a big pile while the guy who had Andrew's duffel bag emptied its contents and placed the bag on the pile as well. Someone else forcibly took off his shoes.

"Hey, what are you doing?"

"Quiet!"

The shoes also went on the growing pile, along with other junk. One of them poured some kerosene from a little container, and another lit the pile with a match, creating a smoldering, foul-smelling fire which gave out billows of thick black smoke.

There was a reason for all this. Laser guided rockets and bombs were being developed during the time of the Indochina war, where they were tested against real targets, mostly caves in Laos. It was this technology that killed four hundred people in the cave at Tam Piu, but the peasant armies of Vietnam and Laos had soon learned how to counter this sophisticated weaponry with a match and a pile of rubbish. Thick smoke scattered the laser beam that directed the rocket to its target, and without guidance, it would shoot back up into the air out of control. Unfortunately for those at Tam Piu a year before, they never got to learn that trick.

"Bai, bai!"

That accomplished, they made their way deeper into the cave. The ceiling became lower and Andrew, taller than the rest, had to bend down. In the darkness he smelled smoke, not from the burning rubbish outside, but wood smoke from a campfire within the tunnel, and it caused his eyes to smart and tear. The passageway eventually opened up into a large cavern, softly illuminated by a fire, and where close to a hundred people were sitting and squatting. The mysterious farmers of the rice fields in the valley were at last revealed.

Andrew squatted down with the rest of them, and the difference between prisoner and captors soon became indistinct. Having been untied, he accepted a small bamboo pipe from a man on his right, took a few puffs, and coughed. This prompted amused laughter from those around him. Among the crowd, was a little boy who stared at him persistently with wide eyes. Whenever Andrew looked back at him, he would turn away and giggle shyly, covering a bashful smile with the back of his hand.

"Listen—a horse!" Andrew then did the trick his father used to do for him, clapping his hands and slapping his knees, making a sound imitating a horse's gallop, which to the Laotians was uproariously funny, their loud laughter resounding in the cave at such a volume as to drown out the noises of devastation outside. This seemed to break a spell. One mother repeatedly murmured something to her small daughter, at times pointing to Andrew, then feigned an attempt to hand the child over to him. The little girl hung onto her mother's paa-sin in a desperate panic, wailing in fright, and there were more raucous guffaws at her expense.

That these people could still have enough buoyancy of spirit to jest in the middle of all this misery touched him deeply.

The bombing went on for the rest of the day and throughout the night. They all slept on bamboo mats, huddled close to keep each other warm.

By the middle of the next morning, there was a respite in the bombing, and Andrew and his escort were off again. This time they were joined by four women, who carried heavy loads, most of it rice, in large baskets pressed on their backs with straps that went across their foreheads, a mode that placed much of the weight upon their necks. A male villager, who seemed to be acting as a guide, led the way. Andrew had eaten well while in the cave, there having been fish and meat and vegetables along with the rice, and the long rest did him some good, so in the beginning he was able to keep up more easily than before. But now, without his shoes, his bare feet inevitably became so cut and bruised that they soon agonized him. Every time his pace slowed, the guy in front would snap his leash, prodding him to move faster. He fell down on one occasion, and got a quick beating for it. The women, relentlessly chewing their betel nut, and who also walked barefoot, had no trouble keeping up in spite of the burdens they bore; of course, they were used to it, and the leathery skin of their soles provided tough armor against the rocks, roots and thorns.

They were heading south. In fact, since the time he had been captured, except for some minor changes in direction, it became evident that they had always been traveling south. Why would they be doing this in the middle of a US-backed offensive? he kept asking himself. It was the rainy season, and according to precedents already set in this seesaw war, it was the enemy's turn to retreat from the Plain of Jars. Andrew guessed that these guys were the vestiges of the last PL/NVA forces left on the Plain, and that they must be cut off from Route 7, their most obvious escape route, by Hmong Special Guerilla Units coming from the north.

The trail that they were following hugged the base of a ridge of mountains, where, as before, access to nearby caves would offer quick shelter in the case of an air strike. The cheerful banter that they had engaged in when they had first set out had by now died down to a labored silence. Some of the soldiers were rolling themselves cigarettes as they were walking, using dried banana leaves as paper.

Another one was busy carving something. They were a motley crew, in varied attire. The more respectable-looking wore frayed khaki uniforms, while others dressed in a hodge-podge of western and Laotian; almost all of them wore sandals made from tires.

They stopped in the middle of the mountain rainforest and picked up a new guide, who, oddly enough, had been waiting for them under a tree, and who was to lead them the rest of the way, the first guide returning to the caves they had left in the morning. They walked for several hours through the jungle at a good clip, but they didn't run, much to Andrew's satisfaction. Still, the burning of the cuts on his feet and the exhausting tedium of the march was beginning to take a toll on him. In the middle of the night they reached a place with a huge hole in the ground, and, after he was once more freed of his ropes, they clambered down into it.

They crawled underground for what seemed like hours, through absolute blackness, and the smell of humus was so rank and moldy that it was suffocating. It wasn't long before his hands became scraped and his knees bruised, adding to the pain of his bleeding feet, yet he consoled himself by empathizing with the women straining with the baskets on their backs.

What the hell were they all doing, scrabbling like rats in the damp rotting earth? Everything he had seen so far on the ground was such utter madness. War. War had a nasty way of changing normal existence into a freakish nightmare, turning mundane routines into perverse extremes that were accepted and accommodated in the struggle to survive.

At last, the tunnel opened up into a large musty chamber, where the man with the Chinese cap gave a shout and knocked twice on a shuttering of small logs set in the earthen ceiling, covering a hole above them. The trapdoor opened and they emerged to find themselves surrounded by a group of soldiers, shadowy figures in the night, in the middle of a forest. Simple thatched structures were vaguely visible in the faint starlight; silhouetted dwellings that were covertly nestled among the bushes. Andrew surmised that this was a base camp, a supply center that sustained the guerillas which operated around it, like the hub of a wheel, connected to other hubs by main supply routes.

The camp itself was a randomly made group of huts and shelters scattered throughout the forest, making it more difficult to spot on recon photos, and more difficult to knock out with tactical bombing. There were crisscrossing trails, camouflaged by snares of vegetation, which made it easy to intercept any penetrating invaders. These paths were quite narrow, so that it was possible for one man with an automatic weapon to defend them.

As the others found their places outside, the soldiers escorted Andrew and the capped officer to one of the larger of the huts. Inside, several men were gathered around a table, studying something by candlelight. One of the uniformed men got up and exchanged words with the Chinese-capped officer, while the rest appropriately walked out. This man, the one remaining in the hut, was dressed in a crisp blue military uniform, complete with an officer's cap, and was apparently the one in charge. He also spoke Lao with a guttural accent.

However, he addressed Andrew in English. "You must be tired. Sit down."

They both took their seats on opposite sides of the table. Even in the feeble glow given off by the candle, Andrew could tell that the man he was face to face with was of lighter complexion than most of the Lao he had seen. He had a rather large, lizard-like mouth and he wore glasses with thick, black, plastic frames, the type that the nerds back in high school used to wear. His thin, slight build added to the semblance of a mild-mannered petty clerk, which uncannily made him appear all the more frightening. Most certainly a North Vietnamese Regular.

"Are you hungry?"

"Yes."

"I'll have some food brought to you. It is only our simple food...yet do not underestimate the sustenance that rice provides. It is the fuel of our armies here in Indochina." His English was so flawless that it was almost menacing. The man gazed at him with an attentiveness that was equally upsetting. "Are there any other problems I can help you with?"

The overtly gracious manner with which this man conducted the conversation made Andrew uneasy. It was a calculated and insidious tactic that interrogators often employ.

"My feet are badly cut. It hurts when I walk."

"Yes. Your face also is not good."

The Vietnamese officer offered him an American cigarette.

"No thanks, I don't smoke."

"You should learn. It is one of the few pleasures we can afford you." He took one himself and lit it.

The man with the floppy cap handed over Andrew's identity cards to the Vietnamese officer, and exited without ado.

"What is your name?" the Vietnamese asked, as he handed to Andrew only the Geneva card, keeping the US Air Force ID. His question was merely a formal confirmation, having already read the name that was printed on the ID.

"Andrew Kozeny," he answered, putting the Geneva card in the same shirt pocket as his index card.

"Polish ancestry?"

"Yes."

This man was no fool. He gave the impression that he was well-educated, and this made Andrew suspect that he was an intelligence officer rather than a military advisor.

"How old are you, twenty-two?"

"Twenty-three."

"You are still young and innocent. Married?"

"No."

"You have a girl waiting for you?"

Andrew paused. "No. Not any more."

"Ah, there is plenty of time. When you get back to America, you will find a nice girl." The Vietnamese opened his mouth into a long, rubbery smile, his tongue arching up to caress his upper lip in a diabolically pensive manner. "Which part of America are you from?"

"Ohio. Small town called Camden."

"Yes, the Midwest. The heart of America. And your parents, what do they do?"

"My father is an insurance salesman. My mother works occasionally as a nurse."

"I'm sure they are very nice people. And you are a good son."

Andrew was becoming impatient with this preliminary chitchat. "Where are you taking me? Hanoi?"

"I wouldn't worry about that for now. Our first concern is to leave the immediate area, which, as you are keenly aware, is becoming very dangerous for us, and you as well."

Andrew decided not to press the matter for now.

The Vietnamese studied him with bemused interest. "Tell me, why did you join the Air Force?"

"I love flying."

"Ah, yes, a magnificent pursuit. And when did you join?"

"In 1963."

"The same year Kennedy was assassinated," the bespectacled Vietnamese noted.

There was a knock on the door followed by the presence of a soldier bearing a tray. The Vietnamese nodded, and the soldier approached and placed little bamboo baskets of sticky rice on the table, as well as a bowl full of chicken stew and the miniature round eggplants that were common in Southeast Asia.

"Do you know why Kennedy was killed?" the Vietnamese continued as the servant soldier departed.

"A madman shot him."

The officer laughed. "You really are an innocent. It doesn't surprise me. Most Americans are unaware of many things. They are placated with material comforts, and distracted by silly television shows, so they accept everything their government does. But not anymore. Now, there are citizens who question the US government and demand that it should be accountable. Your leaders are not happy about that." He proceeded to give the names of places, including universities, and the dates as well, of major antiwar demonstrations, the accuracy of which truly impressed Andrew, who was by now sure that this man was some sort of a political cadre.

"Oh, please, you can go ahead and eat," he said, pointing at the food on the table.

Andrew busied himself with his food while the man with the glasses continued his declamation.

"Some people say that Kennedy was killed over Cuba, because his refusal to allow air cover in the Bay of Pigs angered the right-wing power factions. That is true in a way, but you don't necessarily eliminate people based on what they already did, but more so because of what they might do in the future. Kennedy was killed over the issue of Southeast Asia."

Andrew looked up from his food. "That is just your opinion."

The Vietnamese, for the first time, showed some anger and impatience in his expression and tone. "That is not just my opinion!" he declaimed vehemently. "In 1961, Kennedy and Khrushchev met in Vienna where they both agreed not to get involved in a war in Southeast Asia. A year later came the Cuban Missile crisis; it appeared that even Khrushchev thought your president weak. After the Bay of Pigs, the more aggressive elements in your government felt that he would be too soft on the Indochina issue. Kennedy was in favor of the coalition government with the Pathet Lao."

Whether or not all this was a bunch of lies, one thing was certain. This man, whatever his official function, was attempting to dominate him intellectually. The first step in brainwashing.

Andrew thought hard to match his wit. "Unfortunately, we in the Armed Forces don't have the luxury of speculating on such theories. You know as well as I do that a soldier obeys orders without question. All your philosophizing has no relevance for me. It won't change things."

The Vietnamese grinned, showing yellow, nicotine-stained teeth. "Have you ever heard of Ngo Dinh Diem? The former leader of the puppet government of renegade South Vietnam?"

"I'm not sure I recall..."

"He was a very corrupt and irresponsible tyrant, despised by his own people but backed by your government, so he felt he could do whatever he wanted. His brother, wife, and other relatives ruled with him, and together they oppressed the masses. Three weeks before Kennedy's assassination he was also killed in a coup led by his own military officers, who were encouraged by the State Department and the US embassy, because they now judged him unfit to rule the government that they were backing."

"Coincidence," Andrew scoffed.

"Coincidence? Both Kennedy and Diem, in different ways, were obstacles in your government's imperialistic and militaristic designs at subjugating our country. Your government became so obsessed with our struggle for liberation, so frightened of our heroic revolutionary spirit, that they killed their allies and even their own president. You are too young and ignorant to know these things. Do you even know how many members there are in Congress?"

"I can't remember off the top of my head..."

"If you do not even know your own government," the Vietnamese sharply interrupted, "how can you understand the governments of other nations?" Changing tack, he asked, "Tell me, now that you have been on the ground and have seen the suffering of simple peasants, do you still believe that the bombing campaign of your government is a noble act?"

Andrew thought carefully before answering. He didn't want to reveal his true feelings, for fear that they would consider using him as an instrument of propaganda, or even worse, press him to reveal his knowledge concerning ECM and the F-111. He decided to put on an act of an uncooperative prisoner. "This is war. Civilians are bound to get killed. It's tragic but unavoidable."

"What type of aircraft were you flying?" the officer asked

abruptly.

"According to the Geneva Convention, I am not required to answer that."

The man snickered derisively, his extensive mouth twisting repugnantly. "Oh, you poor innocents. You all use that excuse. Rules. Rules of engagement. Civilized war. Except war was never officially declared against North Vietnam, and as for Lao, there isn't even a war taking place here at all, or didn't they tell you that?"

"Then I am not here," Andrew countered, "and I wasn't flying any airplane."

That sarcasm evidently pissed off the Vietnamese officer. "What type of aircraft were you flying?" he repeated, this time in a much harsher tone.

Andrew decided not to overdo the uncooperative prisoner bit. "F-105 Thunderchief."

The F-105 came in many different flavors. The Thunderchief, or Spud, was a conventional jet bomber of which very little was secret. And it was flown with only one pilot inside.

"*Kee-tua!* Liar!" the man with glasses yelled, in Lao. This switching of languages was a cue for the soldier who was standing behind Andrew to smash the butt of his rifle into the prisoner's back. Andrew's face flew forward and crashed into the bowl of stew he was eating and the bowl rolled off the table to bounce upon the floor.

Andrew sat up, stew dripping off his face.

"How did your aircraft go down?" the Vietnamese queried in English. "There are no AA batteries in that location."

"The hydraulics malfunctioned and I lost control."

"*Kee-tua!* .

Again, another rifle butt in the back, this time harder, and Andrew fell off his chair.

"Take him away!"

Andrew rolled on his side, opened his eyes, and feebly lifted his head. He sat up abruptly, momentarily bewildered, surprised at not being bound up in any fashion. He gathered his knees in his arms, for this position somewhat relieved the aches that were consuming his entire body. To keep his mind off of his discomfort he watched what must have been the cooking detail preparing breakfast.

The stove they used fascinated him. It was made of collapsible pieces of scrap metal, and the chimney seemed to be a helicopter exhaust pipe. This chimney didn't point up, however, but penetrated into the ground, making the smoke pass through a long tunnel to cool it enough so that it wouldn't rise and give their position away. The smoke emerged about a hundred yards away and clung low to the ground. Clever bastards, he thought to himself.

It didn't take them long to get this morning's repast ready: sticky rice and raw wild vegetables. Immediately after breakfast, everyone geared themselves for leaving the camp—it was to be abandoned, since they knew that whether visible or not, it would eventually be bombed in the saturation bombing campaign which had now begun.

There were scores of men, but they weren't going to be traveling together. Instead they broke up into little groups of ten or so and went off in different directions. The group that Andrew was assigned to included both the Vietnamese and the high-ranking Pathet Lao officer with the Chinese cap. It was understandable that they should accompany their precious cargo. They tied him up like before, with the guy behind him holding his leash, then left via one of the camouflaged trails.

Again, it was single file along narrow trails enclosed by impenetrable walls of dense bamboo. In places, the trail was so overgrown that it had to be cleared with machetes by the men in front, and the slow progress was a pleasant departure to the brisk pace that they had adhered to up to now.

They reached a river, the Nam Ngum, Andrew guessed, and it was in flood. He looked at the gurgling, ochre-colored froth indicative of the strong current and wondered how they were going to get across—there was no boat in sight. But they just kept on marching straight into the river. He was frightened following them, especially being trussed up the way he was, but was amazed when he found himself walking, only ankle-deep, on an underwater ramp just beneath the surface made out of logs and stones, stable enough to drive a truck over—a hidden bridge!

The jungle growth was much thinner on the other side. Nonetheless, they continued to march in single file. A fog set in once more and it began raining, first lightly, then heavily, then just steadily. They broke up leafy branches and wore them to protect themselves from the rain, making a similar raincoat for Andrew as well. Still, they didn't break from their march, even for lunch.

They continued to hug the base of a range of mountains that was trending east to west. Renewed air strikes could be heard in the distance, but there was also another, closer, booming series of reports. US howitzers, he suspected, 105-millimeter. It appeared that the Hmong army was closing in. Yet, they didn't halt nor change direction.

It was barely an hour later, shortly after the rain stopped, when, spontaneously, the line halted and broke ranks to stand around a tree where a tube of bamboo hung down from a rope. The guide took out a stick that had been placed inside, and began banging on the bamboo pipe, first slowly, then faster and harder. Four men came out of the jungle, dressed in the usual peasant fashion, holding homemade flintlocks. Home guards, or some type of village militia, Andrew figured. The CIA had also set up village defense units for the opposing side, but he suspected that they weren't as organized as the Pathet Lao's network of local militia, guides and porters.

Greetings were exchanged between the man with the Chinese soldier's cap and the village guerillas, while the guide, like the one before him, begged his leave and went back along the trail they had come on. The Vietnamese officer stood indistinctly, yet purposefully in the background, like an observer. The home guards then led them to a clearing, in the middle of which stood a hut with a crudely fashioned altar inside for the village spirit. Nearby, there was a man sitting on a big boulder wearing a tattered suit jacket. He was a large man for a Lao, with expansive eyes set in a wide, chunky face. He got up and approached the visitors.

After some discussion, he turned in Andrew's direction. "Untie him," he told the guards positioned behind him. To Andrew, he asked, in Lao, "Is it true you speak Lao?"

"Yes."

The man, apparently in his forties, with a face that conveyed paternal benevolence, smiled amicably. "Where did you learn it?"

"In America. A language school for the army."

"You speak very well," the Lao gentleman commented in a genial tone.

The man's friendliness seemed genuine, and Andrew relished it. "I practice speaking Thai, so that helps. I've been in Thailand for almost two years." His wrists now free, he began to rub the soreness from them.

"Yes, in the northeast of Thailand it is the same language."

The Air Force base where Andrew had been stationed, at Udon Tani, had once been part of Laos a hundred years ago, and the language spoken was practically the same.

"By the way, how do you like Thailand?"

"Well, I don't get to see much of it, I'm usually stuck at the base, although I did take a few hikes…"

"Yes, I would imagine with all the bombing, you barely got any chance to relax."

Andrew kept silent, wondering if that was sarcastic and whether the guy was going to continue to be friendly.

"Oh, I am sorry, I should introduce myself. I am the district chairman, Soupanat Chamvong. Would you like to see my village?"

The two of them walked together abreast, the rest of the group trailing behind, in a stilted pretense of showing him around, as if he were some sort of visiting dignitary.

"Of course, this is not the true village, which is called Ban Na," the chairman explained in an avuncular manner. "We had to make one here in the forest, because the planes dropped bombs on us, but Ban Na is not far, just there," the Laotian said, pointing down at the valley to his left.

There were huts ahead of them, but without walls. Rough-and-ready shelters to keep the rain off them. The local denizens, mostly women and children, stood rigid as they approached, and silently watched them come into the village.

The procession stopped, and Andrew was ordered to sit down on a log by the path. The crowd of villagers moved towards him and arranged themselves like an audience in front of a stage, moving delicately, their curiosity tempered with caution. Naked children with potbellies clung to the paa-sins of their mothers, uncomprehendingly watching the band of armed men and their prisoner.

"This man is an American pilot," the chairman announced to the newly forming crowd. "He is one of them who brings the bombs. But it is not his fault. His chiefs made him do it." To Andrew, he asked, "Are you sorry for what you did?"

It was difficult in this situation for Andrew to remain reticent concerning the bombing. Reluctantly, perhaps foolishly, considering the presence of the Vietnamese political cadre, he decided to be honest in front of these humble peasants. "Yes," he answered in Lao.

"Tell, them."

"I am sorry," he told the gathering in their own language.

The sounds of the bombing grew louder, and began to even overshadow the booming of the artillery.

"Where are your shoes?" the village headman asked him, ignoring the clamor of war raging in the distance. He gestured to indicate Andrew's feet, by now bloodied and blue with bruises.

One of the Pathet Lao spoke up, ostensibly explaining the burning of the shoes, at which point the chairman said something in a loud voice, now addressing the crowd. A woman stepped forth and approached the chairman. Her hair was gathered into a dignified bun but her face was severely disfigured from what appeared to be the result of third degree burns. One side of her face was particularly scarred, to the extent that the left side of her mouth was grossly misshapen and there was no skin under her left eye, an unsightly deformity which made it look as if the eye had popped out of its socket. Her injuries were accentuated by purple mottles and streaks, indicating they had only recently healed.

In response to the chairman's appeal, she trotted into one of the huts and came out with a basin of water and a towel. Kneeling in front of Andrew, she bathed his feet. Despite the initial sting, the footbath soothed him beyond all expectation. The woman's touch was especially tender. She was about the same age as his mother, Andrew noted.

The air raids were evidently getting closer and there was some deliberation among the villagers.

"We have to go to the caves now," the chairman declared.

It is hard to imagine anything more frightening than being in the attack path of a jet. The screams of the jets were even more terrifying than the sounds of the blasts. They had all been through this countless times before, and so they ran in a well-practiced reaction.

There were about three caves; all next to each other, and Andrew ran limping, following the woman who had bathed his feet. The cave they entered was much smaller than the one he had been in two nights ago, and it was crowded inside. A bonfire was already burning to divert any rockets.

They gathered themselves into the space available and watched the explosive display taking place outside with a grave silence, until an old man, as if to defy their predicament, broke out with a sad lam which sang of the old days of peace and contentment, of beautiful mountains and fields, of scenes of water buffaloes grazing in the paddocks, of the November harvest, of festivals and children playing. While the singing continued, people took the occasion to find places on the floor to sit down.

After the song finished, there were several simultaneous discussions among them, and like the discussions in the first cave he had been to, all were concerned with what was to become of them and when the war would end. These poor people, he thought, caught in the middle, and they had no idea why. They had no conception of Cold War politics, the Domino theory, or the Marxist axioms of economic determinacy. All they wanted to do was to go back to their rice fields and have everything the way it was before the war. They didn't pay attention too closely to the things going on in Vientiane, leave alone Hanoi, Moscow, Bejing, or Washington. It confused them to think how those things from so far away could arrive at their own little village.

In these past two days, hiding in the caves with the Laotian peasants, Andrew had shared their food, their fears, and their laughter, and so it was natural to more readily identify with them, rather than his former mates who were dropping the bombs. His empathy reassured him that the choice he had made was the right one, the moral one, whatever the final outcome.

Sitting with his legs drawn under his body in lotus fashion, he reached into his shirt pocket and took out the card with the hibiscus petals, looked at it hard and long, and decided it was too risky to keep it on his person. It was lucky for him that his captors had so far not taken any stock of it, and hadn't yet become a subject for interrogation and, ultimately, food for propaganda. On an impulse, he glanced at the disfigured woman who had attended to his feet and who had taken a seat next to him. "Keep this," he told her, handing over the card. He smiled. "It will bring good luck."

For a long moment she looked at him with a mixture of curiosity and concern, and then turned her scarred face away from him to stare out the mouth of the cave.

"Kopjai," she said impassively. "Thank you."

It was in the quiet of the early evening when he was tied up again and told to bai, bai. There was a new local guide with them, as well as two women from the village who would replace the other porters, and one, Andrew happily noticed, was the middle-aged woman with the mangled face.

It was raining again when they started off. It grew to a steady, substantial fall, and despite the branches and plastic sheets that they wore, everyone was soaking wet. They forged ahead, ignoring the continuous pelting, but when a black goat came out of nowhere, there was a complete halt. The Laotians were reluctant to continue, insisting that this was a bad sign. The Vietnamese guy was resolute on this issue, demanding that they proceed. In the end, his willfulness compelled them to march on.

The booming of artillery grew louder and louder through the splashing of the raindrops. An hour later the sounds of helicopters could also be heard, and the group stopped again. The Vietnamese officer and the man with the Chinese cap were discussing something, which Andrew couldn't hear through the din of the helicopters and the clapping of the rain. But he could imagine what was being said, as he himself knew what was taking place just nearby. Either Air America or US Air Force helicopters were leapfrogging Hmong units into position on the mountaintops. The little troupe was about to enter a battlefield.

Most of the men, except the Vietnamese political officer and the guide, divvied up the supplies in the baskets that the women had been carrying. Along with the Chinese-capped officer, these men went on ahead to join the fight. The women porters remained where they were, as well as one of the soldiers who held a Browning automatic rifle, apparently left as an armed guard to watch over Andrew.

It wasn't until moments later that the Vietnamese officer noticed that the guide had disappeared. Having taken advantage of the commotion, he had fled discreetly into the rain. The officer was furious, shouting at the guard, while Andrew looked at the rifle and started to think fast.

The Browning was very heavy, around twenty pounds. This would slow the guy's reaction time. Yes, right now, while they were talking. The rain was thrashing down furiously, whacking the air with a harsh clattering, building up to a crescendo, and booms could be heard from the cannons as they continued firing. The Vietnamese guy, with his open mouth going a mile a minute, was still rebuking the Pathet Lao soldier, but the words were lost in the bedlam. The gathering darkness of the storm had diminished everyone to shadowy silhouettes in the sporadic flickering of the lightning. The rain kept coming down harder and harder in a raging climax. Now, now's the time, do it, just do it!

Andrew sprung up with all the energy he could muster, lunging at the soldier and knocking both him and the Vietnamese officer down. Predictably, the Browning fell out of the soldier's grasp and bounced away on the ground. Andrew stood up and gave the fallen man a kick in his face, only to turn around and see the Vietnamese officer drawing his nine-millimeter revolver. A scream pierced the air and as Andrew looked on, stunned beyond movement, a laden basket came crashing down on the officer's head. The man collapsed from the blow, and Andrew found himself staring into the eyes of the disfigured woman, her resolute face dripping water, her penetrating glance fixed through the downpour. He returned her gaze briefly, before fleeing into the monsoon-drenched forest.

In his panic, with his wrists still tied behind his back, he ran right into the thick of it—blazing flares and smoke grenades which the artillery units fired off to correct their ranges, 105-millimeter shells bursting all around him, the sound of rapid-fire automatic weapons, shadows of men running everywhere, screams and shouts, planes coming in dropping bombs—a deranged chaos blanketed by a dull, immense sea of rain. He dashed through all of this, running the gauntlet, the gauntlet of his life.

Chapter 11

Laos 1990

"Faith is the substance of things hoped for, the evidence of things not seen"
Bible: New Testament: Hebrews 11:1.

Once back in Ponsavan, Dorothy called again to the River View Hotel to pass a message to Mr. Prasert to pass on to Miss Cynthia in the US. The message read: "Checked out the crash sites. Nothing of any substance yet, but investigating some stories."

In the evening she met with Kampeng at the restaurant, the one with all the bomb decorations.

"What Miss Doro-tee want to do now?" he asked, as they sat at their usual table.

"Do you believe that woman's story?"

"Maybe true," he answered in his usual noncommittal way. "Maybe not true. But pilot not your son. Map not show eff one-o-five crash there."

"I know. Even the other map doesn't show any jets that crashed anywhere near that village. Still, that card she showed us is rather strange."

Kampeng was silent.

"The writing on the back reminds me of Andrew's writing."

"You think old woman talk about your son? You also think son crash near Muang Kham. Cannot be same person. He get rescued at Muang Kham. If Vietnamese find rescue party, kill Hmong and take pilot, they go on Route Seven to Nong Het, then to Vinh and Hanoi. Or maybe take him up Route Six, to Sam Neua, place of Pathet Lao. That in east. Would not go from Muang Kham in northeast, cross Plain of Jars back to southwest where American army is."

"I agree. That's why I think he went down twice."

"Twice? You mean two time?"

"Yes. He was shot down over Ban Ban, I mean Muang Kham, and rescued. Then he crashed again further west, in the south. He was captured, that woman with the scars met him, and then he ran away like she said."

Kampeng wanted to say that she was only thinking in this way because she was the man's mother, but that would be too direct and impolite. "No, I don't think. Not on map. What about pilot that get buried? You say that your son also."

"I don't care about the map. And the pilot that was buried was someone else. I think my son ran away from a second crash. In fact, Mr. Kampeng, I think that he may have been assassinated by the CIA."

"Assas...?" Kampeng stuttered, not knowing that word.

"Killed, murdered."

"By CIA? Why Miss Doro-tee think that?"

"Because I got a letter which suggests that a group of men went to look for him, with the objective of killing him."

"Why they do that?"

"I don't know. That's why I've come all the way here to Lao. I want to find out just what happened. I'm not getting answers from the US military."

"If he run away, where he go?" Kampeng asked rhetorically, not believing any of this.

"I believe he went to Pu Khe Mountain, to the top."

"Why he do that?"

"I know my son. He would go there to die. I don't think he had any hope of getting out of his situation."

"Why mountain of Pu Khe?"

"It's the tallest mountain around. He would want to go up, just out of his own feelings."

"Kampeng not understand what Miss Doro-tee want to do."

"I want to visit Pu Khe Mountain."

"No, not possible."

"Yes, it is possible," she corrected him, "just difficult."

"No, very dangerous."

"Chao Fa?" Dorothy anticipated.

"Yes. And too much bombies...also many spirits. Forest spirits."

Dorothy looked down at the table as she thought about what to say next. "Listen, Mr. Kampeng, I understand your reluctance. And I am not saying that you should go with me." She looked up to face him. "I appreciate all that you have done for me. I just ask one last favor. That you find someone who can help me climb that mountain."

"Kampeng not afraid," he asserted, in case that was her insinuation. "But I don't know mountain. You need local person."

"So, you'll help me?"

"Kampeng help, but I don't feel good."

"Why? What's wrong?"

Kampeng couldn't tell her that he felt her safety was his responsibility, that they had taken too many chances already, and that climbing the mountain was absurd.

"You don't know, you don't know," he simply told her.

Kampeng, despite his misgivings, agreed to drive down to Muang Koon, also known as Xieng Khouang town on European maps. It was about fifty kilos, he told her, and of course, the road was bad. He was counting on the hope that Dorothy would eventually give up the idea and realize that going up the mountain was foolhardy.

As they got nearer to Muang Koon, the isolated ridges got closer and closer, and the long flat valleys got narrower, and pretty soon they were amongst somber-looking hills, the larger ones small mountains with knife-like peaks. On the way was the invariable police check that inspected their laissez-passer. It took almost three hours through heat and dust to get there.

Muang Koon was what Dorothy would describe as a one-horse town. Not even that— the term 'town' would be a misnomer. The main street of the settlement was only about a quarter of a mile long, flanked by ramshackle houses and torpid hovels serving as shops. Before the war, it had been a thriving place, a royal capital, and then a provincial center with thousands of people. During the war, it had been a strategic position, because the town, along with the mountains around it, was the gateway to the Plain of Jars. That was why its capture by the Royalist army and Vang Pao's forces was considered so important. The many battles fought over its possession, the bombing, and the shelling by the artillery, eventually destroyed it.

Kampeng stopped the car in front of the market. "You go see temple, very interesting. I look around for someone I know long time ago, maybe he still here. He know mountain."

The temple was across the road from the market, less than a hundred feet from where Kampeng had parked the jeep. It was called Wat Pia Wat, Wat being the Laotian word for temple. She crossed the street, carefully avoiding the abundant pats of buffalo dung. Again, she had to pay one thousand kip to a foxy-faced old man who possessed a ticket book before she could gain entry. There wasn't much of a temple left after the bombs had hit it. With the roof long gone, it was open to the sky and the walls were virtually absent, save for a few remaining pillars. The concrete floor had been recently re-laid, she could tell. The striking thing was the huge, black Buddha image squatting at the other end of the ruins, totally exposed, calmly posing in the open, and which, other than a few shrapnel scars, had been left miraculously unscathed.

"Bomb and cannon hit everything but no touch Buddha," Kampeng said, suddenly appearing behind her.

Dorothy whirled around. "Oh, hello. Where did you go?"

"I find out if my friend here. I find out my friend home. We go now and see him."

They got back into the jeep and drove out of the town for a quarter of an hour before Kampeng pulled it over to the side of the road. "We walk. About three kilo."

They walked up a hill through dry, open woodland, following a well-used trail, then branched off to their left, which led them up another small hill past cleared areas that were blackened by fire.

"Cut, burn," Kampeng elucidated.

Eventually, they came upon a village; twenty or so decrepit huts cluttered together without any apparent organization or orientation. They were frail, pale-yellow structures, perched on skinny poles, their walls constructed of mats woven from split bamboo, their roofs of thatched grass. All of them had an open porch at one end of the house. In the air was a stench composed of wood smoke, dry dung, and rank straw. Dorothy's presence seemed to have caused a bit of a stir, as the few people that were around stared at her in bewilderment, while children, obviously having never seen a European before, stopped their playing and ran to their mothers to cling onto their paa-sins.

"Sabai dee," Dorothy called to them.

They watched her silently, only one woman making a half-hearted reply.

"These people no Lao Loom. They are Lao Toong. Speak different language."

"Lao Loom? Lao Toong?"

"Yes, in Lao there are Lao Loom, Lao Toong, and Lao Soong. Kampeng is Lao Loom, live in valley. Lao Toong live on sides of mountains, and Lao Soong live on top of mountains."

Kampeng approached a group of men who held homemade hoes in their hands and began a conversation, presumably asking for the whereabouts of his friend. Then he led Dorothy over to the shade of a large fig tree. "We wait here, my friend in fields, they send boy to call him."

Dorothy was curious as to how he communicated. "Did they understand what you were saying?"

"Kampeng speak many languages. I speak Kammu."

"But you said these people were Lao Toong."

"Yes, Kammu is Lao Toong. Kammu, Lamet, Sedang...all Lao Toong. Many, many peoples Lao Toong. Just like many peoples Lao

Soong, like Hmong, Yao, Akha."

All of this was beyond Dorothy so she decided to leave it be.

An adolescent boy came and in response to Kampeng's solicitation, led them to one of the houses. On the way, they passed a small thatched structure which was supported by stilts fashioned from bomb casings of CBU dispensers.

"That is where they keep rice," explained Kampeng.

"A granary?"

"Yes, gran-ree," he answered, bending down inspecting the metal post, not really knowing the word she mentioned. He banged on one of the bomb shell legs. "This very good. If wood, maybe after five years have to make again. But this…" He banged on the metal again like a salesman demonstrating his product, "…stay for twenty years."

After arriving at the house, which appeared a bit sturdier than most of the other squalid residences, they climbed up a rickety ladder onto the porch. Dorothy assumed it was the home of Kampeng's friend. Once inside the dimly lit shack, which wobbled slightly as they moved, they underwent similar formalities that they had gone through in the District Chairman's house in Muang Kham: a young girl wearing a kerchief on her head bade them to sit on a mat placed on the floor. Shortly thereafter, an older woman, with a drawn face and buxom body, probably the wife, came in with a tray pressed against her ample stomach and served them Chinese tea, which Dorothy had begun to suspect was the standard Laotian way of welcoming visitors into their homes. Kampeng greeted her by saying something that sounded like 'eh-ruam'.

"Is that hello in Kammu language?" Dorothy asked.

"Yes, like Sabai dee."

The woman smiled at Dorothy, then conversed with Kampeng. From the manner in which Kampeng was responding, Dorothy could tell she was saying something that interested him very much.

"This my friend wife," he then explained. "She say there is some trouble with Chao Fa, near road to Ta Thom."

"What trouble?"

"Chao Fa attack Hmong village. Kill ten people, set village on fire."

"But you said that the Chao Fa are Hmong people. Why do they attack other Hmong?"

"Last week, three Chao Fa walk into village. Want food and some animals. Villagers refuse. Don't want to help Chao Fa. Then there is argument, and villagers kill the Chao Fa. Later more Chao Fa come to punish the villagers."

This shadow of the Chao Fa seemed to be following them everywhere. "Is this near where we are going?"

"Ta Thom near, but not very near. Government send army, Chao Fa run back in forest. Everything quiet now."

That seemed to have been all the news of any general interest. Kampeng then resumed his discourse with the woman of the house, who had since hunkered down to join them on the mat, leaving Dorothy to sit quietly drinking her tea, a diversion insufficient to ward off her boredom. In due time, food was brought, a strange looking mishmash, as well as a plate of odd-looking green leaves and the familiar sticky rice. She ate very little. Despite her repeated attempts, she wasn't getting accustomed to the food. It was all right as a novelty, but as a regular routine it was a letdown. She found herself dreaming of pizza. She was also conscious of the fact that since she had been in Lao, she had lost quite a few pounds, which pleased her, except for the fact that her face, already wrinkled enough, was beginning to look emaciated.

Another half hour went by without event, and Dorothy found herself lapsing into a fit of repeated yawning.

"Where is your friend?"

"He in fields. Coming just now. Fields very far away. Cut and burn farmer have many many fields, all over mountain, far away."

It wasn't long after when the man did indeed arrive. He was dressed in a military uniform and his physical appearance was quite arresting. His dark brown face was long and pear-shaped, and he looked like an absolute madman, with curly hair sticking out of his head as though he had been struck by lightning and with eyes that were badly crossed. Kampeng stood up and the two men embraced. "This my friend, Tanak," Kampeng announced. "He is army man."

The man called Tanak must have known some Lao, for he said 'sabai dee' to her.

The Laotians became involved in a zestful discussion, with Tanak aiming a substantial glance at her from time to time. Dorothy was growing tired of the language barrier, of not having anyone to talk to besides Kampeng and of always hearing things second hand.

Kampeng, as if sensing her feeling of estrangement, attempted to draw her into the conversation. "My friend in army. During war he fight on side of Pathet Lao."

"But you fought on the Royalist side. you're still friends?"

"Of course. War is over. We all Lao peoples."

Despite the fact that Kampeng knew English and that they had already spent a good deal of time talking to each other, Dorothy realized she still didn't know him, still couldn't figure him out.

"Tanak agree, say he will take us up mountain, tomorrow."

"Us? Are you going also?"

"Of course. Tanak don't know English like me. And tonight we have *baa-see*."

"Baa-see? Is that a special dish?"

"It is ceremony to keep us well and pray to *pii*."

"Pee?"

"Yes. It is good to have baa-see before going on important journey. And we go to Pu Khe, where there many *pii*."

"I still don't understand what a pee is," she complained.

"*He-roo-oy*," Tanak, the Kammu, clarified.

"Kammu people call them He-roo-oy. They are in trees, in rivers, and in wild places in mountains. Some pii make sickness or bring bad luck. There are pii also inside people, inside everyone."

"Inside people?"

"Yes. They try to get out. Then you not feel well."

"They? How many are inside a person?" She was beginning to get interested in this.

"Thirty-two."

"Thirty-two?"

"Yes. Those pii we call *kwan*, the ones inside everyone."

She wondered how they came up with the number thirty-two. She didn't know at that time that it was the approximate number of organs in a human body.

"Lao Toong, like Kammu peoples, are first peoples in Lao, come before anyone. They close to land. They are experts with pii."

"*He-roo-oy*," Tanak corrected.

"So the Kammu are among the original inhabitants of Lao?"

Kampeng didn't understand her question, particularly the word 'inhabitants', but nevertheless he continued undaunted. "That is why we go on mountain together with Kammu man. Only Kammu and Hmong on Pu Khe. No Lao Loom go on mountain, except forest monks, *Pra Baa*, who also have special power over pii."

"*He-roo-oy*," Tanak insisted emphatically.

She figured out that pii were something like spirits, and there were different types.

The rest of the afternoon was uneventful, and the only two things that Dorothy did was to lie down on a mat and fall asleep, and afterwards, take a bath in a little area in the back of the house, concealed by a high bamboo partition. The bath of course was of the bucket and ladle type. She finished dressing in a little room assigned to her and not long after was led to a fairly large timber structure that lacked stilts, but stood directly on the ground, apparently the village meeting hall.

Tanak entered with several villagers carrying a beautiful silver urn. Sitting snugly inside it was the *bai-see*, a cone elaborately fashioned out of banana leaves, and sprouting a small bouquet of flowers, candles, and several sticks of burning incense. Dorothy noticed that there was a multitude of thin white strings dangling from the stems of the flowers. Tanak placed this elegant centerpiece on a small wicker table. Women, chatting vivaciously, brought fruits, bowls of chicken, rice, eggs, and bottles of that deadly rice whiskey, and placed them on the table around the urn.

The hall began to get crowded. Everyone sat down on the floor around the table as the main 'priest' arrived, an elderly man who wore a white silk-like sash.

"*Ikoon,*" Tanak promptly pointed out with reverence.

After the priest, or ikoon, sat down, he lit the candles that were placed among the flowers and began a monotonic chant. As he did so, the people nearest the table reached out and touched the urn. Others behind folded their hands in prayer, and Dorothy aptly followed suit. Once this solemn monologue was completed, Dorothy, along with Kampeng and Tanak, were urged to move up front.

The prayers, Dorothy learned later, were entreating the house spirits to protect them, and the forest spirits to allow them to pass unharmed. The ikoon, apparently finished with his grave recitation, looked up at them.

"Do what I do," Kampeng told her.

Luckily for her, he was first. He raised his left hand as if to shield his cheek and extended his right, into which the ikoon placed an egg. Then the ikoon took one of the white strings and tied it around Kampeng's wrist, after which he did something that looked like he was rubbing it into his skin. Other people were touching Kampeng while this was happening. When it was Dorothy's turn, she could feel a multitude of hands on her and looked around to see everyone was touching each other, all connected to her. It all seemed so mystical. She looked at the white cotton string around her wrist. It was just an ordinary piece of string, and she now understood the strings she had first noticed around Kampeng's wrist and around the wrists of the bridal couple at the wedding ceremony.

The trio got up after the procedure to let others take their turn at receiving the cotton bracelets. Dorothy wondered what she should do with the chicken leg the ikoon had put in her hand.

"Eat it," instructed Kampeng.

The party climaxed with everyone eating, accompanied by lots of laughter and gaiety. Dorothy was surprised that she was really enjoying the food, which included what she thought to be a tasty buffalo stew (later Kampeng was to reveal to her that it was porcupine). Some people were passing around glasses of lao-kao. She really didn't want to, remembering her last experience with the stuff, but she felt she couldn't refuse, given the circumstances. She should have known that this wasn't to be a serious, sober, grave ritual, but yet another occasion to have fun. The house was packed with people, and of course, plenty of kids too. The little ones smiled and giggled, as they looked on at their parents being carried away with all the merrymaking.

And what would a party be without music? A man appeared in the doorway making wonderfully strange shrieking sounds on a bamboo panpipe that looked like bagpipes without the bag. He was blowing passionately, stomping his feet on the wood floor. People got up and danced around in hypnotic circles, clapping their hands in a steady throbbing rhythm.

When it was over, Dorothy, not being too drunk, thought the baa-see had been a rather fine idea.

Fortunately, Dorothy had had a great sleep, and even though the bedding wasn't as plushy as that at the house in Sieng Di, she was beginning to realize just how comfortable sleeping on the floor was. Around five in the morning Kampeng woke her up. Even at such an early hour they still managed to eat breakfast, which in Laos, didn't seem any different than the food served for lunch or supper, namely, sticky rice.

They set off, first driving as far as possible to get as close as they could to the mountain. As the dawn was making its appearance, they left the jeep and trundled off into the woods. Dorothy had made sure to generously spread insect repellent all over her body, and even on her clothes, for she knew that dengue fever was a common malady in the Laotian jungle, and the mosquitoes that carried it were day biters. She offered some of the foul-smelling liquid to her comrades, who declined.

They embarked upon an ascending path to the melody of morning birdcalls. At first, they went through little obscure villages that displayed limited activity in the early hours, but by eight o'clock, they had reached an area that was fairly uninhabited. Still, there were cut trees and blackened patches that bespoke of human presence. By nine o'clock, even that was missing, and she felt she had arrived at a point of no return.

It was going to be a warm day she realized. She took off her bush shirt, which she had worn over a baggy tank top, and tied it around her waist, as they trudged over a roughly hewn trail through nondescript dry-leafed bushes and tall, willowy banyan trees. Dorothy was relieved that the climb so far wasn't too steep, and grateful that Kampeng and Tanak were taking a rather slow, methodical pace. The two Laotians carried all the supplies, including the water. Both men, dressed in shorts and sleeveless T-shirts, posed a picture that was a striking contrast to her own overdressed, white, flabby body, for their sinewy frames were forged of taut muscles and large veins, rippling against their shining brown skin.

With a gentler slope, the vegetation changed to very tall grass, higher than the corn in Ohio, and having a very scratchy texture.

"Is this elephant grass?" Dorothy asked.

"Yes," answered Kampeng. "More elephant grass now than before war. Because of much bombing."

Once out of the grass, they found themselves in a jumble of palm trees and wild banana trees and the way became more declivitous. Kampeng began to sing a lam, a bittersweet and sorrowful sound. He was a good singer, his voice melodious and heartfelt, and the song seemed to imbue a purpose to their trekking. And though his crooning helped her to put a swing in her step, she was soon discomforted by the straps of her daypack, which began to irritate the tops of her shoulders in spite of the light weight.

The sun grew stronger and Dorothy was now dripping with sweat. The air was smothering, like a hot, damp rag on her face. With labored breathing, she followed the two men going up, staring down at the ground and putting one step ahead of the other, wondering when they were going to decide to stop for a rest. "Are we going to rest anytime soon?"

"We go little more, then rest. Best way to walk in forest is walk slow, but not stop much."

While the men chatted, Dorothy battled her growing fatigue, and her doubts as well. What did she expect to find here? The original plan was to talk to people, not traipse in isolated woods. But she had run out of ideas and still had plenty of time left on her visa. As long as she was doing something, exhausting all possibilities, however unlikely, she could go home knowing she had tried her best. Still, the idea of just turning around and going back was becoming a more and more appealing option with every step.

Walking up, and then down, into a broad ravine filled with a thick growth of bamboo, they finally stopped. They had been walking for six hours.

"Trail end here. Now we go into jungle. First rest."

They brought out little plastic bags of pre-cooked sticky rice, along with fried meat, and an assortment of fruits. They ate quietly, Kampeng and Tanak sharing only a few terse words. After they had finished eating, the two men set about cutting down some of the bamboo stalks.

"What's that for?" Dorothy queried

"For cooking," Kampeng explained.

Dorothy leaned against a tree and closed her eyes while the Laotian men went about their task of collecting bamboo stems. It wasn't long before she went off into a little dream. She was at Elizabeth's house playing bridge, when they stopped the game to watch an episode of 'The Golden Girls'. Joan was there too; laughing as she usually did at every line of dialogue, even the straight ones.

A big fat fly landed on her nose and woke her up. Opening her eyes she was startled to see Tanak, a glazed look in his crossed eyes, poised with a machete over her head. This couldn't be happening she thought, as he swung down at her. She ducked, and a moment later, marveling at still being alive and intact, she peeked out from her hands that had instinctively covered her face, and watched Tanak as he picked up a wriggling, gigantic centipede, minus its head. It was a repulsive creature; its segmented body an inch wide and almost a foot long, with all these legs. Kampeng came over to scrutinize, and words were exchanged with Tanak, who then flung the thing into the bushes.

"Oh, you very lucky," Kampeng informed her. "If bite you, you die in one hour."

She wished he hadn't told her that. She abruptly stood up, slapping the dirt off her safari trousers and looking around for any more frightful creatures which might be lurking around. "Are there snakes here as well?"

"Oh, many, many snakes. Watch out for bamboo snakes, hang in branches."

It was less than fifteen minutes before they were on their way again.

"We must hurry," Kampeng said. "Must reach before get dark."

"Reach where?"

"Place to sleep."

Crossing the floor of the vegetated washout, the gurgling of a small brook could be heard. Kampeng told her that they would drink all the remaining water in their containers and refill here. "No water up high," he gravely announced. Then, as they were filling their containers, he said, "Walking in dry season, there little water and food in forest, but easier to walk, and no leeches."

"Leeches?"

"Yes, disappear in dry season, but when rain, they too many. The green ones very bad. Like to climb up. Go in your eyes and mouth, and you don't know."

She scrunched up her face. "Uugh!"

They climbed out of the ravine and continued to clamber past more bamboo. There still seemed to be a trail.

"I thought you said the trail ended?"

"This animal trail," he told her.

But soon, that too disappeared, as the tropical growth became thicker on all sides. In the dense, dim jungle, everything looked ominous, and there were creepy sounds as well, such as the creaking of the trees and the rattan, which had long stems that reached out and intertwined. Above, leaves and branches meshed to form a vegetative roof, which the sun could only pierce with isolated shafts of sunbeams. Red and black barked trees rose like pillars to a height of a hundred feet or more in the pale aquarium-like light. Around their trunks were vines as thick as a man's arms, clasped and coiled in grotesque fashion, and from their high branches lianas hung like rotten ropes. The scent of fecund soil was primal, and the oppressive silence exaggerated the splashing sounds of the undergrowth that Kampeng and Tanak were hacking at to clear the way. Once again, she found herself questioning the prudence of her decision. Her qualms grew stronger as they came upon a minor chasm, carved out by a dry, boulder-filled streambed, above which spanned a huge log, the only obvious way to proceed. With her terrible sense of balance, she knew that there was no way she could walk across it without falling. Kampeng and Tanak strode across it nonchalantly, then proceeded up the other side. It was only then that it occurred to them to look back to see how she was doing.

She was still on the far side, deciding how she was going to tackle this obstacle. She realized there was only one sure way. She sat and straddled the log and pushed herself along as if she were playing leapfrog or Johnny-ride-the-pony.

The pair of Laotian men looked on disbelievingly. "What is matter? Cannot walk across?" Kampeng inquired incredulously.

"You do it your way, and I'll do it mine."

Of course, her way was a bit slower, and they had to obligingly wait for her to get to the other side. It was embarrassing too, because what she was doing wasn't ladylike.

But they made no comment as they continued.

The going got slower, with Kampeng and Tanak doing most of the work cutting a swath through the jungle vegetation, while she herself followed at a leisurely pace. Still, being on her feet for such a long time was tiring, and she plodded on with aching monotony. Despite Kampeng's remark about there being no trail, they were proceeding along a path of some sort, albeit very overgrown. He explained later that it was one that hadn't been used for a very long time, perhaps since the time of the war when the Pathet Lao had utilized it.

Not long after, they were climbing up steep walls of earth full of tree roots, which they used to pull themselves up, and the hike began to get exhausting. The exertion caused Dorothy to pant heavily, and even the Laotians were quiet from the physical effort. Mercifully, the terrain eventually leveled out, and the undergrowth became sparser, as they arrived at a forest of teak and mahogany. Daylight grew dimmer, but they continued.

"We must hurry, it will be dark soon," Kampeng warned.

"Why can't we stop here for the day?" Dorothy asked. She didn't know how much longer she could go on, and the straps of her little pack were starting to cut into her skin.

"No, not safe."

The men picked up the pace, and Dorothy stumbled along behind, numb with weariness, her throat parched with thirst, her tank top plastered to her skin like shrink-wrap. The salt from her perspiration not only made the strap cuts on her shoulders burn painfully, but also dripped into her eyes, irritating them as well. In the face of all these discomforts, she resolved to hide her fatigue and distress from her comrades, lest Kampeng admonish her with reminders of his original disapproval of this trip. But eventually her alertness dwindled to such a low level that it became obvious that she was on her last legs. She found herself blundering into obstacles, and her gait had turned into a careless lurch, like that of someone drunk.

The piping of the cicadas and crickets had already announced the onset of twilight when they came upon a small bare patch under the trees.

"This is where we stay for night."

Dorothy practically emanated with relief. Her body felt like it had been battered all over with twenty-pound sledgehammers. "Thank God!" she exclaimed rather loudly.

"Shsss!" Kampeng was cautioning her to be quiet.

"What's wrong?"

"Don't speak too loud. Attract spirits. You know? If they attack you, take your *kwan*. Then get sick and die."

"They hear us talking?"

"Yes. But Kampeng and Tanak speak forest spirit language, so they don't know what we say".

The first thing that Tanak did was rummage through his little knapsack and come out with incense sticks, some food and lao-kao, and a couple of strange figurines. Meanwhile, Kampeng went into the forest to collect wood. He came back after only a few minutes with a couple of small logs and other flat pieces, which he handed over to Tanak. Dorothy watched their activities sitting on a rock drinking from her water bottle and periodically plucking her sticky shirt from her skin. It became apparent that the two men were constructing a miniature altar, upon which the figurines and burning incense were placed. That done, Tanak went around the perimeter of their campsite placing lighted incense sticks in appropriate places and pouring small amounts of lao-kao on the ground, as Kampeng went back into the forest to collect more wood. She, on her part, felt that all these precautions were unnecessary, but she tactfully kept her thoughts to herself.

Dusk had settled in, and the forest surroundings took on an eerie appearance in the shadowy gloom. Scores of fireflies sparkled in the air around them, adding to a fairyland atmosphere. She admittedly felt more secure when the fire got going.

Tanak took one of the bamboo stems he had cut down in the afternoon, while Kampeng stripped pieces off another and plaited it into a grid. Water was poured into the tube, the mesh of strips then inserted halfway down and uncooked rice put in. The little lattice was needed to support the rice, since sticky rice was a special type of rice that, if one boiled it, turned into an unpalatable mush. It had to be steamed instead. The bamboo cylinder with the rice was then placed on the fire. They repeated this for two more bamboo stems, and by then, it was quite dark.

They squatted around the fire, inevitably staring into the hypnotic flames.

"I happy to go on mountain," Kampeng declared to no one in particular. "Make me feel like young man again."

"I feel just the opposite," Dorothy countered. "This trip is reminding me that I'm an old woman."

"Tomorrow afternoon we reach cave."

"A cave?"

"Yes, near top of mountain. Sacred cave. Cave is where Miss Doro-tee want to go, yes?"

"Yes, of course, that's probably where Andrew would go if he saw it."

"Where you think he go before?"

"I didn't realize there was a cave."

"You want to walk around mountain, look for bones, you don't know there is cave?"

"Yes, well I knew there must have been something…"

She was interrupted by a horrible scream; similar to the one she had heard in the jungle where the truck had broken down on the way to Ponsavan.

Kampeng and Tanak talked excitedly to each other. "You hear?" Kampeng asked Dorothy.

"Sounds like that gra-tair animal," she offered.

"No, pii."

"*He-roo-oy,*" corrected Tanak.

Silence followed.

When Dorothy was a young girl she remembered going camping and listening to ghost stories by the campfire. Now, almost a lifetime later and on the other side of the world, she was doing the same thing again.

Tanak kept checking the rice until it was pronounced ready for consumption. They ate it with dried beef and some wild weeds that Tanak had collected. After the routine smoking of cigarettes at the end of the meal, the two men put more wood on the fire, prepared beds of leaves for themselves, and laid out a blanket for Dorothy. They then went about spreading ashes around their sleeping spots. The ashes were to stop the ants, Kampeng explained.

Kampeng and Tanak continued to talk quietly to each other while lying down, but Dorothy, against the background noise of their hushed chatter, dropped off into a deep sleep and remained there until boisterous shrieking entered her dreams. She opened her eyes, saw the dark forest night, but the shrieking was still going on. She sat up in an abrupt motion.

The two men were awake as well. "Sleep good?" Kampeng asked.

"What on earth is that racket? Pee? Herooey?"

"What is 'rak-et'?"

"I mean all that noise."

"Monkeys," was the explanation from Kampeng. "They wake up forest. That is their job."

"Well they do their job well, I'm certainly awake."

They had their breakfast of sticky rice, then collected their things and set out for the second day's journey, one full of new dangers for Dorothy. These took the form of loose gravel and slippery leaves, which nullified the traction of her expensive hiking boots, despite the claims made of the Tracto-Grip soles. She slid and slipped with almost every step and occasionally fell down on her butt, making her cuss in pain.

It wasn't until midmorning when they finally got out of the oppressing jungle, entering a beautiful meadow full of giant black butterflies and ornamented with scattered tropical pine trees, their branches bending upwards, rather than the sad-looking, downward-pointing limbs of the North American variety. The sunshine was bright and sharp, and the view in front of them was spectacular, a vertical wall of blue-gray limestone, streaked with yellow and black lines. This was the 'head' of the mountain that Dorothy had seen from afar, and the most incredible thing about it was an oval cave, uncannily shaped like an eye, peering out from the middle of the cliff. It gave her a flushed, prickling sensation, just looking at it. Not only her, but all of them stared fixedly at the elliptical black hole, not saying anything. What was even weirder was the bright spot in the center that appeared like a white pupil.

"What is that white spot, in the middle, that makes it look like an eye?"

Kampeng discussed this with Tanak before giving an answer. "It is hole in roof. Light go down and light up rock inside."

They stood gaping for a few more seconds.

"Next part very difficult," Kampeng warned.

He wasn't kidding either. They had to scramble over small boulders and scale even bigger ones. This was a much more demanding workout than she had ever had to undergo at Jack La Lane's. She had to continually use all of her limbs—arms as well as legs—to push herself up and over repeatedly to surmount the craggy rocks, making her feel as if she was reaching the limit of her physical capabilities. The Laotian men were very patient; she knew that if they wanted to, they could have leapt over the rocks like a pair of mountain goats, but purposefully restrained their pace to stay near her.

Even though the going was difficult, draining all of her strength, not to mention the bruises and scrapes from banging her legs against the rocks, it was child's play compared to what was up ahead. It was Dorothy's worst nightmare—a narrow, winding ledge etched out against the limestone wall. She kept her fears to herself as they made their way against the cliff face. Soon, however, Kampeng realized her phobia, watching her as she clung tightly to the wall making little frightened murmurings from time to time.

"Don't be afraid, Kampeng here, I no let you fall."

The whole way, both of her guides were very concerned for her, going very slowly, constantly looking back at her, with Kampeng periodically asking if she was okay. Time passed at the same speed that they did, at a snail's pace, gradually placing them in the shadow of the late afternoon, and they were still on this dam cliff. She inched herself on, persuading herself that she could get through this without any major problems. That is, until she reached a noticeable break in the ledge, which had to be traversed by making a wide sideways stride over a significant gap, very gingerly. Moving gingerly wasn't one of Dorothy's most proficient skills, and her immediate response was to freeze.

Kampeng, already on the other side, stretched out his arm. "Take my hand."

Dorothy was reluctant, but Kampeng's voice was forceful.

"Take my hand," he repeated.

Her legs began to tremble uncontrollably.

"Take my hand," he said a third time.

She did so, putting all her faith, and her life, in the hands of this swarthy Indochinese man that she had only known for a couple of weeks and attempted to make the breach, but of course, being so tense, she slipped and fell. Kampeng went down with her for a brief, yet endless moment, before managing to grab hold of a bush growing out of a rock, stopping their fall. They both hung dangling while Tanak came over and helped to lift Kampeng, and her as well, back onto the ledge.

Kampeng looked at her with a smile radiating his own relief. "See", he said panting, "I tell you Kampeng no let you fall."

She could have kissed his dark rough face.

After that, the ledge widened and Dorothy was able to move a bit more confidently, as the constricted path expanded onto a broad shelf. Tanak suddenly stopped, looked at the sky, then turned around and mentioned something to Kampeng. Kampeng, in response, looked at his watch.

"We wait here," he informed Dorothy.

The entrance to the cave was only about a hundred feet from where they were standing.

"Why do we have to wait when we're so close?"

Kampeng didn't answer her, so she looked out at the view. On one side were companion mountain peaks, some a blazing orange, others a pastel purple in the shadows of the setting sun. To her left was the glorious expanse of the Plain of Jars, enveloped in a nebulous light brown haze.

"Listen," Kampeng said cryptically.

Almost imperceptibly, a sound started to vibrate from deep within the mountain itself, gradually turning into a high-pitched murmur, like wind in a tunnel, growing so loud Kampeng could hardly hear Dorothy when she tried to ask him what it was. The whole effect was as if the mountain were exhaling. Suddenly, the two Laotians abruptly pointed at the mouth of the cave, and Dorothy could see what she had first imagined to be thick black smoke issuing forth and shooting up into the air. No, it wasn't smoke, it couldn't be smoke, for it contorted, gyrated, and spiraled upward in a spinning choreography that could only be made by animate creatures—bats, millions of bats! A thick, dense gush of little black bodies continued to stream upwards, breaking free in penumbral swarms streaking across the evening sky, eventually fanning out. The bats poured forth from the cave for a full twenty minutes before the exodus brusquely stopped.

Tanak said something in an authoritative tone.

"Always at this time," Kampeng translated.

Once this incredible event had taken its course, it was deemed an appropriate time to enter the cave. It was refreshingly cool inside. They passed by the 'eyeball', a globule of limestone on a pedestal, and descended down a shaft floored by boulders, carefully scrambling over the sharp-edged rocks until they arrived at the majestic cavern below, which was enchantingly lit by the daylight pouring out of the cave mouth above them. There were hollow sounds of water dripping and plopping all around them, and to Dorothy, all these sights and sounds elicited scenes from Jules Verne's Journey to the Center of the Earth. After passing through this remarkable rock chamber they then entered into a dark, narrow, subterranean passage.

Tanak and Dorothy had their flashlights on, and immediately in front of them, the shadows of little creatures could be seen slithering into the darkness. The floor of the cave was slippery and muddy, and as they went further in, the water increased until it was up to their ankles. The air got colder and damper, causing her to shiver. It was darker than dark; a true absence of light of any kind, and Dorothy definitely did not like this, especially when the water started to reach her knees. The sounds of their sloshing were amplified in the close confines, reverberating off the walls and roof. The subterranean corridor got wider and they soon ran into a wall that had two entrances.

"Where do we go now?" Dorothy asked, immediately taken aback by the booming resonance of her voice inside the cave.

Tanak pointed to the left portal.

"Tanak say we go left."

"So I gathered." Their voices continued to bounce off the walls in exaggerated echoes.

It wasn't long before they realized that the left gallery wasn't taking them anywhere, as it turned out to be a dead end. They reversed their direction, exited, and tried the right entrance. It was smaller, and Dorothy had to bend down as they proceeded. The damp, dank tunnel smelled of mildew and mold and wet earth, but at least the water had gone some other way, for they were now treading upon exposed mud. She thought her eyes were playing tricks on her, for she could make out a faint glow ahead of them. Her nose seemed to be conspiring against her too, for she could detect the sweet fragrance of incense.

"This is right way," said Kampeng.

"What's that light?" she asked.

"This is right way," he repeated.

And then, the most unearthly sight she had ever seen. They were inside a huge chamber where several flaming torches were placed in selected spots on the floor; the bulbous geological formations on the cavern walls flickering like supernatural apparitions in the ghoulish glow. The sight of the torches sent tingles up her spine, for it indicated a mysterious human presence, and it suggested something out of the occult.

"My God! Who keeps the torches and incense going?" she inquired.

"Before, old monk stay here. I don't know now. See?" he directed her, aiming his flashlight at a simple bed low to the ground and made of branches and woven bamboo. "Maybe monks from Forest Temple still come here and light torches. Forest Temple not far from here."

They advanced cautiously. Stalactites hanging off the roof and stalagmites rising from the floor, gave the impression of teeth, making it seem as if they were entering the jaws of a mythical behemoth.

"Oh my goodness!" she cried, dropping the flashlight from her hands, which made a sharp metallic crash as it hit the ground.

There he was, over twenty feet long, lying on his side, his huge head resting in his right hand, a serene face smiling in a paternal, patronizing way, his whole body shining a celestial gold in the dull glow of the torches. It was a cast image of a reclining Buddha, and in front of it was an assortment of offerings, vases and little urns, garlands, statues of elephants, flowers and incense.

They approached, awestruck, no longer in single file, but abreast, like Dorothy and her comrades going to meet the Wizard. She strode over to the Buddha and the offerings in front of it, to get a better look. When she deemed she was close enough, she stopped and sat on her haunches, peering at all the lovely paraphernalia glowing in the sepulchral firelight. There were little Buddha images plastered with flickering leaves of gold, and various golden tiered umbrellas, which were a series of shimmering concentric rings attached to an upright axis. So many beautiful vases, she marveled, some porcelain, some brass. Inside one brass vase, a small silver chain flashed leadenly in the weak amber light. For some inexplicable reason, she was drawn to this relatively unattractive bauble. She stared at the chain for some time, before being overcome with an irresistible urge to touch it and pick it up. She swiped it into her hand and held it before her. Suspended on the chain was a rectangular piece of metal with rounded corners, revolving as it hung from her hand. It spun left, then right, clockwise, then counter-clockwise, and as it turned she could pick out the various Roman letters, in capital, which had been imprinted on its dull metal-gray surface. She spotted an 'N', then a 'D', a 'Y' an 'A'...

Her mind reeled and her heart fell, flipping and somersaulting like a helpless stone in a torrent of turbulent emotion. She clutched the silver necklace firmly to her breast. Her eyes closed and her mouth opened wide, but no sound could get past a huge lump which blocked her throat except for wretched choking noises. It was then that Kampeng and Tanak ascertained that something was going on with Dorothy in front of the reclining Buddha.

They came over and watched her, her body heaving in a silent fit, rocking back and forth as if pumping to get a cry out that wouldn't come out, and then it came, an icy congealing wail that expanded to fill the entire cavern. "M-MU-MU-AY-AY-AY... S-UH-UH-N!"

Neither of the two men knew what to do, though Kampeng felt obligated to find out what was wrong. "Miss Doro-tee, what is matter?"

She raised her hand, offering up the dog tag, which he took.

He immediately understood. "Where Miss Doro-tee get this?"

In the midst of her emotional fit, she managed to point mutely at the brass vase. Kampeng looked over to inspect it, put his hand in and came out with a Geneva Convention identification card.

Dorothy turned around, and noticing Kampeng, lunged to touch and kiss his feet. He abruptly grabbed her and held her firmly. It took a few more minutes before Dorothy calmed down enough to listen.

"In morning we go to Forest Temple," he told her, "maybe they know. Tonight we sleep here, okay?"

Dorothy nodded her head in silent tear-filled concurrence.

Chapter 12

Laos 1969

"With renunciation, life begins"
Amelia Barr, novelist, 1913

How he had gotten out of the battle zone alive, out of the wanton annihilation that was taking place all around him, he didn't know. It was pure luck. With no time to think, he had run through a frenzied fury of fire and rain, fleeing terror-crazed out of the mouth of hell. Shrapnel was flying everywhere, and soldiers were shooting at anything moving, but he just seemed to have dashed through it all unharmed. He continued to run into the forest, the ground ripping his bare feet, the thorny bushes clawing at his already shredded clothes. His hands were still tied behind his back, depriving him of balance, and inevitably, he fell down smacking his face on the ground. There was no other choice but to worm his way through the mud and look for some means of getting the ropes off. Wallowing through the wet earth on his knees, he found a tree to lean against where he sat and strained to free his hands, the friction of the ropes burning his skin as he struggled. The rain was slashing at him, whacking his head and stinging the nape of his neck, coming down in a deluge that threatened to wash everything away, as if competing with the man-made madness of war raging through the mountains and valleys.

Soaked with rain, the wetness helped to lubricate his wrists and make the ropes soggy enough to lose strength, and after many minutes of painstaking effort, his hands slipped out unfettered. Just in time, for through the loud clattering of the raindrops, he distinctly heard the voices of men approaching. He had been fortunate so far, in that he had skirted the perimeter of the battle, a battle that was now expanding, threatening to enclose him in its murderous rampage.

He had to quickly figure out what was going on. The Hmong held the hills, the communist forces were retreating. The voices he heard were above him, so they must be the Hmong coming down in pursuit. The only way was to slip behind them. Near to where he was sitting was the mouth of a confined gorge that ran to the south. None of the fleeing Vietnamese and Pathet Lao would be foolish enough to enter there. If he could get deep enough inside it, he could climb up the side and into the mountains that flanked it. Hopefully, by then the Hmong would have completely abandoned their mountain top positions in their advance onto the Plain. As for what he would do after that, he had no idea.

The rain, he realized, was his friend, obscuring everything into a bleary, unfocussed film. But he couldn't take the chance of getting up and running past the men, who were now too close. He quickly dug a shallow pit out of the soft ground and covered himself with mud. Unless they stepped directly on top of him, he would be unnoticeable, for they weren't expecting to run into anyone on this slope.

He heard them striding past, and caught a glimpse of their dim outlines, moving at a fast pace through the jungle. Snuggled, wet and motionless, he waited and waited until he felt that there would be no more soldiers coming off the mountain, lying in an indeterminate limbo, until the calm that followed assured him that it was safe. He got up cautiously and reconnoitered his surroundings before slowly making off into the gorge, crouching stealthily as he walked.

The rain had died down to an ineffectual drizzle and soon stopped in the late afternoon, as did the sounds of the fighting, and the world was finally quiet. Hiking through the riverine growth of bushes and fig trees, he moved without anything driving him other than the instinct to survive, although his brain was telling him that it was pointless. It now became apparent to him that his original plan of a northwest escape route was pure folly. In this dispirited state, he wandered aimlessly, each step an exhaustive effort, and his only desire now was to go up and die on top of the mountains, to gaze down at inspiring scenery, and to make his peace with God.

The sun came out, and the jungle steamed, coming alive with insects and birds. He took a side canyon up toward its head, clambering over the boulders and fallen tree trunks that gorged its channel until it led him to the base of a ridge, which he ascended with some difficulty. At the top, the view was breathtaking. The menacing rain clouds had been replaced by innocuous balls of white fluff in an azure sky, as if nature had completely forgotten its rage of the previous few hours. The ridge he was on was one of a series of peaks in a range that trended east to west. Immediately to his east was an extraordinary crest that looked like a human head. In the middle of its bleak, gray face was an eye-shaped black spot that could only be a cave. It seemed to call to him. That's where he would go.

To get there, he had to traverse a karstic landscape, steep and jagged ridges interspersed with irregular protuberant rocks. It took him hours to climb over rows of razor-sharp crags, and to slither through the crevasses between them. Approaching his destination, he witnessed an amazing spectacle of millions of bats emerging from the eye-shaped cave, embarking for their nightly feeding, an ageless ritual undisturbed by man's trivial activities of war and destruction.

Once at the cliff face, he had to scale a precarious rock ledge, which was a dangerous thing to do in his condition, weak and dizzy from fatigue and hunger. But the view spurred him on. On one side were companion mountain peaks, some a blazing orange, others a pastel purple in the shadows of the setting sun. To his left, off in the distance, was the prized expanse of the Plain of Jars, tragically enveloped in the nebulous haze of war.

Slowly but persistently, he edged his way to the mouth of the cave, then entered through its eerily-shaped opening. He passed by a globule of rock on a pedestal and descended down a shaft floored by boulders, scrambling over the slabs and stones until he reached the majestic cavern below, enchantingly lit by the daylight pouring in through the mouth of the cave above him. There were hollow sounds of water dripping and plopping all around him. After passing through this remarkable rock chamber he entered into a dark, narrow, subterranean passage.

Immediately in front of him, the sounds of little creatures could be heard slithering into the darkness. The floor of the cave was slippery and muddy, and as he went further in, the water increased until it was up to his ankles. It was darker than dark, a true absence of light of any kind, and without a flashlight or torch, he moved through blindly as the water started to reach his knees. This should have been a frightening experience, but for some strange reason, Andrew wasn't afraid. On the contrary, he felt comforted, as if he had at last arrived at a place where he could hide from the terrors of the world. Amazingly, his hunger and fatigue were gone.

The tinny sounds of his sloshing in the water were amplified in the narrow confines, reverberating off the walls and roof. The echoes told him that the subterranean corridor must be getting wider, but he soon ran into a wall, painfully bumping his nose and forehead. He groped along and felt an empty space, large enough to walk through. At the head of this passageway, there seemed to be a light, and he could smell the scent of incense, welcoming him, beckoning him onwards. He could see quite easily now; his eyes had already become accustomed to the pitch black, which was now gradually being replaced by the glow in front of him. The passageway spilled out into a huge cavern lit by torches, and oddly enough this didn't surprise him, nor did the magnificent reclining Buddha with its ornamented altar. For reasons beyond rational comprehension, he was almost expecting this, and more than that, his desire for death had abruptly dissipated.

A somber chant arose out of the silence, bouncing off the walls, and startling the living daylights out of him.

"*Namo Tassa Bhagavato Arahato Samma Sambuddhasa.* Homage to the Exalted One, Perfectly Enlightened by Himself."

Andrew whirled around in the direction of the chant.

Just to the left of the Buddha image, sitting in lotus fashion on a simple bed that was low to the ground and made of branches and woven bamboo, was an old man who appeared to be as ancient as the cave he dwelled in, his head shaven, dressed in the orange robes of a monk. Recovering from his initial fright, Andrew, now inundated with a reverent awe, drew nearer, taking slow, astonished steps. He got down on his knees, and, while resting his haunches on his heels, studied this strange figure. The aged man's visage, despite being partially hidden in dancing shadows, contained a timeless repose, an assuring conviction that had the power to quell all of life's calamities. In the old man's hands was a big palm leaf, and as he chanted his eyes remained fixed on what he was doing—stenciling the leaf carefully, drawing perhaps, with a wooden stick that had a needle on the end.

Andrew waited for the priest to raise his head and face him, but the old man merely continued with his labor in a calm and serene manner, ignoring him, his resonant psalmody undiminished. A few minutes passed, and then, without any caveat, he abruptly ceased his chanting. Andrew took that opportunity to greet him.

What do you say to a hermit monk? "Sabai dee, *Luang Paw*." Hope you are well Venerable Father.

"Sabai dee," the old man said, who still didn't deign to look up from his handiwork. His composure was impressive, almost inhuman. "You have come to visit the Cave of the Enlightened One?" he asked in Lao.

"*Doi, kanoi,*" Andrew responded using the polite, subservient reply. "Yes, master."

"You are welcome."

"Thank you, Venerable Father." The cave, along with this person that he had found inside it, was a significant turn of events he felt. Everything that had transpired before was no longer relevant, except in the context of leading him here, to this final destination.

As the hermit didn't give an indication of initiating any further conversation, Andrew boldly prompted him. "May I ask, how long have you been here?"

"Many years," the old man answered, still sketching his picture. "I do not remember."

"How do you eat?"

It was only then that the priest finally raised his head. He had a tightly drawn, hoary face, bony and furrowed, which in full view was, strangely enough, fearsome, yet curiously reassuring. "The monks from the Forest Temple come here to bring me food. They have devotees who cultivate for them, and they share some of the harvest with me, but rice is very little these days."

"There is a war outside," Andrew informed him. "They are taking people away, out of Xieng Khouang. Soon, there will be no more rice."

"When the rice stops, I will die. Then they must send someone else to take care of the Buddha image, to wash it, and keep the candles and incense lit."

"Are you not lonely here?" Andrew asked.

The old priest put on a face of confounded incredulity, as if Andrew had missed something obvious. "There is stillness, a stillness filled with everything, yet I cling to nothing, therefore I cannot be lonely."

There was a lull in their dialogue, as Andrew pondered this cryptic answer.

"Why have you come here?" the old man asked him. Apparently, this question was more important than who Andrew was.

"I ran away from the war," Andrew told him.

"You are a soldier?"

"I was a pilot of one of the planes that brings the bombs."

"Why did you run away?"

Was the monk testing him? "I don't want to bring harm to anyone. If I didn't run away, I would still be dropping bombs and killing women and children."

"It is good you feel this way," the monk said. "Respect for life is one of the first steps one can take before entering the Sublime Way of Life."

"The war should stop," Andrew declared to him, thinking he had finally found a willing ear to sympathize with his dilemma. 'There's so much suffering going on. It is madness. I ask you, as a holy man, if there is a Supreme Being, why doesn't he step in and end it?"

"Do the fish see the water?"

"The fish...see water?"

"Do the worms in the dung heap see the dung they borrow through? Does humanity see the world? You, my son, are but a thin thread, interwoven with many threads of all colors, but you cannot see the tapestry of which you are a part. You are only one note in a song that you cannot hear. Suffering, is the world, and the world is the same as suffering."

"Are you saying that to be alive is merely to suffer?"

"Yes, it is the first of the Four Noble truths."

Andrew bowed his head down, and silently agreed. Everything he had seen while down on the ground in Laos had substantially attested to what the monk was saying. "I wish to stay here with you. I would like you to teach me more."

Perhaps under different circumstances this might have been an irrational wish, but with the war raging outside, this subterranean chamber actually seemed to be the sanest place to be. "I will help you take care of the Buddha image, and go outside to bring you food."

"You may stay as long as you wish, I cannot turn you away."

"But is there enough food for the both of us?"

"The monks from the Forest Temple will be coming here to visit with me on the full moon day. They will be bringing more rice."

Something was puzzling Andrew. "How do you tell what day it is?"

"I count the days by the bats. They make a great noise when they leave the cave to eat, which, like myself, is once a day."

That reply made sense to Andrew, who now looked at the reclining Buddha and all the devoted offerings. He wished he had something, even a candle, to place at the altar, to somehow say thanks for having been delivered from his hitherto hopeless ordeal. "I have nothing to give to the Buddha."

"That is not the Buddha, it is merely an image, and those offerings are only objects. When you say you have nothing, you mean you have no material things, and that is good, it is how it should be. But you still have your life."

"Yes," Andrew agreed. His life, perhaps a new one, who could tell? He got up and walked toward the large golden icon, not cognizant that he was being disrespectful by being above the monk, then knelt down at the altar, before the Buddha statue and all its attendant artifacts glimmering in the elegiac glow of the torches. He took his dog tag from around his neck and placed it in one of the vases. He took out his Geneva identity card from his shirt pocket and put that in as well.

"My life," he muttered to himself.

They had gone through the jungle for two weeks, surviving on emergency rations and the wild produce of the forest, of which the Hmong were well-versed. During that time, Anatoly had found Botkin harder and harder to deal with. He was a condescending, egotistical son-of-bitch, who didn't make any effort at even basic camaraderie. What irked Anatoly more was that he was unprofessional, at least in the terms that had been defined for him, Stephen Anatoly, as a Marine, as a First Force Reconnaissance Marine. Botkin had no regard for orders, acted as if he were oblivious to standard procedures and improvised whenever he liked. When he made radio contact, he would report that they were to follow a certain course of action, and then changed it as he went along. While Anatoly could appreciate the natural instincts of a hunter, there still existed a chain of command that should be informed of your whereabouts and your intended strategies.

His personal habits were just as distasteful to Anatoly. He never took the few opportunities to bathe, claiming that it made a man soft. See how tough the Hmong are, and they don't bathe, he gloated. At mealtimes he would make smacking sounds when he ate, and spoke with his mouth full, so that food would drop out of it. Then he would make large belching sounds with his mouth wide open, exaggerating them on purpose.

The worst part was the nightly drinking. Botkin had brought along his own stock of Canadian rye, but he would also dive into the Hmong's rice whiskey, and get into a state of complete delirium. And Anatoly would have to listen to his bullshit all night long.

Hopefully, the mission would end soon. They had been tracking this pilot guy faithfully, although this meant going up and down and around in circles, because that's just what he did. That is, until the trail went consistently down the valley where they found it visibly bound up with the passage of others.

Captured, they all agreed.

They followed the new trail now, which wasn't too hard, since it either went along established paths, or ones that were noticeably hacked out. They then traveled over the rice fields. Apparently the Pathet Lao hadn't been concerned about leaving clues behind, since they were in a hurry trying to get their asses out of there. They passed some sort of hideout with trenches and then an abandoned base camp. The trail eventually led them to a tree with a bamboo tube hanging from a branch. It contained a long stick inside it.

"Bang on it," Botkin told one of the Hmong.

The Hmong just looked at him quizzically.

Botkin went through a pantomime of banging the bamboo with the stick, after which the soldier got the idea.

Immediately after sounding the crude bell, they found places to hide in the dense understory on the fringes of the clearing, before the village militia, only four men, predictably came out to investigate. The commando team skulked noiselessly behind the forest growth in predatory concealment, waiting for the right moment. As the home guards looked around baffled, the Hmong sprang from their hiding places, and with a minimum of grappling, disarmed the four men.

They didn't kill them, because they had been previously instructed not to.

"Tie them around the trees."

Again, the head Hmong commando jutted his head in puzzlement.

Botkin made movements with the rope he now had in his hands, simulating a circular motion. All of them immediately understood and accepted the rope he offered out to them.

What a fucking intelligence operative, thought Anatoly. Doesn't even know the language of the people he's been working with for the past few years. And why the hell did he wear those dark sunglasses when it was cloudy, and they were mostly in enclosed forest? Did he think he was fucking cool or something?

Botkin took off those same wire-rimmed sunglasses and put them in his shirt pocket before going into a knapsack that one of the Hmong trackers had on his back. He took out a long stretch of detonating cord and a trigger box.

"Ever play pop-the-fucking-weasel?" he asked his captive audience, although he knew they didn't understand a single word he said. He then proceeded to tie the cord around one of the prisoner's necks. One could tell that by his calm demeanor, the village militia guy didn't know what a detonating cord was. Botkin instructed his men to get down, by gesticulating with his hands palms down, then, from behind the shelter of a large bush, he fired the triggering box. The man's head shattered like a ripe pumpkin into a multitude of bloody fragments of skull and brains, some of them splashing on the other prisoners tied up nearby. Blood spurted out of the body's headless neck like a red fountain, while the body itself jerked and twitched with the lifeless responses of disturbed neurons.

Anatoly didn't appreciate this line of interrogation, especially in the context of his feelings about his last mission, where he had to slice open those women.

"Okay, talk," Botkin commanded to the rest of the prisoners, who were now in a hell of a panic. He beckoned to one of his men, and then put the back of his right hand to his mouth, opening and closing his fingers repeatedly against his thumb, like a child would imitate a duck quacking. The Hmong soldier evidently comprehended this sign, as he went over and started questioning one of the captives, who, along with the others, was screaming his head off and practically convulsing in a frenzied fit of terror.

Anatoly, ignoring the shrieking wails of the men tied to the tree, couldn't restrain his urge to be captious. "You don't know Hmong language, and you don't know Laotian either?" he asked Botkin in a reproving tone. Anatoly himself had mastered Vietnamese, not so much for speaking purposes, but to be able to eavesdrop while on intelligence gathering missions.

"I know some Lao," Botkin stated in defense of himself.

Anatoly didn't believe him.

"But I make it a rule not to grill prisoners directly. Why should I let them know that I understand their language?"

After some time, the interrogator, ostensibly satisfied with the information received, faced Botkin and proceeded to communicate with him using a mixture of sign language and enigmatic sketchings on the ground. Botkin picked up a stick and answered in the same manner, drawing in the dirt.

What a joke, thought Anatoly.

But Botkin was apparently used to this odd form of dialogue. "The Benny pilot's been captured alright," he told Anatoly. "They're headed to Sieng Khouang. They hope they can get east under cover of the retreating forces." He turned to the rest of the hunting squad. "Shoot them."

The Hmong knew these words without requiring any signs, and the other three prisoners, in the flash of a moment, had bullets shot through their heads. Then Botkin distributed cards, which had a drawing of a green skull with red eyes dripping blood. The soldiers nailed these through the middle of the corpses' foreheads, through the pituitary gland, the third eye of the Buddhists, producing horrible crunching sounds as they did so. After another gesticulation on the part of Botkin, who was now making motions stabbing at his abdomen, they carved an arc through the torsos of the dead bodies with long silver knives. They then removed the livers, causing blood to spew all around. The commandos, not being in the least squeamish in using their hands to rip out the organs, threw them on the ground while some of the soldiers were so rabid as to stomp on the dismembered body parts. They wiped their bloodied hands on the leaves and foliage nearby.

Some Buddhists believe that without an intact liver, one cannot enter heaven.

Anatoly didn't approve of these last actions any more than the pop-the-weasel game. He felt they were unnecessary as the information had already been gathered, and the witnesses to the presence of the team had already been terminated.

"Let's get a move on," ordered Botkin.

From that day forward, Anatoly's repugnance for Botkin developed into hatred. A few weeks later it almost came to a head.

It was evening and they had already pitched camp. It was the usual campsite setting, with small hidden piles of dry branches laid out along the perimeter, placed so that they would crackle and snap if an intruder inadvertently stepped on them, and with four guards patrolling the four quadrants. And it was the usual entertainment as well—a drunken Botkin antagonizing a younger, sober Marine Anatoly, who was dutifully taking his sniper rifle apart and cleaning it.

"You don't like my style, do you, Marine?"

Anatoly gave out an embittered sigh, yet managed to answer him with phlegmatic toleration. "You are the intelligence part of the team...Sir. I have never intervened, nor have I hindered any of your actions...Sir."

"Still, you don't agree with them, do you?"

"I don't think that the nailing of cards in the heads of corpses, nor the mutilation of dead bodies is necessary...Sir."

"That's called psy-ops. You mean to tell me that you never played that game?"

"Yes, I have been on missions involving psychological operations…Sir."

"You don't like that part of the job, do you?"

Anatoly couldn't get that young girl and her mother out of his mind. "No, sir."

"But you sure like your weapons, don't you, Marine?" Botkin queried, pointing to the rifle that Anatoly was attending to.

"A Marine is instructed to take care of his weapon…Sir." Why was this asshole riding him, he was only doing his job. Did this shithead not want him to do his job; did he want him to be a fuck up like he was?

"Okay, okay," Botkin laughed, "at ease…Marine." He was standing, but just barely, wavering around without a sense of balance, his left hand loosely clutching a bottle of Seagram's Seven.

He was disgusting, thought Anatoly, who was now in a mood to tell this bastard off. "I also feel that terminating those monks was unnecessary and could have compromised our mission…Sir." Anatoly was now referring to another incident that had taken place just that morning, when Botkin had the Hmong mow down four monks who were walking in the forest. He had just gotten over that sordid day with the peasant soldiers, when Botkin had to go and kill more people unnecessarily—monks for God's sake, holy men. Even if Anatoly wasn't a Buddhist, he still felt it was almost the same as killing Christian priests.

"Listen, shithead, all these monks around here are Pathet Lao spies. Maybe they spotted us…"

"I don't think so…Sir"

"Well, whether they did or not, they for sure won't be telling anyone now, will they?"

Anatoly was silent as he began putting his weapon back together.

"First Force Recon. Think you're hot shit. Tougher than Special Forces, better than Navy Seals. Stupid little cunts."

Anatoly mustered all of his regimental composure to ignore this.

"Hey, I'm talking to you, Marine!"

Anatoly was just putting in the last pieces. He finished this task before looking up. Even his deadpan expression couldn't hide the glare of hate in his eyes. "Begging your pardon, sir, but I request that you not address me as Marine...SIR!"

"Oh yeah, why the hell not?"

"Because I feel you are using the term in a disrespectful, derogatory manner, not deserving of the Corps...SIR!"

Botkin laughed. Then he took another swig from the bottle and sat down on one of the little Hmong stools that they traveled with. He was still laughing as he sat down. He lit up a Lucky Strike, then blew the smoke out in Anatoly's direction before he resumed chuckling to himself. "Heh heh heh."

Anatoly had his weapon assembled already.

Botkin continued to laugh, before he managed to pause and say, "Heh heh, Corps and Country."

Anatoly stared at him, hard and resolute. "God, Country, Corps, SIR!""

Botkin eyeballed him back, challenging the young marine's defiance. "Fuck you! And fuck your fucking Marine Corps!"

Anatoly stood up in a shot, aimed his weapon and disarmed the safety.

"Go, ahead," Botkin taunted. '

The moment of anger had passed, leaving Anatoly feeling oafish and ashamed, ashamed that he had lost control, and to have behaved in such a dishonorable manner. It was the worst breach of military conduct he could imagine, a total loss of restraint and discipline, and all brought on by this alcoholic wash-up from the CIA. He put the rifle down, completely abashed and humbled.

"Ah, unwind, Marine, I'm just busting your balls. Actually, I deserve to be killed. But don't you do it. You'll get in trouble for it...Let the enemy do it, it's their job."

Anatoly lowered his face. "Begging your pardon, sir, you have every right to report me, sir."

"Ah, forget it. I'm a drunken...asshole. But I was trained this way, you know...to be an animal, just like you were trained to be one."

"Begging your pardon, sir, I was trained to be a Marine, sir."

Botkin continued as if he didn't hear Anatoly's reply. "You know, these people, they ain't so bad..."

What the hell was he saying now, wondered Anatoly.

"They got heart, I have to give them that. Worthy fuckin' adversaries...worthy fuckin'..." He broke his speech to give out a loud belch. "They got balls, the little bastards...and you know...and you know...and, you know what, I think Buddhism is probably the most sophist...sophisticle-focated, fucking religion in the world..." Botkin raised the bottle of Seagrams to his lips to indulge in another long pull.

Anatoly gave up trying to follow the direction of this maudlin drivel.

"More than...more than..." Botkin's head dropped limply in a boozy stupor. It was nearly a full minute before he raised it and continued what he had wanted to say, "...This may sound fucking weird, but I would like to be...to be... reborn as one of 'em. And sometimes, I think, yeah...yeah, I'm tired of war, all this bullshit..."

Silence, as a drunken Botkin collected his drunken thoughts, his head shifting left and right, stoned out of his mind. "I'm fucking tired of killing."

Anatoly, feeling extremely drained since his own episode of unprofessional emotion, just nodded his head, humoring the booze-sodden paramilitary man. God, how he wished for this mission to end.

"I would like my life to change," Botkin rambled on. "I ain't got no relatives, no wife...I wouldn't mind being a monk even...you know?"

But Anatoly didn't know. He didn't know how someone who had just murdered four monks in cold blood could have a change of heart only hours later, and decide to become a monk himself, unless of course that someone wasn't playing with a full deck.

"Sometimes, I even think that I'm doing wrong, could you believe that?"

Anatoly didn't answer, repulsed by the disjointed contradictions Botkin was making, incoherent psychotic nonsense originating from the fringes of an inebriated mind.

"One of these days, I'm gonna make it up...gonna make it up...gonna be a monk and do right."

Anatoly just stared at him, wondering what he had done to be assigned this mission, to have to endure this sickening, pathetic, drunken wacko. He had no respect for him. And respect was something he needed to feel toward his commanding officer, a quality that was a requisite in the Marine Corps, especially First Force.

"Do you believe that a person's life can change?" Botkin suddenly asked. "I mean, really change... like become the total opposite? To just go against all the things they try to teach you?"

For this seemingly philosophical question, Anatoly somehow found an answer. "Yes, sir, I believe so...It can happen in a flash of a moment...Sir."

Botkin seemed to ponder this briefly, before passing out.

That night, Botkin sort of freaked out. He was rolling around in his bed, yelling out "No, no! Oh man, fucking blood, oh shit, my...my, my blood..." Then he started groaning like a woman getting laid. Not long after, he began a nightlong session of puking. It was pitiful. Poor Anatoly could get no sleep.

"I gotta stay away from that rice whiskey," Botkin said in apology the next morning, in between further bouts of retching.

Chapter 13

Laos 1990

"The truth is really an ambition which is beyond us"
Peter Ustinov, British actor, writer, director, 1990

Dorothy hadn't slept very well. It wasn't due to discomfort, for they had given her the makeshift bed once used by the resident monk, while Kampeng and Tanak had laid on the hard, cold, damp, rock floor. She was certainly grateful for that. But her mind had remained awake trying to picture the events that had set her son upon this journey, a journey that now they were attempting to retrace. Would he be with the monks in the Forest Temple, hidden away from the world? And if not, if he had left for yet another destination, would there be anyone there who knew where he would have gone? Why did the military send a team to kill him, what had he done? Did Anatoly's group catch up with him, or did the communists go after him and put him in prison?

Mercifully, the hypnotic dripping of water plopping into pools, combined with her exhaustion, eventually escorted her into a deep sleep. It was probably morning when the Laotians woke her, although she couldn't tell for sure, being inside the bowels of the earth. It felt like morning anyway.

Leaving the cave, they took a different route, again on a ledge-like path, but this one went off towards the west. Once more, they had to travel over bare, rugged terrain of eroded limestone, where the rocky boulder-strewn ground dictated their route, before they crossed into grassy meadows and then back into the forest. Going down for Dorothy was, as she expected, a bit more challenging to her poor sense of balance than coming up had been, but her determination overcame this and allowed the Laotian men to set a fast pace down the mountain. She reckoned they were going down at twice the rate they had used journeying on the way up, and while keeping to their stride, she felt an uncomfortable strain on her aged knees. Moreover, the blisters on the balls of her feet were beginning to sting.

The two men abruptly stopped, looking and pointing at something on the ground. Dorothy came over and glanced down, and at first she couldn't make out anything, but then she noticed a large, round, circular depression.

"*Chao Baa,*" announced Tanak.

"Chao Baa," Kampeng told Dorothy.

"Ah, yes, Chao Baa," she concurred, feigning her ignorance. "What is Chao Baa, is that an elephant?' She felt that it was a good guess, since it looked like an animal spoor, and only an elephant could make one like that. Further evidence of the beast was provided by several piles of grapefruit-sized balls of fibrous dung just ahead.

"Chao Baa is Prince of Forest. He ride elephant. He is *saksit*, and he go even at night, not afraid of spirits. You cannot kill him."

"Saksit?"

"Yes, very holy, powerful person, much wise."

It must be some sort of local legend, Dorothy surmised.

"See," Kampeng pointed out, indicating with his arm a noticeable swath of trampled vegetation that veered off to the right. "He go that way."

The discussion ended when Tanak lumbered off down the hill, in a different direction from the pachyderm's tracks, which was much to Dorothy's relief, for she wasn't eager to run into any mystical figures on elephant-back.

She and Kampeng followed their Kammu guide, making their way through thick growths of mahogany trees whose firm trunks offered invaluable opportunities for holding onto. Her companions asked her if she needed to stop for lunch, and she declined, which seemed to please them, and so on they went. But by mid-afternoon, the heat, together with the energy drain from the day's trek, persuaded all of them to halt for a rest. They were in an area full of tamarind trees, laden with the pods that they called makham, many of them lying on the ground. Kampeng and Tanak collected them and showed Dorothy just how to eat it. Inside was a sweet and gummy paste surrounding the seeds. The two men gathered more bamboo and cooked sticky rice, which they ate with the makham. Then Tanak used a slingshot to kill a small bird, which they roasted, but Dorothy would not eat it.

Somewhere between four and five o'clock they set out again. It was getting dark when Kampeng informed Dorothy that they would have to stop for the night. She noticed that the two Laotian men were in better spirits than they had been in before, and that at least some of their elation, according to Kampeng, was owing to the belief that this part of the jungle had very few pii. Furthermore, they were getting closer to the Forest Temple, which they seemed to think offered some protection against the mischievous ghosts.

But that couldn't be the full explanation. With the rice on the fire, they broke out the lao-kao and were making a time of it. Pretty soon, they were up singing songs and dancing around, not caring whether or not they aroused the forest spirits.

Kampeng, a bit tipsy, ceased his dancing to address her. "We do good. Everybody in Lao look for bones of MIA. Nobody find, very few. But we will find, Kampeng and Miss Doro-tee. We will find son's bones. You very wise Miss Doro-tee. I, Kampeng, respect you."

It was then that she realized that Kampeng was sharing in her success, and that it was almost as important to him as it was to her.

"Let me have some of that," she requested, pointing to the bottle of rice whiskey in his hand.

In due time, she was dancing along, with Tanak and Kampeng singing obscure, raucous songs in Kammu and Lao languages, maybe even forest spirit language, all of which sounded the same to her.

For Dorothy, it was a true celebration. She had come to Lao, knowing virtually nothing, and, in a million to one shot, had found her son's dog tag and identity card in a mysterious cave in the remote jungle, which could have been undiscovered forever without her intervention. She finally had confirmation that her son had been alive on the ground, and at least had made it to that cave. She had a sense of renewed hope; what she would find out at this forest temple they were heading for could help unlock the secret. And of course, she, being his mother, held out a furtive yearning that he would be there, waiting for her, after all these years.

Tanak brought out some dried fish that he had been saving, and they ate that with the rice. Not much later, Dorothy was sound asleep, snoring in her blanket.

In the morning, they didn't have breakfast, one of the reasons being they had run out of rice. Dorothy was grateful that she didn't have any sort of a hangover. In fact, to the contrary, she felt great, even without her morning coffee, and was understandably anxious to reach their destination. There was a noticeable spring in her step as they continued the journey, winding their way down into a forested valley. Notwithstanding her enthusiasm, she was a bit disconcerted when they approached a rickety footbridge suspended over a little river.

It was cleverly built, this little bridge, but made for people with a better sense of balance than she had, for it wasn't easy to walk across it. There were two large truck chassises, no doubt relics from the war, one on each side of the river, standing up on their front ends, serving as posts. Connecting them were two pairs of wire cables, one pair at the top and another pair at the bottom — a peasant's version of a suspension bridge. Straddled across the bottom pair of cables were wooden slats and pieces of timber of various shapes and sizes, loosely attached by thin binding wire, thus forming a surface to walk upon. They had to cross the bridge by holding onto the top cables to keep from falling, as they tottered and teetered on the swaying, wobbly framework. She took it step by step, Kampeng constantly asking her how she was doing. She looked down at the stream below them, which seemed fairly placid, and she reasoned out that even if she fell in, it wasn't life threatening. This gave her enough confidence to move on until she reached the other side.

From the footbridge, it took only two more hours of walking through dark woodland before they arrived at an incredible place that could only be the Forest Temple. It was an oasis of tranquil splendor, like a fairyland carved out of the jungle, adorned with graceful bodhi trees, fragrant frangipani, and idyllic, large-leafed palms. Two monks with shaved heads, wearing their Grecian, saffron-colored robes, came out to receive them at the arched, ornate wooden gate.

Kampeng made the usual complaisant greetings, and they led the way to the sim, a typical Buddhist temple, a delightfully decorative structure capped with a stack of flowing elegant roofs and pleasant oriental porticos running along its sides. The outside walls were adorned with myriad tiny pieces of colored tiles glinting in the sunlight and arranged in intricate mosaic patterns. Adding to its beauty was an aspect of timelessness.

"Tanak, will go back now," Kampeng notified Dorothy. "This place not far from Route Four. He beg ride back, then bring car. We meet on road. Save much time."

Tanak begged his leave rather awkwardly from Dorothy and left the courtyard, as she and Kampeng made their entrance into the temple, escorted by the young monks.

Dorothy followed Kampeng's example and took off her shoes before going in. Inside was dark and cool, and the round wooden pillars, as well as an elaborate framework of rafters, were also embellished with thousands of small pieces of brightly colored porcelain. On the walls were faded pastel murals depicting the horrors of Buddhist hell, which were actually based on the ancient punishments meted out to criminals in India around two and a half thousand years ago—gory scenes of mutilation and the pouring of horrible liquids down people's throats. It was a bit too morbid for Dorothy's taste. The peaceful beauty of the large brass Buddha and the spiritual altar at the end of the temple were much more appealing. There was a long boat-shaped candleholder in front of the statue, and the smell of beeswax from the burning candles planted along its length gave out a sweet aroma.

They were beckoned to sit on a mat laid out in the middle of the hall, while their hosts departed, leaving them in the hallowed silence, waiting for something. Kampeng explained.

"They go to call Abbot, he very old and was in Forest Temple before war."

Three more young monks wandered in with unrestrained expressions of welcome on their faces and proceeded to sit down on the floor opposite them, their pearly-white teeth flashing from behind wide smiles. With their flowing robes, they gave the impression of hairless cherubs.

"My monk name Santikaro," the one in the middle declared.

"You speak English!" Dorothy exclaimed, surprised.

"Yes, little. Abbot teach me. Was your name?"

"Dorothy."

"Doro-tee," he repeated, reflectively.

"The Abbott taught you? He knows English?" she asked the young monk.

"Yes, farang come long time ago and teach Abbott."

"A farang?"

"Yes."

Andrew! She thought to herself. "Did you ever see this man, the farang?"

"No, that many year ago. I baby."

"No, I mean recently?"

"Rees-antlee? Rees-antlee what mean?"

"*Dang tair ma yuu ni*, since you came here," Kampeng interjected.

"No. But I see Chao Baa once. He also farang."

"The man who rides an elephant? He is a farang?"

"Yes."

This Chao Baa guy was a white man? Was this the same guy that

Nigel Coddington spoke of at the Nam Pu Bar? Could Andrew be this Chao Baa? Dorothy thought to give it a shot. She pulled out Andrew's photograph that she had brought from home, as well as his Geneva Identity card. "Does he look like Chao Baa?"

She handed the pictures over to the bald-headed boy in robes. The other two monks crowded around him, staring over his shoulder at the pictures, and then all of them burst into laughter shaking their heads negatively.

"I guess not," she remarked despairingly, taking the pictures back.

An older monk entered and announced to Kampeng that the Abbott was ready to receive them. Accordingly, they left the sim and proceeded outside onto the sunlit portico, where there was a slight delay as they waited for Dorothy to lace up her hiking boots before they could cross the serene courtyard. She wondered why she had bothered, since she was required to remove her shoes once again prior to entering the little timber shack on stilts that they were brought to. Within this dark, cramped hut sat an old monk perched on a high bench, his legs crossed underneath him, his back remarkably straight and erect. Immediately to his right was a tiered altar table with various paraphernalia including little Buddha images. Several sticks that had oval-shapes at the end, which she presumed to be some type of fan, were standing in the corner.

The Buddhist priest himself appeared very ancient, with a withered, sapless face that resembled a skull with only the barest covering of skin. What was totally out of place, even comical, was the fact that he was wearing very dark-colored, wire-rimmed sunglasses.

Dorothy quickly sat on the floor while Kampeng made a supplicating gesture that was almost embarrassing for her to witness, putting his hands down and bowing his head to the floor three times. Before he could get a chance to address this venerable figure, Dorothy, heedless of Laotian propriety, took the risk of talking to the holy man directly.

"Sabai dee," she greeted.

"Sabai dee," replied the old monk.

"I was told that you speak English. Is this true?"

"It true." As he spoke, he remained motionless, staring out into an undefined distance, not bothering to look her way. "You are farang woman," he stated.

She thought that it was rather obvious. "Yes."

"Why you come here?"

"I am trying to find out what happened to my son. He was a pilot during the war and he crashed. He may have been captured, but then later he escaped. He went to the cave on Pu Khe. I found his dog tag and identity cards there. I thought that maybe, he may have come here, after leaving the cave I mean."

"Excuse, you speak fast, I no understand."

Kampeng, using Lao, reiterated.

"Cave of Enlightened One?" the old monk asked.

"Yes, I guess that would be the one." She went into her bag, to again take out the photo and the card. "Here are some pictures…"

Kampeng gently grabbed her arm as she offered them out. "No, Abbott not see, he blind."

"Oh," she uttered, feeling like an idiot. That's the reason for the sunglasses, she realized.

"I blind, I cannot see pictures," the monk disclosed.

"Yes, I'm sorry."

"No sorry. You think it problem, but it help me see many thing that other who have eyes not see."

Dorothy paused a second before her next question. "Do you remember a farang who came here during the war?"

"Yes."

"That was my son, Andrew!"

"He name, your son, it An-drrroo?"

"Yes!" she cried out, exhilarated.

"That it not what he say. He say he name Ree-chart."

"Richard?"

"Yes, Ree-chart Jon-sown."

"Johnson? Was he a pilot?"

"No, he work for eiii-veee-et."

"I, V, et?"

"Yes, he is waa-lun-tia, he come to help poor people..."

IVS, International Voluntary Services, Dorothy quickly ascertained.

"... but they want him say about peoples who not like American, and call plane make bomb peoples. He not like, he no do."

"Where is this Richard Johnson now?"

"I cannot say."

"You don't know where he is?"

The monk was disconcertingly quiet, choosing not to answer her.

"This man, does he now ride an elephant?" Dorothy asked, a question out of the blue.

"Yes, he go around look bombs."

"Is he the Chao Baa?"

"Yes." The monk answered. "I believe he know your son. Go talk to him."

"Where can I find him?'

"Go to Ta Vieng, Ban Ling Kao."

Dorothy was puzzled by the monk's behavior. Before it seemed he was unwilling to reveal Johnson's whereabouts. He must have had a change of heart. "Ban Ling Kao?" she asked for confirmation.

"Yes."

"Have you seen him recently?"

"Rees-antlee, what mean?"

Kampeng translated.

"Yes," the old monk confirmed. Then, pointing to his wire-rimmed sunglasses, he added, "He give me sun-glat."

It took several hours of fighting their way through intransigent forest growth to get to a little dirt track, and when they got there, there was no sign of Tanak with the jeep. They found a tree to sit under, Kampeng insisting defensively to Dorothy that Tanak would soon arrive.

During the hike down the mountain, they had avoided talking to each other, doing so only when absolutely necessary, ever since their quarrel that had ensued shortly after leaving the temple. It had started when Dorothy asked him what the plan was, and he had replied that it was to return to Ponsavan. She offered an alternative, and that was, to find Richard Johnson, the Chao Baa. Not possible, Kampeng had said. Possible, but difficult, Dorothy had retorted. Too dangerous, too many Chao Fa bandits, he told her. She in turn rejected that argument. If Richard Johnson could move about unharmed, why couldn't they, she queried. Because he is Chao Baa, that's why, was the answer. What is so special about the Chao Baa? Ah you don't know, you don't know. After which, a sullen silence had grown between them. The unsettling reticence endured as they sat in the shade of a thick growth of trees that flanked the dirt road.

"Kampeng," Dorothy petitioned once again, "the monk said that this Chao Baa knows what happened."

Kampeng gave no comment.

"Do you believe this man has knowledge about what happened to Andrew?"

"Chao Baa know many things, maybe he know. But where he stay, in Ta Vieng area, not safe."

"Is Ta Vieng far?"

"Not so far. We take this little road, we go Route Four. Then, three hours in jeep. But no can go in. Army won't let you go. It border of Special Region Saisamboun."

"Special region? Why special?"

"Many Chao Fa. Many army. Like war zone."

Just then, they heard a low drone approaching, and moments later, Tanak zipped up with the jeep in a cloud of dust. The engine stopped and the door flew open. Enthusiastic greetings were exchanged between the two Laotians followed by a rather demonstrative discussion.

Kampeng then turned toward Dorothy with a condescending

frown. "Okay, we go, but don't be dis-loosened if army no let us go," he barked with a tone sounding that failure was inevitable.

"I promise. And thank you, Kampeng."

Kampeng took over the driving, and he drove fast and rough over a laterite road that climbed up and down through an endless series of hairpin bends. He was correct in saying that it wasn't very far, that is, if one came to that conclusion by looking at the odometer. But the condition of the grueling switchbacks made it seem farther than it was. Over three hours of battling stony inclines and sand filled ruts, and they still hadn't reached Tang Vieng.

"Chao Fa, Chao Baa, Chao Fa, Chao Baa," Dorothy kept repeating to herself as the jeep bounced along the dirt track. "What does 'Chao' mean?" she asked Kampeng.

"Chao mean Prince."

"And Fa?"

"Fa mean 'sky'."

"So Chao Fa means Prince of the Sky."

"Yes."

"Then Chao Baa is also a prince, a prince of what?"

"Prince of Forest."

"And the Chao Fa don't attack him? Why is that, do they like him?"

Kampeng laughed in a low-keyed manner. "No, no. They afraid him."

"The Sky Princes are afraid of the Forest Prince?" She didn't understand all this mythical mumbo jumbo.

Tanak jumped into the conversation by chattering away to Kampeng.

"Tanak say government let Chao Baa live in forest, because he tell Chao Fa to stop fighting."

"Yes, but why are the Chao Fa afraid of him?"

Her question instigated a more vigorous discussion. It seemed to Dorothy that Tanak the Kammu spoke with a greater tone of authority than Kampeng, the lowland Lao, and therefore probably knew more about the issue.

Kampeng began to summarize for her. "He have power over forest pii..."

"Heroo-ey!" Tanak corrected.

"...and also nobody can kill him. If you shoot, the bullets fly away from him, if you stab him with knife, the knife breaks."

"I don't believe any of that. The Chao Baa is just a man, an American who went a bit nutty."

"No, it true!" Kampeng insisted emphatically. "He *thevada*."

"What is tay-va-daa?

"Like angel. He wear special magic..." He stopped to verify a few points with Tanak, "...he wear *pra kroo-ung*, and he have magic tattoo all over body."

"What is a pra kroo-ung?" she asked.

"It is little Buddha image, he pin it inside his robe."

"Oh, like an amulet."

"Yes, omelet."

"And what are the tattoos for?"

"They protect his body. That why no bullets or knives can hurt him."

It was pointless to argue that all of this was mere superstition, since the Laotians obviously believed it as though it were a part of their religion. Dorothy did concede, however, that there could be a grain of truth hidden somewhere beneath these layers of fables, so she had nothing to lose by inquiring further.

"And how does the Chao Baa kill his enemies?" she quizzed, expecting something akin to a golden sword or even using thunderbolts, or just maybe, an M-79 grenade launcher.

"Chao Baa not kill. Chao Baa cannot kill, not even insect..."

"You mean with all his power he can't kill a bug!" she interrupted, not getting the answer she expected.

"Chao Baa is monk. Cannot kill any animal. No eat meat, only plants," Kampeng explained.

"He's actually a Buddhist monk?"

"*Jao, jao*, yes," he confirmed.

Their conversation was prematurely terminated by something that the two men spotted up ahead. As foreseen, there was a checkpoint, but nothing like the other ones she had been through before. There was barbed wire all around, as well as concrete bunkers and large cylindrical objects tied around some of the trees. Rockets, Kampeng pointed out to her.

Three armed men in camouflage fatigues came to the barbed-wire fence to inspect them. One of them addressed Kampeng. After a few words, Kampeng asked Dorothy for her passport and her laissez-passer, which he then handed out the window over to the approaching soldier for inspection. A few minutes of silence passed as the young guard perused the documents. He was shaking his head 'no'. He handed the passport and paper back to Kampeng and there was more conversation, this time with Tanak joining in, but it was to no avail, for it suddenly ended when the soldier clutched his AK-47 in a menacing manner, and said something like 'bye! bye!' in a very harsh voice.

As Kampeng started the engine, Dorothy suddenly opened the door and got out. The guards, all three of them, jumped nervously. Undaunted, she walked towards them with a vehement-looking face, waving her passport and papers in the air.

Her eyes were glaring. "I am a Mennonite Doctor, and the Chao Baa has called me to tend to someone seriously ill!" Knowing they couldn't comprehend what she was saying, she spoke brusquely and authoritatively, endeavoring to use all the magic words she thought the soldiers might respond to: Mennonites, Chao Baa…"If you don't let me through, there is going to be a lot of trouble around here, and I am sure that you will get the worst punishment!"

Kampeng, from within the vehicle, made a liberal translation of what she had said. Tanak opened the door slowly with his hands raised in the air and made his own contribution to the discussion. In all likelihood he was identifying himself as a fellow soldier. The guard who had looked over the papers shot a soliciting glance at his comrades, then nodded his head. To Kampeng he said something terse and then abruptly left.

"He say we go see Commanding Officer. These two soldiers take us there," Kampeng announced, referring to the two other guys with the automatic weapons.

They were led up the hill to a large wooden house, perched on poles in the typical Laotian style, where they were made to wait outside. The first guard, who had taken off before them, was already there, and was ostensibly informing the C.O. of the visitors. Shortly, the Commanding Officer appeared on the side porch, stripped to the waist, his lower body clad only in a sarong, his flabby chest exposed. He was short, in his early thirties, but very stern looking with a severe frown. Dark skin, high cheekbones, slanted eyes, lustrous black hair. He took the cigarette butt out of his mouth and threw it disdainfully on the ground, then folded his arms and tucked his hands into his armpits, peering at Dorothy from beneath beetled brows. His body was rigid, apparently with annoyance.

She hoped he wasn't too upset at being disturbed.

He spoke first to Tanak, who subsequently pointed to Kampeng. The half-naked army officer turned his attention toward Kampeng, questioning him in Lao. Dorothy distinctly heard the word 'Mennonite'.

Kampeng nodded his head, saying "*Jao, jao*, yes."

The Laotian army officer switched his gaze back to Dorothy and switched language as well, addressing her in English. "You Mennonite doctor?"

"No."

He looked back at Kampeng with irritation.

Kampeng smiled sheepishly. "She Mennonite doctor before," he tried to explain, "but now she travel guide writer," Kampeng struggled in English, hoping this time Dorothy would get the cue, shooting an imploring glance to Dorothy, pleading to agree...

"It true?" the commanding officer asked Dorothy.

"No."

Kampeng bowed his head, shaking it in besetment.

"Why you come here?" the army officer bayed harshly, now visibly angry.

"My son was a pilot in the war. The US government cannot tell me what happened to him. I have traveled all the way to Lao to find out. I have been told he was captured by the Pathet Lao, then escaped. I found his identity card and dog tag in the Cave of the Enlightened One on the Pu Khe Mountain. I thought that perhaps he found his way to the Forest Temple, but instead I found out that Richard Johnson, the Chao Baa, was the only farang who arrived there. I believe that this man knows what happened to my son and I wish to see him to ask him about this. Will you not let us through?"

"*Yang?* What did she say?" he asked Kampeng, understanding only a smidgen of what she had said.

Kampeng explained to him using their own language.

"Come inside," the army officer beckoned.

Once inside the house, the army officer shed his official authority and became a simple friendly human being. Even his face changed: boyish, chocolate-colored, with sympathetic eyes. He told them his name was Sousat, a Major in the army, and he introduced Dorothy to his wife and children. All of them were invited to sit down on the mat laid on the floor and share the meal that the family had been partaking of before their arrival. There was fish and vegetables and, of course, the ever-present khao nee-oh, sticky rice.

After the meal, the Major lit up a cigarette, offering others to Kampeng and Tanak. "Road ahead very dangerous. You cannot go. You understand?" he told Dorothy in a benevolent manner. "I no want anything bad to happen."

"Major Sousat, I am an old woman whose husband is dead, and with my only child missing and presumed dead. I have nothing else to live for except to find out what happened to him."

Major Sousat pondered this seriously for a few suspenseful moments. "I sorry. You cannot go." He put the cigarette out, then, after a short interval of embarrassing silence, surprisingly lit up another one only a moment later.

Dorothy, out of impulse, grabbed this new cigarette out of his mouth.

Kampeng was shocked, and Tanak even gasped aloud.

Dorothy, falling into her former role as a health worker, chastised Major Sousat. "You are smoking too much."

The major looked at her bewildered, while Kampeng and Tanak both turned their heads, ashamed at her action.

Strangely enough, instead of getting angry, the army officer actually smiled, and rather warmly at that. Even Dorothy didn't expect such a response.

"You not Mennonite doctor?" he questioned again, still grinning, but now trying to understand her reaction to his smoking.

"I was a nurse once."

He laughed, implicitly cueing everyone else to laugh as well.

"Okay," he said abruptly, with a new tone in his voice. "I will go find Mr. Ree-chart, the Chao Baa," he told her, reaching a compromise. "I will speak to him and ask him to come here. That is only thing I can do. You wait here as my guest in my house. I come back this evening, or maybe tomorrow."

"Thank you, you are most kind."

Dorothy sat on the porch of the wooden house, gazing at the stern mountains around her. Major Sousat had been gone for several hours. The sun was setting, escorted by fiery streaks of red that raced across the sky and gilded the edges of far-flung clouds. Dragonflies and other flying insects skipped through the air, their translucent wings glittering in the horizontal rays. Kampeng and Tanak were down below, playing a game with the soldiers that looked like a mix between badminton and soccer; where one had to use one's foot to kick a little shuttle-cock thing over the net. Their spirited whooping grew more subdued as the day withered away into dusk, and finally died with the night.

They ate supper by the glow of little paraffin lamps; Sousat's wife had cooked an omelet especially for her. Soon her bedding was laid out, and Dorothy, more tired than she had realized, fell into a wearied sleep.

Major Sousat came back in the morning, alone. He wore a grave expression. He sat down where they were having breakfast.

"I speak to Chao Baa, Mr. Ree-chart. He say he very busy man and cannot come. He tell me story of your son. Some men come during war, from Army and CIA, and they kill your son. Then take body. They kill him because he crash his plane and run away from the war. He tell me that they want to kill him, Mr. Ree-chart, too, because he see what they do. So he run away. He afraid to go back to America. And he no want to talk to anyone, he still afraid. He say you go back and forget, like he try to forget."

Dorothy bowed her head, despondent.

"I sorry," said Major Sousat.

Dorothy turned away from him. There was nothing to do now but drive back to Ponsavan and get on a plane to Vientiane.

"Yes, so am I," she said dispiritedly.

Looking out the window of the Y-12 turboprop, down at the tawny, denuded landscape of the Plain of Jars, Dorothy finally understood what saturation bombing really meant. The countryside was littered with craters of all sizes, everywhere, as far as the eye could see. It only exacerbated her melancholy spirits and her disappointment at not meeting with Richard Johnson personally. His refusal to see her angered her, as well as making her feel dejected. Was it really that, or was it the news that had come from him, news that brusquely extinguished her secret hopes? Had she been longing for more than merely finding out the truth? From the beginning, this whole affair had revived the aching memory of her son, forcing her to dwell upon her deceased child so much, that, for the first time in many years, she missed him and hungered for him to come back to her, alive.

The search for the truth was over. It only remained to pack her bags and leave.

From Wattay Airport in Vientiane, they took a tuk tuk to the Riverview Hotel. Kampeng didn't alight from the vehicle. He too was feeling down, her somber mood having affected him as well.

"I sorry, Miss Doro-tee."

"Don't be sorry, Kampeng," she said, taking her bags. "I have a lot more now than I had before I came to Lao. Being in your country has made me richer in many ways. It was the experience of my life, and I am truly grateful. But most of all, I found a friend. A loyal, trusted friend. I shall never forget you. You are a good man, Kampeng. Thank you for everything."

Kampeng, in spite of himself, was touched. "I also glad to meet you. I never know farang woman before. If all like you, then farang men very lucky."

It was the greatest complement she had ever received. Not even anything Bill had ever said to her could match it.

"I will come in the evening, if you want," he said.

"Yes, we can have a last meal together. And I will give you my address in the US, so we can keep in touch."

"Yes, Kampeng would like that very much. And I give Miss Doro-tee my address. See you later." Then, to the tuk tuk driver, he shouted, "Bai, bai!"

Inside the lobby, she was warmly greeted by the hotel staff, and she was forced to give a fainthearted smile in spite of her rueful mood.

"Oh, many messages for Miss Doro-tee," the young concierge told her, reaching behind the counter and handing her a stack of slips. She stood at the counter, reading through them. They were all messages from Cynthia, offering words of encouragement and also informing her that she was continuing her investigations. The last one completely caught her off balance. "Oh, my God!" she exclaimed to herself, "Cynthia is coming here!"

"That message is already old," said a female voice behind her. "I've already arrived."

Dorothy whirled around to find herself face to face with Cynthia.

There she was, standing right in front of her, smiling indulgently, looking a bit outlandish done up like a Laotian woman, with a sleeveless white blouse and a shiny purple paa-sin. "You didn't think I was just going to sit at home, did you? I'm a freelance journalist. I couldn't resist."

"Cynthia! I'm so happy to see you!"

The two women hugged each other affectionately, Dorothy reluctant to release her grip.

"Let's go up to my room, it's right next to yours," suggested Cindy, sensing that Dorothy was on the verge of tears. "We have a lot to talk about."

They climbed up the stairs to Cynthia's room, two doors down from Dorothy's. Cynthia reached into her bra for the keys and fumbled with the doorknob for a few seconds.

"I love your haircut," Cindy praised, as they walked in. "You look good in short hair, like Mary Martin as Peter Pan."

"Peter Pan was a boy who never grew old. Look at me!" She stopped to inspect herself in the dresser mirror. "My face looks like a Halloween mask!"

"Stop that! It's not that bad, a bit thinner perhaps…here, come sit on the bed."

Dorothy took a spot next to Cynthia, adjacent to the night table.

Once seated, Cynthia recounted the details of her arrival in Bangkok. Dorothy at first tried to interrupt her to give out her own news, but Cynthia's loquaciousness was unstoppable. She described meeting with Prasert, who had briefed her and helped her in much the same way as he had helped Dorothy, and she also went on to succinctly narrate other aspects of her trip. She couldn't wait to disclose some of the information she had obtained in the US before her departure. Dorothy waited with a self-assured patience, knowing that she herself was the bearer of the real bombshell news.

But Cynthia continued relentlessly. "I managed to finally get the names of the pilots who went down. Andrew's plane is the one that crashed in Ban Ban. In the database his status is listed as 'recovered', which means he was rescued."

"Yes, I know all that."

"You do? How?"

Finally given a chance, Dorothy expounded on her visit to Muang Kham and her discussions with the villagers regarding a pilot who had hidden in the hole with them, and how he had wept after the bombing. Then she herself burst into tears and fell into Cindy's arms, crying out that she knew they were talking about Andrew.

"Oh Dot, I'm sorry."

Remaining within Cynthia's embrace, she related the peasant woman's story about the prisoner of the Pathet Lao, a pilot who had given the woman a card that held a pressed flower. She explained how that story, based solely on a hunch, had led her up Pu Khe Mountain where she found Andrew's dog tag and identity card in a Buddhist cave. She broke from Cynthia's hold and went hurriedly over to her bags to retrieve the items and handed them over for her to inspect.

Cynthia took the dog tag and Geneva Identity Card, one in each hand and gazed at them alternately with wide eyes. "This is incredible!" She looked up at Dorothy with amazement. "You have really turned out to be a first-class investigator, Dorothy Kozeny! I'm more than impressed. Nothing that I have ever done in my career could hold water to what you have accomplished here. I can't believe it!" She continued to look at the things in her hand, with a rapt expression. "So he must have gone down twice," Cynthia concluded.

"Yes," Dorothy replied, plopping back on the bed and bursting into tears again. Cynthia consoled her by reaching over her and giving her a Kleenex from the box on the night table. While Dorothy sniffled, Cynthia carried on, adding more bits of information she had obtained.

"That's the same conclusion I came to. The report that he had been rescued only deepened the mystery for me," Cynthia went on to say. "I decided to grab the bull by the horns and deal with the sons of bitches directly. I went to the CIA, and confronted them using all my resources. I looked up ex-operatives who participated in the secret war and some other ex-paramilitary advisors. I even found some ex-pilots who flew for Air America. They weren't talking, either because they truly didn't know what I was talking about, or because they weren't willing to discuss it. After all that turned up zilch, I thought to myself, who else was intimately involved in the ground operations? USAID, of course, the US Agency for International Development. They were under contract to the CIA, doing the logistical work, under cover of humanitarian aid, helping to organize supplies to be airlifted by Air America. Some of my informants who had been here during the war told me that, when it came to the work in the field, they used volunteers from the International Voluntary Services, which was the pre-cursor to the Peace Corps. I followed that lead and got hold of a few people, but again nothing turned up. However I did manage to hear of a very strange story, one that might be related to our own. There was this guy, called Richard Johnson..."

"Yes, I know."

"You do? You know that too? What do you know?"

"Cynthia, Andrew really was murdered by the CIA. Richard Johnson was there, he was a witness."

"He was? How the hell did you find that out?"

"He told me."

"He told you? Dot, that's not possible."

"Well, he told me through someone else, actually. It's only hearsay I know, but that's all we have to go on."

"Who was the someone else who relayed this information?"

"A Major Sousat, the commanding officer in charge of the Ta Vieng army post. They wouldn't let me through to see him personally..."

"See who personally?"

"Richard Johnson. You see..." she stopped for a sniffle "...he remained here after the war and rides around on an elephant looking for unexploded bombs…"

"Dorothy, that just isn't possible. Richard Johnson is dead."

Dorothy sat dumbstruck. Her search for the truth was not over. There seemed to be no end to the web of lies and deceit. "Dead?" she asked, as perplexed as ever.

"Yes. The story I got was that he was murdered; his throat was slit from ear to ear. They said it was the Pathet Lao who killed him. Now here's the interesting part. I went to visit the parents, and they told me that Richard wasn't cooperating with the CIA, who of course were the people that he was ultimately working for, whether intentionally or not. He was supposed to provide intelligence, and help to call air strikes…"

"Well that's exactly what he told the monk at the Forest Temple!"

"He, who?"

"Richard Johnson!"

"Dot, I just told you Richard Johnson is dead, his parents positively identified the body."

"Well, then who…" Dorothy broke off in mid-sentence as Nigel Coddington's words welled up from the back of her mind and replayed themselves— "…name's Johnson, or some other…with his knowledge of explosives, and the fact that he's been here since the war, … some sort of rogue operative leftover from the CIA…the odd guise, … a form of psychological warfare…to make the locals fear him…seems to have some power over the Chao Fa. He's about the only outsider that can enter their territory at will. All the more reason to suspect he's an ex CIA fellow…"

It came to her as an epiphany, a sudden flash of realization that illumined her thoughts with blazoned clarity. The man who claimed to be Richard Johnson, the Chao Baa, was none other than Robert Botkin, the man who had helped to murder her son.

Chapter 14

Laos 1990

"The truth is rarely pure and never simple."
Oscar Wilde, playwright, 1898

"Cynthia! It's Botkin!"

"Botkin?"

"The man who rides around on an elephant and claims to be Richard Johnson, I believe that is Robert Botkin."

"But Botkin is also dead."

"How do you know that? You told me they never found the body. If it's like everything else, which from the beginning has never been what it seemed to be, then his death is also questionable. It's all illusions, secrets, tricks and lies, oh Cynthia..."

"Wait a minute, Dot, get a grip on yourself..."

"And that's why he wouldn't come to see me!" She slapped her hand hard on the night table, almost knocking the lamp down. "He couldn't face me!"

"What makes you think this guy is Botkin?"

"Well, who else would go around masquerading as Johnson? And who else would know about Johnson, how he wasn't cooperating in their secret war?"

"Did he mention that?"

"The old monk in the forest temple knows all this. How would the monk know if Johnson, I mean Botkin, didn't tell him so himself? And who else would know what happened to Andrew? I'm surprised he was man enough to tell the truth and confess it."

"Hmmm..." Cindy hummed reflectively, opening her mind up to the possibility. "Probably figures you won't be believed if you reported it."

"Cynthia, didn't you tell me that Botkin used to go around with a shaven head?"

"Yes..."

"Well so does this man. He tells everyone he's a monk, can't kill any living thing, oh the gall of this despicable bastard! Oops, I'm sorry."

"It's okay, Dot, you're allowed to cuss in moments like these," Cindy said sarcastically. "Interesting theory, though..."

The telephone rang, startling them. Cindy picked it up. "Hello?"

"Yes, Miss Doro-tee there?"

"Yes, one moment." She handed the phone to Dorothy

"Who is it?" Dorothy asked Cynthia, before putting the receiver to her ear.

"It's reception."

"Hello?"

"Oh I call your room, you not there, so I try Miss Sin-dee room," the tinny voice said. "Mr. Kampeng, he here to see you."

"Please tell him to come up to room 135." She no longer cared about appearances, and anyway, there were two women in the room and it wouldn't look so bad. Or so she figured. "It's Kampeng," she told Cindy.

"Who?"

"Kampeng, the man who's helped me since I arrived."

"Oh yes, yes."

"He was in the war, fighting for the American backed side," Dorothy stated. "Perhaps he might know about Botkin."

A knock on the door.

"Come in, Kampeng," Dorothy shouted.

The door opened up slowly and cautiously, and Kampeng stepped into the room in a similar circumspect manner.

"Kampeng this is my..." she almost said daughter-in-law, "...friend, Cynthia."

"Just call me Cindy, it's easier," Cynthia said, standing up and holding out her hand.

Kampeng shook her hand. "My name Kampeng. How you do."

"Fine. Sit down, please, sit down."

As Cindy resumed her place, he sat in the chair against the wall facing the two women on the bed.

Dorothy was eager to inform him of their hypothesis. "Kampeng, we were just discussing Richard Johnson, the Chao Baa. Except we think the Chao Baa is not Richard Johnson."

"Then who he is?"

"When you were in the war, did you know any American advisors? From the CIA?"

"Yes, many."

"Did you ever hear of a Robert Botkin?"

Kampeng compressed his face in thought. "No, I don't know."

Cynthia intervened. "What about 'Bobby Bo'?"

"Oh, yes Bobby Bo." His expression opened up mirthfully as he chuckled at the recollection. "Crazy man. Like killing too much." He laughed again. "Ha, ha! He say soldiers in Royal Lao Army is bunch of woman's private parts. Lao soldier don't want to fight, always running away. He speak truth...Then get drunk and say he want to be Buddhist. He want to go buat pra and be monk. We laugh. Oh, Bobby Bo...He even shave head, like monk. He have codename. Mr. Sheen. He wear white shirt like mine." He pulled at his tightly fitting white T-shirt.

"I would imagine that his had a few less holes in it," Cynthia quipped.

"Did he like to wear sunglasses?" Dorothy queried.

"Oh yes. Wear all time, even when sky cloudy. Inside house too."

"Kampeng, we believe that Bobby Bo is the Chao Baa," Cynthia announced.

"Oh no, cannot be."

"Why not?" Dorothy questioned.

"Chao Baa don't want to kill. Bobby Bo kill too much."

"Have you ever seen the Chao Baa?" Cynthia asked.

"No, I never see."

"Dot," Cynthia asked, "how many days left on your visa?"

Dorothy fumbled in her handbag for her passport, which she flipped open to examine. "In twenty-three days I have to leave the country."

"That should be enough time. We'll try to get a flight tomorrow."

"Where Miss Sin-dee and Miss Doro-tee go?"

"We're going back to the Plain of Jars to find the Chao Baa," Dorothy announced. "You don't have to go with us, Kampeng."

He leaned forward, resting his elbows on his thighs, his hands clasped together. "If Miss Doro-tee go, then Kampeng must go," he said soberly.

"Is it possible to get a flight tomorrow?" Cynthia asked exuberantly. Then without waiting for an answer, she said, "Oh well, if we can't, maybe we can go by road."

"Oh, no!" Dorothy protested. "I'm not going through that again!"

"Maybe get flight," Kampeng offered, "they change schedule since problem last time; now two flights Xieng Khouang every day. We try tomorrow."

"Let's keep our fingers crossed," said Cynthia.

Not only was the food very good, Cynthia had commented, but cheap too. They were at a restaurant finishing off a repast that consisted of fried noodles, grilled chicken, lop, and of course, there was sticky rice as well, which Dorothy didn't bother with. Shortly afterwards, once Cynthia and Kampeng had smoked their after dinner cigarettes, Cynthia announced that she was off to the Nam Pu Bar for a drink.

"What a fine idea," agreed Dorothy. "I'll join you. Kampeng, would you like to come along?"

Before he could reply, Cynthia interjected, "Sorry Dot, but I would prefer to go alone. I need to be free to mingle, if you can catch my meaning."

Dorothy was a bit hurt by that, and it made her realize that she really didn't know Cynthia at all after all these years. Her explanation seemed to be a tacit way of saying she was going to look for a man to share her bed. And of course, Dorothy, being an old bag, would cramp her style. "Of course, I understand," she responded coldly.

Kampeng looked on curiously.

Cindy gave Dorothy a wry smile. "Not mad at me, are you?"

"Of course not," she lied.

"See you tomorrow," Cindy said standing up. "Don't wait up for me," She winked as she said that, only affirming Dorothy's suspicions.

Kampeng walked Dorothy back to her hotel, where she said goodnight and ascended to her room to turn in early.

It was the middle of the night when incessant banging on her door shattered her sleep.

"Who is it?" she asked groggily from her bed.

"Dot, it's me, Cindy."

But she wasn't alone, for Dorothy heard a male voice saying something she couldn't make out, followed by a 'shush' from Cynthia.

Dorothy wasn't about to open the door if she was with a strange man. "Go to bed. It's late," she admonished. She felt like adding, 'you got what you wanted', but thought the better of it.

"Dot, open up, please, it's important."

"Very important!" the man said loudly, obviously drunk.

"Sssh!" Cynthia rebuked him. "Please, Dot, open up, everything's okay."

Dorothy didn't think so, but she got up to open the door anyway, seeing as she had very little choice.

Cindy stumbled in with an inebriated young Caucasian, clearly younger than Cynthia, about half her age, his black-framed glasses hanging lopsided on his face, a pleasant yet banal face with small features—small eyes, small nose, small mouth…It seemed he needed Cynthia's help to stand up, for he was slouching heavily with his arm around her shoulder. His buttoned shirt was half out of his pants and his breath stank of stale beer.

"Here, sit down," Cindy told her new acquaintance, directing him to the chair by the wall.

Dorothy was clutching at her nightgown, inhibited by the presence of the stranger. "Cynthia, what on earth is going on?"

"Dot, meet Jeffrey," she introduced. "Jeffrey Heller. Jeffrey, meet Dot."

Slumped in his chair, the young man suddenly whipped his head up, banging it inadvertently against the wall. He was bombed out of his skull. "Heloo, Dot. Dot-ta-ta-dot-ta-dot." Then he laughed stupidly.

"Honestly, Cynthia, you could have done better than that," Dorothy reprimanded, ashamed of her.

"No, I don't think so. In fact, I did much better than expected." Cindy didn't appear as drunk as he was. "He's a great catch."

"If I were you, I'd throw him back."

"Throw me, throw me," he parroted fatuously, stretching his arms out and lunging at Cindy. She let him wrap them around her waist, tolerating him like an indulgent mother.

"Jeffrey," she addressed him. "Tell Dot what you're researching."

He let go of her and with ineffectual, ludicrous aplomb, he attempted to straighten the eyeglasses on his head, before sitting back in the chair in a hopelessly stilted attitude. "Cog-anitive disss...oh...nance," he slurred. "Cognitive...dissonance," he said again with greater clarity.

"What?" Dorothy asked, scrunching up her face.

"A fancy term for mental conflicts," Cindy explained. She once again spoke to Heller. "Yes, but more specifically, what are you doing here?"

The young man didn't answer. Instead he began rubbing his face vigorously, which caused his glasses to fall off. Cynthia promptly picked them up.

"Jeffrey," she addressed him, bending over him and stroking his hair, as if talking to a child. "Do you want to go and wash your face with cold water?"

He uncovered his face to look at her, then buried it into the cleavage of her breasts. "You have beautiful tits," he said from the depths of her bosom.

"Dot, give me a hand."

The two women struggled to get him to his feet and lead him to the bathroom.

"Why is he so drunk?" Dorothy asked disapprovingly.

"That's my fault. I was 'lubricating him'. He wasn't talking otherwise."

The cold water seemed to sober him a bit. "I'm drunk!" he announced to himself, somewhat surprised, once the two women had doused him.

"Do you know where he's staying?" Dorothy asked. "Maybe you should take him back to his hotel. In his state, I don't think he'll be able to, you know...do anything tonight."

"Why, Dot! How naughty of you! I wasn't looking to get laid; I went to the Nam Pu to snoop around. Here, lets get him back in the chair."

His attempts at walking were improving, but still somewhat somnambulant. "I drank too much," he acknowledged apologetically, as they helped him back into the main room.

"You'll be okay. Here. Sit back down. Now, tell Dot what you're doing here."

Sitting in the chair, he accepted his spectacles from Cynthia and again made an attempt to adjust them. "I'm writing my thesis."

"What's it about?" Cindy asked rhetorically, since she already knew, but wanted him to declare it aloud.

"Personality alteration as a mechanism for resolving cognitive dissonance..."

Dorothy was impressed that he got such a mouthful out, considering his condition.

"...And the eclectics of karmic manifestations..."

Cindy exhaled with impatience.

"...Found in Buddhist mythology."

His recitation was apparently finished, with Dorothy not comprehending any more than she did before.

"Dammit, Jeff," Cindy scolded, "Tell her!"

But evidently there was more.

"...Case study: The Legend of the Chao Baa."

There was a dramatic silence until Cindy turned around with a victorious smile. "He'll sleep in my room," she announced, "on the floor. I'm not going to let him out of my sight. We're going to take him with us."

"We are? Suppose he doesn't want to go?"

"Oh, he'll wanna go alright," she stated with wicked assurance.

The next morning, Dorothy, on Cynthia's instructions, had to hurriedly get in touch with Kampeng to tell him to purchase four airplane tickets rather than three, as someone else was coming along. She couldn't help feeling guilty about this, as the young man was still asleep in Cindy's room when she went downstairs, and he clearly had no idea that he was about to go anywhere today. She also had difficulty in explaining just who this person was to Kampeng, who in the end merely accepted the request.

In the hotel restaurant, Cindy and Jeff Heller were drinking coffee, both dressed comfortably in T-shirts and jeans.

"I'm really sorry about last night," he apologized as Dorothy took a chair opposite. "I normally don't drink that much."

"Never mind." She almost found herself saying 'bo ben yang'. "How are you feeling this morning?"

"Like a piece of..." he stopped himself, "...not so hot, but getting better." He looked Dorothy in the eyes. "I just want you to know that I didn't do anything improper with your daughter last night."

"My daughter?"

Cindy, behind Heller's back, put a conspiratorial finger to her mouth.

"Yes," Dorothy said. "Well she's a grown woman, and she is free to do what she likes."

"I also appreciate you inviting me along to Xieng Khouang and paying my expenses. My grant money is very little, and I had to go there anyway, sooner or later. You see; there are indications that the story of the Chao Baa takes place somewhere near the Plain of Jars."

"Yes, we are aware of that."

"Cindy tells me that the both of you are also interested in the legend."

"Yes."

"We think it's fascinating," Cindy broke in. "And we want to devote our whole vacation to finding out more about it."

As the conversation progressed, it was revealed that Heller was a graduate student from the University of Hawaii, and he was conducting this study in conjunction with the East-West Center in Honolulu. He had been to Lao PDR once before, but didn't get much co-operation from the authorities, who in fact went out of their way to discourage him, so this time he was going to do the research more covertly, and therefore he advised everyone to keep it a secret.

"Your secret is safe with us," Dorothy pledged. "Where is it in Xieng Khouang Province that you want to go?" she asked him.

"Actually, to be honest, I have no idea. Where I originally wanted to go isn't on any map."

"Yes, well I know that problem," Dorothy sympathized. She was examining his face, which depicted a mien of innocence. He wasn't handsome, but he was cute in a way, certainly huggable. She felt some remorse at the way she and Cynthia were treating him. Hence she tried to be more cordial and sincere. "Tell me, Jeff, what will you do after your thesis?"

"Gee, I don't know. I never thought about it. I mean, the end of my thesis, it's been so hard to get any information, I'm starting to think I'll never finish it. I don't know," he commented in a fey manner, getting back to the original question. "Maybe come back here and become a monk." He laughed self-consciously.

She noticed Cynthia's face angling up in smiling recognition, prompting Dorothy to turn her head behind her. Kampeng was coming towards them, a big grin displaying his large, square teeth.

"I get them," he proclaimed. "Four tickets. For today, three o'crock."

"You've done well, Kampeng," Cynthia commended.

Dorothy felt a twinge of resentment at Cynthia's remark, since Kampeng was her associate...comrade...buddy...His actions weren't required to meet Cynthia's approval.

Kampeng took a seat next to Dorothy.

"Would you like some coffee?" she offered.

"Yes, preeze."

"Mr. Kampeng," Heller addressed, as Dorothy filled a cup, "Dot and Cindy told me that you know of the Chao Baa."

"Yes, I hear about Chao Baa."

"Have you ever heard of the Village of the White Monkey?"

"No, I never hear."

"Have you ever seen him? The Chao Baa, I mean."

"No," interrupted Dorothy, "he's never seen him." She was starting to feel uncomfortable about the direction this conversation was taking, though she wasn't quite sure why.

Now it was Cynthia's turn. "Kampeng, people say that nobody can kill him. What do you think?"

"It true. Cannot kill him."

"Is he an *arahant*?" Heller asked.

"Yes," Kampeng answered.

"Does the Chao Baa have the ability to fly with his sacred elephant?" Cynthia asked in an overly eager manner.

"Yes, they can fly."

Cynthia turned towards Heller and giggled. "Sounds like a Laotian version of 'Tarzan meets Dumbo'," she caustically commented.

That was enough for Dorothy. "I think we should change the topic." The condescending tone of this discussion was infuriating her. She felt they were mocking him. "Mr. Kampeng is my friend and I won't have you treat him as some subject in an anthropological study!"

"Sorry, Dot," Cynthia atoned.

"What is anso-potaa-jikle?" Kampeng inquired.

"Bo pen yang," Dorothy told him.

The breakfast of eggs and toast came, and they ate without further inquiries concerning the Chao Baa.

On the airplane, the turbulence didn't detract from the exhilaration Dorothy got from the view out the window. Down below, the Vientiane floodplain was charmingly laid out with brilliant green rice paddies and ponds that flashed with reflected sunlight. As the plane crossed to the edge of the Mekong Valley, she looked out at celestial cumulus clouds, dazzling white fluffs floating on their way up the steep rise to the highlands. Once over the mountains, however, everything became enveloped in a brown-gray sooty haze.

"They've started to burn the vegetation on the mountains," Heller pointed out to Dorothy, sitting across the aisle. "Slash and burn agriculture." Then, from out of nowhere, he asked her, "Do you get airsick?"

"Not yet, why?"

"Think you can read something?" He handed her what looked like a bound report. "This is the main basis for my dissertation. Turn to page twenty-five. There is a condensed version of the legend, written by a monk in Vientiane, who is compiling a collection of such stories. He gave it to me in secret. It won't be included in the final compilation. He said the government didn't want it to get published with the others. It's funny; it was the only story they censored. I got it translated from Lao language into English in California, from one of the exiles who emigrated."

She took the manuscript, then fumbled for her reading glasses.

The Legend of the Chao Baa
As recorded by Maha Metta Suriwong
Author's note: The following is only draft of oral reports which not

yet cross-referenced to fullest extent to capacity. Many of people from Xieng Khouang are sources of this story, and only common elements is taken to be written here.

Not quite understanding that, she read on, and in spite of the bouncing of the airplane and the poor English, became totally absorbed:

The Chao Baa was evil man in previous life. He kill many men. He was a fierce warrior and very brave. But he was not wise. So he was reborn with bad Karma. First he get reborn in a strange land to become a stranger. He is farang with farang name, Ree Chart Jon Soon. Then he come back to kill his own people and he don't know. Then when he knows, he is filled with such sadness as to break his heart. So he become a monk to try to expiate for all the bad Karma he accumulated. He is given monk name Sunnata.

Dorothy pondered over the word 'expiate' before continuing.

He is a Pra for years studying the Damma. He become very religious and very excellent monk. Then the evil giants find him and take him away. They want him to stop being monk and become their slave. But Sunnata refuses. So they decide they must kill him. They kill him and put him in the ground. But the next day they dig up the ground and found him still alive. So they kill him and bury him again. Every time they kill him and bury him, he doesn't die. Seven times they try, and seven times he live. So then they say become our slave, and he finally says yes. So he become their slave and then he is good to them so they say you are a good slave, you can marry. Now he forget being a holy man and he want to have family and be ordinary person. He live in Village of White Monkey and be farmer. He farm and also he could predict the future and heal sick people. Everyone like him.

But he not consume all the bad Karma. His years not enough as monk. So the bad Karma come back to him. The spirits take away his son, and bad prince take away his wife and daughter. So now he has nothing, he become monk again.

Then a holy man in Lat Buak tell Pra Sunnata that to expiate the bad Karma, he must fight his own armies and defeat them. Also he has to go through the fields of fire. Only then will bad Karma be expelled. Indra gives to him Akanee the brave elephant to help him fight the evil princes and go through the fire fields. Indra also give both of them power to fly, as Pra Sunnata is very holy and has much merit.

Holy man also tell him now you are not Pra Sunnatta, you are Prince of the Forest, the Chao Baa (my Italics), and you must protect people. You have to live in the forest rest of your life and protect people. Only then will the bad Karma be consumed. So Chao Baa fight his own armies, who try to kill him. But they cannot kill him. They shoot him, but he fly away, then he chase them out of villages. He turns fire fields into tung naa (rice paddy – my inclusion). He tell people now you will have food.

"Who is Indra?" Dorothy asked.

Heller answered her, but in a manner that would soon get on Dorothy's nerves. He would always give a long spiel before getting to the point. "Theravada Buddhism puts emphasis on how one should live one's life. It doesn't offer much in the way of cosmology. So, many of the Gods are borrowed from Hinduism. Indra is the chief god in the lowest heaven."

Just when she thought he was finished, he went on.

"It's also interesting to note, that the name of the elephant that Indra gives to him is called Akanee. That's the name of the God of Fire. He was noted for dispelling war."

"Oh," Dorothy muttered, trying to be polite despite her lack of interest in these arcane details.

But he still wasn't finished. "It's even more fascinating, in light of my thesis, that when this guy becomes a monk, he takes the name of Sunnata, which in both Pali and Sanskrit means 'voidness', or 'denial of self'."

They were now over the rim of the mountain range, entering the basin land of Tung Hai Hin, the Plain of Jars. The clouds disappeared, but the haze of fire smoke blurred the scenery below.

The airplane made an abrupt descent that terminated Heller's discourse and two minutes later they landed at the Ponsavan airstrip. They took one of the many tuk tuks that were waiting outside the miniature airport building, ending up at the same guesthouse that Dorothy had stayed in during her last visit. Kampeng left them there in order to try and procure the same Russian jeep.

During their late afternoon stroll, Cindy and Jeff seemed to share an almost childlike enthusiasm over Ponsavan, whipping out their 35-millimeter cameras and taking pictures of just about everything, in contrast to Dorothy's lackadaisical indifference. Her impression of the town hadn't changed. It was as she remembered it: ugly, chalky, plane-faced structures in a place that baked in scalding sunshine throughout the day, until cooled by a bath of expanding shadows in the evening. Besides all the military-looking vehicles, endless hordes of motorcycles and scooters would parade up and down the overly wide lanes, splashing a perpetual spray of dust, so that the box-like buildings wore the same tan colors as the sandy streets. Her image of Ponsavan was nothing more than a cubistic blur in dingy shades of brown and buff, and the pedestrians ambling by were equally indistinct.

Towards evening, they were to meet Kampeng at the same restaurant that he and Dorothy had frequented previously, the one with the décor of bombshells and artillery projectiles, artifacts which seemed to interest Cynthia, who spent some time examining them.

"Hmm. 105-millimeter casings," she commented, inspecting the torpedo-looking things planted in the little garden outside.

Once they were seated at a table, the discussion inevitably centered on the subject of the Chao Baa, which Heller dominated in his self-assumed role of being an authority on the matter.

"It's notable that in the story the character changes his identity three times. First, he's a Western man, then he becomes Pra Sunnata the monk, and then the Chao Baa. Three is a significant number, not only in Buddhism, but figures prominently in many of the animist belief systems as well."

"That's right!" Cynthia emphatically concurred. "The Triple Gems—the Buddha, the Darma, and the Church."

Meanwhile, Dorothy played distractedly with the rice on her plate, feeling depressed. They were denigrating her heartfelt quest, the search for the truth concerning her son's fate, and turning it into an academic pontification.

"Yes," Heller was saying, "but in non-Buddhist rituals as well many of the acts are performed three times, and almost everyone, even most of the hill tribes, considers that a newborn baby doesn't acquire its human soul until after three days have passed."

"Interesting," Cynthia said.

"But seven is also a recurring number. For instance there are seven Nagas, or Naks as they're called in Laotian."

"What?" Cynthia asked.

"They're sacred serpents, but they can change into human form as well. They control the waters of the earth and even protect the Buddha. You might see, in the back of some Buddha statues, the Buddha is sitting on the coils of their body, while seven snake-like heads are hovering over him."

Dorothy stopped fiddling with her spoon, and without checking herself, actually made a contribution to their discourse. "Yes, I've seen that."

"There are also seven heavens."

"Oh," Cynthia exclaimed with a devilish smile, "that's where the expression, seventh heaven comes from."

"Yeah, I think so," Heller concurred, not fully catching her intimation. "So they try to kill this guy seven times, and seven times they fail. You see, although this appears to be a modern legend, it's still consistent with the literary traditions that the Khmer civilization brought from India."

Dorothy, in contrast to her earlier empathy for the young man, now found him boring and pedantic.

"...But what I want to focus on, is the change of personality, the transformation of alter-ego that the hero must undergo to expiate his Karma..."

Now she was enraged. She brought her two fists, still clutching her fork and spoon, down on the table with a force that rattled the plates and cutlery. "HERO!" she shouted, causing everyone else in the restaurant, all of them Laotians, to stare. "THAT MAN..."

"DOT!" Cynthia commanded. "Let's have a private word. Excuse us, Jeff."

Jeff Heller's face dropped, his jaw hanging limp in mild shock. He didn't realize he had said anything bad. The two women got up and went outside onto the dusty street.

"Dot, what the hell is wrong with you?"

"How can he call that man a hero, the man who killed my son?"

"Dot, get a hold on yourself. He doesn't know what we're doing here. Don't blow our cover."

"Yes, our cover, I mustn't forget," she retorted sardonically. "For you, this is just another journalistic assignment, but for me, it's my life. You don't know what it's like to lose a child. You wouldn't know, you were never a mother..." She suddenly halted her harangue in mid-sentence, struck with stabbing regret over her unkind uttering.

Cynthia's mouth had already turned down into a trembling pout, tears making glistening tracks down her cheeks. She looked away from Dorothy. "I loved him too, you know."

"Oh, I'm sorry, Cindy. I didn't mean it. I'm just tired and tense and..."

They hugged each other as Heller came outside, and, viewing the scene, he suddenly felt responsible for whatever had just transpired.

"I'm sorry if I said anything wrong," he repented.

"No, it's alright," Dorothy assured him, composing herself. "It's only women things." In a timely deliverance from this emotionally awkward scene, Kampeng noisily pulled up with the Russian jeep.

The two women let go of each other.

"Sorry, I late," he said, slamming the door shut and coming around from the driver's side. "Kampeng change oil."

They lumbered back inside the restaurant, Kampeng's presence having a mollifying effect on any further emotional undertones, so that they were able to confer pragmatically about their strategy in the hunt for the Chao Baa.

"How are we going to get past that army checkpoint, with that Major Sousat?" Dorothy wanted to know.

"Ah yes, Kampeng have plan. We go another way, you know, small road, no army, no police. There is small road, go off from Route Four not far from Muang Koon. It go to Ban Ling Kao. Remember old monk tell us to go there?" he reminded Dorothy. "But sometime not safe," he cautioned. He then paused. "Before, you know, Chao Baa, he live in Ban Ling Kao."

"Excuse me," Heller interrupted, "I know that 'Ban' is the term for village, but what does 'Ling Kao' mean in English?"

"It mean white monkey."

"You said you didn't know it."

"Know what?"

"The Village of the White Monkey."

"Yes, because I don't know it in English. Ling Kao, white monkey, yes."

"But the Village of the White Monkey is a mythical place," Heller objected, "it doesn't exist. It's not on any map."

Dorothy felt a bit smug, now that she had the chance to lecture Heller on the peculiarities of Laotian geography. "That's because of the war. Many villages were destroyed, then rebuilt again with new names."

To her surprise, Kampeng refuted that. "No, Ban Ling Kao build after war. Then, one day, few years ago, Chao Fa attack, people move out. No more Ban Ling Kao."

"Wow, this is truly incredible," Heller blurted out. "We're going to actually visit the Village of the White Monkey. It's a good thing you guys invited me along."

Dorothy wasn't so sure that it was.

They were all in the jeep, bouncing their way out of Ponsavan. The haze from the seasonal burning of the hilltop fields not only dulled the scenery, but also made the air thick and heavy, which, together with the dust, seemed to stick to their skin. As if that wasn't enough discomfort for Dorothy, Heller, in the back seat with Cynthia, unceasingly expounded in a pedagogical voice his esoteric theories concerning the Chao Baa.

"There is an unmistakable parallel between the Chao Baa's story and the story of Mogallana."

"Ah, Mogallana, yes," Kampeng acknowledged as he drove.

"Who?" Cynthia asked.

"The Buddha had two great disciples, Sariputra, known for his wisdom, and Mogallana, who was famous for his mighty mystic powers. In some temples you can see their statues at the altar, paying homage to the statue of the Buddha. Towards the end of Mogallana's life, he was constantly battling with bandits who were sent to kill him, and he used to escape by flying away. In the end though, after realizing that it was his Karma to die for the horrible sins he'd committed in a previous life, he allowed them to beat him to death, and didn't use his magic powers to save himself."

Heller cleared his throat before going on. "It's easy to see the common elements: the Chao Baa also has supernatural powers, including the ability to fly, but despite them both being great holy men, they still had to answer to the bad Karma of a previous life."

Notwithstanding Heller's intellectual haughtiness, Dorothy had perked up her ears. This analysis was certainly consistent with the Chao Baa being Botkin—not the bit about being holy, but having a depraved past. She relished the part about him being beaten to death and privately brooded that Botkin himself should meet with a similar fate.

They came to the turn off, and the asperity of the road conditions imposed a slower pace. The route narrowed into a little track, not much wider than the jeep, with the vegetation at the margins occasionally scraping the sides of the vehicle with that same grating sound as someone running a fingernail against a blackboard. Kampeng's job became more strenuous, as he wrestled with the steering wheel, while the others rocked and jostled uncomfortably in their seats. However, the unpleasant jolting did cause Heller to finally shut up, much to Dorothy's relief.

All the while it was evident that they were going up to a higher elevation. The track got even worse, and their progress was reduced to crawling over an uneven surface of small boulders, which required Kampeng to engage the four-wheel drive.

"Nobody go on this road for long time," explained Kampeng. "It very bad," he added, stating the obvious.

But it was to get worse. Soon, the small boulders they were traversing were hitting the bottom of the vehicle, and he had to maneuver cautiously to avoid damage to the rear axle and fuel tank. There were also deep gullies and creeks, whose steep banks made everyone hold their breath, as Kampeng would guide the jeep down and then climb back out at appallingly declivitous angles. Eventually they came to a stream that couldn't be crossed without a makeshift bridge, one that had already been put in place by other unknown travelers who had gone before. This bridge was merely small logs and raw timbers that were laid side by side, and it didn't look very sturdy.

"Everyone, go out and walk," Kampeng ordered. "I bring car."

They exited the jeep and scrambled down, waded the stream, and climbed up to the other side to watch with suspense as he made the attempt. No sooner had the front wheels trodden on the crude platform, when the loose pieces of wood shifted around, creating large gaps in which the wheels eventually fell through, while the jeep itself hung through the crude structure over the edge of the ravine, hopelessly stuck.

"Oh, great," Dorothy bemoaned.

"I guess we'll have to walk the rest of the way," Cynthia advised.

"How are we gonna get back?" wondered Heller.

Kampeng slowly opened his door to inspect the situation he found himself in. He peered at the displaced logs and shook his head in disgust. He ducked back inside the jeep, bending down and fiddling about until he came out with a jack. This he placed on whatever remained of the bridge, after which he set about placing rocks in front of the rear tires, to circumvent any forward rolling. Once he found a workable and stable position for the jack, he proceeded to jack up the right front wheel, while the others looked on from the far side. Heller aimed his camera and took a memorable photo.

"Why don't you go and help him, Jeffrey?" Cynthia scolded.

"Oh, yeah, right."

All of them ended up crossing back to join the lone Laotian struggling to rectify the predicament. Cynthia, as well as Heller, offered her labor and suggestions, as they tried to return the wandering bits of lumber back into a suitable position underneath the jacked up wheels. Dorothy herself sat down under the shade of a tree by the bank. God, how she was tired of traveling in this country.

It was taking a long time, and it seemed doubtful as to whether they would be able to extricate the vehicle from its ungainly pose. The effort consisted of much parleying and exhortations as they tried to rearrange the disheveled bridge. It was nearing noon, and the sun was getting uncomfortably hot and bright.

"That one, move this way, no, to here!"

"Like this?"

"No, not good, bring to this side."

"Not that way, Jeffrey! Over there!"

"Oh, okay."

"Good, now put that one…"

"Which one? This one?"

"No, that one."

"This one?"

"Yes."

"Take that one away, it no good."

"How about this, Kampeng?" Cynthia asked, holding onto a small log.

"No, that one we put later."

After getting one side of the structure to meet Kampeng's approval, the left wheel of the jeep was now jacked up and the whole rigmarole was repeated. Cynthia, deciding it was time for a cigarette break, came over to sit by Dorothy.

"We're getting there," she announced to her with reserved reassurance.

"Do you think we'll be able to get it out of there?"

"I don't know," Cynthia admitted. "Kampeng seems confident." She lit up her Salem.

Dorothy shrugged. "Yes, I know. Bo ben yang."

A pause as Cynthia puffed pensively on her cigarette.

"I've been thinking," Dorothy said. "The Lao government is authoritarian and very conservative. How can they permit someone going around, claiming he's the Lord of the Forest, and making people believe he has magical powers? It doesn't make sense. You would think they would arrest someone like that, especially considering his background as an ex-CIA."

"That's a very good point. I've also given this some thought. You know who Kaysone Pomvihan is, don't you?"

"Isn't he the Prime Minister or something?"

"Yes. He was the real leader of the Pathet Lao, the guy calling the signals from the caves in Sam Neua. After the revolution he became the Secretary of the Party, and that makes his word virtual law."

Dorothy was getting fed up that every time she asked anybody a question, she had to listen to a sermon before the answer was eventually delivered. "What does all this have to do with the Chao Baa?"

"I'm getting to that. Just listen. Kaysone is in very bad health now. In fact, it's rumored that he is dying. It is also well-known that he often visits this famous monk just outside of Vientiane, a monk who had been arrested four years ago and put in prison, because people claimed he had great magic and could fly as well. After spending two years in prison, the authorities admitted that they had made a mistake and released him, not long before Kaysone started to seek his services for healing and religious blessings. It's likely that the order to exonerate the old priest came from him directly. Now, the most powerful man in the government prostrates himself before a venerated monk. So you see, by setting this example, it was as if Kaysone had decreed that all such figures should not only be tolerated, but respected as well."

"Laos is so complicated," Dorothy griped. "I don't think I'll ever understand it."

"Plus, we shouldn't rule out the possibility that the Chao Baa has his own patrons in the government."

"Patrons?"

"Yes, you know, contacts, people protecting him. Especially since he's helping in his own way to control the Chao Fa insurgents."

The roar of the jeep was heard and both women looked up. Kampeng had put it in reverse and was backing it off the bridge.

"YAAY!" everyone cheered.

Once the vehicle was safely on firm ground again, preparations were made to re-fashion the bridge in a new and improved way. Kampeng foraged for rattan, which everyone, including Dorothy, helped to lash and fasten the timbers with. It was mid-afternoon when Kampeng's second attempt to cross the new bridge turned out to be successful, with everyone boarding in high spirits.

However, they didn't get very far before the track narrowed to a point which didn't permit the vehicle to proceed further.

Kampeng started to back the jeep up. "I think I pass place." Slowly, meticulously, he guided the jeep backwards. Making a U-turn was out of the question.

"I don't understand," Cynthia blurted, "what place did we pass?"

"It not far," Kampeng assured, his left hand controlling the steering wheel, while he strained to peer rearward.

"It might be faster if we walked."

"Yes, we can walk," he confirmed.

"Where are we going?" Dorothy wondered.

"Small trail. Lead to Hmong village. People there know how to get to Ban Ling Kao."

Kampeng stopped the vehicle, switched off the ignition, and they all disembarked.

"Is it okay to leave the car here?" Cynthia asked.

"Bo ben yang," Kampeng replied.

"We've done this sort of thing before," Dorothy assured her.

It took about a half-hour of hiking back along the track before Kampeng announced, "I think here." He glanced around the spot until he was sure. "Yes, here."

After walking into the thick vegetative growth, it could be seen that there actually was a path, albeit barely discernible. It was very overgrown and hard to follow, tunneled under a dense web of cluttered, untamed vines. Kampeng had to stop a few times to ensure they were still on it. It was rough going as they pushed away the tentacle-like foliage from their bodies whilst they advanced. Not helping any was the fact that the sun was getting lower on the horizon, and the pale light and translucent shadows further obscured the way. They climbed up the jungle hillside until, inevitably, Kampeng reached a spot where indecision set in.

"We stop here for rest," he declared.

Nobody objected to that. They had been walking for almost two hours and they were grimy, sweaty, and aching. Cindy and Heller put down the knapsacks they were carrying, and took seats on the ground. Their T-shirts were stained wet with perspiration. Kampeng explored on ahead to see if he could pick up the trail.

"Isn't this exciting, Dot?" Cynthia asked Dorothy, expecting agreement.

"No. I've already done this and it loses its flavor the second time around. I'm tired and I can't wait to get home."

She didn't feel like sitting down with them and engaging in trivial conversation. She too, set about foraging for the trail. Fortuitously, she found it. "Over here!" she hollered.

Suddenly excited about her discovery, she trudged ahead.

"Miss Doro-tee, where you go?" she heard Kampeng shout.

The path curved around through thick bushes, then seemed to open up a bit. It was much more perceptible at this point.

"Over here!" she yelled back.

As the trail wound to the left she came around a curve and that's when she saw it right in front of her. She screamed, "Aahhhhhhhh! Aahhhhhh! Aahhhhhh!"

Within seconds Kampeng was behind her. "It okay—bo ben yang."

Heller joined them. "Oh wow! Spirit Gates!"

Cynthia had also arrived. "What is that?" she shouted, referring to what they were all looking at.

"Spirit Gates," Heller repeated. He took hold of his camera and clicked the shutter. Cynthia followed suit.

In front of them stood two poles, connected by a rope that spanned the trail. Inserted into the strands of rope were carved wooden knives, as well as the thing that had made Dorothy scream, a severed dog's head, and a bloody set of paws, which also hung from the line.

"Yes," Kampeng confirmed. "Hmong do this during time of 'peanut spots'."

"Peanut spots?" Cynthia asked, flabbergasted, putting her camera down.

"Yes, very bad. All over body. Also bleed. People get fever, die."

"But, Kampeng," Dorothy interjected, now over her initial shock, "there aren't any more peanut spots."

"Yes, you right, Miss Doro-tee."

"So you know about peanut spots?" Heller inquired, with a newfound respect for Dorothy's erudition.

"Yes, of course."

"Well I don't," complained Cynthia.

"Smallpox," Dorothy answered curtly. She had been a nurse. She knew these things. "It's been eradicated for several years now. Why the gate?"

Kampeng tried to explain the existence of the structure. "They don't take down. Leave them to fall down by themselves." But in the end he really couldn't. "This one new. I no understand."

"Who doesn't take them down?" Cynthia demanded to know.

"The Hmong," Heller responded.

"We not allowed go further," informed Kampeng. "If we go past it, have to pay fine of one pig."

"Well, what are we going to do?" Cynthia questioned. "It's blocking the path. And we don't have any pigs on us."

"Yes, this is village we want to go. Maybe they take money instead."

"This is their way of quarantining the area during epidemics," Dorothy said. "Do you think there is a sickness in the village?" she asked Kampeng.

Kampeng looked around him, inspecting his surroundings like a bloodhound sniffing his way. "Does Miss Doro-tee want to continue?"

Dorothy felt a warm camaraderie towards this Laotian man. By asking her to make the decision, he was acknowledging that her wishes had precedence over anybody else's. It was also a re-affirmation of the original partnership, for it was her and Kampeng who had started this pilgrimage and who had already gone through several adventures of their own.

"Unless you think it unwise, I say we enter the village."

Kampeng's response was to walk ahead, with Dorothy just a step behind him.

"Wait! I gotta get the knapsacks!" Heller remonstrated.

So they waited for Jeff and Cindy to get the packs and return, then they proceeded forward, bending low as they ducked under the rope of the spirit gate, following the path into the Hmong village.

They trudged on wordlessly, until Kampeng suddenly stopped and extended his arm in back of him in a protective manner, stopping Dorothy also. From out of nowhere, stood two armed men, stock still like statues, dressed in what looked like black pajamas, pointing big guns at them. Kampeng addressed them, apparently in their own language.

"Oh, shit," murmured Cynthia from behind.

Kampeng outstretched both his arms, smiling broadly to allay the strange men's fears while continuing to talk to them.

They answered back in a coarse manner that was alarming, yet they visibly loosened the grip on their weapons. That seemed a good sign. Dorothy was nervous, but she trusted Kampeng.

"Are they the Chao Fa?" Heller whispered, loud enough for Kampeng to hear.

"No," Kampeng answered during a break in the discussion with the Hmong. "If they Chao Fa, we dead already."

The palaver between Kampeng and the two men resumed, while everyone waited in suspense. Finally, he turned toward his companions. "It okay, they will take us."

The tribesmen slung their guns over their shoulders phlegmatically and turned to walk into the forest, with the troupe of strangers following.

It was only a matter of minutes before they arrived at the village, a squalid settlement crudely placed in the thick of the jungle. The houses were low structures that sat directly on the ground with walls of vertical wooden planks; their gabled roofs made of thatch or split bamboo. They were built in groups along curved lines following the contours, hidden in the trees. Amongst the houses were numerous corrals fenced with logs, where water buffaloes languidly chewed cud, and huge, hairy, grunting gray pigs sniffed the ground for food, all of which filled the air with acrid animal odors.

The men of the village, some having discussions while standing, others squatting on the ground, abruptly terminated their conversations and stared with suspicion at the strangers passing by. Young girls, sitting outside their houses on the little slabs of wood that served as stools, stopped their embroidering to gape at them. Most of the villagers were dressed in indigo cotton clothes, the men with short jackets and baggy trousers, the women in pleated skirts with elaborate multicolored designs, although some of the women also wore trousers.

"White Hmong," Heller commented to Cindy in a low voice. "See the women wearing pants like the men. Also Green Hmong, the women with the pleated skirts. A mixed village, huh, not typical, not typical at all."

Many of the kids, however, were dressed in western T-shirts and shorts, with faded and torn nylon jackets. Their first response at the sight of the farangs was to stand frozen, before timorously fleeing to a safer distance.

The two Hmong 'home guards', as Cynthia had referred to them, led them through the village until they stopped at one of the larger houses, where they were made to wait outside. A few mothers with babies in slings on their backs stood around looking at them, the infants adoringly garbed with tasseled caps.

"Look, you see the marks on the babies' foreheads?" Heller pointed out. "They make them with soot from the fire. Keeps the spirits from bothering their kids and making them sick. Also, the tassels on their caps are made for the same reason."

"They're so cute," Cindy lauded, smiling warmly. She couldn't resist taking a quick photo, zooming in on their faces.

The Hmong mothers smiled back, and some giggled bashfully, not insulted at being photographed.

"Okay," Kampeng said abruptly, as the two soldiers came back outside and made a motion for them to enter, "we go inside now."

The interior of the house was dark and low, and smelled strongly of smoke from the cooking fire burning inside a clay stove, which was set in the back room, evidently the kitchen. The floor was of packed and smoothed earth. The room that they were in was at the core of the house, and there were merely curtains partitioning off other rooms to the side. Furnishings were minimal: low stools of wood and a low table around which were gathered roughly ten individuals, men, women, and children, who were in the middle of their evening meal. The visitors were invited to sit down on the floor.

"It certainly is crowded in here," Cynthia commented.

Again Heller had an answer. "Yes, it's not uncommon for the married sons to remain living with their parents, bringing their wife and children to the home, and all of them living under a single roof."

The people who had been eating paused their meal to study the visitors with expressionless faces before resuming their munching. The children would continue to take furtive glances and then quickly look away, while the adults discreetly ignored the newcomers. Nobody spoke at first, and the sounds of chewing and lips smacking prevailed until Kampeng initiated a discussion. It was obvious to Dorothy by now that Kampeng could speak quite a bit of the Hmong language, as well as Kammu and English. He had really turned out to be an invaluable guide.

There was one old woman standing by the far wall, in front of a shelf full of various bowls. She was lighting incense and candles and uttering what sounded like incantations.

"She's informing the house spirits that strangers have arrived," Heller said. "Just in case any spirits from the jungle followed us here, they're asking for the house spirits' protection."

The meal apparently over, everyone got up as a few of the girls, who wore blue woolen scarves wrapped around their heads, cleared the wooden bowls and dishes off the table.

"This is the house of the village chief," Kampeng informed his farang comrades.

As if on cue, one of the side curtains fluttered open and emerging from behind the drape was a nuggety, toothless old man wearing a

European style shirt and a sarong. On his head was a black turban-like headdress.

The old man sat down in front of them on one of those upright slabs of wood that was a Hmong stool. He muttered a Hmong greeting to Kampeng, and then, directing his gaze to the farangs, said *"Comment allez vous?"*

Another French speaker! Dorothy was pleased, and so was Cynthia, for she knew French as well.

Both women answered him in enthusiastic French, but after that, the Hmong chief reverted back to Kampeng in Hmong language to hear the reason for their presence. The elderly gent kept nodding his head in interest, and then, when the old man seemed to have been satisfied, their short dialogue ended, affording Kampeng the opportunity to make introductions.

"This is chief of village. His name is Moua Tor. I tell him we want to go to Ban Ling Kao, and to meet Chao Baa. He ask why, so I want to know what I tell him."

Dorothy, instead of relaying her message through Kampeng, made the bold initiative of addressing Moua Tor directly. *"Parlez vous Francais, nes pas?"* she asked to confirm.

"An petite peu," he replied.

She told him in French that she was trying to find out about her son, an American pilot who had crashed during the war, and was certain that the Chao Baa knew about it.

The old man just nodded his head.

After that, Dorothy didn't know what to say, so Cynthia took over.

"Do you know where we could find the Chao Baa?"

He looked at her with a staid face. "His wanderings are a secret," the old man replied. "He could be anywhere out there." He waved his arm across the room to emphasize this point.

"Do you remember him from the time of the war?" Dorothy broke in. "When he was with the CIA army?"

Moua Tor put on an expression indicating befuddlement. It

wasn't due to his limited French, but rather it was the content of the question that confused him. "I don't think Chao Baa fight for *l'armee clandestine.*"

"You don't remember seeing him during the war?" Dorothy inquired further.

"Why me to remember? If he was CIA, I don't know. My people do not join *l'armee clandestine.* We fight against them."

Cindy put a hand on Dorothy's arm, signaling that a consultation was in order. "Dot, wait. Not all the Hmong fought in the secret army."

"People came to me," Moua Tor continued, "some Hmong from the Vang clan, and there were farang with them. They told me that the farang would give me money if I fight on their side. I tell them I take no side and we just want to be left alone. They tell me that I must kill Pathet Lao. I tell them I don't want to kill anybody. So they shoot me." He paused to lift up his shirt and show them his scar. "At that time I was local king. So they killed my daughter, my princess, and then they attack the village. We had to get our guns to defend ourselves. We drove them away."

A silence followed. The old man then began a conversation with Kampeng, more than likely a reiteration of what they had just discussed in French. Cindy on her part filled Heller in, who had been sitting quietly for once, mainly because he didn't know any French.

"Oh, yes," Kampeng suddenly said in English, "the chief he tell me that the village make the Spirit Gates to keep out the Chao Fa. He say Chao Fa same same secret army. He say if they come here, he kill them. Headman no like Chao Fa."

The girls whose heads were swathed in the blue scarves re-entered the house bearing large trays, one full of corncobs. The others had bowls of chicken soup and rice.

The food was appreciated, for they were truly hungry, not having had lunch. While eating there was more discussion between Kampeng and the headman.

"Moua Tor say he get someone to take us tomorrow morning. We sleep here. In jungle no one walk at night."

As they nibbled on the last of the corn, a man, rather tall for a Hmong, stood in the doorway, begging permission to enter. He walked in, cloaked in black, with what looked like a black cowboy hat, and both his attire and regal manner called to mind a swash-buckling figure, like a Southeast Asian Zorro. Once he had finished talking to the chief, he exchanged a few words with Kampeng and then sat down.

"This is man who come with us tomorrow," Kampeng announced. "He know English."

"Hello," the man said, using his English. He was a good-looking man in his late thirties, early forties, although his eyes were unusually small, like little slits, pushed into the hollow recesses formed by his bulging, high cheekbones. Yet in spite of their modest size, they emitted a dark intensity that was unsettling. "My name Ly Feng."

The three Americans said hello back.

"How do you know English?" Cindy asked.

"During war, I fight with Americans. They teach me."

Heller turned to Cindy. "But I thought you told me that this village fought against the Americans?"

"That true," the Hmong answered for her. "Ly Feng not from here."

"Oh," uttered Dorothy

"Chao Baa bring me here."

"What?" she exclaimed. "You know him?'

"Yes. We in *seminaa* together."

"You hear that Dot?" Cynthia exclaimed. "Seminar, a re-education camp. Now things make more sense. They caught the S.O.B and put him in a labor camp. After they broke his spirit and made sure he towed the line, they let him go."

"A slave of the evil giants!" Heller blurted out, referring to the story.

Ly Feng looked at them, not comprehending their babble.

Cynthia was rummaging through her knapsack and came out with a passport-sized photo. "Does he look like the Chao Baa?"

It was a snapshot of Robert Botkin, alias Mr. Sheen, which Cynthia had managed to obtain from one of her many contacts.

He took the picture and studied it, for quite a long time it seemed.

Heller was completely thunderstruck by all this fuss. "Hey, you guys are acting like you're looking for a real person."

Both Dorothy and Cynthia shouted at him in unison, "Yes!"

"Dot, show him the picture of Andy," urged Cynthia.

"What? It's no use Cynthia, I already tried that. Andrew is not the Chao Baa."

"Will you just show him! In my business you learn not to leave out any possibility, you have to cover all the angles."

Dorothy reluctantly went into her bag to retrieve the photograph. "Maybe this man?" she asked Ly Feng as she handed him the second photo.

Now he examined both of the snapshots. His gaze went from one picture to the other, while they all waited with baited breath. Kampeng himself was peering over the man's shoulder to also get a better look. The old headman, meanwhile, sat quietly entertained, despite the fact that he couldn't understand what was going on. Heller was also just as perplexed.

Ly Feng continued to inspect the two photographs. "I think it this man." He gave back one of the snaps. It was the one of Botkin. "But maybe not. I not sure."

"That man," Cindy proclaimed, holding up the photo, "is named Robert Botkin, Bobby Bo. You may have known him as Mr. Sheen."

Ly Feng's eyes opened wider in recognition. "Yes, I think it him."

"Where can we find him?" Cynthia continued, becoming impassioned, as she always did when hot on the trail.

"You want to see Chao Baa?"

"Yes."

"Not easy. He live in forest. Always move around."

"But you said he brought you here," Cindy pointed out, not missing a thing.

"Yes."

"If he brought you here, you must be his friend. You must know where he stays, isn't that so?"

Ly Feng didn't reply to that.

Cindy realized she was being too direct and aggressive. She would try another approach, to get in through the back door so to speak. "We want to go to Ban Ling Kao, because we think we might be able to meet him somewhere around there. Do you think that is a good idea?"

"Yes. He like to go there sometime. He think of home."

"Mr. Feng," Dorothy addressed, "Did the Chao Baa bring you here when you got out of prison?"

"No. Many years after. Three years ago. When he tell village to make Spirit Gates."

Heller was all ears, trying to figure out what was going on.

Cindy's turn again. "Mr. Feng, did you fight together with the Chao Baa, Mr. Sheen, during the war?"

Ly Feng turned to Kampeng and started talking in Lao. He couldn't handle the zealous interrogation he was undergoing at the hands of the two farang women. He decided he wouldn't talk to them directly. He had tried to be polite by speaking their language and now they were harassing him.

Kampeng spoke on his behalf. "He say he tired. He go now. Get sleep. Leave early tomorrow. We also sleep."

The man got up, gave a weak smile and departed.

Outside, the village was dimly illuminated with the scant, grayish glow of dusk. Heller was standing with Cynthia, attempting to find out what her and her mother were up to, but she brushed him off with a tone intended to keep his curiosity at bay. So instead he decided to leave it be for the moment and try to soften her up first.

"Wow, look at this!" he exclaimed, pointing to an antediluvian-looking contraption.

Cynthia smoked her cigarette while Heller gave a discourse on the primitive corn grinder, two large circular slabs of cut stone that sat on a hollow rock platform. The top slab was hooked up to an elaborate series of wooden shafts. He even went so far as to demonstrate how it worked, amusing an audience of peeping kids standing around them. By turning what appeared to be a handle, the top slab revolved against the stationary bottom one, a setup designed to crush and grind anything in between them. As the stone wheel turned abrasively, the kids laughed and cheered in admiration at the farang who apparently knew how to grind corn. Shortly after that, Kampeng urged them inside.

Four low bamboo beds, about a foot off the floor, had been brought out for the visitors to sleep on. The farangs got busy rummaging in their knapsacks and bags to fetch what they needed: toothbrushes, toilet paper, and other sundries. They did this by flashlight, as all the lamps in the house, as well as the cooking fire, had been extinguished.

"Why is everyone going to bed so early?" Cynthia asked.

"Most people who live in the jungle like to eat before it gets dark," Heller explained to her, "after which they put out the lights and fires. The spirit world is the converse of the human world. Our night is their day, so about this time, I guess, the spirits are waking up. The lights and the smell of food would attract them. If there's any leftover food they would find it and eat it, and then if you ate such food, you would become half-spirit yourself," he stated, lying down on his bed, which was conveniently located next to hers.

Kampeng was soon snoring robustly, deep within an imperturbable slumber. Heller and Cynthia continued to chatter for a while, and their murmured whisperings were often punctuated by Cindy's giggles, keeping Dorothy awake. Eventually, the long, event-filled day claimed their energies, and they all fell fast asleep.

They were woken up the next morning by Ly Feng, who was

carrying an automatic rifle, and after a hasty re-packing of their bags, all of them set off into the pallid light of dawn.

"How long will it take us to reach Ban Ling Kao?" Dorothy asked Kampeng as they began their trek.

"Two days. We will sleep in forest for one night."

Cynthia was talking with Heller. "AK-47," she told him, pointing to the gun slung over Ly Feng's shoulder. "Hope he doesn't have to use it."

Leaving the village, they passed by fields of stalk-like plants some with bulbous buds, and others that were in full bloom, making a pretty scene with white, purple, and rose-colored flowers rippling in the breeze. In the distance were numerous women amongst the flowers who appeared to be running their hands up and down the stalks.

"Opium," Cynthia announced. "They use this little knife to slit the plant and let the sap out."

The poppy fields ended and the wilderness began. They hiked through the jungle, first up and then down. In the beginning, this excursion promised to be easier than the trip to Pu Khe had been, for the trail here was in better condition, which suggested it was used quite frequently. But this didn't make Dorothy feel any less tired. She had come to the conclusion that she had had enough of this jungle trekking to last the rest of her life. On the other hand, Jeff and Cindy seemed to be in good spirits, buoyantly bantering, cooing and laughing. It was becoming apparent that the two were growing fond of each other.

As they descended, the jungle growth became denser. Stepping over rocks and roots had caused Dorothy's dormant blisters to painfully wake up from their weeklong respite. It was then that she realized they would have to walk back as well, and with that thought, her purpose faltered. They could go all the way to this supposedly mythical village and still not find Botkin. They could walk for days, even months, without ever finding him. This whole idea was a feckless waste of time, energy, and trouble.

At one point Heller and Cynthia ambled a little ways off the trail to admire a tree festooned with resplendent orchids, and naturally, to take pictures of it.

"Stay on trail!" Ly Feng shouted at them.

They obeyed his instruction, but not without Cynthia wanting to know why. "You think there is Chao Fa here?" she asked.

"No. Too close to Moua Tor's village. But bombies are everywhere."

"What?" Heller vociferated.

"Cluster Bombs," Dorothy told him, glad at the chance to lecture him. "About the size of a small ball, but very deadly."

Resuming the way, Kampeng and Ly Feng talked non-stop in low whispers as they led the little troupe in single file through the undergrowth. In the rear, Jeff and Cindy, delighting in the hike, were exuberantly loquacious. Dorothy, in the middle, was quiet, lacking the energy to make idle conversation. The only consolation she had were the beautiful views of lovely green mountains that confronted them whenever they climbed out of the thick vegetation.

It grew hot and humid even before they stopped for lunch, which they eventually did in a shady grove of forest figs, the whining of the cicadas reaching a feverish pitch. Of course, the cooking of rice in bamboo containers fascinated both Cynthia and Heller, who again seemed determined to document it with photographs, and their bubbly enthusiasm over this whole trip was depressing Dorothy. Why was that, she wondered to herself.

"Laos is such a gorgeous country," Cynthia concluded, sitting together with Heller on a large rock. "Isn't it, Dot?"

"Yes," she answered in a wearied tone.

"What's the matter, Dot? Are you tired?"

"Yes, I suppose so. I feel drained, emotionally as well as physically."

Heller also showed his concern. "You want me to carry your pack for you?"

Dorothy smiled. He really was sweet, despite his motor mouth.

"No, that's okay, Jeff. Thank you anyway, it's very kind of you."

Kampeng began to dish out the lunch on the big teak leaves that served as their plates.

Eating the rice with her hands, Cynthia was indeed having a good time. Right now she had a wide, self-satisfied smile on her face as she confessed, "I haven't had an experience like this since I went trekking in Borneo four years ago."

"You were in Borneo?" Heller asked her, and that started off a conversation concerning ancient civilizations that built great irrigation canals etc etc., a topic which once again excluded Dorothy, who sat quietly, picking at her rice until it was time to move on.

In the afternoon, however, while treading through the thick forest, everyone's chitchat evaporated into silence as the heat of the day grew stronger. The thick odor of the tropical jungle filled their nostrils, and that familiar feeling of fatigue was once again haunting Dorothy. The light dimmed to a greenish gloom in an airless hothouse. Even Heller was quiet.

When they finally stopped for the night, Ly Feng told them that they weren't far, only a half-day's walk away, and they should arrive before lunch the next day.

The usual preparations were made for cooking.

"I don't understand," Heller said out of the blue, while waiting for the rice to boil in their bamboo vessels. "How come some Hmong fought on the American side, and other Hmong with the communists?"

Cynthia, squatting on the ground next to him, was more than willing to answer his question. "That's because there was a rivalry between two clans, a rivalry that the French created. The Lo were always the dominating clan in Xieng Khouang, but the French put the Ly clan in charge to counter their power. Isn't that right, Mr. Feng?"

"It start before French," he argued. "Ly Touby, he marry daughter of Lo Blia Faydang. Touby, he beat her, and she run back to father. Then she die. Faydang then hate Touby. But French put Touby in charge. Faydang get mad, join Viet Minh and fight French. Then join Pathet Lao and fight American, while Touby and his people go with CIA army."

The history lesson was deferred until Kampeng finished dishing out the rice on their leafy dishes.

"What clan are you, Mr. Feng?" Dorothy asked as they ate.

"I am Ly of course."

"That's right," Heller remembered, "the clan name comes first. Ly Feng."

Cynthia posed a question of her own. "The Hmong who formed the Chao Fa are from those families that fought for the CIA. You also fought for the CIA. So how come you didn't join the Chao Fa?"

"I join," he countered.

A disquieting halt to the conversation developed, until Kampeng managed to clarify matters.

"He Chao Fa before, but now no more."

Dorothy jumped in. "Why did you leave the Chao Fa, Mr. Feng?" she demanded to know.

"Chao Baa, he tell me to leave."

"And so you listen to what the Chao Baa tells you?"

"Yes."

"Why?"

"I try to kill Chao Baa, but I can't, he…more powerful, and after that he not angry with me. He not kill me."

Dorothy was beginning to get worked up. She knew what Ly Feng would say next, and she would argue it. If there was nothing else that she could accomplish while here in Laos, she would at least strive to ruin Botkin's reputation and shatter the myth that he had created for himself.

"Do you think the Chao Baa is a good man?"

"No. He great man."

"No, he is not. He is a coward, a murderer…"

Cynthia placed a firm arm on her. "Dot, take it easy…"

Dorothy was still ranting "…an evil man who tricks simple

people and hides behind a wall of lies!"

Ly Feng turned to face Dorothy with a grave countenance. "Ah, you don't know, you don't know," was all he said.

These differences of opinion put a dampener on their evening meal, which was taken in an almost hostile silence. When they had finished eating, they curled up in their blankets, mostly for protection against insects rather than for warmth, with Jeff and Cindy picking a spot together a discreet distance away from the others.

"Do not go too far," Ly Feng warned.

During the night there was another incident which would once again arouse Dorothy's ire. In the darkness, the sound of Cindy's moaning grew to sharp little cries, which made her sound as if she were in distress. But she wasn't in distress, was she? Dorothy surmised angrily to herself. They were doing it, with all of us here. Didn't they have any shame?

Apparently it was bothering Kampeng as well, for he was tossing and turning. Dorothy felt she had to apologize for them.

"I'm sorry, Kampeng. They have no manners."

"They will attract the attention of the spirits."

But Ly Feng wasn't troubled. "Don't worry. It is normal. That is the way our girls and boys do it."

Waking up at an ungodly hour, before the sun was barely over the horizon, wasn't really that difficult when sleeping in the jungle. For Dorothy, she was getting quite used to it. She sat up and regarded the misty morning with some apprehension, as if something ominous was afoot. She couldn't shake this negative feeling, even as the two Laotian men dotingly served breakfast of coffee and rice. Cindy and Heller wandered over hand in hand, behaving in the overly solicitous manner characteristic of new lovers. The sanguine prattle that they engaged in while sipping their coffee did nothing to lift Dorothy's spirits.

As they made preparations to leave their bivouac, Cynthia squatted by Dorothy, who was lacing her hiking boots.

"Never judge a book by its cover," she giggled impishly, "I mean, to look at him, you wouldn't think he was such an animal."

"Cynthia, aren't you ashamed? Everyone could hear you."

"Really? Were we that loud? I thought we were far enough away. I'm sorry."

"You could have attracted the bad spirits."

"That loud?"

"Bo ben yang," Dorothy told her, not wishing to discuss it further. "Let's get going." She stood up and struggled with her pack, but Cynthia still felt the need to explain her actions.

"Listen, Dot, don't be angry. I know this trip isn't exactly a fun-filled vacation for you, but for me, I can't let the romance and adventure get by me. I'm forty-one already, and I want to grab as much out of this life while I still can. You only go around once in this world."

Heller appeared out of nowhere and propped his head between the two women. "Not if you're a Buddhist," he joked blithely. He was, understandably, in a wonderful mood, with a mawkish grin on his face. He drew near to Cindy and held her hand while he gave her an affectionate peck on the cheek.

Why was she so upset, Dorothy asked herself. Did she still consider Cynthia to be Andrew's sweetheart? It was a mistake to have brought Heller along. Even Cynthia. The both of them, instead of providing pleasant company, were making things complicated.

Underway once more, they moved through a wonderland of greenery. Above them a lattice of vegetation formed a hanging garden of ferns, creepers and orchids. The light all around them was a pale lime, as if they were walking through a giant experimental arboretum. Loud rustling sounds gave them a sudden fright.

"Bo pen yang," assured Kampeng. "Only monkeys."

In due course, they ascended a steep slope and no one, not even the Laotians, could spare a breath for talking. As if in compensation, the forest growth thinned and the air became cooler and less oppressive. They continued to climb until the terrain leveled off into a flat shelf. There, they came upon a cleared area where they saw several huts on stilts, apparently abandoned. Heller broke from the rest of the group to run among the middle of these crude structures.

"Yes, yes," he cried, "the Village of the White Monkey!"

"No," Ly Feng called out, "this not village. Before, it *seminaa* camp. No more now."

"But there isn't any fence," Cynthia observed.

"Yes, no fence," Kampeng said. "This different re-education. This work camp. More freedom, but still prisoner."

Heller walked back disappointed, a bit abashed at his hasty enthusiasm.

Ly Feng offered another piece of local lore. "Chao Baa, he stay here, he prisoner in this seminaa before he live in Ban Ling Kao."

Passing the deserted labor camp, they were soon descending down a tree-covered slope. Down below was a grassy valley, where circular patterns of vegetation and dusky ponds reflected the bomb-cratered terrain. Cynthia astutely pointed this out.

"See how the land has been carved out by the bombing?"

"Oh yeah," remarked Heller.

Ly Feng halted for a moment. "You can see from here, down in valley. That is where Ban Ling Kao be before."

From where they stood, it didn't look like much. Just a lowland forest with patches. On the far side, however, there were soft green squares, apparently fallow fields. Towering over the distant meadows was a series of rain-sculptured mountains, with thick jungle growing around sheer rock faces. The dark hill nearest the settlement had a huge barren hollow, a glaring red wound hewed out of its side, as if a giant's mouth had bitten into it.

"There was a landslide there," Cynthia noticed, pointing to the broad scar on the hillside.

"Oh, yeah," Heller whined, gazing with interest.

"Yes, mountain fall," Ly Feng affirmed, "many years ago when it rain too much. Chao Baa, he save village."

So he has power over the forces of nature as well, Dorothy noted scornfully. This man was exceptionally insidious. The way he had beguiled the populace was almost frightening. "And just how did he do that, Mr. Ly?" she questioned mordantly.

"He know before it happen, he make village people leave homes to come up here," Ly answered.

Kampeng supported this statement. "He see in dream," he affirmed.

After that Ly Feng cued them to move along by walking ahead with a renewed pace.

They picked their way down the mountainside and reached the bottom in less than an hour. Now they could see that the area they were in had indeed once been a settlement. There were crude lanes and criss-crossing paths, smoothed out spots, and standing timbers that marked former dwellings, most of them charred black by fire.

Heller was entranced. "The Village of the White Monkey, yes?" he asked for confirmation.

"Yes."

Walking through the ghost village was eerie. It held an atmosphere of foreboding, which was due in part to the strange color of the sky, now a reddish hue from the smoke of distant burning fields.

Astonishingly, they came upon one compound that was relatively intact, with two houses on stilts—a large, clapboard one made of timbers, and a smaller hut made with bamboo. There was also a granary and a pen, presumably for water buffalo.

"I think this where Chao Baa live before," Ly Feng disclosed.

Both Heller and Cynthia tore away from the group to enter the compound.

Underneath the bigger house was a large, remarkable-looking, wooden device with a complicated framework.

"What's that under the house?" Cynthia crowed out interrogatively.

"Hey, it looks like a homemade loom, for weaving!" Heller interjected.

Ly Feng commanded them to stop. "Do not go inside!"

"But there might be some clues," Cynthia objected.

"I just wanted to look at the loom," Heller pleaded.

"No one go in," Ly Feng restated.

After taking a few quick shots with their 35-millimeters, they turned back reluctantly, not wanting to upset their guide, who also happened to be carrying a big gun.

Further on they came upon another undisturbed structure, a large one made of wood with a corrugated iron roof, surrounded by a walled compound.

"This is the village temple, isn't it?" Dorothy inquired.

"Yes, Chao Fa army not go in temple," the Hmong guide told them. "This also end of village."

Beyond the temple they could see that the forest began again.

"So what do we do now? Wait for the Chao Baa to come?" Cynthia wanted to know.

Ly Feng looked up into the great mountain range behind the derelict village. "Chao Baa has small house in mountain. Sometime go there. He never come down here."

"That's it! That's where we want to go!" Cynthia fervently exclaimed.

"Very dangerous," he warned.

No one said anything for a while, and in those moments Dorothy was aware of a sick feeling in her stomach. She wasn't so sure that she wanted to continue with this mission, growing more tremulous at meeting Botkin the closer that she got to him.

"Miss Doro-tee want to go?" Kampeng asked her.

She didn't reply, but instead walked away.

"Dot?" Cynthia was about to go to her but Kampeng lightly touched her arm.

"She want to be alone," he intuited.

As she walked, Dorothy fumbled in her shirt pocket for her Xanax, and taking a swig from her water bottle, swallowed one of the pills. She had come so far, but now all she wanted to do was to go home, admitting to herself that she didn't have the strength or courage to face this man. She couldn't forgive him, and confronting him wouldn't bring Andrew back. It was pointless. After a few minutes of self-deliberation, she turned around and walked back to the rest of the group.

"Cynthia?"

"Yes, Dot?"

"What should we do?"

"Whatever you think we should do, we're all behind you."

Maybe it was the way Cynthia had said that, or maybe it was the Xanax kicking in, or maybe it was some new untapped resolve emerging. Whatever the reason, she steeled herself to face the unknown ahead of her. "Let's go."

Just as everyone turned to forge ahead, Heller blurted out, "Hey, aren't we going to have lunch? I'm starving."

It was a sensible idea that no one had considered in the high drama of the moment. It was nearly midday, and this was as good a place as any, probably better than what they would find where they were going. Not only because the temple compound afforded a rather attractive and comfortable spot, but, as Heller was to suggest next, "There's a hell of a lot of fruit trees around here."

Although it was still the dry season, the fruit trees at the temple bore bananas, mangos, papaya, and other exotic fruits. Enthusiastically, they picked, poked, and threw stones at these to bring them down. Gorging themselves on their harvest they found no need to cook rice.

But despite Heller's brilliant suggestion, he managed to put his foot in his mouth once again. Luckily, they were sitting on the ground quite a good distance away from Kampeng and Ly Feng, who had gotten up to talk among themselves.

"You know," Heller said, "if this guy really exists, then that makes my thesis even more relevant. He's a living example of how cognitive dissonance resolves itself through changes in identity and personality. This could lead to a major study."

"Oh shut up, Jeffrey!" Cindy grumbled disdainfully.

"I'm sorry," he said, naturally surprised, and hurt by her harsh tone.

Half of Dorothy said 'Hurray', while the other half felt guilty.

"From now on, I won't say anything." He himself was angry, and fed up that these two women weren't being truthful with him. "I'll be just like you, and not tell you any of my secrets."

Deceit was something that Dorothy had never before practiced. Heller wasn't to blame.

"No, Jeff, you're right," she said contritely. "I'm sorry. It's true that we haven't been honest with you. I apologize. Forgive me. Cynthia, apologize to Jeffrey."

"I'm sorry, Jeff." She leaned over, gave him a hug and kissed him on his cheek, an act that touched Dorothy who looked on, making her eyes a bit moist.

"I'm trying to find out what happened to my son," Dorothy confessed. "He was an Air Force pilot, who supposedly was shot down, and they gave me some ashes and bone fragments, and to make a long story short, I found out that they weren't his remains. We have some evidence that leads us to believe he was assassinated by the CIA, and we also believe that this man who masquerades as the Chao Baa was one of the men assigned to kill him."

Heller was amazed. "Oh wow, why didn't you tell me that in the first place?" Then, thinking about his own request for secrecy, regarding his own, what now seemed petty, endeavors, he discreetly understood. "Never mind, I understand."

It was Cindy's occasion to confess. "And to make this a really poignant situation, I'm not Dot's daughter. I was Andy's fiancée, and I feel responsible, because I was against the war, and I put a lot of pressure on him, and, I think I made him desert. I think I made him ditch his plane."

"Cynthia! You think you were responsible for him crashing his plane?" This notion had actually been with Dorothy for some time now, though she never wanted to admit it, even to herself.

"Yes, that's what I believe, Dot. He went down just a month after

I had sent him that last letter which condemned what he was doing. In that letter I told him it was over between us. Once he deserted, they sent the assassination team because he knew things that could compromise the air war, and they couldn't risk him being captured by the enemy. All the signs point to that."

They all were quiet after that.

"I'm sorry," Heller said again. "I didn't know any of this. I'm sorry if I've been insensitive."

Cynthia hugged him for the second time. Straightening up, she said to Dorothy, "Dot, do you think you can handle facing him? I mean, I think that's the problem you're dealing with right now, isn't it?"

Dorothy turned her face to gaze abstractedly in another direction. "Yes."

"Listen to me, Dot. I have to tell you what's been on my mind for some time now. We don't know that Botkin killed Andy. In fact, I have a theory that he did the opposite—I think he tried to save him."

"Cynthia, you can't be serious."

Cindy grew animated at the chance to explain her conjecture. "Remember in Anatoly's scribbles he said, and I quote, 'Botkin got weird on me and I had to carry out the mission in my own way.' Remember that?"

"Yes, I remember asking you about that."

"This is what I've pieced together: Botkin is a schizo, not a stable personality, he flips out from being in the jungle too long with Buddhists, feels repulsed by all the horrible things he's done and decides he doesn't want to kill anymore. He backs out when it comes time to do Andy in, maybe tries to stop Anatoly, but Anatoly carries out the objective. Botkin, meanwhile, has to run away, because he's just fucked his life up, being that all he knows is how to be a frigging gladiator. Also the conflicts in his mind, they must have been incredible. And that's why I decided to kidnap Jeffrey, I thought he might be useful."

"Useful?" Heller's face now showed a touch of disgust. "Kidnap?

So that's what it was?"

"I'm sorry, Jeff."

For the third time she gave him a hug, but he wasn't receptive. In fact, he resisted her embrace and got up to go away and sulk.

Cindy sighed dejectedly. "Why can't I stop myself from being a bitch?"

"You're not a bitch, Cynthia!" Dorothy objected fervidly. "It's a normal spat. Go and beg forgiveness for treating him the way you did and start all over. Believe me, I know these things. Hell," she said in spite of herself, "I was married for thirty-seven years." For some inexplicable reason, she now felt she had an interest in the success of their romance.

The two women held hands for a brief moment, before Cindy got up to console her young lover.

"Okay!" Kampeng shouted brusquely from where he was standing. "We go!"

Moving ahead into the forest, all of them lapsed into an uneasy wordlessness. Adding to the disconsolate mood of the farangs was the taciturn caution of the two Laotian men escorting them. All this imparted a somber aspect to the afternoon. Or perhaps it was the way the day was getting darker from the unearthly haze brought on by the smoke of the burning fields. At times they were able see some of these fires, irregular patches and serpentine lines glowing on the mountaintops, whenever they reached a point where they could observe what was around them.

They halted at one such spot that afforded a panoramic view. Huge hogbacks of sedimentary rocks angled down like cleaved tables, their surfaces encrusted with a broken covering of forest. There were also broad massifs, boldly erect with mighty faces carved out of their limestone cliffs. The mountains seemed endless, hordes of them, all shapes and sizes, jumbled amongst each other until they faded in the blur of the horizon. The expanse of sky above them dimly radiated a bizarre, dirty-pink hue.

"Weird, huh, the way the fires make the sky reddish?" Heller remarked needlessly.

"Yeah," Cindy concurred. "Looks like a Martian sky."

When Ly Feng deemed it was time to move on, they once again descended to re-enter the jungle. For most of the excursion the little troupe were enclosed by walls of vegetation, and this, together with the spongy humus underfoot, succeeded in completely absorbing all sound. Even the sharp plashing sounds they made in their struggle with the underbrush were hollow and muffled. Other noises were amplified disproportionately, especially the scuttling of unseen creatures among the fallen leaves which gave out an unsettling clatter. Thorns and branches tore at their clothes as they made their way through, their heads bowed down in growing weariness. There was no breeze, and the air pressed heavily upon them. Cindy looked up, and what she saw made her suddenly stop. "Holy shit, look at that!"

Above them were gigantic spiders clinging onto their dangling webs, which were strung out over the high foliage. Their hideous bodies were several inches long.

"No worry, they no bother you," Kampeng assured condescendingly, in a tone that indicated they weren't to dawdle on account of such trite things. Cynthia, however, deemed it worthy enough to take a picture.

It seemed like forever, picking their way through the murky, overgrown forest, yet there was still light enough to continue, and continue they did, in a tedious rhythm through the entangled path, until their leader, Ly Feng, abruptly halted.

"Somebody else in forest," he understated in a low voice. "Ahead of us, and behind us also."

Dorothy couldn't accept this. She didn't need any more melodrama than what the situation had already provided.

"How do you know?" Cindy asked.

Kampeng explained. "Ly Feng know Forest Spirit language. Kampeng also know. We not alone."

"Jungle too quiet," Ly feng added in a low whisper.

"What should we do?" Heller cried out, obviously spooked as well.

"Shush!" Ly Feng warned. "Follow me."

They had only taken a few steps when a dreadful noise stopped them in their tracks.

It was a sinister bellow that clearly communicated a threat, the sound of a great beast roaring its defiance. Unnervingly, its distance or direction wasn't easy to pinpoint—it seemed to emanate from everywhere, a penetrating resonance that bounced off every surface of the tropical rainforest.

"That is Chao Baa's elephant," Ly Feng said with conviction.

From somewhere out there, another resounding call reached them, one that shook the dark wilderness with its fury and challenge, hurling shrill vibrations that rattled the air.

Dorothy was suddenly seized with an uncontrollable fear. It is hard to imagine how frightful that inhuman noise was in the middle of the jungle. This augmented the terror she already had of finally coming face to face with him, the Chao Baa, the evil Robert Botkin. She felt that uncomfortable sensation of her heart beating stiffly, constricting her as it increased its tempo. She became short of breath, and her body started to shake, symptoms she had experienced countless times before. Despite the Xanax she had taken, she was having a panic attack. Losing her wits, she bolted back the way they had come.

"Miss Dor-tee!" Kampeng shouted. "Where you go?" He chased after her.

As she ran she heard another shrieking trumpeting of the elephant, and she made an irrational response by going to the nearest tree and hugging onto it for dear life.

After that, what happened next she would never be able to recall with utmost certainty.

They came out of nowhere, these strange figures dressed in black. Kampeng was running forward, yelling, "Miss Doro-tee!" when a loud crack echoed through the forest and a big red spot appeared on the front of Kampeng's white T-shirt, from which his blood erupted in spurts. She could see Kampeng's eyes bulging wide before he fell forward, flopping lifelessly to the ground.

She was telling herself that this wasn't happening, she was dreaming.

One of these men in black approached the fallen body, turned it over and began smashing the head with the butt of his large gun. The violence of the act made her scream. She pressed herself so hard against the tree that the rough bark cut into her cheeks. Tighter and tighter she gripped the tree, as if to get inside it and hide from the horror.

This isn't happening.

Another of the black-garbed figures came toward her brandishing a long knife that was so long that it was almost a sword. He grabbed her hair and yanked her head back, making her lose her hold on the tree, and all she could see was that huge knife about to cut open her throat. Her body went into spasms, convulsing in the shock that she was about to experience her own death. This thought so numbed her that she didn't hear the crashing sounds behind her.

This wasn't happening.

She found herself suddenly released from her assailant's grasp, falling to the floor and looking up at an incredible scene. The man who had been trying to slit her throat was now in midair, coiled up in the trunk of a huge elephant looming before her, a horrible crazed beast with these big, pointy, sharp tusks. There was a bald-headed, emaciated-looking man with sunglasses sitting on top of the creature, screaming furiously, his arms and shoulders blue-green with tattoos, the rest of his body covered in orange-colored robes.

This isn't happening, it's not happening.

The elephant finally let his captive down, who immediately took off in a panic. The elephant then lifted up its leg and the man who must be the Chao Baa stepped down on it and came towards her as she made a frantic effort to stand up. He approached her arrogantly, purposefully, whipping off his sunglasses, revealing his fierce eyes.

Dorothy did the only thing she was able to do under the circumstances.

She fainted.

Book II

The Legend of the Chao Baa

Chapter 15

Laos 1990 / Laos 1970 - 1976

"The trouble with life is that we lead it forwards and understand it backwards."
Soren Kierkegaard, Danish philosopher, circa 1840's

"What should we do about this woman?"

The Chao Baa turned around and took a few steps away from Major Sousat, his hands clasped behind his back, his orange robes swaying about his body as he walked, and with his head bowed in deep pensiveness. He halted stiffly, pausing to give out a barely audible sigh of vacillation as he looked up at the forest around him, a forest that had once appeared serene and soothing, but now loomed dark and somber. The mountains behind his crude timber dwelling seemed to stare down at him with scorn, as if admonishing him for a life of lies. For over twenty years he had lived in the Lao People's Democratic Republic, having been reborn into another being, totally cutoff from any connections to a bygone world that was literally a lifetime away. Until now.

It was understandable then, how this new turn of events forced him to reflect upon the course his life had taken during that time, a course that was quite extraordinary, yet inextricably bound up with the history of the young impoverished nation that had become his home. The crossroads where it had all started, taking shelter with the monks at the Forest Temple, back in the beginning of 1970...

In those days, the war over the Plain of Jars had become a marathon arm wrestle between the communists backed by Vietnam and the rightist forces backed by the US. A tenacious struggle, each side pressing forward, then resisting the opponent's renewed force, back and forth, until by the beginning of 1970, it had become clear that a turning point had been reached, and the right arm was trembling, going down in a gradual, agonizing defeat.

In February of 1970, the Pathet Lao and North Vietnamese overran the Plain of Jars and swept across the area all the way to Muong Soui, retaking it. Vang Pao withdrew his troops from the eastern side. For years there had been talk of B-52 strikes, though Washington had consistently refused to authorize them. But given the deteriorating situation, Nixon finally approved the use of these weapons of mass destruction, airplanes as large as commercial airliners, each carrying fifty tons of bombs, the perfect tool to carry out saturation bombing.

The B-52s were to no avail, however. Sam Thong had fallen, and the CIA-Hmong headquarters at Long Chieng was under siege. For the rest of the war, they did all they could do just to hang on.

At thirty thousand feet you couldn't see nor hear them, and so the terror unleashed by a B-52 drop seems to come from out of nowhere and into everywhere. All at once, the entire horizon erupted into blazing destruction with an ear-shattering din that ripped the air and jostled the ground, a tsunami-like wave of explosions pummeling everything in its path, advancing over the ground as an unstoppable force, threatening to engulf him.

Oh shit, nowhere to hide! He dived into a steep stream gully and cowered in fear, knowing that he was in the hands of fate. There was nothing else he could do. The bombs were two thousand pounders, and if any landed closer than a football field away from him, he was surely a goner. He heard objects whistling past him, felt the whizzing of the air above him…the pressure waves were so intense they seemed to originate from inside him, rattling him like a limp rag and blowing his ears out. He remembered he was praying to God.

It was over almost as abruptly as it had begun, only minutes. He knew it was over, because B-52s don't turn around for another strike.

He staggered to his feet, warily listening, watching, waiting.

Climbing out of the streambed, he walked through a smoking wasteland, through a netherworld where the earth had been turned over hundreds of times, a chaos of scattered heaps of soil, broken rock, and shattered trees. And with no other option but to go on, he kept on walking. He stumbled in a daze for almost two days before he finally arrived at a place that defied belief.

It was amazing, not only because this place had escaped the bombing, but also because he had no idea of how he had gotten here. It was an oasis of tranquil splendor, like a fairyland carved out of the jungle, adorned with graceful bodhi trees, fragrant frangipani, and idyllic, large-leafed palms. The Forest Temple.

Two monks with shaven heads, wearing their Grecian, saffron-colored robes, spotted him by the timber gate and came out to receive him.

He was still quite fazed and, not conscious of it, muttered to himself in English. "How the hell did the B-52s miss this place?"

"Yang-kee?" one of them asked him.

He looked at the young, bald-headed monk, still trying to get his bearings on reality, still slowly surfacing from his stupor of wonderment. "Yang, what?" he asked.

"Kon American?"

He took a lengthy moment before answering. *"Jao. Suu* Richard."

"Ree-chart?" the youthful bonze parroted. His comrade stood behind him, silent, with expressionless eyes.

"Jao. Richard Johnson."

"Jon-sown?" he echoed again for confirmation.

"Jao."

"Why have you come to the Forest Temple?"

Why? How the hell did he know? He stumbled on it, that's all. *"Bo huu.* I don't know."

"You are welcome if you wish to enter. There is food if you are hungry."

"Yes."

He walked behind the robed twosome to enter the becalmed

courtyard, who in turn accompanied him to an open-sided gazebo, a structure they referred to as the *sala*, which enclosed a small table made of stone, and where he was told to wait. In spite of his unusual appearance—his torn clothes, haggard looks, and a head that was as bald as theirs and much more clean-shaven than his face—the young priests displayed no detectable reaction to his enigmatic arrival. The pair of monks departed stoically, leaving him alone for a few minutes, until a timid boy around ten years of age showed up bearing a tray laden with bowls of sticky rice and a green vegetable soup, as well as a glass and a bottle of water. As soon as these items were set down on the rock-hewn table, he pounced on the food, not bothering with the courtesy of waiting for the boy to leave, and ate greedily until nothing was left. Upon finishing his meal, he leaned back on the bench of the gazebo and began a chorus of belching, then reached into his shirt pocket for a packet of Lucky Strikes. He took one out and lit it, and with the first few draws of it he coughed violently.

"Oh man, I don't think I need these." He promptly threw the half-finished butt on the ground.

Just then, one of the monks returned, the one who had previously done all the talking. "It is best you see the abbot first, if you would like to stay here," he advised.

So he got up from the bench and loped along in a careless, jaunty gait, in comical contrast to the prim step of the young monk, until they came to the abbot's hut. He trod heavily up the rickety bamboo ladder and, following the example of his escort, took his shoes off before entering. He walked in upright, and that was his first mistake.

The monk who had led him there was already on his knees, and he grabbed Ree-chart's arm to pull him down. "Be respectful! You cannot be higher than the abbot."

As Ree-chart got down to his knees, the monk crawled a short distance forward on all fours and stopped at a deferential distance before placing his palms down and bringing his forehead to the floor three times. The object of his veneration was a gaunt old man in an orange toga, who sat cross-legged in a ceremonious posture upon a platform made of wickered bamboo, his back resting upon a cushion positioned against the wall. Two huge candles, three feet high, stood on each side of the platform, framing his motionless figure in the flickering firelight. The elderly priest was so thin that, in his robes, he literally looked like a bag of bones.

"Venerable Kru Jarun, I've come to inform you of our visitor, who wishes to stay here."

The old man on the platform bent himself forward to get a better look at the stranger. His hollow, bony face folded into a severe scowl. "And why do you wish to stay here?" he asked the stranger directly. "For refuge? Or do you wish to learn the teachings of the Enlightened One?" His booming voice didn't seem to fit his frail appearance.

"Both," the stranger replied.

The abbot leaned back upon his cushion. "That is an honest answer. I warn you, however, that if you are seeking refuge, the only place you will find it will be in yourself." The old priest pursed his withered lips and gave him a long meaningful look. "Very well, I have no objections. Pra Boon will see to your needs. In turn, you will obey Pra Boon's every instruction. Is that agreed?"

"I agree."

"You may leave."

So that was it? No 'who are you' or 'where do you come from'?

"Aren't you interested in knowing who I am?" the stranger boldly asked.

"Interested?" the elderly priest repeated rhetorically. "Interest implies clinging to the mundane world of men. I have no such interest. As for who you really are, and where you came from, I will know soon enough. The reason why you have arrived here at our temple is another matter, and that can only be answered by knowing your Karma. Go now."

The younger monk prostrated himself again three times, then

crawled backwards on his knees. The farang called Ree-chart made a clumsy attempt to do the same.

Once outside, Ree-chart Jon-sown dumped out the pack of Lucky Strikes, shaking out the cigarettes, and then crumpling up the packet to throw it aggressively to one side.

"Would you like to look around our monastery?" the monk, Pra Boon, asked, ignoring what the strange bald-headed farang had just done.

He was shown the *kuti*, where the monks lived, basic bamboo huts on stilts, and the *sim*, the large hall that housed the Buddha image and where most of the religious ceremonies were held. The outside of this latter building was as beautiful as that of any temple, with its cascading curved roofs and elegant porticos running along the sides. The interior of the sim was dark and simple, but with a quiet beauty, fashioned from timber. The wooden beams and columns were of unfinished teak and mahogany, but they had little intricate designs painted on them. A massive golden Buddha image sat magnificently at the end of the hall, imperially imposing its presence over scores of smaller statues, tiered umbrellas, and other artifacts that surrounded it, including a long gondola-shaped candleholder with the heads of dragons on each end. The smells of incense and beeswax were pervasive.

Departing the sim, they resumed their walk around the compound, where Pra Boon pointed out the bell tower, an attractively ornamental structure that looked like a small-scale, oriental version of a lighthouse, and which accommodated both a giant drum and a large bronze-colored gong. In another corner of the compound was a vegetable garden. Throughout the grounds were numerous skinny dogs hanging about: lying, prowling, and scavenging, for the most part, miserable creatures with their fur eaten away in patches of skin disease.

During this little tour, he also saw at least five ratty-looking kids scurrying about, all of them boys.

"Where do these children come from?"

"They are the *dekvat*, the temple children. All monasteries have temple boys. I myself was once a dekvat in the temple of my own village. Of course, you must mean, here, in the middle of the war, it is surprising to see them. Is that what you are asking?"

"Yeah, I guess so," the American replied in English. In Lao he answered "Men, men," which was a local way of responding affirmatively.

"These children were found wandering the mountains. They are orphans of the war. We took them in."

"They're all boys."

"Yes, girls cannot stay with monks in the monastery. We took the girls to the Pathet Lao, who promised they would take care of them."

Evening had come, and the last of the daylight was silently departing. Timely enough, he was shown Pra Boon's kuti, where he himself would stay. It was a flimsy structure made entirely out of bamboo, and with a faded cotton curtain down the middle of the interior already in place as a partition. Almost as soon as Pra Boon had made the new sleeping place, Ree-chart laid down in it and fell into a deep sleep.

He was awakened by the sound of gongs; a repetitive bonging that started slowly then increased its frequency until it became a din that resonated throughout the night air. He raised his upper body, sluggishly emerging from his slumber, to discover that it was quite dark. What the hell was going on in the middle of the night? In a few minutes the din stopped, and he was soon resuming his snore-filled sleep. But his snooze was again interrupted some time later by a somber, effusive droning coming from the sim. The monks were chanting. This lasted for a much longer time and it was at least an hour before he could doze off again.

When Pra Boon came to wake him up, it was daylight already.

"Do you wish to have breakfast, or do you prefer to continue sleeping?"

"What time is it?"

"Seven in the morning."

"Give me a few minutes."

One of the temple boys entered, bringing him a basin of water and a towel. Jon-sown forced himself to stand up, and, after washing his face, stepped outside to stand on the frail, wobbly porch, contemplating his new surroundings. Hands akimbo, he took in the view, studying the balmy trees, the simple buildings, and the peculiar robed figures sauntering demurely in the foreground.

This was the end of the line, he told himself; his sanctuary, for better or worse, the final destination, where he could lose himself in a lifetime of obscurity.

"I'm really lucky," he thought aloud, "to find a place like this…in the middle of all this shit…It's what I wanted, wasn't it?"

His morning meal of rice was brought, which he ate rather rapaciously. With his belly full, he set about strolling around the place, feeling awkward, not knowing what to do with himself. No one seemed particularly interested in him, although this indifference appeared congruous with the general atmosphere that prevailed here, for there was very little discussion among any of them. He surmised that there must be an unspoken rule that kept idle chatter to a minimum. This quiet composure was uncanny in the midst of the war raging outside. Even the kids were quite subdued. The monotonic mantras of the monks, which they intoned several times throughout the day, were the only stimulating activities that took place here. That, and the gong ringing.

The men in robes did a little light work in the mornings, but it was apparent that they relied on the dekvat boys to perform most of the chores, including the tending of the vegetable garden. The priests actually spent most of their time inside the sim. Consequently, he had both his lunch and supper alone. And when he finally returned to the hut in the evening, the only conversation Pra Boon made was to ask him if he was comfortable enough. After that, the monk lay down to sleep, leaving Ree-chart little choice but to do the same.

It wasn't long, however, before the man who called himself

Richard Johnson began to understand the schedule of the monks, and he eventually synchronized himself to start and end the day at the same times that they did. Within a day or two, he would go to the sim with them at four thirty in the morning and listen to their chanting. Then he would have breakfast with them, which, compared to other temples in populated villages, was very meager: small portions of sticky rice with assorted indigenous vegetables. Yet, even the scant rice available impressed him, and at breakfast on the third morning, Jon-sown felt impelled to inquire about its source.

"I know that you people have a small garden, and also that many of these vegetables, like these small eggplants, can be found in the forest, but where does the rice come from?" he asked Pra Boon, who was sitting next to him.

"The villagers at Ban Suk grow it for us. Do you know Ban Suk, just below Ta Vieng?"

"I have heard of it. But that's far!"

"Yes, they bring it here by buffalo cart."

"Through a war zone?"

"They are protected."

That protection probably involved the Pathet Lao. "I don't think there's anyone left around here after all the bombing. Maybe there isn't anyone at Ban Suk anymore."

"We have enough in the granary to keep us for another four months. You have seen the granary at the back?"

"Yes. But what will you do when the rice runs out?"

"I don't know. The abbot will tell us."

Four months, and then no food!

"And Ree-chart," Pra boon continued, "you are stuffing the food in your mouth and smacking your lips, which is indicative of greed. When eating, as in all things, you should be mindful. Watch our example and follow it."

"I'll keep that in mind," Ree-chart punned sarcastically while chewing rather loudly.

"And as well do not speak with your mouth full of food."

After breakfast, the monks normally chanted again, and then there was a short work period in which he would help the monks in their tasks. While raking leaves near the sim, which was the ceremonial hall that housed the Buddha image, he looked up to watch a few of the young boys galloping about on the bare field in front of the temple grounds. They were playing a three-man-team version of soccer, each side with a goalie, one striker, and one defender. The goals consisted of two bamboo posts stuck in the ground. Standing near one of the makeshift goals was an older boy. The kid was smoking a cigarette! Where the hell would he get a cigarette around here? Ree-chart walked over to see if it was one of the Lucky Strikes that he had discarded the day he had arrived, and as he drew nearer his suspicions were confirmed.

He grabbed the cigarette out of the boy's mouth. "That's not good for you." He threw the cigarette on the ground and crushed it with his foot.

The boy looked at him, startled and cowering, as Ree-chart, his anger having passed, walked awkwardly away.

Barely a week after finding sanctuary at the temple, the strange farang had asked for a private audience with the abbot.

"I would like to be a monk, sir."

There was a brief silence as the abbot deliberated this matter in his head. "Perhaps you better start as an *Upasok*," the old priest advised.

"An Upasok?"

"Yes. Like a trainee, so to speak. You must receive the eight precepts. That is more than what a layman receives, who only needs to accept five, but much less than those of a monk."

"How many precepts must a monk follow?" he asked, now having some doubts.

"A monk must adhere to two hundred and twenty-seven rules. Do you think that you could manage that?"

"I'm willing to try."

"If your period as an Upasok proves satisfactory for you, I will consider ordaining you. The first thing you will have to do is to learn Pali. I will inform Pra Boon to instruct you. In the beginning you memorize just enough to repeat the important phrases. All of our rituals involve Pali, which is the language of the Buddha. If you still decide to become a monk, you will need to have a good command of it."

"I understand."

It took him only three days to learn by rote the questions and answers. He took the eight precepts in the abbot's kuti.

Pra Boon handed the abbot his ceremonial fan, a large, decorated, oval sheet of bamboo attached to a stick. Hiding his face behind this fan, the old priest began chanting, "*Namo Tassa Bhagavato Arahato Samma Sambuddhasa*. Homage to the Exalted One, Perfectly Enlightened by Himself." The abbot recited this three times.

After that, Ree-chart himself had to request the eight precepts in Pali, "aham bhante tisarena…"

The Venerable Kru Jarun then listed the precepts one by one, and Ree-chart was obliged to repeat:

"I undertake to abstain from:

Taking life

Taking what is not given

Unchastity

False speech

Intoxicants which cause a careless frame of mind

From sleeping in a high sleeping place

Taking food at the wrong time (after twelve noon)

Dancing, music, visiting shows, flowers, makeup, the wearing of ornaments and decorations…"

As an Upasok, he helped out with the daily chores just as he was doing before: fetching water from the spring up the hill and refilling the water jars, mopping the floors of the sim and the other gathering halls, watering the garden and the trees, and sweeping the leaves from the courtyard. The temple boys assisted him in these work assignments; including the kid whom he had caught smoking a cigarette, and whom he had found out from the other monks was called Sousat.

In addition to the physical labor, he took lessons in Pali, as well as learning the most basic chanting formulas, and of course, the fundamentals of the *Damma*, the Buddha's teachings.

Only a few days after becoming an Upasok, during their usual work period after breakfast, Pra Boon asked him to help in cleaning the *chedi*'s at the corner of the temple grounds. A chedi was a memorial where the ashes of notable people were enshrined, a four-sided, tapering, concrete spire that vaguely mimicked the outlines of a lotus bud. Most of them held the remains of old monks who had passed away, but one of them, Pra Boon explained, did not encase any ashes inside. It was in remembrance of four monks who had disappeared several months ago after departing for the Cave of the Enlightened One.

"Do you believe they died?" Jon-sown inquired.

"Yes, it is certain."

"How do you know for sure? Maybe they were captured, or they just ran away from the fighting."

"Our Abbot, the Venerable Kru Jarun, told us that they were killed."

He grew nervous at this pronouncement. "How can he know? Did he go out and find their bodies?"

"No, he doesn't have to do that. He has mastered the art of 'perceiving'."

"Perceiving? What is that?"

"He has the ability to make his mind one-pointed, and therefore can know things which are hidden from ordinary men."

This made him even more uncomfortable.

"He has also seen their spirits," the monk continued. "They told him that they would like us to find their bodies so that they can be cremated. Now they are pii dai hong, spirits that died wrongly, but would like to be released from wandering and be reborn as humans.

The abbot has explained all this to us."

"And you believe him?"

Pra Boon looked at him with an expression of incredulity. "Of course! A monk cannot lie, certainly not the abbot!"

For the rest of the day, the matter of the four monks pestered his mind, and to further add to his uneasiness, towards evening, he was ominously summoned by the abbot.

He made the ritual subservient entrance crawling on all fours and then kowtowing, which by now he had learned to do less awkwardly, and after a few disquieting minutes, the hitherto motionless abbot stirred uneasily on his little platform.

"You have seen the chedi?" the old priest stated, rather than asked.

"Which one?" Upasok Ree-chart retorted.

"You know which one."

The abbot's presence was difficult to ignore. It was his imperious concentration of attention, as if he could see right through you. When the old priest spoke, his words seemed to issue forth from a boundless reservoir of conviction.

"In memory of the four monks who disappeared? Yes, I did. Did Pra Boon tell you?"

"Pra Boon does not need to tell me."

There followed a heavy, unsettling stillness, as the old man stiffened, his eyes glassy and distant. His lips appeared to be moving, but no words came out. Then his body relaxed, but he still didn't say anything.

A minute or two passed before the abbot finally spoke. "I have no wish to perceive who you are. But you do know where the bodies of the four monks are, do you not?"

There was another pause as Ree-chart looked down at the floor. "Tell me," he beseeched, without looking up, "Can someone who has killed still be ordained as a monk?"

"Anyone who meets the thirty-two physical criteria, and is not in financial obligation, and has the consent of relatives, can be ordained. Whether or not it is someone who has killed, or anyone else for that matter, whoever can enter the *Sangha* must meet those conditions."

Jon-sown took that answer as a 'Yes'. He looked up at the abbot. "Tomorrow I can take whoever you choose, and lead them to where the bodies are."

"You will go with Pra Boon, Pra Kan, and Pra Ayan. You will bring the corpses back here for cremation. You are dismissed."

He made the five-point prostration, which by now he had also learned to do, with elbows and palms on the floor, lowering his head to the back of his crossed hands three times. Then he crawled backwards on his knees to exit the abbot's abode.

The next morning he set out with the three young monks chosen by the abbot on their long journey through the mountain jungle. Regardless of the physical hardships, they made good progress without any grievance, keeping up a silent, steady pace. Although they were young, maybe late teens or early twenties, they were not intimidated by marching barefoot through the wilderness. After all, Ree-chart reasoned, they were trained as forest monks, weren't they? Their gait was brisk, their temperament subdued and phlegmatic, walking at a uniform speed with their hands reverently clasped in front of them. Their composed demeanor was in hilarious counterpoint to the farang's angry tromping, his fierce stabbing at the vegetation blocking his way, and the loud expletives issuing from his mouth whenever he stumbled. The monks themselves didn't complain, nor did they seem to need much food or water, since they only consumed these things once a day at midmorning.

"Pra Boon," Ree-chart addressed, as they made their way on the murky, overgrown trail, "do you ever wonder where I came from?"

Pra Boon replied without turning around, keeping to his constant step. "Sometimes I do. But it is not my place to ask." His voice was bizarrely muted by the dense jungle foliage.

"And you're not wondering now, how it is that I am leading you to the bodies of the four monks?"

Pra Boon was silent.

But from behind Jon-sown, Pra Ayan, the youngest of the monks, took up the challenge. "Whatever explanation you offer, Ree-chart, the answer ultimately lies with our Karma."

They were wordless for the rest of the day as they hiked through a wet greenery of tropical growth, listening to the screeching of birds and other animal sounds. Trees soared out of sight, their tops obscured by the sloping, twisting vines that hung halfway up. Immense ferns sprouted ubiquitously around them, even from within the dark recesses of the underbrush. The jungle grew steamy, and although the monks didn't seem to shed a drop of sweat, Jon-sown himself was constantly lifting up the lower part of his torn T-shirt to wipe his grimy face. As evening set upon them, however, the monks were eager to stop. The three of them immediately took places on the mulch-strewn ground, folding their legs into lotus positions to begin their chanting, leaving Jon-sown alone to collect firewood. After hastily getting the fire going, he sat down facing them and waited for them to finish their melodious mumbling, whereupon he taunted them with a question.

"Are you afraid of the ghosts, the *pii dai hong*?"

"Fear is a human emotion," stated Pra Boon, the light from the fire playing on his glabrous visage. "We must discipline ourselves from clinging to all such feelings. They are hindrances to spiritual development."

Pra Kan spoke up. "These men who were killed were monks, skilled in *Vipassana* meditation. They understand their death as a result of the Law of Karma, and do not hold grudges. They would not be as vengeful as the pii dai hong of an ordinary layman."

"Besides," Pra Ayan broke in, "We have protective amulets pinned on the insides of our robes." He unfolded a piece of his robe to show him. It was a ceramic Buddha image encased in glass. "We are not allowed to wear them on our necks, since a monk must not adorn himself, but we can wear them like this."

Having deemed the discussion to be over, the monks resumed their prayer positions and began their chanting anew, which was to last a good part of the night. He suspected they really were doing it to keep the spirits away, including those of the four dead monks. In any case, further conversation was out of the question and he soon fell asleep to their hypnotic timbre.

The morning also began with their chanting. Following forty-five minutes or so of this, they were ready to continue on through the wilderness. As they got closer to their destination, Jon-sown was forced to slow the pace so that he could remember the more subtle details of the spot where the bodies were. They crossed a clearly defined path, and that's when he knew they were near. Jon-sown did not lead them along this path, but strayed up-gradient through the jungle growth. He reconnoitered his way in a series of overlapping circles in the manner reminiscent of a hunter, scanning through the underbrush, with the monks behind him silent and unquestioning. After a period of wandering around like this, they eventually found the bodies, or rather the bones, since most of the flesh and viscera had already been consumed by ants.

The three monks immediately got down on the ground cross-legged and chanted. He himself took this opportunity to cut down two long poles of bamboo. Then there was the rather unpleasant task of putting the remains inside the nylon sacks that they had brought with them. What made it more distasteful was the fact that all the tendons and ligaments had already rotted away and the corpses would break up into pieces as they attempted to put them in the sacks. In addition, there were swarms of biting red ants all over the decayed flesh and bones. Johnson avoided looking at the grisly skulls, whereas none of the monks seemed to be bothered by this gruesome duty.

They tied the sacks to the poles, two to each pole. With Pra Boon and Johnson shouldering one pole, and Pra Ayan and Pra Kan the other, they embarked on their return journey. It was an unpleasant and arduous hike. Fortunately, because the corpses were in such an advanced state of decay, they were dried out, so they were light-weight, and didn't smell too badly.

On their return trip they didn't stop, choosing to brave the forest spirits rather than sleep next to the corpses. The monks chanted incessantly the whole way back through the dark jungle. They arrived at the temple in the middle of the night, thoroughly exhausted, though they had to put the corpses into the temple mortuary before they could get to bed.

In the morning, after breakfast, all of the monks, together with the abbot, gathered at the mortuary, a lightless mud brick shelter that stank of mold. Ree-chart was there too.

There were a total of eleven monks at this temple, and he had yet to know all their names. However, the fact that it was an odd number was a good thing, Pra Kan had assured him, although he hadn't explained why.

Inside the mortuary, they examined the decayed bones, which, at the abbot's instruction, had been obscenely splayed out, undignified, on the ground.

"Hmm, they appear to be in the eighth stage of decomposition already," the abbot declared.

"What does that mean, Venerable Father?" asked Ree-chart.

"The Buddha describes corpses in nine stages of successive decomposition. These here," he said, pointing to the dead monks' remains, "could make ideal objects for meditation. We shall hold such a session, to meditate upon the impermanence of all things. This will be done before all other preparations for their cremation, to be held tomorrow."

"Excuse sir, Venerable Father," interrupted Pra Ayan, "should we not cremate immediately, given the circumstances of their death?" He was alluding to the fact that they had been murdered.

"Why do you question my decision? Is it that you are afraid of their spirits? These corpses were taken from the forest without incident, and now they are within the sacred confines of the temple grounds. What kind of forest monk do you expect to be if you fear the spirits of the dead?"

Pra Ayan bowed his head with an expression of a whipped dog.

"Now then, we will meet here after the afternoon chanting session." He turned to Jon-sown. "Ree-chart, please come with me to my kuti."

"Venerable Father, I don't understand," Ree-chart blurted as they walked away, "these are the bodies of your brethren, your comrades, and you want to treat them as objects of meditation. I find that a bit heartless."

"You are right, you don't understand. They are just corpses, with no more life than a pile of rocks. It is the same fate that awaits all of us." His frail body lost in the immense folds of his sagging robes, the abbot nevertheless walked at a pretty brisk clip. He spun his head sideways to give Jon-sown a scornful glance. "I see as well, that you lack respect. Why do you walk at my side? A layman, even a subordinate monk, should walk a step behind me."

"Sorry, Venerable Father," he apologized, now lagging a step behind.

Inside the hut, the abbot took his chair. Jon-sown got on his knees and kowtowed three times.

"Now then, you have succeeded in your mission. The monks have already begun talking about you. You have managed to create an air of mystery around you, and I see it is just the beginning."

"Beginning of what?"

"Never mind. It is your Karma I am talking about. But that is not why I called you here." The abbot shifted himself in his chair and continued. "Ree-chart Jon-sown worked for ei-vee-et in the village of Nong Hak, just to the south of here. He was an American who liked to help people, and though his superiors wanted him to call in the airplanes to bomb, he did not. Is this the person whom you claim to be?"

He now realized how clever the abbot was. The Venerable Kru Jarun did not want him to break the eight precepts he had recently taken. Answering yes was actually stating the truth, despite the fact that he wasn't the real Richard Johnson. He only claimed to be.

"Yes."

"Claiming to be someone whom you are not is speaking falsely. Do not continue to do so. On my part, I will not question you further on this matter."

"Yes, Venerable Father."

With a leniency not typical of the Venerable Father, he tactfully changed the subject. "Now then, do you still wish to be ordained?"

"Yes, Venerable Father."

"Do you think you will be ready to answer the questions in Pali, in four days?"

"Yes, I can manage."

"Very well. You must have your head shaved the evening before the ceremony. I see that you are accustomed to having a hairless head, but the stubble is beginning to re-appear. We need to remove that. Start off with a fresh head so to speak."

"Yes, Venerable Father."

"That is all, you may go."

He made his exiting bow and crawled backwards on his knees out the door.

That night, as they lay down upon their sleeping mats, he asked Pra Boon if he really believed in spirits.

"Yes, of course."

"Have you ever seen one?"

"No. Although a human can, on certain occasions, see them, it is very difficult, unless they want to show themselves to you. But the dogs can see them."

"The dogs can see them?"

"Yes, you will hear them howling tonight no doubt. Good night, Upasok Ree-chart."

"Good night," he replied. But it was a long while before he could get to sleep.

A few hours later, in the middle of the night, the dogs did indeed make a ruckus, first barking like mad and then breaking into a chorus of howls. Jon-sown woke up in a fright, the hairs on the back of his neck standing on end.

"Pra Boon, listen, you hear the dogs?"

"Yes," came the drowsy reply.

"It's the ghosts!"

"Yes. Now please let me sleep."

Jon-sown turned on his side and pulled the cotton sheet all the way over his head until the commotion died down and thereafter drifted off into unconsciousness. Sometime later, he again opened his eyes, and this time he found Pra Boon looking at him with a rather concerned expression.

"Are you well, Upasok Ree-chart?"

"I'm not sure."

"You were making a great deal of noise in your sleep."

"I had a nightmare."

"Do you often have bad dreams?"

"Yes. Almost every night."

"Don't let them trouble you. They will soon cease. Sleep now."

For the rest of the night, Jon-sown slept like a baby.

The normal program of the monks was slightly altered on the following day. First of all, there was the meditation over the corpses in the mortuary, which lasted quite a few hours. Ree-chart, not obligated to attend, opted on staying away, keeping himself busy with his usual morning chores. He got Sousat, the older dekvat, to help him with most of the work.

"How old are you, Sousat?" he asked the kid as they were filling the water jars, which were kept in a small, dark, musty room in the back of the sim.

"Fourteen."

There was a lull for a while after this initial exchange. The boy did not look up in acknowledgement, but remained taciturn, putting down his bucket and grabbing another to pour into the large earthen vessel.

"Are you afraid of me?" the farang asked a few minutes later.

The boy silently continued his task, lifting his pail as if he were the only one in the lightless, dank storage room.

"How come you don't speak to me when we work together? Is it because I got mad and took the cigarette away from you?"

Still, the boy remained tightlipped.

"Where are you from?"

Out of respect alone, Sousat was required to answer that question. "Lat Bai."

"How did you get here, at the Forest Temple?"

The boy suddenly became effusive, with a hint of impudence in his tone. "First airplanes bomb the road, then the whole village. My parents died with all my brothers and sisters, so I ran away. A monk takes me and brings me here."

"I'm sorry about that."

Now the pause in their conversation was clearly awkward.

"How come you speak Lao?" the boy boldly asked, but even now not daring to look at the farang.

"I've been around here for some time. I talk to people. I listen, I speak." He was trying to be as vague as possible.

"You are not a monk," Sousat said abruptly.

"No, but I'm going to be one soon."

"You are a farang."

"Yes, I know."

His curiosity aroused, Sousat forgot his temerity and finally looked up. "Can a farang be a monk?"

"The abbot told me that I could become one. Would you like to be a monk someday?"

"No. I cannot be a monk. I am of the Black Tai people, we are not Buddhists."

Jon-sown didn't know what to say after that, and it was his turn to look away embarrassed. They carried on the rest of their work in silence.

Later, in the waning afternoon, was the cremation of the monks. Jon-sown had helped the dekvats in making the coffins, using crude saws and other implements, but wasn't allowed to help prepare the corpses since he himself wasn't a monk. The robes of the dead priests were collected and gathered into a pile by Pra Ayan. Then the boxes containing the remains were placed on a platform barely clearing a large, carefully arranged funeral pyre. The Venerable Pra Kru Jarun gave a thirty-minute speech on death and impermanence, and after that the monks chanted briefly.

The Venerable Pra Kru Jarun then ordered Sousat to light the fire.

"Venerable Father, perhaps it is best if one of the monks lights the fire," Jon-sown offered, thinking that such a gesture would honor the deceased.

The abbot gave out a long-suffering sigh of forbearance, as if gathering up his patience. "No, my son, a monk cannot light the fire, because the wood contains many sentient beings."

"Spirits?"

"No, ants, spiders, and other creatures. We are not permitted to kill them. Because you have taken the eight precepts, I would not even ask you to light it. By the way, you will choose one of the robes as your own, as you will need it for your ordination." He pointed to the pile Pra Ayan had prepared.

"Venerable Father, is it right that I take the robes of a dead man?"

The abbot turned around and looked at him, trying to control his annoyance. "If it were not right, would I suggest that you do so? It is good that you question things, but sometimes your questions border on insult. I hope in time, and by learning mindfulness, you will learn to restrain this urge. Since you have asked, however, I will explain. During the Buddha's time, and for many years following his death, the monks used to look for pieces of cloth in the cremation grounds and in graveyards. Cloth was very scarce and expensive. They would sew the bits and pieces together and dye them. Those were the robes that they wore. So, consider taking the robes of a dead monk as adherence to a great tradition."

"Yes, Venerable Father."

Sousat lit the fire; apparently with some experience of having done it before, for soon it was a roaring blaze. As the corpses burned up the monks chanted in Pali:

"Alas, transient are all compounded things

Having arisen they cease

Being born, they die

The cessation of all compounding is true happiness."

After that, they watched the flames of the bonfire in silence. The dekvat tended to it, ensuring that it burned steadily, and later retrieved the burned bone shards, which the monks placed in bronze urns.

Two days after that, just as they were having their breakfast, their only meal of the day, an incredible sound boomed in the valley. It sounded like music. Everyone ran out of the eating hall. It was definitely music, with a war cry ring to it, and as it came closer, Johnson could recognize it as the *Ride of the Valkyries*, by Wagner. The sound of the airplane blasting this music could also be heard. He looked up and noticed it was a Twin Otter, with giant speakers attached to the fuselage. Small objects were being jettisoned which floated down like confetti, while the German opera blared on at an ear-splitting volume. The air was filled with items that were the size and shape of little cards, and as they fluttered down to the ground everyone ran over to investigate. When Pra Boon picked one up, he screamed, terrified, flailing his hand that touched it. A couple of other monks did the same, throwing the cards down, yelling, and holding their right hands by the wrists as if they were alien growths that they desperately wanted to chop off. Was it some chemical weapon that burned upon contact?

Jon-sown didn't think so. He bent over and picked up one of the cards. There was a picture of a naked oriental girl standing in stiletto high-heels, with beautiful oval tits, a softly rounded ass, and a shaved pussy with the vaginal lips in full view. The card said, "Surrender and Meet Bubble Gum." Ree-chart laughed so hard it shocked the monks.

Such a charade was known in CIA circles as a 'Loud Mouth' mission. But couldn't those assholes in charge of psychological operations come up with anything better than this? And as for hitting the target, they couldn't have been more off the mark.

For monks, females were the enemies of religious life. It was forbidden for a woman, even a little girl, to have the slightest physical contact with a monk, and vice versa. If a woman wants to give an object to a monk, she must place it on a cloth, rather than hand it to him directly. This taboo extended to animals as well. A female dog, for instance, could not be petted or touched by a monk.

The abbot had to come out and assure the affected monks that touching the card was not in any violation of monkly ethics, but under no circumstances were they to look at the pictures.

Afterwards, Jon-sown and the dekvats were charged with collecting the cards and burning them in a trash heap, although he was convinced that the boys kept a few copies for themselves.

Notwithstanding the unexpected interruption in the temple's routine, Jon-sown continued preparing for his ordination. Pra Boon and Pra Ayan were chosen to be his teachers, and also to serve as his questioners during the ceremony itself, while the abbot was to be the ordainer. The day before the ceremony, his head was shaved, which didn't take long, since he himself had already shaved it about five weeks ago, before he ever arrived at the temple. After the shaving, he was given a white sarong and a lacy see-through robe, which he had to admit, he felt silly wearing.

On the morning of the ceremony, they formed a procession, with the abbot in front, followed by Ree-chart with his two teachers, Pra Boon and Pra Ayan, and with the dekvat bringing up the rear. One of the kids carried a big leather drum, which he banged on in slow solemn beats—dum...dum...dum... The little parade walked around the sim in a clockwise direction, making three trips around, symbolic of the Triple Gems. Before entering, Ree-chart had to prostrate himself before the shrine of the temple's guardian spirit. After that, they all entered the dark hall of the sim, the monks taking their positions on a raised platform, sitting in lotus fashion in a single line to the left of the large Buddha image. The abbot took his seat in the ornate preaching chair. Ree-chart approached him on his knees carrying one of the dead monk's robes in his forearms, his hands palm to palm in a prayer-like attitude. The abbot took the robes from him as Ree-chart made the triple obeisance, putting his head to the floor three times.

In Pali, he announced, "Venerable Sir, I go for Refuge to the Lord..."

The abbot hid his face behind his ceremonial fan and chanted, the rest of the monks accompanying his loud, clear, dominant voice. At one point Ree-chart was taken away to the back by his two teachers, who helped him out of his white robes, and into the robes he had brought, the official orange robes of a monk. When they returned to the platform, his teachers became interrogators.

"Are you a human being?" they asked him in Pali.

"Yes, Venerable Sirs, I am a human being," he replied, likewise in Pali.

"Are you a man?"

"Yes, Venerable Sirs."

"Are you a free man, and not a slave?"

"Yes..."

"Are you in debt?"

"No, Venerable Sirs."

"Do you have ulcer, ringworm, epilepsy or consumption?"

"No, Venerable Sirs, I do not."

"Are you at least twenty years old?"

"Yes, Venerable Sirs."

"Do you have your parents' permission?"

He hesitated at this question, even though beforehand he was told it was okay to answer yes to it in the present circumstances. He was sure his mother wouldn't mind.

"Yes, Venerable Sirs."

There was more chanting as he took a small silver vessel and poured water into a small silver chalice. This concluded the ceremony. He was given the monk name of Sunnatta, which meant voidness of self, and thus became a member of the holy Sangha.

His life was now that of a monk. As part of his initiation, the abbot assigned him the job of ringing the gong at 3.45 in the morning, which was supposed to wake everyone up for morning prayers. He couldn't help but suspect that perhaps the Venerable Kru Jarun had taken some sort of perverse glee in giving him this task. He was presented with an ancient, rusted alarm clock that seemed to be possessed by the essence of the abbot himself; appearing decrepit, it ticked on with an obstinate precision. At first, he would set the clock according to his own Seiko wrist watch (which he still kept but was not allowed to wear), though he was told that after a short period of practice with Vipassana meditation, he wouldn't even need the clock, but would automatically wake up at the right time.

And so, immediately after waking up, he had to go outside in the pitch black and climb up the rickety ladder inside the tower, then hit the huge brass gong with a 20-pound mallet, forty times, increasing the tempo every seven hits. The vibrations made his arms shudder along with the gong. The noise would also set the temple dogs barking and howling.

In the beginning he also had trouble keeping his robe on. A monk's robe consists of the outer robe as well as a sarong underneath, which was held up by tying a cord around the waist, though whenever he tried to dress himself, he would invariably end up looking like a sack of rice. The other monks were very kind however, in showing him how to put them on, to sit and walk in the robes, and most importantly, to make the triple bow without them falling off.

At 4.30 in the morning all the monks would assemble in the sim for their first session of chanting. After the morning prayers, they ate their breakfast, their only meal of the day, then tended to simple meditative chores around the temple until it was time for more chanting. Then more light work, followed by another chanting period. In the early afternoons were lessons in Vipassana meditation. The new farang monk, Pra Sunnata, got special instruction from the abbot, who started him off with the basics.

First, he would get a lecture from the abbot. "The object of meditation is to rid the mind of defilements, namely, greed, aversion, and ignorance. It is based on a method developed by the Buddha himself, which is called the Four Foundations of Mindfulness. Pra Sunnata, can you name the Four Foundations?" he asked him.

"Mindfulness concerning the body, sensations, the mind, and ideas."

"Very good. Now then, we are ready to begin with the first stage of walking meditation. Stand up, and recite to yourself 'standing' five times. Make sure to bring the mindfulness from the top of the forehead down to your feet, and then from your feet back up to your forehead."

Pra Sunnata did as instructed.

"Now, as you lift your right foot, recite to yourself, 'right goes thus', slowly moving your right foot forward. Now do the same with the left foot, reciting 'left goes thus'."

The abbot, watching his new pupil, became agitated. "No, no, not like that! You are moving too fast. If you walk so quickly, the Truth will be hidden by your movements."

"The Truth, Venerable Father? What is the Truth?"

"When your mindfulness becomes good, you will know what the Truth is. Now, after five or six steps, turn while reciting 'turning' five times, then again recite 'standing' five times and continue."

He was made to practice this for an hour, after which he had to practice reclining meditation, which he did by lying on the floor, his right hand on his abdomen, reciting 'rising' as he inhaled, and 'falling' as he exhaled. As required by this exercise, he had to try to notice if he fell asleep with his belly rising or falling.

There were the special days of worship, called *wan pra*, which, like the Christian Sundays, occurred roughly four times a month. They were more like Moondays, rather than Sundays, for they followed the cycle of the moon. On two of these days, the full moon and the new moon, the Pattimoka, the two hundred and twenty-seven rules of the monks, were recited. Only three of the monks at the Forest Temple—the abbot, Pra Boon, and old Pra Suk—knew these by heart, and they could recite them word for word, while the other monks only listened, for it took many years to learn the Pattimoka. At his first attendance of such an occasion, just before the actual recitation, the abbot tested Pra Sunnata with a question.

"Pra Sunnata, can you name the Four Parajikas, the cardinal sins whereby a monk is automatically expelled from the Sangha?"

Pra Sunnata, without hesitation, answered in Pali:

"A monk completing sexual intercourse with a living being is no longer a monk.

A monk who intentionally kills another human being is no longer a monk.

A monk who boasts about his magical powers is no longer a monk.

A monk stealing an object worth more than five masaka is no longer a monk."

"Very good."

"Venerable Father, how much is a masaka?"

The old priest tilted his head in the air while making a mental calculation. "About ten kip. But to be on the safe side, don't steal anything, regardless of its value."

"Yes, Venerable Father."

Then there was religious instruction. One day they were discussing the Law of Karma.

"It is the law of cause and effect," the abbot was saying. "Karma is an action associated with intention, and every such action has a consequence which must be expiated."

"Venerable Father," Pra Sunnata asked, "what would be the karmic result of killing someone?"

"That varies on the seriousness. Sometimes its effect is immediate and can be experienced in the present life. In other cases, the effect is evident in the next life. For example, the person who has created such Karma in a previous life may die early in the next one. Or, the victim may be reborn and kill his murderer. However, if one is as heedless as to kill a monk, it is possible that he will go to hell."

"Even if the murderer feels guilty for what he did and repents? Even if he becomes a monk and promises to never kill again?"

"Do not bring your Christian beliefs with you into the Sangha. We do not encourage guilt; it is a hindrance to spiritual development. There is no forgiveness either, Karma must be expiated, one way or another."

Pra Sunnata sat silently throughout the rest of the discussion.

The days passed, and Pra Sunnata became more and more proficient in his monkly skills, his chanting, his knowledge of the Damma, and most importantly, his meditation. He had progressed quickly to the fourth stage of walking meditation, whereby he had to concentrate and recite all the details of his movements associated with each step: heel up, lifting, moving, treading. He was astounded at the results such simple concentration yielded, and how the awareness of every movement seemed to bring him closer to a newer, truer reality. This was what was called Mindfulness. He learned Mindfulness regarding the three types of sensations, pleasant, painful, and neutral, and to recite 'feeling pain', and 'feeling pleasant', until these sensations dissipated, putting into practice the concept that there was nothing to cling to. He trained himself in Mindfulness regarding thoughts—learning to discern a greedy thought, a deluded thought, a thought with hatred, an unmindful thought, or a thought that wasn't free. He even learned not to gulp down his food and not to speak with his mouth full—to eat with mindfulness.

"The instructions of the Buddha, all 84,000 of them," the abbot had told him, "can be summarized in one word—mindfulness."

"Venerable Father, why is the mind so restless when I try to meditate?"

"It is restless all of the time. That is why the Buddha compared it to a monkey. You are only aware of it when you are trying to control it."

Despite the rigors of the training, he actually enjoyed the meditation. He could see the power in 'mindfulness'. In truth, it wasn't so difficult for him, as in his previous life he had, albeit in a different sense, to concentrate, to know everything going on around him in the work that he had formerly been engaged in. But there was so much more in meditation. He found that all his aggressive urges were atrophying, withering away in a medium of serenity. The effect was physical as well as mental, and he reasoned that it was due to a willful regulation of the body's hormones—adrenaline for instance—since he discerned an overall decrease in his heart rate and breathing. That could very well be why, he reflected, that the pituitary gland was considered such an important organ in Buddhist philosophy, for it was the master gland that controlled the hormones and was directly linked to the brain. That was probably how it all worked.

By the second month of his monkhood, he began to experience a sensation of inner satisfaction bathing his soul and thoroughly remolding his thoughts and actions. He became more subdued and objective, and his powers of observation were becoming enhanced.

Perhaps the most significant effect of his new life as a religious mystic was that his old life became extraneous. As the bits and pieces of his original personality broke off and fell away, he began casting off the memories that belonged to his former identity. He no longer had to be Richard Johnson. He no longer had to be himself. He no longer had to be anybody. He soon became truly person-less, silencing the voice in his head that had once made him spuriously consider himself as the center of existence. All that had preceded his time in the Forest Temple was rendered immaterial, banished forever from his mind.

And, as Pra Boon had foretold, the nightmares stopped coming.

One pleasant, sunny morning, while sitting on the bench in the sala, he spotted Sousat hobbling away from the kuti, the huts of the monks. Concerned about the boy's limping, he called him over.

"What is wrong with your foot?"

The boy stopped in mid-stride. "I hurt my ankle getting firewood."

"I am sorry," the American monk said. "If it isn't healed you should rest it."

The boy limped over, because, as he was called, he must approach out of deference. "No, it is much better now."

Sousat, although not a Buddhist, respectfully sat on the ground, rather than on the bench, so that he was lower than Pra Sunnata. Being at the temple had conditioned his behavior. He even addressed the monks as a Buddhist would.

"Reverend Brother, you are a monk now. Do you like it?"

"Yes, very much."

"How long will you be a monk?"

"I don't know."

Sousat had by now grown accustomed to this stranger who lived among them, and his feelings had evolved from apprehension into curiosity. "Where is your home?" he asked.

"Here, at the temple."

"No, I mean before. Where do you come from?"

"America."

"Will you go back there after the war?"

"No."

The boy bowed his head contemplatively down at the ground. A moment of thoughtful silence passed by. "Reverend Brother, will the war end?" he asked, looking up again.

"Yes, all things must end."

Sousat returned his gaze to the ground, picked up a twig and idly poked at the dirt. "Why are the Americans fighting here?"

"It's very complicated. It is a war. It is not the first, and it won't be the last." Pra Sunnata felt a bit impotent at not giving the boy a more definitive answer, especially in light of the fact that the kid's family had been wiped out. To compensate, he gave out a weak smile. "But don't worry, it will end, soon. Before you even think of marriage."

There was a short silence after that.

Pra Sunnata, for reasons as yet unknown to him, discerned a bond growing between them. He sensed that their futures were linked somehow. "Sousat, what do you think you will do when the war stops?"

"I don't know, Reverend Brother."

"Let us make a pact. That whatever happens, whichever side wins, if we get separated, then we must try to find each other again. Maybe I could help you in the future with any problems you might face."

"Would you really help me?"

"Of course I would. Even if it meant my life."

The boy believed him, but he still had to ask, "Why would you do that?"

"I don't know. I like you." He didn't want to admit that he felt guilty over the fact that it was American bombs that had been responsible for the boy's plight. Guilt was a hindrance to spiritual development.

"I hope we don't get separated," the boy said.

The gong rang for the evening prayers, and Pra Sunnata had to excuse himself.

It was a wan pra of the full moon, an evening when the Pattimoka was recited. Pra Suk was soliloquizing for the benefit of all. He was up to the fifth category of precepts, the *pacit-tiya*, the ninety-second rule, when the B-52s hit.

The ground shuddered violently, heaving beneath them with the shock waves of the bombardment, ruthlessly shaking the sim and causing one of the beams to fall in a horrendous crash, with clouds of dust billowing throughout the hall. The air cracked and ripped, releasing an immense roaring that enveloped everything. All the monks, including Pra Suk, got up and ran senselessly towards the entrance, while at the same time the temple boys shot in like a swarm of bees. The two groups passed each other, neither noticing the presence of the other, nor questioning the opposite direction each were heading in. It was utter frenzy. The abbot got up shouting, "Where are you going?" to the panicked monks who were already almost out the door, while the dekvat prostrated and cowered at the Venerable Father's feet. Outside, not far from the temple, horizontal blasts cleared the jungle of trees and sent geysers of soil into the air.

The abbot turned around to see Pra Sunnata, still facing the Buddha image, chanting away, though he couldn't hear his chants over the bedlam of the bombing. The monks eventually ran back into the temple, still in disarray. They dived in front of the Buddha image and bowed down in a frenzy of kowtowing. Hardly a minute passed after that, when the bombing stopped.

In the deathly silence that followed, Pra Sunnata's voice boomed out the one hundred and twentieth rule. The rest of the monks resumed their positions, while the abbot returned to his chair. Pra Sunnata was continuing with the Pattimoka, already on the seventh category of precepts. A half-hour later, the whole of the Pattimoka had been recited. It took years to learn the Pattimoka, and yet the American monk had been able to accomplish it within a few months.

The abbot ascended from his chair and walked over to Pra Sunnata. Although he was a bent old man, he seemed to loom over him like a giant.

"It is as I thought. You are destined to be an extraordinary man."

After that, despite being a junior monk, Pra Sunnatta was looked upon with great respect and awe. His knowledge of the Damma and his meditation skills soon surpassed most of the monks, and equaled those of Pra Boon and Pra Suk. It was only the abbot who could truly claim to be his superior. But when the abbot approached Pra Sunnata to teach him English, even that relationship became reversed, with the Venerable Kru Jarun as the student, and Pra Sunnata as the teacher.

And so it was, Pra Sunnata offering English lessons to the abbot, using USAID-donated textbooks that had been kept in the temple for years. Unexpectedly, Sousat asked to attend as well, and the abbot had no objections to the dekvat sitting in.

It was during one of these classes, a few months later, that the Pathet Lao arrived.

They were a large group, mostly Laotians, but including a score or so of Vietnamese soldiers, yet nobody heard or saw them until they were practically at the entrance to the temple. A spokesman dressed in a black uniform and a floppy Chinese-style cap came forward accompanied by a handful of officers, while the rest remained just outside the grounds.

The abbot closed his English book shut, guardedly got up and peered out the window of his hut with circumspect concern.

"You better go and hide yourself," the abbot told the American monk, turning away from the window. "Your presence here might be questioned."

Pra Sunnata discreetly left the abbot's kuti and walked quickly over to the mortuary. Sousat faithfully followed, shutting the door behind him as they entered inside. Both of them watched silently out the little window as the Pathet Lao officers confronted the abbot, now standing outside his hut with the rest of the monks gathered protectively around him.

"We have come to take you to the liberated zone in Sam Neua," they heard the leader say. "It isn't safe here."

"We have been at this temple throughout the war," the abbot answered, "and as you can see, we are still here, continuing the

Buddha's teachings. The Pathet Lao also came two years ago, offering the same sanctuary, but we refused it. We thank you for considering our welfare, but we must refuse once again."

The Pathet Lao didn't want to antagonize the monks, since many of them in Xieng Khouang had been sympathetic to their cause, and often supplied valuable intelligence. In turn they tried to protect them as best they could. "As you wish. But we insist the children must come with us."

"Very well." The abbot turned to the rest of the monks. "Any of you who wish to leave, may also go."

Three of the monks took this option.

Meanwhile, inside the dank smelling mortuary, Pra Sunnata turned to Sousat. "You better go."

Sousat hesitated. "I don't want to leave. This place has become my home."

"Go, Sousat, they'll take you to a safer place than here. We will meet again after the war, when there is peace."

The boy, with some hesitation, opened the door, gave Pra Sunnata a brief, disheartened glance, and walked out without looking back.

Pra Sunnata himself was to spend six more years as a monk in the Forest Temple, a period which irrevocably shaped his person and behavior, preparing him for the antithetical life ahead of him. His religious life completely embraced him, providing all the answers he had been previously seeking. He found himself entering an existence of peace, tranquility, and harmonious bliss, his heart freed from misery and upheaval. The temple had been, as he had predicted when he had first arrived, the perfect place to destroy all the vestiges of his past life. All that he had been before becoming a holy man was eventually effaced, now meaningless in light of the immemorial wisdom of the Damma. The sole meaning to his being became locked to his newfound faith.

And so, when his religious vocation was abruptly terminated by the political tempest that was brewing, his identity had already been entrenched in the role of a Buddhist monk, an impenetrable shield that could not be pierced by the mundane events of humanity. He believed that he had finally found the refuge within him, a conviction that would remain even after being forcefully taken away by the victorious revolutionaries.

Chapter 16

Camden, Ohio, 1969 - 1979

"And grief stirs, and the deft heart lies impotent "
Philip Larkin (1922–1986), British poet

Bill Kozeny was in the kitchen scraping off the peeling coat of old paint that covered the backyard door, so that he could paint it anew, while Dorothy, a few feet away was doing the dishes.

"You know, Dot, if I would have painted this dang door a few years ago I wouldn't have to do all this scraping. It's really tedious."

"Well, look at it this way dear, it will look much nicer in the end than just painting over the old coat."

He turned around. "Thanks for looking on the bright side," he said, his chubby face folded in a smile that accentuated his ruddy cheeks. It was a jolly face, a face that once made Dorothy quip that he reminded her of Santa Claus, without the beard and flowing hair, particularly in light of his cheerful demeanor that could easily match that of Saint Nick himself. In fact, at Christmas time when Andrew was young, Bill Kozeny was the most popular Santa Claus in the neighborhood.

Going back to his task, he asked, "you're on the graveyard shift, tonight, aren't you?'

"Yes, I go on at eleven. Dr. Stevens is picking me up, you remember him, that pleasant young intern, just got out of med school?"

"Oh yeah, nice young fella. Bit chubby."

"You should be the one to talk." She turned around to jab her finger into his paunch.

"Hey I'm old already," he declared chuckling. "When we were teenagers you said I had a physique like Johnny Weissmuller."

"No, I said you had a barrel chest like Johnny Weissmuller."

"Same thing."

"No, it's not. Looks more like two barrels now."

They both worked at their chores in silence for the next few minutes, with Bill apparently thinking about something. "I know you love your work Dot, but I really don't like it when you work late like that. I told you I'm getting promoted, so then maybe you can just work part time or something."

Sensing that she stopped her washing up and was looking at him he turned around to face her. "What?" he asked, smiling sheepishly, suspecting she was about to deliver one of her bombshell lines. He was right.

"I love you Bill."

"What's that for?"

"For...I don't know...for being Bill."

They hugged one another.

These were the moments they needed; to keep them strong, sane, safe...easing the stress they both felt but never mentioned: the worry over their son. It was a strategy that worked. Until that flash of a moment.

The doorbell rang.

"I'll get it Dot."

He put the scraper on the stove and walked past his wife into the short foyer that separated the kitchen from the living room, and passed the staircase on the right that led to the upstairs bedrooms, hurrying to the front door.

When he opened the door he was confronted by two men in black military uniforms with white trimming, and even had white caps and gloves to match the trim. With somber faces, they took off their caps. Bill Kozeny stood frozen, divining why they were there. His jowls flushed red. The officers barely had the chance to get out "Good afternoon, sir", when he shut the door in their faces, turned around and, like a zombie, walked up the bedroom staircase.

"Who is it, Bill?" Dorothy asked walking down the same hallway, wiping her hands with a dishrag. She looked up the stairs. "Bill?

Bill?"

She hung the dishrag on the banister. Then went to the door and opened it. The officers were still standing there, young handsome men in their crisp dress uniforms. Dorothy smiled, for no good reason other than a reflex she had when opening the door to visitors.

"Are you Mrs. Ko-zany-nee," the one on the left asked, as if making sure he had the right pronunciation.

With her smile now frozen on her face, she nodded her head up and down.

"We're from the Air Force Casualty Office. I'm really and truly sorry to inform you that your son Andrew was killed in action while serving his country."

Dorothy continued to nod her head up and down, her smile puckering into a stupefied frown.

The man on the right handed her a white envelope. "The details are in there. How to get the remains, his personal effects…"

She accepted the envelope, still nodding her head up and down, mechanically, the frown slowly melting into a grimace agape with shock.

"We're truly sorry Ma'am." They put their caps back on and turned around. Dorothy shut the door, and slowly moved her body to come face to face with the grandfather clock in the living room corner. She remained standing with a rigid face for a few moments, gazing unfocused at the clock, before she collapsed to her knees, and wailed "NO-OH-OH-NO-OH-OH!"

Bill Kozeny ran down the stairs like a maniac, blubbering loudly, "DOT OH DOT" He scooped her in his arms, and locked in an embrace of anguish, cried along with her.

Someone was knocking at the door, a persistent, official-sounding knock.

Cynthia Sorenson stomped to the door, dressed only in a large oversized, faded denim shirt, apparently a man's shirt, wearing nothing underneath. Her blonde hair swayed with indignant impatience, as the knocking continued. "Alright I'm coming already!"

She opened the door to a man in a plain, ready-to-wear black suit, wearing a moderately brimmed felt hat. He removed this hat and held it in both hands. His hair was short and neat, diminishing to stubble on both sides near his ears. He had a very full face, longer than it was wide, with an insincere smile on it. She knew he was a fucking pig even before he flashed his badge and ID, contained in one of those leather card holders that they just love to flip open with authority, which, predictably, he did. "Agent Jacobi, FBI."

"Can I help you?"

"May I speak to you for a moment?" He still had that stupid smile on his face.

"What's it about?" she asked standing in the doorway, her hand still on the door, ready to close it.

"Please, I need to speak to you for only a moment."

"Well you're speaking to me now, aren't you?"

"Can I come in?"

"No."

"It's just a routine matter," he stated in a rather genial tone. "Believe me, I'm such a low-level guy, they never send me on anything really important."

"So, what is it?"

"I just want to confirm something, then I'll be on my way."

"Yes?"

"Do you know an Andrew Kozeny? Lt. Andrew Kozeny?"

"Why, has anything happened to him?" Now he finally did have her attention.

"I'm sorry, you mean you don't know?"

"Know what?" she asked, alarmed.

"He's been killed in action. Can I come in for a moment?"

She opened the door wider to let him in, trying to keep her mind from racing off to other places, images and memories coming from out of nowhere now flooding her mind with confusion and sadness.

"Thanks," he said, stepping inside. He darted his head this way and that, taking in his surroundings. "Quite a big house. You live with other students?"

Of course he knew who she lived with.

"Just my...friend", she told him, closing the door. Her half-hearted tone exposed her distraction.

"Is your friend here at the moment?"

"No, he's...at work."

He walked to the center wall of the living room, with his back to her, towards an ornamental fireplace over which hung a large framed poster of John Lennon's face, draped with flowing brown hair and wearing the trademark, granny-style, wire-rimmed spectacles. "Oh fantastic," he declared, staring long and hard at it. "I love that guy, such a genius." He remained standing, looking at it, for almost a minute it seemed. "I am the Walrus," he chuckled. "Koo-Koo-Ka-Joo..." He then abruptly turned around. "Mind if I sit down?"

"Go ahead," she said, almost under her breath, now obviously disturbed by his presence.

The only things to sit on were brightly colored, amoeba-looking beanbag chairs, a fashion among the hippy kids of the time. He plopped down on one and tugged at his trousers to relieve the tautness, revealing his white sweat-socks encased in Buster Brown loafers. Cindy sat on another, protecting herself by pulling down the bottom of her shirt, folding her arms and closing her legs tightly together.

They sat for a moment before Cynthia asked, "So, is there anything else you need to tell me? Like what happened for instance?" She was irritated now, having had her feelings touched by a stranger, a fucking fascist peon for that matter, and struggled to fight off her emotions lest she risked being naked in front of him.

"Well, my main reason for coming here was to confirm that you knew him. What was your relationship with Lt. Kozeny?"

"The fact that you're here means you know that already. He was my ex-boyfriend."

"Look, I'm sorry. Just doing my job. And presuming things is not a part of it. Just confirming." He paused and looked awkwardly at the floor, still holding his hat. "Actually, I just wanted to ask you if you had kept any letters you got from him."

"Why? To tie up any loose ends?"

He jerked his head up. "I don't know what you mean."

She was angry enough to give him a lecture and disclose that she knew all about Laos, before checking herself. "I think I would like you to leave now. If you want any more of my time, then next time come with a warrant."

He put his hat on his head and slapped his palms on his knees, before raising himself up. "Okay, I understand."

She also got up to show him to the door.

As he walked out he shot a glance over his shoulder. "My condolences," he said glibly, re-flashing that deceitful smile he had when he first arrived, then tipped his hat and turned around to walk back to his black sedan parked in front of the house.

She closed the door forcefully, then covered her face with her hands and cried into them, sobbing with overwhelming guilt and shame. She knew that the Pathet Lao and Vietnamese forces hadn't killed Andy. She had.

Agent Jacobi never came back. But two other guys did. And they had a warrant.

For the Kozeny's, the time following the news of Andrew's death was too morose to describe, life depreciating into strings of intermittent breakdowns that came without warning, one after another. Like the day they had the memorial in Hustleton Park, where an Air force Major handed over the ashes in a beautiful gilded box, adorned with a gold plate inscribed with Andrew's name, rank, and the phrase 'died with honor serving his country'. When they got home, Bill went upstairs, complaining of a headache. Dorothy, left to her own devices, pondered where she should put the box that held

Andrew's remains. She decided to place it in the middle of the ornamental shelf on the back wall, and to that end she had to arrange the small vases of flowers and other knick-knacks to make room for it. In the evening, after Bill had come downstairs, and upon seeing it there, asked in a criticizing tone, "Why did you put it there?"

"I didn't know where else to put it. Is there something wrong with it being on the shelf?"

"It's morbid...it's paganistic."

She walked over to him and asked him sternly, "Don't you want to remember your son?"

He stretched out his arm to point at the box. "That's not my son!" he stated, raising his voice. "I mean...what are we supposed to do? Say 'Hello, Andrew, how are you doing in your little box'!"

Dorothy stood trembling uncontrollably. She was frightened. The man in front of her was not her husband of twenty-four years, but a stranger, cruel and hurtful. "How can you say such things to me," she hollered back, fighting to restrain her tears. Heartache battled with anger. Anger was dominating. She tore out at him. "You are a selfish, stupid, weak, self-pitying shell of a man!"

Dorothy honestly did not know where those words came from, but it was too late to send them back. Heartache overthrew anger in the end. "Oh Bill I'm sorry, I'm sorry!"

Bill Kozeny turned around and slumped in his armchair. "You're right. I'm a spineless piece of dirt, just feeling sorry for myself, not thinking about your own pain."

She went over to kneel on the side of the armchair, took his hand and kissed the back of it. "No, you're not, it's just grief making us act this way. They told us this would happen."

He was crying quietly now. "I know, I know."

A month later, because the presence of the box in the house made Bill uncomfortable, they made arrangements to have it buried at the cemetery run by the Veterans Administration on the edge of town, next to the plots their own caskets would someday occupy, plots that they were entitled to because Bill was a WWII vet.

Then there was the time a few weeks later when Dorothy noticed Bill standing by the large front window in the living room, for almost an hour it seemed, sometimes making little noises that sounded like hiccups. She couldn't take it anymore, so she walked over to him.

"Bill, what's the matter?"

"I keep thinking I'm going to see him come to the front door."

"Oh, Bill!"

"I'm sorry, Dot," he sniffled. "I can't help it. It's like my arm was cut off. A part of me is gone. Can't ever get it back."

Now she was crying, despite all she told herself, to just accept, to be strong for him, and not show the immensity of her own bereavement.

"I'm sorry, Dot," he repeated. He held her, so tightly that she was honestly afraid he would crush her with the strength of his emotion. "I'm so weak and selfish," he blubbered. "You were his mother for God's sake. I should be the strong one; a husband should be there for his wife. Forgive me."

Dorothy paused her crying to suggest, "I think we should see Father Wolanska again."

This suggestion was to precipitate significant events. Even though, in the beginning, Bill was not accommodating.

"I know it's hard," Father Wolanska told them, "but you have to get on with your lives, you have no choice." He was a cheerful-looking man in his mid sixties, with a narrow face that could barely contain his wide mouth. He reminded Dorothy of Fred Astaire.

"The life I knew had a son in it," Bill said bitterly.

"Well, the next one could have as well you know," Father Wolanska said with an impish grin.

The Kozeny's squinted at him, as if trying to confirm what they had just heard, and then looked at each other.

"It's too late," Bill said.

Father Wolanska turned to Dorothy. "Are you still, 'of the month?'"

Dorothy blushed. "Yes."

Father Wolanska clapped his hands in the air. "There you go! All you need is a little help from God." He then gave out a naughty wink. "The rest is up to you."

Sex was not a main ingredient of their marriage, at least not the way it was when they were still young and passionate. Once a month had been their frequency in later years. Of course, since the news of Andrew's death, it became more like never. But they tried. More importantly, Bill tried. Candles, baths together, even sexy movies. But he couldn't do it. Despite repeated attempts, it appeared that it was not a case of ill-timed happenstance, but rather chronic impotency. All he could say was that he was sorry.

That year they attended the annual Thanksgiving Dinner given by the Polish American Union, because they were told by Father Wolanska and the other therapists that they occasionally saw, that they needed social interaction to aid the healing process. Dorothy, towards the end of the dinner, perhaps out of desperation, confided to Elizabeth Malazinsky about her and Bill's failed attempts at baby-making. Maybe she disclosed this intimate matter to her because Elizabeth seemed to be a clever person who always came up with good ideas. This time was no exception. She said the house was too depressing a place, reminding them of Andrew, and suggested that she and Bill go on a cruise to the Caribbean. She knew a travel agent that could arrange the passage, all the hotels, everything.

They decided to take the cruise to the Bahamas on their 25th wedding anniversary, and it was during this holiday that they reclaimed the ardor they once had for each other, and sure enough they had the best sex in years. Dorothy even got pregnant. But instead of turning out to be a blessing, it was another ordeal of grief, and almost ended in tragedy. Dorothy had a miscarriage, and the doctor said she was lucky, because it was an ectotopic pregnancy and the embryo had implanted itself in one of her fallopian tubes, and if she hadn't aborted she would have died.

"It was a sign," Bill assured her.

They never had sex again.

So once more, they returned to their disheartening existence, made even worse by the recent trauma, and life again was still punctuated with sudden and unforeseen episodes of emotional scenes. Like the time Cynthia's mother called.

The telephone rang, the one on the wall in the kitchen. Dorothy picked it up. From her end it sounded like this:

"Hello…oh yes…oh my, how are you?" A long pause. "Yes, yes, thank you…oh I know…" Another long pause. "Well, we're doing ok under the circumstances…thank you…yes, we certainly know how close your daughter was…what? No! Really! What? Really? "A third, even longer pause. "Yes…we will do that…yes…we should…thank you, Sylvia. Bye."

Dorothy hung up the phone. "Bill, that was Sylvia Sorenson. Cynthia has just been arrested for pot."

Bill was staring glassy-eyed at a Cleveland Indians baseball game.

"Did you hear me Bill? Cynthia was arrested…they said it was marijuana, but Cynthia told her mother they planted it and were actually after some documents…did you hear me Bill?"

"I always liked Cynthia…The Earth Child," he said, as if that ended the matter.

She returned to her sink full of dishes. She was scrubbing them briskly when she said loudly enough for Bill to hear, "I wished Andrew had smoked pot…been a hippy, like Cynthia…we could have yelled at him…nagged at him to cut his hair…grounded him if he went to a sit-in…thrown him out of the house if he brought drugs in here…could have done anything…if he were alive…" She threw the plate she was washing into the sink, shattering it. Then she broke down and cried.

Bill leapt out of his armchair and ran over to console her.

"I'm sorry, I'm sorry!" she sobbed over and over.

"It's okay, it's okay."

For a while, it seemed that they were always doing that—apologizing to each other.

Not long after that, came the day of Bill's confession, a purging of something that had been inside of him for awhile. They were watching the Carol Burnett Show on the television, he in the armchair, she on the sofa, when he suddenly said, "I never told you about the war."

Dorothy could never forget the day he came home, debarking from the ship; she stood there in ecstatic expectation. When they found each other, before he even kissed her, he told her, "Don't ever ask me about it."

"I won't," she promised. And for the next thirty years, she had kept her promise.

Now, looking at him nestled in his armchair, she responded, "I never asked."

"Yeah, well you should know about it." A pause. "I was a coward." Another pause. "I don't know if I was more scared of killing than of dying…not like Andrew. He was a hero. He redeemed me. With the price of his life."

"Oh Bill, don't fret over that. you're here with me now. I don't care if you're not a hero." She wasn't quite sure whether that might have been the wrong thing to say.

"My point exactly."

Now she was.

As the years passed, they grew accustomed to the continual pain in their hearts, like one resigned to having a chronically sore back. Bill no longer went out on the road, as he was finally promoted to Sales Manager. Dorothy resumed her nursing job at St Boniface Hospital. The couple became regular churchgoers for awhile, but soon stopped because Bill was averse to socializing beyond occasional, token greetings. His once effusive and bubbly personality changed to a dull, sheepish cordiality, and he was tired of people seeing the resignation in his face, which made them look at him with a certain amount of pity. As a result, Bill and Dorothy didn't go out much, not even for a casual meal at a restaurant.

The permanent absence of their son had created a vacuum, one which they filled with themselves, becoming closer and more supportive of each other. During the day, they became absorbed in their work. In the evenings, they would update each other with a daily report on the things that had happened. At night in bed, despite the lack of sex, they fell asleep in each other's arms. In the end they accepted that they had only themselves.

Chapter 17

Laos 1976

"Some persons have asked me when they will be allowed to leave the re-education centers and return home. I cannot answer this question, nor fix a deadline for their release. It is like asking a doctor how long he is going to keep his patient."

LPRP Politburo member Poumi Vongchivit, January 6, 1977

For three more years, the B-52s rained bombs on the Plain of Jars.

In December 1972, in order to pressure the intransigent Vietnamese at the Peace Talks, Nixon, Kissinger, and the military decided to embark upon the Christmas bombing of Hanoi. The eleven days of continuous bombing by over one hundred B-52s also affected the Plain of Jars, for it was the place to drop unused ordnance on the way back from these missions. Scores of two-thousand-pound bombs fell from the sky each day, pounding the land into oblivion. Amidst this manmade hell of destruction, the Forest Temple continued to endure virtually unscathed. It was a minor miracle.

But the darkest hour is always before the dawn. The war was actually nearing its end. Within a month of the signing of the Paris Peace Treaty between the United States and Vietnam, effectively ending the Vietnam War, the warring factions in Laos signed a treaty of their own under the auspices of the American Embassy, which provided for a ceasefire effective February 22, 1973. There was to be the formation of a coalition government, the third and last coalition attempt in Lao history.

In the countryside and in the towns, people were relieved. For the next two years there was peace, and they could go about their lives undisturbed by the horrors of war that had plagued them for three decades.

The monks in the Forest Temple didn't realize what was happening politically, but they did sense the quiet. News eventually got to them that the war was over, and that a peace treaty had been signed. Still, no one had as yet returned to the Plain of Jars.

Two years later, in 1975, the LPRP decided to change its strategy of cooperation when it became clear that the Khmer Rouge were about to take Phnom Penh, and that Saigon was falling under a North Vietnamese offensive. They felt they should take advantage of the momentum of communist victories in Vietnam and Cambodia, for it presented an opportune occasion to remove their political adversaries now, while they had the chance. Through carefully orchestrated rallies, street protests, and worker strikes, the right-wing elements in the government were denounced and those that remained were soon to be rounded up and sent to re-education camps. In May 1975, the CIA airlifted Vang Pao out of Long Chieng. The remains of his army took up arms, preparing themselves to fight a guerilla war in the jungle, many regrouping to form the Chao Fa. A mass exodus of the country's educated elite, including civil servants, technicians, teachers and doctors, fled the country. The US also terminated all aid money. Laos was now on its own.

On December 2, 1975, the Lao People's Liberation Party announced the birth of a new nation, the Lao People's Democratic Republic. And, as any mother could tell you, birth is a painful experience.

The economy fell apart at the seams once US aid money was cut off. Thailand closed its border, effectively blockading the flow of goods to landlocked Laos.

To make matters worse, the revolutionary zeal of the new leaders made life miserable for the populace. LPRP cadres became unduly focused on the lifestyles of the people, and their first priority was to mold the 'new socialist man and woman'. Forms of dress, music, and dancing, all came under official scrutiny.

Neither was the Sangha, the Buddhist clergy, spared this inimical inquisition. Cadres, political officers sent by the party, told monks to stop preaching the Law of Karma. One's fate wasn't a result of the sins of a previous life, but determined by the unjust system of capitalist production. They discouraged the idea of obtaining merit for a better rebirth, which one mainly got through feeding the monks and donating to the temple. The government condemned these offerings as a wasteful expenditure of the agricultural surplus which should go to the state instead. Monks were pressured into maintaining gardens to feed themselves instead of living like parasites off the people, and the faithful were prohibited from giving the monks food on their morning alms round.

In March of 1976, in this campaign to subjugate the Buddhist church, the LPRP cadres came to the Forest Temple near Pu Khe and discovered Pra Sunnata, the American monk.

All of the monks were in a meditating session, sitting cross-legged and focusing on their abdomens rising and falling, so they didn't hear the strangers approaching. The communist officials and their soldiers had been respectfully waiting outside for a few minutes already, when, not getting any response, they impatiently barged into the sim. The abbot broke his concentration and slowly stood up, then discreetly stepped toward them with restrained vexation.

"Come with me," he told them. He marched out of the sim with a determined stride surprising for his age, one in which the cadres didn't anticipate. They followed him on a reflex, without realizing that he was ordering them, so persuasive was his authority.

Outside, he turned to them, "Can you not see we are meditating?"

The apparent leader of the group, in his floppy cap that was a hallmark of the revolutionaries, rebutted him. "Yes, it is precisely the reason why we have come. Such idle practices must stop. We are ordering you to leave this place, and take up residence in Ban Ling Kao."

"I have never heard of such a village."

"The villagers of Ban Suk have come back to rebuild their homes.

They have renamed their village. It is the closest settlement to this temple, and we require you to go there and serve the people."

"We are perfectly content to remain here. If the villagers have come back, they will help us as they were doing before."

"No!" the cadre hollered out with a fierce grimace. "They will no longer support lazy, feudalistic leeches who live off the blood and sweat of the peasant. From now on you will live and toil among the people, and you will assist in educating them in the socialist manner of thinking. Your role is to help the Party bring modern development."

"So," the abbot uttered contemptuously, "you would like to change things. To remove traditions that are thousands of years old. To abandon the Buddha's teachings and become involved in worldly matters such as politics. This cannot be."

"It will be. All forms of backward superstition must disappear. Lao is to become a modern nation, a socialist nation. You will inform the other monks, that they are to be ready in ten minutes. We will escort you personally to the village."

The abbot noted the heavily armed soldiers that had come with the cadres. Resistance didn't appear to be an option. He swiveled around with reluctant capitulation and stepped gravely back into the sim. Less than a minute later, all the monks filed out.

Pra Sunnata was spotted immediately. The leader strode briskly towards him. *"Jao men pai?* Who are you?"

"That is Pra Sunnata," the abbot answered from behind.

"Let him speak! *Vao pasa Lao ben, bo?* Can you speak Lao?"

"Vao ben. Yes, I can."

"Who are you?" the cadre repeated.

"As the abbot told you, I am Pra Sunnata."

The cadre slapped him hard on the face. The other monks gasped, shocked at the physical violation of a monk. It appeared that, because Pra Sunnata was a farang, the cadre felt he wasn't a genuine monk. "You mean to be insolent?" He turned to the rest of them. "Go and collect your belongings." To Pra Sunnata, he said,

"You also."

The monks went to their huts under the watchful supervision of the armed soldiers. The cadre stayed close by Pra Sunnata, who, along with Pra Boon, was made to stand to one side of their kuti while the soldiers went through their things. They eventually found the clothes that Jon-sown had worn when he had first arrived at the temple, and ultimately, a business card that was left in the shirt pocket, which one soldier dutifully handed over to the cadre. He looked at it, but couldn't read the English. On the flip side, however, the information was written in Lao script.

"Ei-vee-et? You are a CIA spy!" He gave him another slap, this time with the back of his hand, cracking Pra Sunnata's lip and causing him to stumble a few steps backwards to bang against the shaky bamboo wall. Pra Boon stopped arranging his belongings and looked up at the scene with alarm evident in his face.

"Hurry up!" the cadre ordered.

The articles, having been inspected, were handed back to the owners, and Pra Boon and Pra Sunnata were made to leave the kuti. The other monks as well were similarly ordered outside of their respective huts and then ushered into single file, whereupon they were forcibly evacuated out of the temple grounds.

They walked for the rest of the day, silently resigned, through the forest, until they came out of the mountain jungle and onto Route 4, where a large Soviet-made truck was waiting, full of soldiers, half of them Vietnamese. Surprisingly, the LPRP officers showed enough respect for the old abbot as to allow him to ride in the cab, while the other monks were directed to clamber up onto the crowded back. The truck drove on for a couple of hours along the dusty, uneven, laterite road, until they came upon a small track which they followed for some time. Eventually, they stopped at a site where several raised bamboo houses stood planted among the trees. There, the monks were ordered to disembark.

"Not you," the cadre told Pra Sunnata.

The monks, under the leadership of the cadre and some soldiers, entered the village, while Pra Sunnata was made to wait in the truck. Apparently, there must have been some sort of meeting going on, for the cadre, accompanied by the abbot, came back nearly an hour later.

"Bai, bai!" the cadre shouted as he opened the door to the cab. The driver dutifully started the engine.

The abbot, standing by the side of the road, looked up at Pra Sunnata, who remained alone, apart from the soldiers in the bed of the truck. "Go well, my son," the old priest bid, in a voice as close to a shout that mindfulness would allow. "And do not be worried, for I have perceived that we shall meet again."

"Yes, Venerable Father. I shall endure whatever awaits me with Mindfulness."

The vehicle stormed off with a violent lurch. Pra Sunnata could still see the Venerable Pra Kru Jarun, framed by the wake of billowing dust, a motionless, spindly shadow, dwarfed by the huge mahogany trees that stood over him.

The truck ultimately came down off the mountains at Muang Koon, and then crossed the Plain of Jars. At Ponsavan, it took a left on Route 7, heading into the hills near Khang Kai. It was well into the night when they arrived at a compound cordoned off by a high fence laced with barbed wire, girding several large barracks made of timber, their angular shapes ominously cut out against the backdrop of a still, star-studded, black velvet sky.

Once off the truck, he was led to another smaller building that was constructed of concrete breezeblocks and housed several austere offices. Inside one of them, were several men sitting at a table. A gas lamp illuminated the room with a blinding glare; its hissing nearly deafening in the stillness. One of the seated men was a farang in full dress military attire.

This European leaned back in a swiveling, office-type reclining chair, the light from the lamp causing his nose to cast a shadow on his far cheek. The hair on his head was a silver fuzz that seemed translucent in the yellow-white light, while his eyes, despite them being buried in the pink jowls of his beefy face, issued a concentrated gaze. He gently rocked himself in the chair, deliberately producing invidious creaking sounds as he studied Pra Sunnata. The verbal silence that he imposed amplified the squeaks of the chair as well as the hissing of the lamp and was calculated to heighten any sense of suspense and dread that the captive may be experiencing. But for Pra Sunnata, who was by now quite capable of maintaining a temperament of equanimity, these staged effects were of little consequence.

The Laotian cadre, the leader of the group that had arrived at the temple, handed this paunchy, self-assured farang the IVS business card.

"American?" the European officer asked in English, not deigning to look at the card, but preferring to keep his eyes on his prisoner. The man spoke with an unmistakable tinge of accent.

"Yes."

The fat farang then looked down at what was handed him. "Iz diz your card?"

His inflection was more like that of a German, not a Russian. "Iz diz your card?" he repeated in a louder voice, impatient with the slight delay in response.

Pra Sunnata pondered this question for another moment. As a monk, he couldn't lie. For all practical purposes, the card did indeed belong to him.

"IZ DIZ YOUR CARD?"

"Yes."

The officer stared at Pra Sunnata for a few deliberating moments. "Richard Johnson...Hmm...IVS, Nong Hak." He continued to rock his chair, apparently relishing in the grating sounds it produced. "You stay here and become monk. Why?"

"I believe in the Damma. And I had wanted to be a monk for a long time."

The farang officer leaned forward, and putting his right elbow on the table, rested his chin in his hand, somewhat perplexed at this predicament. A noisy stream of air issued out of his mouth, as if to express his discontent at being delivered such a problem at this late hour. His eyes darted to look at the card again, then shot back up at Johnson.

"Why you dun't go back to Amereeka? Or Thailand? You can be monk in Thailand. Why you stay here?"

Pra Sunnata's face was impassive as he answered, "Back in the United States, I would be considered a traitor. Even in Thailand, it might be too dangerous for me."

"I don't believe you."

"It is true. A monk cannot lie."

The East German threw his torso back into the chair and laughed contemptuously. "Ha, ha, ha! A monk is human being, and human being will lie to protect himself, to survive. Monk or no monk."

Pra Sunnata avoided a reply to that.

"Let him wait outside," he instructed the Laotians, pointing to the door.

Outside, under the watch of two guards, Pra Sunnata could hear them discussing his case in a mixture of German, English, Lao, and Vietnamese. A quarter of an hour later, all of the men came out of the office and confronted the man in their custody.

"We have unusual situation here," the East German officer told him. "You are to be kept in isolation. Under no circumstances will you have contact with the other inmates until we find out who you are and what you do here."

After that pronouncement he was taken by two of the guards, who persistently pushed and nudged him along as they headed to the fence on the edge of the compound, where they abruptly stopped.

"*Niyo! Niyo!*" he was ordered.

Pra Sunnata lifted up his sabong, his inner sarong, and began to urinate. When he was finished, he was prodded back towards the barracks and then shoved into one of the other offices in the same building where he had been questioned. As he stumbled inside, the door was slammed shut and locked behind him, leaving him in the dark, lampless room.

He lay down on the cold, hard cement floor, and began to recite "Rising, Falling," in time with the motions of his belly, and soon fell into a deep sleep.

He awoke on his own at four in the morning. He stood up, and immediately began his walking meditation: right heel up, lifting leg, moving leg forward, treading, left heel up...

When, about an hour later, the guards who came to wake him opened the door and shined their flashlights inside, they were so taken aback at seeing him walk toward them that they raised their AK-47s. "*Yut, yut!*"

Pra Sunnata halted his movements instantly.

One of the guards threw in a small bundle, the clothes that Pra Sunnata had not worn for six years. "*Pian!* Change!"

He obediently removed his robes and put on the shirt and trousers, under their scrupulous eyes. Without further ado, they took hold of each of his arms and led him around the back of the building, where they came upon a shadowy figure leaning on what looked like a sledge hammer and in front of whom was a large flat rock. One of the guards violently slapped at Pra Sunnata's right leg.

"*Yoke! Yoke!* Lift!"

He placed his foot on the rock, and two semi-circular bands of iron were fixed around his ankle, joined by the blacksmith hammering a bolt through the clasp. The same was done to the other leg, and after that they shackled both his ankles together with a heavy chain.

"*Bai, bai!*" They punched at his back, jostling him forward.

He shambled along, the chain that bound his legs clanging noisily, as the guard on his left withdrew his machete from its scabbard and handed it to him. The forced march continued past the sentries at the gate and into the surrounding woods, with Pra

Sunnata clumsily taking short, sliding steps, awkwardly holding the machete. The sky above them glowed a pale gray blue, signaling that the dawn was about to break, and cueing the forest birds to begin their sunrise calls. But the peacefulness of the morning was distant and artificial.

They hadn't gone very far when they stopped at a dense stand of bamboo, whereupon the guards ordered him to start cutting the poles. "*Het viak!* Work!"

Pra Sunnata refused. "I am a monk," he told them. "I cannot labor thusly."

He was answered with a gun butt striking his chest and knocking him down; as he fell, he saw stars floating around inside his head, then slowly surfaced in a sensation of aching around his midsection. "Feeling pain," he grunted to himself.

"*Luk koon!* Get up!" they shouted at him. "Cut the bamboo!"

As he got up, they waited a few patient moments before repeating their order to cut down the bamboo, and again he refused.

"Cut it!"

"I cannot."

Once more he was struck down on the ground. The guards were young, seventeen or so, and were of hill-tribe origins. When he refused for the third time their impatience grew into frustration and they proceeded to pummel him with their gun butts and kick him with their boots. Having sufficiently relieved themselves of their anger, they dragged him to his feet and forced him to waddle ungracefully back to the compound, bruised and bloody, lurching and stumbling along the way.

In the prison yard, the light of daybreak was sufficient enough to make out other prisoners shuffling past, some with ripped shirts, others half-naked, wearing shredded, soiled shorts, all of them bound with leg irons, and who, with hollow, gray faces, stared in amazement at this new arrival, this farang, who apparently had already received his first beating.

The two young guards led him into the same office where he had been questioned the night before. The East German officer wasn't present. This time he faced a Vietnamese, in a blue military uniform, standing behind the table, and a Laotian, in the black pajamas of the Lao Liberation army, seated in a chair, and who, Sunnata was to shortly find out, was the Commandant of the prison he was brought to, Camp 07.

"You refuse to work?" asked the Laotian. Even in a sitting position one could see he was short and stout, a fat little midget, and it was almost laughingly farcical the way he was hunched over the table. His acne-scored, dark-complexioned face held beady eyes and fish-like lips, bringing to mind a mobster figure from one of the gangster movies of the 1940s.

Pra Sunnata, trying to stand erect, only managed to barely control his wavering.

"Why don't you cooperate, and do what the guards tell you?"

"I am a monk," Pra Sunnata slurred, still wobbling, "it is not permitted for a monk to work in the same manner as ordinary people."

"If you don't work, we will punish you severely."

"I am a member of the Sangha. I cannot go against its rules."

"And what about our rules? You think they don't apply to you? Perhaps we should prove to you that indeed they do." The Laotian turned towards the Vietnamese officer standing next to him, a grim expressionless man in an officer's cap, who eventually nodded his head as if approving something.

The Laotian spoke to the guards. "Put him in the hole."

They took him outside toward a corner of the compound, again in full sight of the other prisoners who were mulling around in the yard. Not far from the edge of the fence was a wooden trapdoor set in the ground, which was lifted open by the guards, revealing a deep, dark pit. Straight away, an overpowering moldy stench wafted out. Inside could be seen a bamboo ladder, and predictably enough, Pra Sunnata was ordered to descend it to the bottom. They withdrew the ladder and closed the door, leaving him in utter blackness.

The pit was a simple but effective torture chamber, filled with an absolute murkiness and putrid, foul-smelling odors. The typical response to a person left there would be unfathomable horror, and five minutes would be more than enough to have someone pleading to be let out. But Pra Sunnata, who had learned to master control of his mind and body, wasn't typical. The narrowness of his confines prevented him from lying down, and so he sat cross-legged to engage in sitting meditation, his left hand upon his lap, his right hand on top, both palms up. Focusing on his navel, he noted the rising and falling motions of his breathing, but was distracted by the throbbing of his contusions and cuts. Engaging Mindfulness regarding sensations, he recited to himself 'feeling pain', until he could no longer feel it.

They kept him in there for the rest of the day, with the hot moist air becoming so thick that breathing itself was an exertion. "Breathing," he intoned to himself, putting his body in automatic mode, marveling at how it extracted whatever oxygen it could in the seemingly airless environment. By evening it became cooler, but the initial relief gave way to a bone-penetrating chill that furtively seeped in, and he had to focus his concentration on the cessation of his shivering. "Feeling cold," he recited.

Nighttime was also the time when hundreds of huge cockroaches became active, and they would crawl upon him and bite his skin, apparently used to the taste of human flesh from the bodies, both living and dead, that had been confined in here before. Mosquitoes and ants also showed up to feed on him. In the end, his contemplative energies were efficacious in removing the avulsion he initially experienced, aware that these creatures were animated by the same life forces that flowed within himself, and he continued to sit passively motionless. In his mind, however, he struggled against a growing painful stiffness and sought to drive out his other bodily discomforts caused by lack of food and water. Eventually he entered into another plane of being, where such physical things were without significance.

At daybreak, twenty-four hours later, the door opened, startling him out of his disembodied wanderings. The Laotian Commandant looked down at him. "Will you work today?"

Pra Sunnata, upon his return to the material world, didn't feel it was necessary to raise his head and face his tormentors, who had shown themselves deaf to his asseverations. "I cannot work so long as I remain a member of the Sangha," he said to the earthen wall in front of him.

Boom! The door slammed shut.

The hours passed, through the morning, the hot afternoon, the waning evening. During the day, the hole in the ground was an oven that was steadily cooking the life out of him; at night a refrigerator keeping him like a piece of dead meat for the insect inhabitants to nibble on. Each individual moment stretched into a trial of endurance. "Feeling thirsty, feeling hungry," he repeated in his mind, over and over, in a silent chant, reminding himself that these painful sensations were temporary. After arising, and existing, they must eventually cease. Some time later, all his bodily distress disappeared, as he once again revisited the incorporeal realm that he had journeyed to on the previous night.

The next morning they didn't even bother to open the door. Instead, a round, saucer-sized aperture in the middle of the door opened up. An eye with a bushy eyebrow appeared in the center of the peephole. "Have you changed your mind yet?"

Pra Sunnata mustered all his energy to answer in a cracked, hoarse voice, "A monk...cannot...work."

The aperture was closed with a sharp thump.

He sat in the darkness, and noticing that the morning condensation had made the ground moist, took a handful of mud and put it in his mouth, sucking on it like a piece of candy. It was the only water he could get, but it was enough to keep his tongue from swelling and to keep him alive, at least for the time being.

By now, all the prisoners were aware of what was going on, piecing together the little they had seen with the fragments of gossip they exchanged with some of the guards. It became a hot topic in a place where people literally died of boredom and drudgery. So, quite naturally, many of them occupied their idle time in the evenings, huddled on the floor in their dark barracks, deliberating upon the subject of the farang in the hole.

"This is the third day," someone said.

"How long do you think he will last?" asked another.

"Remember Sisana, he lasted the longest in the hole. Five days. On the sixth day, they opened the door to find his corpse," remarked a third.

"This man is a farang. How long can a farang last without food and water?"

"Yes, but I heard he's a monk."

"What's the difference, a monk is a man. Even a monk needs to drink water, and to breathe the air."

"He isn't an ordinary monk," came a voice behind them.

They turned to look at the young guard sitting in the corner, smoking a cigarette. "He's different."

"Why do you say that?" they asked, surprised at his intervention in their conversation.

"Because I know him." The guard stubbed out his cigarette, got up, and walked away.

In the hole, Pra Sunnata strove to control his mind, but he was losing it instead. Fantastic colors danced and leapt all around him, and strange sounds reverberated in his head. There were also voices, telling him to let go, that he had reached Nirvana. He knew what was happening—it was a Mara, one of the devils, trying to deceive him, to obstruct the way to stillness. "Leave me," he ordered faintly in the darkness. There was another voice as well, this one above him, addressing him by his priestly title, over and over again.

"*Luang Pi*, Reverend Brother!"

"Leave me," Pra Sunnata whispered under his breath.

"Reverend Brother, it's me, Sousat! Remember me, Sousat?" the voice repeated.

Something dropped from above and hit him on the head, bringing him back to his sense of the physical world. It was a package wrapped in banana leaves. He looked up, and the hallucinatory visions dissipated.

"Take it, it is rice," he heard in the darkness. "I have some water also. But you have to give me the bottle back."

Now he could make out something. It was a plastic liter bottle of water, coming down on a string.

He grabbed at the bottle and drained it down his throat. It was a good thing he had been filling his mouth with wet mud, for the sudden ingurgitation of liquid would have otherwise fatally choked him. When he finished the water he looked up and called out in a low voice, "Sousat!"

"Yes, be quiet. You must also eat the banana leaves that I wrapped the food with. Don't forget. Otherwise they will know you were given something. I will come back with another bottle of water, but that is all I can do for you now."

The bottle jerked up and ascended through the hole, the aperture in the door closing with a harsh sounding thud. Pra Sunnata succumbed to a moment of joy and relief, but quickly admonished himself for it. "Feeling happiness," he recited, with the purpose of dispelling it.

Sousat managed to give this assistance for the next few nights, and Pra Sunnata was once again able to summon his mental vigor sufficiently enough to continue his meditation in earnest. These two factors, physical sustenance and spiritual ascendancy, allowed him to survive the hole longer than anyone else had at Re-education Camp 07. However, the food and water also brought new problems, for what goes in, at least some comes out. This meant urinating and defecating in the tiny area available, which he began to do on the fourth day. The stench of ammonia and hydrogen sulfide, in a hole where there was little air to begin with, was soon suffocating. Pra

Sunnata tackled this problem, again, with Mindfulness, recalling his knowledge of the six external sense fields: seeing, hearing, smelling, tasting, touching, and ideas. Although to an undisciplined mind, the odor was repulsive, he learned to accept it as a neutral phenomenon, for aversion, along with greed and ignorance, was one of the mental defilements.

"Smelling," he repeated over and over to himself.

Whenever they would check on him in the morning, the Commandant and guards wouldn't even open the peephole, so deterred were they by the reeking fumes, but instead would shout their questions from outside the door. If he answered, it meant he was still alive, and if the answer was still no, he would remain in there. They didn't ponder at length how he could be excreting without food and water, even though the others that had been confined in the hole had stopped after a day or two. They reckoned that the constitution of farangs, who had generally larger, meatier bodies, contained a lot more excess excrement in them than a more diminutive Laotian.

Time dissolved into an ether of vacuity. Now and then, his concentration would be broken by incredible feelings of enjoyment with the Damma, cognizant that this was the most profound meditation session he had ever experienced. But even this wasn't the correct objective, being indicative of greed, and he sought to bridle such perceptions, to silence once again that little voice in his head, the ego. The mind is a restless monkey, the Buddha had said. The goal was to control it, and he directed all of his efforts into doing so.

The darkness and silence of the sealed pit served not as a punitive deterrent, but as a helpful means of removing distractions, where sensory deprivation allowed the mind's eye to see past the veil of its physical fetters. His consciousness was soon reduced to a life force, a person-less, unfeeling energy, oblivious to everything but itself, focused only on its own subsistence. Upon attaining this state, he remained there for a length of time that had no obvious end.

It was just before noon of the seventh day when the door finally opened, and Pra Sunnata was rushed back into the tangible world of human beings with an abrupt rending and tearing of time and space; a shift so sudden, so violent and abrupt, it gave him a sensation of nausea that triggered a fit of gagging and choking. The sunshine blinded him painfully, even after he had shut his eyes, but the fresh air eventually revived him. The ladder was lowered, and he was ordered to get out. It took great effort just to stand on his legs, an exertion that required a full ten minutes, his hands reaching out to the earth wall for support, with his captors diligently waiting up at the brim. He grabbed onto the ladder and he took it one step at a time, pausing, concentrating…heel up, lifting leg… Near the top the guards assisted him out, and practically dragged him all the way to the office of the Commandant.

They plopped him down in a chair on the veranda just outside the door. He was given a cup of water to drink, which he took to his lips, half of which spilled down his neck and shirt as his arms trembled with uncontrollable spasms.

Inside the office, a group of men were deliberating around the table, including the Vietnamese officer and the East German, who had come back from wherever he had gone. In addition there was a newcomer: a Laotian dressed in an expensive black business suit, collared shirt, and a tie made of Italian silk. The nasty little pipsqueak Commandant was sitting next to him, deferentially quiet. The East German was blabbering away in English, which the Vietnamese, apparently multilingual, was busily translating into Lao.

"You have made a great mistake here. You did not listen to what I told you," the East German was saying. "We come here to assist you in these matters, and you don't listen." The Vietnamese was frantically repeating this in Lao, trying to keep pace with the farang's truculent chiding. "I said he must have low profile!" The German slapped his hand down on the table. "But you make martyr of him. Now you have three choices. You can execute him, but even in death

404

his memory remains to cause trouble in future. Anyway, that is not option, until we assess his intelligence value. You can remove him from here and bring him to another camp, but that does not solve problem. Or you can treat him like everyone else, as if he is no one special. Now, isolation no longer possible. Everybody know he is here."

The men around the table finally took notice that the subject of their conference was outside. The man in the business suit called out, "Bring him here."

Pra Sunnata was lifted up out of his chair, hauled inside, and deposited into another chair in front of the wooden table.

The man in the well-cut suit stood up and walked around the table, approaching slowly until he eventually cambered over him. His dusky face was large, round, and looming, and his carefully combed hair glistened under a thick layer of pomade. Furry eyebrows capped his heavily lidded, ruminating eyes. He stood over him for what seemed an inordinate amount of time, until his puckered, dignified mouth opened into a warm, almost amiable, smile. "Hello," he said in English. He lifted Pra Sunnata's chin up in order to look him in the face. "Do you remember me?"

Pra Sunnata stared back at him with a pitiful expression of exhaustion. He studied the man's visage, but didn't recognize it in the least. As he was still a monk, he couldn't lie, even if it might prove advantageous to do so. "No."

"But I remember you. The village of Nong Hak? I was in the unit there. Of course, you look a little different with no hair and after being so badly treated, which, by the way, I apologize for." The Lao gentleman turned to his associates. "If this man is actually Richard Johnson, he is a hero of the revolution. Have him bathed and fed. He must recuperate."

As the prisoner was helped up and escorted out of the room, the Commandant remarked, "But he refuses to work."

"Wait," the visiting Lao official called out, halting the guards. "Is this true?" he asked the man he thought was Johnson.

Pra Sunnata nodded his head yes.

"Why is that?"

"I am a monk," he said under his breath, with the little strength he had.

"What was that?" the man in the suit questioned, thinking he hadn't heard correctly.

The Commandant intervened. "He claims he's a monk."

"A monk? Really? That will not do. We have no need for a monk here. This place," he spread his arms out, as if lovingly embracing the camp's surroundings, "should be considered a school. It is for re-education. Here, we teach practice, as well as theory. Physical labor is the practical part. You must participate in this."

The farang they assumed was Johnson shook his head left and right in refusal.

"Perhaps if you disrobe, leave the priesthood, you would be able to join our student community, yes?"

Despite his enfeebled state, his mind, as well as his heart, still possessed an exceptional clarity. These people were in control now; there was no doubt about that. If he continued to resist them, he could possibly die. And since he was conscious of this, was he not taking his own life, and thereby breaking a parajika rule? Is dying for a cause such as refusing to work, egoistic? Maybe so. In that sense alone, Pra Sunnata didn't see that he had much of a choice. "Yes," he conceded in a very low voice, indicating his agreement with a resigned nod as well, in case they didn't hear his reply.

"Very well, we will arrange it. If you do well here, I will see about placing you in a more pleasant situation. Go and rest and think about what we have discussed."

After the prisoner was taken away, the Lao dignitary addressed the others. "I am impressed. A man of commitment. That is the type of person the Party wants. Such a man only needs to be pointed in the right direction. Think of the propaganda value. Of course, we at the Ministry of the Interior must be assured of this man's identity. Do not keep him in isolation. Put him in with the rest and let them work together, and make him attend the classes as well. A man has social needs in addition to the material needs, and he will start talking about himself to the others. You can monitor what he tells them. But whatever happens, make sure he stays alive for the time being."

"Finally, somebody has right idea," agreed the East German.

The East German went on to predict that, in the beginning, this American monk wouldn't be accepted into the prisoner community, and that the camp authorities shouldn't expect any reliable information for at least a month or more. The others will fear him like the plague, he said. It takes time to build trust, he explained.

The man was obviously well-experienced in prison psychology, for truly no one would speak to Pra Sunnata when he was first brought to the main 'student's quarters', a dark, windowless, clapboard shack. No one would even sit anywhere near him. This was a major feat, considering the circumstances. There were over one hundred men squeezed inside, and to lie down they had to carefully arrange themselves, economizing space as best they could. Somehow they managed to find the extra space necessary as to maintain an invisible barrier; the nearest person to him was never closer than three feet away.

In the morning when the inmates woke up, they would find him sitting in a lotus position, with his hands in a prayer gesture, chanting to himself, and in perfect Pali no less! To chant by oneself was very difficult and required one to know the words by heart. How could this farang be so advanced in the monkhood as to chant so impressively? It was too odd to be believable.

This was a Russian trick, they determined. It was too clever and devious for the Laotians, even the Vietnamese. Everybody's suspicions increased when the farang was allowed to stay behind and rest, while they had to go off and work at five o'clock in the morning. Then there was a rumor that he was getting extra food.

But the rumor-mongering changed tack after he was taken away and wasn't seen again.

Perhaps he really was an American. A pilot? A CIA advisor left behind to spy?

Where had they taken him?

Some of them thought the authorities had taken him to Vientiane for an interrogation by Russian KGBs.

They killed him, one person said.

No, no, they moved him to Sop Hao, argued another. Sop Hao was the most notorious of the re-education camps.

Maybe he was taken to Hanoi, maybe Russia, offered yet someone else.

In reality, Pra Sunnata was being delivered to the newly formed temple in the newly formed village of Ban Ling Kao, the Village of the White Monkey.

The temple was simple in design, roughly square in plan and made of timber, with a four-sided, pyramid-shaped roof covered with red and black wooden shingles. A labor force of detainees, encamped just across the valley in a Mobile Work Camp, a more lenient form of 're-education', had helped the villagers construct it. As Ban Ling Kao was small, newly settled, and relatively poor, the monastery wasn't fashioned in the grand exotic style seen in the larger villages and towns. It sat in a small, clean compound that was rather bare, having only newly planted seedlings as trees. To be disordained at this particular temple, which was a long journey from Re-education Camp 07, was a special request of Pra Sunnata, who was benevolently granted this favor by the Ministry official.

There, Pra Boon met with him. He looked much older, and his once youthful face now wore the tribulations of hastened maturity.

"Pra Sunnata, perhaps it is a clinging emotion, but I am really happy to see you. You look ill. Are you of good health?"

"I am well enough. Yourself, and the others?"

"We are also well enough."

The leader of the group that accompanied Pra Sunnata interrupted their mutual salutations, having deemed it unnecessary to offer any of his own. He wanted to get to the matter forthwith. "Are you the abbot of this temple?"

"Yes," Pra Boon answered.

Pra Sunnata was startled by the reply. "Where is the Venerable Kru Jarun?" he asked, concerned that Pra Boon had ascended to take the old man's place.

Pra Boon frowned, in spite of himself. "He does not participate actively in this temple. He stays in his room and meditates. I myself understand him, it is different now."

"This man would like to leave the Sangha," the cadre announced brusquely, feeling enough time had been wasted in sentimental chitchat.

"Is this true?" Pra Boon asked Pra Sunnata.

"Yes, Pra Boon, I want to disrobe."

It wasn't too difficult a decision. Entering the priesthood wasn't a permanent commitment, nor was leaving it. It was permissible to rejoin the Church again at a future time. Pra Sunnata sensed that for the next portion of his life, he would be spending it as a layman, the same as an ordinary struggling Laotian.

"But we must choose an auspicious day, otherwise you may be plagued by bad luck," Pra Boon pointed out. "The Venerable Kru Jarun is the only one who has sufficient knowledge of astrology to suggest the proper time."

"Never mind that," interjected the communist cadre. "We do it today."

Pra Boon faced the man resolutely. "Today is not possible. It must be done at sunrise. So you must stay at least for the night."

It was a grueling five-hour drive to get here, and the temptation of sleeping at the temple and getting a good meal and a good sleep before making the return trip was too tempting an offer to refuse. These considerations were enough to disintegrate the expeditious mood of the cadre, who eventually agreed.

It had to be so. Because it was a tradition that the day before leaving the priesthood, the disrobing monk must take leave of his fellow monks by prostrating before them and asking forgiveness for any grievances that he may have committed. In the evening, all the monks were called and Pra Sunnata bowed down to each of them, and then went off to the hut of the Venerable Kru Jarun to do the same.

After the gesture of asking forgiveness, Pra Sunnata sat cross-legged listening to the old abbot's advice.

"I do not know your birth date, so I cannot calculate the proper day for your disrobement. Tomorrow may not be a good day."

"I have no choice, Venerable Father."

The Venerable Kru Jarun folded his hands together, signaling he was about to say something important. "The next few years will be difficult for you, as it will be for all of us."

Pra Sunnata faced the abbot. It was at this time that he had first noticed the gray patches in the whites of the old man's eyes. "I accept the Law of Karma," he swore steadfastly.

The abbot hummed a note of doubt. "Hmmm. There will come a time when you will not."

"Is that what you perceive?"

"Yes, but never mind that for now." He changed the subject. "You understand that I am semi-retired now, so Pra Boon will perform the ceremony of disordination."

"I understand."

The abbot has cataracts, Pra Sunnata realized.

"Very well. Remember, you may depart from us, but we will never depart from you."

"I understand, Venerable Father." And with that, Pra Sunnata took his leave.

A man should leave the priesthood at sunrise because it symbolized ritual rebirth, of being born anew. Pra Sunnata crawled forward bearing the offering tray of flowers, candles and incense, and bowed three times in front of the Buddha image while Pra Boon filled his begging bowl with water. Holding a lit candle, Pra Boon let it drip wax into the water as he chanted the thousands of years old

Pali incantations. He then dipped a brush of twigs and leaves into this holy water and sprinkled Pra Sunnata, who had to state three times that he wanted to leave the order.

"I leave the Sangha, please regard me as a layman."

Following the thrice-fold utterance of this proclamation, he was told to bathe, and then come back to Pra Boon, where he was asked to recite the Five Precepts. As a final gesture, Pra Boon tied a plain cotton string around his neck to protect him.

After six years of having invested his identity into the role of a religious disciple, Pra Sunnata was no longer a monk.

So, when he was brought back to the Re-education Camp two days later, everybody's previous theories regarding his ill-fated demise were repudiated.

In fact, the distrust grew, and there was even a new rumor that the time he had spent down in the hole had been staged. One of the prisoners came up with the story that he had been taken out when no one was around, given lots of food and water, and periodically put back inside to make it look like he was in the hole all that time. No one could survive down there for seven days!

He remained a pariah, even though he now went out to work with them, at first, collecting firewood and fetching water from a brook that ran close by. Sometimes he was given the job of cleaning the houses of the guards, as well as running small errands. It was the light stuff, the other inmates noted, not the grueling duties that they had been given when they themselves had first arrived. Then he was put back in leg irons and sent into the forest, cutting down trees and hauling them back to camp. It was his first taste of what was truly hard labor. He had to use a crude axe that rattled his hands when he struck with it, and whose head popped off numerous times during the day, and a handmade cross saw which required a synchronized stroke from the two men pulling it to prevent the teeth from snagging. He, along with a group of others, would drag the logs back to camp using chains. It was arduous work given only to the strongest and healthiest of the men, and at the end of the day every joint and muscle in his body ached. However, the silent hostility of the other prisoners was actually more difficult to bear. It was fine enough to be alone when one was actually physically alone, but speechless contempt in the presence of other human beings was unsettling, even for an ex-monk. Later on he was assigned to road repair, which was just as backbreaking as the logging work, but still no one talked to him.

The prisoners just couldn't resolve how to view this stranger. Furthermore, they noticed that he seemed to be very close to one of the guards, the kid called Sousat, who talked to him regularly, and who also tried to spread the word among the inmates that this farang was some type of hero. Moreover, the farang was still putting on this monk act, chanting and doing meditation exercises as well. All of their misgivings were re-affirmed when the assignments for bomb-clearing activities were given out.

The farang actually volunteered. Volunteered, can you believe that? When asked why he wanted to go, he had replied that since the Americans dropped the bombs, and he was an American, it was only fitting that he should go out and help clear the area. And of course, his request was refused and he was given the task of fixing the Commandant's house instead. It was all a rehearsed scene, the prisoners concluded, just like the 'hole' business. In the evening, after receiving word that two of the inmates picked for bomb clearing had died from accidentally triggering off hidden bombies, their bitterness was misdirected at this enigmatic farang, whom they now were convinced was a planted informer. What was an American doing here among them anyway?

Sunnata, being socially alienated, once again turned towards meditation, indifferent to the fact that he was no longer a Pra, and it became the key to his survival. He also took the opportunity to understand the other inmates and what they were going through.

In Laos at this time, the re-education camps came in many different varieties and flavors. There were the mobile work groups, whose members lived outside and had a fair degree of freedom. And there were the seminars, which were short-term courses of indoctrination about the policies of the Party. Then there were the high-security camps, at least one in each Province, which were virtual prisons, and where those who were considered the greatest threat to the revolution were incarcerated. Re-education Camp 07, where he had found himself, was one such institution. The prisoners at these camps were the once powerful politicians and military leaders of the old regime, the ones who would gain the most should the present government be overthrown.

Laotian society and culture, over and above the recent revolution, was of too gentle a nature to carry out mass executions like those in neighboring Cambodia. In Laos, there were no killing fields. And so, the enemies of the State, real or imagined, were gathered into these camps to remain until such time that it was deemed they had finally conformed to the revolutionary point of view. Either that, or remain in captivity until they conveniently died on their own, a fate that could easily be met given the abysmal conditions in these detention centers. It was almost as bad as one of the Buddhist Hells.

Their abode was a smelly, airless, undersized shack with no lights or windows. There were no sleeping mats; each person had to find their own place on the dirty, bare floor. Everyone also had to shave their heads to control the problems of lice and fleas. For Sunnata, this was just as well, since this act was redolent of his religious vows, but for the other inmates, it only served to remind them that they were nothing more than convicts.

Food for the day was a cupful of rice with some salt and only a liter of water for drinking. In the rice, there were maggots that Sunnata had to carefully remove, as he was still opposed to the taking of life, while the other prisoners didn't bother, but were rather grateful for this extra protein source. Sometimes there was a tin of canned meat shared between five or six persons, although Sunnata couldn't eat this. A few of the inmates used to catch lizards and rats to eat, but if they were found out, they were punished, as such behavior was judged to be primitive. Hunger and thirst were persistent torments that would gnaw at them in all their waking moments.

Despite the meager diet, the physical labor that they were expected to perform was exhausting, and the guards would often beat someone who, in their opinion, was slacking off. Digging roads, hauling heavy skids of machinery, felling trees, and carrying bricks were some of the duties that they were compelled to render. Their ankles were shackled to each other by chains, which after a time, cut into the skin, leaving open sores. If someone took ill, they were in real trouble, for there was no medicine.

In fact, ill health was practically guaranteed by the inadequate food rations. Many men exhibited swollen necks, arms, and legs, indicating Vitamin B deficiency, and some of them were actually suffering from beriberi. Missing teeth, and the numerous cases of bone fractures, suggested scurvy, so there wasn't much in the way of Vitamin C either. Cuts didn't heal, but became sores and ulcers. Quite a few of the men had chronic, lung-ripping coughs, a symptom of pneumonia.

But the psychological hardships were usually the most difficult to endure. The prisoners were formerly wealthy and influential, living the good life, but now they had nothing, nothing but hopelessness. The guards constantly reminded them that they were on the bottom now, forced to bow in submission to young hill-tribe boys with guns, who had to be addressed as comrade.

In this regard, Sunnata was more fortunate than the rest, for he didn't have a past to brood about. He had spent six years successfully obliterating it. As for the physical hardships, the time he had experienced in the hole had only made him stronger and had summoned new energies to overcome the weaknesses that all sensations brought.

Meanwhile the others continued to suffer. Each night was marked by someone sobbing and moaning, and almost every week at least one person died. The pattern was always the same. The person would become quiet and melancholy, maybe get a bit nutty, develop a fever and get delirious, grow weaker, and ultimately expire. Sunnata knew they were dying of despair.

It was the issue of food, although indirectly, that led to the second incident involving Sunnata, causing him to inadvertently step into the limelight once again. One morning, during their routine of queuing at the long concrete water trough set at the side of the barracks, the inmates crowding lethargically around to splash water on themselves, their only bath of the day, a guard approached one of the prisoners and grabbed his jaw, forcing him to open his mouth, and ordered him to remove what was inside. The prisoner put his hands to his mouth and pulled out brown shards of what was probably once the wings of a large cockroach, as well as spiny fragments of legs. The guard slapped the man hard and pushed him on the ground, while the other prisoners were made to line up and watch the forthcoming disciplinary action.

The guards tied the man's hands behind his back, and as he lay face down in the dirt, they circled him, each of them brandishing a long bamboo cane. They walked around slowly, purposefully, their steps noisily mashing the sandy ground, when they suddenly stopped. All at once they brought down their clubs simultaneously, flailing the man, the blows making disgusting smacking sounds that rose above the wretched man's shrieks. As abruptly as it began, the attack ended. Once more they promenaded around the fallen figure, and like before, they stopped. This time they did nothing, but waited silently before continuing their circumambulation. They kept up this game, marching methodically around in a circle, alternately beating him and doing nothing, until the braced anticipation alone became the torture. The rest of the prisoners remained standing around watching this display, as if they were also being punished by proxy. After some time, the beatings became fiercer, and the man's skin burst and cracked open in bloody gashes. And while Sunnata himself didn't truly object to the flagellation, since such inflicted suffering was within the bounds of the degenerate nature of misguided human beings, he soon grew disturbed that the victim was on the verge of being beaten to death. The taking of life was in violation of the Five Precepts, and therefore, as a religious man, he couldn't allow that to happen. That was the real reason, not mere squeamishness, why he broke from the ranks to stand over the beaten man.

"Cease now or you will cause his death!"

At first, this absurd intervention caught everyone off balance, but the men with the canes soon recovered from their surprise and struck him down. As they raised their clubs to fully deliver their vengeance, a voice commanded them to desist.

"Yut!"

It was Sousat, and he was aiming his assault rifle at the ring of guards. "Any punishment of this man must be sanctioned by the Commandant himself."

Only a second or so elapsed, giving them enough time to realize that indeed this was true, leading them to throw down their canes in wordless acquiescence. A few of them then busied themselves with dragging the beaten prisoner by his feet, the blood smearing the earth in a trail behind his broken body. The rest accompanied Sousat as Sunnata was brought to the Commandant's office.

They explained to the Commandant what had occurred.

"Seeing as you are so concerned with the welfare of this prisoner, you will now be personally responsible for his well-being. Dismissed."

And that was the extent of his punishment. In addition to his normal work duties, Sunnata had to nurse the man, whose name was Pantavong, back to health, tending to his wounds to prevent infection and ensuring that he ate his daily cupful of dirty rice. Although this was a burden, it was hardly the type of punishment meted out for defiance of authority. If, in fact, the whole thing was staged, as some speculated, the performance was being carried to ridiculous heights. Otherwise the American was indeed a genuine oddity that not even the authorities knew how to handle. Whispered, yet heated debates continued to take place concerning his interment in the camp. And if the inmates were confused before about the American prisoner, by now they were becoming truly dumbfounded.

In the afternoons, classes were held, which also took on a form of mental punishment. These were conducted in Building Four, the only other building besides the administrative office that was made of cinder blocks. The seminar room was a long room painted a drab bile green, with pillars supporting the roof and a multitude of long-bladed ceiling fans, which whirred around in syncopated swishes, but only succeeded in shifting the dense hot air. The tables they sat at were arranged in a long line from one end of the room to the other.

The teacher was ignorant and uneducated, and the lessons often deteriorated into a screaming tirade. He would shout out questions and then answer them himself. They had to sing songs with inane words such as: "We sold our country to the imperialists, but the heroic revolutionaries took it back to protect the motherland! Shame on us, hurray for the revolutionaries!"

One class was particularly memorable because of two events. The East German had come back for another visit and elected to sit in on the class, along with a high-ranking Vietnamese officer. The other notable incident occurred when Sunnata, for the third time, broke the low profile he had originally wanted to maintain and caused a major scene with the teacher.

There was one Hmong in the class that the teacher often liked to pick on.

"Why did you fight for the Americans? Because you are stupid, that is why! Say you are stupid."

The Hmong wouldn't say it.

The teacher slapped him hard on the head. "Say you are stupid!"

As the teacher was about to strike him again, Sunnata raised his hand, then stood up without being told to. "Comrade teacher, sir, I think it would be instructive to explain the division between certain groups of Hmong and the intervention of the CIA. Otherwise he won't know that he is stupid."

The instructor glared at him in outraged disbelief. If looks could kill, Sunnata would have surely been dead. The teacher, dressed in a floppy cap and green uniform, forgot the Hmong prisoner and strode purposely over to the insolent American like a lion spotting a newer and tastier quarry. He was determined not to lose face, particularly with the visitors present in the room.

All the 'students' who were dozing or daydreaming, suddenly woke from their reverie, taking a morbid interest in the confrontation that was about to occur.

"It is you, who is the stupid one," the teacher told him as he approached.

"I am neither stupid nor clever," Sunnata replied, still playing the Buddhist monk.

"Get on the floor, on all fours, facing the wall."

He did so without hesitation. Once in this position, the teacher kicked him hard in the buttocks, and he fell forward, his face smacking painfully on the concrete floor.

The East German murmured something to the Commandant, who then stood up.

"The class is terminated," the Commandant announced, "everyone return to the barracks."

All of the inmates promptly stood up, gave submissive nops to the teacher, then turned and gave another one to the Commandant and his visitors, before filing out of the hall in an orderly fashion.

The class had been stopped because the East German, and to some extent, the Vietnamese officer, were already disgusted at the teacher's performance. Also, perhaps the East German, being a European, didn't enjoy watching a farang get a boot in the ass.

Whatever the reason, the instructor was relieved of his teaching duties forthwith. Not only that, but the whole structure and philosophy of the classes changed. It became more like a school. Within a week, a new teacher had come from Vientiane, who in the mornings would hand out documents that the 'students' were supposed to read. In the evenings there was a discussion and a written test. The prisoners had to pass the test and convince the teacher that they wholeheartedly accepted the party's line. They were taught the history of the Indochinese communist movement from its inception up to the time of the Lao revolution that had taken place a year ago. Much of it was Vietnamese history, Sunnata noted. The biographies of the leaders of the revolution were also expounded upon, as well as the main battles of the war, of which they were expected to memorize the names, why they were fought, and how many died. They had to know the fundamentals of Marxist-Leninism and the history of the communist-run government right down to the last Central Committee decision.

At least half of the prisoners thought it was all a bunch of crap. But almost all of them agreed that the American in their midst had the power, in his own quiet way, to change things. Significantly, there had also been a parallel development that curtailed the guards' power to administer beatings offhandedly, ostensibly because it was now considered reactionary behavior. It was all because of him, the American who acts like a monk, they murmured amongst themselves. Some began to get so curious about him that they sought out Sousat, the guard who knew him before, and who only confirmed to them that this farang was a natural born leader. Sousat further convinced them that indeed it was true, that Sunnata had actually spent seven days in the hole, without respite. He naturally omitted, however, the role he had played in helping him.

Sunnata's fellow inmates now sensed that his chanting in the mornings was sincere, and not a put-on show. This man had truly been a practicing monk. They observed him when he did his sitting and walking meditation, and some were bold enough to ask for lessons. It wasn't long before a Vipassana meditation group was formed, practicing together before they lay down to sleep and upon waking up in the early morning. They found him a modest, yet engaging fellow, always willing to bend an ear to listen to their afflictions and to assuage their anguish and hardship. Despite his protestations, they addressed him as Luang Pi, Reverend Brother.

"I have left the Sangha, I am no longer a Pra," he would tell them. "Please call me Sunnata." But they found the habit hard to break.

Still, to his relief, no one as yet questioned him about what he had been doing in Lao so as to end up in a high-security re-education camp. In fact, there seemed to be an unwritten rule that no one talked about himself, unless he wanted to.

Oddly enough, it was someone outside his meditation group, the tall, handsome-looking Hmong who had been persecuted in the classroom and subsequently defended by Sunnata, who was the first to broach the subject of the past.

"That was interesting, what you said in the class a few weeks ago, about division of Hmong," he told him candidly in Lao. "There is a guard here, he is a Hmong, guarding me. I am also a Hmong, but I am his prisoner. That is division."

"Do you ever talk to this guard?" Sunnata wanted to know.

"No, when we meet, he is very cruel towards me. He is from the Lo clan, and I am from the Ly."

"Try to talk to him. Be polite to him, not belligerent."

"I cannot do that. The more he taunts me, the more I want to kill him."

"When Hmong kill Hmong," Sunnata said, "that is real division."

The young man scrunched up his face and looked at Sunnata with a vague recognition. "Are you CIA?" he abruptly asked him. "Sky Man?"

Sunnata mulled over this for a moment, then shook his head. "No."

"My name," the Hmong informed him, "is Ly Feng. I used to work for 'Mr. Hog'. Do you know him?"

"No, I don't."

"But you remind me of someone. You look like 'Mr. Sheen'. Are you Mr. Sheen?"

Before Sunnata could answer, a loud yell sounded from the back of the barracks room. "SHIT ON YOUR FUCKING ANCESTORS, YOU DOGS!"

Someone was standing up in the back, and others got up to try and restrain him. It was Pantavong, the man that had been caught eating the cockroach and whom Sunnata had taken care of.

"SONS OF WHORES!" he went on shouting.

"What is wrong with Pantavong?" Sunnata asked.

"Pantavong," Ly Feng told him, "was a big general in the north. He had made a lot of money in the opium trade. Now he has nothing."

"He still has his life," the former monk, Sunnata, preached.

Pantavong was eventually brought down to the floor, making ugly groaning protests.

"Perhaps, but I don't think for too much longer," retorted Ly Feng. And with that pronouncement the Hmong got up and wove his way through the reclining bodies to return to his sleeping place.

The days passed, the hard labor continued unabated, and despondency remained chronic. Each dismal moment of misery melded into the next and deadened one's sensibilities until, like the tolerance one builds up to drugs, they no longer cringed from the anguish. But underneath their emotional numbness were oozing wounds that drained their mental and spiritual fortitude. One by one they fell victim to fatal depression.

The man called Pantavong wasn't the only one who was losing it. One evening, one of the inmates came over to Sunnata. "Luang Pi, Reverend Brother!"

"Please, call me Sunnata, but do not address me as a monk."

"Yes, Ai Sunnata. Come, and look at poor Savang, we think he is dying. We don't know the sacred chants to the degree that you do. Would you pray over him?"

"Yes, of course." Sunnata got up from his place, and made his way towards a group huddled around a man on the floor.

He appeared to be suffering under the typical delirium that preceded death in this place. His body trembled in fits and starts, and he was babbling incoherently.

"I assume this man is a Buddhist, and that he has spent some time in the Sangha."

All Buddhist men were expected to spend at least one Pansa, the Buddhist Lenten period, as a monk before getting married, to gain merit for their mothers.

They remained in respectful silence as they nodded affirmatively.

Sunnata knelt down by the afflicted prisoner and brought his face close. "Savang, can you hear me?"

"Agh, agh…"

"Think about your ordination. Remember the time when you were a Pra."

"Pra…Pra…Mair, Mother…Mair…Mother help me…"

"Listen to me…are you listening?"

"Yes…yes…Pra…Mair, oh Mair help me."

"You must clear your mind. Think of the Sangha, the Damma, and the Buddha. Clear your mind of corrupt things. If you die in a greedy state of mind, you will become a hungry ghost, if you die with thoughts of hatred, you may be reborn in hell. If your thoughts are deluded, you may be reborn in the realm of beasts. You should free your mind from these impurities. You must not die in bewilderment. Repeat after me. Namo!"

"Na…Namo…"

"Again, Namo!"

"Na…mo."

"*Natti santi param sukham*—there is no happiness greater than peace."

"Natti…santi…param…sukham…"

Having put the man's mind in the proper condition, Sunnata began his chanting. He stayed all night with Savang, chanting over him until he expired in the early morning hours.

Sunnata's valuable knowledge of Pali incantations, and his role in providing the spiritual comfort to a dying man, raised his status among the prison population to a new level. However, this was seen as a threat by the camp authorities. The emergence of such a spiritual leader, and the group sessions he was holding, were all hinting at conditions amenable to producing an organized rebellion. The Commandant inevitably had the man they thought was Johnson brought before him to explain his actions.

"What are these little meetings you are having in the barracks in the evenings?"

"They are not meetings, Comrade Commandant, they are lessons in Vipassana meditation. It gives the men hope, sir."

"Hope? We do not want them to have hope. With hope they will be clutching at the past. That is dangerous. We want them to change their way of thinking."

Sunnata knew it was foolish to argue. "I understand, sir."

"You will stop such activities forthwith."

"Yes, sir."

"Go back to the barracks."

Sunnata sheepishly gave a nop and left.

After that discussion with the Commandant, and the breakup of the meditation groups, the camp administration was prepared to look upon Johnson in a more positive light. Although he clearly had considerable influence with the other inmates, he didn't appear to be actively encouraging it. He spoke sparingly, and went about his labor during the day in an industrious and cooperative manner. He was also doing well in his classes, and the teacher was writing favorable reports about him. And indeed it was true, for Sunnata really did enjoy the classes; at least they provided the occasion to exercise his mind. He especially liked the movies they showed. The one about the caves of Sam Neua was fascinating—how the caves had been organized into large meeting rooms, even hospitals and schools, as well as multiple chambers for individual dwellings, a virtual underground city that enabled them to survive and run a parallel government in the midst of daily saturation bombing.

And surprisingly, he found Marxist-Leninist theory quite interesting, though it was more like a Waldenesque fantasy that only idealized the mundane material world, and so to him, it wasn't much different than capitalism. Of course, these latter opinions he kept to himself.

In fact, Sunnata was the best student in the class. The others resented the propaganda they were forced to swallow, letting their pride interfere with their common sense. The instructor could discern those who were refusing to accept the program's content, and in many cases, it was rather obvious.

The teacher would often single someone out and test his sentiments. "Now, tell me, after reviewing the events that have led to the revolution, what is your opinion of the Party's policy?"

Many were still obstinate. "I don't know. I have no opinion."

This was clearly not the response desired.

In contrast, Sunnata, the star pupil, would answer, "It seems the Party has constructed an effective strategy to bring about the changes needed for successfully socializing the means of production."

The other inmates didn't understand Sunnata's attitude. On the other hand, he didn't understand theirs.

"Why don't you just say what the teacher wants to hear?" he would advise them. "It's your only hope of eventually getting out of here."

They would stare back at him, their ashen faces lacking any expression. "We will never leave this place," some said with despair.

In spite of Sunnata's own advice, however, he managed to strain the newly formed good relations he had developed with the camp authorities by confronting them on an issue that was to embroil the entire prison community in a tense drama. It was the issue of the dead that were buried outside the compound, and the need for their cremation.

The recent death of Savang, and his subsequent burial, brought this matter to Sunnata's attention. It provided the opportunity for him to reflect on the score or so graves that already existed: slightly raised mounds of earth with no markers just beyond the camp fence. After considering this for a time, he decided to request a meeting with the Commandant to discuss this problem.

Sunnata, not having been granted permission to enter, was standing outside in front of the Commandant's door under the watch of the guard who had brought him.

"What is it you want to see me about?" the Commandant asked through the open doorway, while reading something on his desk. He didn't deign to look up, nor did he feel it necessary for Sunnata to come inside.

"Comrade Sir, I have heard that some of those who have died here have been buried for over a year."

The Commandant still didn't bother to glance at him. "What concern is that to you?" he asked rhetorically, his eyes still fixed on the papers before him.

"The bodies need to be cremated, Comrade Sir."

"That would be a valuable waste of firewood."

"If they are not cremated, their souls will wander about. They may be vengeful. They require cremation to be released for rebirth."

The Commandant finally looked up, his fleshy, tuna-fish lips twitching with a menacing vexation. "You are being insubordinate! After I had the courtesy and generosity to reply to you, you refuse my answer! Go back to the barracks before I decide to punish you!"

The guard grasped Sunnata's arm and led him away.

This was all it took. Like a little seed that is planted, the mention of the spirits of the dead sprouted an unspoken apprehension that gradually grew into a spreading foliage of fear. The guard who overheard the discussion with the Commandant began to gossip to the other guards about this, and it became the new subject of conversation during their leisurely moments. Although half of them weren't Buddhist, the hill-tribe guards had all been brought up to believe in spirits, and all agreed that if a spirit was once a Buddhist, it should be appeased in the Buddhist way.

The prisoners also became agitated. The struggle for their own daily survival had so far kept them from dwelling too much on those that were already gone and buried, but now that it was out in the open, they couldn't help but give this some thought. In this morbid atmosphere, they grew quieter and talked less. At night, Sunnata's usual chanting took on a more ominous tone. Pantavong, the ex-general who was slowly going mad, amplified the communal sense of dread by his nightly outbursts, which were becoming more frequent and upsetting, almost as if he were channeling their fear. On some nights he would talk to himself loudly, keeping everyone awake. They didn't need this extra distraction. They had enough problems with the mosquitoes and the ants, not to mention the rats, repulsive things with long shrew-like snouts and malevolent eyes that shined in the dark, and who bit their feet as they slept. Now it was becoming almost impossible to get the little sleep that they formerly could, their insomnia turning their nights into long ordeals of tormented thinking, and thinking too much was their greatest enemy in a place like this. This added stress served to intensify the already existing psychological pressures of living in an isolated camp in overcrowded conditions.

Once this uneasiness started to accelerate, some of the prisoners came to Sunnata with their holy amulets for him to bless. They wanted protection from the spirits.

"I am no longer a monk," he protested.

"But you still have the power. You have accumulated a lot of good Karma. The communists forced you to disrobe, but in your heart you are still a monk."

So he gave in to their demands and uttered the sacred Pali spells over their amulets, ending the recitation by blowing on them sharply, in accordance with the proscribed formula. Even Sousat, influenced by his years in the Forest Temple, came to Sunnata for 'charging up' the power of the amulet that the Venerable Kru Jarun had given him years before.

But not everyone had amulets. This created a source of tension. One morning, as everyone groggily woke up to another day of toil, one of them shouted, "Who has taken it? My amulet!" The distraught man then attempted to physically search those who had slept next to him, and they roughly brushed him off, irate and offended. A scuffle broke out as he began screaming and shouting, making such a scene that he had to be taken away by the guards.

The guards were also swayed by fear, especially after having noticed that Sousat had a protective charm. Now they all wanted one. If these were Buddhist ghosts, it required Buddhist magic. Some guards would get a prisoner and forcibly take his amulet from him, which would lead to minor brawls breaking out.

Sunnata's presence, once again, had fomented a crisis in the camp.

It wasn't long before the Commandant became aware of the disturbing undertones going on within his domain. His frustration with the man he knew as Johnson was barely controllable. Despite the farang's promise that he wouldn't stir things up, it now seemed as if he was trying to create some sort of uprising. If it weren't for the instructions of the official from the Ministry of the Interior, he would have executed this trouble-making bastard long ago. He decided to have Johnson make a public announcement to deny the existence of spirits.

They were all called to stand in assembly outside the barracks. Aptly enough, it was a dismal looking day, overcast with a gunmetal gray sky, and with a chilly breeze that pierced through their shredded clothes and into their bones as they stood raggedly at attention.

The Commandant began with a little speech. "If we ever hope to become a modern nation, we must rid ourselves of the primitive beliefs of ghosts and demons. Your behavior is disappointing, to say the least. We expect more from you than this childish nonsense. You are going backwards instead of forwards." He turned to Sunnata, who was standing a few steps in front of the assembly. "Face them, and tell them that there are no evil spirits here."

Sunnata, now feeling responsible for the situation, turned around and stated in a loud, clear voice, "There are no evil spirits here."

"You see, even the one who started all this admits this. It was just a devilish ruse of this American Imperialist to trick you." He walked over to Sunnata. "Are you sorry for the trouble you have caused?"

"I am sorry."

The Commandant addressed the group. "Consider this matter finished. Back inside!"

But it was too late.

The next morning, the hysteria became irreversible when they found one of the camp dogs dead, its legs stretched out stiff, its mouth wide open exposing its teeth and tongue, and the eyes popping out as if in utter terror. In all likelihood the dog had had a fatal encounter with a cobra, but the mood of the camp wasn't conducive to considering such rational explanations.

Nobody said anything. They went about their onerous tasks of the day silent and somber, their bland faces belying their fear. Adding fuel to the fire was Pantavong. He had already been confined to the barracks for two days running, because he couldn't even perform the simplest tasks, so demented he had become. That night, he began screaming, for no discernible reason, "AAY! AAY AAY…"

As usual, his neighbors had to get up and calm him down, but tonight he was proving to be uncontrollable.

"AAY! AAY!" he kept screaming.

Sunnata stood up, and the inmates parted the way for him. "Pin him down."

Four guys jumped him and held him on the floor.

"Give me your shirt," he ordered the man standing closest to him, who quickly removed it.

Placing the shirt over Pantavong's face, Sunnata began chanting in Pali. Fortunately it didn't take too long; they had to endure another twenty minutes of his ranting before the madman became pacified. Sunnata, having finally put the man at ease, returned to his sleeping place, and everyone else went back to their spots as well.

"Somebody should kill Pantavong and put him out of his misery," one of them grumbled as they lay back down.

But Pantavong wasn't the only one who was on the edge. During the following night, just as most of the inmates had gone off in a tender, commiserating slumber, another unnerving event occurred. Without warning, the still, dark night was suddenly and violently ripped open with machine gun fire, followed by bloodcurdling screams, then more rounds from the AK-47. Everyone jumped up terrified, looking around with wide eyes into the darkness of the sleeping hall. There followed a ghostly quiet. Once they all had recovered from their shock, they began to murmur timorously amongst themselves. A minute or two later, the double bolted doors flew open and the Commandant, holding a kerosene lantern and dressed only in his sleeping sarong, burst into the barracks. He pointed to Sunnata. "YOU! Come with me."

Apparently, what had happened was that one of the guards had heard something, which could have been a small animal in the bushes, or an errant breeze rustling the leaves. In any case he had become spooked and fired his weapon to chase away the evil spirits. The Commandant had run out of his house, questioned the panicked guard, and then, after getting his explanation, had proceeded to slap the living shit out of him.

Now the Commandant was pushing and shoving Sunnata all the way to the middle of the compound. Once he decided they had gone far enough, the Commandant reached up and grabbed him by the left ear to make him halt. Maintaining his grip on the ear he shook and yanked Sunnatta's head like it was a yo-yo on a string. "You have caused me to lose my sleep. Now you will not have yours." He let go but slapped him hard on the temple as he did so. He then ordered one of the other guards to watch over him. "He is to stand up all night. If he sits down, shoot him. That is my order. If he sits down, shoot him," he repeated for emphasis. "Is that understood?"

"Yes, Comrade Sir."

As Sunnata's luck would have it, the young guard assigned this duty was none other than Sousat.

"Why are you always getting into trouble?" he asked after the Commandant had departed. "And I have to help you all the time," he complained.

Sunnata, without expression, stated, "It is your Karma."

"It is bad Karma." Sousat looked down at the ground. "You can sit down if you want."

"What if the Commandant sees me?"

"He won't come out again."

So Sunnata sat down on the ground cross-legged and engaged himself in sitting meditation.

Of course he made sure that by five o'clock in the morning he was already standing up again.

Shortly before dawn, after the usual day's work assignments were given out, Sunnata still stood under Sousat's charge.

When all of the inmates had been dispatched, the Commandant strode over to him in a leisurely manner, a manner meant to convey that he was free now to give him all of his attention. Sousat was subsequently replaced by two other soldiers.

The Commandant put his face nose-to-nose with Sunnata's. "You are very clever, aren't you?"

"No, sir."

The little man began shouting in a fit of ecstatic rage. "YES YOU ARE!" He stood on his tiptoes as he yelled in his face. "YES YOU ARE!" he repeated, staring hard, his eyes black with fury. "Thinking of ways to disrupt the camp. And if you are thinking, that means you have too much energy. We shall reduce it."

A host of other guards came over. Together they marched him out of the compound, and then proceeded along a trail that led into the rice fields, with the Commandant walking a few steps in front, leading the way with his fat little body making an obscene swagger. They stopped at the last paddy basin, in the middle of which was a crude wooden plough that lay abandoned.

"I am a realistic man. I know you do not have the strength of a water buffalo, so I give you a basin that has been ploughed already. Although, I must say, it has been a long time since then. Perhaps it needs to be done again." He extended his right arm, pointing to the middle of the field. The soldiers grabbed Sunnata and took him to the plough, to which he was bound from the back, hitched like a human ox. Two guards held the handles to drive it.

"Pull it!" the Commandant ordered.

Sunnata strained, and the initial effort was excruciating. At first the thing didn't budge, but once he got the blades sliding it became easier. He stepped forward with resolve and mindfulness. Left heel up...lifting leg...moving forward...treading...right heel up... Every muscle in his body, from his face to his feet, stretched themselves tautly in exertion, while sweat poured down his torso in rivulets. He grappled with the plough until he had done the full sixty feet of the basin, the whole of the first furrow.

"Continue!"

Now he had to turn the plough around and go in the other direction. The guards didn't help him at all. After struggling, stumbling, wheezing, and groaning, he managed to position it and began the second furrow. When he reached the end of the second furrow, the Commandant yelled out, "Stop! Come here."

The guards unhitched him, and Sunnata limped over, not realizing that something important was about to happen to him.

"Prostrate before me, and apologize."

Sunnata, still panting from the effort, looked him straight in the eyes. Something snapped, and he experienced a flashback to his former self. "Fuck you," he spat out in English.

The Commandant didn't know much English, but he knew what 'fuck you' meant. He immediately gave Sunnata a swift kick in the groin.

As Sunnata doubled over, he could hear the Commandant shout. "Go and pull it!"

He was roughly brought to his feet and made to turn the plough again to do another furrow. When he had completed it, he was called for the second time. Once more he refused the command to beg forgiveness, but this time his defiance was silent. Another furrow later, Sunnata acquiesced and obeyed.

But it wasn't over. After they had brought him back to the compound, he was told to stand, the guards being ordered to shoot him if he sat down. And so through the afternoon he stood. The physical pain, however, wasn't as agonizing as the torment caused by his own disillusionment. He had spent more than Six Pansas, over seventy-two cycles of the moon, as a member in the sacred Sangha, and it had all been negated in one afternoon. It made him realize that he still hadn't received the Damma entirely into his heart, and since that was the only thing that gave meaning to his life at that point, his sense of loss was overwhelming. How could he have forgotten the most valuable thing he possessed? To have become so pathetic as to throw it all away in a flash of anger?

He chastised himself mercilessly. Pride and ego had risen up like demons, tempting him with the repulsive thought of taking life and reminding him of his former self, for at one point he had felt the desire to kill the Commandant. After the countless hours of Vipassana Meditation, he was still so corrupt as to succumb to hate and ill will. He silently chanted the *sadeng abbat*, the Monk's Confession.

The events of the past week precipitated another visit by the official from the Ministry of the Interior. On that day, another fateful day for the future Chao Baa, Sunnata had already been called to the Commandant's office and was standing outside the door when the Soviet Mi-14 helicopter landed in the middle of the compound, creating a haze of dust. Sousat had been summoned as well.

The visiting dignitaries disembarked and walked towards the admin block with a gait that reflected a grave and pressing business. The Ministry official, once again nattily dressed in a dark suit, was in a foul mood, as revealed by the sour, saturnine look on his face. He had good reason to be. The plan to take the farang out of isolation had backfired, not only because it had led to major disruptions in the running of the camp, but also because there was still no information forthcoming that could uncover the identity of this character. The gossip of the inmates and guards had yielded nothing helpful whatsoever.

Accompanying the Lao official was another farang, this time unmistakably a Russian. They entered the office to sit together behind the large mahogany table, alongside the Commandant. The others let the Ministry official do all the talking. He questioned Sousat first.

"You knew this man before?"

"Yes, sir."

"Where did you meet this man?"

"At the Forest Temple, near Pu Khe."

"What were you doing there?"

"I was a temple boy."

"And that is where you first saw this man?"

"Yes, sir."

"What was his name at that time?"

"Ree-chart...Jon-sown. But later, after becoming a monk, we call him, Sunnata."

"This man had never told you where he had come from, and how he found his way to the temple?"

"No, sir."

The Ministry official turned to the Commandant and the Soviet advisor. "It is the same story that the monks disclosed. It seems that no one had ever been interested enough to ask him."

He returned his attention to Sousat. "Very well, you may go." Sousat saluted and exited.

"Bring him in here!"

The guards shoved Sunnata into the room.

The official pursed his lips gravely and stared at the farang with glowering scorn. "We have compiled a small list of those people who we think you might be. Why can't you just make it easy and tell us who you are?"

Sunnata remained reticent.

"Would you like to take a look at the list? Perhaps, you have truly forgotten who you once were. Maybe the names would jolt your memory." He motioned for Sunnata to pick up the piece of paper on the table.

Sunnata held the paper in his hand and studied it halfheartedly. Many of those on the list were pilots, as well as some civilians, and a few CIA men. One name stuck out clearly and caused him to flinch. Robert William Botkin, Paramilitary Division, Central Intelligence Agency.

He was no longer a monk. To speak falsely meant only breaking one of the Five Precepts of a layman. He decided he would try not to lie, but that he would do so if necessary. "Richard Johnson's name is not there."

"We believe Mr. Johnson is dead. We approached the American Embassy concerning the whereabouts of Richard Johnson and that is the information they communicated to us. He died seven years ago. We are also of the opinion that you have knowledge of his death. Isn't that so?"

Sunnata didn't answer.

"You take the identity of a dead man, don't tell us anything truthful about your past. Naturally, under these circumstances we are not in a position to inform your government concerning your presence here. Is that what you wish?"

"Yes."

There was no comment to that.

The Russian finally spoke up. He looked at Sunnata with a hard, expressionless face; his impassive, cold blue eyes narrowing in a focused scowl as he addressed him in brutally accented English, full of discordant stresses on all the wrong syllables.

"I personally believe that you are an ex-CIA advisor. What has taken place here in this camp could only be attributed to an *agent provocateur*. You have managed to subvert the authority in this camp by manipulating the guards as well as the prisoners. You have done this clandestinely, concealing your motives, using subtle psychological methods which are the trademark of a professional.

"There are three possible explanations," he continued. "You are truly Richard Johnson, yet the American authorities actually believe you are dead. In which case you may have staged your own," he paused for emphasis, "murder. Just why you would do such a thing is not easily understandable. Another scenario is that you are an imposter, using Johnson's identity as a cover. Now why would you do that, unless you are a planted spy monitoring the events going on in this country? But then why would the US government compromise your mission by discrediting your cover? And then, not even asking us why we were querying them? I would think they would have wanted you out of here as soon as possible to retrieve whatever intelligence you have gathered up to this point. So even that theory has weaknesses. The third possibility is that you fear the American government because of some act that would be considered a crime in their eyes, possibly traitorous. Yet, you do not cooperate and confide in us. I feel that only a thorough interrogation will lead us to the truth."

The Ministry man leaned forward and said, "We have no choice but to remove you from here. We shall take you to one of our special schools in Sam Neua. We will make sure you have contact with no one. There, we will concentrate on extracting what you are hiding. We won't repeat the same mistake we have made here. Wait outside."

He was ordered to stand in the vicinity of the helicopter until such time that the official entourage was ready to depart. He was to be personally delivered to Sop Hao, Camp 01, a reputed hellhole.

The meeting inside the Commandant's office lasted for another hour. As the camp prisoners shambled back into the compound, returning from their laboring outside, they peered at Sunnata, standing alone in the courtyard, with concerned curiosity. No one, not even the guards, noticed crazy Pantavong slipping out of the barracks.

When the group of dignitaries withdrew from the office and began their walk towards the chopper, Pantavong crept up behind them. It happened so fast there was no time to react. Somehow he managed to jerk the automatic pistol out of the holster of the Soviet officer, pushing him to the ground; he then grabbed the man from the Ministry around the neck and placed him in a standing headlock, threatening him with the pistol while keeping their bodies close. "TAKE ME TO THAILAND OR I'LL KILL YOU ALL!"

At first no one knew what to do. Then all the guards raised their guns.

"Do not shoot!" ordered the Commandant.

The AK-47 was a durable and powerful combat weapon, but it wasn't very accurate. There was no way they could pick Pantavong off without endangering the Ministry official. Even if they were successful in hitting the target, there was no telling what the bullet would do once inside his body. It could twist and turn and exit out of an unpredictable spot, possibly boring through his hostage as well. Shooting him from behind was therefore not an acceptable solution either. It was a standoff.

Time seemed to halt melodramatically, as everyone stood motionless in the glaring sunlight, their shadows crisp and black upon the incandescent red sand. It became quiet enough to hear a grain of rice drop.

"TAKE ME TO THAILAND!" Pantavong shouted a second time.

"Pantavong!" someone called out. It was Sunnata. "Listen to me!"

Pantavong whirred about, clinging to his hostage. "You! You, farang monk, don't interfere! I am leaving here, one way or another."

Sunnata slowly walked toward him.

"Stop, or I'll shoot you!" He pointed the gun in his direction.

Sunnata continued to draw near, undaunted. "I am not afraid to die. If that should happen, then it is my Karma. I cannot escape my Karma. Neither can you."

"Yut, yut! Stop! Stop, I said, stop now!"

"Release that man first."

Pantavong may have been crazy, but he wasn't stupid. "If I release him, they will immediately kill me," he argued, referring to the twenty odd soldiers who had their guns trained on him.

"And if you shoot him, they will also kill you. Either way, you are going to die, there is no way out of that. But you have a choice. If you kill this man before you die, you will have increased your bad Karma for your next life. You will be reborn in the Realm of the Beasts. You would only be punishing yourself…"

"Do not come any closer!"

It was eerie, the way the situation had turned all those that were looking on, the guards, the prisoners, the officials, into frozen spectators, as still as figures in a wax museum; a hushed performance in front of a captive audience, the two players performing alone in this scene, the stage a dusty, desolate courtyard.

Sunnata kept approaching, his steps deliberate and full of authority. "…But if you spare his life, you will earn much merit, by showing mercy and compassion just before your moment of death."

Pantavong didn't say anything. He was becoming confused. He again put the gun to the Ministry man's head, then extended his trembling arm to aim it once more at Sunnata. He continued to do this, alternately jutting it against his captives head, then flinging his arm back out to point the gun at the man coming nearer, as if seized in the grip of bewildering uncertainty. The beads of sweat on his forehead glistened in the hot afternoon sun; his breathing grew rapid and desperate.

"Listen to me, Pantavong," Sunnata shouted, getting closer, "do not die in bewilderment. Free your mind of impurities, especially hate and ill will. Think of the Buddha and the Damma, say the sacred words..."

The gunman took his aim off Sunnata and pointed it at the head of his captive with a manner of finality. It appeared he had made his decision.

"*Namo Tassa Bhagavato Arahato Samma Sambuddhasa ...*" Sunnata chanted.

Pantavong abruptly shoved his hostage down to the ground, put the gun to his own head and shouted "Namo!" then pulled the trigger and—bang!—his brains spouted out the side of his head in a crimson cloud of blood and tissue. The only sound after that was the thud of his body hitting the ground.

Chapter 18

Laos 1977

"Friends die for us to bury, and live for us to feed"
Laotian proverb

For him to die that day, the day that Pantavong had gone berserk, was just not his Karma, neither was it for him to be sent to the notorious Sop Hao. On the contrary, the events of that day were to play an important part in the life of the future Chao Baa. Just before the Great Famine of '77, the man whom the authorities had only known as Sunnata, alias Richard Johnson, was assigned to Mobile Work Force 333, not far from the village of Ban Ling Kao, the Village of the White Monkey.

The bureaucrat from the Ministry of the Interior had indeed taken note of the incontrovertible power this peculiar farang had displayed. The man's quiet authority and cool command of the situation should have been all the more reason to have him kept in isolation and have him investigated further. Such a person could pose a potential threat. The Ministry official couldn't bring himself to make such a decision, however, since this man had saved his life while endangering his own. That created a durable bond between them that could never be broken. So he risked his career and relied on his faith that Johnson, Sunnata, or whoever he was, wasn't a threat to the state, despite the extraordinary influence the man could hold over people. Consequently, the official did just the opposite of what good sense dictated: he rewarded him by placing him in a form of detention that meant less hardship and more freedom.

As for Sunnata himself, the nine months he had been inside Re-education Camp 07 had been a time of intense emotions, where he himself had been the center of attention. To be such a phenomenal figure wasn't his design. It was at odds with the goal of eliminating the ego, the voidness of self, equanimity and calmness. The episodes at the camp had exhausted him spiritually, even mortified him, and all he wanted now was to be an unnoticeable nobody.

There was no fence around Mobile Work Force 333. There were no barracks either. The detainees had to build their own houses on an allocated piece of land and the guards' houses as well. Most of these dwellings were lined up in two rows facing each other, although a few were scattered in the woods behind. The detention camp was situated in an isolated spot, but it had a scenic view, on top of a large hill. Down below was a grassy valley, where circular patterns of vegetation and dusky ponds reflected the bomb-cratered terrain. Far off on the other side, were the wooden and bamboo houses of Ban Ling Kao, and in their wake, the green checkerboard mosaic of the villagers' rice paddies. A series of rain-sculptured mountains, with thick jungle growing around sheer rock faces, was just behind, towering over the sleepy hamlet. The dark hill nearest the settlement stood out obtrusively in that it had a conspicuously naked patch of ground presumably deforested by the villagers. This cleared area was in the shape of a rounded triangle pointing downwards and had a small crack in the earth near the top.

In addition to constructing their own dwellings, the prisoners also had to grow their own food, for they weren't fed. It was like being a frontiersman really, since the detainees had to virtually build something out of nothing. Naturally, the first few prisoners were helped by the guards, but after that they had to help each other. They worked the land collectively, as in a commune. When Sunnata first arrived, obviously he didn't have a house, so he relied on the hospitality of one of the inhabitants, old Potisat, who invited him to stay in his home, a bamboo hut on stilts.

He was brought to the compound one sunny afternoon, accompanied by a small contingent of soldiers. They were met by the camp's guards, who led them straight to Potisat, he being the eldest among the detainees.

Potisat stood in the doorway, dressed in his best clothes, a green

Western-style, short-sleeved buttoned shirt and a striped sarong that he only wore on special occasions. He wasn't surprised at first to see a farang, although he was a bit confused by the way he was clothed: in a shabby shirt and torn trousers, and his shaven head was also out of character. He had seen farangs before, Russian advisors in military uniforms that would stop at the camp on their way to somewhere else to have a look around the place. But when they informed him that the farang, named Ree-chart Jon-sown, was to be a new member of the Mobile Work Force, he couldn't fathom how that could be. Of course, he knew well enough not to inquire from the guards. He would, in due course, find out from the European himself.

After greeting each other with prayer-like nops, the old man set about brewing some green Chinese tea while the soldiers rested on the veranda, which was a bamboo platform at one end of the house. As they sat in the customary cross-legged position, with each foot resting on the opposite thigh, they sipped their tea and engaged in minor chitchat, mostly concerning the weather, notably the unusual coolness and strong winds that were atypical for that time of the year. Sunnata himself was quiet, taking in the sight of the austere settlement shimmering in an effulgent sunlight. He sat thoroughly passive, keeping his thoughts to the minimum possible. He didn't ponder too much on what destiny awaited him here, as he was apt at preventing his mind from wandering too far, a habit not only developed from his years of meditation, but from his survival of Camp 07. Yet he couldn't restrain himself from gazing at the few men who strolled by on the path in front of Potisat's little dwelling: their torn shirts and faded sarongs gave them a ragged appearance, but they seemed strong and healthy.

The soldiers eventually begged their leave and drove off in their Russian jeep, while the camp guards returned to their huts, leaving the two men alone on the little veranda.

"Do you speak Lao?" Potisat asked, wearing an inquisitive expression. He was a handsome man in spite of his age, endowed with a square, proportioned, and congenial face, which by now, had become thoroughly creased. His thin lips framed a wide mouth that seemed suited for eloquent conversation. His short gray hair added an air of distinction, yet his eyes bore a sprightly twinkle.

Sunnata looked at him with a blank face. "Jao. Yes."

"Are you French?" Potisat figured that was a good guess, since many Frenchman had remained throughout the war, most of them having taken Lao wives, committed to setting up new lives for themselves here in Laos.

"No, I am an American."

"An American? A prisoner of war?"

What should he say to that? As little as possible he decided. "No, not really. I joined the monks at the Forest Temple and the cadres found me there. They didn't know what to do with me, so they put me in Re-education Camp number seven."

The old man was chewing on areca nuts wrapped in betel leaves, which gave his teeth a reddish hue and caused him to spit a lot. "How did you come to the temple?"

Again, he had to pause to contemplate his answer. "I was involved in the war, but I decided it was wrong, so I ran away and became a monk."

"Why don't they send you back to America? They could at least send you to Thailand and from there you can get back home."

"It's complicated. Besides, I don't want to go back."

"You want to stay in Lao? Why? You have a Lao wife here?"

This question momentarily broke Sunnata's indifference, and even caused him to smile slightly, for the idea of intimacy with a woman seemed so absurd to him. "No, I was a monk, I told you already."

"A married man can still be a monk," Potisat pointed out. "Although, if he remains one for too long his wife will forget him." Potisat grinned mischievously, exposing his dark-stained teeth and then turned his head to expectorate in a rather burnished tin spittoon.

"And you, Uncle?" Sunnata asked, addressing him in the respectful kinship term used in the villages.

"That's a long story. My life was interrupted by the war. My sons were forcibly taken to fight on the Royalist side. Now they are dead, all three of them. My wife died of malaria in the refugee camps just before the end of the war. I am alone now."

He was quiet for a while, before going on to describe other aspects of his life. From his verbal ruminations, it came out that Potisat possessed a wealth of information concerning customs and tradition. He had been, and still considered himself to be, a maw pii, a ritual specialist, and the man in charge of ceremonies to appease the spirits, including the pii ban, the village spirit. This may have been the reason why he was called 'Old' Potisat, though he really wasn't that elderly, being only in his mid-fifties. He was originally from Lat Buak, a market settlement in the hills north of Ponsavan, not far from the Nam Ngum River. In 1970, along with everybody else, he had been forcibly evacuated by the CIA army and brought to a refugee camp on the Vientiane Plain. Five years later, he returned to the Plain of Jars to help rebuild his village.

"When I first came back, I couldn't recognize this place," he told Sunnata. "No more trees, the bomb craters everywhere, the whole Plain of Jars black and silent. Even the wild animals were gone. But it's getting better now."

He then narrated how shortly afterwards, he fell out with the local cadre, whom the government had sent to mobilize the people in the creation of the new socialist state. The cadre prevented the old man from conducting many of the rites that were reputed to be important in village life. Arguments between the two of them were frequent, and on several occasions, Potisat actually threatened him publicly with retribution by the spirits. It was clear that Potisat needed to be re-educated.

"And so, now, my life continues here in this place," he forlornly concluded. "I only hope it doesn't end here."

Three other men were approaching the house. Potisat called out to them, and he and Sunnata rose to their feet.

Everyone put their hands together and bowed their heads, giving a nop to each other.

"Sabai dee, sabai dee, sabai dee," they all exchanged.

Once the men had climbed up to the little hut, Potisat did the honors of introducing each other. The men's names were Mat, Wattana, and Oun, all of them in their thirties. Mat was a small scrawny fellow with spectacles and an intellectual manner, while Wattana was a brutish man, whose block-shaped face appeared even blockier by the crewcut he sported. The third person, Oun, was a short swarthy guy with greasy hair and exceptionally high cheekbones.

"This is..." Potisat turned toward Sunnata. "What should I call you? Ree-chart, or..."

"Please, call me by my Pali name, Sunnata," he entreated.

"Were you a monk?" Mat asked, a bit stupefied.

"*Sern nang*, let's sit down," the old man suggested.

They sat on the veranda and listened to Sunnata's brief explanations, a condensed version similar to the one he had given to Potisat.

"Tomorrow, we must start building this man a house," Potisat announced.

The three visitors, after enthusiastically agreeing to offer their help, went on to elucidate the routine of the Mobile Work Force. The residents of the camp, they explained, were organized into migratory units that performed public works, helping to build village houses and repair bombed-out buildings. They had to help in clearing the land for paddy and in building simple irrigation systems, and sometimes transplanting and harvesting rice in the fields of others as well as their own. Political re-education classes were held three nights a week, and the syllabus was pretty much the same as that recently given at Re-education Camp 07. They had weekends free, and they could travel within the province during those two days and visit friends. Friends were important, and the way they had survived was by winning the confidence of the villagers and gaining their sympathy. That was how one could get extra food and herbal medicines. Relatives were allowed to visit. It was even possible to obtain special permission for your wife and family to live with you, although that wasn't an option commonly practiced.

The American, whom they would call Sunnata, described the more extreme conditions at Re-education Camp 07 and all of them shuddered, glad that they were fortunate enough to have escaped that fate.

Despite their efforts at making him feel welcome, he saw through them, to a core of gloom underneath their happy facade. The work camp wasn't a severe castigation, but rather a slow, gradual acquiescence to the power of the state. The detainees were more like exiles than typical prisoners, trying to make the most of the situation, lapsing into a passive resignation, and hoping for the day when they would truly be free.

As evening approached, Oun and Wattana left, while Mat stayed to have dinner with Potisat and his guest. After the meal, Sunnata fell asleep to the soft tones of the Laotians' chatter.

The building of Sunnata's house was much more involved than the construction of a simple shack would lead one to expect, and it served as an important first lesson in local customs for Sunnata. Before anything else, they had to erect a shrine and conduct rites to placate the spirits who were considered the true owners of the land. Special charts had to be consulted, astrological calculations had to be made, and special poles had to be chosen. Unsurprisingly, it was Potisat who was in charge of all these hallowed formalities. In addition, the house couldn't lie along a north-south direction, as it would offend the sun. And the ladder to the house had to have an odd number of steps to prevent the evil spirits from climbing up.

It was also mandatory to have a baa-see ceremony to welcome him, which was held on the evening of the third day, with the other detainees holding onto him as the sacred strings were tied to his wrists.

All these proceedings made him realize that he still didn't fully understand much of Lao at all, having spent all of his time in isolated and extreme situations—in the chaos of the battlefield, in the seclusion of a remote temple, and in the internment of a prison camp. Like that time six years ago when he wandered into the Forest Temple, he once again saw the need to flush out the assumptions of the past and start with a clean slate. If he was to remain in Lao, living among its people, he had a lot more to learn. But what posed as an even greater challenge was that he might have to learn more about himself.

On his fourth day in the Mobile Work Force, Sunnata accompanied a team of detainees on his first assignment outside. He was given a pair of shorts and a haggard-looking shirt, as well as a hat to keep the sun off him—a funnel-shaped, reed-woven hat called a goop, a style brought over by the Vietnamese. In contrast to the inmates at Re-education Camp 07, the men weren't fettered with leg irons and only a minimal number of guards accompanied them. When Sunnata asked if anyone had ever run away, one of the men told him yes, just once. He was caught, but then never seen again. After that, nobody else had made another attempt.

For the first few weeks his work assignment was to build a small bridge over a nearby gully, which entailed stabilizing the slopes of the banks and laying timbers for the structure. When the bridge had been completed, the team was disbanded to join other crews in less demanding labor. During this period, he was taught how to make a rope from rattan vines, how to dig a well and line the walls with bricks, to make a diversion weir using stones and branches. He prepared his own rice fields, constructed the paddy dikes, and mastered the art of plowing with a water buffalo. At first the shocks and chafing from the wooden handles of the plow caused ugly, painful blisters to develop. It took some time before his hands could grow the calluses of a genuine plow handler.

Simple things, like matches, were hard to come by. When it came time to start a fire using a flint—a special quartz rock with colored streaks—Sunnata surprised the Laotians by doing it without any guidance, for it was something he had seen the dekvats do at the Forest Temple.

Considering that he now had a house, he still spent most of his time at Potisat's place. He relied on the old gent's generosity in order to eat, and that of others who contributed food for him. The Laotians, in general, seemed amicable and commiserating, but only to a certain degree. There was still a dark, private layer that he couldn't gain access to. This was fine by him, since he too had difficulty in relating too closely to them. When Sunnata began to get work assignments in the village of Ban Ling Kao, he benefited from the charity and compassion of the villagers as well, although in the beginning they were afraid to even talk to him.

While the village looked deceptively near from atop their hill, it was a twenty-minute walk down the mountain, and another half-hour to get across the valley. The way back was over an hour's walk, for they had to climb back up the slope to their camp.

In the late afternoon of his first day in this village, after a day of planting trees, Sunnata was given permission to visit the wat to greet the monks that had once been his colleagues at the Forest Temple. It had been almost a year since he had seen them, since the time he had been made to disrobe. Strolling through the village now, Sunnata noted that Ban Ling Kao had subsequently grown a great deal larger.

Mat had chosen to accompany him.

Walking along the main lane of the hamlet, greetings were reciprocated with the other passersby that the pair had come upon, all of them taken aback by the sight of a Caucasian among them. Naturally, they were all inquisitive and some were actually bold enough to stop and ask Mat what such a person was doing here. Mat, who seemed to be well-known in the village, did all the talking. None of them questioned Sunnata's presence too deeply, however, since the government's paranoia concerning any criticism or discontent could easily cause a person to be branded as an enemy of the state. Too much conversation was a dangerous thing, and the villagers learned to keep to themselves and say little. Nonetheless, with regard to Sunnata, it would take at least another six months before the turned heads and startled looks would desist.

A refreshing evening breeze was blowing through the village, which made the banana trees murmur sibilantly. The sky was a beautiful blue dome, with puffs of cloud being pushed along by a wind that blew in a parallel world above. As they continued their stroll, they passed by a house with a dilapidated roof, in front of which were several bowls perched on low stools, as well as a large water jar sitting on the ground near the road.

"What is that? What it is it for?" Sunnata asked, referring to the earthen pots.

"Water and food for whoever passes by. It is what many women do to make merit."

"So a woman lives there?"

"Yes, Jampaa, and her father Kampoon."

"She is not married?"

"No."

"They should get someone to fix their roof."

Upon arriving at the temple, they were greeted warmly by Pra Boon and the rest of the monks, who were grateful to see Sunnata, their former brother of the clergy. For Sunnata, the feeling was mutual. Six years together in a religious community wasn't an experience that could easily be discarded. And, strangely enough, a growing sense of loneliness was developing now that he was in the outside world of ordinary people.

The visitors were given food, after which Sunnata asked for an audience with the Venerable Kru Jarun. He was told that the Venerable Father wasn't present, but had gone off to the mountains to meditate and wouldn't be back for five more days. Sunnata was disappointed, for he was the one he had been most anxious to see.

Despite the dispassion required of a monk, he had grown to love the old man like a father. Naturally, he was concerned about his welfare, wondering what the old monk would eat in the wilderness, but they assured him that the revered master had done this countless times before and always returned stronger than ever. The pair then bid farewell and departed.

On the way back, when passing the house with the water jar and the bowls of food outside, Sunnata asked Mat if he would like to eat some more rice.

"No, my belly is full."

"Let's go and eat a little. Let's give that woman a chance to make merit."

There was a plastic ladle in the water jar. They drank some water in turn, and then ate a little rice from the bowls, and as they drank some more water, she appeared above them, emerging from the doorway on the raised wooden balcony of the house. She was carrying a large reed basket that she held close to her body and was dressed in a white sleeveless blouse that exposed her buff-colored arms and a blue cotton paa-sin that was wrapped around her shapely midriff. Sunnata, without realizing it, studied her as she proceeded to collect the washing, which was suspended from a horizontal bamboo pole that ran along the edge of the roof. She went about her task with a practiced deftness, methodically plucking the clothes off the pole. Her hair was done in a bun, with a few stray wisps dangling fetchingly against her creamy beige cheeks. Even from where he was standing, there was something about her that bewitched him, and he felt powerless to shut it out.

"Sabai dee. Kopjai lai lai nawng sao. Hello. Thank you very much little sister."

"Bo pen yang," she replied, still snatching at the laundry with an undue urgency that forestalled her from turning around.

With her basket full, she picked it up, set to go back inside.

"Your roof needs to be re-done," he blurted out. "The rains will be here soon."

She flicked her head to glance at him, revealing a splendid, softly rounded face, with high, regal cheekbones that caused her eyes to curve alluringly upwards. "How much will you charge?"

"One *mun* of rice," he answered with a feeble aplomb. One mun weighed about twenty-five pounds.

Turning her body to face him fully, she gave him her answer. "That's a bit high." But actually the price he gave was less than usual. She continued standing, apparently reconsidering. "Agreed," she said finally. Her crescent-shaped lips formed a smile as she spoke, brightening her winsome looks, and endowing her with a wistful beauty. To Sunnata it was like the halo of dawn over the horizon. But the glow soon faded.

"When can you start?" she asked, with a tone that was more business-like than coquettish. She didn't appear at all surprised to be addressing a farang in a remote village in post war Laos, one who could speak Lao nevertheless.

He was caught off guard by the fluttering of his heart. It had been so long since he had felt anything like this. It made him feel guilty, yet he couldn't repress this unexpected hormonal reaction. God, she was beautiful! "Uh, uh, I don't know," he stammered, looking up at her.

"Well, it better be soon. As you mentioned, the rains are drawing near."

"Yes, sister, thank you, sister," he answered, walking away with Mat, unable to take his eyes off her.

"That was a poor deal you struck," Mat told him. "Of course we will have to give a percentage to the guards."

"Bo pen yang. That doesn't matter."

That night he couldn't sleep. He was facing a crisis, his first since he had stepped out of the war and into the forest temple.

Desire. Not lust, certainly not—he felt he could never again degenerate to such a base level. Something else, something positive and natural. Yet it was wrong, grating against all he had been taught as a monk. For seven years he hadn't desired anything other than the voidness of self, convinced that everything else was an illusion. But after all his efforts to obliterate it, the physical world of feeling still persisted undeterred. Was the aesthetic life actually the illusion and everything else real? Could one really dispossess the ego?

Doubt. Doubt was another hindrance to spiritual progress.

The Mind is a restless monkey.

He placed his hand on his stomach. "Rising...falling," he intoned to himself until he finally fell asleep.

It was a normal practice for the detainees to get extra work outside the camp over and above their usual assignments, and in fact it was a rather common way to supplement what they received from their own subsistence farming. This private work had to be done on their free time, namely weekends, and had to be approved. Once the camp's authorities were informed, a team of four, Sunnata, Oun, Mat, and Potisat, chose next weekend for the roofing of Jampaa and Kampoon's house. This required them to collect the materials, mainly ramie grass and branches, during the week, as well as making the pieces of thatch, activities which they busied themselves with in the evenings after their usual work.

They had set a realistic goal of two days to finish the roof. On the first day, Sunnata, in spite of himself, was greatly disappointed to find that Jampaa wasn't there, having gone to the market at Ta Vieng, a three-hour walk from Ban Ling Kao.

"She went to buy salt and cooking oil, trading with the paa-sins she has woven," he heard her father, Kampoon, tell the other men.

It was then that Sunnata spotted the large loom in the space underneath the house.

"Only four men? Is that enough labor?" Kampoon demanded to know.

Potisat countered with a question of his own. "Do you think this is the first roof I have ever thatched?"

Kampoon's reply was merely a low snort. He wasn't exactly a

cheery fellow, for he never smiled, but constantly chewed areca nuts wrapped in betel leaves and never looked anyone directly in the face. He was a balding man with sunken cheeks that hung like deflated bags, and shifty eyes that skittered nervously. Framing his thin upper lip was a threadlike gray mustache, and baubles of spittle would gleam distractingly in the corners of his mouth. He asked Potisat how long they would take to finish, and then mumbled that one mun of rice was an exorbitant price to fix a roof. What he really was annoyed at was that they had approached his daughter in making this arrangement, as he was the one in charge of the household.

Amidst Kampoon's grumblings, Sunnata and Oun proceeded to climb on top of the roof, where they began to tear down the old thatch, tossing the pieces to the ground. As they worked, Sunnata learned from snippets of conversation with Oun that Kampoon was the head of the Village Committee and was a stern man that had to be reckoned with concerning anything to do with village affairs. Sunnata now saw a possible reason why men would avoid courting his daughter.

It wasn't until mid-morning that the old thatch had been completely removed. For the next phase, Potisat and Mat would hand the panels of new thatch to the two men on top, who fastened them to the bamboo framework, with Oun constantly checking Sunnata's ties. Shortly after noon, they stopped to have a lunch of sticky rice and pak boong, fried stems and leaves of the Morning Glory plant.

Their meal finished, they continued working until the sun was a fading orange ball just above the jagged horizon. Oun and Sunnata descended from the roof.

"All that remains is the chicken's breastbone," Potisat declared.

Sunnata wasn't sure what that meant. "What?"

"Where the two parts of the roof join together at the top."

"Oh, yes."

Just then, Jampaa appeared, back from her long journey, bearing a large basket on her back supported by a strap that ran across her forehead. Sunnata self-consciously brushed the dirt and debris from his person and also from his hair, which he noted was now getting as long as that of an ordinary man.

"Sabai dee," she beckoned to all. With her basket still hanging from her head, she gave a nop to everyone, putting her hands palm to palm up to her nose. All of the men returned the gesture, even Potisat, who was clearly her elder.

"You have done a lot today," she said, removing the strap from her head and placing her basket down. "The work was easier than I thought. Maybe one mun was too high a price." Now that her head was free of the basket strap, strands of her long, glistening black hair floated aloft in the breeze, exposing the exquisitely curved line of her jaw.

Sunnata, quelling the abashment over his disheveled looks, boldly answered her. "Excuse us, Little Sister, but we spent all week making the panels of thatch, so we have actually done a lot more work in addition to what we have done today."

She turned her head in his direction. Her wide, pear-shaped eyes had a sultry, almost feline effect that gave him an unexpected thrill. "I didn't know that farang knew how to make thatches. Is that how you make roofs in your country, the same as in Lao?" she asked with a disarming smile. Was her question sincere, or was she teasing him?

"No, they taught me," he replied with a simpering grin. He made a gesture with his arms referring to his friends. "They are good teachers."

"I am sure you are a good pupil as well." She looked up at the roof again. "It seems to be a fine job." Then she squatted on the ground, her sarong taut on her haunches, and lifted her basket, repositioning the strap around her head. He couldn't keep from staring at her as she stood up and climbed the ladder to her house.

How could a mere woman affect him like this? Was he being tested?

"I think Sunnata is enjoying the fragrance of a flower," Wattana ribbed as they walked away. The others chortled with laughter, while Sunnata himself smiled sheepishly.

Wattana had joked in a pun, for the girl's name, Jampaa, meant Frangipani, the flower of tears, sadness, and love. Sunnata wondered why she was given such a name, since for him she seemed, outwardly at least, to be full of smiles and a serene happiness. Love, however, did seem to be appropriate.

In the following days, Sunnata went about his daily routines in a quandary. This matter of the woman had caught him unawares. He had never had it in his mind to look for female companionship, leave alone romance. He didn't enjoy the internal tension that this preoccupation over Jampaa was causing him, and even his meditation practices were proving ineffective in warding it off. He was at a loss about what to do, and consequently, sleep came with difficulty when he retired for the night in his little bamboo shack. He tried to convince himself that, as with all ephemeral things of the physical world, it would soon pass and fade away. He hoped so, anyway.

The chicken's breastbone only required half a morning to cover. Although Jampaa was at home all this time, she seemed to be busy with innumerable chores, including the cooking of the afternoon rice, so that Sunnata hardly caught a glimpse of her.

When their work was completed, the men were invited to sit with Kampoon and eat together. The bowls of chili sauce and pla dek, as well as two baskets of sticky rice, were already arranged on the mat. Sunnata partook of the meal, but abstained from eating the fish.

By now he had learned a few more things about Jampaa's father. Kampoon revealed himself to be a pragmatic man who spoke little, and who didn't see much difference between the old and new regimes, except that now there were more committees and less money for the temple. During the war, he was the headman for Ban Suk and in charge of the village self-defense unit for the Pathet Lao. He lost both his sons in engagements with Vang Pao's army, in curious contrast to Potisat, whose sons died fighting for the other side. His wife was killed by a bombi when they first returned in '75. She was digging a new garden and she hit the thing with a hoe. There was only Jampaa left to him. He had a few brothers and sisters, but they had so far remained on the Vientiane Plain, still afraid to come back.

As the men engaged in conversation, Sunnata himself fell quiet. Soon the topic turned to the weather.

"It is too cool for this time of year. It is always the hottest around New Year, and that's getting closer."

New Year in Lao is in April.

"I hope this doesn't mean a drought," bemoaned Kampoon.

Jampaa came in to take the plates away, and Sunnata naturally watched her. As she bent down to take the bowls, her long, dark, silky hair fell appealingly across her shoulders. His eyes followed her all the way out the back door to the kitchen.

"It is important to have a big Rocket Festival this year," Potisat asserted.

The Rocket Festival involved shooting elaborate homemade rockets into the sky to bring rain. There was also a lot of singing, dancing, drinking and eating.

"Well," Kampoon grumbled, "you know the way things are now; I don't think they will allow it. The government doesn't want to see costly and extravagant festivals."

The discussion continued but Jampaa was still out of sight. It was only when they departed that he saw her again, outside the house, balancing a shoulder pole with two buckets of water on each end. She put down her burden to give a nop goodbye. He had only said two words to her the whole day, and that was Sabai dee.

Before returning to the camp, the three Laotians decided to stop at another villager's house, someone they suspected might have some ooh, which was sweet rice wine. Sunnata instead elected to see the Venerable Kru Jarun at the vat, who was reported to have returned from his retreat in the forest.

He entered the old priest's kuti on his hands and knees. Pra Kru Jarun, sitting cross-legged on a little platform, put the book down he was reading as Sunnata made the five-point prostration.

"How does it feel to be a layman again?" Kru Jarun asked.

"Very mundane, Venerable Father." Sunnata replied, hoping his answer would please the old monk. He also noticed that the gray patches in the Venerable Father's eyes had grown bigger.

"How many precepts have you broken already?"

"At least one, sir. I have taken intoxicants." Sunnata had been obligated to partake in a few glasses of lao kao at his baa-see ceremony.

The old master then did something strange. He smiled. "It is only the beginning. There are more profound temptations which await you. You know what I am alluding to, don't you?"

"I'm not sure, Venerable Father."

"You must taste life, just like Prince Gautama, the Buddha, did."

Gautama, the rich prince, had everything, till he saw the futility of worldly things, when he gave it all up and set out on the path of enlightenment.

Kru Jarun's smile wilted abruptly as he continued with a cautionary monition. "You will inevitably suffer as a consequence."

"Yes, Venerable Father." This topic was making Sunnata uncomfortable, and he sought to change it. He respectfully paused before asking, "How was your meditation in the forest, Venerable Father?"

"Very fruitful."

Sunnata noticed that the book Kru Jarun had put down was a sixth-grade English textbook. "I see you still study the English books on your own. You have not given up now that you don't have a teacher?"

"I do not have enough time for it these days. But I remember all that I have learned." He then went on to demonstrate. "My name Kru Jarun," he said in less than perfect English, "I am monk in Lao. I want learning Inglit. My teacher it American." Switching back to Lao, he asked, "How was that?"

"Very good, Venerable Father."

"Inglit has such odd letters; it gives me a headache to read them."

Certainly, reading would be painful, given the worsening condition of his eyes. "And your health?" Sunnata inquired. "I mean, your eyes seem to be…"

"Bo pen yang. Never mind. I can still see you. And other things as well."

After that, there was an awkward abeyance.

"I am happier now that I am here," Sunnata said, dispelling the silence. "And it is fortunate that we are near each other."

"Yes. But I myself will go back to the Forest Temple. Most of the monks will remain here to try and serve the community and to safeguard the Damma during this time of uncertainty."

"You should stay here until the end of Pansa," Sunnata advised, "when we harvest the rice. After that the villagers could feed you at the temple."

"There will be no harvest this year."

"Excuse me, Venerable Father? No harvest?"

"There will be no rain this year."

Sunnata didn't know what to say to this rather drastic proclamation.

"And the year after that, there will be too much rain. There will be floods and destruction."

Nor had he been prepared to hear yet another apocalyptic statement. What was most frightening was that his faith in Pra Kru Jarun convinced him that these things were, without a doubt, going to happen.

"Have you perceived these events during your meditation in the forest?"

"Yes. But they are not unnatural. They are in accord with the first of the Noble Truths."

"Yes," Sunnata concurred. "Existence is suffering."

All the signs of drought were there. It was growing cooler and drier instead of hotter and more humid. The wind picked up, blowing fine dust from the thirsty soil. But still people waited. It wasn't that unusual for the rains to be late.

In the meantime, the Mobile Work Force teams had plenty to do and were often in Ban Ling Kao on assignments. Whenever Sunnata found himself in the village, he would pass by Jampaa's house hoping to catch a glimpse of her, and find an excuse to say hello. Although he reproached himself for such foolish, shameful behavior and for discounting all he had embraced as a monk, an irrational craving was driving him, disintegrating his once stolid restraint. On a few of these idle strolls, he had run into Kampoon, the father, who would merely offer a reluctant Sabai dee. But eventually he did catch up with her. She was in the shaded space underneath their raised house, busy at her loom.

"Sabai dee," he called, heading towards her.

"Sabai dee," she replied, giving him only a fleeting glimpse.

He walked over to her weaving machine. "That is a very beautiful paa-sin you are making."

"How can you tell? It is not finished yet." She didn't seem to appreciate the complement, nor did she look at him, but instead kept her eyes on her handiwork.

He edged toward her, as close as he dared to, feigning an absorbed examination of the cloth draped upon the loom. He could smell the earthy fragrance of her rampant, luxuriant hair and was overcome with a barely controllable urge to nuzzle her soft cheek. Where was this desire coming from? He sought for something to say. "But it will be beautiful when it's finished, I'm sure."

He could see she was now smiling modestly, although she still didn't face him. "Kopjai," she said.

Out of politeness, he drew his head away from hers. It dawned on him that they had never introduced themselves, nor had anyone else introduced them to each other. "You are called Jampaa, aren't you?"

"Yes. And you are Sunnata, yes?"

He felt inflated that she knew his name. "Yes."

"That is a Pali word," she noted. "It sounds like the name of a monk."

"Yes, it is."

"Were you once a monk?" She had indeed heard the story already, but given the nature of village gossip, she wanted to confirm this from the source himself.

"Yes."

She laughed. It was a pleasant dulcet sound, yet in spite of that, he felt self-conscious.

"What is funny?"

"A farang monk. And you speak Lao very well, so it means you have been in Lao for many years."

"Yes."

There was a lull in the conversation while he watched her, fascinated at her operation of the loom, her hands swiftly and adroitly manipulating the spindles, her feet working the pedals in coordinated movements. The wooden bars of the loom responded by rocking back and forth like a clockwork mechanism.

"Why are you here?" she suddenly said.

"Because I wanted to talk to you. I like you."

She shook her head embarrassed, and she laughed bashfully. "No, I mean in Ban Ling Kao, in seminaa."

"Oh," he blurted, feeling a bit stupid. "I want to stay in Lao and they don't know what else to do with me."

"You want to stay in Lao? I don't believe it. Why don't you go back to your own country? I hear it is very rich, and you could live a wonderful life, and not be poor like us."

"My life is finished there. The war finished it."

"What about your family, your parents?" She hesitated purposefully before continuing, "Your wife..."

"I am not married, I have no wife."

There was another anxious pause in their conversation as she rearranged a thread that was growing slack. After correcting this problem, she finally turned to face him and made a strange request. "Show me your hands."

He put his hands out.

"No, with the palms up."

He reversed the position of his hands, and she held them in hers while tracing the lines on his fingers and palms. He felt a tingling throughout his body as she touched him. It was an effort to hide his excitement.

"You have beautiful hands," she said.

"Thank you."

"Were you a soldier?" she asked, still studying the lines of his palms.

"Not really, but something like that."

"An event changed your life. You ran away from the war, but you are not a coward. Your decision was one of wisdom and compassion." She released his hands.

"Is that all that you see?" he asked, disappointed that she had let go, causing him to lose the touch of her.

"It is enough for now," she told him, brushing a long lock of her hair away from her forehead.

She spun away from him with a serious face and resumed her weaving.

"Why do they call this place the Village of the White Monkey?" he asked, to steer the conversation to a more neutral topic.

"Oh. That is because the first villagers to come back from the camps in Vientiane had seen a white monkey in the forests near the mountains. Even I myself have seen him many times."

"Have you really?"

"Yes. I used to call him, and he would appear. Although I haven't seen him for a while, he may have gone elsewhere," she said wistfully.

"You could call him? How?"

She smiled. "That is my secret."

"Have you ever tried to catch him?"

He must have said something wrong, for her manner changed into one of reproach. "Oh no, never. We Laotians have a belief that any white animal is the incarnation of an enlightened being. That is why a fisherman will throw back a white catfish, no matter how big."

Just then Kampoon, her father, approached them and greeted Sunnata with a tone that unmistakably conveyed disapproval. The old man then ignored him, speaking to his daughter about how the grass and leaves for the water buffalo were getting low, and she should fetch some in the woods before it got dark. Although Sunnata entertained thoughts of accompanying her, he knew that it would be considered improper, and so he made some offhand excuse to go on his way.

He walked back to the work camp, straying off the established trail so that he wouldn't bump into anyone. He made an attempt at walking meditation, lifting leg, heel up, bringing leg down...and just as he was becoming mindful, he tripped over a stone, which broke his concentration. So he took a seat on the ground and began to chant, but the sound of his voice was false and hollow. In his frustration he ran his hands through his greasy hair, the abundance of which served as another reminder that he was no longer a monk. Had all those years been merely a phase that he had gone through?

Desire is the cause of all suffering.

Kru Jarun was right. He was suffering already.

"WHO AM I?" he yelled out to the forest around him.

New year, Song Kran, April 13, arrived. It marked the beginning of the agricultural season, and it was also a time of cleaning one's house and possessions, of starting life anew. The Buddha image had been carried out of the sim of the temple and placed on a platform outside for the faithful to come and anoint with perfumed water and scented paste. In the homes, elderly family members solemnly sat for the custom of *lot nam*, having water poured over them by their younger relatives, who in turn begged them to be forgiven for any wrong doings. Young kids and teenagers would stand outside their houses and gleefully throw buckets of water on passersby, although this year there wasn't too much of this play, as water was becoming scarce. People put on their best clothes, and women took out the silk paa-sins that they kept for wearing on special days. But the celebrations that year were subdued, due to the state's policy on avoiding wasteful consumption, and the growing fears that famine was ahead. The brewing of alcohol from rice was discouraged, and so, as there was very little liquor, the partying was minimal. The detainees at the work camp were given three days off.

Song Kran passed and the sixth lunar month began without any sign of rain. Each new day was hot and dry, exactly like the one before it. June came and there was still no change. The heat was like a vengeful serpent, slithering down the mountains, strangling everything in its grip. The rice fields, covered with the parched stubble from last year's crop, baked under a relentless sun. At night the heat lightning in the horizon taunted everyone with false hopes, but it soon became evident that this was going to be a waterless year.

A village meeting was held, and the chief guard of Mobile Camp 333, as well as Potisat, attended. It was decided that emergency measures should be taken to avert disaster. The people were to be mobilized in digging canals from the stream they called the Nam Vang and in making spring boxes with stones and bamboo pipes to get water from seeps emerging at the sides of the closest mountains. These schemes weren't able to reach into every homestead, and the only alternative for many was to carry water from miles away. Long cavalcades of men, women, and children could be seen coming and going bearing shoulder poles laden with buckets, walking carefully to avoid spilling even a drop. Others pushed and pulled wooden carts loaded with containers. The villagers felt that they were fortunate to have the extra labor that Mobile Work Force 333 provided, but soon, the 333 teams were dispatched to other outlying villages, as far afield as Ta Vieng and beyond. The detainees weren't happy about this, as it was somewhat inconvenient, since sleeping and bathing were awkward in the houses of strangers, and food was scant. For Sunnata, there was the added dolor of being deprived of the chance to see Jampaa, however limited those occasions were.

It turned out that it was to be another month before he saw her again. He had just come from Ban Na Nat where his team had been building irrigation ditches, and this was his day off. He strolled through the village, walking up and down the main lane, passing her house repeatedly with the aim of catching her outside. It was only a matter of time when eventually he met her along the path.

"Sabai dee, Little Sister."

"Sabai dee, Elder Brother."

Her face looked thinner and paler.

"How are you and your father faring under this drought?"

"We are fine. We have enough rice in the granary for two more months."

"What will you do after that?"

"I will try to buy rice with the paa-sins I weave. Otherwise we will eat taro root and yams. I planted them last dry season and they are ready now. And you?"

"I'm not worried. I'll get by somehow."

They reached her house.

"Goodbye, Ai Sunnata. Good luck."

"Soke dee, good luck."

On his return trip across the valley, he felt depressed. Ahead of him, emerging from the woods, young men and women were trekking up the trail from the banks of the Nam Vang. They were singing folk songs of courtship, totally oblivious to his presence behind them, and this only served to deepen his melancholy.

The new turn his life had taken had eroded his pious attitudes, and he was once more becoming a victim of the same clinging desires that ordinary people felt. No longer encased within a religious community, he needed something else to hold on to. Yet, whatever contentment the villagers got out of this hard life, he himself had no access to. He couldn't get further than a casual conversation with Jampaa. And why should he? What could it possibly lead to? He reasoned out that it was hopeless. He was still basically a prisoner, who owned nothing but the rags on his body. What did he have to offer her? The slowly surfacing fantasy of being with her, to possess her, was a corruption of his once finely honed discipline. Perhaps he should take up meditation again to try and extinguish this longing, which arose out of lust and ego, mental defilements that were transient and deceptive.

He was too lethargic, however, to restart his meditation practice, and he no longer had any interest in contemplating the illusory nature of the world. His time in Ban Ling Kao, apart from his infatuation with Jampaa, had placed him in the company of the genial, gentle country folk, who, despite hardships, had the courage to be happy. The joy in their lives sprang from their families and village, for they regarded their families as the focus for their existence, and their village as the center of their unaffected world. He himself had neither family nor home, things that he was now beginning to hunger for.

Thinking along those lines only made him lonelier. In the evenings he would sit on the porch of his bamboo house and stare into the distance at the cozy stilted houses, spread out among the stands of bamboo and the clumps of palm trees, then look up at that bare patch on the slope of the mountain behind. To amuse himself, he imagined a face in that bald spot, a bland, anonymous personage with no identity, like himself, with the cleft in the upper right corner as a single, unpaired eyebrow. He was just like that errant, misfit eyebrow, he felt. Unmatched, unpaired, alone without a partner.

His sense of self had come back, and with it, the memories, and even worse, the nightmares. He was gradually returning to the person he once was, and he was scared. He would wake up in the middle of the night, frightened by an unknown, intangible enemy; a nameless fear lurking in the shadows of his subconscious.

The growing misery of the oncoming drought didn't make his

emotional struggles any easier. As the dry season continued, he and the rest of the detainees did what the villagers were doing to try and secure food. They dug up crickets in the forest and caught cicadas by poking branches into the trees. The guards would even lend them their guns to go hunting after mongoose, civets, and birds. Sunnata, out of his own increasing frailty, began to eat some of these things.

The rains eventually did come, but too little and too late. The prophecy of the Venerable Pra Kru Jarun had so far proven to be true.

Chapter 19

Laos 1977

"Moving of th' earth brings harms and fears"
John Donne, poet, A Valedicton: Forbidding Mourning, 1896

In 1977, the leadership of the Lao People's Revolutionary Party pushed ahead with a program of radical social change at a pace that overwhelmed the ordinary Laotian, the government's lofty ambitions far outweighing their inadequate ability. Most of the political officers in the countryside were uneducated and inexperienced, and, as there wasn't much money to do anything of any substance, they directed their energies on propaganda. Loudspeaker systems were set up in Vientiane and in the provincial capitals, broadcasting incessant political exhortations. But even these fell into disrepair, with no funds to maintain them.

Vientiane had its own special problems. The former presence of the Americans and their supply of dollars had created markets for alcohol, prostitution, gambling, and drugs. The city had become spoilt with decadence. It was a mess that required drastic action. All prostitutes, gamblers, thieves, and drug addicts were collected and sent to two islands in the reservoir of the Nam Ngum dam, named like restrooms, Gentlemen and Ladies Islands. There, they were to be rehabilitated and released within one year.

A miniature army of thousands of Vietnamese soldiers remained in Laos. Security was a main concern. In some areas, there was still a war going on. The remnants of Vang Pao's army fought fierce pitched battles with government troops at Pu Khan, Nam Sen, and the Muang Cha River. But they had help. The concentration of Lao refugees in large, overcrowded camps just across the Mekong made them potential bases for insurgents who could infiltrate back into Lao PDR as a rebel force. The new Lao leaders were truly worried.

Even nature turned against the new Lao state. In 1977, there was a severe drought, with food scarcity becoming an imminent threat, and as a result, the Lao government had no alternative but to appeal to international humanitarian aid to avoid widespread starvation.

The next year, in 1978, the opposite happened, when there was too much rain, and the excessive precipitation caused widespread flooding. In some areas, half the rice crop was inundated.

The rural peasants were somehow not surprised at these two years of disaster. After all, their seasonal rituals to appease the water deities had been prohibited, and so naturally the water gods, the Nak serpents, were understandably peeved.

For those in Ban Ling Kao, it was at the beginning of 1978 when the effects of the drought were becoming serious. Some of the villagers had temporarily left their farms to go on caravans to the Nam Ngum River, where they would camp out and fish, preparing the pla dek that would see them through the year. Most of those who went stayed until April, after which they headed for home to make ready the rice fields once again, in the hopes that this year would be better than the last.

Arriving back in Ban Ling Kao, they were met with a new development brought about by the government. The cadres were initiating a drive for agricultural collectivization, which entailed the formation of communes, where all the people were to farm together and share the harvest based on a work point system. Whereas the party leaders had instructed the cadres that joining these co-operatives was to be on a voluntary basis, many of these young and inexperienced political officers abused their authority and threatened the unwilling with the punishment of re-education. In Ban Ling Kao, the cadre sent to the village, and the ambitious co-operative officer from the district, were so tyrannical that they encouraged the co-operatives to forcefully take over adjacent plots without any remuneration, and the same practice was applied to draft animals and plows.

Resentment in the village grew. Some chopped down their fruit trees and destroyed their yam gardens for fear the co-operative would take those too. In the wake of all this hysteria, many villagers slaughtered their chickens, ducks, and pigs, and held grand feasts to consume the meat, again, because they thought their animals would be seized. Others hastily took what cattle they had and sold it for rice at Muang Koon or Ponsavan. In the end, only half of the villagers joined the Ban Ling Kao Co-operative.

Amidst all this confusion, it started to rain. The first showers arrived early, as if to make up for the poor performance of last year. They commenced a pattern of coming at least once, sometimes twice a day, growing in intensity as the weeks passed. In the beginning, despite the controversy over the co-operatives, everyone was elated. The drought had ended. Rain had finally come. After awhile, though...people wished that it would let up just a little bit. Many hadn't yet finished plowing, the early rains having thrown them off schedule. Soon it was difficult, if not ineffectual, to work the land in the wet conditions, especially after the paddy basins started to fill up. A good proportion of the seedlings that had been sown got waterlogged.

The sun disappeared, and the villagers didn't see it again. The sky took on various themes of gray: gunmetal gray that signaled an impending storm; charcoal grey while a tempest was raging; and the drab monotonous gray in between, the cycle repeating over and over while everything, including the air, became soaked and sopping wet.

Added to all this was the fact that, even during a normal rainy season, Ban Ling Kao, like most rural villages in Laos, was practically cut off from the outside world. Travel in and out of the area soon became impossible.

The constant grayness of the skies matched Sunnata's mood. The detainees had been busy working on their own co-operative farm and weren't sent outside. Even on the weekends, Sunnata, becoming increasingly glum, remained within the confines of the camp. He didn't socialize much anymore, and the others, concerned, tried to ask him if he was okay. Yes, he was fine, he would answer them laconically. His reserved demeanor inhibited any further inquiries. It was impossible to explain to them the inner struggles he was going through—how that now, no longer a monk engaged in stripping off his selflessness, he needed a new, virgin identity to fend off the memories of the previous one. He needed something to keep the nightmares away.

In the evenings, whenever it didn't rain, he would still sit outside his house, and try to take comfort in the peaceful view of the countryside. He continually found himself gazing at that naked spot on the mountain, barren like his soul, he felt. The crack in the earth in the top right corner stood out more than ever, and it appeared to be bigger. Perhaps it was swelling along with his sadness.

As the monsoon season progressed, the rain continued, and when it came time for transplanting, it was apparent that the rain had been too much. Transplanting the bundles of young seedlings was normally done in a soaked paddy, but the basins already had over a foot of water in them, and the whole process became a messy, frustrating exercise. Doubts about this year's harvest were beginning to arise.

Then the really big storms came.

The usual convectional thunderstorms that marked the rainy season were soon being augmented by gales coming from the east. The typhoons that originated from the South China Sea were typically stopped by the great Annamite Range that separated Lao from Vietnam, but this season they came barreling over, driven by mighty winds that posed a threat to those who lived in houses made merely of bamboo and thatch. A couple of these houses were blown over, including some at the work camp, and many families had to take shelter with their neighbors. Great peals of thunder, which accompanied the blinding flashes of lightning, made it seem as if the Plain of Jars was under bombardment once again. Then mercifully, a lull in the monsoons offered a welcome respite.

It was on one of these few calm mornings, that Sunnata stood outside and vigorously rubbed salt on the insides of his mouth, the local way of brushing one's teeth, and while doing so he happened to take a casual glance at the mountains. He stared at that stark, cleared blot on the slope, the one with the breach in the earth. He stopped rubbing his gums, taking his hand out of his mouth, and slowly straightened his back to get a better look, absorbed in what he beheld.

It had gotten bigger, no doubt about it. The fissure now extended almost halfway across the top. He felt a chill tingling in his spine.

Fortunately it was a Saturday, and he was free. He would go down to the village immediately and talk to Kampoon, Jampaa's father, who was also the village headman.

Crossing the valley wasn't easy since it had been flooded for several weeks now. In fact, it was dangerous, due to the submerged bomb craters, many of which were over ten feet in depth. The detainees, along with the villagers, had staked poles in the ground to demarcate safe routes of passage, yet despite these markers, two children and one old woman had inadvertently strayed into the deep parts and drowned.

It took him over an hour to slosh his way through the valley, his pace fruitlessly trying to match the urgency he felt. When he reached Kampoon's house, he was both relieved and proud to see that the thatched roof they had put up last year had survived the battering by the elements, except for a small section near the back corner. He brushed off his tattered shorts, removed his rubber sandals, and climbed the ladder to the veranda.

Kampoon had just finished breakfast. He was sitting on the floor smoking a cigarette rolled in a banana leaf.

Sunnata, out of respect, bent his back as he entered. "Sabai dee, Lung. Hello Uncle, are you well?"

"Sabai dee. I am well."

"Forgive me. I hope I didn't interrupt your morning meal," he apologized, still hunched over.

"No, I have finished."

Jampaa made an appearance through the doorway at the rear of the house. "Sabai dee."

"Sabai dee," he replied as he sat on the floor opposite her father.

She approached to collect the woven basket, half full of sticky rice, and her father's bowl, then exited.

Kampoon remained silent, puffing on his cigarette.

"I have something important I would like to discuss with you," Sunnata announced timidly.

"Er." That meant 'yes' in Lao.

"People must leave this village before it rains again. They should stay with us, at the Mobile Work Camp, at the top of the hill."

Kampoon ceased his puffing, looked at Sunnata with harsh eyes, and exclaimed, "Yang? What? I don't understand what you are saying."

"The side of the mountain is going to come down on top of the village."

Kampoon stared at him with his mouth agape. He didn't like this farang, never trusted his presence here. He was a prisoner, an American, probably ex-CIA. He didn't know why they didn't get him out of the country, or why they just didn't keep him locked up in Vieng Chan. Neither did he appreciate the fact that this man and his daughter seemed to have some mutual interest in each other.

"You are a madman," he proclaimed scornfully.

Just then, Jampaa reappeared, standing in the doorway to the kitchen with her arms folded across her bosom.

"No, it is going to happen," Sunnata insisted. "Perhaps, the ancestors are angry that you didn't have a ritual at the village altar this year."

Of course, he could have explained that the excessive precipitation had created a critical pore water pressure in the soil, and that shear failure was inevitable. But he didn't think that Kampoon would buy that.

"Excuse, please," Jampaa interjected, "Father, one of the water buffaloes has a bad sore on his back. I applied some coal tar on the wound to keep the flies off, but I think it is getting worse. Can you please come and look at it and advise me?"

Kampoon got up and followed his daughter out.

Sunnata sat there, sensing that he blew the whole thing with the spirits of the ancestor story. He honestly didn't know about such matters. But he did know that the mountainside was going to come down, sooner or later.

Kampoon came back, alone, but didn't sit down. "Let's go outside so you can show me what you are talking about."

Outside, Sunnata indicated to the old man the rent in the earth, explained how water was going in there and flowing somewhere under the ground, eroding underneath, and how the whole slab was going to eventually come floating down like a raft on water.

"The next rains, you say?"

"Yes."

"Agreed. I will arrange for people to take shelter. It cannot be sooner than tomorrow, so let us hope it doesn't rain tonight."

"Yes, thank you."

Sunnata gave a nop and departed. On the way back he couldn't help feeling pleased with himself, proud of how his persuasiveness had convinced the old man. Then it struck him that it wasn't he who swayed him, but Jampaa, his daughter. She must have said something to him in private. That whole story about the sore on the buffalo's back was nothing more than a crock of bull.

There was a continual light rain throughout the day. Sunnata informed Potisat of his apprehension concerning the stability of the deforested slope. The old man requested a meeting with the head of the guards whereby Sunnata was given the opportunity to explain the situation. They then gathered all the detainees together and told them to prepare their houses for the coming visitors. There were about twenty families living in Ban Ling Kao, over one hundred people, and luckily there were enough huts in the camp to provide shelter for all of them, which meant four to five extra persons per house. Kampoon, as village headman, arrived in the late morning to discuss the arrangements with the guards and detainees. Everyone in the village had been told, and they were now in the process of collecting their things. Naturally, there were a few skeptics who insisted on staying put, but that was their own affair, as Kampoon wouldn't force anyone to leave.

The rain lasted until late afternoon, when the sun broke through the clouds. By evening it was still clear, but some of the more frightened villagers arrived at the camp, electing not to wait another day before evacuating. The next morning, the rest of the village came to the work camp in one large group, including Kampoon and his daughter. People were distributed according to the sizes of the individual dwellings, and efforts were made to keep families together. After everyone found a place, they began to assemble outside, where various campfires were started, and pots of rice and food were soon simmering away. By noon, the gay chattering of the crowd generated a festive atmosphere, evoking a sense of community reminiscent of the times they had spent in the caves during the war.

Inevitably, the rice whisky and sweet rice wine were passed around. Someone had had the foresight to bring a ken, a large bamboo panpipe, and its shrilly panting initiated the singing and dancing. Potisat, that old rogue, displayed his talents as a maw lam, a singer of ballads, by launching into a tune that praised the sky, the mountains and the rivers. Then, much to Sunnata's delight, it was Jampaa's turn.

He, along with the rest of the crowd, watched transfixed as her body swayed with her arms outstretched, her hands gyrating in a delicate rhythm. With her eyes closed, her voice quivering with emotion, it was as if she were possessed. The melody that welled up from deep inside her was almost unearthly; a haunting plea to the supernatural forces to take pity on the helpless mortals whose suffering was endless.

The dancing of the lamvong followed and, with Jampaa as his

partner, Sunnata was in seventh heaven. Everyone, in fact, was having such a wonderful time that they forgot why they had come in the first place. That is, until about four o'clock, when the sky began to darken.

There were several strata of clouds, and the lowest of these advanced swiftly over the land with the impetus and menacing intent of a marauding army. The rain began in a fury, scattering the group and sending them fleeing to the shelter of their assigned houses.

This was to be the storm of storms. Lightning flashed several times a second, as if a demented maniac were playing with a light switch—on off, on off…Some of the flashes were followed by horrendous cracks and booms that shook the bamboo huts with their rumbling vibrations, while others gave out no sound at all, torturing the villagers as they constantly braced themselves for the noise with every blinding flash, never knowing when it would come, keeping them in an adrenaline-filled suspense. Soon, the searing white flickering alone was enough to petrify them. The wind whistled, howled, and roared as it whipped through the crevices in their shelters, and the raindrops were so large and fell with such velocity that they sounded like solid objects crashing against the walls and roofs.

Huddled inside, nervous parents consoled their young children who were soon crying. It was hard to subdue them when some adults were moaning and wailing as well. In an almost malevolent fashion, the intensity of the tempest would ease up, offering false hopes that were soon snatched away as the storm would only rise up again with renewed ferocity. Hours went by, and it just wouldn't end. Nobody got any sleep that night.

Just before sunrise, it stopped, having exhausted its vengeful energy.

That morning, emerging from the huts, they were met with a dawn as quiet and peaceful as any, bathed in a crisp and clear sunshine. The gale that had raged during the night seemed as if it had merely been a bad dream. The villagers looked down from the edge of the cliff and saw everything as it was before; the side of the mountain still where it should be, and the houses of Ban Ling Kao still intact, sitting peacefully among the palm and bamboo groves.

Many of them laughed with relief. But for others, the jocularity of the day before and the terrors of the night that followed were forgotten, and they began to grumble and bitch about being inconvenienced like this over a false alarm. They had struggled across the flooded valley for hours, carrying their children as well as their belongings, and all for nothing. Kampoon was more indignant than the rest, for the farang had made a fool out of him in front of all the villagers.

He approached Sunnata, barely able to control his ire. "The next time you have a vision, keep it to yourself!" he chided.

Jampaa, standing behind her father, sent Sunnata a sympathetic look.

Some people were already collecting their things and making haste to go back to their homes.

"No, wait, you can't go back yet, it is still dangerous."

"That mountain will still be standing there when my grandchildren have grandchildren," someone retorted.

"If that storm couldn't bring the mountain down, nothing will," another man snapped.

No amount of cajoling could deter the majority of people who were intent on going back down. They formed a disgruntled procession, carrying their possessions, their chagrin showing through their low mumbling. Sunnata followed them down, entreating them to remain at the work force camp. He ran to where Kampoon and Jampaa were making their way down.

"Please, don't go, the mountainside will come down, I know it."

"Get away from us," Kampoon shouted.

He grabbed Jampaa's hand, in spite of himself, and blocked their way. "I cannot let you go."

Kampoon was furious. "What business is it of yours? How dare you touch my daughter in my presence!"

Sunnata released Jampaa's hand.

"I know all about the trouble you caused in Seminaa Seven at Khang Kai," Kampoon continued. "Now you want to start trouble here in our village, as if we didn't have enough problems of our own already. I also see through your scheming. You have confused my daughter, and you are trying to use her to acquire land, my land, which is her inheritance, but it won't work, because I am requesting the province to have you removed from here. Now get out of the way!"

There was a motion on the bare mountain slope across the way, noiseless and instantaneous. Only a few would later claim that they actually saw it. What happened next was scarcely believable. As if by means of a powerful and malicious sorcery, solid earth was turned into liquid, and a hideous river of mud suddenly materialized before their eyes, pouring down the mountain in a harsh, drawn out, wind-like whisper. Moving a hundred miles an hour, it crashed its way down the slope, engulfing trees along the way. They watched, horrified, the women screaming and the men wailing, as the torrent of earth swept down and bulldozed through the village, smothering the houses in its path, finally stopping in the middle of the valley. After that there was a shocked silence, shortly broken by doleful weeping. Within seconds, over half of the village of Ban Ling Kao had been destroyed.

Sunnata, the mysterious farang, had once again inadvertently drawn attention to himself, further fueling the legend he was to become.

Chapter 20

Laos 1978 - 1980

*"The new regime is like a turning wheel: you do something good for it,
and you will get something good in return."*
Laotian citizen in the Vientiane area, circa mid 1980s

1978 was a depressing year for everyone in the Lao People's
Democratic Republic. The restrictions on trade, the political indoctrination, the threats from ham-fisted cadres, the deadly bombies,
and even the weather, were slapping the populace on all sides.

In Vientiane, the leaders of the government were also disillusioned. Things were just not working out as they had planned, and
worse still; the people were full of discontent. For security reasons
alone, they couldn't afford to let the growing resentment of citizens
fuel a rebellion. They already had their hands full with the
remaining guerillas leftover from Vang Pao's army, who had based
themselves on the slopes of Pu Bia, the highest mountain in Laos,
less than fifty miles away from Ban Ling Kao. They now called
themselves the Chao Fa, the Princes of the Sky, and held secret
rituals designed to make them invincible and their opponents
powerless. These practices weren't sufficient to ward off the troops
of the Lao army and the heavily armed Vietnamese contingent, leave
alone the helicopter gunships and bomb-dropping Migs. Yet the
battle at Pu Bia didn't mean the end of the Chao Fa. It only scattered
them into the countryside.

Nevertheless, the socialist leaders couldn't ignore mounting
opposition from the ordinary peasants and townsfolk. The cooperative program was a disaster. The hard-line approach was proving
to be a failure. They had to make peace with the people. Even the
Vietnamese and the Soviets told them so. At the advice of their 'big
brothers', the Party was to take a slightly different approach.

In 1979, there came the Seventh Resolution, a piece of legislation that brought liberal reforms, reversing the tide of oppressive policies. Laws were passed that halted the cooperative campaign, encouraged private businesses, and relaxed restrictions on the movement of goods and citizens, thus ushering in a new chapter for the Laotian people.

In Ban Ling Kao, the end of 1978 was a time for picking up the pieces. There was much work to do in the reconstruction of their half-buried village, and whatever of the harvest that could be salvaged from the devastated rice fields had to be cut and threshed.

For the villagers, despite their efforts at encouraging each other, rebuilding their homes and working in their ruined rice fields were tasks that broke their hearts. What made it worse was that the avalanche of mud had carried many lethal bombies into the area, a tract that previously had been cleared years before at the cost of several lives. Now that dreadful work had to be carried out yet again, and the cleaning up of the earthen debris caused more casualties among the residents, further dampening their morale.

Sunnata, along with the rest of the detainees of the mobile work camp, was engaged full time in these activities, and as he participated in this labor, he tried to maintain as low a profile as possible while in the village, but it wasn't easy after the incident of the landslide. He again had become a figure of awe and mystique, and now more than ever, it appeared impossible to lead an ordinary life among the peasants. Interaction with the common folk became strained and distant, so in response he himself avoided talking to people. In the case of Kampoon, the coolness was mutual, for the village headman was bitter that the saving of the villagers' lives had been at the expense of his own authority and respect, which he felt the stranger's intervention had already undermined.

Potisat was one of the few who, instead of shrinking in his presence, actually grew closer to Sunnata. Potisat felt that this man had the gift, and the old spirit master had resolved to take him under his wing. The stranger was to be his protégé, so to speak, to whom he would divulge the secrets of the trade. Potisat also had the self-interested motive of wanting to appear associated with Sunnata's successful prediction of the landslide disaster. Sunnata, being a Caucasian in one of the most remote places in Asia, already stuck out like a sore thumb, even without the episode of the landslide, and Potisat's attentions only amplified the situation. In spite of his better judgment, he succumbed to the urgings of the old man and accompanied him in the performance of various rites. The reconstruction of the houses and the remaking of the paddy lands provided repeated opportunities to conduct the house-building ritual and the propitiatory blessing of the fields.

In time, Sunnata actually became interested in the belief systems of the Laotians; it was a diversion that occupied his mind and kept him from thinking too much about his own inner quandary. He was soon made to understand just who all these deities were that had to be placated. He learned the names of the nine different Chao Ti, the guardian spirits, each accorded to different types of land use. There was the guardian spirit of the rice fields, and another one for an individual household, a different one for the granary, still another for rivers and swamps, and one for the buffalo pens. One of the Chao Ti, Dammahora, was one that Sunnata had been made familiar with during his time as a monk, for it was the guardian spirit of temples.

He learned how to make magical drawings, and to interpret the mystical charts, such as the 'three-in-lion' and 'twelve directions' diagrams. The intricacies of the baa-see ceremony were also revealed to him. He had to know about the thirty-two kwan inside a person that corresponded to the thirty-two physical qualities of the body, and the spells used to bind these kwan to the person when tying the sacred strings, so that they wouldn't escape and cause the person illness. He was also taught how to call the spirits of the sky, and the incantations used to beseech the Nak serpents. Potisat also spent a great deal of time teaching Sunnata how to make complicated astrological calculations.

During the first part of 1979, Sunnata was involved in many of these traditional rites, but it conflicted with his plan to steer clear of Jampaa. Whatever differences of opinion existed between himself and Kampoon, he agreed with him that contact with his daughter should be avoided. Sunnata, as Potisat's apprentice, found this hard to do. At the festival of Boon Koon Kao, Jampaa was the principal officiate, conducting the rituals of thanksgiving to the fertility gods of the soil. He and Potisat also had a part to play, and it was difficult for Sunnata and Jampaa to ignore each other's presence. They greeted each other coldly and conversed only when absolutely necessary.

Not long after that, came the *Pii-bawb* scare.

Once it took hold, people changed. Before the sun set, all the villagers made sure they were in their homes. When it became dark, they bolted their doors. No one dared to walk at night. There was a pii-bawb in the village.

Uncle Gah's son, Koon, a lanky youth who detested work, was coming back from a session of social drinking with friends in an abandoned field when he found a nice tree to doze under before confronting his parents at home. Upon waking up, he squatted for a second and spotted a frog with his insides eaten out. The sight was sobering enough for him to let out a shout and run the rest of the way home.

Auntie Bua, a stout old widow with a penchant for muttering to herself, woke up as usual shortly before dawn. She ambled about her dark bamboo hut in her characteristic rickety fashion, getting dressed and making herself her morning tea. Despite her peculiarities, her survival of a long and troubled life, in addition to a caring and loving nature, earned her much respect in the village. So, when she frantically related what happened next, much credence was given to her story. She ventured out to tend to her two water buffaloes, and shortly thereafter gave out a gasp—all the dung from her buffalo pen had disappeared!

Compounding all this, several homesteads began losing chickens mysteriously. And while all these strange things were happening, Uncle Pon caught a fever and began to talk strangely.

In the village, it was easy to be frightened. There were no lights, except for little tin lamps filled with a kapok wick dipped in kerosene. At night, while walking, you could hear someone coming long before you could see the person. It might be your neighbor, or then again it just might be a pii-bawb or some other evil thing. There were no televisions or radios to provide pleasant distractions, only the sounds of the night around them.

But it was more than this. The restiveness that followed was just a symptom of what everyone had been through. Displaced by war, forced into co-operatives, blown up by sleeping bomblets, punished by the weather, and nearly buried by the mountain, the villagers were vulnerable to hysteria. Life was full of incomprehensible dangers.

Dealing with pii-bawbs was the job of the maw pii, Laotian ghost busters, and their duty was to cure people who had the unhappy misfortune of being infected with it. The pii bawb was a maleficent spirit that entered one's anus and devoured one's entrails, including the liver. The condition was contagious—the pii bawb could leave that host and go into another, and if the person couldn't be cured, there was pressure to send him or her out of the village. Sunnata felt obliged to dispel these beliefs. But what choice did the common people have in the absence of medicines or doctors? After all, there were indeed cases of successful recovery following a shaman's ceremony, perhaps owing to a placebo effect. If one believed they were getting well, the mind could cure the body. He himself believed in the monk's version of exorcism, the one he had performed for Pantivong in Camp 07, for the Pali chanting soothed those in distress and offered relevant guidance on how to deal with suffering.

Because the pii-bawb were usually blamed for diseases that

caused delirium, Sunnata surmised that the real culprit was probably malaria or dengue fever. Fortunately for the victims, Potisat must have inferred this himself, for there was a potion he forced his patients to drink, made from leaves which contained substantial amounts of quinine, an effective medicine for the malarial parasite.

"During the day," Potisat explained, "the pii bawb is inside the person, chewing on his liver, gnawing at his kidneys, and when he eats up everything inside, that's when the person dies."

They were on their way to what was to be Sunnata's first experience with a pii bawb, walking down a side path in the ethereal glow of twilight. Potisat was bare-chested, dressed only in a pakima. This was done with the obvious intention of showing off the impressive tattoos all over his gaunt body. In Southeast Asia, tattoos were more than bodily decorations, for the images and enigmatic figures contained powerful magic. Consistent with this, the tattoo artists who make them were invariably monks or spiritualists.

"But at night," he continued, "the pii bawb leaves the person's body and scampers about full of mischief and evil, and usually feeds on chickens or frogs or dung, but if it finds a person who is sick and weak, he rushes right up into their anus."

Sunnata was carrying the bowl of holy water that had already been sacralized with dripping candle wax before their departure from the camp. "Uncle Potisat, how do you ensure that it doesn't go into someone else when you drive the spirit out?"

"Don't worry. With the spells Potisat has learned from a great master in Luang Prabang, it will leave the village and never come back."

By the time they arrived at the house of the patient, poor Uncle Pon, a small crowd had already gathered outside. Some of them were throwing stones at the walls and shouting "Pii Bawb get out of our village!" But they became quiet once the maw pii and his assistant approached.

Potisat lifted up his pakima and tucked the hem in at the waist, revealing even more potent tattoos on his thighs, which everyone gasped at. He closed his eyes and muttered secret words. He pawed the ground like a charging buffalo, then scrambled urgently up the ladder with Sunnata following close behind.

The first thing that Potisat did upon entering the sick man's room was to beat him with a stick. Then he took the bowl from Sunnata and threw some water on him. "Bathe in the holy water!" The man on the floor continued to thrash about, until Potisat grabbed him by the wrists and put his face nose-to-nose with his. "Do you fear me?"

"Yes, yes, I fear you," the feverish man said in a weak voice. "Please, let me go."

Potisat did indeed let go of the man's wrist, but then began to pummel the man's chest with his fists. Then he forced his patient to drink the special herbal medicine, before dowsing him again with holy water. The last step involved screaming. "OOOOh," Potisat bellowed, after which he turned to Sunnata. "Okay, we can go now."

The crowd was still standing with agitated expectation at the front of the house, awed by the commotion they heard, and thus eager for a report.

"Did you see it?" Potisat asked the crowd. "Horrible, a floating head with no body, only his intestines dangling down. Horrible! But don't worry, it's gone now. Let the poor man rest."

This was exactly what everyone wanted to hear, and their wild applause confirmed their approval.

The next day the sick man's fever had diminished and he began to eat again. Another dose of Potisat's unique brew and he was cured completely. Soon after, the Pii-Bawb panic died down.

The next big social event was Bang Fai, the Rocket Festival. Large rockets, some over three feet in length, were sent soaring into the air to petition the heavens for rain before exploding in bright flames to the accompaniment of great cheers from the onlookers. But it was Jampaa, once again displaying some fireworks of her own, who served as the highlight of the celebrations, singing and prancing through the crowd like a diva summoning her followers.

She capered among the throng of villagers, her arms outstretched and undulating in fluid, tantalizing waves, her hands fluttering like a pair of butterflies in a mating dance. She threw her head back as she cried out, her powerful piercing voice like the wailing of the wind, intoning a plaintive ballad to beg for rain.

"Oh rainwater, uh-uh-uh-uh,
Stand long in our rice fields,
With rainwater, uh- uh-uh-uh,
Let my paa-sin be soaked..."

Sunnata fell in love with her all over again, hopelessly and irreversibly, negating all his recent efforts at abstaining from earthly desire. He could no longer resist the feelings he had been suppressing for the past few months.

The crowd clapped in time to her lyrical ode, while musicians played ken panpipes, traditional fiddles, bamboo xylophones, and drums and gongs of various sizes. Before long, she was leading them all in a lissome dance, a spirited Indochinese ballet with bodies swaying and arms in the air. Somehow Sunnata couldn't get into the jubilant mood that everyone else was taking pleasure in. Nearly every man had a partner to share in his rhapsody, and although there were a number of women eager to dance with him, he only wanted Jampaa. To avert his dilemma, Sunnata slipped away unnoticed.

He found a quiet palm tree to sit under, though the music, singing, and laughter relentlessly wafted through the evening air to follow him, as if in derision. He picked up a stick and began to poke at the sandy ground, drawing circles. Without warning, he was struck by a lurid flashback, horrible images of blood and fire, of unspeakable violence and atrocities. A sensation of spinning caused his body to collapse and he lost consciousness, but not entirely; he could see himself on the ground, gripped by shuddering spasms as if he were having a seizure. It must have lasted less than a minute he reckoned, before he had come to.

He raised himself up. He was shivering uncontrollably. Although he had been having flashbacks for the past year, they weren't as forceful as this one. It was like having one of his nightmares while still awake. He must be getting weaker. All the strength he had gained through meditation was waning low, and the threat of returning to his old self was looming real. But a sense of self also requires a future, and he had none.

To his amazement, a familiar pain emerged—grief! His face contracted in a grimace and his eyes flooded with tears. "Oh God!" He covered his face and sobbed like a frightened child.

"Who am I? What am I doing here?"

But this strange emotional fit passed as quickly as it came. He stopped his crying and wiped his eyes with his arms. After that, he just sat there, looking at a pair of wrens in the tree above him, and listening to their chirping with a dull and listless frame of mind.

It must have been at least another hour that he had sat, sullenly, under that tree, when he noticed, much to his consternation, that Jampaa was approaching him. He abruptly stood up.

"Sabai dee," she greeted, with an uncertain smile.

"Sabai dee."

"You seem sad, Ai Sunnata. Is there something wrong?"

He didn't have a ready answer for her. He didn't know what to say, other than, "Yes."

She avoided his gaze and looked down at the ground. Her hair had been brushed back and was bound in a long, tassel-like ponytail, exposing her entire oval face, which was left free to impose all of its beauty. Her bearing was mute and contrite, for she sensed what was troubling him. This only made it more difficult.

He had to be frank. "I have feelings for you, Jampaa."

She didn't look up, but stood idly gazing at her own bare feet.

"I love you," he blurted. "I want to marry you."

With her head still bowed down, she asked, "Even if it means suffering and pain?"

"Yes. My heart leaves me little choice. I can't see how I could suffer more than I am suffering now."

She finally lifted her head, their eyes locking for a long exquisite moment, which gave him the sensation of falling.

She smiled shyly. "Go and see my father." She then quickly turned around to go back to the festivities.

Sunnata, walking back to the work camp, was torn between elation and diffidence. Her reply, that he should see her father, was an implicit yes; she wanted to be his wife. But the thought of discussing this with her father seemed a formidable and unpleasant hurdle to get over. Kampoon didn't like him, plain and simple. And technically, he was still a prisoner of the state. Would he be allowed to take a wife?

Later in the evening he sought out Potisat for counsel on these issues, in the privacy of Potisat's bamboo shack.

"Oh ho!" the old gent whooped. "I was wondering when you would ask her. I don't see any problem about getting married, but you will need to ask permission from the district, and in your case, maybe the provincial authorities, or even the Ministry. I admit this is a little awkward, since Kampoon, as the chairman of the village, has to be the one to submit the request."

"I have to talk to him anyway, since he is her father."

"You cannot do that! It is unthinkable!"

"But she told me to see her father."

"She did not mean for you to go personally. It is not done like that. That would be disrespectful, an insult beyond belief. You must send someone to speak on your behalf. And, of course, Potisat will go and represent you."

"Thank you, Uncle. I wouldn't want anyone else but you to do this for me. I just feel guilty about giving you such a difficult task. Her father hates me."

Potisat guffawed, showing his black, betel-stained teeth. "Don't worry about that. You will pay me for my efforts. That is customary. And Kampoon should be no problem. All fathers are stern with their daughter's husbands. Besides, he needs you."

That last statement confused Sunnata. "Needs me?"

"His sons are dead. He has a lot of land but no one to work it. He gave most of it to the co-operative, which was good for him, because it made him appear a model citizen. But now with the new laws, the co-operative is breaking up, and he will get his land back. What will he do with it, if he doesn't have enough family labor to farm it? If he hires workers or rents it out, he will fear being branded as a feudal landlord, a capitalist."

Sunnata was impressed with Potisat's analysis. "I see. If I marry Jampaa, then he can give the land to us and save face."

"What?" Potisat exclaimed, incredulous. "No, not like that. The land will belong to him until he dies."

"I don't understand."

"You don't, do you? You better know what you are getting into. When a man gets married, he goes to live in his wife's home, where he works for his father-in-law, who now gains an extra helping hand. The new husband has no say in family matters; he only labors under the father's authority. It is when a wife's younger sister takes a husband that the first couple can move out and start on their own. The last daughter to get married, together with her husband, stay in her home and take care of the parents until they die. They inherit the house and the remaining land. In Jampaa's case, she is the only daughter, so you will remain under her father's roof until he passes away. Then you get everything."

Sunnata had no idea that this is what marrying Jampaa would entail. He was beginning to have doubts. Instead of living happily ever after in their own cozy little bamboo hut, it might turn out to be quite a dismal proposition. Now, he thought that he finally understood her question to him about suffering and pain, and he couldn't go back on the answer he gave her. He would go to hell and back with her. It would still be better than being apart.

The next day, as if in response to the rockets and Jampaa's singing, soft rain showers anointed the land.

About this time, Sunnata received a letter from Sousat, who was currently in Vientiane, undergoing officer's training. In three months he would graduate and automatically become a lieutenant in the Lao People's Liberation Army. In addition, his application for membership in the Lao People's Revolutionary Party was being processed and its approval was imminent. He was very happy and thanked Sunnata for bringing him luck.

Sousat had good reason to be happy. At that time in Lao PDR, the only means of upward social mobility was through the army, and even more so, through the Party. He had come a long way since Sunnata had first met him as a temple boy nine years ago, and he seemed bound for a promising future.

Sunnata replied to the letter saying he was happy for him. He also informed him of his plans to get married, and asked if he could put in a good word for him to his uncle on the Provincial Committee in case permission from the authorities got caught up in bureaucratic red tape.

Shortly before Potisat was to meet with Kampoon concerning the marriage negotiations, another development took place—the Venerable Kru Jarun, after nearly two years of being away, had returned to Ban Ling Kao. Sunnata immediately went to see him at the village temple.

Inside the old priest's kuti, Sunnata sat in a kneeling position, with his knees on the floor, his rear end resting on his heels.

"I am glad to see you are well, Venerable Father. I was worried over the hardships you might have endured at the Forest Temple, alone all this time."

"I did not stay long in the Forest. I fasted for seven days, and then journeyed to all the surrounding villages, where I witnessed for myself the suffering of the past two years. And even as they suffered, the people were still generous to share what they had, so as to help me survive, and through their acts of charity they have gained much merit."

When he sensed that the holy man had finished speaking, he decided to tell him, "We in Ban Ling Kao have also suffered, Venerable Father."

The old monk leaned forward and squinted at Sunnata. His eyes were getting worse. "I, of course, know about your vision concerning the earth movement..."

"It was not a vision, Venerable Father, it was..."

"...and of your new association with Potisat, who is teaching you ancient rituals and magic spells." Kru Jarun's tone sounded foreboding.

"Do you disapprove, Venerable Father?"

"I neither approve, nor disapprove. I only advise you to be mindful in everything you undertake. You should be aware of who this man is. He was once a revered monk, but was later expelled from the order."

"Expelled? He broke one of the parajika rules?"

"Yes."

Sunnata wondered if Potisat, while a monk, killed someone.

"No, he did not kill anyone, either when he was a monk, or before," Venerable Kru Jarun answered, reading Sunnata's thoughts. "He was disrobed because he boasted of his magical powers. That is a serious offense, and that alone should make you wary."

"Yes, Venerable Father."

"Furthermore, it is rumored that this man has used namman prai in his practices. If that is true, he should be considered a very dangerous man."

This made Sunnata shudder with revulsion. Namman prai was fluid extracted from the skulls of corpses of those who died inauspiciously, most commonly a woman who died during childbirth, and whose pi dai hong were the most vengeful of all. It is used in only the more notorious forms of black magic.

"I also know that you are contemplating marriage."

"Yes."

Pra Kru Jarun was silent for a moment.

"Are you not happy for me?" Sunnata asked.

"I am neither happy nor sad. Again, I advise you to be heedful of your actions. Through the deceptions that emotions bring, you are seeking an identity, a self, which you know deep in your heart and from your own experiences is a fleeting sensation, a temporary distraction that, when it is finally gone, causes great pain. A man who has a wife and family is inextricably tied to the mundane existence of the material world, which invariably means suffering. You must be ready to accept the consequences."

"I thought perhaps you would attend the wedding and chant blessings for us."

"Invite Pra Boon and the other monks for the ritual blessings. I myself cannot do so, for I perceive your Karma. Do not attempt to question me on this matter."

"Yes, Venerable Father."

"I also know that you no longer practice meditation."

Sunnata bowed his head down.

"Do not feel guilty, guilt is a hindrance to spiritual progress. I only point out that it is a mistake to think that because you are now a layman, that you do not need to meditate. It is a waste for someone like you, who has the knowledge, to neglect it."

"Yes, Venerable Father."

"Before you go, I want to inform you that at the end of Pansa this year, I will return to the Forest Temple, and take any devout person, monk or layman, with me. Since the government has loosened its control of the Sangha, the villagers can once more come and sustain our work there, as it was done before. You yourself will make this decision whether or not to come with me, although I already foresee your answer."

"Yes, Venerable Father."

"Now, it is nearing the time for the evening prayers. You must leave, for it is the night for reciting the Pattimoka, and no layman should be present."

Sunnata couldn't help but feel that this last comment was a deliberate jibe. "Yes, Venerable Father." He made the five-point prostration, bowing his head to the floor three times, then crawled backwards out the door.

He was waiting nervously the whole day. It was a Sunday, and being his day off, there was nothing he could think of doing to occupy his mind. Potisat had left in the morning with two earthen pots, one of rice, the other filled with areca nuts and betel leaves, to arbitrate with Kampoon over the betrothal of his daughter.

Sunnata had time enough to worry over what Pra Kru Jarun had said about Potisat, making him view the old man in a different light. He now regarded him as more than just an amusingly rakish fellow, but as someone who should be treated with caution. To be expelled from the monkhood carried a stigma, and the use of namman prai would reveal the man to be lacking in compunction and capable of performing malicious deeds. If Potisat's dark past was known to others, sending him as his emissary for a marriage proposal would be an insult, as it required a person with an unblemished reputation. Still, at this late juncture, he couldn't change his mind about this without arousing Potisat's suspicions.

It wasn't until mid-afternoon when Potisat came back, still carrying the pots, which meant that Kampoon didn't accept them, which meant that Kampoon didn't accept the marriage proposal.

"He wants to talk to you first," Potisat reported. "Very unusual indeed. Go now, so you don't have to return at night. There is no moon tonight, and it will be dark."

Sunnata made the trek down the hill and across the valley with anxious trepidation. Forty-five minutes later he found himself in front of the house of the woman he loved and summoned his courage to face her father.

Kampoon was outside, sitting cross-legged on a mat in the soft evening light, shredding tobacco.

"Sabai dee," Sunnata greeted as he nopped, quickly sitting down on the ground.

"Sabai dee," the old man responded, darting a quick glance to him before resuming his work.

Sunnata didn't know what to say, so he just sat watching him.

Kampoon sharpened his machete against a grinding stone, then went back to shredding more tobacco. He would tighten the tobacco into a wad, then feed it through a small hole in a piece of wood, shaving the leaves as they emerged. His movements were rigid and severe, reflecting his mood.

"Uncle, I was told you wanted to speak to me."

Kampoon finally stopped his work and brought his head up. He looked at Sunnata with eyes that seemed to drill right through him. "My daughter is the only family I have. She is already over two cycles in age, and she should have been married by now."

Two cycles equaled twenty-four years.

Kampoon continued. "But she is a headstrong girl and has refused all her suitors. Now that she is a grown woman, she is more difficult to control. I know she needs a husband, and I need a son-in-law. I do not have anyone to plow the fields. At first she would go and try to plow, but I had to stop her. It is shameful. Even a widow hires a man to do that work." Kampoon stanched his flow of words to carry on compressing rolls of tobacco leaves, apparently contemplating what he was about to say next. "She is also a *Nang Tiam*, a fortune teller, and after the revolution, I had to protect her and try to restrain her from practicing these things. I didn't want my daughter to be taken away. Do you understand what I am saying?"

"Yes, Uncle."

Sunnata understood all too well. The new government feared spirit mediums, because they often acted as the conduit for people's feelings. Moreover, being possessed by historical figures of the past, they had the potential to speak through deceased right wing Royalist personages whom the revolutionaries had removed from power. Worse still, in the role of fortunetellers, they might prophesize the downfall of the new regime. Their behavior was unpredictable, and thus their séances were prohibited, and many of them were rounded up in the first few years of the revolution.

"Now you come along, a strange farang" complained Kampoon. "Obviously, the government considers you a troublemaker, otherwise, why would you be here in a seminar camp. Before, you were in Camp Seven, which is for more dangerous people. On top of that, you are a controversial figure; some say you are a magician, or even an angel. You use a monk name, which is not your original name. I don't know who you are or what you did, but I do know that as the village headman, I don't need any more controversy than I already have with my daughter. But more importantly, my daughter doesn't need it. I am just trying to protect her. That is why I don't think it would be a good idea for you to marry her. Do you understand?"

"Yes, Uncle." Sunnata gave Kampoon's words some thought. There was definitely more to this than he had originally considered. But he discerned that Jampaa herself must be aware of all these implications. How did she feel about it?

He had to know. "I will withdraw my request of marriage, but only if Nang Jampaa agrees."

"I will tell her."

"I will leave now, Uncle. If things change, you can inform Uncle Potisat."

In the morning of the next day, Potisat received word that he should go back, and to make sure to bring the earthen pots with him. It appeared that Jampaa, willful as ever, was determined to marry the farang with the monk name.

Each day, Kampoon, like everybody else in Southeast Asia, made offerings to the spirits of his ancestors. The altar was typically a shelf on the wall, always the easterly wall, where the ashes of the departed were kept, along with ornamental receptacles for flowers, incense, and candles. If there were any pictures of the deceased, they were also placed on the shelf. In the evenings, usually before retiring to bed, people prayed to their forebears and gave them a daily report of the goings on in the household. In his summary of the day, Kampoon omitted anything about his daughter being engaged to the farang, because he felt they would be furious about it. He would have to break it to them gently. After all, there was no need to upset them needlessly since it had to be approved first by the province, and that just might not happen.

He figured that the authorities would be reluctant to grant permission, since this man was a foreigner and had been an inmate at Camp 07. But he was wrong. The Provincial Committee chairman informed him that because the groom wasn't a citizen of Lao PDR, the request had to go up to the level of the Ministry, then assured him that there shouldn't be any problem. And in truth there was none. For this matter was handled by Sousat's uncle and was subsequently directed to the Ministry official whose life Sunnata had saved at Camp 07. The official was pleased at this new turn of events, mainly because it assured him that this man could now be put in a position which would preclude him from making trouble. A man with a family was vulnerable, and likely to think twice before doing anything stupid. Marriage would domesticate, and thus neutralize this man whose past remained a mystery.

Therefore, not only was permission for marriage granted, but Sunnata was to be released from Mobile Work Force 333 to be upgraded to a Closely Guarded Citizen, and was allowed to move into his wife's home with the stipulation that he wasn't to leave the village without permission. This should be rather easy to enforce since it virtually placed the farang in the custody of Kampoon, who was the chairman of the village committee, as well as the bride's father.

Kampoon, once informed of this decision, had no choice but to break the news to the ancestors that a newcomer would be joining the household.

The rains were good that season, and the harvest promised to be plentiful. The raucous croaking of frogs was like music to the ears of the Lao country folk, who would catch the amphibious critters and make tasty dishes out of them. In the freshness of the early mornings, children were gleeful as they scooped up fish and little crabs from the newly formed paddy basins, and their parents, the rural farmers, were optimistic about the tidings of the new year. Everyone couldn't help but get the feeling that this year was going to be a good one. In this upbeat mood, the villagers saw the wedding of Jampaa and Sunnata as a propitious sign, and all were looking forward to it with great anticipation.

In a community as small as Ban Ling Kao, such an event as a wedding served as one of the highlights of village life, and the nature of this particular union only made it more special. There was a noisy, boisterous parade to the bride's house, accompanied by the sounds of drums and gongs, full of children racing around excitedly, and various four-legged animals that the villagers had donated as wedding gifts.

Drawing up in front of the house, Sunnata saw his bride, sitting demurely on the porch surrounded by doting old crones. Her hair was bound into a topknot with a bejeweled silver headband, and she was beautifully dressed in a sarong of sky blue, the color of sincerity, and a sash that hung from her right shoulder across her bosom, pink in color, symbolizing love and loyalty.

The wedding itself was full of rituals, involving both the monks and then Potisat as the community spiritualist. The final part of the ceremony was the part that Sunnata liked the best, called the 'arranging of the pillows'. The couple were led to the sleeping place, where the brideprice and 'love leaves' were placed in the middle. They had to lie down together, trying not to bump their heads, which would prophesize a marriage plagued by incessant quarreling, and then they were made to listen to the rules expected of husband and wife. Besides the usual homily to love and respect, cherish and obey, they were informed of the prohibitions against sex on the days of wan pra and during menstrual periods, and were reminded to pay daily homage to the ancestors.

After this they were free to join the party which had already been going on for hours, full of frequent bursts of Laotian yodeling: "Hoy-oy-oy-oy-oy-ooy!" Sunnata was touched to tears, witnessing how fully the community shared his own joy.

That night drums and gongs sounded throughout the village. Sunnata and Jampaa were husband and wife.

There was no doubt that it was an auspicious year. The rains were perfect, in both amount and timing, and unlike the year before, when the skies were continually dark and foreboding, the sun did manage to come out from time to time, and on those days, it was so beautiful that it was almost unreal. The old bomb craters, lined with koy trees and bamboo along their rims, were filled with green water blooming with gorgeous lotus blossoms, while hornbills and parrots warbled their melodious mating calls. Life was easier after the government had relaxed its totalitarian laws, and people were at liberty to do as they did before. To top everything off, like icing on a cake, Jampaa, the revered daughter of the village, had finally gotten married after all these years, and furthermore, to Sunnata, the mystical stranger.

For Sunnata, his wishes had really come true, since he not only had Jampaa as his lover, his wife, and his partner, but he also had a foundation upon which to build a normal life, and a new and wonderful sense of self that was defined by this relationship. He had forgotten what it was like to have a woman, although having Jampaa wasn't like anything he had experienced with a woman before. Every time they made love, it was with the same profound feelings he enjoyed on his wedding night, a complete physical and emotional fulfillment. However, married life wasn't without some minor short-comings.

Even though they were husband and wife, they still addressed each other as Little Sister and Big Brother. He was having some frustration in trying to teach her how to kiss, for osculating mouth to mouth was a totally alien concept in Lao culture. The Laotian version of kissing was fondly rubbing cheeks, which he liked, but longed for more than that. And of course, being in the same house as her father, they had to be quiet. After the harvest, he would suggest building their own sleeping hut on the compound. Although, even then, they would still have to be a bit subdued in their vocal expressions of lovemaking, for Sunnata rightly reckoned that loud moaning and grunting would probably not be looked on favorably by the spirits of the ancestors.

The ancestors, though, seemed to have approved the marriage. This is what Kampoon, her father, had surmised, even though he too was a bit uncomfortable knowing that the farang and his daughter were copulating under his roof.

Frequently, visitors came by to consult with Jampaa, mostly older women. She would read their palms and study the lines on their face and long discussions ensued which excluded Sunnata. Many times, this took place in the evenings, which was when, having been away from her all day; he had relished spending some time with her alone.

Kampoon, being the administrative leader and one of the elders of the community, had his guests as well. Men came over almost every night to sit in the large main room of the house, or sometimes out on the veranda, chewing betel leaves and smoking hand-rolled tobacco while talking about farming, the weather, land disputes, and other village concerns.

The relationship between Sunnata and Kampoon didn't mellow as Sunnata had hoped. It would take some time, he figured. The old man was curt and impersonal, and he rarely spoke to Sunnata, but rather communicated to him indirectly through his daughter, forcing Sunnata to do the same. It was a bit of a strain really. And Jampaa, instead of smoothing things out, only made them worse.

As the transplanting of the rice seedlings had already been completed, there was not a great deal of farm work to be done until harvest, for paddy rice didn't require much weeding. When Kampoon sought work for Sunnata to do, it had to be approved by Jampaa. She didn't want Sunnata to help her father when he went fishing, for she didn't want her husband to break the precept that prohibited the taking of life. Kampoon, because of the paucity of labor in his own household, had accumulated a labor debt with several of his neighbors. During transplanting, before the marriage, many people had given him a hand, but when it came time for him to reciprocate the gesture, there was previously only himself and his daughter that could return the help. Kampoon, now that he had an extra worker in his son-in-law, sought to pay back in kind by sending Sunnata to whoever needed him. But when the request came to help make repairs on Uncle Gayo's house, Jampaa forbade her husband to go, for Uncle Gayo was a drunkard and there would be more drinking than actual working. Despite Kampoon's outward show of sternness and authority, Jampaa actually bullied him, and Sunnata soon realized who the real boss was. This wasn't the typical behavior of a Laotian girl, overriding her father's authority in this manner. Then again, Jampaa wasn't typical. She had always been difficult, her father admitted, but now that she was a married woman, she had become more assertive. This was only in the privacy of their own home, however; in public she always deferred to her father out of respect.

Sunnata had to be given neutral tasks, such as going into the woods to make charcoal, or harvest the gum from her father's chamcha trees.

Similar to Kampoon, Sunnata would also clash with Jampaa's unyielding obstinacy on numerous occasions, which inevitably led to their first marital spat. It was over his attempt to prohibit her from going into the forest to gather wild foods. Several times a month, groups of women would move slowly through the forest, foraging for herbs and other natural things useful for the family...but it was dangerous because of the bombies. There had already been two casualties that year, with one woman dead, and the other maimed. When Jampaa refused to comply with his order not to go into the forest, Sunnata attempted to restrain her physically by grabbing her. She wrenched herself free and went anyway in defiance of his will.

After that, they didn't speak to each other for several days, and Sunnata even found himself doubting the prudence of his decision to get married. Now both his wife and her father weren't talking to him, and this social isolation in the very home he lived in made him feel like the stranger that he was. In the end he had to apologize, telling her that it was only because he loved her, which she naturally understood, so she easily forgave him.

Kampoon and Sunnata weren't the only men who, in one way or another, had to answer to her. Jampaa was also head of the Woman's League chapter of the village. If it became known that a man was beating his wife, Jampaa would rush over and give the husband a severe scolding. Needless to say, incidents of wife beating were rare in Ban Ling Kao.

Jampaa, besides her weaving and forest gathering, tended her garden, in which she grew the many vegetables and legumes needed to sustain her and her husband's vegetarian diet. She also had chickens, not for their meat, but for the eggs. Eggs were one of the things that she had deemed permissible to eat.

"Have you ever eaten eggs baked in the sand?" she asked him, as they lay on their sleeping mat, embracing each other. They often talked about trifling things when they went to bed, just to have the pleasure of hearing each other's voices.

"No. Can you really cook them that way?" He smiled, full of affection for her. She was always trying to entertain him, to please him, to teach him new things.

"Yes, when the sun is strong, the ground gets very hot. I will make them for you when the dry season comes again," she said softly. They were whispering, as it was a bit late and they didn't want to wake her father.

There was a soft, lovely rain falling, a mellow pattering on the thatches of the roof. He held his new wife tightly. All the hardships of the day were forgotten at night, the time when her pliant, warm body was next to his, their arms around each other.

"Little Sister, why are you so beautiful?"

She laughed. "What a silly question. It's my Karma. And anyway, I will be old and ugly soon enough."

"You know that you're my whole world now, don't you?"

She gazed at him with a smile full of meaning. "I knew that we would be married," she confessed.

"You did? When did you first know that?" He gave her cheek a loving kiss.

"That day you came to see me, and I was at my loom. I read your palms. I saw it in your hands."

"You knew from the lines in my palms?"

"Yes."

His interest evoked, he raised his head and supported it with his hand, his elbow propped on the mat. He looked at her attentively. "What else did they say?"

"You will be a great man."

"Really!" he exclaimed, laughing.

"Sshh! Be quiet. It's late."

"I know one way we can be quiet. Let's practice kissing."

He pulled her under him and they put their mouths together, rubbing and nibbling at each other lips. It wasn't long before Sunnata became aroused.

"Little Sister, my beautiful wife, can we not build our own sleeping hut?"

"Yes. Give me some time to persuade my father."

To Sunnata, that meant it was as good as done. They then celebrated their decision by making love.

As it turned out, permission from Kampoon to build the hut was given the very next day. Of course it was to be in the compound, only a short distance from the main house. With the help of some of the detainees from the work camp, the little shack on stilts, notwithstanding all the building rites, was completed in three days.

One morning, about two months after they had been married, Sunnata rose from his sleep in the pre-dawn darkness. Jampaa wasn't there; her place on the sleeping mat was vacant. She had presumably gotten up already to cook breakfast for the monks, who would pass by at first light with their begging bowls. Every morning, just after sunrise, she would make Sunnata kneel outside with her, so that they could make the offering together.

He entered the bathing area, a bamboo-fenced space out back under the trees, and gave himself a quick dousing. He knew he had about an hour before the holy men would reach their house.

These days he dressed like any other Laotian man, in a pakima wrapped around his waist, and a baggy sleeveless shirt, both woven by his wife, and when he worked outside he wore a goop, the same conical-styled hat that he had worn as a detainee in the work camp. As well as the clothes, he had also adapted to the Laotian outlook on life: disregarding the past and not dwelling on the future, but to take life day by day, an outlook that well suited him.

Fully attired, except for the cone hat, which he held in his hands, he made to leave the compound. As he walked past the kitchen, which was a room at the back of her father's house, she stepped out on the veranda and called out to him. "Sabai dee, Big Brother! Where are you going?"

"Sabai dee, Little Sister. I am going to let the buffaloes out."

"I've already taken them to the fields," she shouted back.

"Oh." He wondered why she had done a task that was normally his. "Then I'll collect some more firewood."

"There is enough already."

"Oh. That means I can get an early start. Father has sent me to help Uncle Chat mend the yoke for his buffaloes. I can leave after the morning offering. If there is some rice left I can take it with me and eat on my way over there."

She put her hands on her hips. "You are not going anywhere to work today. It is my birthday. I want you to take me to the market at Muang Koon."

He looked at her standing on the veranda, as a warm feeling of cheerfulness filled him. "Well, happy birthday, Little Sister!" he hollered out to her.

"Kopjai."

"How old are you now?"

"Never mind," she shouted back. "I am older than two dogs, and that is all you need to know."

That meant she had seen two Year of the Dog's and was older than twenty-four.

Leaving the village in Jampaa's company never required approval from her father, despite the fact that he was in his custody. Jampaa's influence was overriding in these cases.

To get to Muang Koon required boarding a rot duk-duk, a cart that was hitched to a little tractor-like contraption with long handles for steering. It took several hours of bumping along to get there. At the market, Jampaa was without restraint, buying all sorts of little birds, and two large buckets of live fish. She carried the buckets on a shoulder pole, while Sunnata carried a big cumbersome basket on his back, filled with bamboo birdcages. He wondered where they were going, and why she had bought all these animals, since eating meat in her household was taboo. But she wouldn't answer his questions. They left the settlement and continued walking towards the hills.

"Where are we going?" He was tired and his back was hurting him. He also didn't enjoy watching his wife treading laboriously under her own heavy burdens.

"We're almost there."

They finally stopped beside a small stream. She put the pole and buckets down. She removed one of the buckets from the wooden boom, and carried it on her head to the bank of the stream, where she dumped it into the water and released the fish, while her husband watched, amazed.

"Go fish!" Jampaa proclaimed giggling, "swim back home." She did the same with the other bucket. Then she went over to the big basket, and with Sunnata's help, let out all the birds from their cages, one by one. "Fly birds, fly back home."

They stood watching the birds flying away for a few moments.

"I do this every birthday," she explained.

Sunnata, his eyes wet with love for her, took her hand and squeezed it. "Happy Birthday, Little Sister."

As the days passed, Sunnata, besides learning how to live in a peasant home with his wife and father-in-law, also began to figure out just how the village was run. Kampoon was officially the village president, although the people still called him the village father, the old term that had been thrown out by the new regime. His job was to mediate the discussions of the village committee, a few sessions of which Sunnata, because of the esteem he now held in the community, was allowed to observe. Kampoon's role of arbitrator wasn't easy, for decisions had to be made unanimously, which meant he had to get everyone to agree. Kampoon would remold the conflicting arguments to convince the dissenters, without bossing them or pressuring them. This he did rather adroitly, and Sunnata's respect for his father-in-law grew, as the meetings always ended in mutual understanding and solidarity. On some occasions, however, a cadre representing the Party would take part, and the participants wouldn't express themselves quite so candidly. Usually, this was of little consequence, since after the official left, the villagers tended to do what they wanted to do anyway.

In their attitude towards Sunnata, the local people viewed him less and less as a farang, and more and more like a Laotian, whom they came to believe had been reborn, by some quirk of fate, as a Caucasian in America, and whose Karma finally brought him back home. His fluent Lao, and his now formidable knowledge of indigenous customs, facilitated this sentiment. He was rather grateful to be encouraged in this fashion by the opinions of his neighbors, as it made it easier to regard himself as a certified citizen of Ban Ling Kao. And something would occur in the very near future that would further fortify these notions.

Awk Pansa, the day marking the end of Lent, arrived as the rains departed. The air was delightfully filled with the sweet fragrance of the ripening rice crop. It was now that time of year to hold the Katin ceremony, which entailed making new robes to give to the monks. Everyone in the village was busy weaving, dying, cutting, and sewing, and naturally, Jampaa was playing a prominent role, frantically working her loom, running around here and there assisting in the dying and the cutting. They only had one day to complete this work, as the robes had to be ready by dusk.

She was walking hurriedly, bringing a pile of dyed and cut cloth to the old women who formed the sewing group just a few houses away, when she slowed to a halt, tottered, and collapsed on the ground right in front of them. All the women trotted over to see if she was okay, and Sunnata, in the all-male cutting group, threw down his knife, and jumped up to join them. He slipped his hands under her, and, as he raised her head, she regained consciousness, albeit a bit confused, looking at him with a weak smile. "I think maybe I am doing too much. I need to rest," she said calmly.

Sunnata put his lips to her forehead to check for a fever. There seemed to be none. "Yes, you have to rest," he told her, picking her up in his arms to carry her home.

The next morning, Sunnata woke up to the sounds of her vomiting over the side of their sleeping mat. He roused himself to see the back of her head, her hair in that lovely morning frazzle that he had always found so appealing.

"What is it, Little Sister?"

"It is normal," she said, without turning around, then heaved up again.

"No, it is not. Yesterday you faint, and now you are vomiting. You are not well."

"Not long ago I had a dream, so I am sure."

"What dream? Sure of what?"

Her retching apparently finished, she turned her head to face him. She was smiling. "A *winyan* has settled inside me."

A winyan was a human spirit waiting to be reborn.

"What?" He was flabbergasted, thinking that maybe he knew what she was talking about, that she was pregnant, but he wasn't sure.

"It is a boy."

Now it was Sunnata who felt faint. "Are you sure?"

"I just told you. You don't believe me?"

He wondered why he was so overwhelmed, since it was a natural event that was bound to happen, a normal consequence of nature. Still, he couldn't get over the feeling that it was something magical, beyond comprehension. They embraced, and Sunnata felt a warmth in his heart that he had never known before.

Harvest time was near, and the sparrows had to be kept away. The children would sit on the raised makeshift shelters erected in the middle of the fields, using slingshots to knock the little birds out of the sky, or otherwise run in the paddies making loud noises to chase them. All the farmers got together for the customary drawing of lots to decide the sequence of fields to work in. It was a critical operation, and the faster they could do it, the less the birds would eat and the more rice everyone would have. They placed palm leaves that had numbers stenciled on them into a big earthen pot, and each household head would reach in and pick one. The lower a number the farmer drew, the sooner his field would be harvested, for all of them came to work the paddies together, not moving to the next farmer's crop until finished with the previous one. This was the way they had done it for as far back as anyone could remember.

They worked through the day and through the night as well, leaning over, tilting their cone-hatted heads, swinging their arms left and right, scythes and sickles and machetes hacking away to the accompaniment of songs and jokes, which gave heart to those engaged in the demanding work. Sunnata himself was assigned the evening shift, which he didn't mind, preferring the coolness of the night canopy to the burning rays of the sun. The puddles in the paddies would glisten like broken glass in the moonlight. And he would listen amusedly to the villager's jesting.

"Hey, look at me, I'm a madman with a long blade!"

"A long one you say? We will have to ask your wife!"

Peals of laughter under a starry night.

"What about a song? We who work at night are deprived of good singers. Those in the daytime have Nang Jampaa and Lung Potisat."

"I can sing," one young man responded.

"That may be, Poumi, but like a frog!"

There were more guffaws. The youth ignored them, and proceeded to croon the opening lines of a lively harvesting song. They all joined in.

It was true that Jampaa did sing beautiful lams during the day shift while she worked. Sunnata didn't want her to go to the fields given her delicate condition, but she wouldn't hear of it. Of course there was no way that he could stop her. Most women worked in the fields until the final month of pregnancy.

The harvesting lasted several weeks, during which time a noticeable paunch began to develop on Jampaa's tummy. The older women had known about her condition long before, more by the color of her cheeks than by the slight bulge in her paa-sin. They came to pay regular visits, full of pampering. They made sure that she was taking all the right precautions, including the adherence to a special diet for pregnant women and the wearing of special talismans. One couldn't be too cautious in these matters, since a woman who dies in childbirth is one of the most cursed things that could happen. Soon it became the talk of the village about the baby that was on the way. This was truly a lucky year.

As if to bear this out, the harvest was beyond everyone's expectations. Threshing, the separation of the grains from the cut stems, began in earnest. This was done by placing the stems in a pile and beating them with sticks. Sunnata wouldn't allow Jampaa to do this work, and neither would the other villagers, who came over in turns and helped to thresh the rice for Kampoon's household. After that, the grains were stored in their granaries, entrusting the rice goddess to keep it safe from rats and bugs.

January came. At home, Kampoon's attitude towards his son-in-law changed radically. He had already noted that Sunnata was a hard worker who never complained, and who always showed proper respect, never questioning his authority. It was also obvious how devoted the married couple were to each other. Now, about to be a grandfather and to finally witness the continuation of the family line, his fondness for Sunnata grew until it equaled the love one had for one's own son. And indeed, as required by custom, Sunnata no longer addressed Kampoon directly as Uncle, but as Father. The marriage had turned out to be a grand thing after all, and Kampoon spoke enthusiastically about it in each evening's progress report to the ancestors.

As for Sunnata, his transformation from holy man to family man was well-advanced. He confined his thoughts only to the present, a strategy that he had been practicing for years now, and made easier by the more pleasant developments that were now taking place. Other than occasional moments of anxiety, he managed to disclaim any memories that lacked relevance to his present situation. If he had been having any nightmares, he didn't remember them upon awakening.

Watching Jampaa's pregnancy develop, he began to make preparations. Every day before embarking on his normal work, in the wee hours before sunrise, and in the evenings as well, he would go into the forest, select the proper trees, and cut them down. He was interested only in wood that would burn steadily for a long time. He would use one of the water buffaloes to drag the pile of logs back home, where he would chop the wood into even shaped blocks, carefully stack it, and cover it with a thorny branch to keep evil spirits away. This was to be the wood for his wife's 'lying in at the fire', which would begin immediately after birth, and last from seven to fifteen days. In accordance with this, he also prepared the oven near their sleeping place, constructing it with banana leaves and earth.

The New Year celebrations in April were particularly festive that year. It was the year of the Monkey—1980 in the Western world, and the year 2524 on the Lao Buddhist calendar. It was to be the year that Sunnata and Jampaa had their first child.

It was in the evening, when he was chopping the last of the wood, when Kampoon called out. "Sunnata, get the midwife, it is time!"

He ran over to Auntie Bua's place, and the both of them hurried back to the scene as fast as they could, constrained somewhat by Auntie Bua's arthritic legs. Other people heard the news and followed close on their heels. It was to be a long night. Despite Jampaa's moaning over the violent contractions, the sounds of which made poor Sunnata cringe, the baby didn't seem ready to come out. He vicariously experienced his wife's pain, but he was powerless to do anything about it. Auntie Bua wouldn't allow him inside the room, so he remained outside and peeked through the door to see her lying across Jampaa's belly, trying to force the baby out. Kampoon came to Sunnata and led him away from the doorway.

"Don't worry, my son. It was like that with her mother as well. The first one is always the most difficult." He put his arm around Sunnata's shoulder and escorted him to the main house, where other men from the village were sitting on the veranda, all in a merry mood, drinking lao-kao.

"Here, sit down and have a drink," one of them said, "you look as nervous as a mongoose cornered by a pack of hunting dogs."

Sunnata was reluctant.

"Go ahead," Kampoon ordered, "consider it medicine for the nerves."

No sooner did he sit down and swill the contents of the glass, when a young girl came running over, loudly announcing, "Auntie Jampaa has had the baby, Auntie Jampaa has had the baby! It's a boy!"

Sunnata rose to his feet, perhaps a little bit too abruptly, for this time he did actually faint. Kampoon, laughing with joy, caught his son-in-law's falling body just before his head was about to hit the floor.

There were now several women attending to things. The umbilical cord had already been cut with a special ritual knife, and Auntie Bua, as the head midwife, was holding the baby, sucking on his face, removing the mucous from his nose and mouth, after which he gave out a loud, hearty cry. People clapped their hands and cheered as she presented the baby briefly to his mother, after which she placed him on a reed-woven winnowing tray.

Sunnata, together with his father-in-law, went over to gaze at the infant, before turning to look at his wife. "He's beautiful," he told her, his eyes moist with elation, his mouth stretched in a besotted grin.

The afterbirth came, and the placenta was collected, salted, and put into a jar, which was ceremoniously handed over to Sunnata.

"We must keep it for three days," Kampoon told him. "Then we will plant it underneath the frangipani tree out front."

Sunnata nodded his head knowingly, and then gave back the jar to his father-in-law so that he could go to the stove that he had built weeks earlier and light the fire. The bamboo platform on which Jampaa lay was brought as close as possible over to the oven. It had been decided that she would stay by the fire for nine days, which would minimize the blood clots, and it was the job of both Sunnata and Kampoon to ensure it was kept burning steadily.

After three days the child was ceremoniously accepted into the world. Auntie Bua and Potisat were appointed to conduct the ritual, held inside the main wooden house of Kampoon. The little baby was placed upon a large winnowing tray, which Auntie Bua moved in a clockwise, circular motion three times, repeating, "Three days a child of the spirits, fourth day human child, who will receive this child?" Potisat was the one who took the child and tied a string of cotton thread around the infant's right wrist to bind its new soul. He then bumped the baby softly on the floor to familiarize him to the fact that he has come into a harsh and difficult world. When the ceremony was finished, Sunnata went and got the bottled placenta, now three days old, took it out of the jar and buried it in a prepared hole underneath the frangipani tree that stood in the front of the compound. The little boy's fate was now bound with the state of this tree; if the tree thrived, the boy would be healthy and happy.

In consultation with the monks, the boy was given a name, which had to be selected with care, since a wrong choice could adversely affect the child's health. Even though some might claim it was a name more suitable for a girl, he was given the name of Santipop, which meant Peace. Of course they couldn't call him by this name until the child grew older, and worthy of the quality the name inferred. The evil spirits as well had to be deceived into thinking there was no child in the house, which they might want to take away in death, so his play name was chosen. Therefore, during his tender years they were to address him as Ling, the little Monkey.

Chapter 21

Camden, Ohio, 1980-1986

"The house seems heavier, now that they have gone away..."
John Ashbery (b. 1927), U.S. poet

Bill is not the same she thought. He's distracted. Or something. Reflecting on this, Dorothy realized that this had been her imagining for almost a year now. But it was becoming more real. Going out the door and forgetting your car keys is not an unusual sign. But doing that about twice a week was not normal. What was even more portending was his announcement one day, "Dot, I'm going to teach you how to drive."

"Well, I would love to learn, but why did you decide that now?"

"You never know," he said.

Actually, it was a wonderful idea. Dorothy loved the lessons, and Bill was unusually focused, and as well, very patient with her. So every day when he came home from work, they would spend an hour with Dorothy at the control of their Oldsmobile Delta 88, a rather big car that took her several weeks to master. Uncannily, or perhaps not, the timing was perfect. Because after two months of lessons, when Dorothy had just become proficient, Bill had a massive stroke.

Dorothy got a call from his office, saying he had collapsed at work and was rushed to the hospital. She practically flew out the door and commandeered the Delta 88, despite not getting her license yet.

The stroke left Bill Kozeny appearing as a vegetable, for he could not talk nor move any part of his body, save his head. The doctor said this was not a good sign, and had him on a respirator just in case. But the doctor did note that he was cognizant, responding to 'no-yes' questions by nodding his head. She looked at her husband, lying motionless upon the hospital bed, heartbroken to see him so helpless.

Over the next few days, Bill's condition improved greatly, but motor loss was considerable the doctor had said. Bill was actually attempting to say words, although the pronunciation was so bad it rather sounded like incomprehensible syllabic noises. But when he spoke these utterances, he would gaze at Dorothy fervidly, trying in frustration to communicate the meaning.

One week later came the day of decision. Bill could stay at the Veterans Hospital, the Hospital Director had said, whereupon all costs would be paid by the government according to the VA bill, or she could take him home, providing she realized that any cost of home-care would be borne by her. The decision was easy for Dorothy, Bill was coming home. She wasn't ready to spend the rest of her life alone.

Obviously, the first day was the hardest. The hospital had sent two orderlies to help her bring him up the stairs in his wheel chair. Ascending to their bedroom, Dorothy felt despondent knowing that he would probably never go out of the bounds of this part of the house again, as bringing a wheelchair down those stairs was beyond her capacity. That's why she almost collapsed in relief when the orderlies told her, "Ma'am, if you should require assistance in the event of an emergency, you can call the hospital and they will send a paramedic and an orderly. Also, once a week, you are allowed to use hospital orderlies to accompany you and your husband outside of the house, provided that such outings are limited to four hours. Thank you and have a good day Ma'm."

Dorothy was so elated at the words that she fished in her pocketbook for a tip.

One of the white-clothed orderlies held up his hand in protest. "No Ma'am, that is not necessary, we're proud of our work. Your husband was a veteran."

The most difficult thing was comprehending what his needs were.

One word that she had already deciphered was that 'frwee…pu, pu,p' meant 'sleep'. The next most urgent matter eluded her however, the first time she heard it.

He was still in his wheelchair. "T, ta, t…ta… ta, t, t…ta…ta."

"What is it Bill?"

"Ttt…ta…ttt…ta…ta," he repeated, over and over, shaking his head violently.

"Tea, you want tea?"

His face crinkled into a grimace, with tears rolling down his ample cheeks. His upper body was heaving.

That's when Dorothy noticed the dripping. He had urinated in his trousers. 'Ta' meant toilet.

"Oh dear Bill!" she hugged him. "Never mind, we'll fix that up."

So her first instance of lifting him out of the wheelchair presented itself. He still had one good arm which he slung over her shoulder, and she bore him like a sack and brought him to the bathroom, his lifeless feet dragging the floor. With a small struggle she removed his clothes, and with an even bigger struggle, through careful and slow positioning, got him into the bathtub.

Acts such as these became the core of her life. Every simple need of Bill's became a physical ordeal for her, lifting and carrying his unresponsive bulk. But Dorothy was soon able to manage these things routinely. After all, she was a nurse. And her reward at the end of the day was well worth the price. At night in bed, she would hold him, as if he were the same Bill she had always known. And she was grateful for that.

But before long, less than two months later, even that small, hard-won prize was denied her, for Bill soon died from a second stroke.

She was bringing him tea when she saw him lying still on the bed, his face a bluish white. She knew he was dead. She dropped the tray with the coffee cups and thermos and flung herself on the bed.

"Please don't leave me, Bill!"

But he had already left.

In this next phase of her life, the new tribulation Dorothy had to endure was loneliness, as the little family that she once had was now gone, leaving her alone with an emptiness that engulfed her. To make it worse, she also tried to get her job back, her position as nurse that she quit when Bill had his stroke. But the hospital had a new policy that any new nurses had to be younger than thirty-five, and they apologetically refused.

This only amplified her dismal frame of mind. She even experienced moments where her thoughts shifted to suicidal, borne out of a yearning to follow the path leading to wherever her son and husband had gone. These ideas of doing herself in were too shameful to disclose to her casual friends. There was only Father Wolanska. One day, going to the church to light candles for Andrew, and now for Bill as well, she bolstered herself to see him in the confessional.

She entered the dark booth, and heard Father Wolanska slide open the shutter.

"Bless me Father for I have sinned. It has been…" She honestly didn't remember how long, "…a long time since my last confession."

"Yes," he acknowledged, waiting for her to continue.

"Father, this is Dorothy." She stopped there.

"Yes, I know."

Silence.

He took her stillness as a cue for him to help her get her words out. "You came to me because you're troubled. I know what you're going through. Don't be afraid to talk to me."

"I have had bad thoughts." She paused. "About dying, even killing myself."

"Nothing to be ashamed about. It is natural. Not a sin. God knows your pain."

She was struggling now, resisting the urge to break down. "He's doing to me what he did to Job!" she moaned tearfully.

"Come now, Dorothy. God has more than you to think about." He hesitated, apparently reflecting. "I will give you a perfect example. My mother died when I was eight years old. She was vacuuming when she collapsed right in front of me. I was devastated after that and I too blamed God. As it turned out, she was riddled with cancer, some of which went to her brain, and by taking her at that moment he spared her much suffering."

"Well, wasn't he the one who gave her the cancer in the first place?"

"No, not at all!" he rebutted, a bit sternly. "Sickness and death are not from God, they arise out of Original Sin, inherited from Adam and Eve."

Dorothy did not reply to that.

"I don't think a theological debate will help you. Don't seek answers to justify your anger; that would be fruitless."

"So, are you saying Bill was spared from pain?"

"You tell me."

"Maybe you're right. He never got past the grief of losing Andrew. But what about Andrew, what was he spared from? He wasn't sick."

"No, I would say in that case, God did have a hand in that. But you should look at it this way—Andrew's death was almost certainly in the course of saving many lives. And I am sure that his sacrifice has been rewarded with a rightful place in Heaven."

"Why doesn't he take me then? I have nothing left to live for."

"I think God knows the answer to that better than you and I. Again, I'll tell you about what happened to me. The death of my mother made me question my faith and for years I too wanted to know why. To make a long story short, it led me on a spiritual journey where the destination was the Church. And here I am, helping people in His name, people like you." He paused.

She waited, sensing he was not finished.

"So, to answer your question, I believe that God has a special plan for you. That's why."

She thanked him, made the sign of the cross, and exited.

Despite the fact that Dorothy had no idea what God's plan was, her little talk with Father Wolanska helped her to at least make some attempt at improving her quality of life. She began to seek out her friends who, in the beginning, had been willing to comfort her right after Bill's death but whom she eventually drove away with her bouts of melancholy. When she apologized to them for being so cold, they told her that there was no need to do that and that they understood. They affirmed that they were there for her anytime, for any reason, to give the support she needed.

At first she didn't want to overdo it—friendly phone calls, intermittent casual visits. There was still a bit of awkwardness in their company.

But her efforts were not enough. She would have these lapses, where she would remain motionless in one place catatonically. One day she was standing, staring out the front window, looking at nothing in particular, when an overwhelming terror swept over her. Her heart starting galloping, pounding out of her chest. She became dizzy and fell against the window pane. She knew she was having a heart attack. She propped herself, turned and walked only two steps before she slumped to the floor. She desperately crawled to the end table with the telephone. She was thinking, is this God's plan? Isn't it what I wanted?

But she was scared. So scared that she reached for the phone and dialed 911. "Help me, I'm dying…147 Grace Drive, Northwoods…" After that, she passed out, and the next thing she knew she was in an ambulance, with a handsome paramedic looking down at her.

"Don't worry Ma'am, you're alright now."

They carried her stretcher out of the vehicle, slid her onto a gurney, which they wheeled briskly into the Emergency Room, with all those neon tube lights streaming by her, then transferred her to a draped cubicle and hooked her up to all these machines. They closed the curtain.

She lay there, frightened, confused, for a full fifteen minutes.

A young girl, dark, with long dark hair, and a clipboard in one hand and a pen in her other, opened the curtain..

"Ma'am? Can we have your name please?"

She gave it out, even spelling her surname, very slowly.

"And do you have insurance Ma'am?"

"Yes. Happy Life."

"Your customer number?"

"I don't remember…"

A middle-aged, sandy-haired doctor with a cheerful face walked by on his way to somewhere else, when he briskly changed course and strode to the gurney she was lying in. The young girl promptly left.

"So, how ya feeling?"

"Better."

"Yeah, you're all right now. Came in, pulse a bit high, blood pressure a bit low, but now, normal. No problem with your heart. You probably had some allergic reaction, maybe something you ate, or…just a panic attack."

"A what?"

He ignored her question. "Tell me, did you eat anything strange or new just before this happened?"

"No."

"Been under any stress lately?"

"Well, I just recently lost my husband."

"I see. Any children?"

"I had a son, but he died in the Vietnam War."

"All alone then?"

"Yes."

"Uh, uh."

"Doctor, just what happened to me?"

"Well, I think you just had a panic attack. Nothing to worry about, not life-threatening."

"But I wasn't panicking. Just looking out the window."

"Yeah, that's how they happen. Just comes from the back of your mind. I'll prescribe something for you. If you feel that such an attack is coming on again, just take one pill, and you'll feel better. You can pick up the prescription at the admin counter, then you can go home."

He made to leave, but before he exited he made a half turn. "You might want to try joining a gym or something; exercise will help to relieve some of your anxiety." He was about to leave once more when he did a double take and looked at her again. "And maybe think about getting a pet."

"A pet?"

"Yeah," he grinned, "to keep you company."

The next day, Dorothy set out to follow the advice the doctor gave her: first joining the Jack La Lane Fitness Center over on Rosedale, then going to the animal shelter on Harley Street. At first she was thinking about a dog, but then, after weighing the pros and cons, decided that a dog would be too much responsibility. Not only the physical chores: taking it out, bathing it, getting shots from the vet...but dogs also demanded a lot of love and attention, and her heart was not ready for that yet. And so, a cat it was.

She took him home, not really a kitten, but a young, gray, feline ball of fur. In the living room, she released him from his little cage and held him as she went to sit on Bill's armchair (it would always be Bill's armchair, regardless), with the cat on her lap.

She looked down at him. "So what do we call you then? I know, Felix!" She then began to sing the cartoon song, "Felix the Cat, the wonderful wonderful cat, oh the things he does..." at this point she forgot the words, "...duh-da duh-da, duh duddy-da duh-da-duh!"

He must have agreed on the name. He was purring loudly as she petted him.

The exercise and pet strategies were working quite well. Dorothy had moments of contentment and peace of mind. Sometimes she even found herself humming aloud. She decided to include her garden in this new set of activities. Not really her garden. Bill's garden. He had put more work into it than me, she reflected. So that created an extra motivation. She would make it beautiful for him.

It took a shorter time than she expected before the backyard was blooming again with poinsettias, crocuses, irises, and even Mexican sage. She was so proud she invited Elizabeth and her mother Trudy, and one of Elizabeth's friends, Joan, to come and see. That day witnessed the birth of what would become their Saturday evening bridge parties, when Elizabeth, sitting, drinking coffee in Dorothy's living room, began touting the joys of the game and remembering the fun times she used to have playing it before her divorce. They all agreed it was a great idea, and then ordered a pizza to celebrate. Elizabeth offered to hold the bridge party at her house since it was centrally located for the rest of them, and even volunteered to make cheesecake for those occasions. But Dorothy objected to the last offer, saying they should all take turns baking, and they might get tired of cheesecake every week. Dorothy would bring one of her famous pies whenever it was her turn.

The game really was a lot of fun, especially in the learning stages.

"Joan, you're the dummy," Trudy announced the first night of play.

"Why do I have to be the dummy?"

"Because Trudy won the auction, and you're her partner," Elizabeth explained.

"But then I don't get to play."

"Watch television then."

The set was always on, one of those portable ones with a handle for carrying it, perched upon Elizabeth's kitchen counter.

This social event now completed Dorothy's life, and the pie-making added one more task that helped to keep her mind from wandering onto gloomy paths. However, there were still embarrassing moments when she was with her friends, for it always seemed to her that they felt sorry for her. One of those nights had to do with the news about the death of Cynthia's parents. She had just left the bathroom when she heard them whispering around the kitchen table that served as the venue for their card game. She wondered why they were speaking in such low tones, so she halted, attempting to eavesdrop.

"Isn't that terrible?"

"Yeah, drunk driver, hit them head on."

"So Cynthia's not selling the house?"

"Nope. Not even going to rent it. She wants to keep it for herself."

"But she's never here!"

"Anyway, don't tell Dorothy," she heard Elizabeth say, "She has enough emotional baggage as it is, what with all she's been through."

When the conversation finished, Dorothy joined them with feigned buoyancy. "I'm getting peckish. How about that cheesecake?"

But soon after arriving home, she had her second panic attack, and hurried to get the Xanax the doctor prescribed her, and to her relief it worked as he promised. Once she was relaxed, she was strong enough to go and retrieve the large envelope that held Andrew's personal effects. It was something she should have done long ago. For inside, were two letters from Cynthia as well as a gold ring that Cynthia gave Andrew when they were still teenage lovers. Dorothy had lost contact with her ever since she had gone to school in California. Upon surreptitiously hearing the news that Cynthia would keep the house in Camden, she finally had a destination to send those things to.

While inspecting the items she suddenly became puzzled. Odd, she had never dwelled on it before. There were only two letters from Cynthia, compared to the scores that she and Bill had written. She took the letters out of their envelopes, but only to read the dates at the top, averting her eyes from the rest, as reading them would be dangerous for her emotional stability. The last letter was dated in Cynthia's handwriting as September 3, 1968. That would be about the end of Andrew's first tour. She didn't remember their breakup to be as far back as that. She quickly returned the contents and stuck to her original objective, preparing a parcel to send through the post.

Then came the hysteria over the serial killer. Two young women were found dead, strangled, apparently having been raped. A dangerous psychopath was on the loose. It was hard to believe such a thing would happen in a small town like Camden, where its generally provincial atmosphere made it even more vulnerable to fear. Dorothy and her companions even considered canceling their bridge games.

"Nonsense," Trudy said, "he's after young girls, he wouldn't be interested in old bags like us."

"Speak for yourself," Elizabeth retorted. "Now stop gossiping and play. Dorothy you lead the trick, you won the last one."

And so their weekly ritual continued.

A couple of weeks later there was a break in the case, and the police were seeking a man for questioning. But then, an even stranger incident arose.

They were sitting at their usual places at Elizabeth's kitchen table.

"That's it!" Joan declared. "One hundred and four points, we win!"

"And don't forget fifty for the insult," Trudy her partner, reminded her. "It was a doubled contract."

"Oh my God!" Elizabeth suddenly shouted. "It's Father Wolanska, he's on TV! They're arresting him!"

They all turned their chairs toward the television set. What apparently had transpired was that the chief suspect for the murders, knowing he was about to be apprehended, had fled to the Catholic Church on Harmony Road where Father Wolanska was the pastor, pleading for sanctuary, which of course the old priest had granted, on condition the man beseech God to provide him the strength to give himself up. The police then came to the church on a tip they got, but the man escaped through the back door of the rectory. Father Wolanska was to be charged with aiding and abetting.

The women watched him being led away, handcuffed, by two plainclothes officers, during the live coverage of this breaking story.

So much for God's plan, Dorothy thought cynically.

"That's disgusting," Trudy said with a contemptuous tone. "He's a priest for God's sake. He was doing his duty, a priest's duty. He's not a criminal."

"Well, you have to draw the line somewhere," Joan countered.

This precipitated a debate over the morality of Father Wolanska's actions, and while it was going on, Dorothy sat quietly, her eyes still glued to the screen. Father Wolanska and his escorts stopped, so that he could give out a statement to the multitude of reporters waving microphones in his face. But he wasn't looking at them. Instead, he stared straight into the cameras to address the TV audience. Dorothy shuddered, for it seemed he was focusing his gaze on her.

"We should all remember that ultimately, Judgment, Punishment, and Forgiveness lie under the provenance of Our Lord God."

Then they pulled him away.

That night Dorothy had her third panic attack.

After that, life became comfortably mundane, with no traumatic events to disrupt the harmony of her now well-established routines, and accordingly the panic attacks disappeared. Dorothy kept busy during the day, what with shopping, gardening, cooking and baking, her soap operas during the afternoons and workouts in the evenings. At night, she would watch television and have phone conversations with her friends, long talks that inflated her telephone bill. Besides their Saturday night bridge games, the four women often exchanged visits and went out to dine and see the latest films together. Bill's pension and life insurance provided more than she could use, and all of her needs were well taken care of.

Over the next few years she became whole again; a functioning, even conscientious human being. As the saying goes, 'All wounds heal with time', and this was certainly true of Dorothy. Of course the scars were still there, they were permanent. But at least she had finally found peace in her heart. That is, until that fateful morning when the envelope from Rockland arrived.

Chapter 22

Laos 1980 - 1985

"All sentient beings are dependent on their Karma."
The Buddha, circa 500 BC

The adopted American whom they called Sunnata was now firmly entrenched in his life as a Laotian peasant. He had a home and a family—a wife, a father-in-law, and a baby boy—and there was land to farm as well, for Kampoon prematurely handed over Jampaa's inheritance shortly after becoming a grandfather.

This was only a formality, however, designed to demonstrate Kampoon's unquestionable endorsement of his son-in-law. The couple still remained within her father's compound and things went on pretty much as they had before, all working together to improve the lot of their common household. Except now, Sunnata had a greater voice in things and was granted the status of a fully active citizen of the community, the head of his own sub-household. He was now addressed as Ling's Father, rather than Brother Sunnata. And everyone in Ban Ling Kao agreed that this was how it should be, for he was regarded as a meritorious man who rose above his peers.

Sunnata's son, Ling, spent his babyhood in a relaxed environment, coddled with love and affection, not only from mama, papa, and granddad, but from everyone else in the community, all of them having adopted themselves as honorary relatives, and who made the least excuse to come and visit.

Ling was taught to walk, speak, and control his excretory functions without punishment and was met with practically no restrictions other than those designed to keep him away from harm. He ate when he was hungry, and slept when he felt tired, activities which he did well. At night he would sleep with his parents on the same sleeping mat, which was the norm for young Laotian children. He grew bigger and healthier by the day and showed a precocious aptitude for learning, and on top of that, rarely cried. He became an avid crawler, and to prevent him from falling off the veranda necessitated constant vigilance, and Jampaa joked that it was like trying to get a live crab to stay on a tray. Every step he took when he first aspired to walk was rewarded with lavish praise.

Even at this delicate age, Ling was taught to nop to people in greeting, and to nop whenever he received things, even the milk from Jampaa's breast. Of course they had to take his two little arms and help him to put his hands together, but by the time he was one year old he was able to perform this on his own. They also taught him to *grap*, to kowtow, a posture he would later need in his religious life. His first attempts were so cute, as he would often end up rolling over on his side. The toddler, if he was awake at that time in the evening, would be present with his mama, papa, and granddad when they paid daily homage to the ancestor spirits, which gave him ample opportunities to practice the supplicating gestures in imitation of the adults.

When he began to talk, it was as if the real magic was beginning. Sunnata was struck with the realization that the fruit of the love between him and Jampaa had resulted in the creation of a miniature human being.

Meanwhile, the frangipani tree where Ling's afterbirth was buried, burgeoned with myriad green leaves and blossomed with more flowers than anyone could ever remember.

All in all, people were happy despite the hard life. The little Laotian village of Ban Ling Kao survived through the inhabitants' own reciprocal support for each other. When someone needed a house built, all the able-bodied men would come to lend a hand, the only payment being a good meal and some potent lao-kao. The most severe form of drudgery was transplanting. The seedlings had to be uprooted and packed into bundles, then taken to the paddies, where one had to spend the day with back bent over, planting them with care. As with harvesting, they drew lots to see whose farm everyone would work on first. This activity required laboring under a hot sun for ten hours a day, seven days a week, for about six weeks. But it was a small price to pay for having food for the rest of the year.

In addition to farming, the villagers were fairly self-sufficient in almost all their daily needs. Wives and daughters wove clothes, and many of the men were amateur blacksmiths, forging their own tools and implements using homemade bellows in their compounds. For the really big jobs, they would go to see Kang, the master blacksmith of Ban Ling Kao, a dark-skinned, rough-hewn man with long stringy hair and drooping eyes. And if there was anything else lacking in the village, there were always the markets at Ta Vieng and Muang Koon.

Despite life's rigors, the vitality of the peasants, and the interactions between them, preserved an atmosphere of orderly contentment. However, there were times when this calmness was disrupted, usually precipitated by the excessive drunkenness that occurred among them. It was the only form of recreation the men had, and on frequent occasions it resulted in ugly scenes. Sunnata once found Uncle Kem's son lying in the road, thoroughly inebriated and having been beaten up by his fellow drinking mates. The story was that he had been parading around shouting obscene insults at them in his crazed drunken stupor, and they had retaliated in an equally senseless manner. Sunnata had flung him over his shoulder to bring him home and tend to his bruises.

Sunnata himself was happy enough cultivating rice to feed his family, living without newspapers, nurturing little ambition beyond achieving the satisfaction of a peaceable life; a life geared to the seasons, punctuated by feast days, religious festivals, and harvest celebrations. Over the course of his farming labors, his new way of life molded him to fit in its pattern. As time passed, everything that had gone before faded into a hazy dream; his former experiences became obscure, and the present was real and true. Old memories were safely shut out by this new, gratifying mode of existence.

He loved watching his son growing up, talking with him and teaching him new things. At two years old the boy was advanced in his language skills, perhaps because of the constant attention he got from many adults. He was a beautiful boy with bright brown eyes, shiny black hair, and creamy beige skin. His button nose and sweet little lips made him all the more endearing. Sunnata's favorite play activity was to pretend he was a wild animal, ready to gobble him up and then bury his face in Ling's little midsection, snarling and nibbling, the little boy's trills of laughter sweeping over him in exhilarating ripples. The toddler was physically active as well, running here and there, climbing up things, and generally exploring his environment. It amused his mother Jampaa that the boy sometimes literally lived up to his name, Monkey.

Jampaa was also something special. Like a thousand-armed angel, she could put everything in its proper order, organizing her household and ensuring that all her family's needs were met. She not only provided a warm home life, but also gave Sunnata the status he needed to live in village society. Through her advice and edifying support, she had made it possible for him to strike roots in this land, roots that were nourished by their unified labor.

He rediscovered the love he could have for a woman. Each and every sound she made endeared her to him: the bok-bok sounds she made as she pounded condiments with her mortar and pestle, the rocking and creaking of her loom, and the singing she often did in accompaniment to her tasks.

At times he would cover his face in his hands, afraid to believe that happiness had come to him at last.

And just when he thought he couldn't possibly be any happier, Jampaa became pregnant again. Nine months later, they had a little girl. After consulting the monks, they named her Yee-Sai, with the play name of Nok, which meant Bird. Now mom and dad shared their sleeping mat with two children, with Ling in the middle between them, and the infant Nok at Jampaa's side, close to her breast. The coziness of his family was an indescribable joy.

All this made him forget what he had previously been taught concerning the transient, impermanent nature of the world.

The first reminder was the illness of Jampaa's father. The old man was always thirsty, and even though he ate like a horse, he was losing weight and always griping that he was hungry. He needed to relieve himself several times an hour and complained of tingling in his feet. Sunnata initially thought that perhaps Kampoon had worms, so he gave him a special tea to drink in the evenings. It didn't help. Eventually the old man became bedridden, too weak to do the simplest chores. Sunnata was obliged to remain at home, mainly because Kampoon needed to be helped to the toilet, and preferred Sunnata to his daughter in carrying out this task. The old man was urinating blood, and afterwards Sunnata noticed that swarms of ants would congregate wherever Kampoon had pissed. He soon figured out that there was sugar in the bloody urine—it was kidney failure brought on by diabetes. One evening, it was becoming clear that he was about to go. They sat on the floor around his sleeping mat, along with friends and relatives, the low flame of the kapok wick emitting a dying glow. He spoke to Sunnata.

His voice was low, hoarse, and halting. "Forgive me... my son."

"For what, Father?"

"I did not...treat you well...especially...in the beginning."

"I cannot forgive you. I cannot forgive someone who has been a loving responsible father to his daughter. I cannot forgive when there is nothing to forgive."

"You are...a good man. I have...been...lucky...my daughter... she always knew...she is so wise..."

Sunnata took the hand of his young son and bundled up his baby daughter to show the both of them to Kampoon. "They will remember you, and carry our family on even after our own deaths."

"I have...been lucky," Kampoon repeated. "To die like this...is to...die rich."

After that he talked no more. He shortly fell into a coma, and then expired.

Jampaa didn't shed any tears, for that was considered to bring bad luck, and the crying of relatives could make it difficult for the deceased to depart this existence.

The body was placed in a coffin and kept in the house for seven days, as was the custom. In front of the coffin was a small table with a brass bowl full of incense sticks and candles, and during mealtimes, some food and drink was placed on the little table. Each person who came to pay his or her last respects would knock on one end of the coffin.

Jampaa ensured that her father was accorded the full treatment for a Buddhist funeral. Each morning nine monks would come and be given breakfast, then they would chant holding a sai sin, the sacred string, tied to a Buddha image, which passed through their hands and was attached to the coffin.

"Alas, transient are all compounded things, having arisen they cease, being born they die. The cessation of all compounding is true happiness."

In the evenings four monks would come to chant the Abidhamma, faces hidden by ceremonial fans.

Jampaa assisted Sunnata in preparing the body for cremation. The corpse was bathed in cold water, then hot water, and anointed with fragrant oils. Before being taken to the temple, the body was bound—a loop around the neck to signify breaking the tie to children, binding the feet to break the tie to wealth, and tying the hands as well to break the tie to one's spouse. The coffin was passed out the window so that Kampoon's spirit wouldn't realize he was being taken away, and loaded onto a buffalo cart. The procession to the temple began, with the monks in front holding the sacred string attached to the coffin, followed by Sunnata and Jampaa, also holding onto the sai sin. A group of young men pulled and pushed the cart, and people were gathered as they made their way to the temple. Everyone in the village attended the cremation.

Afterwards, Kampoon's ashes were collected in an urn and joined the others on the ancestor altar in their house.

Not long after, there was some good news. Mobile Work Force 333 across the valley was to be shut down, and the detainees, most of them having been there for the past seven years, were to be freed to return to their homes. This was happening in many parts of the country, for the camps were expensive to maintain and the need for them was questionable. The government was 'downsizing' the re-education process.

Potisat was to return to Lat Buak, and Mat was going back to Luang Prabang, while Oun would go to his home in Champassak in the south. Wattana, however, had found a sweetheart in the village and would follow in Sunnata's footsteps and remain in Ban Ling Kao. Sunnata himself was now given permission to travel outside the village if he needed to, although he couldn't go out of the Province. He was informed of this new development by Sousat, now a Captain and a member of the Party.

He came to pay his condolences to them regarding the death of Kampoon, and also to see Sunnata's new family. He apologized for not being able to attend the wedding and not visiting sooner. He praised the children as beautiful and strong. He was happy for Sunnata, and he was also happy that next month he was going to be posted to Ta Vieng, which was nearby, and not only that, he was getting married as well. He then went on to describe the deteriorating security in the region. Bandits, who were calling themselves Chao Fa, were operating in the mountains all around the Plain of Jars. There were several fatal encounters already, where travelers had been ambushed and killed. He advised caution to anyone who was considering a journey out of the area and told Sunnata to spread the word.

Kampoon wasn't the only person who died that year. Death was an unwanted, yet perennial resident of Ban Ling Kao. It wasn't just the aged, however. Infant mortality was high, and it wasn't uncommon that babies would die within days of being born. Nor was it uncommon for young children to succumb to malaria and other fatal illnesses. Every year there were more casualties resulting from the little grenades of the cluster bomb units dropped over a decade ago. Just a month after Kampoon's cremation, an eight-year-old girl was killed by a half-buried bomblet on her way back from collecting firewood. In clearing the land for the new school, despite the ritual placation of spirits by Sunnata and the blessings performed by a chapter of monks, one worker was seriously injured by an explosion and had to be taken to the hospital at Ponsavan.

When Potisat came to say goodbye to Sunnata, he consequently left to him his position as medicine man and ritualist. In this capacity, Sunnata became very busy, and he was confronted with sickness and suffering at least several times a month, and with death several times a year. He would come home after attending to his patients, sometimes late at night, and rub his cheek against the cheeks of his sleeping children, and hug his wife. On these occasions he was often beleaguered with anxiety and found himself praying to Kampoon and the other ancestors to protect his family. There were all sorts of dangers out there.

Being the village witch doctor did have its moments of satisfaction, however, for the knowledge of medicinal herbs he had acquired, combined with his own skills in first aid, led to the recovery of many of his patients. But there were still several ailments that he felt powerless to deal with. One was hemorrhagic dengue fever.

Many of the victims were kids. They would be lying there, shivering, blood trickling from their noses and mouths, bloody rashes over their bodies, and groaning from intense body aches. Their parents sat around them with helpless expressions on their faces trying to comfort them. To the villagers, it was a clear case of Pii Bawb.

At first he didn't know what to do, for he had never seen such a horrible thing. He chanted, he recited magical formulas, he bathed them in the holy water. Then he started to use his head.

The illness seemed to be concentrated at the edge of the village closest to the paddy fields, which held standing water, so it was probably carried by mosquitoes. In some homes there would be several family members who were struck within days of each other, implying that the mosquitoes could carry the disease from one person to another. The blood coming out of the extremities of those afflicted, and in their urine and feces, only reinforced the idea that their insides were being eaten out. Some of the severe cases lost blood pressure and went into shock, leading to convulsions, the sight of which startled those who witnessed it, and confirming to them that it was a demonic possession. Sunnata believed that he had finally unmasked the true identity of the Pii Bawb.

The only advice he could initially give was that those with the fever should drink plenty of fluids, a whole water-jar a day if possible, with salt in it, and not to administer aspirin, for he knew that would make the bleeding worse. Only the strong would survive with this minimal treatment, but many, the very young and the very old, weren't strong enough. They needed plasma drips.

Sunnata sent someone to Ta Vieng with a message to Sousat, who had now taken up his new post there, informing him that he needed a vehicle to take the sick to Ponsavan. A pickup truck arrived the next day and took those in the most serious condition, and this was consistent with the people's belief that those who couldn't be cured of the Pii Bawb should leave the village.

Meanwhile, the village administrative committee held an emergency meeting for all adults at Sunnata's request…he informed the gathering on what to do to rid the village of the Pii Bawb for good. He explained that this particular evil spirit hid itself in mosquitoes. He distributed an ointment to those present, and told them about the plant that it was derived from and how to prepare more of the paste when they ran out of it. They were to spread this on their skin and the skin of their children, so that the mosquitoes wouldn't bite. He then ordered all vegetation at the edge of the paddy land to be cleared. Finally, he instructed them to burn coconut husks under all the trees and bushes in their compounds, and especially inside the house, to repel mosquitoes.

Within one week, the Pii Bawb left the village completely. Those sent to Ponsavan came back cured. It was clear to all that Sunnata was a great and powerful *maw pii* who had rid them of a horrible affliction. And Sunnata, as an ex-monk, felt a certain self-respect, for his advocacy had accomplished this without directly killing one mosquito.

One day, Sunnata traipsed along the paddy dikes with his young son, filled with a simple happiness that he often felt on such leisurely walks. It was a glorious morning, fresh, and full of life. The ponds in the basins were like mirrors reflecting the clouds in the sky, and the green blades of the rice plants emerging through the water were gilded with early morning dew, glimmering like silver tinsel. Above them, a pair of herons streamed by, soaring with dignified grace.

"Paw, Paw wait. Wait me."

"Er." Sunnata stopped to let his son, now four years old, catch up to him. "Do you want me to carry you?"

"No, Paw. I walk fast. Faster than Nok. She walks slow."

"Yes, but she is still little."

"Am I big, Paw?"

His Paw, his Daddy, laughed. "Well, you are bigger than Nok."

"But not big like you, Paw."

"Don't worry. You will be soon enough."

"And I will be big man, yes, Paw? Like you?"

Sunnata crouched down to face his son. He looked into his doe-like inquisitive eyes, then tousled his hair and kissed him on his little forehead. "No son, not like me...you're going to be a better man than me." He stood up and took his boy's tiny hand as they continued walking.

Sunnata, together with his neighbors, had recently constructed a well, powered by a makeshift windmill. They used bamboo as pipes for distributing the water. The new system would enable them to grow rice during the dry season. Yesterday, Uncle Som had complained that no water was getting through. Sunnata was thinking that maybe the wind hadn't been strong enough to achieve the pressure required to bring it to the fields. Or perhaps there was an obstruction.

They had reached the end of the paddy land and were now in the meadows in front of the mountain forest. Sunnata slowly traced the pipeline, looking for anything that seemed abnormal. His son let go of his hand and ran up ahead, trying to catch a large black butterfly.

"Ling, stay with Paw. Come back here."

The youngster, realizing the butterfly was beyond his grasp, turned around obediently, and walked toward his father.

As Sunnata looked in the direction of his son, he saw something that caught his attention. It was a pool of water where there had been none before. He headed for it, meeting his son along the way. They strolled together to the spot. The pipes were disconnected, probably trodden on by one of the water buffaloes, as there were a few hoof marks around. The water was gushing out, eroding the soil around it.

Sunnata bent over to examine the damaged section. It was less than a minute, maybe twenty seconds or so, when he heard his son cry out "Luk bawn! A ball!"

It was the prettiest thing Ling had ever seen. A round thing, bright yellow.

Sunnata turned around to see his son, about fifty feet away, stooping to pick something up.

Sunnata jumped up. "NO, LING NO!"

An awful blast. The boy never heard his warning.

Sunnata, instinctively running to protect his child, didn't feel the shrapnel grazing his head, penetrating his shoulder, piercing his leg. He stumbled from these blows as well as the shock of the detonation, which made him fall, and then he crawled frantically on his hands and knees. In front of him was a bloody mass of flesh that just seconds ago had been his son.

Jampaa had been carrying firewood, several hundred yards

away, when her ears caught the dull thud of the explosion. She dropped her load and ran panicked to where she saw a cloud of dust. Her fears were confirmed when she heard the horrifying wail of her husband.

In those days, a child under seven years of age wasn't cremated, but buried with special rites somewhere outside the village. To prevent the corpse's spirit from proving troublesome to society at large, such as causing nightmares in the community, Sunnata had to perform a special ritual to coax his child's spirit into an earthenware vessel. What made this act unbearably difficult was that he had to hide any inkling of sorrow. The fact that he could do this at all was due to the bravery of his wife Jampaa, who witnessed the ceremony with a grave countenance, yet one that was devoid of tears. This was in stark contrast to what had transpired on the night of Ling's death, when they had gone to the paddy fields out of earshot of the village to wail and moan together, to release the pain that gripped them. But grief still ravaged them, consuming every corner of their souls, and it required a colossal effort to conceal this.

Sunnata invoked Ling's spirit with calm affection, talking to him in a sweet voice as though he were there in front of him, after which, he tightly closed the vessel, chanted powerful spells, and attached the appropriate magical drawings. Uncle Som offered his oxcart to take the couple and fellow mourners to the Nam Ngum River to place the vessel in its flowing waters, while Auntie Bua would take care of Nok, their baby girl.

It was, of course, a solemn and painful journey. Except for the periodic jolting of the cart and the jangle of the bamboo pipes hanging around the necks of the oxen, there was only a morbid silence.

It seemed like ages before they reached the river. Solemnly, the couple jointly waded into the water and placed the vessel to float on the current, which would carry their boy's soul to the Mekong, and then, hopefully, out to sea.

That night, returning from the Nam Ngum River, was almost as bad as the day that Sunnata had carried the bloody body of their son back to the house. Jampaa cried all night, and Sunnata, naturally, cried along with her as he held her tightly. It was only through sheer mental and emotional exhaustion that the crying died down to a whimpering and they both fell asleep.

Meanwhile, Auntie Bua, in her sixty-odd years in life, had seen her share of suffering and sorrow in this world, including the tragic loss of her own as well as other people's children. She knew that any time now, Jampaa, as a mother, through a gap in her cloud cover of bereavement, would realize that she had another child who wasn't with her, and would, in a desperate frenzy, come to fetch her. Sure enough, Jampaa appeared at her door later that night. "Sabai dee, Auntie Bua. I've come for my baby."

Little Nok was still awake, on the floor, her mouth smeared with *khao bat*, a sweet, sticky rice treat. Her hands were full of the gooey desert as well. Jampaa bundled her up in her arms and cried, "My baby, my baby."

Sunnata stood in the doorway. "Thank you, Auntie Bua."

"Bo ben yang. If there's anything else I can do, I am here for you. You are all my children now."

The couple gave her a nop, with little Nok cuddled on Jampaa's shoulder.

The sense of loss at the death of one's child can be more tormenting than the most severe physical pain. With physical pain, the mind is so distracted by the negative stimuli, that it cannot produce thoughts. With emotional pain, this is not so. The mind is able to dwell on it, irritating the wound until it becomes a festering sore. And while Sunnata, during his tenure as a monk, had learned how to nullify bodily distress, the agony that was crushing him now was a new sensation he didn't know how to cope with.

It was to be expected that both of them would be more sullen during this period of mourning, but Sunnata was weaker in controlling the anger and bitterness that accompanied his grief. He became overprotective with his daughter, to the point that he didn't want her out of the compound. If she started scratching at the dirt in her innocent play, he would scoop her up and bring her into the house, and the child, not comprehending the intimidating urgency of his actions, would start bawling. After that, he and Jampaa would have an argument, he accusing her of not watching the child properly, and on one occasion, she, in the heat of their quarrel, reminded him that she wasn't the one who was with Ling when he was killed. Of course she regretted what she said as soon as the words had left her mouth and she fell to her knees, weeping, pleading forgiveness. Siezed with overwhelming guilt, he got down on his knees along with her, telling her that it was he who should be asking forgiveness.

Soon after that, only a few weeks after setting the boy's spirit free on the river, Sunnata noticed that the leaves of the frangipani tree where Ling's afterbirth had been buried were yellowing and there were no flowers. It now only served as a tormenting reminder to Sunnata of his immeasurable loss. He resolved to chop it down. He went into the space beneath the house, retrieved his axe, and commenced sharpening it with his grinding stone. Then he stalked over to the tree and attacked it with all the rancor contained inside him. Swing, chop, bang, swing chop, bang. He found swear words in English welling up from the recesses of his mind and coming out of his mouth. "Fucking bombs, fucking bombs, fucking war..." swing chop bang.

Jampaa ran out onto the porch. "Stop! Stop!"

He ceased his assault on the tree to look up at her.

Her face grimaced in anguish as she cried out once more, "Stop it!" Then she ran back into the house wailing.

He stood there, panting from his exertion and recovering his senses. He looked at the axe in his hands and felt like an idiot. Throwing it down on the ground, he climbed up the ladder and entered the house, where he found his wife sobbing on the floor. He held her, apologizing over and over again.

For a while, it seemed that they were always doing that—apologizing to each other.

All of the other citizens of Ban Ling Kao, while busy with their own struggles of life, couldn't help but share in the grief of Sunnata and Jampaa. The little boy Ling had represented their own hopes and aspirations for the future. His death could only be an inauspicious sign of what was ahead. It worried them. What did this mean? Certainly, Sunnata, as the village spirit master, wasn't failing in his duties to attend and appease the spirits. The tragedy must have been brought about by Karma from a past life of misdeeds, they concluded; it was the only theory that could explain it. It wouldn't be the first time that a great holy man with supernatural powers was brought down in such a way. Was that not the case of Mogallana as well? The greatest of Buddha's disciples, who could fly through the air and perform other wonders, was eventually beaten to death by ordinary bandits because of his sins in a previous life.

But what about Jampaa? She was being punished as well. And the boy? Why should he suffer from the Karma of his parents? Only karmic sharing could account for his death. They must have all done evil together in their former existences.

All these uncertainties made it difficult for them to console the bereaved couple without revealing their own concerns. And it became increasingly difficult to ask Sunnata to come and help when they had a problem, or required a ritual to be performed.

Sunnata abetted this sentiment by his aloofness toward anyone else and their problems. His behavior made it plain that he wasn't interested. Rather, he became preoccupied with his own current activities, some of which appeared bizarre and arcane. He would rarely venture out of his compound and seemed to be busy all day, with the sounds of banging coming from his backyard. Even his wife didn't understand what he was up to. The only person he seemed keen to talk to was Kang, the blacksmith. He went to visit him at least once, sometimes twice a day. Naturally, the other villagers would come over to Kang's shop, a nondescript hut, to interrogate the old man.

"He is building something," Kang would tell them.

"What is he building?"

"I don't know yet, he hasn't told me. But I think it will be a great machine."

"What will it do?"

Kang looked up with his sullen, sagging eyes, his long stringy hair fixed as if waxed. "I don't know. He hasn't told me."

Sunnata couldn't stop himself from thinking about the death of his son and of the other children and adults who had been victims of the bombies, and, consequently, couldn't stop himself from thinking how to devise a way to avert such tragedies. It grew into a tenacious obsession, and pondering about it, to the degree that he did, estranged himself from his wife, as well as his baby daughter. He became absorbed by the plan that was developing bit by bit in his mind to the point where nothing else mattered. It may have been mere sublimation, a way to divert his grief, but to him it was a plan; more than a plan, it was a vision. It was the blueprint for a flailer.

A flailer is a device that clears mined areas by setting off all the hidden explosives, usually by disturbing the ground in some way. This contrivance was progressively taking shape in Sunnata's head, and he found himself designing a new feature each day. He would go to Uncle Kang, draw it on the ground, and explain to the blacksmith the dimensions desired. Back at home, he would fiddle with the pieces Kang had fabricated, fitting them together. His wife didn't favor this new hobby. It frightened her.

It was true that Sunnata grew indifferent over other matters that should have been considered of more immediate importance to the family. The paddy dikes needed repairing, and he was supposed to be organizing help to re-thatch the roof before the rains. At mealtimes, the only thing he talked about was making his new invention. Jampaa wasn't angry over this, for she intuited that this was all part of his Karma of being a great man, but it made her lonely. She was finding it hard, for what she needed now was a partner, and to be healed with the comfort that only he was capable of providing.

Not long after, there was another visit by Sousat, this time to offer his condolences, having heard about the tragedy. The reason he hadn't come sooner, he apologetically explained, was because he had been away on a military operation against the Chao Fa in the neighboring Special Region Saisaboun. The couple invited him to stay for lunch. During the meal he lamented the fact that there were still many bombie's lying about since the war, and how scores of children, as well as adults, had already been killed. This provided Sunnata with an opening gambit. He described his new idea to the young army officer and asked if it was possible for him to acquire a truck to test it out. Sousat, sympathetic to Sunnata's loss, didn't have the heart to refuse him, yet didn't promise him either. "I'll see what I can do," he told him.

The connections he designed were on the outside, the male pipes having hooks, the females having loops; one twist and they're connected, so it could easily be taken apart and reassembled, making it portable.

"Tomorrow is Boon Pavet," she was saying.

He stirred briefly from his reverie. "Huh?"

"I said tomorrow is Boon Pavet. We have to go to the temple early in the morning."

"Yes, Nok's Mother, we will go."

But his thoughts pulled him away again.

The best thing was that the frame was made with a titanium alloy that had been salvaged from a downed jet from the war, and which he had sent Kang to buy at the market in Muang Koon.

"Did you hear me?"

"Yes. What?"

"Nothing."

"No, you asked me something. I didn't hear it."

"It was nothing."

The meal over, she began to remove the bowls and the baskets of sticky rice.

It was often like this. He was always somewhere else.

More and more of his time was devoted to his flailer. A few additional weeks went by before he finally had it fully assembled. The whole village was abuzz with talk of Sunnata's new machine to clear the bombies, and people came by to gape at it. To a Western eye it looked like a giant hand-pushed lawn mower. To a Laotian eye, it was totally incomprehensible.

It had two series of metal wheels, one axle on the ground, the other up in the air, and each wheel below was connected to a corresponding one above by a vertical bar, like a crankshaft, resembling the wheels of an old-fashioned locomotive. Long chains hung from the top wheels. It was very long, or, more correctly speaking, it was wide, since it rolled perpendicular to its length, like a wide plow, he explained, except it was pushed, not pulled. There was a bar in front that held a suspended blade, so that it could knock down small trees and uproot bushes. In the back was a shield that ran along its width, to deflect the shrapnel and protect whoever was behind it. There was also a long shank that served as a hitch to the vehicle that would drive it.

In the end Sousat did manage to provide a truck, a Russian troop carrier. He brought it over personally, as he was curious to see how this thing would work. He chuckled in admiration when he saw it.

"You are very clever, Nok's father."

"It is portable as well," Sunnata elucidated. "Takes about a half hour to put it together, and the same for breaking it down. And lightweight too."

To demonstrate, he took the thing apart with the help of a local youth whom he had been training, showing Sousat the various pieces and how they connected. The components were loaded onto the bed of the truck, which scores of village men had already boarded in order to see the show, and Sunnata directed the driver to the western boundary of the paddy fields. After the unit was assembled and connected to the tow hitch on the back of the truck, the driver put the gears in reverse, and, guided by Sunnata, drove backwards pushing the flailer over a fallow field. The chains on the top set of wheels whipped around to pound the ground, as the men in the back of the truck laughed with excitement. The blade at the front of the thing mowed down the bushes and small trees. Sousat was impressed by the flexibility of the device, conforming as it did to the irregularities of the terrain.

"The axle segments are connected with ball joints," Sunnata shouted to Sousat over the roar of the diesel engine. "You can adjust the width by varying the number of middle sections when you put it together."

"I see you have given much thought to this," Sousat commended. He then proceeded to light up a cigarette.

There was a loud explosion and everyone in the back dived down in panic. Sousat dropped his as yet unlit cigarette. The startled driver halted the truck.

"It works!" Sunnata yelled, a satisfied grin on his face.

The crowd in the truck recovered from their alarm to cheer heartily.

They rode around like this for an hour, setting off one other bombie before returning to Sunnata's compound.

As the bomb clearer was unhitched, Sousat climbed back into the cab of the truck for his return journey to Ta Vieng. "The only problem," he told Sunnata, after lighting another cigarette, "is that you require a truck full-time, and a soldier to drive it. We don't have any to spare. We were lucky to get this one today."

"Well, I'll leave that up to you to sort out. Now that you see what it can do, maybe you could convince someone of the need."

"Er," was Sousat's response, although his tone didn't sound hopeful.

The trial run that day had been the climax for Sunnata's hobby, for the flailer after that just sat idle inside his compound. He eventually returned to the ordinary routine of his life, and with that, sank back into a lugubrious depression. Now that he had nothing to occupy his mind, he was once again a victim of a sadness he couldn't control, and this only made him feel guilty, since he couldn't yet conquer his moroseness so as to give his wife and daughter the full love and devotion they needed.

One night, while lying on their mat, baby Nok asleep between them, Jampaa confronted Sunnata with a serious request. "*Paw Nok, yak hai jao buat pra.* Nok's Father, I want you to get ordained. I want you to become a monk again."

Sunnata was slightly taken aback. When a man is in mourning for a deceased relative, it wasn't uncommon for him to join the Sangha for a short time, usually ten days or so, to make merit for the soul of the departed. However, as far as he had been made to understand, this wasn't normally done in the case of a small child. "It is not customary for a young child. But I will do it, if you wish."

"No, I want you to do it to make merit for me, as well as Ling's soul."

This disturbed him. She was making a rather morbid plea, if he indeed understood correctly what she was getting at. Buddhist mothers, not being able to join the priesthood themselves, depended on their unmarried sons to be ordained, to make merit for them. It was like being a monk by proxy. In Jampaa's case, she would have relied on Ling, if he hadn't been killed.

"Nok's Mother, please don't say that. We will have another son. There is still plenty of time."

"I cannot wait."

"Why?"

She didn't respond to that.

"That means I must remain a monk until the end of Pansa? I won't be able to be with you."

"Even now you are not with us."

She was right about him not being there for them—in spirit anyway. Moreover, he and Jampaa hadn't made love since Ling's death.

"Do not worry," she said with a weak smile, "we will visit you every day at the temple."

Sunnata mulled this over. Joining the monkhood to reflect upon life was a natural choice, one which was frequently practiced. He could no longer consider it as a lifelong commitment to seeking the truth, as he had with the earlier outlook he had adopted at the Forest Temple. At this time, he still felt that such a path was no longer open to him, as he had a family, but still, being a monk would at least offer a period of spiritual healing. Three months was just long enough. Perhaps Jampaa was right. She usually was. It would do him some good, by shaming him out of his self-pity and to stop him longing for the dead, and to give his love to the living.

"I shall do it. For you, and our family."

As it turned out, it wasn't only for him and his family, but also for the whole village. The people couldn't imagine a more wonderful event than to have Sunnata rejoin the order and serve as one of their monks. Some felt it was long overdue, and the village would benefit from all the beneficial Karma that he would generate by being a holy man once again, this time in their very own temple. The significance of little Ling's death was now clear—it was a sign telling Sunnata he had to take this path to the priesthood. The donning of the orange robes could only augment his magical potency and protective powers. Being a priest during Pansa was especially efficacious, since it was a time of much chanting and religious activity among both the clergy and devout laypeople.

These feelings were unequivocally expressed by the fanfare that accompanied the formalities leading up to his ordination. In fact it was quite unusual, since such public displays were normally reserved for those entering the priesthood for the first time in their lives, typically unmarried men joining during Khao Pansa. This holiday atmosphere, which enticed the whole community to join in, was Jampaa's doing. She spent over a week making the *prasat*, a four-foot-high ornamental tower made out of palm leaves and beeswax, embellished with flowers, incense and candles, and took great pains in collecting and preparing the gifts that were to be presented at the temple. There was a small party when Jampa cut his hair and shaved his head.

All this fuss made Sunnata uneasy, because she was arranging his ordination in the same manner as a mother would organize the ordination of her son, rather than her husband. At first this saddened him. It was only later that he realized why she felt it had to be done this way.

Early the next morning there was a great procession, and anyone who could walk, crawl, or be helped along was in it. All of the houses in Ban Ling Kao were emptied as their occupants joined the parade making its way to the temple. Leading them was a host of dancers and musicians, who were banging drums, clanging cymbals, and leaving no doubt as to the greatness of the affair. Sunnata was carried on burly Wattana's shoulders, with various men putting their hands on his back to help support him, while others held a large orange parasol to shade him. Jampaa carried the monk's robes that she had made for him and his new alms bowl. When they reached the monastery grounds, they marched pompously around the temple in a clockwise direction. The crowd was exuberantly clapping their hands to the slow, purposeful rhythm of the music, singing and laughing, some bursting forth with that yodeling cheer of the Laotians, wide smiles on all their faces.

It was then that he finally understood that this occasion was a celebration for the entire village, to purge everyone of their grief and worry and to renew all of their hopes.

The third time around the temple, Sunnata got off of Wattana's shoulders, and prostrated himself in front of the shrine of the guardian spirit of the temple. Just before entering the temple, Sunnata reached into a basket and scattered fake coins to symbolize his rejection of the material world. As he tossed them into the air, everyone scrambled in excited merriment to catch or pick them up off the ground, as these were considered good luck charms.

The solemn ceremony inside the sim lasted less than an hour. When it was over, Pra Sunnata was once again a monk, to once again live in the temple.

Back at home, Jampaa took the holy water that had been blessed during the sacred ceremony and performed the yaat nam, pouring it under the frangipani tree to share the hallowed merit with the soul of her little boy.

Every morning, when it was light enough to see the lines in the palms of their hands, the monks would leave the temple and walk in a single file on their alms round through the village. It was hard for him not to feel a special warm joy when he passed his own house, where Jampaa would be kneeling on a mat outside the bamboo fence, holding a basket of food to offer to the holy men in robes. His daughter would be there too, with her long locks and wide, inquiring eyes, sitting on the mat beside her. As each priest approached her in turn, Jampaa would spoon out a portion of sticky rice and deposit cooked vegetables, pre-packaged in banana leaves, into the begging bowl. There was no direct eye contact, and when the monk received his food he would say a blessing in Pali before passing on. Sunnata himself didn't behave any differently on his turn, although he secretly wished he could tell her how much he loved her. He would always remember her like that, kneeling in pious devotion, head bowed in veneration, making her offering to the disciples of the Buddha.

Pra Sunnata, however, didn't spend all his time pining to be with his family. He took this opportunity to relearn his religious skills and knowledge, such as preaching from the sermons written on palm leaves in the sacred *tham* script. All the things that a monk was expected to know and perform were coming back to him, including his proficiency in meditation. He often led a chapter of monks in the ritual blessings of the paddy fields, and was often invited into people's homes to conduct private chanting sessions. Jampaa was one of those who requested such liturgies. Pra Sunnata couldn't go by himself to his own house, for there were no other males in residence there, and it wasn't allowed for a monk to have private conversations with a woman out of earshot of a third person. Pra Boon, and one or two others would accompany him. And of course Sunnata couldn't hold his two-year-old daughter, for she was a female.

Notwithstanding these restrictions, he did indeed find personal fulfillment in his return to the austere life of the Buddhist priest. In addition, there was also the satisfaction of serving his community. Unlike his time in the isolated Forest Temple years ago, his term as a monk in Ban Ling Kao made him aware of the role the temple played in the lives of his fellow peasants. But more importantly, this was also a time of healing for him. Again, he was confronted with the problems and personal tragedies of the people who came to him for consolation and advice. Suffering always seemed to be around; it rarely took time off. Through witnessing the anguish of others, he began to accept the fact that his son's death was the result of the mysterious workings of the Law of Karma, and his bitterness consequently diminished.

Still, he couldn't wait for the end of Lent, when he could return to his wife and daughter and start all over again.

In the years ahead, during his weaker moments, he would remember the last conversation he would ever have with his wife.

It was two days before Awk Pansa, the end of Lent, after which he could leave the order and go back home. They were sitting at the *sala*, the gazebo, outside in front of the monks' huts, with one of the younger monks standing close by. She sat on the ground, out of respect for Pra Sunnata's monkly status. As always, she came with the baby.

"How are you, *Luang Pi*, Reverend Brother?"

"I am fine, Nok's Mother."

Two-year-old Nok got up to toddle off somewhere.

"Nok, Nok!" Jampaa ordered. "*Ma ni!* Come here!"

"Let her go," Pra Sunnata said. "The temple boys will play with her."

And indeed, a ten-year-old dekvat came out of nowhere to intercept her and began amusing her with innocuous diversions. It wasn't a matter of childish antics. They had to be careful where she wandered, for there were monks around.

"She is very naughty," Jampaa told him. "She always gets her way."

"Just like her mother."

Jampaa laughed, self-consciously covering her mouth with the back of her hand.

Sunnata didn't break his deadpan expression, for it wasn't appropriate for a monk to laugh.

Jampaa, now composed, informed him, "Tomorrow I will go to Ta Vieng to buy kerosene for our lamps, and also salt."

"Can you not send someone? Your needs must be little, since it is a small household now."

"That is true Luang Pi, but the fact is I am going for others as well. Auntie Bua's legs have been paining her and many others are preparing for Awk Pansa, so I volunteered to go."

"Can't they send someone else?"

"Yes, there are others. I am not going alone. We are trading for the whole village. About four of us, I think."

"You will leave the baby with Auntie Bua?"

"No, Auntie Bua can't walk very well, and you know children at Nok's age. You have to run around after them at times. I'll take her with me."

"The roads are not safe these days."

"I understand, Reverend Brother, but it has been quiet recently. The bandits always prefer the rainy season, and now that it is over, I don't think it is a risk."

"How will you go?"

"There is a *rot kaban* coming from Ban Na Nat."

A rot kaban was a pickup truck.

A lull in their dialogue followed. Sunnata was looking at his daughter who was rolling a ball back and forth with the temple boy.

"In two days you will be my husband again," she said.

Sunnata was silent. He didn't want to show his joy, for that would have been unseemly, wearing as he was, the orange robes.

"I am proud of you, Pra Sunnata."

"And I am proud of you, Nok's Mother."

The evening of the next day, Pra Sunnata thought that his wife would have found some excuse to come to the temple, in order to inform him of her arrival back from Ta Vieng. But she didn't come. He tried to sleep, although her failure to show up was bothering him, leaving him anxious. He had to revert to his sleeping meditation.

He, along with the other monks, went on their alms round the next morning. As they drew near his house, he noticed with trepidation that Jampaa wasn't outside ready to make the offering. This could only mean that she wasn't there, for no matter how late she had come back, she wouldn't have failed to wake to make merit. It was difficult for him to hide his distress as they continued on their way to receive the donation of others kneeling up ahead. He felt a sudden sense of dread forming in his stomach, and on the verge of being sick, he had to discipline himself to drive out the apprehension. And he had a tough time back at the temple trying to eat his food at the communal breakfast with the rest of the monks.

It was midmorning when Pra Sunnata heard the sound of a vehicle, and then a second later, a woman's scream tore through the air. He briskly stepped down the ladder of his kuti to find himself face to face with Captain Sousat.

"I am sorry, Reverend Brother."

Pra Sunnata ran past him to get to the pickup truck parked in the courtyard, now surrounded by a throng of villagers wailing and moaning. As he approached, the crowd grew subdued and parted the way for him in a manner that was overly conciliatory, further increasing his panic. In the back of the pickup were five bodies piled up for delivery to the temple mortuary. Uncle Tem, Auntie Tongsy, Auntie Piew... Jampaa. The other was the little body of his two-year-old daughter.

Pra Sunnata quickly put the back of his hand to cover his mouth and fought off a feeling of dizziness.

"Chao Fa," Sousat declared behind him.

Jampaa's corpse was pale, and both her mouth and her eyes were wide open. His baby girl had her eyes closed, but she was covered with blood.

Shock can numb a person's feelings. Pra Sunnata, at first, didn't feel anything but that icy numbness. He drifted off somewhere, a place he couldn't fathom, an anywhere, an anywhere from here at this particular moment, then gradually surfaced back up into the brutal reality that confronted him, his eyes slowly focusing on the host of people staring at him with some sort of expectation. Again, he was put in a position where he couldn't show his emotions. The families of the other victims were also there, looking at him with distraught faces. He didn't know it then, but this scene would become an important part of his legend. The fact that he didn't break down and show tears was an inspiration to them all to summon their courage, to stoically accept this monumental tragedy.

He swallowed hard before addressing the crowd. "Tomorrow is Awk Pansa, and the ceremony of Pavarana. We will have a chance to make much merit for our departed loved ones. Go home now and grieve quietly. Find solace in the words of the Buddha, and in the Damma."

He turned to Sousat, and said rather coldly, "Why didn't someone close her eyes?" Despite the affected impassivity of his tone, he was dying inside. Sousat could detect this.

"I am sorry, Reverend Brother," he repeated. It wasn't easy for him either. "But we only thought to collect the bodies and bring them here as soon as possible."

"Understood," was all Sunnata said.

A corpse couldn't be brought into a house. It was bad luck. If a person were to die outside the home, the body had to be brought to the temple. Even Sousat, who wasn't a Buddhist, knew this.

The crowd slowly drifted away from the jeep, but many were reluctant to leave the temple grounds. Some of the men finally led away the weeping women.

Pra Sunnata, to his relief, noticed Pra Boon at his side.

"Reverend Father," Pra Sunnata addressed him, "I beg you to see to this matter. It is beyond my capacity."

Pra Boon put his hand on his friend's shoulder. "Yes, of course, Pra Sunnata, you may go."

He walked out of the temple grounds with an aggressive gait, past the paddy fields, past the meadows, past the open woodlands, where he entered the forest and walked further into it for a time that he couldn't remember, before he stopped and dropped to his knees. Despite the words that he had given to the bereaved, he himself couldn't follow his own advice.

It was here, in an obscure spot in the forest, kneeling on the ground, where he screamed in protest to the sky. "I CANNOT DO IT! I CANNOT DETACH MYSELF FROM THIS PAIN!"

He flung his face unto the ground and broke into sobs. "I am not worthy," he wept, "not worthy of the robes I wear, please, please release me." He had no idea to whom he was addressing. "Please, please," he blubbered, his eyes stinging from a teeming stream of tears.

"I am sorry for any wrong doing I've done," he whimpered in submission. "WHY MUST OTHERS PAY THE PRICE OF MY SINS?" he shouted.

He began to pummel the ground with his fists, grunting in an uncontrollable rage as he did so, punching the soil so hard that he bruised his hands. "UGH, UGH, UGH, UGH..."

It went on like this for hours, alternating between moaning, yelling, and beating the ground.

He couldn't accept it, couldn't accept the fact that everything in his life, including its very purpose, had been taken away from him. All he had been living for was gone. The anguish was unbearable, smothering him, as if he were drowning in a deep, dark pool of loneliness and desolation. But no matter how much he cried, how much he remonstrated, how much he struggled, he couldn't escape the murky waters of despair. And there was nothing that could be done to reverse what happened. Eventually he just sat there, catatonically.

He fruitlessly sought solace in clinging to his recollections, images that he wished would come back and become real: Jampa chasing him with a wooden spoon after he tried to pull off her paasin while she was cooking, the both of them giggling uncontrollably...Nok crawling on all fours, cornering the cat, hollering 'Meow meow'...Ling beating a stick on the floor of the hut to drive a cobra out, and he and Jampaa, relieved at the snake's rapid exit, praising the young boy for his bravery...even simple things, like himself fixing the door, sitting on the mat eating with his family...things that no longer had any future. His children growing up, he and Jampaa aging together in a warm solidarity of an old couple that had seen life together... none of this was to be, their course violently aborted.

It was getting dark. He came to his senses and realized they would be looking for him. He resolved to go back to the temple.

Tomorrow was Awk Pansa and the Paravana ceremony. All of the village would attend, even the relatives of the deceased. But could he face them as a dispassionate monk? Perhaps not, but his absence would generate an even bigger controversy. If he could just get through one more day he could be free, free of being everyone's saint.

That night required all of his mental discipline to chant and meditate. He didn't sleep.

The Pavarana ceremony was important—when people brought large amounts of water to be blessed in order to have their personal holy water for the year. Pra Sunnata absorbed himself in the chanting, but it was a mechanical act, put on for everyone's benefit. He himself was far away, in a place where there were no thoughts, no pain. But the devout were praying earnestly, in the belief that he was charging up their jars of water, making it sacred with the powers of healing.

The ceremony was also the occasion whereby the younger priests who had joined for the Lenten period asked to depart from the Sangha. And as these young men announced their leave-taking from the priesthood, Pra Sunnata himself now saw no reason for him to disrobe, for he had nothing to go back to. Searching for answers, straining to see past his grief, he knew he was destined to remain a monk.

At the conclusion of the service, people poured some of the holy water under a tree to share merit with other beings, the living and the dead, especially those just killed by the Chao Fa. After the ceremony, Pra Sunnata retreated hastily to his quarters. He couldn't escape yet. There was still one more thing he had to do.

When people died through the violence of others, the bodies were to be cremated as soon as possible. That same afternoon, the under-taker, Uncle Fak, helped the monks prepare the bodies. Pra Sunnata had decided to break with convention and place the little corpse of his baby daughter in the same coffin as her mother. He took one last look at Jampaa's face before putting her hands together palm to palm, placing a lotus flower between them.

The next day, the entire village was present at the cremation. Each of the bodies was consumed in the blaze of their individual funeral pyres, disintegrating along with Sunnata's life as a layman. When the fire had died down to a smolder, he collected the bones and ashes of his wife and child, putting them in a small wooden box. After waiting for everyone to depart, he left the temple grounds alone and wandered back to the house where he once knew happiness, to shed the last vestiges of a life that would henceforth only exist as a memory.

He was greeted by emptiness. Outside, there lay the contraption he had made for bomb clearing, his flailer, appearing stupid and vain. And as he stared at the house, he took note of the bamboo pole Jampaa had used for drying the laundry, how it was bare, hanging without purpose. The broom made of palm leaves she used for sweeping the compound wasn't outside in its usual place, and her loom under the house now sat dormant, missing the beautiful hands that once gave it motion, fated to remain silent and unmoving forever. He reminisced over her pet sayings, her poetic songs, her optimistic smile. The image of her, with baby Nok riding on her hip, returning from the market, was still fresh in his mind.

Holding onto the box of ashes, he walked out of the village, into the forest and up into the mountains. He climbed up for hours, his stride slow, grave, and mindful.

When the trail ended, he scrambled over the loose boulders and hugged the base of the cliff until he found an easy way up onto a saddle surrounded by jagged pinnacles. He chose to go up the tallest of these. Reaching the top, he stood solemnly, letting himself be buffeted by the evening winds, his robes flapping briskly about him. The sun disappeared under the land, throwing a golden spray in its wake, showering the mountains. He opened the lid to the box, and as a gust blew by he threw the ashes into the air.

"Fly home my loved ones," he called out, his eyes filling with tears, "fly back home."

After that Pra Sunnata disappeared. It would be a long time before anyone would ever see him again, when he would finally emerge as the Chao Baa.

Chapter 23

Laos 1985 - 1986

"A man may be born, but in order to be born he must first die, and in order to die he must first awake"
George Gurdjieff, Greek-Armenian mystic, date unknown

There was only one place he could go now. Trekking through the mountains, totally alone, but with an unstoppable firmness of mind, he headed toward the area of the Forest Temple, carrying only a cloth bag wrapped on a long stick. All he could think about was seeing, or rather, confronting, the Venerable Kru Jarun.

It took two days for him to reach, engaging in his walking meditation, stopping only for short periods to forage for the wild foods of the forest and to take short naps. When he arrived, the young monks that were present greeted him timidly, taken aback at his abrupt, unannounced arrival. All of them were new disciples gathered from various villages in the region, but there were a few, from Ban Ling Kao, that recognized him, and they bowed their heads down as he strode past. He made only a curt acknowledgement with a slight nod of his own head as he marched emphatically towards the kuti of Kru Jarun.

He entered on his knees, but didn't say anything. He made the triple kowtow required of him but remained silent as he looked at the old monk, sitting cross-legged on his platform. Kru Jarun's eyes no longer had pupils, being covered with a sickly gray growth. He was totally blind. Pra Sunnata felt he should announce his presence, but before he could do so, Kru Jarun addressed him.

"I have been waiting for you."

"Yes, without a doubt you knew I would come," Pra Sunnata challenged.

The old priest made no reply.

"In fact, you know a lot of things," Pra Sunnata continued, with a hint of impudence in his voice. "You know a lot of things before they happen. And you knew that everyone in my family would die, didn't you?"

Kru Jarun was silent.

"You do not wish to answer me?"

"Your rudeness betrays the anger in your heart. You feel that I am to blame?"

"No, of course not..."

Kru Jarun leaned forward, grasping the armrests of his chair tightly. "Welcome to the world of suffering," the abbot interjected, his face stern, his rheumy, pupil-less eyes nonetheless shining with authority. "Is that not what you yourself wanted? Yet you come to me seeking answers. The answer lies within you."

"Why did my wife and children have to die?"

"I once told you that in order to analyze the Law of Karma you must practice Vipassana Meditation, using the Four Foundations of Mindfulness. It is up to you. I cannot help you. You know what you must do."

It became clear, without any further words, that this conversation was over. Pra Sunnata prostrated himself three times and crawled away.

He left the Forest Temple as abruptly as he had come, heading into the forest with no particular destination in mind.

When he felt he was far enough away, he slowed his pace and began to walk more mindfully—heel up, lifting leg, moving leg forward, bringing leg down, treading...He did this until the light of day grew dim, then looked for a clear spot to sit. Eventually he came upon a boulder surrounded by tall trees and perched himself upon it to engage in sitting meditation, which he undertook for the whole of the night. In the morning, he went on his way, again, walking with mindfulness.

This was the pattern he followed for several days, continuing without sleep, losing himself deep in the montane forest. He knew what to do whenever he felt he was about to be overcome with drowsiness, for he had been taught long ago by Kru Jarun. He would focus on the pit of his stomach and mentally recite, "Feeling drowsy", and the fatigue would soon disappear. Sometimes he would break from his meditation to dig up wild tubers and bamboo shoots, eat jik leaves and other edible vegetation, and pick dry-season fruits.

Thus, he wandered through the jungle barefooted, dressed in his robes, carrying his cloth bag wrapped onto the end of a stick, which held only a water bottle, a razor, his boke with flint and wick, and a bowl.

On the seventh day he found himself in front of a cave way up on a gray, stone-faced mountainside, and he knew that it was here where he should stop. He put down his stick and undid the cloth, spreading it on the ground in front of the mouth of the cave, whereupon he proceeded with the appropriate Pali chants to consecrate the site as his temple. At this cave, he would practice the Thirteen Austerities; the rest of his life to be devoted to being an aesthetic monk, to do nothing but meditate and fast. His objective wasn't necessarily to achieve the power of perceiving, for he was no longer interested in analyzing the Law of Karma, no longer interested in knowing why things happened as they did. All he wanted now was to remove all clinging, to detach himself totally from the illusory world that had deluded his mind, cheated him, and which had made him suffer; a world which was ephemeral and evanescent, and only led to pain in the endless cycle of birth and death. More than ever, the teachings of the Buddha, the Damma, rang true and clear in his mind's eye.

The regimen he would follow would be to fast for seven days, chanting continuously, then gather foods and eat for one day. Using his flint, he would make a fire and prepare a soup with herbs and tree bark. Then he would resume his fasting. He would rely on his mental powers to survive, though he wasn't really concerned with his physical well-being, whether he died of starvation or not, but only with seeking the Truth. The Truth would make him free.

During the days of his fasting and chanting, what he experienced were sensations and perceptions that aren't easy to describe. Suffice it to say that he was totally absorbed in his explorations through the inner doors of his soul, searching for the meaning of existence, when, on the third day of the third week, some stimulus from outside, for hours it seemed, was persistently distracting him. He had no choice but to break his exquisitely satisfying trance to take note of what it was that insisted on diverting his attention. There was some kind of chirping sound behind him, which was now circling around to his side. He eventually found himself looking into the eyes of a small monkey, the color of his fur an unbelievably pure white.

There followed a few seconds of mutual staring, after which the little primate ran off. It wasn't long however, before it came back with a handful of berries, which the creature deposited a few feet in front of him. It then sat on its haunches and resumed its wary gaze.

Intrigued by the peculiar behavior of the animal, Pra Sunnata leaned forward and extended his arm to take some of the berries, which made the monkey jump up and take a new position further away. The brightly colored genitals revealed it to be a male.

Was this truly the mythical Ling Kao, the White Monkey? He smiled at it, wondering if the creature could recognize the good-natured message that a human smile conveyed. He also wondered how it would react to a human voice. "You are the Ling Kao, the White Monkey."

The animal remained motionless.

"Are you an enlightened being on your way to a higher plane of existence?" he asked it, continuing with his smile. In contrast to his previous desire for solitude, he found the presence of the monkey quite comforting.

As Pra Sunnata munched on the berries, the monkey got up and walked over to a small shrub, which he adeptly ascended, standing on his hind legs making shrieking sounds. After a few seconds of this chirruping he scampered down quickly and paced over to his original position. He did this repeatedly and Pra Sunnata tried to ascertain what was going on in the monkey's mind. Then he realized that the creature was probably, in its own way, wondering the same thing as regards to the human he was face to face with.

"May I call you Ling?"

The monkey stopped its agitated ambling, as if sensing it was being addressed.

"I once had a son named after you," he told the animal. "Perhaps our Karma is bound together?"

Of course, the monkey had no answer for that.

After a few more minutes or so of watching him, the monkey, without any forewarning, abruptly took off back into the forest. Pra Sunnata couldn't help conceding to a sort of disappointment, which in turn only made him feel worse, for he was clinging again, clinging to companionship, companionship with an animal no less. How hard it was, to strip oneself of attachments and emotions. It had taken the Buddha five hundred lifetimes to detach his selfness and escape the cycle of birth and death before he reached the state of Nirvana, never to be reborn again. Would he himself ever be able to achieve such a goal in this one lifetime?

Pra Sunnata waited for the rest of the afternoon, but the monkey didn't come back. The creature probably had its own agenda, perhaps to rejoin his fellow monkeys or his mate, the novelty of the human in the bright orange robes apparently wearing off.

But for Pra Sunnata the effect that the monkey had upon him did not wear off. He couldn't regain the discipline required for his meditation, and eventually gave in to the temptation of wandering around in hopes of finding the strange animal. Although he spent the rest of the daylight hours and the whole of the next morning reconnoitering the area, there was no sign of any monkey, white or otherwise. He even entertained the notion that perhaps the animal didn't exist, but was merely a hallucination brought on by the intense meditation and lack of food and sleep.

Whether real or an illusion, the end result was tangible enough. The vision of the White Monkey had brought him back into the physical world, and worse, it elicited memories of Jampaa and his family. It was clear that he could no longer continue this practice of being an aesthetic. Loneliness engulfed him, and he felt himself to be an insignificant speck in the vast embrace of the jungle.

He meandered about until he found an animal trail, soon recognizing where he was. This in due course brought him to a path that he knew would take him back to the village. Still trying to be mindful, he took this path. He wanted to go home, refusing to believe that it didn't exist.

Upon reaching Ban Ling Kao, he was shocked at what he had come upon: the village had been razed to the ground and consequently abandoned, many of the houses torn asunder into smoldering ruins. The wreckage was everywhere, with personal possessions—clothes, pots, burned mattresses—scattered among the pieces of timber as if the inhabitants had been fleeing from a ghastly cataclysm. The emptiness and havoc jolted him out of any equanimity he might have gained in the forest. Instead of finding comfort in the company of his fellow human beings, he had entered upon a scene of devastation that revoked his life in Ban Ling Kao with a savage finality, for now the entire village had been wiped out.

He walked down once familiar lanes, now made alien by their altered state of destruction. Strikingly, in his own compound, both Kampoon's house and the little hut that he had shared with Jampaa and the children appeared to be untouched. The flailer was in the yard lying undisturbed. Jampaa's loom was still nestled under the main house.

Further ahead, the temple was one of the few other structures standing intact, in front of which were parked two large military trucks. In the courtyard were five or six loosely erected tents with soldiers milling about. The two sentries at the entrance to the monastery wouldn't let him go in. So he stood outside the main gate and questioned them.

"What has happened to my village?"

"Chao Fa," one of them answered.

The war had never finished, Pra Sunnata thought to himself. Bombs, armed guerillas, death, destruction. It wasn't Karma, it was the evil of men. And all he had managed to do was feel sorry for himself, seeking solace in solitary meditation.

No, he protested... he couldn't be a holy man, for he still had an aggressive vitality that wouldn't permit him to just walk away, not again, not this time. He concluded that he was still too young to reject the world, too impassioned to regard it passively. He felt that this turn of events was guiding him to a new purpose for his being, and consequently, realized what he must do to carry it out.

The sound of an approaching vehicle made him turn around. A Russian jeep pulled up in front of him and Captain Sousat promptly jumped out, not bothering with opening the door. "Pra Sunnata, we were wondering where you had gone. You see the work of the Chao Fa? They are becoming very bold, but we are going to punish them. Come inside."

Now, in the presence of Captain Sousat, the sentries let him through.

"We are using the temple grounds as a temporary base," he explained, walking hurriedly. "I am sorry that we have to occupy it. I know for you Buddhists it is not right to have armed men within the compound, but we have no choice, as it is the most defensible position in the village and tactical considerations have priority. This is nothing less than war."

"Where is everyone?"

"They have fled. Some have gone to Lat Sen, and other villages in the middle of Tung Hai Hin."

The two men climbed up one of the larger huts, formerly the abbot's kuti. Sitting at a table placed on the porch, Pra Sunnata asked the army captain if he knew the reason for the attack.

"They do not want people in the area. They want Xieng Khouang for themselves."

Pra Sunnata considered this for a few moments. What could cause such a curse over this place, for people to be repeatedly driven away by violence?

Sousat broke up his thoughts. "I am making arrangements to leave for Ponsavan," he said, lighting up a cigarette. "I will leave within the hour. I am receiving reinforcements with troops from Muong Soui."

"How are you going?"

"A helicopter is coming to take me."

"May I also go?"

Sousat folded his hands on the table and looked down at them, the blue smoke from the cigarette between his fingers streaming lazily upwards, as he silently contemplated the request. There was indeed an available seat in the chopper, but it was against army policy to carry civilians. Yet, it was difficult for him to deny Pra Sunnata anything. "What are you going to do in Ponsavan?"

"What am I going to do here?"

"I understand. But you should realize that not even Ponsavan is safe these days."

"I will be traveling on to Lat Buak."

"That is a risk."

"It is one I must take."

"Why are you going to Lat Buak?" Sousat asked. He felt he had a right to know.

"To visit an old acquaintance."

He chose to walk along the road, realizing it was dangerous, a prime place for a possible ambush. But he was in a hurry; if he could get a lift from a passing vehicle, all the better. Much to his dismay, however, no vehicles passed the whole of the morning. During the trip in the helicopter, Sousat had warned him that only the week before, the Chao Fa had surrounded Ponsavan and laid siege to it for two days before the army arrived. The bandits had run away without battling the army, but not before threatening all the shopkeepers and making off with much money and goods. Several people were killed. It was no wonder then that people were afraid to travel.

It was mid-afternoon when he finally got a lift from an army jeep that was on patrol through the back roads leading to Muong Soui. From the spot on the road where they picked him up it was only an hour's ride to Lat Buak, a sparse settlement in a broad, undulating depression, sheltered amidst pine-covered hills. They dropped him off at the market, a large one that gave the hamlet its name, Lat being short for *talat*, the Laotian word for market. It wasn't far from here that Potisat's ramshackle bamboo house was located, in an isolated spot in the bordering woods.

Potisat was outside on his veranda, wearing a faded orange buttoned shirt and undersized trousers, the legs of which stopped just below his calves. He held a makeshift broom in his hand and was busy sweeping his porch. At the sight of Pra Sunnata approaching, the old man leaned the broom against the wall and gave him a respectful nop. "Sabai dee. I am honored by your visit."

Pra Sunnata put his hands up to return the gesture. "Sabai dee, Lung Potisat."

Potisat lowered his hands and put on a sad face. "I am sorry Pra Sunnata. I heard about the tragedies of your family. I know how it feels to be alone in this world, as my many years alone have taught me. *Sern nai huan.* Welcome into my house. At least tonight we will not be alone."

"It is not only ourselves who must endure suffering," Pra Sunnata said. "Ban Ling Kao has been destroyed. Some have died, the rest have fled their homes."

"Really!" Potisat exclaimed, stunned. "So these troubles are in the south as well?" He looked up and swept his gaze across the surrounding mountains. "They are encircling us." Then, in a solemn, determined tone, he declared, "It is good you have come. We must use this time together to enlist the help of the spirits."

After climbing up the ladder onto the porch, Pra Sunnata was welcomed inside the little shack. "I am warming some tea," the old man told him. "Please, sit down," he invited, leaving him for a moment.

As he took his seat on the floor, Potisat came back with a kettle and two glasses. "You have come to see me about something," he said, pouring the tea.

"I believe you know how to make tattoos, with all the appropriate spells. There has been much talk, as far away as Ponsavan, that says you put great magic into your designs."

Potisat took his place on the mat and remained reticent, looking down into his glass, sipping his drink.

"Is that not true?"

"Do you wish to be tattooed, Pra Sunnata?"

"Yes. All over. Every type that you know, including the most powerful."

The old man now looked him in the eyes, showing concern. "Why do you want to do this?"

"That is my affair."

"Very well."

"I have nothing to pay you."

"That is not a problem. But an offering must be made to the 'teachers', the original possessors of the sacred knowledge. I will do so at my expense. We will start tomorrow, Saturday, a day when the spirits are strong."

That night, Pra Sunnata stayed with Potisat to share a sleeping place on the floor. Potisat didn't have his evening meal in deference to his guest, who was a monk and wasn't allowed to eat after noon.

In the early morning, Pra Sunnata stood in the back room that Potisat used for his tattooing operations, amidst the sordid bric-a-brac that the old man employed in his trade. He busied himself by glancing at the various bottles of inks and fluids that were tidily lined up on a shelf on the wall.

"I have many inks to choose from," said Potisat, entering, "but I recommend the gall of python, which is the strongest and most durable and never comes out, not even if, after your death, the skin is removed from your corpse and dried. It will still be there."

Pra Sunnata fixed his gaze on a small bottle of cloudy gray liquid. He whirled around and grabbed Potisat's wrist, squeezing it hard, causing the old man to double over with pain. With his other hand he reached for the bottle and practically shoved it in Potisat's face. "Is this *namman prai?*" Namman prai was the fluid extracted from corpses.

Potisat shook his head vehemently, with his mouth agape in horror. "No, no!"

"Then what is it?"

"*Namman nanga.*" Namman nanga was sesame seed oil, used to make invisible tattoos, for those, like army officers and government officials, who wished to conceal the fact that they had been tattooed, since it was officially looked down upon.

Pra Sunnata composed himself, letting go of Potisat's wrist and returning the bottle to its place.

"It is a vicious rumor," Potisat stated in defense, rubbing his wrist. "I have never used such bad magic."

"Were you ever a monk?"

"Yes."

"Why did you leave the order?"

"I was made to disrobe. They said I was using magic to achieve power. The other monks were afraid of me, and they wanted me to leave." He paused, as his face slipped into a dreary expression. "'The animal's meat I have not eaten, nor sat upon its skin, yet its bones hang around my neck'." Potisat was reciting a Lao saying that meant he was being falsely accused of a wrong he hadn't committed.

"I am sorry."

Potisat straightened up and retook his air of dignity. "No, it is better that it is out in the open. We are about to perform a serious rite that requires trust and purity of heart. There can be no barriers between us."

They knelt down facing toward the east, lighting incense and candles upon a little wooden altar and then offering flowers to the 'teachers'—those who, in the dim past, had passed down the secret art of tattooing.

"The first thing we shall do," Potisat announced when they had finished their reverent tribute, "is to mark the tongue."

Pra Sunnata opened his mouth while Potisat made a perfunctory jab with the tattoo needle.

"Already, some of the beneficial power is pervading your body through the saliva. Now we will begin with your back. I will create Hanuman, the Monkey God."

Pra Sunnata lay face down on the mat while Potisat guided the instrument using his thumb and index finger, making rhythmical, powerful strokes in order to pierce the skin, pausing often to refill with ink. During the whole time he recited magic formulae.

Pra Sunnata himself had to chant, "*ehi ehi samma*, Oh, come, come properly."

Although it was a painful process, Pra Sunnata had very little difficulty in detaching himself, as he wasn't an ordinary man, but one who was well-versed with the faculty of mindfulness and self-discipline. And while it was generally accepted that only an area of about twelve square inches could be covered in any one session in order to let the swelling of the recently tattooed skin subside, he insisted that Potisat should continue. It would be a lot of work to cover his body and he didn't want to delay any longer than necessary. The tattooing lasted most of the day, with only a brief interlude for lunch.

That evening, while drinking tea, Potisat once again interrogated him as to the purpose of the tattoos. "Why do you desire such a thing?"

"I wish to be feared."

"By whom?"

"By the Chao Fa."

"Why?"

"I must be allowed to travel freely, for there is something I need to do."

"If you want the Chao Fa to fear you, you have done well to come to Old Potisat. I will create figures that will strike terror in their hearts. On your arms we shall put great snakes."

"Snakes?"

"Yes, many Hmong fear snakes. Among the Chao Fa, there will be at least some who will tremble at the sight. And we must shave your chest, to put a magnificent tiger there. All men fear the tiger; it is a symbol of unmatched power."

Over the next few days, they continued this grave undertaking with sessions lasting for hours, which seemed to drain Potisat more than Pra Sunnata. Whenever he finished a design, Potisat would rub his fingers in the blood and ink that welled up from the wounds and say a final spell before blowing with all his might upon his handiwork. At the end of it all, Pra Sunnata had the image of the Buddha surrounded by mystical diagrams on the crown of his head, fierce snakes upon his arms, an awesome tiger on his chest, Hanuman and other heroes of the Ramayana epic on his back, and mythical creatures and cryptic drawings on his legs. Then, to charge up all the tattoos, they held a sacred ceremony with more offerings to the 'teachers'. Potisat pierced the top of Pra Sunnata's head with a jab of his needle, empowering all the tattoos, the potency of which now resided in his body.

The old man sighed with relief after that. He was greatly fatigued, for he had never before been called upon to perform such a marathon tattooing. He was more than impressed, rather in awe, of Pra Sunnata's incredible stamina to have endured it.

"You are the most courageous man I have ever met," he told him. "I confess to you that, although I never knew why, I have always feared you. Now I know. Your soul force is very strong. I have no doubt that even the Chao Fa will learn to fear you."

"My main problem," Pra Sunnata said, "is that I do not know the Hmong language. Not a word of it. Whenever I had to deal with them, I would be forced to make gestures with my hands and even draw things on the ground."

"I know their language. I can teach you. It should be no trouble for you to learn only the most basic words. If you wish to pose as an intimidating figure, you should speak as little as possible so that you remain mysterious."

"You are right."

"You will need a new name," Potisat told him.

"A new name?"

"Yes, one that will command respect. Just to be called Pra is not enough."

Pra Sunnata thought about this. Potisat was correct, for what he himself was doing with all these tattoos was none other than psychological operations. He might as well go all the way on this. Potisat would have been a good psy-ops advisor, he thought to himself.

"So what name do you suggest?"

Potisat put on a thoughtful face. "Well, since they are the army of the Prince of the Sky, you could be the Prince of the Forest. They may be the Chao Fa, but you are the Chao Baa."

Such a name would be treading on dangerous ground as regards the Buddhist Church.

"With a name like that one," Pra Sunnata argued, "I could be accused of boasting of supernatural powers. It is not befitting a monk." He could already foresee the disapproval of the Venerable Kru Jarun.

"Perhaps not, but it seems that whatever it is you want to do is just as contentious. You will have to take the same risks that I did when I was a priest, then accept the consequences. Otherwise I would advise you not to do anything that is outside the ordinary monastic life. If your task is so important, then you should disrobe first. You can always take the vows again when you have finished."

"No, I need the protective power of the robes behind me. My goal is only to promote peace."

The two men fell into a contemplative silence. Pra Sunnata put down his tea, got up, and went to stand outside on the porch. A reposing breeze caressed his face, as if to quell his anxious thoughts. The natural world, the world outside the petty, ignorant struggles of human beings, seemed to be in a peaceful order. He looked at the scintillating stars hanging in the night sky as if they could offer him some supreme counsel. The crickets were chirping their shrilly plain-chant, unperturbed.

It was true that some of the things he might end up doing in the near future could lead to his excommunication, but he saw no other alternative. He wouldn't kill anyone, or otherwise intentionally cause death to any living creature, and he would be careful not to make claims to any magical force. The populace, especially the Chao Fa, would have to believe in his potency on their own.

He stepped back into the hut as Potisat was clearing the kettle and cups. He stood in the doorway and announced to the old man, "Very well. From now on, I shall be called the Chao Baa."

Several weeks later, the security threat in the region had diffused. Pra Sunnata found it ironic, yet understandable, that the guerillas were using the same tactics that they had used during the war, going out on the offensive during the rains and retreating during the dry season.

He himself was waiting to have a meeting with Sousat, and to that purpose he had sent a message to the commander at Muong Soui to radio the Captain, telling him to come to Lat Buak the next time he was in the area.

He didn't have to wait long. Within a few days Sousat showed up in a jeep driven by a corporal. As the Captain ascended upon the porch, Potisat discretely exited out of his own hut, leaving the two men alone.

Captain Sousat, before even getting a chance to remove his officer's cap, stood, shocked, with his hands on his hips. "What have you done to your body? I don't understand it, Reverend Brother."

"Sousat, from now on, you are to address me as the Prince of the Forest."

Sousat looked at him, incredulous, finding it hard to take his eyes off all the tattoos. Of course he, as a Captain in the army, would not address him in any such manner. He made an acerbic face. "Chao Baa? Or Chao Bah?" Bah, with the same sound but a higher tone than Baa, meant crazy. Sousat honestly felt that the tragic loss of his family had caused Pra Sunnata to flip. "You are mad. Why do you have all these tattoos?"

"Are they not impressive?"

The facetiousness of that last remark angered the army Captain. "It is a lowly, superstitious custom. You have degraded yourself." Sousat removed his right hand from his hip to point his finger at Pra Sunnata in a reproachful manner. "I warn you, even though we have been friends, I will not hesitate to have you arrested if you go around claiming you are the Prince of anything. We have enough lunatic princes in the area," he castigated, referring to the Princes of the Sky.

"I need your help."

"My help? You are always coming to me for help. I have helped you enough. Now I will help you one last time, by locking you up, if you do not cease your foolish talk." His friendship with this strange farang was becoming a burden. Before, as a kid, he had nothing to lose, but now as an adult, a Captain in the army and a member of the Party, he risked a lot by helping him.

The Chao Baa ignored the Captain's caustic threats. "I need you to find me an elephant and bring it here."

Sousat's eyebrows leapt upward in mortified astonishment. There was no longer any doubt in his mind. He swiveled his body abruptly and gave a command to the corporal. "Bring the old man here."

Potisat, who was sitting outside under a tree, stood up, frightened, as the soldier approached him.

"Leave him out of this," the Chao Baa entreated firmly inside the hut, "it does not concern him."

"Are you ordering me?"

"No. But he has nothing to do with this. He only made the tattoos at my request."

Captain Sousat turned his attention to Potisat, now before him, being held in the grip of the corporal. "What spells have you put on this man? He has become deranged."

"Sousat," the Chao Baa interjected, "I need the elephant for the machine that blows up the bombies. You saw it work. You said the only problem was a truck. I don't need a truck. Not if I have an elephant."

Potisat was trembling. "I do not know what he is talking about. I only made the tattoos. I have done nothing wrong."

"An elephant is even better than a truck," the Chao Baa continued. "It can travel through the jungle to inaccessible places you would never be able to drive to, even up and down mountains."

"Let him go," Sousat barked to the corporal, referring to the old man.

Potisat, free of the soldier's constraint, brushed himself off with exaggerated affectation and walked off the porch in a huff.

The Captain turned around to look at Sunnata with an expression of newfound interest. "I am listening."

"An elephant can knock down a tree. It should have no problem pushing the machine."

Sousat chewed on his lip pensively while considering this, then fished a cigarette out of his breast pocket. "Why do you want to be called the Chao Baa?" he asked, before putting the cigarette in his mouth and lighting it.

"Psychological warfare," the tattooed monk replied, speaking in English.

"*Sai-ko*...what?"

"That day, at the forest temple, during the war, the airplane came with music and announcements, and they dropped pictures of that naked girl, 'Bubble Gum', do you remember?" The Chao Baa then smiled before continuing. "I know you kept one of the pictures."

"That was a long time ago. I was a boy."

"That was psychological warfare. That will be my weapon against the Chao Fa since I cannot kill or cause violence. It will be my only weapon."

Sousat screwed up his face in bewilderment, causing him to prematurely exhale his cigarette smoke. "You want to play music and show them pictures of naked women?" He honestly didn't understand what Pra Sunnata was getting at.

"No. The tattoos, the name, even the elephant. I want them to believe that I have great magic, and that I cannot be killed. Wherever I go, I want them to flee the area."

"It is a stupid idea. The Provincial authorities would never permit it."

"Your uncle is still on the committee in charge of security, is he not?"

"I cannot ask him to allow such a thing. The Ministry of the Interior will hear of it, and they will be outraged. Not only you and me, but the entire Provincial Committee will end up in re-education."

"Not necessarily. You forget that I have a patron in the Ministry. I shall write him a letter explaining what I intend to do. You know who he is; you can take it to him personally. If he sends a reply allowing it, you will approach your uncle."

"If the Ministry condones such a thing, I will ask my uncle."

"And get me my elephant?"

Sousat violently coughed up cigarette smoke. "Where am I going to get an elephant from?" he asked, once he had recovered from his hacking. "There are no longer any in Xieng Khouang. Then you will need a teacher, to train you, as well as the animal."

"You can get both from Sayabouri Province."

Sousat puffed in exasperation. "Anything else you want?"

"Yes, sunglasses."

"Sunglasses?"

"Yes, the type the CIA advisors used to wear, the round dark ones with the metal frames. I'm sure they can be found in Vieng Chan, in the small shops on the side streets. At least two pairs."

"Two? Why? You want the elephant to wear them as well?"

Momentarily forgetting Mindfulness, Pra Sunnata chuckled heartily in spite of being a monk, putting his palm to his mouth in embarrassment, and relieved that Sousat had regained his sense of humor. But Sousat wasn't mirthful. He hadn't intended his sarcasm to be funny.

"No," Pra Sunnata said, regaining his composure. "The Venerable Kru Jarun is blinded with cataracts. I thought of giving him a pair."

"Hmmph." Sousat threw down his butt and then walked off the porch back to the vehicle where the corporal was waiting behind the steering wheel. As Sousat banged his door shut, the Chao Baa added one more thing.

"Oh, Captain Sousat."

"Yes?"

"The elephant…make sure it is a male."

"Oh, yes, that's right. You can't ride on top of a female, can you? You are a monk."

Now it was only a matter of passing the time, waiting for the reply from the Ministry of the Interior. Pra Sunnata, still in the process of transforming himself into the Chao Baa, took this opportunity to deal with one other requirement. He sent Potisat on an errand to procure pieces of bomb casing from spent cluster bomb dispensers, which were everywhere to be found, and to bring them to the local blacksmith to forge into amulets with figures of the Buddha engraved upon them. While they were being made, he took lessons in the Hmong language from Potisat. He himself didn't venture out of the hut and hid himself whenever visitors came to call. He didn't want anyone to see him, much like the caterpillar hiding in its cocoon during its mysterious metamorphosis into a butterfly.

"What do you intend to do with all these amulets?" Potisat asked

572

one day, perplexed. "They are large and heavy, and as a monk, you cannot hang them around your neck."

The both of them were studying the seven oval pieces of cast metal, beautifully etched with various Buddha images and magical unaloms.

"I will pin them to the inside of my robe."

"But why are they so large? And why do you need so many?"

"I want to protect my chest," the Chao Baa explained. "It is not foolproof, but it is the best I can do."

"I still do not understand."

The Chao Baa explained. "Even though I am no longer a soldier, I can remember a few things. In a firefight, combatants tend to aim for the chest, since it is the easiest target to hit, especially when both you and the target are running around. When I eventually bump into the Chao Fa, they will no doubt try to shoot me. Of course, if I catch it in my arm or leg, then it's all over. They will see blood and know I am not invincible."

"But the tattoos will protect you just as well."

The Chao Baa forced a wry grin. "I'm not taking any chances."

About one month later, the reply from the Ministry came, and in a most dramatic way.

It was mid-morning when an army jeep pulled up and two soldiers disembarked with imperious haste, strode boldly into Potisat's hut, grabbed the would-be Chao Baa roughly, dragged him out of the hut, and placed him forcefully into the vehicle. He didn't even get the chance to say goodbye to Potisat.

Nobody spoke to him, although he reasoned they were taking him to Ponsavan. Yet, they didn't stop at Ponsavan, but instead drove speedily through it. They passed Khang Kai and then took a little side road that the Chao Baa, Pra Sunnata, and the alias Richard Johnson all knew only too well. It was the road to Re-education Camp 07.

He shuddered as they reached the iron gates, which a sentry, after examining the papers handed to him by the driver, opened to let them through. They drove up to what he remembered was the administrative building where the camp Commandant used to have his office. They ordered him out of the vehicle, marched him to the veranda in front of the office, and then made him stand at attention. The official from the Ministry of the Interior, as ebulliently attired as ever, emerged from the doorway. Despite the ten-year interval that had passed since Pra Sunnata had last seen him, he didn't appear to have noticeably aged.

They stood facing each other for a few tense moments. Finally, the government man broke the ice and grinned. "All these years, we have never known each other's names. If you tell me yours, I will tell you mine."

"I am Pra Sunnata, who wishes to be the Chao Baa."

The grin disappeared from the man's face, replaced by a stern frown. Then, without any foretoken, his face changed once again, this time into one of amusement, smirking conspiringly. "You, despite your monk's robes, are a very cunning man. Maybe your idea will work."

At that moment, Captain Sousat came out of the room and appeared at the side of the Ministry official.

The government man continued to address him. "Don't feel sad about this place. It is closed down now. The most stubborn were sent on to Sop Hao. The others have been transferred to Mobile Work Units."

"I am neither sad nor happy," Pra Sunnata, the Chao Baa, assured him.

"I appreciate your discreetness," the official went on. "It means that you respect me. Giving Captain Sousat the responsibility of ensuring the receipt of your letter is very admirable. It also shows that the Captain is trustworthy himself. He never revealed my identity to you."

"I have no need to know it," the Chao Baa told him.

"I am a vice minister now," the man said. "You may call me Mr.

Nim." He gave the Chao Baa a cold, hard look. "I must admit you do look quite formidable with all those tattoos. Do you really think they can stop a bullet?"

"No. But as long as the Chao Fa think so, I will be alright."

Mr. Nim laughed heartily. "Come with me."

The three of them walked around to the back of the building into the main courtyard, where a large elephant stood indolently in the scanty shade of a mango tree. Except for the swishing of its tufted tail, it didn't move.

In front of the beast was a short, round, human figure of muscular stature, dressed in ragged shorts and a baggy blue denim shirt, a straw hat perched upon his head. He gave a respectful nop as they approached, then took off his hat.

"Sabai dee."

"Sabai dee, Sabai dee, Sabai dee."

"This is the *kwan* who will teach you," Sousat informed Pra Sunnata. "He is also the owner of the elephant. He is called Saree. Kwan Saree."

Kwan was the Laotian title for a mahout, an elephant driver.

The two men nodded to each other. Kwan Saree had a dark, rotund, pockmarked face, keen with a prehensile tenacity. His smile bared large brown teeth. He appeared to be at least in his mid-forties. With his hat off, his hair hung limply in a fringe of bangs over his craggy brow in a mop-like fashion, bestowing him with a comic resemblance to Moe in the Three Stooges. Except that this fellow was rather smiley. Even now he had a big grin on his face.

"You will remain here for as long as you require training," Mr. Nim said. "I must leave immediately. Before I go, I need to tell you that we in Vientiane will be looking the other way as long as you do not create too much controversy. Should you do so, we will stop your activities forthwith and give you a new home in Sop Hao. Do you understand?"

"Perfectly."

"Good luck."

"Thank you."

It was only when Mr. Nim from the Ministry walked off to a corner of the courtyard that the Chao Baa noticed the helicopter. Although Sousat accompanied the official to the aircraft, he didn't board it. Instead, after watching it take off, he walked back to where the Chao Baa and Kwan Saree were standing, also looking at the helicopter as it departed clangorously in a swirl of dust.

"I myself will be leaving tomorrow afternoon," Sousat informed them. "Before I go," he told the Chao Baa, "I expect to see you riding atop of this elephant. Tomorrow," he emphasized.

Kwan Saree let loose with a malicious sort of laugh.

The Chao Baa looked at the beast, an imposing mass nearly ten feet tall at the shoulders, and he guessed it must have weighed around five tons. A huge, dome-shaped head was joined to an enormous slaty-gray body. A scattering of stiff, wire-like bristles emerged from its thick hide. It was a fully-grown male with two yellow mottled tusks that curved upwards to a sharp point, and which issued from bulging, fleshy sockets at the top of a long, drooping mouth. In between them, its serpentine trunk swayed desultorily. It continually flapped its large leafy ears, while its small eye shifted in its socket to focus on him, exposing an unexpected, yet intense, consciousness behind it, giving him an eerie sensation.

"It has been a long time since I have had any amusement," Sousat said, shaking a cigarette out of a pack. "I deserve to be entertained."

Kwan Saree broke out in another, naughty, wicked little chortle. Then he plucked a thin sliver of bamboo out of his shirt pocket and stuck it in his ear, twirling it with his fingers.

"How old is he?" the Chao Baa inquired.

"Thirty-four," Saree answered, his head cocked while cleaning his ear.

"That sounds old."

"No, he is in his prime. An elephant can live until seventy years of age."

The Chao Baa noticed something that disturbed him. The

elephant's back legs were fettered with shackles. Ironic, considering that he too, had been bound in that same manner while he was an inmate here at this same spot just a decade ago. "Why are his legs tied with chains?"

Kwan Saree pulled the twig out of his ear and addressed him. "That is to discourage him from wandering off. Also, he tends to kick people he doesn't like, and I'm not sure that he is going to like you, or the Captain," he chuckled with a big toothed smirk. "So, the first thing we have to do is to make introductions." He pointed to the elephant. "This is Akanee." He then talked to the animal. "Akanee, say 'sabai dee'."

The elephant bent both its forelegs to make a curtsey-like motion, vigorously nodding its head up and down.

Both the Chao Baa and Sousat could not refrain from smiling in amazement.

"Akanee," Kwan Saree continued, "this is Pra Sunnata."

"The Chao Baa," Pra Sunnata corrected.

"Yes, Pra Sunnata, the Chao Baa."

The elephant extended its trunk forward to sniff at him, moving down to his feet. The Chao Baa could feel its wet breath tickling his toes.

"Let him smell you," Kwan Saree told him. "That is how he will know you. Elephants can't see too good, but they can smell something ten miles away. When meeting someone for the first time, they usually prefer to smell the feet first."

Kwan Saree went over to a large bunch of bananas that was just out of reach of the elephant. He broke off a few of the fruits. "Feed him. Let him know you are a friend." He handed the Chao Baa the bananas.

No sooner were the bananas in his hands than the animal greedily stuck out its trunk, attempting to grab the food out of his grasp. The Chao Baa pulled back.

"Do not take what is not offered to you," he admonished the elephant.

This sent Kwan Saree into a convulsive fit of laughter. "Very good!"

The Chao Baa broke off a banana and held his hand out. Akanee's trunk extended forward, disclosing two pink nostrils and a finger-like extension at the tip, before it wrapped around his hand and deftly removed its contents. The tough skin had a rough, warm feel, and the tight grip it exerted indicated the potential strength of the leathery appendage. He realized that the elephant could use it to easily snap a man in half. And the huge tusks were even more formidable weapons. So when the animal made a low rumbling noise that sounded like a tiger growling, the Chao Baa naturally got nervous and stepped back.

This provided another occasion for Saree to snicker haughtily. "Don't be scared. He is purring. It means he is happy."

He continued to feed the animal one fruit at a time until there were no more left in his hand. The elephant stuffed the fruits in the back of its mouth, making sibilant squishy sounds as it chewed.

"Now you can touch him. Pet his trunk."

The Chao Baa did so. Meanwhile, Saree drew near and murmured something to the elephant, which made the creature open its mouth wide. A fleshy pink lump rose up from the lower jaw.

"Stroke his tongue. Elephants like that."

He caressed the hot moist tongue, feeling a bit strange while doing so.

The whole afternoon was spent in this fashion, the Chao Baa touching the animal in various places, to facilitate getting to know each other better, with Saree behind him tittering annoyingly. Sousat looked on, while smoking his cigarettes.

By early evening, Saree decided that it was enough. "It is time for him to be left alone to eat. You will help me take him into the forest. Come." He directed the Chao Baa to a pile of chains on the ground behind the tree. Actually it was a single length of chain, a very long one. The Chao Baa helped to drag it close to the elephant, while Saree took the first portion of it and slung it over Akanee's back, repeating this maneuver until the entire length had been folded and draped upon the animal.

"You will have to learn to do that yourself," he told the Chao Baa. "*Song!*" he shouted to the elephant.

The elephant raised its left foreleg, bending it at the knee, and Saree stepped up on it, then launched himself upwards to sit just behind the elephant's head. Without being told, the animal brusquely swung its immense body around, compelling both the Chao Baa and Sousat to quickly get out of its way. It then marched forward with a slow supercilious gait, as if oblivious to everything except its own motion. The elephant and its rider, along with the two men on foot, left the courtyard and headed out of the main gate, which the guard rather hastily opened, to enter the forest that surrounded the camp. Sousat and the Chao Baa walked behind the huge rocking backside of the lumbering beast, its tufted tail swaying to and fro. As the creature walked, it defecated with heedless indifference, the pulpy brown balls plopping in front of the two men in the elephant's wake.

Following one of the well-used trails, one wide enough to accommodate the animal's girth, they soon came to a small running stream where they stopped to let the pachyderm drink. Its trunk extended out and dipped into the water, sucking it up, then coiled back to deliver the fluid to its mouth.

"Akanee drinks thirty gallons of water a day. If he fills his trunk up, he can suck up ten gallons at a time. But he won't drink dirty water. Or water that is too still and clear."

"Why won't he drink clear water?" Sousat asked.

"He doesn't like to see his reflection."

For some reason that the Chao Baa didn't want to acknowledge, that statement disturbed him.

After the animal had apparently taken its fill, they walked for about another half an hour through the woods before Saree halted the elephant and got down. He then proceeded to unravel the chain it had been carrying on its back.

"You must ensure that Akanee gets enough feeding time," Saree declared firmly. "He eats more than ten *mun* a day."

That meant nearly three hundred pounds!

"You, Chao Baa," he called disdainfully, "a Kwan always starts off as *Kwan din.*" 'Din' was the Laotian word for foot, and a Kwan Din was assigned the job of chaining the elephant's feet. "Undo the shackles, but don't remove them. You will see a hook. Then attach this end of the chain."

The Chao Baa bent down and drew near to the enormous, pillar-like hind legs, slightly apprehensive, remembering what Saree had said about the animal's penchant for kicking. But during the procedure the creature appeared docile enough.

Saree himself went over to a thick tree and wrapped the other end of the chain around it. "You must tether the animal, otherwise in the morning you will not find him."

"Why is that?" the Chao Baa asked, concerned. He didn't realize that his having an elephant required it to be a captive.

"An elephant can smell its favorite foods from miles away. It will wander in search of it. Also, it is a wild beast. It is not like a dog, or even a buffalo. It can go back at any time to the forest and live comfortably, without the need for a human master."

"You mean he will run away?" Sousat asked.

"Yes."

With the animal secured, they made their return trip back to the camp, Saree now as well on foot.

"Oh, yes, one important thing that I must tell the both of you," Kwan Saree informed them. "Do not approach Akanee without me being present. He might attack you."

"That behavior must change," the Chao Baa remonstrated. "Soon I will have to be alone with him."

Kwan Saree made no comment.

That night wasn't a pleasant one for Pra Sunnata. They had to sleep together in the same room on makeshift beds in one of the former offices. It wasn't the matter of the beds that made him uncomfortable, since he chose to sleep on a mat on the floor, as it was forbidden for a monk to sleep in a high sleeping place. But rather, it was the company. Saree and Sousat were heavily indulging in lao-kao and were in the process of getting sloshed. He himself felt like leaving them to it, but he didn't want to appear impolite, and some of what Saree was discussing was of interest to him. Sousat, a bit tipsy, seemed to be apologizing, despite his rank as an army Captain.

Through their drunken conversations, the Chao Baa learned that Saree, in contrast to his outward conviviality, was bitter about this project. He hadn't been given a choice about coming here, and it wasn't fair that he should be forced to do so. He was also angry that his younger brother, his usual assistant, hadn't been allowed to come along. It took at least two men, preferably three, to control a male elephant, he protested in a slurred voice.

The Chao Baa broke into their discussion. "But I need to command him by myself, alone."

Saree looked at him, his jaw hanging limply in intoxication. "Not possible."

"I cannot risk another person's life. The work I will be doing is dangerous, and in the places where I am going there may be people who will try to kill me."

"I wouldn't worry about that," Saree advised. "The elephant just might try to kill you first."

The initial test came the next morning. They had already fetched Akanee from the forest and were now in the camp compound, ready for the first lesson.

"There are two ways to mount an elephant. You will learn the easy way first. The command is '*Mop'*." Kwan Saree turned his attention to the pachyderm. "Mop!" he shouted.

Akanee the elephant stretched his legs forward, bringing the anterior portion of his body near to the ground, as if he was kowtowing. Saree swung himself over just behind the head, after which the elephant raised itself up. "Mop!" the Kwan repeated.

The animal redid the motion, and Saree slipped himself off onto the ground.

"Now you try it. Mop!"

The animal obeyed, and the Chao Baa, hesitating for a split second, forced himself to get on the beast, which then stood up immediately. Despite his being a monk, he couldn't suppress a thrilling exhilaration, perched high atop the huge mammal.

"Akanee listens to verbal commands, but you can also control him by kicking him lightly behind the ears. Do that now, just tap him behind both ears," Saree instructed, while walking away.

To the Chao Baa's astonishment the elephant began to walk forward.

Sousat, who had been watching, threw down his cigarette butt to clap his hands. "Very good, Pra Sunnata, I am proud of you!" he cheered, laughing.

"*Yut!*" Saree shouted and the elephant halted. "Keep nudging him with your feet."

The Chao Baa did so, but the animal didn't move. "He's not obeying."

"Yes he is. He is obeying me. I told him to stop. That is just to let you know that you haven't done anything yet. Would you like to try the other way of getting down? It is a bit harder."

"Yes, I think I can manage."

"*Song, song!*"

As the animal offered its raised foreleg to provide a foothold, the Chao Baa stepped awkwardly upon it and jumped down.

Saree reached into a wooden holster he wore on his belt and pulled out a stick that had a barbed metal hook on the end. "This is the *takaw*. You must learn how to use it. The trick is not to be too rough, but he should feel it. Hit him with it just behind the ear." He then took out a slingshot from the back of his pocket. "And this is your 'remote control', for when you are on the ground. Use sharp pebbles, and aim for the head, where it can really sting him a bit."

"I cannot use such things to inflict pain on a poor beast."

Kwan Saree gave out another of his infamous bursts of laughter. "Then you cannot ride an elephant. All kwan use the takaw and the slingshot." Saree smiled, seemingly pleased that the Chao Baa would be a failure at elephant driving.

Sousat intervened. "Pra Sunnata, I advise you to listen to this man. He is an expert and we have taken great trouble to bring him and his elephant here."

"Can I at least try without these things?"

Saree was once again twiddling a little twig in his ear. "Song, Song!"

The pachyderm responded by lifting its foreleg, and the Chao Baa stepped up on it and clambered back on to the neck.

"Let us just practice sitting on the neck for today. Bai, Bai!" he ordered the elephant, who lurched forward in slow plodding footfalls.

"Sooner or later," the master Kwan insisted from down below, "you will need to use the takaw. Believe me I know, I have been with Akanee since I was nine years old."

For two hours all they did was parade around the compound. Sousat eventually got bored and left, while the Chao Baa remained atop the creature, the muscles in his legs becoming stiff and painful.

"Okay, that's enough," Saree declared. "Mop!"

Akanee bent down, and the Chao Baa slid off. He could hardly stand, leave alone walk.

"You will have to get your legs in shape. That will be one of the first things you must master. After lunch you will continue."

It seemed that it was time for Akanee's lunch as well, for Saree brought over a pile of palm leaves and dumped it on the ground. The elephant took a bunch of the leaves with its trunk and repeatedly whipped it against its body before putting it in its mouth.

"Does he always play with his food?" the Chao Baa asked, knowing his question would cause Saree to give out his habitual laugh.

Saree did indeed chuckle. "He does that to remove dirt and insects. He is a strict vegetarian and doesn't eat meat, not even insects. Like you, a monk!" he guffawed.

After deeming the vegetation clean enough, the elephant crammed it into its mouth, grinding it with its giant molars, the lower jaw moving back and forth slothfully.

While they were feeding the animal, Sousat returned with an announcement. "I will be leaving in a short while. Come with me, I need to show you something before I go."

All three of them headed towards one of the larger barracks, the very same wooden shelter that Pra Sunnata had spent time in as a prisoner. Inside was dark and musty, and empty, save for a pile of hay, banana leaves, and other foodstuffs for the elephant, and, in the opposite corner, the flailer that Sunnata had made almost a year ago, completely assembled.

"We were not sure how to dismantle it," Sousat reported, "so we just dumped it on the back of a truck and brought it here. I will be coming back to visit you in a few weeks, and I would be most pleased if I can see you and your elephant pushing that thing."

In addition to the flailer, were various ropes, sheets of canvas, wooden blocks, and a metal chest, the type used for armaments.

"What is in there?" the Chao Baa asked, pointing to the metal box.

Sousat flipped the latch up and threw open the lid. Inside were a few dozen hand grenades. "For practice," he explained.

"Practice?"

Kwan Saree spoke up from behind him. "My elephant has never heard a bomb blast. He will undoubtedly be upset when he does."

The training continued for the next several weeks. Among other things, the Chao Baa learned how to bathe the elephant, a lesson that took place in one of the water-filled bomb craters nearby. The command to get the elephant to lie down in the water was 'Lap long!'

With the animal in this position, both he and Kwan Saree capered around on the back of the half-submerged beast, scrubbing hard with lengths of creepers and branches. This was to be done at least once, if possible, twice a day. In addition, the elephant shouldn't work hard in the afternoons and it should stay out of strong sunlight as much as possible, for an overheated elephant becomes irritable, and dangerous.

The Chao Baa was lectured about not overworking the animal. Three or four days of work at most, then two days of rest. When the Chao Baa asked what kind of work Saree was talking about, Saree told him that Akanee had been used as a logging elephant.

The Chao Baa raised a point. "I don't expect Akanee to labor as strenuous as that. Besides pushing the flailer, he will just be walking."

"When you are as heavy as an elephant, even walking is work. For the first day, do not make him journey farther than ten miles, and on the second day, only half that. During the hot season even less."

The Chao Baa was informed of another important issue—musth—when a male elephant is in heat.

"You know, he wants to bum-bum," Saree said laughing, intertwining the fingers of his two hands and banging his palms together, crudely imitating copulation. "He gets stimulated by oil leaking from the little holes on each side of the head, between the eye and the ear, and during that time, for a period of about a month, an elephant will go crazy."

The Chao Baa gawked at the huge maleness between Akanee's hind legs. He had noticed it before, but had never really paid much attention to it.

"One remedy they use in the logging camps," Saree continued, "is to overwork the elephant and give him very little to eat. Then he becomes too tired to run amok. But that is dangerous, especially for someone like you who has no experience. It is best to just tie him to a tree and make sure he is tied up good with extra chains."

In addition to these frequent orations educating him about Akanee's habits, and his likes and dislikes, the Chao Baa was given practical lessons. He was made to give instructions to the animal regarding walking control: moving fast, slow, forwards, backwards and sideways, and telling the animal to turn by nudging his foot in the back of one ear. He was taught how to make the elephant accept things and take things with his trunk. Of course, for Akanee, all this was child's play, inasmuch as the elephant had already been trained to do all of these things from the time he was a three-year-old calf.

But the lessons didn't always go smoothly. On some occasions Akanee wouldn't respond to commands, not even those of Kwan Saree.

"You see, sometimes he is stubborn," Saree explained, "and that is when you need to use the takaw. You have to show him you are the master. You must always remind him of that. It sounds cruel, but it is a fact. It is not his wish to work for humans. It is only through our superiority that we dominate and control the elephants."

"So that makes Akanee nothing more than a slave," The Chao Baa protested.

"I told you before that it is not the same as dogs who want to be with their owner, or even cows or buffaloes, which willingly walk back to the farm. An elephant will make a decision. Most of the time that decision is to return to the wild. But sometimes an elephant can love its Kwan so much that it will come back. They are almost like people."

"Perhaps we should let him rest. It is getting hot," the Chao Baa said, still seated on the elephant's neck. "Song!"

Stepping on the offered foreleg, he got down.

As they walked back to the admin building, Saree suddenly said, "Before we go on with any more training, it's time I tell you a little more about Akanee... that way if you want to change your mind, we will not have wasted too much time."

Back in their room, the story of Akanee was revealed to the Chao Baa.

During the 1960s Saree, wishing to escape the escalating war, took his elephant to look for logging work in the mountains of neighboring Thailand. At that time, Akanee the elephant was just a teenager, but despite being already quite large and strong, he had to start off with light work, mostly as a baggage carrier. Soon, however, there was a call to increase production, and Saree and his elephant were given more arduous tasks, such as skidding logs and unblocking jams in the stream. Akanee, tired and overworked, soon became difficult to manage. Saree had requested a less demanding workload, but his protests had fallen on deaf ears. Unfortunately, Saree himself shortly became very ill with malaria and Akanee was assigned to another kwan. Even more unfortunate, Akanee was approaching his musth period. The substitute kwan attempted to work the animal out of it, but it didn't work. One day Akanee went on a rampage, killing the kwan and three others, trampling and goring them to death.

"You don't ever want to see an enraged elephant," Saree told him. "In his fury, Akanee went on to mangle the corpses of those he killed, smashing them and kicking them with his foot, and stabbing with his tusks, until I was called from my sickbed. You see how an elephant is like a human? The only other creature that would continue to pummel something that was already dead, solely out of anger and hate, is a human. It took me a while to calm him down."

The two men became silent as the Chao Baa reflected upon this sad story. If an elephant was subject to the same emotions as a human being, similar mental defilements, could it also not benefit from Vipassana meditation? Obviously, he didn't expect the elephant to sit in a lotus position and chant sacred Pali texts, but he himself, being a monk, could do it for the both of them. The beneficial power generated would certainly embrace the beast. He decided to voice these thoughts, even though he was sure that Kwan Saree would laugh his head off.

"I shall begin to meditate with the elephant, so that we can sense each other's feelings," he announced.

Surprisingly, Kwan Saree didn't laugh. "That is a very good idea," he noted. "In fact, I only agreed to give up my elephant because you are a monk. Of course, I also know that they would have made my life miserable if I didn't co-operate, but in the end I gave him to you because I would gain merit. So you will chant blessings for me as well, no?"

"Yes."

Every morning henceforth, after the elephant was fetched from the forest, but before each day's practice, the Chao Baa would sit in front of Akanee, chanting, meditating, and then chanting again.

Whereas the Chao Baa and the elephant soon became comfortable with each other and could accomplish many routine tasks, the training grew more demanding. Saree had insisted that he take the elephant through the rounds of logging exercises, despite the Chao Baa's objections that they wouldn't need such skills, which were, furthermore, extraneous to the work that they would actually be undertaking. But the master kwan was adamant that the Chao Baa should know everything that the animal was capable of, since it might prove useful in the jungle. For this purpose, there was a pile of large thick logs that had been cut several years ago when the prison camp was in operation, and which were still lying in the compound.

Hauling logs with chains, pushing them into a stack, lifting them up with Akanee's trunk and tusks, were among the required drills. There was one act to perform that the Chao Baa thought wasn't possible, and was stunned when Saree had ordered it to be carried out.

"Make him walk across it!" Saree was shouting.

A big log was laid out on the ground, and Saree wanted him to order the elephant to traverse it.

"He can't possibly do it. I myself can barely walk across it."

"Do you think this is the first time for him? He has done it before, many times. It is only your own fear and doubts that make you hesitate. I can command him myself, but I want you to give the order."

The Chao Baa gently nudged the heels of his feet behind the elephant's flapping ears, the signal for moving straight ahead. "Bai, bai!"

Akanee stepped up onto the log with his right foot, then swung his left one in front of it, advancing forward, then carried out similar motions for his hind legs until all four of his feet were up on the log. Slowly but surely, one foot went in front of another, hind legs and forelegs moving in tandem, the prodigious mammal balancing himself in a four-legged tightrope act. The Chao Baa sat breathlessly atop the pachyderm, amazed at the nimbleness of its hulk.

"Make him halt," Saree ordered.

"Yut."

The elephant stood still just as they reached halfway across, his four legs in single file upon the log, unwavering.

"Make him turn around."

"Are you insane?"

"Order him to turn around!"

He had to trust Kwan Saree as much as he trusted the elephant. He gave Akanee the signal, and the elephant maneuvered his legs in a complicated, methodical fashion, turning its body slowly, patiently shifting position with incredible fastidiousness, until they faced the way they had come. This act filled the Chao Baa with an inspired thrill and a great respect for both Akanee and his teacher.

When the animal walked off the log, he ordered it to stop, so he could get off. Both he and Kwan Saree agreed that a reward of sugarcane was in order.

The Chao Baa also had to take lessons that didn't require the elephant's presence. They skipped the one about the gathering and cooking of wild foods in the forest, since, having been a forest monk, he was already well-versed in such survival craft. They instead concentrated on rope tying, using special knots frequently employed by logging men.

Following all this, the time came to teach Akanee to push the flailer. First, they had to make modifications to the hitch, and using wooden blocks and parts of the logging harness, they fashioned it so that the tow bar could be strapped around the elephant's head. For a cushion against the animal's forehead they used sheets of dried bark that had been beaten to a soft texture.

"*Bai, Bai, Nangut!*" 'Nangut' was the command to push with his head.

Akanee, being the intelligent animal that he was, didn't find this duty particularly challenging, and he easily rolled the flailer all over the courtyard.

But that was the easy part. The hard part was getting him used to the sound of explosions. Of course Kwan Saree would have nothing to do with the grenades, and so the Chao Baa, being an ex-military man, was automatically assigned the duty of handling the munitions. He stood in the corner of the compound, at first a considerable distance from the elephant, arming the grenades and tossing them over the fence. Predictably, the animal was shaken up, swaying its great head back and forth in agitation, flailing its trunk wildly and shifting its feet nervously while snorting and bellowing. Repeating this exercise over the next few days however, subdued the animal's response. There followed phases in which Akanee was brought closer and closer to the source of the explosions, so that by the time Sousat returned to the camp to monitor their progress, they were ready for a full dress rehearsal. The flailer was attached to Akanee's head with the Chao Baa riding him, while Sousat had the job of pulling the pins from the grenades and tossing them a short distance in front of the advancing bomb-clearing contraption. At the sound of the first blast, Akanee stopped and shook his head in elephantine displeasure, but the Chao Baa tenaciously ordered him to continue.

In the end, the flailer test was deemed a success, and Sousat offered hearty congratulations.

"Oh, by the way," Sousat called as the Chao Baa had dismounted, "is this what you wanted?" He handed him two pairs of black-lensed, wire-rimmed sunglasses.

The Chao Baa took them in his hands and examined them. "Perfect."

Up to now, it seemed that this crazy plan would actually come to fruition, but there was still one more test, the most crucial, upon which everything depended. If this last hurdle couldn't be surmounted, all of the effort thus far expended would be for naught, and the whole idea would have to be abandoned.

So, in the early morning of the next day, the Chao Baa rose from his sleep at the usual time of four-thirty to say his morning prayers, except that on this occasion he didn't sit and chant as he typically did. He combined his praying with walking meditation, walking into the forest to where Akanee had been taken to forage.

The pachyderm had smelled him long before he arrived and let loose with a frightening roar, indicating his location. As the Chao Baa approached him in the dusky light of dawn, Akanee showed signs of uneasiness. His ears flapped nervously, and he was swinging his trunk fitfully.

"It is just you and me now, Akanee. I am your new master. That is how it is going to be from now on. You must accept this." He drew nearer to the elephant, who stepped back cautiously. When he felt he was close enough, the Chao Baa sat on the ground in the lotus position and began his chanting and sitting meditation. Akanee eventually became more relaxed and resumed his browsing. After an hour or so, the Chao Baa undid the chain from the tree Akanee was tied to, and confronted him.

"Song, song!"

A profound happiness swelled in the Chao Baa's heart as Akanee offered his right foreleg, bending it to make the expected step for him. He mounted the beast and rode him back to the camp, only occasionally scolding the animal whenever it was tempted to wander off the trail to nibble at leaves.

"Bai, Bai!" he shouted, but he didn't use the takaw.

When Kwan Saree saw him parading the elephant into the compound, he was truly impressed. As the Chao Baa stopped Akanee in front of him, he had to voice his admiration. "You are the only man besides myself who has ever controlled this elephant. Not even my brother is able to be alone with him. Because of this, you have earned the right to receive the secret knowledge. We shall begin today."

Naturally, as with every other serious endeavor undertaken in Southeast Asia, there were rituals involved, and that was also the case in the relationship between man and elephant. Many of them pertained to the separation of the calf from its mother, and the initial training that followed, which were conducted only once, and therefore were no longer relevant for Akanee, since he had already been through them. But there were two other important rites that had to be performed repeatedly with an adult elephant, and the Chao Baa was required to know them in order to ensure the well-being of both himself and his charge.

The first one that he learned to perform was the familiar baa-see ceremony, but elephant style. This was done to bind the souls of man and beast together, much like the baa-see performed between intimate friends. A plate containing a banana, some sticky rice, an egg, and flowers, was placed on Akanee's head. Saree held a sacred string tied to this plate, incanting the sacred spells, while the Chao Baa touched the side of the elephant with both hands. Once completed, Akanee formally belonged to his new master.

The second ceremony to be learned was one that the Chao Baa should carry out after any lengthy separation between them. It was called *koo-at*, and its purpose was to cleanse the elephant of any mischievous forest spirits that the creature might have picked up in its wanderings which could affect its health or behavior in a negative way.

The remaining 'secret knowledge' that Saree imparted to the

Chao Baa, had to do with the forest spirit culture.

"It is not enough that you have been a forest monk, meditating in the wild mountains," Saree lectured him. "Under those conditions, the forest spirits are fearful of the power of your chanting, and you are not directly interfering with them. But if you are actively working or hunting, you must take precautions, since your actions may provoke their jealous natures. You must make the appropriate offerings and speak the special forest spirit language. I myself have been taught by the Kammu."

And so, the lessons continued.

It took another month for him to end his course with Kwan Saree, after which the metamorphosis was complete. He was now equipped to be a true elephant man of the jungle, ready to emerge from his chrysalis and to make his appearance as the Prince of the Forest.

Chapter 24

Laos 1986 - 1988

*"Happy is the man who hath never known what it is to taste of fame —
to have it is a purgatory, to want it is a Hell!"*
Edward Bulwer-Lytton, English author and politician, 1843

By 1985, the US and Lao PDR were talking to each other. In fact, they had never really stopped talking to each other. Unlike Vietnam and Cambodia, the US had kept diplomatic relations with the Laotian government throughout the years following the war, despite the fact that there was no ambassador in Vientiane. Now, however, they were talking a lot more. One obvious concern was the MIA issue, since out of the five hundred and eighty-five pilots who went missing after being shot down in Laos, only ten ever returned. American and Lao officials made their first joint excavation, at the site of a downed C-130 in Pakxe in 1985.

In 1986, the Fourth Party Congress endorsed the 'New Economic Mechanism', which signaled a new era for the Lao PDR. Socializing the means of production was a concept that went out the window. Now, 'profit' became the new catchword. The Lao kip was allowed to find its own level against international currencies. Laws were passed encouraging foreign capital investment.

The broadcast system setup in Vientiane and other provincial capitals no longer droned with political rhetoric, propaganda being replaced by announcements of temple festivals and the current prices of agricultural produce.

In the Soviet Union, Mikhail Gorbechov announced the philosophies of glasnost and perestroika, and Lao PDR followed a similar course. Although the Party leaders in Vientiane never publicly announced that they were no longer a communist country, terms such as socialism, Marxist-Leninism, and class struggle were never heard again in government speeches. In 1989, the first tourists in fourteen years entered Laos.

With the collapse of the Soviet Union in 1990, communism was history.

The furtive plan of creating the mythical figure of the Chao Baa was due to the maneuverings, willful or not, of six men: Potisat, the ritualist medicine man; Mr. Nim, the official from the Ministry of the Interior; Captain Sousat of the Lao People's Liberation Army; Sousat's uncle on the Xieng Khouang Provincial Committee; Kwan Saree, the master elephant keeper; and Pra Sunnata, the American monk.

From their efforts, a legend was born.

It was in 1987 that the Chao Baa made his famous trek across the Plain of Jars. He started in Khang Kai. He rode into the settlement, a tattooed, shaven-headed, farang monk with sunglasses, atop Akanee, who himself was regally adorned with markings and designs painted with white lime and golden tumeric all over his expansive body. The rattling of the chains as the great beast dragged a skid carrying the disassembled flailer was enough to draw attention in advance of their passage. People gathered around this extraordinary spectacle as the monk announced, "I am the Chao Baa. My goal is to clear the land of the bombi, so that we can continue to farm and live without the fear of death lurking in the ground. I only ask that you help feed my elephant."

The Chao Baa, after ensuring he had made the desired impression, proceeded to the temple hall with the crowd trailing curiously behind. Once there, he requested an urgent meeting with the village administrative committee in order to outline his plan and state his requirements. After he had explained what he could do to clear the fields, the community leaders listed the areas they deemed a priority. Everyone had to make a donation to provide food for his elephant—bananas, grass, rice stubble, fruits, sugarcane, palm leaves... if rice, it was to be unhusked grains—hulled rice would swell in his belly when he drank water and would incapacitate the elephant.

The whole affair was treated as an extremely auspicious event, an unexpected, yet remarkable occasion to make tons of merit by offering aid to this pair. For not only was the Chao Baa a monk, a holy man of the robes, but his companion Akanee was venerated as well, as an animal of special significance held in divine reverence. The Buddha himself, in one of his earlier lifetimes, had been reincarnated as a white elephant. Thus, not only was Akanee amply fed, but he was fed with religious devotion.

He and his master, the Chao Baa, were camped out about a mile away from the main residential area, near a great pond that was fed by subterranean water, called Nam Long. The people came in a steady stream pulling and pushing carts of fodder, all in exuberant spirits, as if a traveling circus had come to town. The Chao Baa facilitated this carnival atmosphere by having Akanee 'say' Sabai dee repeatedly, the elephant bending down and nodding his head, each time evoking a chorus of cheers and laughter from the growing crowd. The Chao Baa was proud of how well-behaved Akanee was with all these noisy humans around, and his affection for his elephant grew very warm. He gauged Akanee's mood so well that he allowed small groups of men to walk under his belly three times for good luck. Some people approached the elephant in an attempt to pet his trunk. This proved to be a great deal of fun for everyone, as he would send out his serpentine snout in a curious rush to sniff his new acquaintances, which would send them scurrying away in thrilled laughter.

Akanee seemed to be eating it up. So was the Chao Baa, in contrast to the impassive demeanor he struggled to present. With a stoic expression that belied his joy, he made Akanee perform tricks, such as picking up a berry with his trunk. The children's faces were agape with wonder.

Everyone else was similarly enthralled. It had been a long time since anyone had seen an elephant in Xieng Khouang Province, and for the younger ones who had never seen one; the sight of such a remarkable beast was unprecedented.

A jolly old man with a ken danced around the elephant blowing a tune on his instrument. When he jokingly offered the beast the bamboo pan pipe, Akanee called his bluff and snatched it out of his hands with his trunk, positioned it accordingly, and began producing absurd shrieking sounds, all the while bobbing his head up and down, and shuffling his legs as if in a dance. This sent his audience into hysterics, and was even a surprise to the Chao Baa, for it was a trick taught to Akanee by drunken elephant-drivers in a logging camp many years ago.

The next day, a gathering equaling the throng of the day before came to watch the man-elephant duo perform the task of bomb clearing. Witnessing Akanee pushing the flailer was truly impressive, and when, after twenty minutes or so, the first bomblet was fired off, there was a dramatic moment as the elephant stopped and waggled his head in refusal, until the monk commanding him compelled him to carry on. Everybody cheered.

It was similar wherever they went: Ban Nam Tom, Lat Huong, Ban Dongdam, and Khosi, all the way to Muang Koon, they paraded and worked. It took them six months to cross the Tung Hai Hin.

His most serious work hadn't yet begun, but he already had a name. Everything was going according to plan.

He had elected to follow Route Four, and didn't deviate much from the beaten path. His sketch maps, which had successfully guided him to the fields that he had previously cleared, were easily interpretable. But now that he was entering sparsely populated mountainous country, he would have to rely more on the compass and topographical maps that Sousat had provided to supplement the crude notes he was making. The records and maps were necessary because he had to eventually show the army the exact areas that had been de-mined. It was the fertile upland valleys in the mountains that had been most affected by the bombing, and herein lay the most important task of the Chao Baa.

The duo climbed into the foothills, the landscape dotted with short ornamental pine trees, as the sun began its journey across the sky. The elephant walked with a soporific swaying of his ponderous body, nodding his head rhythmically with every step and leaving a trail of dung which passed out of his anus every hour or so.

Before they reached the thick jungle in the interior of the mountains, Akanee started to act a bit funny. He halted for no apparent reason, refusing to go on.

"Bai, Akanee. Bai!"

The only response was a constant flinging of his trunk and a snort that sounded ominous. The Chao Baa didn't want to use the takaw, nor did he want to shout too harshly, for that would mean he was losing control. But why was he losing control? From his seat on the beast's neck, he leaned over to inspect the orifice of the musth glands at the side of the animal's huge head and noticed to his dismay that they were glistening wet. Akanee had eaten well while in the villages on the Plain—apparently too well. The rich food had stimulated him into entering musth. The Chao Baa took out a feather from his cloth bag and reaching down, worked the stem of it into the hole of each of the temporal glands, just as Kwan Saree had taught him, hoping to let out the oil and relieve the pressure. The relaxed waving of his ears indicated the animal's satisfaction, and soon Akanee was once again willing to obey his master. But this would only buy some time. He had to make it to where there was enough vegetative growth so that the five-ton pachyderm could be tied up before he became a threat. They also had to get out of the sun before it got too high, as a hot elephant in musth would be twice as perilous.

They entered the forest cover just in time. When the Chao Baa gave the order for dismounting, Akanee didn't offer up his leg. Instead he ambled his body in a confused manner, backing up, moving forward, turning, all the while shaking his head disconcertingly. The oil from the temporal glands was now trickling down the cheeks, leaving a trace that ran down to his mouth. As the elephant staggered around uncontrollably, the Chao Baa had to do all he could to keep from falling off.

"Akanee, song, song!" he repeated, his distress growing. He composed himself and began to chant. The elephant stopped its agitation, and attempted to raise its leg several times, before providing the Chao Baa a chance to get down.

Once on the ground, he made haste to grab the chain on the elephant's back and reel it out. The chain became undone and fell to the ground in a loud jangling, just as the elephant turned its head toward him menacingly. There was a red tint in the brute's eyes, which Saree had warned him signified anger. Struggling to attach the chain to the shackles on the hind legs, a giant foot swung out at him, and the Chao Baa fell to the ground to avoid the blow. The creature whirled and lowered its head, aiming its tusks, but for some reason didn't charge him. Instead, he lifted his head up again and raised his trunk to trumpet maddeningly. The Chao Baa, taking an immense risk, scurried underneath the bulky body with the end of the chain in his hand, wrapped it quickly around the thick ankle, and found the hook just before the creature raised its leg in protest. Running out from under the belly of the beast, he went for the other end of the chain and that's when Akanee charged him. The Chao Baa ran behind a thick tree that shook from the blow of the elephant's head, the tusks protruding from each side of the broad tree trunk, wavering in the air as if searching for him. The animal, however, appeared to be momentarily dazed from the impact, and the Chao Baa worked fast to wrap the chain around the tree and secure it. Then he ran to safety beyond the extent of the tether.

It was a dreadful experience. Roaring, screaming, trumpeting, a deranged Akanee incessantly smashed his head against the tree, while his helpless and pitying master looked on with shock, anguished over the thought that Akanee would fatally injure himself. It took an immeasurable amount of discipline for the Chao Baa to finally still his own emotions and meditate through all the maddening chaos the beast was creating. It wasn't long after, that the tree creaked loudly, then yowled as its wood was being ripped apart. No long able to withstand the battering, it finally fell with a stark crash.

Now lacking an object to vent his frustration, Akanee began fighting with the chain that remained secured to the stump, charging to pull it taught, straining the links until, inevitably, they snapped. Freed of his constraints, the elephant dashed dementedly into the dense jungle, and the Chao Baa, breaking from his chanting, knew there was nothing he could do. The animal's fury was still audible for many minutes, until, after a few anguishing seconds, there remained only a stony silence.

He had lost his elephant.

He continued to chant and meditate, in an effort to dispel the depression that was threatening to overcome him. Taunting voices inside his head reminded him that he had failed. The idea of the Chao Baa was an inane, ludicrous farce. Worse still, was the possibility that the crazed behemoth might kill someone it encountered in the forest, or that the beast would kill itself in its senseless state, and whatever blood that would be spilt would be on his hands. He would have broken a parajika rule and be forced to disrobe. There would be nothing left to him.

Doubt, worry, anxiety, guilt...they were all hindrances to spiritual development, so he tried his best to shut them out. But he couldn't, for he was well aware that this situation was totally his doing, confounded with a purpose that was unclear, even to him, and could only be judged as some vague, selfish, self-serving plan to find expression for his own disappointment at the cards that life had dealt him.

He struggled for two days like this, wandering aimlessly in a state of repentant misgiving, before he resolved to come to his senses and look for food. The last of the rice donated by the villagers was gone. He would have to live on the stems of edible trees and wild tubers.

Using his flint, he made a fire and cooked a broth of herbs and tree bark. Sitting alone in the dark forest, watching the fire flickering and listening to the soft hiss of his soup brewing, he thought how pointless everything was. He couldn't suppress his sense of loss over the elephant, and found it ironic that less than a year ago, in a forest similar to this one, he had been mourning for the loss of his family.

One week passed, and during that week the rains began. The Chao Baa took shelter in a cave, extremely weak from lack of sufficient food. His bodily health, however, wasn't a concern to him, and he even welcomed death. But he also knew that he had a duty to stay alive, and so he did all he could, in a mechanical way, to ensure his survival to the best of his ability. In a few days there would be bamboo shoots and mushrooms sprouting from the forest floor, and he would consume them to sustain himself. Until then, he would pray and meditate.

A few days later, while gathering up the sprouting vegetation, he heard Akanee roaring. It wasn't the maniacal roar of a musth elephant, but of an elephant that smelled and recognized the presence of his mahout.

"Akanee!" he shouted. "Akanee." He followed the bellowing and soon met his elephant trudging laboriously out of the murky forest.

Only someone close to an elephant could ascertain its state by looking at it. Akanee was fatigued and hungry. Most importantly, he had regained his sanity. The red glare in his eyes was gone, replaced by a tired, enfeebled stare.

"I am sorry," the Chao Baa apologized.

That night, the Chao Baa performed the koo-at ceremony, to cleanse the animal of any bad spirits that it might have picked up in its wanderings.

While there was enough food for Akanee, there wasn't enough for the Chao Baa, who was slowly getting weaker. He would have to rely on the strength unleashed by Vipassana meditation, practicing the Four Foundations of Mindfulness, which he found he could easily do while riding atop the gently undulating hulk of his elephant. When the rains were in full swing, food would be more plentiful. However, before embarking any further, the Chao Baa thought it wise to visit and consult the Venerable Kru Jarun, the abbot of the Forest Temple. He knew that a severe castigation was awaiting him, but he also knew that there was an unspoken obligation to report to him. Moreover, there would be some rice and other foods at the temple, which he desperately needed to sustain himself if he was to go much further.

The Chao Baa sat on top of his elephant as they proceeded stolidly through the thick vegetation of the forest, with cataracts of streaming foliage brushing him as they went. The intermittent storms that they got caught up in didn't stop them, and they marched imperturbably into the swirling sheets of rain around them, water dripping off Akanee's tusks and sleeting off his back.

They stuck to the trails, which were no problem for Akanee, even with the mud from the daily rain. Had there been no paths, the elephant would have created one by forging headlong into the forest, knocking down whatever was in the way. The animal had the ability to go through almost impenetrable jungle, and, being exceptionally sure-footed, could climb the most precipitous slopes. The elephant was a perfect mountain vehicle, the Chao Baa concluded, egotistically contented at the brilliance of his own foresight. While reveling in his self-satisfaction, his first confrontation with the Chao Fa was about to unfold.

A bone chilling fog had descended upon them, enshrouding the forest, and before long, Akanee slowed his gait without being told to, pointing his trunk in the air, and then growling. He had smelled men, unfamiliar men. The Chao Baa waited a few moments before urging his elephant to resume the way. The animal agreed to proceed, but kept his trunk in the air, sniffing the area.

It was shortly after that, when moving shadows appeared on the edge of a steep pass, ominous silhouettes outlined against the crags within the diaphanous mist of dawn, slowly coming into focus.

There were about five of them, dressed all in black, with baggy pants and loosely fitted shirts and bulky black turbans on their heads, brandishing M16s.

They were as stunned as he was at this chance encounter. Under more typical circumstances there would have been no hesitation for these rebels to deal harshly with anyone they didn't know, and death would have been a certainty. But they didn't know how to react to such a strange sight.

The Chao Baa quickly seized the moment to his advantage and went on the offensive. "What you do here?" he asked in his broken Hmong. He halted his elephant, as the men stood stuck in their tracks, speechless.

"What are you doing here?" one of them, having recovered from his initial surprise, retorted.

Although a monk should restrain from feeling anger, the Chao Baa took umbrage at the hubris of these men, in spite of his effort to retain equanimity. He understood that the Chao Fa renegades were just as much victims of war as everyone else and consequently suffered from severe mental defilements, yet he was upset that they were so near the Forest Temple. It alarmed him.

"You are Chao Fa," he acknowledged. "But I am Chao Baa, and you are on my land."

At that point, another of them shouted something that was incomprehensible to the Chao Baa. It was something to the effect of 'you crazy monk we will kill you'.

Remembering the advice of Potisat to say as little as possible, he used one of the departing phrases of the Hmong language and made his exit.

"We shall meet again," he said, as he ordered his pachyderm to continue ahead.

It was a fateful moment as they let him depart, the Chao Fa bandits standing stock-still in the road, mouths agape, looking back at the elephant and his bizarre rider.

He had decided that to arrive at the Forest Temple riding an elephant would be too ostentatious an entrance, not in harmony with the serene ambiance required of a monastery, so he tethered Akanee, and walked the rest of the way, about a half-mile, on foot. Luckily, the younger monks were involved in their chanting inside the sim; he discreetly circumvented around the sacred hall to get to the kuti of the Venerable Father.

The sightless old monk knew who it was that had come in to see him, but waited for the Chao Baa to finish making his obligatory prostration.

"Your sense of self has increased since we last met," he bellowed in his typical fashion, belying his frail appearance. "That is not progressing, it is going backwards."

"I am still learning, and practicing, Venerable Father."

"From now on you should address me as Venerable Grandfather. I think it is time that I deserve such a title. I am getting quite old, you know."

"Yes, Venerable Grandfather."

"Come closer, so that I may touch you."

The Chao Baa crawled within touching distance. The old man's hands rubbed across his body.

"Why do you have so many tattoos?" Kru Jarun asked.

"To protect me."

"From what? From delusion? Do you really believe that ink protects you? Only resolute faith can shield you, if you have the strength to possess it."

"I have that as well."

"Do you? Do you presume to have supernatural powers too?

"No, I…"

"Do you feel the white monkey told you to embark on this current charade of yours?"

How did he know all these intimate moments of his life?

"You can see everything, Venerable Grandfather," the Chao Baa acknowledged, "by making your mind one-pointed, and perceiving things that are hidden to ordinary men, so why do you need to taunt me?"

"No, I cannot see everything," Kru Jarun said, "but just because my eyes are rotting, as all compounded things must rot, that does not mean I cannot see anything at all."

There was an embarrassed silence after that.

"So what is the Chao Baa?" the saintly abbot asked, dispelling the pronounced quiet. "Avenging priest, or warrior monk? Either of those is a contradiction in terms."

"But what about the stories in the Pali Canon?" the Chao Baa challenged, "and the Jataka tales, the disciples of the Buddha doing battle with evil giants..."

"Those were stories meant for those unable to grasp the higher truth of the Damma, to provide inspiration for their faith, not as an example to follow."

"What then, are the obligations of a monk?"

"To cultivate goodness," Kru Jarun answered.

"I feel that in my own way, I am cultivating goodness."

"In your own way? Those are significant words, for they are an admission that you are a rogue monk, even a heretic. You, who are so fond of the Jataka stories, would do well to recall the fate of Devadatta." Devadatta was a relative of the Buddha, whom he tried to kill in order to form his own version of the Buddhist Church.

The old man paused to make a sour face. "You should be disrobed."

"Forgive me, Venerable Grandfather..."

"...but I know," he went on, not willing to hear any appeal, "that should I advocate your dismissal from the Sangha, I would be opposed, for even though the state has disengaged itself from the church, I perceive that this matter has the support of certain highly placed people. You are a politician it seems, as well as a monk. Or maybe just a politician."

"Forgive me..."

"There is no forgiveness, so there should be no guilt. It is only

Karma."

"Then you agree that it is my Karma?"

"Yes, but be heedful. It may well be bad Karma."

A lapse ensued in their discourse, as the Chao Baa had nothing further to say in defense of himself. "May I receive some food here at the temple?"

"Yes, and your beast of burden as well, which, by the way, I permit you to bring here into the temple grounds."

Naturally, he knew about the elephant.

"Yes, Venerable Grandfather. Let him browse first."

"We shall feed him rice and bananas, for he is a special creature, beloved by the Buddha, who experienced its existence in a previous life."

"Yes, Venerable Grandfather."

"You willingly expose it to danger, while involving yourself in the mundane foils of men. If you cause its death, you will have created a great sin."

"Yes, Venerable Grandfather." He could see that the abbot was still angry with him, so he changed the subject, attempting to mollify his irritation. "Excuse me, Venerable Grandfather, but I have a gift for you which I wish to place on your head."

"What is it?"

"Spectacles."

"But I cannot see, with or without them, and so, what is their purpose?"

"They are 'sun-glat'."

"What kind of spectacles are those?"

"They are dark."

"Why? To hide my eyes?"

"Yes."

"Why? Are my eyes repulsive?"

"Yes."

"Good. They provide an effective opportunity to practice mindfulness concerning aversion."

Baa made his exit as the astonished Hmong villagers watched him and his elephant saunter into the woods.

Clearing the upland valleys hadn't been an easy exercise, for some of the trees that had taken root in the fallow fields were already too firm to be mowed down by the flailer, even with Akanee as the motive force behind it. They had, on many occasions, needed to tie ropes around them and uproot them using Akanee's great strength, and the ones that could be salvaged the Chao Baa would replant at the edges of the meadows. This particular spot where they were now verging upon didn't appear too difficult, for the larger trees were widely spaced, and the flailer could probably make it through most of the area without removing them. The bushes in between them normally posed no problems.

Once the flailer was re-assembled, he placed the cushion of beaten bark on Akanee's head and securely hitched the harness, and, after mounting him, gave the command, "Nangut!"

Akanee planted his feet firmly, then lunged forward with all his weight to drive the bomb clearer over the bramble and thicket in front. The Chao Baa ordered him to back up and move forward again. They would repeat this maneuver until the patch was bare enough for the whipping chains to be effective. It was tedious work, and it would probably take several weeks to clear this valley.

An hour into this hard labor, Akanee paused to emit a low growl. Someone was approaching. The Chao Baa looked up and noticed distant figures working in the swidden fields on the hillsides. "It is alright Akanee, they are just villagers in their fields. Nangut!" And without further ado, the pair continued their labor.

Soon it began to drizzle, and the dark clouds colliding into the mountain peaks foretold of heavier rain on the way.

Akanee stopped his task abruptly and shook his head up and down, still apparently troubled, prompting the Chao Baa to survey his surroundings. Amidst the hillside vegetation he spotted a troupe of men making their way down a mountain on their eastern flank, a boy holding a flag leading the way, which made it easy to follow them with his eyes, despite the group's intermittent disappearance in the cover of the shrubs. Their gait indicated that they were carrying weapons. He hastily disengaged the harness from the elephant's head and ordered him to turn and walk towards the oncoming party. The time had arrived for the inevitable showdown.

Marching slowly in their direction, he noted the sensation of adrenaline causing his heartbeat to accelerate and his breathing to become rapid. "Feeling nervous," he recited to himself, hoping to make his mind still. He knew that Akanee was feeling the same tenseness.

"Easy, Akanee. If we do this right, we'll only have to do it once. I will try to keep you out of harm's way."

The strange group had reached the valley floor and was now in more open ground. Still, the Chao Baa and his elephant continued to walk forward to meet them. The boy leading them stopped to plant the flag in the ground, and the Chao Baa knew that this signaled the imminent attack. He directed Akanee to wait and hold ground.

There were nine of them and he could make out their guns now — eight looked like M16s, and one was an AK-47. While any one bullet might not prove fatal to his elephant, a fusillade could inflict lethal injuries, especially considering that the medicinal herbs of the forest might not be sufficient to prevent septicemia, a leading cause of death for Asian elephants.

Akanee shifted his feet uneasily and snorted.

"Hold it," the Chao Baa instructed.

They were bringing their weapons to shoulder height, continuing to advance.

Akanee resumed jogging from foot to foot, his trunk fluttering nervously.

"Hold it," the Chao Baa repeated.

The men drew closer, and when he guessed that he and Akanee were within the range of accuracy of the enemy's weapons, he outstretched his arms as if in supplication to the sky and tilted his head back as far as it could go. By doing this, he would be tempting them to aim for the chest.

"I AM CHAO BAA!" he screamed to the heavens. Then, for added effect, he began to babble in the forest spirit language that Kwan Saree had taught him.

The Chao Fa guerillas took aim and let loose with a burst of automatic fire.

Almost immediately, a heavy thud hit his chest, as if he had been struck with a battering ram, and he was forcibly swept off the elephant to land in the bushes, suddenly unable to breathe. Akanee instinctively flew into a murderous rage and charged at the black garbed figures, who then ran for their lives, a few of them throwing down their guns in their panicked flight.

The Chao Baa, in profound pain, struggled to get up. He knew that Akanee, going at thirty miles an hour, would overrun them and thrash at least one to death. He couldn't allow that. Unable even to draw in a breath, he applied his full mental strength to holler out "YUT!"

Akanee slowed his rush and cantered to a halt.

"Ma ni! Ma ni! Come here!"

The elephant struggled to bridle his own instincts for defense, giving his head an abrupt shake, before eventually succumbing to an impalpable trust he had developed for his master. With reluctant resignation, he turned slothfully around to return.

The Chao Baa made an effort to walk, but the discomfort in his chest was debilitating. A rib or two was probably broken, and perhaps his left lung had collapsed, because it hurt so much to breathe. Nevertheless, the amulets had saved his life. Despite his injured state, he wanted to pursue his assailants, to finish this once and for all, to strike them with such terror that they would never think of challenging him again.

"Mop!" he requested of Akanee, now standing next to him. This was the easy way to get up, as the elephant bowed down, enabling his rider to crawl upon his neck.

Slowly, with painstaking effort, the Chao Ba slid his body over the great animal's hide. "Bai!"

He could see them scrambling up the slope. The boy was clinging on the neck of one of them, the child most likely frightened out of his wits, and the burden caused the man carrying him to trail behind. They were the logical ones to go after, and assuming that the boy was a shaman, he would make a prized catch. He would take this underage priest away from the Chao Fa and turn him back into a little boy.

He ordered Akanee to proceed at a swift stride, and the animal trotted toward their quarry. Reaching the slopes, the elephant effortlessly trampled over the bushes to make a beeline towards the pair clambering up the rugged ground. The Chao Baa held his injured side, as the jostling shot sharp pangs of agony into his chest.

After only minutes, they had already gained on them considerably, the man and boy being no match for an elephant in rugged terrain. The Chao Baa signaled with his feet to slow down. Akanee fell into a more relaxed pace, as the hunted strove frantically to escape their hunters. When the shadow of the great pachyderm loomed over them, the man stopped and turned to face them, holding the sniveling boy close to his chest. The Chao Baa checked his elephant to stand in front of them.

"Give me boy!" the Chao Baa demanded in broken Hmong. He was making a great effort in hiding his pain, which would reveal the truth about his ordinary mortality and sabotage the façade of invulnerability.

"No! Spare him! Kill me only!" the man pleaded. The kid was clutching on to him for dear life, bawling his head off.

"I no kill," the Chao Baa told him.

The man's face opened up into an expression of incredulity. "I know you!" he shouted in Lao language. "You remember me?"

The Chao Baa, upon closer examination, did indeed recognize him. "Yes. I don't remember your name, but I know your face. We were together in Camp 07."

"Yes, my name is Ly Feng."

"Mop!" he told his elephant, and Akanee bowed down, enabling the Chao Baa to disembark. He stood face to face with the Chao Fa fighter. "They released you?"

Ly Feng put the boy down, who restrained his crying, sensing that perhaps he was no longer in grave danger. Still, he held on to the man's leg.

"No," Ly Feng admitted. "I was transferred to a Mobile Work Force. Remember the advice you gave me, about being nice to the Hmong guard? I followed it, and we became friends. He helped me by saying good things to the Commandant and I was re-located."

"How did you get out?"

"They let you go out, if you ask permission. So I asked them to let me go to my home village to get married and see my sick uncle and they agreed, but told me to come back in one week. But I didn't go back."

"You joined the Chao Fa instead?"

"Yes."

"That was a mistake. I cannot let you go."

The Hmong guerilla looked down at the young boy, before returning his gaze. "What will you do with us?"

"I will take you to a village just south of here. You will remain there in the custody of the headman. The boy also."

Ly Feng gazed earnestly at the Chao Baa. "Your powers are increased. Now you are immortal. At least two bullets struck your heart, yet you are alive."

The Chao Baa made no comment upon that statement. "Let us go now," he enjoined, "for I am in haste. You will tell me where the Chao Fa encampment is, the one you came from, and who your leader is."

The headman, Moua Tor, was ardently cooperative in taking the two Chao Fa into his charge, and moreover, he behooved all the villagers into donating food to the farang monk and his brave tusker.

Fortunately for Akanee, the Hmong grew as much corn as they did rice, so that he was able to get a special treat, for corn was among the elephant's most favorite foods. There was nearly two hundred pounds of it. This time, though, the Chao Baa would ensure that Akanee wouldn't overindulge in high calorie foodstuffs by regulating such desserts, for he didn't want the both of them to go through another musth episode.

But the severity of the journey that was before them would limit the likelihood that Akanee would have any surplus energy available to get lustful, as the route they were going to take was straight up and down three mountains. The Chao Baa knew this was a route that an ordinary man wouldn't embark upon, for although it was a shorter distance than skirting the shoulders of the slopes, it would actually take longer (for a human) because of the arduousness of the topography. Perhaps, it wasn't even possible. For an elephant, however, this wasn't a relevant consideration. Akanee could go straight up the steepest mountain. Thus, the strategy was to 'head'em off at the pass'. The flailer was to be left in the village for the time being, as the task of dealing with the armed renegades had now become the immediate priority.

The Chao Baa had been in great pain for quite a while. Because he had to interact with other people while in the village, the most he could do was to suppress any outward show of his discomfort by taking short breaths and gritting his teeth. Now that he was alone with Akanee, he could remove the upper portion of his robe and inspect his wounds. There were two large, dark-purple welts on each side of his chest, indicating the impact of the thick amulets that had been struck. One amulet was partially shattered and the marks on his skin indicated that there was some shrapnel imbedded. Ly Feng was right. Two bullets had met the target. He had been lucky. Nevertheless, he would have to apply some of the special ointment he kept with him to prevent his wounds going septic, and to practice the Four Foundations of Mindfulness to deal with the pain, while trusting to the automatic pilot of his elephant.

Passively mounted upon Akanee's back, his goal was to thoroughly remove all the negative stimuli. "Feeling pain," he noted to himself, taking deeper breaths that provoked the irritation in his sore ribs. Less than two hours later, the agony had subsided.

They had already reached the first mountain pass when the clouds that had been threatening all day finally decided to pour forth. The battering rain soaked everything and created a horrendous din, but it didn't affect their progress in any way; Akanee plodding on in stolid persistency, with the Chao Baa on top of him, sopping wet, chanting sacred prayers sonorously in Pali.

The descent was, in contrast to the placid tenacity of the pair, a bit exciting. The grade was steep, the soil slippery. The 'elephant fly', the Chao Baa would later refer to Akanee, alluding to his sticky footholds in the slickest muck and the severest incline. Down they went; slowly, surely, definitely. Once in the flat, forested valley below, the Chao Baa told Akanee to go faster. He wasn't afraid of overworking his beast, as the temperature was cool and damp, and he would push him as much as he deemed feasible. Besides, there was a well-worn trail here, which meant that the path was safe from bombies. There may not be any more trails ahead, he reckoned, so it was better to take advantage of them now. The track climbed up the other side, and they resumed following it as the rain died down to a drizzle. The path ended at a spring in the mountainside, providing Akanee the opportunity to guzzle his daily requirement of thirty gallons of water. Herein, they were in no-man's land.

The Chao Baa and Akanee had been involved in the task of bombi clearing for almost a year now. Akanee had by this time acquired the ability to scent out the plastic and chemical filler of the cluster bomb units. They were composed of synthetic organic compounds that became volatile in the hot tropical sun, producing vapors undetectable to a human nose, but were a foul-smelling odor to the keen olfactory senses of the elephant. So, in a sense, they sniffed their way through the thick mountain jungle, the elephant's trunk probing the ground vigorously as if it was an independent organism.

According to the lectures of Kwan Saree, an elephant 'saw' the world outside through its senses of smelling and hearing, and so could remember a place just by the way it smelled and sounded. To this purpose, Akanee would swing his trunk and flap his ears, analyzing the subtle yet telltale scents and noises of his environment, adding details to the map in his head. When Akanee was confident enough, they would trudge ahead, unstoppable, the Chao Baa sitting on his neck, chanting prayers unceasingly; *Namo tasso arahato...Namo tasso...bhagavato... samma... sammabuddhasa...* The elephant was more than accustomed to listening to his master's resonant droning; and in fact, it actually soothed him.

Reaching the shelf near the summit of mountain number two, the Chao Baa decided that a rest stop was in order, and he took the opportunity of surveying the land around them. It was about an hour before sunset, and the sun was a red ball burning through the fragile cloud cover in the west, casting a soft light that burnished row upon row of razor-edged summits that swept in every direction, making them shine a mellow gold. From his seat on top of the elephant, he looked at the glorious scenery around him. Before he could stifle it, he was touched by a slight sensation of euphoria.

"I do not need to feel such happiness," he said to himself, looking at the lavish display that confronted him. He turned around slowly, painfully, and reached into the huge reed-woven basket strapped to Akanee's back and took out several ears of corn and some cassava tubers. The elephant coiled his trunk backwards, eagerly accepting the delicacies, emitting a high-pitched squawk that indicated his happiness. After the snack, they would descend into the jungle below and camp out where Akanee could browse.

An hour later they stopped, a quarter of the way down. The Chao Baa felt guilty when he tethered Akanee. The animal hadn't only shown loyalty, but risked his life by going after the armed men who had intended to cause harm to his master.

"Enjoy it, my faithful friend," he said, as the elephant extended its trunk to accept another snack.

While an elephant does take some naps when it is standing idle, it really only lies down to sleep for about four hours a day, from around midnight until the early hours before dawn. That was all the sleep that the Chao Baa needed as well, so by four-thirty in the morning they were on their way again.

Down the mountain, through the highland fog, and across the valley. This valley was narrower than the one of yesterday, and much more difficult to get through. They trod cautiously, the elephant smelling their way around the bombed-out area, while the Chao Baa murmured his customary Buddhist scriptures. They rested for only a few minutes by a stream, enough time for Akanee to drink his fill.

Up on the other side, it was approaching mid-afternoon, but still the sun didn't show itself. Instead, the sky grew darker, and it began to rain. In due course, it became quite tempestuous. Still, they ambled on ahead, reaching just below the summit of mountain number three. But this was where their trek was apparently blocked by a seemingly insurmountable obstacle.

Between this peak and the next, there was a formidable chasm. Sheer limestone cliffs dominated the side of the mountain that they were on, and getting to the valley beyond, where Ly Feng had told him the Chao Fa had encamped, seemed impossible.

He studied the precipice below them. To their right, the rock face bulged outward into a gentler angle, and while it could be a bit scary, it was definitely possible given Akanee's sure-footedness. Where that part of the mountain ended, the chasm narrowed into a fissure, which he judged to be forty or fifty feet across. Whether a thousand feet or ten feet, it was just as impassable.

No, that wasn't quite true, he realized. He ordered Akanee to turn around and re-enter the forest they had just come out of. Once they were back in thick jungle, he stopped and got down, but this time he didn't bother to tether his animal.

He walked around for a bit, until he found what he was looking for. It was a tree, one that he had never bothered to learn the name of, yet it was one that he saw often. It stood nearly one hundred feet high and was bare of branches except at the very top, which he figured he and Akanee could sidestep once they were over on the other side. Its impressively thick trunk promised sufficient strength. Yes, this will do, he decided. He knelt down and said prayers to the tree, asking forgiveness for having to kill it and knock it down. While this act was totally in accordance with Buddhist principles, it was actually a placation typical of the hill tribes, notably the Hmong.

As Akanee munched away on leaves and wild fruits, the Chao Baa, using his flint, started a fire at the foot of the tree that would dry out and weaken the sturdy trunk. The bark singed black, then caught fire. He retrieved an axe from his sack of tools and, struggling with his pain, hacked away making notches all around the trunk to further weaken the wood. He kept the fire going most of the night.

In the morning, he had Akanee pull it down. It wasn't easy, as the Chao Baa had to augment the elephant's efforts by further chopping with his axe. It took over three hours of hard work, but in the end, the tree submitted. It couldn't withstand the power of an elephant that had been used to dragging one and a half tons. The tree didn't come dashing down, but rather stumbled to its knees, so to speak, slipping off its weakened base, then inclining until it got caught up in the canopy of the adjoining trees. It had to be pulled down to the ground, a task that Akanee was equally capable of.

Hauling it wasn't normally a problem either for this mighty beast. Except this time they were going down a rock face, and the log continually tried to roll away. The Chao Baa had to bind it crosswise, securing both ends with chains so that it was dragged broadside, which tended to reduce its errant wanderings. They descended carefully, the obtuse angle downwards affecting him with vertigo, but which didn't appear to disturb the elephant. They were heading for a spot where a lone craggy tree stood. They would need this tree as well, to help position the log that would be their bridge.

Making the situation more treacherous was the weather, as the calm morning, in repeat of yesterday's pattern, changed into a violent afternoon. The wind picked up, and the sky started to rage with an awesome outburst; the flashes from the thunderbolts, fervidly engaged in the electric swordplay above them, were blinding in their intensity, and the clattering that followed was equally heart stopping.

When they got as close as they could to the rim of the cliff, the Chao Baa ordered Akanee to turn around in a tight circle so that the log would be positioned near the edge, roughly perpendicular to the crevasse. He disembarked and reeled out the chain from the elephant's back and secured one end around the leading portion of the log, the tip closest to the cliff. This was to be the anchor line, the other end of which he loosely wrapped around the lone tree. As soon as it was coiled round the tree he pulled on the chain until there was sufficient length to attach it firmly to Akanee's shoulder harness. Thus, the chain formed a crude tackle line, a narrow loop that ran from the far end of the log, once around the tree, and running forward again fastened to the elephant. He realized that he had to make bushings to allow the chain to slip around the tree trunk. Trimming some of the harder branches off the log, he whittled them with his knife, fashioning them into smooth cylinders, which he subsequently inserted in the ring around the tree.

The idea was for Akanee to push the log towards the cliff with his head, while the anchor line would prevent the log from nosing down and plummeting into the canyon, even after a considerable length had cleared the ground and would be hanging in midair. This shouldn't be too difficult, he reckoned, as the lighter, tapered end was the leading end, while the heavier base would remain on the side that they were now on.

The lightning and thunder continued their tumultuous movements, attempting to rip the sky apart. The Chao Baa worked in haste, for the rain had yet to come, and he would dread making the crossing under wet conditions.

"Nangut!"

Akanee bent his massive head down, and with it, shoved the log forward, the chain slipping around the tree trunk in jerky movements. So far, the rigging appeared to be working satisfactorily.

"Nangut!"

Akanee repeated the motion, pushing with his head, again and again, the far end of the log gradually moving forward and rising up at an angle with every nudge as the anchor line grew taut, and it wasn't long before the log had edged over the brim.

The Chao Baa had to be sure of the distances, however. For this to work, the anchor line needed to be kept taut, and this was achieved by the pulling action of the elephant as he advanced in the direction of the gorge. If, however, Akanee were to run out of room and reach the brink before the log spanned the gap, the log would dip down and dangle uselessly. Given the system that he had set up, it would be difficult to resolve such a predicament, a scenario that could possibly endanger his elephant's life; and his as well.

"Nangut!"

As it turned out, the Chao Baa had calculated correctly. The leading end arrived on the other side, the log tilting at a thirty-degree angle above the ground, and so now the anchor line could be slackened by having the elephant walk backwards. The log plopped down into place, albeit rolling somewhat askew. This could be corrected by Akanee pushing it at a compensating angle, which he was subsequently ordered to do.

This feat, as remarkable as it seemed, was something that Kwan Saree had demonstrated to the Chao Baa during his training and was an assignment that Akanee had performed previously on a few occasions in his logging career.

But how strong was this impromptu catwalk? Could it hold up under the weight of a five-ton elephant?

The moment of truth therefore, came when they had to venture across it. The foul weather persisted in acting against them, as the storm in the mountains now grew more turbulent, with the rain finally starting to hammer down.

"Bai, bai!" he screamed above the roar of the elements.

One step, two steps...the animal never hesitated and soon all four legs were upon the log. The huge beast gingerly made its way forward, and now they were about to reach the end of the ground and the beginning of the canyon.

A brilliant flash, and then—bang! A great crash of thunder shook the mountains. Raindrops pelted them with stinging ferocity. As they advanced, suspended over the abyss, the Chao Baa thought he could hear the wood creak. "Feeling fear," he kept reciting to himself, and then began to chant in earnest.

Step by step, one huge foot over the other, the wind whipping at them as they inched their way, they proceeded, precariously hovering in space. The Chao Baa stopped his chanting, amazed at the composure of this magnificent animal, crossing the sky on a log that a human would be shimmying in sheer terror. He eyed the chasm beneath them, aghast at the depth of it. Another flash of lightning lit the rocky scene below, and he was filled with momentous exhilaration, drunk with a thrill that drowned all his fears, and gave him an adrenaline rush that he hadn't experienced since he had been a combatant in the war...

The heavens lit up with another bolt of raw electricity and trembled with another resounding peal. Gusts of air and rain slapped at them, as the elephant treaded his way on the narrow walkway with unwavering certitude, only one false step away from plunging thousands of feet.

There was no doubt in the Chao Baa's mind now that they would make it. They were already halfway across, and the second half of this perilous passage went by so quickly that he found himself wishing that there had been more. As they arrived on the other side, the elephant casually stepped off the log and continued on solid ground. Akanee, strolling nonchalantly with a bearing of unruffled demeanor, was nothing short of spectacular.

Perhaps it was the fact that he had been alone with Akanee in the forest for so long, or maybe it was due to the intense emotional experiences they had just been through, that precipitated the Chao Baa in having a long, one-sided conversation with his elephant.

"You follow me blindly. You don't know why, you only do as I say. You risk your life on my command, never questioning. Your faith and courage are greater than my own."

It was a struggle to speak; yet it helped take his mind off the oppressive pain in his chest that he had to incessantly control.

The elephant looked at him for a moment, before arching his trunk upwards to pull down a branch to eat. The animal's tough hide rippled in response to troublesome insects, as if it were an indifferent gesture of dismissal at the Chao Baa's sentimental babbling.

"Who are you? Are you a great being? You are capable of such mindful concentration, surpassing the greatest monk, trusting in your own Karma. Are you a thevada?" A thevada was a Buddhist angel.

The elephant gave no notice that he was being spoken to, concerned instead with filling his stomach.

"No wonder you are revered."

In his initial plans, he had considered the elephant as a mere means to an end, like a truck, or a piece of machinery. He hadn't had the foresight to consider the possibility that he would get to love the animal. Guilt and sadness swept over him as he sat himself on the ground, engulfed in this emotional dilemma. While brooding in self-pity, he felt the elephant's trunk lightly tapping his head and then giving him playful slaps on the face, as if to cheer him up. He stood up and stroked Akanee's trunk. The animal opened its mouth wide, entreating his human master to pet his thick pink tongue.

Still caressing his beastly companion, he was suddenly impelled to perform the ba-see ceremony to further bind their souls together. He retrieved his begging bowl, and inside it he placed two ears of corn and the last of the bananas, which by now were mushy and overripe. He attached the sacred string to the bowl and held it in his right hand, and with his left hand upon the elephant's flank, recited the hallowed words.

"You are my kindred spirit," he told the animal when the ritual was concluded.

The elephant raised his head, exhaled hard, and then laboriously raised himself up onto his feet. The Chao Baa was already awake.

"It is time for us to go, my brother."

There had been no rain since they had crossed the chasm between the mountains. The sound of the crickets dominated the dark waning night, while the stars burned brightly in the absence of the moon. Slowly, deliberately, the Chao Baa and his elephant quietly descended the side of the mountain in the direction of the bandits' camp.

As they drew nearer to the base of the hill, Akanee, as expected, hesitated. The Chao Baa gently prodded him with his feet. It was nearing sunrise, which, in the contrary world of the dangerous jungle spirits was bedtime for the troublesome ghosts, and the Hmong warriors had deemed it safe to light the morning fire. This helped in locating their approximate position. Through a dense mist that concealed everything around them, the smell of wood smoke became perceptible, and soon after, low voices could be heard.

This was close enough, he decided. He parked his elephant momentarily.

"Yang Jou! I am Chao Baa," he yelled out into the foggy dawn. "I take your shaman. I take boy! Now I come for you!"

The muted mutterings that had been heard previously were replaced by baffled expletives, punctuated by a few distraught shouts. The men at the camp were shocked, since the party of executioners they had sent six days ago hadn't yet returned, and even if they had been unsuccessful, it took at least four days to reach here. How did this man come upon them so quickly?

After his ominous pronouncements, the Chao Baa decided to circle around. Stealthily, man and elephant ambled off to the south through an obscure cover of fog. Stationing themselves in this new spot, he repeated his warnings, "I am coming for you, for all of you, so you may be punished for misdeeds!" He then resumed perambulating around them in a great circle, stopping only to give an occasional shout.

"I am Chao Baa! Put down guns and leave here, or you get punished!"

He didn't know how long he would have to taunt them like this before they would leave the area, but he estimated that he had at least two days until the others, the ones he had frightened off during the first encounter, would arrive.

With sanguine patience, he played this game for several hours, and he admitted that, as wicked as it was, he was enjoying himself. He correctly surmised that the Chao Fa would be too frightened to come out and look for him. As noon approached, however, he resolved to remain quiet, and thus give them a chance to think about abandoning their camp.

It wasn't long after that he heard the loud cawing of a bird. He didn't think much of this at the time, though as it transpired, it was a significant event. Some would consider it luck or mere coincidence, while others who see a deeper meaning to things would call it fate, or divine intervention, or perhaps, Karma. For the bird that was screeching was none other than the Poosu, a great black eagle of the jungle, which the Hmong consider such a dangerous spirit, that to utter its name or even think about it, was simply not done. Its presence invariably signaled death.

Inertly seated on his elephant, he heard a commotion in the camp, and then noted that the voices were trailing away. Were they coming after him, going in the wrong direction, or had they decided to depart for good?

After an hour of hearing only nondescript forest sounds, he elected to chance it and encroach upon the camp. It was a cleared area, with the remnants of the fire in the middle. No one was around. He and his elephant hid among the trees, waiting. But by the time dusk came he was sure they wouldn't come back.

On that night, the Chao Baa thought it best to tether Akanee. He couldn't afford him wandering off in the event that some of the guerillas returned in the morning. If those that had vacated their bivouac caught up with the hit squad on their way back, they could either set off together for another destination, or regroup to return here in full force, encouraged by their increased numbers. There was nothing to do but wait.

The second day passed without anyone showing up, yet the waiting was unnerving. He was on vigilant guard until the sun went down. The fact that people were afraid to walk at night in the jungle was convenient, allowing Akanee to browse and he to chant, meditate, and sleep.

By mid-morning of the next day, Akanee smelt something in the air. Because undue noise was taboo while journeying through the wilderness, the Hmong bandits would be quiet, making it difficult to hear them coming. Although he had spotted two distinct trails that led to the campsite it was still difficult to predict exactly where the men would appear. It was only through Akanee's phenomenal sense of hearing and smell, and the Chao Baa's understanding of his elephant's behavior, that the trajectory of the enemy's approach was discerned. At first the animal would walk in the opposite direction desired, attempting to avoid them, until he understood that his master actually wanted him to follow the scents and sounds.

And sure enough, the men that had been sent to kill him inevitably spilled out of the jungle growth and came face to face with the magical monk and his fantastic creature. They gasped in fright, then turned around to flee. Akanee, upon the Chao Baa's command, pointed his trunk in the air, letting go with an ear-shattering shriek, trumpeting his defiance. The elephant's triumphant war cry echoed in the hills, bouncing back repeatedly.

"I AM CHAO BAA!" screamed the invincible monk.

None of the jungle fighters stuck around to hear anymore, but ran helter-skelter, stumbling and blundering their way through the thick forest, trying to get the hell out of there.

Accounts of this incident would later spread like wildfire throughout the Plain of Jars, and the most popular version recounted how the Chao Baa and his elephant flew over the mountains to chase the Chao Fa. It was the only way they could explain the strange pair appearing in two distant places within such a short span of time. For nearly a year after that event, no Chao Fa were seen anywhere in the vicinity.

Sousat was alerted by shrill cries coming from the sentries below. He grabbed his AK-47 before running urgently out the door, dressed only in his pakima. It was nearing sunset, an unlikely time for a Chao Fa attack, but you could never be certain.

However, the hubbub wasn't due to Chao Fa rebels. It was the reaction to a large male elephant walking into the compound, carrying the limp body of a man in its pair of long curved tusks. The animal came to a halt and tenderly deposited the robed figure upon the ground. It then walked backwards a few steps and waited.

It was only after Sousat had gone to the unconscious man on the ground that the others warily drew near.

"Bring water!" Sousat yelled.

A bowl of water was brought, and the army Captain dumped it on the Chao Baa's face. The afflicted man opened his eyes. "Sou...sat."

"Save your strength. Do not talk. I will take you to Ponsavan immediately."

The Chao Baa grabbed Sousat's arm. "The elephant, must...come with me," he gasped out, his voice slurred with pain. "Must hide us...no one should know."

"Understood. We will take a troop transport truck and cover it with a canvas over the frame."

The night had firmly entrenched itself by the time they departed, Akanee and three hundred pounds of fodder hidden in the bed of the truck, the Chao Baa in the cab leaning deliriously against Sousat.

Once in Ponsavan the patient was attended to by an army doctor, who insisted that X-rays were mandatory. The Chao Baa, in his frail condition, was required to deal with the elephant, getting the beast to disembark from the truck and cajoling him to be tied up in the army compound by strange men. Leaving the elephant there, they proceeded in the dead of night to the home of the radiologist working at Ponsavan hospital, woke him up, and together they surreptitiously entered the hospital to take the X-rays. Both the X-ray technician and the army doctor, just like the soldiers stationed at Ta Vieng, were sworn to secrecy.

The Chao Baa was clandestinely kept at the army base to recuperate. No ribs were broken, but the severe contusions he had suffered had caused a substantial amount of swelling that impaired his breathing. His shrapnel wounds were infected and had led to a fever. He was also undernourished and dehydrated. He was put on a drip and given powerful anti-inflammatory drugs, and within two weeks he was back on his feet.

Within that time, his flailer had been found in the field where he had been attacked and was brought to Ponsavan, since Sousat didn't want him to return to the southern rim of Tung Hai Hin. Instead, he requested the Chao Baa, once he had finished his convalescence, to work in the northeast quadrant and clear the area of bombs and bandits where many of his kinsfolk, the Black Tai, were settled. The Chao Baa unequivocally agreed to do this, glad to be able to repay Sousat in this small way.

While working in that area, there were a few dramatic confrontations similar to the earlier ones in the south, but nobody shot at him. After a few months of playing cat and mouse with the Chao Fa, the rebels left this locality as well, and he was free to clean up the bombed valleys. The overall success of the Chao Baa stratagem now figured prominently in Sousat's career, and another promotion seemed imminent.

The legendary monk and his elephant stayed in the north for eleven months. But eventually the Chao Baa wanted to return to the area around his once existing home of Ban Ling Kao. Not only was his work there as yet unfinished, but Chao Fa renegades had once again become active in the surrounding hills. And so, another furtive drive under the cover of night delivered the monk and his elephant to the district of Ta Vieng.

The fact that the Chao Baa was active on one side of the Plain of Jars and then the other further kindled the rumors concerning his mythical powers. To show up mysteriously here and there, many miles away, without any witness to his passage in the exposed lowlands, lent additional credence to the hypothesis that the saintly monk and his magical elephant flew across the sky.

In the meantime, Sousat had a small house built for him at the edge of the forest, less than a day's walk from the army outpost at Ta Vieng. He needed a home, Sousat insisted, and he shouldn't be perpetually wandering around the jungles like a vagabond savage. At first the Chao Baa resisted Sousat's proposal, saying that he wasn't a vagabond savage, but a forest monk who had given up the material world. Nonsense, Sousat refuted. There was a need to rest from time to time, for, despite what everybody else thought, the Chao Baa was only human.

At the beginning of 1990, Sousat was promoted to the rank of Major. He would take up a more comfortable posting in the provincial capital of Ponsavan in three months' time. Until then, he would remain in Ta Vieng and continue to secure the area while waiting for his replacement.

The house in the forest turned out to be a wise proposal, the Chao Baa finally reckoned, for he himself was beginning to feel his age. He wasn't a young man anymore, and since Akanee seemed at home in the surrounding forest (the elephant was never tethered again), the duo would indeed take rest spells there, which would provide the Chao Baa the opportunity to indulge in his meditation. Besides, there was a vantage point nearby that afforded a view of the valley where Ban Ling Kao was once nestled in.

It was during one such rest period that Sousat arrived on a motorcycle.

"Sabai dee, Major Sousat," the Chao Baa greeted, teasingly stressing Sousat's new rank as he approached.

Sousat didn't respond with the expected smile. Rather, his face was corrugated with deep concern. "I am glad I have found you," he stated without ado, as he dismounted.

"I know what you are going to tell me. There are reports of renewed Chao Fa activity. I heard about what happened near Ta Thom."

The Major shook his head. "No, it is not that. We have already dealt with that problem." He hesitated gravely before his announcement. "There is someone from America who wishes to talk to you."

This statement had a noticeable effect on the Chao Baa, sending shudders down his spine, and he couldn't hide his apprehension from Sousat, who, for the first time that he could remember, actually saw the Chao Baa's face become pale with fright.

"Who is this person?" the Chao Baa asked, vainly attempting to prop up a front of imperturbable aplomb.

"It is a woman who thinks you know something about her son. He was a pilot. She found his dog tag in a cave on Pu Khe."

Sousat watched disbelievingly as the Chao Baa seemed to be afflicted with speechless emotion, revealing that indeed, he knew something. It was embarrassing to see the monk's expression crumple, to look at him swallowing hard, putting a trembling hand to his mouth. Sousat was relieved when the Chao Baa eventually turned around to hide his face.

"You know about this?" Sousat persisted in asking. "His name was...let me see...An-droo..." Sousat took out a folded sheet of paper from his shirt pocket. "Here, you read it. It has been a long time since I have read English writing."

"No, I don't need to read it," the Chao Baa said without turning to face him. He then clasped his hands behind his back and walked a few paces away. He stopped, but remained silent.

"What should we do about the woman?" Sousat asked.

The Chao Baa couldn't answer him. After all these years, he kept thinking to himself, all these years…all these years of joy and suffering and inner meaning, divorced from a past he had long since stopped believing ever existed, a previous life that he had been convinced was dead and expired. It was as if he had scaled a high mountain, only to fall just before reaching the summit, to descend with breakneck acceleration back to where he started. How could this be, after twenty-one years?

No, it is best if she didn't know, for her own sake as well as his.

"What should we do about this woman?" Sousat repeated, now growing impatient. He wanted to get back before dark.

The Chao Baa took a few more steps away from Major Sousat, his hands still clasped behind his back, his orange robes swaying about his body as he walked, and with his head bowed in deep pensiveness. He halted stiffly, pausing to give out a barely audible sigh of vacillation, as he looked up at the forest around him, a forest that had once appeared serene and soothing, but now loomed dark and somber. The mountains behind his crude timber dwelling seemed to stare down at him with scorn, as if admonishing him for a life of lies. Now he was about to tell another. It wasn't a *parajika* violation, which would mean disrobement, but one that he could cleanse himself of during a *sadeng abat* ceremony.

"I will need to meditate upon this, before I can give you my decision."

"How long will that take?"

"You will sleep here, if that's what you are concerned about."

Sousat wasn't happy about this. Yet he realized that this was something serious, and perhaps it did, in fact, require some thought.

The Major was woken up before dawn. Sousat was still rubbing the sleep from his eyes when the Chao Baa announced, "You will tell her that her son was killed by the CIA, because he crashed his plane on purpose and ran away. I was a witness to his murder. They took his body, but I don't know what they did with it. I ran away after that because I knew they would kill me too, and therefore I do not wish to have any contact with Americans because I fear for my life. Tell her to forget the past, as I try to do. You will tell her verbally, as I do not wish to write a message."

Sousat ceased rubbing his eyes to look at him hard. "It is very bad for a monk to lie."

The Chao Baa didn't refute that. "Go quickly, do not delay her any longer."

After Sousat left, a difficult time of mental and emotional struggle followed. The Chao Baa no longer knew what was right, or what was wrong. He felt trapped in a no-win situation. A falsehood can protect as well as harm. What good would the truth do in this situation? It couldn't repeal what had happened, but only bring pain, a pain that he was sentenced to endure for the both of them.

By now, it was too late to reverse the course of things. It was mid-afternoon of the next day, and Sousat must have already arrived and delivered the message. It was done. He had averted a catastrophic confrontation. But he knew that he would never be able to conquer the regret that he had already begun to feel; still not sure that he had made the correct decision.

There was no refuge other than to meditate. But even that was denied to him, for no sooner had he taken his meditation position than a dekvat from the Forest Temple arrived with a letter from the Venerable Grandfather Kru Jarun, which was already a week old.

The message, written in Lao script, said the following:

Today, being the third day of the waxing moon of the fourth lunar cycle, in the year 2533 of our Lord Buddha, a visitor came to the forest temple. She is a woman past childbearing age, still in her prime. I could perceive all this from her voice. I also perceived that she is your mother...your name is Androo...

...if you have received this letter than it means that you have acted

in the way that I suspected you would. But the expedient path which you have chosen will not resolve the issue, for the issue is Karma. No being can escape their Karma. It is your Karma to proceed to the place you once knew as your home. The Chao Baa must die.

Yes, yes, he agreed. That was the solution. He must die. His work was finished here. It was his time to be reborn.

Andrew had denied his own mother. He didn't think himself capable of it, but he did it. The trouble was that he didn't know whether to feel proud or ashamed. It was for the good of all, the most mindful choice. He had already been taught the price of clinging, clinging on to love. It always ended in pain because it was part of the illusionary world.

All things pass away, Mom, so why couldn't you just let me pass away?

It struck him that in his head he referred to her as 'Mom'. A Pandora's box of emotions burst open.

He collapsed to the ground sobbing loudly. It had been years since he cried, ever since he had grieved over his wife and children.

Prostrate on the ground, heaving tearfully, he was made to think back to that day twenty-one years ago, a day that ranked in significance to the day he had signed up for a second tour, to the day he had been on the ground during the bombing at Ban Khoum, to the day he had ditched the F-111. Perhaps, it had been the most significant day of all.

Chapter 26

Laos 1970

"One, two, three, four
We don't want your fucking war"
Slogan of antiwar protesters, late sixties, early seventies USA

In October of 1969, 250,000 antiwar demonstrators marched in front of the White House, chivvying President Nixon, declaring 'Moratorium', an end to the war in Indochina. Cynthia Sorenson and Mitchell Talbot were among those who had camped out on Pennsylvania Avenue.

At that time, Andrew was still in the cave with the old monk in a remote corner of war-torn Laos. The priests from the Forest Temple didn't come on the full moon, as the old man had expected. So Andrew had to go out and forage for wild tubers because the food rations in the cave had run out. Outside of the cave it was quiet, and the rainy season, although winding down, was still providing enough moisture for the forest to yield abundant food.

The monks eventually did come, four of them, another two weeks later. A profusion of apologies issued forth from their leader, the fighting was so intense, he explained, that they hadn't dared to venture out. The monks busily set out to sweep the cave floor and clean the Buddha image. But there wasn't much for them to do, since Andrew had kept himself busy helping the old man with these same chores.

Concerning his case, they had a meeting to resolve this issue. He told him his story, and amidst the discussion that ensued, Andrew had declared that he had already decided to stay with the old monk until the end of the rainy season, in case the Forest Temple monks were late again. He could go out and forage for the Venerable Father if the food ran out, just like he had done this time, he argued, and also help to take care of the Buddha image. He would leave in the dry season to stay at the Forest Temple and ensure that food and necessities were still forthcoming.

There were no objections to this, and the monks, because of the rule that they shouldn't spend the night out of their temple during the Buddhist Lent, hastened to return, despite the lateness of the hour.

Andrew stayed for another three months. Until he had reached this cave, he had been through the most distressing episodes of his life. It wasn't merely the physical suffering he had endured while alone in the wilderness, and in the captivity of the enemy, nor the madness that had been surrounding him. It was the madness within him that had been crushing him.

But now, for some enigmatic reason, he had found peace in this cave.

Andrew regularly swept the cave floor, washed the Buddha image, and relit the incense and candles. He kept the torches going, and refilled the water jugs by collecting the water that dripped off the walls. He was happy to attend to the old priest, who had taught him many things, including much of the Damma, and Pali, the ancient Indian language of Therevada Buddhism.

Andrew, disgusted with his sticky, tangled, and smelly hair that he rarely got the chance to wash, even decided to shave it all off, using a knife and a razor he had borrowed from Puritatto.

The days passed, each one ending with the bats' evening departure. Gradually, Andrew developed feelings towards the old man, not unlike the doting affection of a nephew toward a favorite uncle. Puritatto himself didn't invite such feelings, since they weren't in accordance with equanimity, but he had been so alone for so long that he didn't have the heart to discourage Andrew's caring attentiveness.

This peaceful existence was threatened by something that seemed at first to be an innocent cough. Then Puritatto started to spit up blood, and shortly after that ran a high fever. Bedridden, he was, to all appearances, approaching his end. Evidently, all those years living in a damp cave were finally catching up to him. The monk gave Andrew instructions on how to cremate his body.

"Please don't leave me, Venerable Father," he had pleaded, with tears in his eyes.

"All things, including myself, are transient and impermanent," the old man had said. "Even this cave will crumble along with this mountain, not in our lifetimes, but eventually, within the cycle of death and rebirth, where even mountains and seas come and go."

A day or two after that, the old man expired. It was painful for Andrew to build the funeral pyre, to collect the wood, to anoint the body, and light the fire. After that, Andrew stayed alone for several days in grim solitude; tending to the work of maintaining the cave, trying to observe all the old man had taught him.

During that time the Pathet Lao and North Vietnamese army had come back, in more force than ever. They took over the Plain of Jars once again in their usual annual offensive, but it looked like this time they had planned to stay.

It was shortly after New Year's Day, Andrew reckoned, when he finally left the cave.

It seemed quiet enough in the mountain forest. At times he was kept company by birds and monkeys. As he proceeded, however, it became deathly still. That's when he stumbled upon the corpses.

There were four of them, badly decayed, just about skeletons by now, still wearing their monks' robes. Three were pretty much bunched up in the same area, while the fourth was some distance away, face down; apparently he had been trying to run away. This made Andrew think they had been fired upon. Without a doubt these were the four monks who had come to the cave months ago to bring food to the old man. The poor souls never made it back to the Forest Temple. Andrew didn't wish to hang around and examine the corpses. He made haste to leave the area. Perhaps whoever killed them was still around.

Hours after that, he was overwhelmed with exhaustion and hunger. How many times had he been exhausted and hungry since he had ditched his plane? Bombing, exhaustion, and hunger, that's what this war meant. When was it going to end?

Eventually he decided to take a well-worn path, willing to accede to wherever and whatever it led to. It led to a small village, with a few huts hunkered deep in the forest, heavily covered by forest growth, as well as the occasional palm and banana tree. What stood out in this quiet village, which at that time he didn't realize was called Nong Hak, was a red Chevy pickup truck parked in front of one of the larger and better-built wooden houses.

Andrew, out of an irresistible curiosity, approached the house cautiously and, after ascertaining that there was no one inside, decided to enter it. It was definitely the abode of a farang: Papers were all over the place, including American newspapers, and there were cans of Budweiser lying scattered on the floor. On top of a small table along the wall, a pack of Lucky Strikes was left next to an ashtray overflowing with cigarette butts. At the far end of the house were cupboards and a kerosene-driven refrigerator. As Andrew drew nearer, all of the Buddhist concepts he had recently been taught, all the strict discipline he had managed to instill in himself, were instantly nullified.

"Oh, wow! Cheeze Doodles!" he shouted, in spite of himself, running towards the bag on top of the fridge.

He tore open the bag and began stuffing the crispy orange curls in his mouth. At the same time he began opening the cupboards— jars of peanut butter and cans of tuna fish, and a packet of Oreo cookies. He put the Cheeze Doodles down and attacked the Oreos. While munching, he glanced at the refrigerator and opened the door in anticipation. Amidst the cans of beer, there was an opened jar of peanut butter, and lots of chocolate bars.

Andrew took some of the chocolate bars, as well as the jar of peanut butter, and went over to the table to indulge himself. He opened the jar with one hand and broke off a piece of a Hershey bar with the other, dipping the chocolate into the jar. He crammed the concoction in his mouth, and as he swallowed this delightful morsel, before it even got halfway down his throat, he heard a sound behind him.

"Who the fuck are you? And what the fuck are you doing in my house?"

From the corner of his eye he could see the young man, who was about the same height as he, and with the same dirty-blonde colored hair that Andrew had had before he had shaved it off. And like Andrew, he appeared thin and emaciated, with several days' growth of beard. He was also brandishing a handgun, pointing it at Andrew menacingly. There was panic in his bright blue eyes. "Don't fuck with me, I don't care, even if you're an American, I'll kill you."

Andrew opened his mouth, but didn't know what to say.

"Who are you?" the young man with the gun shouted for the second time, stepping closer. "Who do you work for?"

Andrew was ready to tell him his whole story, but he couldn't, because the peanut butter he had eaten had clogged up his throat. "Waw-waw," was all he could manage, desperately pointing at the earthen water jar in the corner, then miming a drinking motion with his arm.

"Get over by the wall you fucking slime! Do it now!"

Andrew did this, and put his arms up as well.

"Do you know anything about those four dead guys on the trees, one with no head and the others, their skulls pegged with this psycho-crap fucking warfare bullshit!"

He suddenly produced a card and thrust it into Andrew's face. It showed a green skull dripping blood from its eye sockets. "How come I wasn't informed, what's going on?"

"Waw, waw," Andrew pleaded.

"Huh?"

He made exaggerated swallowing sounds with his throat.

"Water?" the man with gun asked.

Andrew nodded his head affirmatively.

"It's over by the water jar in the corner. There's a ladle in it. Walk over there and drink from it very slowly. Any funny stuff, believe me, I'll kill you. For me, better safe than sorry. I think somebody like you should be able to understand that."

Andrew again nodded his head. Then, as the man waved the gun at him, he went over to the water jar to have a drink.

"I'm a United States Air Force pilot," Andrew declared, once his throat opened up. "Well, I used to be, anyway. I didn't want to have anything to do with the bombing, so I ditched my plane and deserted. That was about six months ago."

"Yeah right. You're fucking nuts if you think I'll swallow that bullshit."

Andrew shook his head in exasperation. "No, I guess I wouldn't either."

The young man scrunched up his face in perplexity. "Well fuck me, you're serious, ain't you? Nobody could make up a story like that, not even a CIA spook." The man put down the arm that was holding the gun, which now pointed harmlessly to the floor. "For real?"

"For real."

The young guy's face relaxed into a friendly expression. "I like your hairdo," he said, referring to Andrew's bald head. "I thought you were an operative called Mr. Sheen. He goes around with a shaven head, you know, sort of a psych-out look. So, what's your trip? Trying to be a monk or something?"

"I don't know. Maybe."

"What's your name?"

"Kozeny. Andrew Kozeny."

"Hi, I'm Richard...Johnson." He held out his hand for a handshake, and Andrew took it.

"I work for the International Voluntary Services," Johnson said. "Supposedly in the aid and relief-work business. Been here for five years. So what about you? What's your story? I'm sure it's more interesting than mine—Hey, let's sit down." Richard Johnson put the gun on top of the refrigerator and grabbed two stools in the corner, setting them by the table. Andrew followed his host and sat down.

He told Johnson of his relationship with Cynthia, and about the time he was caught in the middle of the bombing raid near Ban Ban. Told him of his anguish over that, and how he impulsively ditched his aircraft. Told him of his time in the jungle and of being captured by the Pathet Lao, ending with the time he had spent in the cave with Puritatto.

"Wow, that's wild! What a novel that would make!" Without any obvious prompt, he jerked his head around to look in back of him. "Hey, you drink bourbon?" he asked out of the blue, returning his face to Andrew.

Without waiting for an answer, Johnson brusquely got up, went into one of his cupboards and brought out a bottle of Jack Daniel's. "Hey don't worry," he said as he sat back down, loudly thumping his chair. "You can stay here for a while, I'll hide you. Oh, do you need a glass?" he asked as he opened the cap of the Kentucky whiskey.

"Nah," Andrew answered, raising his shoulders in indifference.

Johnson took a gulp from the bottle and handed it to Andrew, who followed suit.

"What about you, Richard? What's it been like for you?"

"Oh man, you won't believe it. The IVS is supposed to be working in the field of humanitarian aid. It's like the Peace Corps. Only we were the first Peace Corps, but we're already ruined, that's why Kennedy had to create a new one."

"Ruined?"

"You kidding? The CIA owns our ass. That's my boss now; I have to answer to them. So our credibility as an aid organization is shot to hell. I've suddenly been recruited as a spy. I'm part of the 'Forward Area Program' and I've been instructed to give out intelligence reports on troop movements, and get this, gauge the sentiments of the villagers. Oh, yeah, now to top it all off..." Johnson looked over his shoulder again. "Let me show you, c'mere."

Johnson got up feverishly once more and Andrew followed him to one of the cupboards. Johnson flung the door open and inside there was a shortwave radio. "I can call in air strikes at my discretion. Unbelievable, hah? An aid worker, who joined for noble reasons, now I'm a fucking Forward Air Guide calling in planes to bomb the peasants...you've been there, you've seen it. Nasty shit, ain't it?" he asked Andrew.

Andrew nodded his head gravely.

They returned to the table, where they continued to swig the Jack Daniel's.

"So why do you stay here?" Andrew asked him.

"If I quit, they'll just send someone else, someone who doesn't know what's going on. If he's real green, he'll shit his pants in this place, maybe call in an air strike every time he hears someone cough."

"So you're sympathetic to the Pathet Lao?"

"Well, not at first, but after being here a while. I fuckin' hate this war. The Lao have every right to kill Americans, including me. But I feel I can still help people here. As soon as I feel I can't, I'll leave."

"You think the Lao might kill you?"

"Nah, the villagers know how I feel, and so do the Pathet Lao. The Pathet Lao themselves even approached me. I told them I was against the war, and they noticed I never called in the planes, so they left me alone. I'm sure I'm good propaganda for them. Of course, the CIA and USAID would call me a traitor. But I can't be responsible for the bombing of these people. Even if somebody threatens to kill me, I won't call in an air strike."

"Who is USAID?" Andrew asked.

Johnson lit up a cigarette. "Want one," he said, offering out the pack.

"Yeah, why not?" Andrew, emboldened by the bourbon, euphoric at meeting another American, a sympathetic one at that, took a cigarette and let Johnson light it.

"USAID," Johnson repeated, as Andrew coughed out the

cigarette smoke. "United States Agency for International Development. Another so-called aid organization. They run everything, don't you know that? They've become the civil service of Laos; they handle the total administration of this country. They literally run Laos. I mean, the US fucking owns this country. Or tries to, anyway. And they took over IVS six years ago."

More swigging of the bourbon, followed by more conversation. Andrew, who had often wondered just what it was that people who smoked cigarettes enjoyed about them, surprisingly found that it went well with the alcohol.

"What did you mean about the guys tied up to the trees?" Andrew asked. "And that card, what's that all about?"

"About three months ago, they found these guys, one of them with his head blown off, tied to some trees. The others were shot, and that card was nailed into their heads. About ten kilometers from here. When I tried to find out what the story was, nobody was talking. So now, I don't trust anybody."

"Who do you think did that? The Pathet Lao?"

"No fucking way, man. The guys that were killed were village militia on the Pathet Lao side. It was Americans, man. Some fucking CIA commando group, either Special Forces or some special unit of Marines."

"Mmm. Do you think they could be after me?"

"After you?"

"The plane I was flying was a new type that they were testing here. Besides that, I'm sort of a high-tech person who knows a lot of other shit. My desertion could very well be considered an intelligence risk. Oh, and there's something else also. About a day's walk from here, not far from the cave I was in, I found four bodies—the monks who had come to visit us in the cave. I think they were shot."

"No shit?"

"Do you think that was the Pathet Lao?"

"Hell, no, all the monks here are sympathetic to the Pathet Lao. You have to be nuts to be rooting for the guys who are bombing the fucking feces out of you."

"Then who…" Andrew turned his head in thought, "wow… they sent an assassination team after me!"

The two young men looked at each other, both astounded at this conclusion.

"Well, holy moly!" Johnson exclaimed. "That might be it! But they must be gone by now. Especially since the Pathet Lao have come back in full force. Don't worry. If those CIA bastards come here, we'll fucking show them. I got another gun, I'll let you have it."

"Thanks."

Andrew couldn't remember the last time he had drunk alcohol. It was probably in Pat Pong, almost a year ago. Or maybe it was the cigarette. He was feeling extremely light-headed. "So, who do you think will win?" he asked with a drunken smirk on his face.

"I don't see any other outcome than the Pathet Lao. They've got the Vietnamese behind them, and they're no joke. What do the Royalists have? The way the Royalists conduct this war; it's like a fucking free-for-all. There are five Military Regions. Each region is run by a separate general and the local ruling family, like warlords. There is no cooperation, no concerted effort…hell, here in Xieng Khouang, Military Region II, is a perfect example. You got Vang Pao's Hmong army, and there is absolutely no communication with the Royal Lao Army. It's just them and the CIA. I'm sure these guys expect to carve out this area for themselves…on the other hand, the Pathet Lao are unified, they got all the hill tribes, including half the Hmong, as well as the lowland Lao on their side. There's no doubt in my mind who will win."

Johnson accepted the bottle handed to him and took a swig. "I'm not really a commie sympathizer," he continued, "but I say it's their affair, let's stay out of it. One thing's for sure, if the commies win, even if they do horrible things, it could never match the horrors of the bombing. So if the victory of the Pathet Lao means an end to the bombing of the Plain of Jars, I say hurray."

"Do your bosses know how you feel?"

"Oh yeah, they know. I try to hide it, but you can't. They can tell."

"They haven't tried to remove you from here?"

"I don't think they know the extent of my cooperation with the enemy. But I heard through the grapevine that when my contract runs out three months from now, they're not going to renew it."

More slugs of Jack Daniel's were exchanged.

"I hear they're gonna authorize B-52s," Johnson said. "They're really pushing it. I think Nixon will rubberstamp it any day now, especially since the Pathet Lao have taken everything back."

"I'm sick of this war."

"Yeah, so am I."

So, quite naturally, they began to reminisce about their lives in America. Andrew, by now definitely drunk, burst out crying when he described his love affair with Cindy. "The best goddamn woman that ever lived," he stated in inebriated remorse.

Johnson, on the other hand, had a different opinion of women, ever since he caught his fiancée giving his roommate a 'blow job'. The rest of his life was dissimilar as well, being born to rich parents in Boston and getting a degree in International Finance from Harvard. Then he swung the conversation into music, asking Andrew if he liked the Beatles, and had he heard their latest album, *Sgt. Pepper's.*

Andrew's head was on the table.

"Oh sorry, man, you must be beat. I got carried away, you know, no one here to talk to. Up you go," Johnson said, walking over and grabbing Andrew by the armpits, "take a cold bath, you'll feel better. I'll cook us something to eat."

Andrew got up and took a cold splash bath that woke him up, and then put on the fresh clothes that Johnson had given him. He noticed that in the breast pocket of the denim shirt was one of Johnson's IVS business cards, as well as a packet of Lucky Strikes and a box of Laotian matches. He didn't bother about taking them out.

Meanwhile, Johnson cooked up some of the ground buffalo meat he had in the freezer. There was even bread to put it in.

"Hey, you wanna wristwatch?" He held his arm out, dangling a Seiko. "It's okay, I got fucking three of them. Fucking CIA's giving them out."

Andrew took the Seiko and put it on his wrist.

After the meal, it was time for bed. Johnson gave Andrew his bed, while he laid out a mat on the floor for himself.

"Bet it's been a long time since you slept in a bed," Johnson commented.

But Andrew didn't respond, having already fallen asleep with his clothes on, so Johnson blew out the kerosene lamps and lay down upon the mat.

Andrew, in the comfort of his bed, was dead to the world. It was a queer thing that he happened to wake up when he did. First, it was his auditory senses that signaled him. He heard some movements, then a sound like someone was gargling and choking at the same time. He opened his eyes, but at first all he could see was blackness. Then the dim outline of figures materialized as his pupils dilated.

A flashlight was turned on, almost blinding him.

"Well, fuck me! I think I got the wrong guy!" one of the figures yelled out.

The flashlight shown down on Richard Johnson, his eyes open and glazed, his hands limp at the base of his throat, where all his blood was pouring out. There was a man standing over him.

"The kill was my job," another voice said from the darkness. "Why did you interfere? You sabotaged this mission, Botkin, you fucking wacko!"

Andrew, very slowly, very quietly, his heart erupting in his chest, reached under his pillow for the gun that Johnson had given him, a Colt Python.

"This isn't him, he must have given him the bed..."

Andrew jumped up with the gun in his hands. "Don't move, I'll blow you away!"

All the shadowy figures stood still. The man with the torch, thinking of blinding him, directed the flashlight into his eyes.

With the light shining in his face, Andrew stiffened his arm and aimed the gun at the space behind the light. At that moment he realized that since he had been out of the cave, he had already broken two precepts—he had taken what hadn't been given to him when he had raided Johnson's house, and he had drunk intoxicants. He was about to break a third, the most serious, the one about killing. His arm began to tremble.

"You can't shoot me, can you?" taunted a figure stepping out of the shadows.

Andrew shifted his arm in that direction. The man still walked forward, not intimidated in the least. Andrew conceded, lowering the gun. "No, I'm through with killing."

The man took the gun from Andrew's unresisting hand. He briefly examined it, and then clicked something. "No, asshole, you can't because you had the safety on." He raised the gun.

Andrew knew it would end like this. It was hopeless from the beginning.

The figure holding the flashlight spoke up again. "Look at the dome he's sportin'," he said, referring to Andrew's shaven head. "He almost looks like me. You can see how I could've made a mistake," the mysterious shadow was explaining. "Hell, anybody could've."

"Yeah right," the man holding the gun said. "Even me." He then swung around unexpectedly and—bang!—shot at the figure holding the flashlight, who crumpled almost instantly, dropping the light on the floor with a thump.

The man lowered the gun. "Fuck you, Botkin."

There followed a most frightening silence.

The gun wielder turned to Andrew. "What's your name by the way," he asked him in an aberrantly casual tone.

"Kozeny, Andrew Kozeny."

"K-O-Z-E-N-Y?" he spelled, for confirmation.

"Yes."

"Where're ya from?"

"Ohio."

"Yeah? Where?" the stranger in the shadows asked belligerently.

"Camden, it's a small town in…"

"Yeah, yeah, okay, now get the fuck atta here."

At thirty thousand feet you couldn't see nor hear them, and so the terror unleashed by a B-52 drop seems to come from out of nowhere and into everywhere. All at once, the entire horizon erupted into blazing destruction with an ear-shattering din that ripped the air and jostled the ground, a tsunami-like wave of explosions pummeling everything in its path, advancing over the ground as an unstoppable force, threatening to engulf him.

Oh shit, nowhere to hide! He dived into a steep stream gully and cowered in fear, knowing that he was in the hands of fate. There was nothing else he could do. The bombs were two thousand pounders, and if any landed closer than a football field away from him, he was surely a goner. He heard objects whistling past him, felt the whizzing of the air above him…the pressure waves were so intense they seemed to originate from inside him, rattling him like a limp rag and blowing his ears out. He remembered he was praying to God.

It was over almost as abruptly as it had begun, only minutes. He knew it was over because B-52s don't turn around for another strike.

He staggered to his feet, warily listening, watching, waiting. Climbing out of the streambed, he walked through a smoking wasteland, through a netherworld where the earth had been turned over hundreds of times, a chaos of scattered heaps of soil, broken rock, and shattered trees. And with no other option but to go on, he kept on walking. He stumbled in a daze for almost two days before he finally arrived at a place that defied belief.

It was amazing, not only because this place had escaped the bombing, but also because he had no idea of how he had gotten here. It was an oasis of tranquil splendor, like a fairyland carved out of the jungle, adorned with graceful bodhi trees, fragrant frangipani, and idyllic, large-leafed palms. The Forest Temple.

Chapter 27

Laos 1990

"It ain't over till the fat lady sings"
American proverb

He redecorated Akanee's body with elaborate designs of concentric circles, six-pointed sun-stars, and sacred unaloms, using lime, tumeric, and ochre. Even the elephant's trunk was ornately bedecked with colorful patterns. His big flappy ears were festooned with garlands of flowers. He looked magnificent.

The Chao Baa himself had chosen to wear one of the many sets of new robes that the villagers had given him during his initial crossing of the Plain of Jars. On this occasion, however, he didn't pin the steel amulets to his inner robe. There was no cheating death this time.

If they were to die together, better to go down gloriously.

"We are bound, my brother," he told the elephant. "Our Karma is linked. Perhaps we shall meet in our next life." As a final touch, he slipped on his wire-rimmed sunglasses. "Mop!"

And with that, the Chao Baa mounted Akanee's neck.

"Bai!"

Akanee, his elephant's mind oblivious to any humanly conceived drama, marched unwittingly ahead, underneath a sky stained red from widespread swidden fires, all the while being soothed by the Chao Baa's chanting.

"Namo tassa, arahato bagavato, samma sambuddhasa..."

They marched for hours over mountain paths. The pace was leisurely, and Akanee tested his master's mood by ambling off the trail to browse for some achua fruits. Much to his satisfaction, he wasn't prevented from doing so, and in one spot where the food was plentiful, a complete halt was ordered, giving the animal plenty of rest while the Chao Baa took in the panoramic view. Huge hogbacks of sedimentary rocks angled down like cleaved tables, their surfaces encrusted with an unbroken covering of forest. There were also broad massifs, boldly erect with mighty faces carved out of their limestone cliffs. The mountains seemed endless, hordes of them, all shapes and sizes, jumbled amongst each other until they faded in the blur of the horizon. The expanse of sky above them dimly radiated a bizarre, dirty-pink hue.

They took their time coming down the mountain, through curtains of dense vegetation, the elephant feeding whenever he wanted to. Andrew, similar to the time when he had ditched the F-111, when he had known it would be the last time he would fly, sensed that this too was a final journey, his last trek together with Akanee.

It was just about midday when they reached the lowland forest enclosing Ban Ling Kao. Perhaps they had an hour before they would reach the deserted village, to face whatever it was that was awaiting them.

But what was awaiting them wasn't as far away as that. The elephant halted without being commanded, lifting his trunk in the air. He had smelled them; the men who wanted to kill them.

"We cannot escape our Karma," he told Akanee. "Bai!"

The elephant resumed his plodding gait, but not without some reluctance. Some time later he stopped again, this time letting out a ferocious roar that tore open the stillness of the jungle and crashed against the hillside. The smell that Akanee sensed was definitely that of the men with guns, the men that shoot at them, the Chao Fa soldiers.

Andrew became more forceful. "Bai, Bai!"

Regardless of the command, Akanee only took a few more steps before he lingered again to bellow out a threatening cry to the enemies he knew were out there, a sound so fearsome that the malice behind it was clearly made known. He had learned to hate the Chao Fa; the very odor of them rankled him.

"Bai! Bai!"

Akanee crashed forward in a swift stride with the purpose of meeting their adversaries head-on. As they stormed out of a thick stand of teak and bamboo, Andrew spotted one of them, dressed in black, holding his weapon. Akanee raised his trunk to the sky to trumpet a fierce war cry.

But there were other people—a man and a woman, both of them farangs, on their knees, holding each other, huddled in fright. The man with the gun threw it down and raised his hands in surrender.

"I Ly Feng, Ly Feng!" the Hmong was shouting. Then he pointed in back of him. "Chao Fa!" he cried, continuing to gesticulate urgently in that direction.

A shot rang out, and Andrew ordered his elephant onward, to bypass the man who was shouting and run ahead at full speed. The great beast barreled through the underbrush, trampling the vegetation in front of them.

He could now see two of them. One was bashing at a limp body on the ground, another was grabbing at another farang, an older woman hanging desperately on to a tree. The man who had been mutilating the corpse took one startled glance at the oncoming duo and ran off in a hasty retreat. The other man was drawing his Hmong sword to slit the woman's throat. This man looked up, frozen in fear as the tattooed monk in sunglasses and the giant elephant bore down upon him.

"Jap! Jap!" the monk with the sunglasses commanded.

Akanee distended his trunk, grabbing the man at the waist, wrapping him in a python-like grip, and lifting him high in the air. The elephant's natural instinct to thrash him into the ground was overwhelming.

"NO, NO, WANG LONG, WANG LONG! PUT HIM DOWN!" Andrew screamed at the top of his lungs.

The elephant hesitated for a long moment before bringing his trunk down and dropping his captive, who scrambled frenziedly to his feet and fled for his life into the jungle.

The farang woman was trying to stand up when he finally got a good look at her. The shock of it jolted him, for although twenty-one years had changed her, he could still recognize the face of his mother. Apparently, she hadn't left for home as she had been advised to do by Sousat, but had obstinately pursued him. He should have known better than to think that he could dismiss so easily a woman who had traveled halfway around the world to find her son.

"Song!" he commanded.

He dismounted, and as he walked towards her, removing his sunglasses, he could see her eyes swelling in recognition. He had absolutely no idea what to say to her, hadn't yet fathomed the emotions the sight of her were to invoke in him, when she swooned and fell to the ground.

He didn't know what to do. He couldn't touch her, as she was a female, so he ordered Akanee to do it. The elephant's trunk tapped at her face, his hot wet breath reviving her. She regained consciousness, sat up, and gazed at Andrew as if she were dreaming, before struggling through her astonishment to stand upright.

"Oh dear God in heaven! Andrew!" She came at him with outstretched arms but he backed away.

"You cannot touch me, Mother! It is forbidden for a woman to touch me. I am a monk."

Dorothy halted in mid-stride, her mouth hanging open in disbelief, stunned by his words. She put down her arms that were meant to hold him, anger slowly welling up in her. She took deep breaths, trying to calm herself before she spoke.

"The first thing that you ever were..." she stopped to gulp in more air, "...when you came into this world..."

She paused, panting fervidly, "...and the last thing...THAT YOU WILL EVER BE WHEN YOU LEAVE IT", she screamed, "IS MY SON!"

Filial love prevailed over religious precepts and they fell into each other's arms, crying their eyes out, quaking with emotion, dropping to their knees without breaking their embrace.

Ly Feng, Cynthia, and Jeff Heller were approaching this scene.

"Oh my God!" Cindy cried. "ANDY!" She ran to them and soon they were all huddled together, the three of them, wailing and touching and hugging, in the middle of the jungle, with the two women running their hands all over the man in the orange robes.

Heller came up to them, dazed and confused. "Hey, what, wait a minute...you, you mean...you mean... you know this guy?"

A considerable time had passed before Dorothy realized that Kampeng was dead, and his body lay on the ground less than a hundred feet away from them.

"Oh my God!" Dorothy cried. "Kampeng!"

She got up and ran over to his prone, lifeless body, and threw her head upon the bloodied chest, sobbing, "Oh, my dear loyal friend, I am sorry, it's all my fault, forgive me, I'm sorry, I'm sorry...you died because of me...forgive me..."

"Poor Kampeng," Cynthia eulogized, tears surfacing in her eyes.

With Cindy and Heller a step behind him, Andrew walked over to tend to his mother. "Mother, please stop crying!"

She looked up at her son, her hair and forehead now stained with Kampeng's blood; her face grimaced with anguish, her tear-filled eyes squinting from the heartache inside her. "How can you say that? He was my friend, the best friend I ever had!" She turned to look again at the body before her, weeping.

Cindy moved forward to try comforting her, but Andrew stayed her with his hand. For him, this was worse than he could have imagined, all this emotion was beginning to engulf him. It hurt him to see his mother in pain like this, and her grief became his. He tried hard to stifle his own tears.

Dorothy was still in the grip of sorrow. "Why did you have to leave us, Kampeng?" she cried out.

Andrew, out of a reflex conditioned by his life in Laos, grabbed her forcefully. "Don't say that! Stop your crying!"

Her sobbing ceased as she looked up at him in shock.

"If you shed tears like that, you will upset his spirit, which will be unwilling to depart!"

Perhaps it was his many years as a monk, or his own experience with grief and death, that enabled him to lecture her with words that rang of faith and conviction.

"I know the pain of loss, Mother, but it was his Karma to die. It is egotistical to think you are the cause, and so your guilt is only delusion. It was his Karma for him to help you find me, and in sacrificing his life to protect you, he has died a noble death and has gained merit that will result in a favorable rebirth. But I must speak to him now and remind him of that, lest he take revenge."

Dorothy's face wrinkled up in an expression of appalled reproof.

"Speak to him? Take revenge? Andrew, HE's DEAD!"

"Is that what you believe?"

"YES!"

She got a spooky sensation when he replied condescendingly, "Ah, you don't know, Mother, you don't know."

She stared at her son, confused, not knowing what to believe.

"Please, Mother, let me do this."

Dorothy rose spontaneously, in order to allow him to kneel over the body and mutter prayers in a strange language. It was at that point that she got a hold of herself, and admitted the possibility that maybe she didn't know. She bowed her head in deference to the intonation of what she surmised to be Buddhist last rites. When Andrew was finished, he went over to his belongings on top of the elephant and came back with several vials, the contents of which he rubbed conscientiously underneath the clothes and over the skin of the corpse.

"We must hurry," Andrew said, "and take him to the Forest Temple to prepare his cremation immediately."

He went back to his bag of things which was strapped to the elephant's side and took out his axe, then hastily set about looking for trees to cut down with Ly Feng, who was now holding his machete and following Andrew dutifully.

"Andrew?" Dorothy cried out in curiosity.

Heller shot a darting glance at the elephant, his mind working. "I think he's going to make us a seat."

"Let's help," Cindy suggested.

Heller, his timidity wearing off, addressed Andrew, "Uh hello, Mr. Chao Baa, sir, can we be of some assistance?"

"His name is Andrew!" Dorothy sternly corrected.

"You can drag what we cut over to Akanee, my elephant."

They set about their tasks without much talking.

It was Andrew who broke the silence when, as Cindy approached to take possession of a small log he had just prepared, he stopped his work and asked her, "Did you have a good life?"

"It was okay I guess…whatever…I didn't get married if that's what you're asking"

"I know."

"Did you divulge that through some divine revelation" she said, confused at her own tone of sarcasm.

"No. I remember you said that your world began and ended with me. That's a rather irreversible decision."

She struggled hard to resist the urge to burst into tears. "I'm happy you remembered that. And what about you, did you have a good life?"

"Cindy," Dorothy said, now within earshot. "I think Andrew will tell us in his own time."

Andrew resumed chopping at a small tree. "Mother, my father is dead, isn't he?"

"Yes."

"He died of grief."

"Yes."

"I am very sorry for the sorrow and pain I caused the both of you."

"It seems you've already forgotten your own words about guilt and Karma."

"I'm trying very hard not to, Mother, under the circumstances."

Dorothy's mind was racing. The journey had culminated into one of mixed emotions of grief and joy for her. She had found her son, an impossible dream come true, but at a terrible cost, the life of dear Kampeng. However, she was beginning to comprehend this thing about Karma. Everything, from the anonymous letter and all of the events that had taken place up to that point, was supposed to happen. She also realized that her whole life had just now been altered irrevocably in only a flash of a moment. She wondered what was next, though she was calmly assured by the thought that whatever her future, Andrew would be in it.

They rode on the back of the elephant, sitting wordlessly on the makeshift platform that Andrew had hastily improvised, while he himself sat on the neck of the beast with Kampeng's corpse, now covered by a crude body-bag of leaves, sprawled across his lap. She was impressed, indeed somewhat in awe of her son, who had exhibited a certain expertise in gathering herbs and other materials from the forest to preserve the corpse, and who now sat waving the flies away from the dead body with a palm frond, mystically focused in a somber chanting. Listening to him babbling in deep low tones, his mind seemingly far away, she thought, who was this man? Was it really Andrew, the boy she had raised in Camden, Ohio? He frightened her, yet, oddly enough, she actually felt proud of him, sensing the greatness of the person he had become.

Eventually, Andrew narrated the account of his life for the past twenty odd years, the women wiping their moist eyes, Heller, open-mouthed in a state of wide-eyed wonder, Ly Feng with a dispassionate face. They listened somberly to his poignant tale, vicariously feeling his loneliness, pain, and despair in the course of his life. One thing was clear throughout: that his suffering, as well as that of all the people of Laos, had one root cause. War.

It took the rest of the day to reach the Forest Temple, and a good portion of the night as well. Ly Feng accompanied them only part of the way, before he announced he would take his leave to return to the Hmong village where they had met two days before. Many thanks were exchanged before he went stately on his way.

Despite the late hour of the night, they didn't have to wake the abbot when they arrived, for they found the Venerable Kru Jarun actually standing at the entrance to the compound.

The old priest, looming motionlessly in the dark, announced in Lao, "We shall be busy for the next few days. We have a cremation, and a disordination to perform."

The next day was Kampeng's cremation. The ashes were placed in an urn, which Dorothy was to give to his family in Vientiane. The day after that, Andrew disrobed, with Dorothy, Cindy, and Heller witnessing the ceremony solemnly. From thereon, Andrew's vocation as a Buddhist monk had been forever ended.

These affairs having been completed, they set out for the army outpost at Ta Vieng. Before they reached it, however, there remained one last duty for Andrew to undertake. This final act was to release Akanee from servitude, a deed that was rendered in the jungle just a couple of hours' walk from the army camp.

"Go back, Akanee, my brother. Go back home."

The elephant loped majestically into the depths of the forest, as if knowing his role in the drama had finished, never once looking back, accepting his rightful reward without any undue gratitude, proud and dignified to the end.

When they arrived at the military quarters, Sousat couldn't bring himself to receive them cordially. In fact he was downright furious.

"You have disobeyed my instructions, and your recklessness has cost the life of a man," he reprimanded Dorothy, insensitive to her grief over Kampeng's death. He was also annoyed that he would have to send a vehicle with an extra driver to pick up the jeep they had abandoned, which, it turned out, actually belonged to an army division stationed in Ponsavan. Andrew had to calm him down, again pointing out the inexorable workings of the Law of Karma.

Once over his initial anger, Sousat was struck with the full implications that the disclosure of the Chao Baa's true identity presented. Over dinner, he listened with engrossed attentiveness to Andrew's story, looking frequently at Dorothy, the undaunted mother, while acknowledging the immensity of this strange saga and the significant part that he, Sousat, had himself unwittingly played.

The next day there was a tearful departure as Dorothy and Cindy, along with Heller, boarded a jeep to take them to Ponsavan for the flight back to Vientiane. Andrew remained behind.

Not long after Andrew's retirement as the Chao Baa, he became an ordinary English teacher at Ponsavan high school, although the tattoos had repeatedly caused him some embarrassment. He wished he hadn't followed Potisat's recommendation about using the gall of python, but it was too late to reverse that decision. Potisat himself, a year later, was found mysteriously murdered in a rice paddy with his head bashed in. No one knows who or why.

Dorothy, meanwhile, had returned to the US, but came back to Lao PDR seven months later as a nurse, employed by, of all people, the Mennonites, somewhat fulfilling the remarks made by Kampeng during their unforgettable journey to the Plain of Jars. Feeling she owed a debt to Kampeng's family, she took on the responsibility of paying the fees for the higher education of his eldest son. While in the country, she and Andrew spent much time together.

Back in Camden, Cynthia went on to write of her adventure as an award-winning fictional novel, entitled *The Plain of Jars*, using a male pen name to further disguise the truth. She ended up marrying Mitchell Talbot, her former Political Science Professor at Berkeley, and who was now a successful investment analyst in Los Angeles. They had one son, whom they named Andrew Richard Sunnata Talbot.

Heller, on the other hand, not only completed his thesis, but wrote a New York Times bestseller, a non-fictional account of the Chao Baa Legend, *Cognitive Dissonance, and the MIA Phenomenon*. In the beginning, both Cindy and Dorothy were furious, because, unlike Cindy, he used true names and revealed everything.

In the end, however, this was a blessing.

Because of the publicity that Heller's book provoked, the case of Lt. Andrew Kozeny attained national prominence and became a hot prime-time TV attraction, serving as the premiere topic of such shows as *48 Hours*, the *Oprah Winfrey Show*, and *20/20*, as well as providing Jay Leno with sufficient material for three months of opening monologues. The military couldn't ignore this case, where previously it had been tucked away conveniently, and the most expedient way to quiet the thing was to grant a full pardon. So Andrew was allowed to repatriate to the US to be near his aging mother. The both of them moved to Minnesota, where he worked as a counselor to Hmong youths from refugee families, who were struggling with the difficulties of living in America.

As for Father Wolanska, incarcerated at the newly opened Mansfield Correctional Institution, God's plan had finally been revealed to him, and every evening he got on his knees in the privacy of his cell, fervently thanking the Lord for rewarding him in his later years in life, giving him his greatest congregation ever, so that he, as a prison chaplain, could tend to those who truly needed spiritual redemption.

And finally, mention must be made concerning the Venerable Pra Kru Jarun. At the time of this writing, the Venerable Kru Jarun is reported to be in very bad health, nearing death. He has claimed that, in spite of his physical suffering, he is not distressed in the least. To the contrary, he can't wait to die, as he is looking forward to his next life, which he perceived, to his utmost satisfaction, would be his last.

Roundfire Books put simply, publish great stories. Whether it's literary or popular, a gentle tale or a pulsating thriller, the connecting theme in all Roundfire fiction titles is that once you pick them up you won't want to put them down.